DELIVERIES

PAUL SMYTH

Deliveries
Copyright © 2020 by Paul Smyth

All rights reserved. No part of this publication may be reproduced, distributed, or transmitted in any form or by any means, including photocopying, recording, or other electronic or mechanical methods, without the prior written permission of the author, except in the case of brief quotations embodied in critical reviews and certain other non-commercial uses permitted by copyright law.

tellwell

Tellwell Talent
www.tellwell.ca

ISBN
978-0-2288-2689-7 (Hardcover)
978-0-2288-2688-0 (Paperback)

Acknowledgements

Typing those first few words of chapter one on a keyboard can feel mighty intimidating. But as a story develops, in my case over several years of casual writing, it becomes clear that support from outside sources is crucial. So, without further ado, there are a few indispensable people worth mentioning who made this book possible: my wife and best friend, Diane, for unending support and encouragement and for reading each raw chapter as it rolled off my printer and enthusiastically asking for the next; my friend and pilot extraordinaire Dave Van Dyke, whose knowledge base was instrumental in assisting with all things flight-related; my brother, Rob, who willingly read my manuscript twice and offered valuable feedback and wondrous incentive to keep going; my three amazing children and all other dear family and friends who associated themselves with a writer who on many days had little idea of where he was going but who thoroughly enjoyed getting there! This tale is dedicated to each and every one of you! Enjoy the read and may God bless you all!

Chapter 1

Sporting dark aviator prescription sunglasses, fifty-three-year-old Paul Jackson squinted from the orange fireball's blinding light, the disc just minutes from sinking behind a chunky veil of bluish-grey clouds. Lowering his gaze, he tried to concentrate on the pre-takeoff checklist despite the brilliant distraction outside his airplane.

"Probably not the smartest night for flying," muttered Paul to his co-pilot. "I say we get in and out as fast as we can. You concur?"

"Copy that," a distracted male voice replied through Paul's dilapidated headset. "I'm good with quick and simple." Fumbling with his twisted seat belt, Paul tried several times to re-latch the buckle to the receptacle but gave up; the clasps consistently failed to connect as snugly as they should. Adding to his frustration, the threadbare seat cushions of his aging Cessna 185 had long ago lost their support, but the added cost of reupholstering was not an affordable priority. To Paul's way of thinking, cosmetic repairs and seat restoration could wait for another day, just so long as the rest of his bird passed its annual inspection and continued allowing him to generate a modest income. Pursing his lips, Paul adjusted his back, legs and buttocks to find what little comfort he could.

Nestled among rows of foothills blanketed with blue spruce trees, Owensville Municipal Airport was considered by many to be a crown jewel for commerce and business travel throughout the region. Flanking both sides of the runway, snug rows of mature poplars grew unhindered, their leaves vying for what remained of the late-day sun as it conceded to an expanding mass of roiling dark clouds farther up the valley. Lingering rays of sunshine reflected off the engine cowling and into Paul's eyes. He blinked several times to moisten his eyes, but they remained gritty and sore from a dreadful night's sleep the night before.

Damp with perspiration, Paul unlatched and opened the window in his side door to vent humid sticky air from the cockpit then wiped his brow with his sleeve as best he could. Finding his place again in the pre-takeoff checklist, he completed each task with robotic-like precision: *Parking Brake -- SET* . . . "Brake is on." *Fuel Selector Valve -- BOTH ON* . . . "Fuel is on both."

Flight Controls -- FREE and CORRECT—With coordinated motion, Paul moved the control yoke in and out, side to side. He jockeyed the rudder pedals back and forth with fatigued, achy feet and peered outside the cockpit. Ailerons, elevator and vertical stabilizer all responded properly with no restrictions.

When it came to prepping his airplane for flight, Paul was typically in the habit of taking his time, as any safety-conscious pilot would be. But with the urgency of this last-minute trip, he found himself fast-tracking through the checklist uncommonly fast. He glanced up and surveyed the western sky. Regrettably, his flight path required a compass heading of two-seven-zero degrees due west: a radial that aligned him with brewing cloud formations and whatever else nature had in store as twilight grabbed for control.

With help from a dash-mounted portable Garmin GPS, Paul would track the twisty Moose River for the scenic half-hour flight. But with weather conditions now deteriorating, he grew concerned about getting back in time for the late supper he had promised his wife. And tonight, Diane planned lasagna and one of her Aunt Verna's matchless apple pies, two favorite culinary delights in the Jackson household.

Reaching up, Paul lowered his visor to counter the sunlight flooding the cockpit. Shoving aside his growing thirst, he berated himself for not packing bottled water as per his usual routine. But on this occasion, pressing circumstances warranted the absence of in-flight comforts, and he vowed to make do during the whirlwind trip.

As Paul forged ahead through the tattered checklist, a sudden twitch in his stomach caused him to wince in pain. *No time for a guilty conscience now,* he promptly decided while tackling the next item: *Stabilizer and Rudder Trim -- SET*—Paul adjusted the trim wheel near his right knee by aligning the notch to the takeoff position. "Flaps set, please and thank-you," he requested of the man beside him.

The co-pilot reached over and toggled the flap lever. "Flaps at twenty."

"Flaps twenty," Paul confirmed as he advanced the red fuel-mixture knob to its full-forward position, followed by the blue control, thus angling the propeller blades flat for take-off. He triple-checked the manifold pressure, RPMs and oil pressure: "Mixture rich, prop high RPM. Check and check."

"Cowl flaps open," mumbled the co-pilot after checking the switch.

"Roger," affirmed Paul.

Witness to his share of rapidly changing mountain weather, Paul hoped the approaching system would stall, or better yet, dissipate altogether. He snickered at the memory of his wife calling him a stubborn-mule bush-pilot because she knew all too well his willingness to push the envelope for the sake of money and a family to spend it on. Diane had preferred he sat this flight out, but from experience, she understood it would take more than thundershowers to ground her headstrong husband.

She was right. Paul in no way wanted to disappoint his friend Jack Ward and the 400 plus guests registered for the weekend at his hideaway resort at Spruce Creek. Jack was expecting the arrival of his cargo—all of which had been jam-packed and tightly secured in the aft section of the departing Cessna, or so Paul hoped—within the hour.

Advancing the throttle to the stops remained one of Paul's favorite aspects of flight. It not only gave him a euphoric rush but also a profound sense of personal well-being. For Paul, nothing compared to the sound of a 300 horsepower Continental engine spooling to full power, its deafening roar undeniably bewitching. All set to go, Paul found himself once again smiling in child-like anticipation.

Contrary to its shoddy appearance, his thirty-five-year-old Cessna 185F proved itself a formidable workhorse. In addition to a pilot and co-pilot station, his plane could accommodate up to four passengers, but for this jaunt, he had removed the rear seats to allow more room for his payload.

The plane's exterior red trim and dulled finish required a significant dose of spit and polish, while its thirty-six-foot wingspan displayed plenty of tiny rock chips and impact dents along the entire leading edge. Fitted with twenty-two-inch-diameter smooth tundra tires, the airplane wasn't the prettiest in the sky, but it was the perfect tool for getting the job done, and Paul cherished the old bird like it was part of his family.

With the checklist complete, Paul folded it up and tucked it into the vinyl slot under his side-door window. The pouch had long ago split, but like the rest of his plane, it was functional. The run-down cockpit was a constant reminder of a lengthy to-do list of repairs, and Paul knew that shortening the list required revenue and above-board profit margins. *Now it's time to make some money,* he thought, *tattered airplane and all.*

"Looks like we're finally good to go," Paul confidently remarked.

Glancing out the front windscreen, Paul watched as stray droplets of rain pinged off the engine cowling. Though he could not hear their impact, the visual reminded him of camping as a child when drizzle from an evening cloudburst would create soft pattering noises against the fabric of his family's tent trailer, followed of course, by his father's repetitive lectures about not touching the canvas because it might start to leak. Such memories brought a short-lived but welcome smile to Paul's lips.

Deliveries

Paul's love of flight began as a youngster, when his father was a student pilot. Every time an aircraft would pass overhead, Paul would crane his neck skyward for a glimpse or run to the nearest window if he was inside. Growing up, he spent countless hours imagining himself gliding through clear blue skies to aerial adventures untold.

On his tenth birthday, Paul's dream of flight became reality when he discovered a folded note inside a birthday card from his parents. Unfolding and then reading the paper, the youth jumped excitedly when he learned that his first airplane ride was at hand. One hour later, the pilot and flight instructor of a four-seat Cessna 172 allowed Paul the unique thrill of placing his small hands on the yoke. In no time, Paul learned how to control roll and pitch, and though his legs were too short to reach the pedals, he watched in fascination as the rudder swung back and forth to control yaw. In the rear seat, Paul's dad grinned from ear to ear knowing that his son would never be the same . . .

An all too familiar voice blasted through Paul's headset, snapping him out of his daydream and back to reality.

"Windsock's almost horizontal, Ace, and we're fighting a nasty crosswind to boot. You sure you can handle that, or do you need me to take over and save you from any additional embarrassment?"

Paul's eyes drifted from the instrument panel straight into the deadpan face of his longtime friend and co-pilot Dave McMurray, the man's expression displaying his usual mischievous grin. Pushing forty-seven, Dave's blue eyes accentuated a face exuding defiant confidence. Paul raised his eyebrows and again wondered how his business partner stuffed his one 190-pound frame into a snug pair of impeccably clean bright-orange coveralls. Adding to the comedic attire, a buzz-cut crop of grey hair sat atop his head, the sides tinged with ash brown diagonal streaks.

Dave's typical choice of flying attire always bewildered Paul. "How is it that a guy who drives a cattle liner by day and airlifts cargo at night is able to stay so clean?" Paul asked. "You look like you belong in a Tide commercial, not in the cockpit of my admittedly grubby bush plane!"

"This is the standard-issue flight suit of elite bush pilots!" Dave happily retorted. "Jealous, are we?"

Paul coughed for emphasis while adjusting his glasses. "Not on your life, amigo! Besides, I take great pride in my tattered jeans, hole-riddled t-shirt and frayed hoodie. Maturity of character is what I like to call this aviator look."

"Yeah, whatever," chuckled Dave while focusing his eyes on the sky.

Clouds floated along quicker now, their peculiar shapes rolling and bumping into one another as if battling for airspace. A seasoned pilot himself, Dave had earned his pilot's licence at twenty-one years of age and had eventually worked his way through various ratings towards his commercial certificate. Despite their professionalism inside the cockpit, Dave seldom passed up an opportunity to badger Paul about his flying prowess, especially when crosswind takeoffs were involved.

"I'm feeling a bit anxious," teased Dave. "Perhaps I should fly this departure. Then, as I see it, we both get to live, and you get to watch and learn from a pro!"

"Thanks for your generous vote of confidence," smirked Paul.

Dave pulled down his visor to counter the sun's insistent glare. "No worries, captain. You know me. I'm simply trying to keep my behind safe!"

"Your orange bottom is the least of my worries. And ten bucks says this takeoff will be smoother than a baby's freshly powdered bottom!"

"In your dreams, mate. I've painstakingly witnessed enough of your pee-my-pants takeoffs, and they're by no means pretty. You better make it twenty!"

Paul rolled his eyes. "You're on, partner. You can pay now if you like."

"Not happening," chided Dave.

Underneath Paul's self-assured exterior, a recurring flashback reared its head, the ugly memory triggering pangs of anxiety when extreme crosswinds were present on the takeoff roll. He had tried repeatedly to overcome this self-induced mind-over-matter obstacle, but the unrelenting memory and post-traumatic stress were formidable beasts to slay. And on this hurried trip, their sharp claws were out.

Almost ten years to the day, Paul launched Airflow Charters, a start-up aviation company consisting of two older-model planes: a single-engine low-wing Piper Archer and his current nearly vintage 1976 Cessna 185. Similar to a favourite pair of worn-out slippers, they both showed their age inside and out, yet were perfectly functional. And because disposable income for restorative upgrades was not yet factored into the fledgling operating budget, the airplanes would have to remain an eyesore for the foreseeable future.

On a blustery Sunday afternoon in late November with Paul flying solo in the Archer, punchy west winds grabbed hold of the plane at the exact moment its wheels lifted from runway 26 at Owensville Municipal Airport. Wrestling with the yoke and pedals, Paul kept the wing level through the initial phase of the climb, but at 300 feet above ground level, or AGL, an unexpected wind shear ultimately resulted in cracking up the fuselage. The aircraft flipped on its side at a steep forty-degree angle, half flying and half plummeting like a thin flat stone.

As the forces of lift departed the airfoil, the right-wingtip sliced into the adjacent snow-covered field. The Piper spun on its axis before skidding to a rough-and-tumble stop beside the runway. Miraculously, Paul walked away with only a few cuts and bruises, not to mention a significant thumping to his pilot-sized pride. Subsequent investigation revealed there was nothing he could have done to avoid the mishap, but the good-natured heckling from Dave began almost immediately. Paul took it all in stride, but he never flew again with quite the same degree of tenacity.

Paul keyed the push-to-talk button on the top of the control yoke. "Owensville tower, Cessna one-eight-five Golf-Foxtrot-Charlie-Sierra, holding short, runway two-six. Ready to go, west departure."

An annoying squeal blared through his headset, causing both pilots to cringe. Paul adjusted the radio's squelch control, but he expected it to have little effect, and he was right. *Terrific*, he thought. *Something else that needs repair with money I don't have.*

Dave glanced towards the four-story, rectangular-shaped control tower: the concrete relic situated to the right of the customs building. Owensville airport wasn't typically busy on weekends, and he wondered how the air traffic control staff put in their time without going stir crazy. *Not something I could do,* he determined.

Seconds later, a soft-spoken male voice responded, his inflection upbeat, professional and reassuringly calm. "Golf-Foxtrot-Charlie-Sierra, Owensville tower, you're cleared for take-off, runway two-six. Winds one-eight-five at twenty-five, gusting to thirty. Altimeter three-zero-three-one."

Paul was about to read back the instructions when the controller spoke again. "Also, be advised we've had a report of heavy rain and moderate chop west of the field on your departure heading." Chop referred to air turbulence, something pilots and passengers seldom appreciated, yet could rarely avoid. "And not that it's any of my business, but can you boys hold off till morning? Radar confirms some questionable goop farther up the valley."

"Negative tower," Paul hastily replied. "We go now or run the risk of not getting in at all. We'll stay low to avoid the 'goop.' Plus, our cargo is time-sensitive." *And so is my wallet,* he muttered.

Dave looked towards his friend: a rare look of concern etched on his face. He tightened his seatbelt and made sure the straps were snug. "You sure about this, captain?" he asked. "We could always do what the man says and try again early tomorrow morning. The suns even supposed to be out."

"It'll be too late by then, Dave," lectured Paul. "And besides, I gave Jack my word that his freight would arrive tonight. According to him, they need it all prepped and set up by early tomorrow. I know it's a rushed trip and the weather sucks, but we've done these runs before. You're not scared you'll soil your underwear, are you? If you're wearing any that is?"

Dave conceded to Paul's logic and smiled. "Flying with you is reason enough to soil my briefs, but I'm with you, foolhardy decision or not."

In truth, Paul had already questioned his motives for this flight and whether his promise to Jack Ward was worth the risk. But the money on this sortie was decent enough, and he had no intention of passing that up because of poor conditions and a nagging conscience.

Paul openly tried to convince himself. "We'll be fine," he flatly stated. "Besides, the plane needs a few upgrades, and I've been promising Diane a new dishwasher for months. You know how it is . . . happy-wife, happy-life."

"Amen to that! And did I hear you say, a *few repairs*? If I was you, I'd forget the fixes. What you really need is a whole new airplane! I'm amazed this tub flies at all!"

Paul's mouth formed a crooked smile. He knew Dave's clowning around meant him no harm, but there was truth to his statement. True the airplane needed work, but its heartbeat was strong and the airframe dependable. More importantly, Paul trusted it with his life and knew that Dave would agree if push came to shove.

"Roger," replied the controller. "Best of luck gentlemen. We'll catch you on the rebound later tonight. Go with your read-back."

"Copy that tower," Paul acknowledged. "Charlie-Sierra cleared for take-off, runway two-six. Altimeter three-zero-three-one. West departure approved. See you on the back-track."

"Read back correct. Safe travels."

Paul completed a final check of the instruments, shrugged his shoulders and inhaled deeply. "Another exciting flight into the boonies," he proclaimed.

But Paul's apprehensions did not go unnoticed by his co-pilot. "I hope the cargo back there is worth it, Ace. I'm on record to say that I don't like the weather and your body language isn't much of a confidence booster." Dave smiled. "I promised Tess I'd be back in time for taco soup, and dare I say it out loud, a Dwayne Johnson movie. So, if you screw this up, you'll have my angry wife in your face and a lot of explaining to do!"

"Now I am worried!" grimaced Paul. "And did you say taco soup? There's actually such a gross thing as liquefied tacos?"

Dave closed his window and secured the latch. "Absolutely, *oh Cap-e-tan*, but with your wimpy taste buds, you wouldn't like how Tess makes it."

"Taco's I can usually handle," insisted Paul. "But pureed tacos? That sounds entirely disgusting and, I imagine, far too hot."

"My point exactly," replied Dave. "Tess makes it spicy, so your sissy palate could never take the heat! Taco soup is for real pilots!"

Gripping the control yoke with his left hand and reaching for the throttle with his right, Paul found it difficult to restrain a smile. There wasn't another pilot on earth he'd rather be flying with. Paul flipped his hand up and whacked Dave on the shoulder while easing his feet off the toe brakes. "Real pilots fly from the left seat," he reminded. "Wannabee aviators ride shotgun, and I believe that's the seat you're in!"

Dave refrained from any counter-argument. If left unchecked, he knew their banter could go on with no end. Gazing skyward, he watched as the last of the sun's rays disappeared behind growing masses of cloud. Rain at the far end of the airport grounds made it tough to spot the end of the sloped runway.

Paul hoisted himself up as far as his seatbelt allowed. Dave watched him advance the throttle just enough to get the wheels moving and the Cessna onto the runway. Paul locked the wheels behind the large painted white numbers, breathed deeply several times and squeezed the tension from his neck.

Dave broke the silence. "Though it goes against my better judgement, I've got your back, Ace. So, let's do this before I change my mind and you faint under the pressure."

Despite oscillating confidence, Paul fabricated a smile and tried to focus on nothing else but the safe completion of the task at hand. He glanced at his co-pilot. "If we stay below the cloud base and follow the river, we should be ..." Paul clutched his chest. "Sorry, Dave, I—"

"You okay, Ace?" asked Dave, his joking suddenly curtailed.

"I'm fine," lied Paul. "It's just a heart palpitation. Likely too much caffeine on an empty stomach. I've had them before. They're harmless."

Dave appeared skeptical, but he let it go. "Wish I had some caffeine in my system now," he yawned. "I missed my king-sized afternoon latte today."

Paul nodded absently while staring at his wife and daughter's photograph. Taped to the sun visor, the image of their smiling faces pricked his conscience, which he tried to shake off. Despite the gut check, casting aside business because of self-doubt wasn't an option either. Paul defiantly tilted his head up and resolved to maintain a stiff upper lip.

"Ready, Dave?" asked Paul with a renewed air of confidence to his voice.

"You have the con," replied Dave. "Let's rock and roll!"

In one fluid motion, Paul increased the throttle and waited for the manifold pressure to spike. He checked the fuel-flow gauge to ensure the plane developed full power, and as the big engine revved up towards 2,700 RPM, the airframe shook with bone-rattling force. He kept his feet on the brakes until content the engine instruments were in the green and precisely where they should be.

Like a racehorse eagerly awaiting its chute to open, the airplane shook with anticipation as Paul shifted his toes from the brakes and sank his heels into the lowest section of the pedals for steering. As the wheels surged forward and the propeller bit into moisture-laden air, something about the acceleration seemed a bit off. Paul knew every creak and rattle his airplane emitted, each telling him something about its health and well-being. It felt now as if the plane was alive and, having sensed its pilot's hesitation to proceed, was choosing to respond with less than maximum enthusiasm. Paul's imagination was playing tricks and he knew it.

Had either pilot glanced out the rear window, they'd have seen a long rooster tail of spray rising and falling in the slipstream. During the take-off roll, Paul used the ailerons to offset crosswinds and help hold the left-wing down until the airplane approached V1, or the commit-to-fly speed.

At sixty-five knots Paul added the tiniest hint of back pressure on the yoke. One-third of the way down the runway, the Cessna's tail wheel relinquished its grip as the main wheels broke free. It was then Paul realized he'd been holding his breath and that his heart was pounding unusually fast. He exhaled what little air remained in his lungs, gulped in a huge amount of oxygen and tried his best to relax.

* * *

The setting sun found the tiniest hole in the clouds to offer one last hurrah. Air Traffic Controller Bruce Macbeth squinted as he watched the departing Cessna climb sluggishly into the tempestuous sky. Its silvery wing resembled a burning strip of magnesium as the low sun glinted off its shiny surface. Through his binoculars, Bruce followed the airplane until it flew out of sight into a wall of ugly grey clouds. He turned away from the window and walked towards the coffee pot with growing apprehension and a knot in his gut. But for the life of him, he couldn't figure out why.

Chapter 2

The telephone receiver felt cold in his hand as Jack Ward spoke to someone from the Rural Utilities Commission. "So, you're absolutely certain the road is still out of commission?" he asked. "Because we're still without power up here, or do any of you people actually give a rat's tail about your customers the way you say you do?"

Moderately frustrated, Jack rubbed his free hand along his rib cage to try to warm up. Glancing out the window, he noticed the sun had already slipped behind Copper Mountain, and the temperature inside his office and the rest of Spruce Creek Lodge was beginning to drop despite it being the first weekend in September. Pausing to listen, he wasn't impressed with the curt reply he received.

"All right then," Jack grumbled. "Thanks for the update. You've got my number, so for heaven's sake keep me posted if anything changes. I've got a very busy day here tomorrow so could use some good news." *As if you'd care.*

Chucking the phone back into its cradle, Jack turned and walked towards his partially open door where a dark uninviting hallway loomed, its cedar walls tinged red from emergency battery-powered lighting. "Of all times for this to happen," he complained to himself, "it has to be this weekend." Jack flung the door open the rest of the way and begrudgingly stepped out.

Thunderstorms had begun pounding the valley late Friday night, their continued ferocity resulting in the troublesome power outage by around four o'clock Saturday morning. Jack remained hopeful that work crews might have had the juice flowing at some point during the day today, but so far nothing. Another serious concern, as if electrical issues weren't enough, was that the only gravel road connecting Spruce Creek to the outside world lay covered in places with gooey concoctions of fallen timber, mud and other such mountain refuse. To Jack's further angst, workmen had yet to arrive because they were dealing with, as he'd been so rudely informed, "Other more pressing issues."

"At least the phones work," fumed Jack while sauntering through the corridor with a brooding headache. It felt to him like a clamp being squeezed around his skull, the pressure in his sinus cavities causing fresh waves of pain. Massaging his seventy-one-year-old deeply creased temples, Jack prowled the lodge for something medicinal to relieve his misery.

Following a mercifully short quest, Jack ended up in the lodge cookhouse where he discovered an expired bottle of ibuprofen and a bevy of kitchen staff surrounded by strategically placed candles and oil lamps. He poured himself a glass of tepid chlorine-infused water and downed two of the red pills as he watched a flurry of busy hands preparing sandwiches and mini pastries.

More and more, Jack questioned his motives for buying this property in the first place. But things had been different back then, and though at first opposed to the idea, his wife's adoration for the lodge grew as did his desire to make her happy. He had a genuine purpose then. Nowadays, though, it seemed that every chore became one he'd rather not have to deal with, and Jack found it difficult not to dredge up the past and want to stay there.

As he sauntered away from the kitchen, Jack reminisced about his late wife and those events that led to the lodge's acquisition. As emotions welled up, his throat constricted. Mildred's death was painfully vivid in his memory, and missing her was oftentimes too distressing to handle . . .

Following a quarter-century career with Sears Department Stores and then retirement, Jack Ward began to explore opportunities to generate income while keeping himself out of a senior's home. This ongoing pursuit resulted in frequent disappointment, not only for himself but also for his patient and long-suffering wife.

Uncertain of what exactly he was searching for, Jack scoured the daily newspaper for inspiration. Through it all, Mil supported her husband with words of gentle encouragement. "You'll find something, dear," she would say. "You have to be patient." Then, lo and behold, one month later on a dreary Sunday morning before church, Mil proved herself right.

Already discouraged, Jack slouched in his chair while parked at their redwood kitchen table. He sipped a hot cup of coffee as he skimmed the classified ads, his eyes searching for the fairy tale golden goose. The sports section had slid off the table and fallen to the floor. Several pages splayed over his moccasins, which he purposely ignored.

Standing behind Jack near the stove, Mildred whipped eggs in a metal bowl with a fork. The appealing aroma of bacon overpowered the acrid smell of burnt toast. Jack almost closed the paper and gave up when his eyes stumbled upon an obscure headline in the lowest corner of the real estate section: "UNIQUE INVESTMENT OPPORTUNITY – Own a Piece of History – Call now for details!" In fine print, contact information and property details were listed for Spruce Creek, a parcel of land Jack knew little about . . .

Constructed in the early 1940s by a small group of wealthy entrepreneurs, Spruce Creek Lodge was situated along the western shore of far-reaching Bayshore Lake, its pine-log exterior walls surrounded by carpets of spruce, fir, and pine trees, their root systems embedded into vast sections of scruffy crown land. Sprinkled with fallen timber, the lake held a notorious reputation for ruining the outboard engine propellers of those daring enough to launch a powered watercraft there. The resplendent landscape attracted anglers, hunters and nature lovers of all ages.

The best method of navigating the deep-toned blue lake was by a canoe or kayak, both of which were made available to lodge guests free of charge. Because of its matchless beauty, Spruce Creek resort became synonymous with trophy-size game and walleye, the facility eventually transforming into a bed and breakfast for people who sought refuge from the daily grind of work and life's ongoing stresses.

But when the economy floundered and more specifically tourism, bookings became less and less, the end result being several failed attempts at ownership by various entrepreneurs, and then finally abandonment. The lodge became nothing more than a memory to those who once enjoyed her restful attributes.

Following two ill-fated years on the commercial real estate market, the property deteriorated to such an extent that its value fell to a fraction of its original listing price. Several "FOR SALE" signs marked the tree-lined entrance leading up to the lodge, their faded words overgrown with grass and thistle. The only regular inhabitant on the property was a common loon, the bird's trill-like call falling on deaf ears as it paddled in the water around the boathouse each morning . . .

Lost in thought, Jack stared at the printed words for several seconds before a flurry of crazy ideas chased away his gloomy thoughts. "Now here's a project I could sink my teeth into!" he whispered. The trick, however, was to figure out how best to approach the subject with Mil. She was never a fan of sidestepping issues and would expect full disclosure and straight-up honesty. So, the more Jack thought about it, the more he became certain there was little to gain by beating around the bush.

"Hey, Mil," Jack finally blurted. He did not wait for her to answer before setting the bait. "The old lodge up at Spruce Creek is for sale . . . or what's left of it." *No reaction. This could go either way.*

Accustomed to her husband's ongoing search, Mildred poured the eggs into a sizzling hot frypan and responded with her customary "Uh-huh" followed immediately by, "Do you want more coffee, dear?"

Expecting her lukewarm response, Jack plucked himself from his chair and walked into the living room. He grabbed the cordless phone off the coffee table and entered the ad's phone number to connect with the listing's Realtor. "Ask not, receive not," he quietly remarked.

Aware of his exploits, Mildred asked from the kitchen, "Why on earth are you pursuing that, Jack? We don't have the money to fix up that old place. Besides, I don't want to move."

Jack shuffled back into the kitchen with the phone pressed to his ear. He smiled at his wife but offered no reply. Shortly thereafter, and in the wake of a one-hour phone call and pages of scribbled notes, Jack finally agreed to a showing with his very reluctant wife in tow. This endeavour eventually led to the serious prospect of ownership, but for Jack, the challenge wasn't so much the restoration process as it was in convincing Mil to climb aboard his "wagon train of insanity," as she aptly called it. She in no uncertain terms had decided that her husband had finally lost every square inch of his mind.

"There's no way I'm spending my retirement years in the middle of nowhere, Jack," lectured Mildred in her school-teacher voice. "The place needs a lifetime of work and a boatload of money. We're too old to take that on."

"Listen, Mil," pleaded Jack. "The last thing I want to do for the next twenty years is to play bridge with the old farts at Golden Age Manor. Please just think about it. That's all I ask."

Mildred couldn't help but chuckle.

"Besides," argued Jack. "I'm sure Doug would love sinking his teeth into the place. It's the type of project he's been looking for, and if we bribe him with a tray of butter shortbread and a bottle or two of scotch, I'm sure he'd discount his services."

Doug McLaren was Jack's newly acquired son-in-law, and a highly respected contractor specializing in home renovations and commercial development. For the past several months, Doug's search for a longer-term project had proven unsuccessful due to an increase in cash-strapped investors and wishful fixer-uppers, so Jack's sudden unilateral decision to bring him to task did little to meet his wife's approval.

"Oh, I'm sure!" replied Mildred. "I can just see you two, a hammer in one hand and a glass of scotch in the other. Nothing would ever get done!"

This time it was Jack who snickered.

Mildred understood all too well her husband's need to putter, and unless Jack immersed himself in carving duck decoys, his inability to hold still for more than five minutes was a well-known fact to all who knew him.

Following substantial debate and bribery for new clothes, Mildred finally agreed to ponder the concept of ownership. Over the next month, she spent a huge amount of time walking the property and acquainting herself with the lodge and its still eye-catching former charm. It wasn't long before Mil formulated her own vision of what Spruce Creek could become, and with subsequent price haggling, discounts and negotiation, the Wards soon found themselves proprietors of a vacation property nobody else would touch.

Over the next six months, Doug's collection of trades people descended on Spruce Creek like bees to an open hive. With every nail driven and shingle replaced, the lodge transformed to its former character and beyond. It was painstakingly restored along with several new and improved female touches.

Jack and Mil spent the bulk of their retirement savings on the project, and with significant financial backing, Spruce Creek Lodge re-opened for business on the seventh of November, Mildred's birthday. As word spread and their client base swelled with new and returning customers, the business flourished. People were booking reservations months in advance.

One afternoon the following spring, Jack and Mil busied themselves with re-staining the rustic pine steps leading up to the main doorway. Mildred grabbed her husband's arm. "You know, Jack," she said. "I thought you were crazy for wanting to buy this place, but I have to tell you, I'm so glad you did. I'm proud of you, proud of us!"

For Jack, seeing his wife this happy was worth every penny spent. "Thanks, Mil. We did a good job, didn't we? Now, aren't you glad you listened to your wise old stiff-necked husband?"

Mildred smirked, cocked her head sideways and broke into a smile. Somehow, she splashed red stain on her chin, hands and white t-shirt, a picture forever etched in Jack's memory. He marvelled at her ability to show an inner joy no matter her circumstances or state of health. In and around the lodge, Mil's faith and her courageous spirit profoundly affected those around her, and every day she exuded a sense of love and peace while battling cancer. She loved to share her Christian beliefs and did so with genuine pride and joy to anyone with an ear to listen and a heart for biblical truth.

Mil would see to it that flowers adorned every nook and cranny not obstructed by rocks and brush. Her short strolls brought her face to face with numerous guests, calling everyone "Dear" and always sharing a kind word or scripture verse. Her innate ability to make people feel welcomed and loved also made her an incredible wife, mother, and grandmother. Her pride in the lodge swelled, but on December sixteenth, two years after acquiring the property, Mildred's life ended at the still youthful age of fifty-nine.

Devastated, Jack agonized over how to go on without her. Mildred's death left a gaping hole in his heart, and he lost the will to go it alone. He even contemplated re-listing the property, but Mil's words rang loudly in his ears. "Now, Jack, you promise that if anything happens to me, you'll keep this place going. Do this for me, Jack? Do you promise?" With tears trickling down his cheeks, Jack cupped his hands into hers and promised . . .

As Jack approached the front lobby, he brushed aside tears and tried to shelve the onslaught of memories. *You've got work to do old boy, and now isn't the time for blubbering.* He switched to business mode while pondering his decision to ask Paul Jackson for help. With the road out and his guests hoping to enjoy weekend festivities and getting their faces on TV, Jack knew he had little choice. And as a self-proclaimed man of action, using air transport was exactly what Mil would have expected him to do.

Centered in the middle of the foyer and ablaze with pine logs, a stunning copper and brick open-hearth fireplace basked the room in warm tones. Long angular shadows danced on the walls behind those standing close to the flame. Despite the power outage, people seemed in good spirits. Almost everyone wore a jacket or pullover sweater, and Jack was sure he saw people's breath as they spoke. *Surely, it's not that cold in here.* But a sudden chill told him otherwise.

On a nearby folding table, guests enjoyed hot chocolate, tea and coffee, bottled water and soft drinks—the hot beverages made possible by several outdoor propane camping stoves the lodge made available to patrons by request. Conversations were abundant given the brisk temperature inside, and Jack wondered if the weekend he spent months planning might not be so big a flop after all.

Throughout the lodge, electric baseboard heaters provided warmth to most of the rooms, but due to the power outage, all the units were inoperative. Certain rooms had wood-burning fireplaces, so guests occupying those suites had less reason to whine about cooler temperatures.

Jack grabbed a Styrofoam cup and poured coffee from one of many ceramic carafes. People noticed him enter the room, and he suddenly felt very self-conscious. He knew folks would be expecting an update on the electricity situation, and because he had nothing good to report, his stomach balled up.

From the other side of the lobby, a pair of young men ambled towards Jack, the shorter of the two wearing knee-length shorts, bright red sandals, and a long-sleeve jersey plastered with bike patches and sponsor logos. His tanned face sported a neatly trimmed beard of a week's growth at best. Wind-blown sandy blond hair complimented a trim physique, and despite the man's casual appearance, his stride looked all business. As they approached, Jack angled away and tried to enjoy a few sips of coffee in private. He remembered the first time he met Matt Hawley years ago, an introduction that would ultimately change Jack's life and the way Spruce Creek Lodge conducted its business . . .

In the months following his wife's death, Jack made the trek into Owensville, as he often did, to meet up with his old friend Tom Sullivan, CFCB Television's Program Manager. Jack would bring donuts and plop himself into one of Tom's office chairs; the two men would drink second-rate coffee and chat about the usual trio—weather, politics, and business.

Unbeknownst to Jack at the time, his beloved lodge would soon undergo a radical transformation, a re-write so to speak of its original mission statement from calm and tranquil to one of spoked wheels, carbon-fibre frames and disc brakes. And such a moderate shift was the last thing on earth Jack ever thought he would agree to.

"Listen, Jack," Tom said. "I appreciate you stopping in, but I've got an unscheduled meeting in a few minutes and fires to put out, so I'll have to cut our visit short. If you don't have any place else you need to be, and I'm sure you likely don't, you're welcome to hang around for a bit."

Not waiting for Jack to reply, Tom grabbed his empty mug and stood up from behind his desk. "Besides, there's a talk show guest in our studio right now that I'd like you to meet. I think you'd find him very interesting."

Jack shrugged his shoulders and laughed. "Well, Tom, contrary to your ill-advised beliefs about me, I do have a resort to run. So, no offence to your guest, but I think I'll scoot back to Spruce Creek."

Tom upped the ante. "This is one of those rare gut feelings I have, Jack, and it's about your business. So, perhaps you'll hear me out?" Tom refilled his coffee and grimaced when he added too much cream. "His name is Matt Hawley, and the kid is a superstar in the world of downhill mountain biking."

Jack glanced up at Tom but showed little interest. "You'll have to hit me with a bigger club," he said through a growing yawn. "A what kind of biker?"

Unfazed by his friend's lack of exuberance, Tom patiently explained. "A mountain biker, Jack. Matt's a well-spoken young man, and when you're around him you can't help but tune in to what he has to say. In addition to being an exceptional rider, I believe he's got the charisma to make a fine politician one day. Though rumour has it he's planning to open a string of bike shops in the not-so-distant future."

Jack focused his eyes outside on a small grove of crab apple trees just beyond Tom's office window. He watched as several pudgy blackbirds gorged on the wrinkled fruit. "And I should care about this why?" he asked vacantly.

Tom continued to plead his case. "Because Jack, even if you don't know the first thing about mountain biking, and I know you don't, this guy might just pique your interest from a business standpoint."

"Guilty," replied Jack. "I know nothing about the sport, and aside from having what I assume is two wheels and handlebars, I don't have the foggiest idea what a mountain bike even looks like."

Tom stirred his coffee. "That you will learn, Jack, I guarantee it. Matt's become a top-level competitor and is racking up victories on the pro circuit. He's a go-to guy for promoting the sport across North America, and now even more recently in parts of Europe."

Unsure of where Tom was going with this, Jack ran his fingers through his thinning grey hair. "I'll ask you this again,

Tom. Why would I care in the slightest about this kid or his chosen career path?"

"Because, Jack, he knows a thing or two about world-class DH course design. And seeing as you own a mountain retreat with a working chair lift already on site, I thought you might be open to something new."

Tom noticed his friend's raised eyebrows, which only spurred him on. "The Freeride and DH circuits are growing in popularity," explained Tom. "And Matt's been a big part of it. The energy drink company Red Bull snatched him up fast by sponsoring his first few years on the pro circuit with—"

"Whoa, Tom. Freeride and DH? I have no idea what you're talking about."

The phone on Tom's desk began to ring. He let it go to voicemail. "DH," replied Tom. "It's an acronym for downhill. These kids rip down a mountain at full throttle on a course that takes them over jumps, through trees and other obstacles. It's a race against the clock. The fastest time wins."

Jack tried to keep up. "And Freeride?"

"Freeride is more related to downhill cycling and dirt jumping. The rider focuses on control and speed, plus an assortment of tricks. It's an exciting spectator sport if you're into that sort of thing."

"You know you sound like a sport's reporter," acknowledged Jack. "And a bad one at that."

Tom sipped his coffee and smirked. "I learned it all from my son!"

Sitting perfectly still, Jack's eyes narrowed as Tom kept running off at the mouth. "Matt's hugged his share of trees over the years and gone over the handle-bars more than once. But that's part of the fun for these kids. Injuries are considered a rite of passage."

"Hug a tree?" asked Jack, his thoughts churning.

Tom smiled. "Hug a tree is essentially a wipeout. It's when bike and rider meet a trunk up close and personal, which in most cases results in a visit to the hospital, like what happened to Matt early last season."

"What happened?" asked Jack curiously.

"He fractured his sternum on the last leg of the finals, and then still insisted on finishing the race!" Tom shook his head. "The kid thought he was invincible until a broken bone forced him off the track."

Jack fished for more information. "Any bike parks around here?" he asked.

"None," answered Tom. "But with its rapid growth in popularity, I believe the region could benefit from one. Plus, as an added bonus for us here, it'd be welcome local content for our weekly sports package."

Tom watched as Jack turned back towards the window, a pensive expression on his face. "Have I finally piqued your interest, Jack?"

Jack collected his thoughts before answering. "Okay, Tom, maybe I can stay a few minutes and talk to the kid as you suggest. Lord knows I've got the space and topography for such a thing. Who knows, perhaps a bike park will inject some new life into the lodge. And like you said, the area could benefit from something like this. As could my bottom line for that matter."

Tom back-peddled for a moment. "Be a challenging drive for larger volumes of people to get up there without major road improvements," he admitted. "You're pretty far from mainstream society, and I'd be concerned about a steady revenue stream for you during the off-season."

"From optimist to pessimist, eh Tom?" Jack stated. "Well, partner, the way I see it, challenges are meant to be conquered. Biking in the summer, skiing in the winter like it used to be before we bought the place. I kill two birds with one stone. Simple as that."

Tom set down his coffee. "You do realize this would require a huge amount of capital investment to pull something like this off?"

"Well," grunted Jack while stretching his arms. "It behooves a wise businessman to ask questions and woo investors. And fortunately, I'm good at both tasks. But let's not get ahead of ourselves, shall we?"

Tom grabbed the doorknob. "Tell you what, Jack, pour yourself another cup of coffee and follow me. I'll introduce you to Matt and maybe you'll be able to convince him to listen to your enthralling business plan."

Jack topped up his coffee and followed Tom into the smaller of two studios, a working space no larger than a double-wide garage, but with high ceilings for a lighting grid and a green screen covering one entire side wall. Three large pedestal-mounted cameras graced the floor with a camera operator behind each one. They stopped their chatter when the boss walked in.

Tom found a director's chair for Jack and positioned him behind the studio cameras, but still with a good view of the set. "Its dark back here, Jack, and there are video cables all over the floor, so until the show ends, please stay in your chair for your own safety." Tom walked up to the set which consisted of a carpeted riser, two easy chairs, a coffee table and a pair of dated brass floor lamps. He exchanged pleasantries with Matt Hawley and the show host before heading for the studio's exit. "Catch up with you in a half-hour, Jack. Enjoy the show."

As Jack stared at Matt Hawley, he pondered Spruce Creek's future and tried to imagine what Mildred would say if she was here: "Have you lost your mind, Jack? A mountain bike park? Perhaps you should nap dear until your head clears." But Jack's thinking was sound, and he believed the lodge needed to move forward with the times and could benefit from something fresh to offset a recent decline in reservations.

When the sports show went to air, and he listened to Matt speak, the freshly implanted vision started to make sense for Jack Ward. Now he needed to figure out a way to implement this cockamamie plan and try to convince the young man on set to help make it happen . . .

For Jack, that day seemed an eternity ago, like a dream that would never come to pass. And yet here he was in a room filled with mountain bikers and enthusiasts and his beloved lodge literally transformed into a full-fledged sports hub for anything with two wheels. Matt Hawley had indeed proved himself invaluable with course design and the construction of wooden freeride structures built into the slopes for riders to test their mettle. And on more than one occasion his unceasing enthusiasm for the project bolstered Jack's moral when there were days he wanted to quit. He owed that young man a great deal more than he could ever repay monetarily.

Jack chugged the rest of his coffee and watched as the two men closed in, their body language suggesting a serious discussion was occurring between them. To Matt's left was Dylan Sullivan, Tom's son. Dylan wore bleached hole-riddled blue jeans and a canary-yellow t-shirt emblazoned with the words, 'EAT-SLEEP-RIDE.' Just shy of six feet, he had wisps of coarse jet-black hair poking out from underneath the brim of a well-used National Hockey League ball cap.

An avid biker himself, Dylan was currently enrolled in his fourth year at the University of Owensville, studying biological sciences. To help offset burgeoning tuition costs, his dad hired him part-time as production assistant for the station's Promotions department. And because of his son's love of biking, it was during an in-studio public service announcement, with Matt as the spokesperson, that Tom made the introduction. Since then, the young men became best of friends and rode together whenever Matt was in town and his schedule allowed for playtime.

When Dylan and Matt stopped uncomfortably close to Jack, he stepped back to regain his personal space. He waited for the bevy of questions he knew was coming. He did not have to wait long.

"So, what's happening, Jack?" asked Matt. "We still able to race tomorrow? Did the TV gear show up yet?"

Before Jack could answer, Dylan chimed in. "Any word on getting the power restored?"

Jack eyed both men warily and smiled. "Well, it's nice to see you boys too," he grunted. "I'll answer your questions in the order they were asked. I hope so, no, and no."

Dylan and Matt shared a puzzled look but said nothing.

"We've got too much vested in this, Matt, to have things fizzle," explained Jack. "As long as the plane arrives with our replacement gear, we'll be okay. But the road's still out which is keeping patrons away, and so is electrical power. So, those are the wild cards right now. That's all I can tell you."

Someone chucked logs onto the fire which released a flurry of sparks into the wide-mouthed flue above. The distraction caused Jack to lose his train of thought. "Now where the blazes was I?" he uttered to Dylan. "Oh, yeah. According to your dad, the TV mobile slash satellite truck has its own generator, so even with the power out we can still send the broadcast signal back to the station for the auction." Jack glanced around the room. "Speaking of Tom, where is your dad anyway?"

Dylan shrugged. "Lying down, I think. He wasn't feeling well."

"Oh terrific," croaked Jack. "Be just my luck for him to come down with something on top of every other problem around here. We can't get to air without him, so I hope he snaps out of it fast!"

Dylan overlooked the negative sentiment in Jack's voice. "When's the plane due in, Mr. Ward?"

Jack's focus shifted to the large picture window near the front entry. Rain trickling down the glass partially obscured a wall of grey clouds hovering low over the lake. Closer to the shoreline, a triple-decker bird feeder swung wildly from the lowest branch of a pine tree. Sparrows aiming to fill their bellies flitted about as they tried to counter the blustery winds so they could land and feed. Jack met Dylan's gaze. "Depends on the weather through the mountains and when they left, but I'd expect them inside of an hour."

Suddenly feeling nauseated, Jack's growing anxiety over the inbound flight began to fester. He had offered Paul Jackson a $500 cash bonus upon completion of the trip, hoping the extra incentive would be enough to entice him to fly regardless of the weather. "You'd be able to buy Diane that dishwasher, Paul," Jack threw in for good measure. But he knew his desire to honour his wife's memory occasionally clouded his judgement, and Jack worried about the ramifications of coercing others to fulfill his own agenda.

Jack swallowed hard and turned away from Dylan and Matt. He faced the crowd, clapped his hands twice and mustered up what little courage he felt he had left. "Ladies and Gentlemen, could I please have a moment of your time?" Jack waited for conversations to die down before continuing. "First off, let me apologize for the situation we find ourselves in. As you know, last night's storm resulted in a power outage here in paradise, which should any of you want to lay blame, I had nothing to do with."

Several people chuckled.

Jack remained straight-faced. "Seems our electricity issues could plague us for the balance of the weekend unless things magically change."

This news resulted in a low chorus of groans throughout the room.

Jack's throat constricted. "To make matters worse, the road into Spruce Creek is temporarily closed due to a mudslide or some such thing, so until repair crews open a path, which I hope is soon, no one gets in or out. And, no, I won't give room discounts for extra nights, so please don't ask."

More grumbling ensued, only louder this time.

"The good news is this," added Jack. "All the television gear we need for tomorrow is being flown in as we speak and should arrive shortly." Jack fought the urge to cross his fingers. "So, with any luck the first annual Mildred Ward charity ride and live auction will go tomorrow as planned."

Jack flinched when someone behind him yelled. "Rock 'n' roll!"

This time laughs rippled through the gathering from front to back.

Jack fielded a few questions while eyeing his watch. He needed to leave for the airstrip right away, and with daylight rapidly fading, the lighting along both sides of the grass runway needed powering up before the plane arrived. Despite the humdrum announcements, he felt pleased that no one blamed him for the ongoing misfortunes of the day, at least to his face. Though for whatever reason, Jack still felt the need to shoulder the responsibility, and he inwardly reprimanded himself for not somehow figuring out a way to have side-stepped the entire mess in the first place.

With no further questions, Jack turned his attention back to his two young friends. He tried to forge another smile but failed miserably. "Well, guys, it's time I head out to the airstrip and wait for the plane to show up. I've got a generator to start and lights to turn on." *And I think there's still a bottle of sherry tucked away in the shed. Goodness knows I could use a sip.*

When Jack excused himself and began walking away, Dylan spoke up. "Feel like some company, Mr. Ward? Matt and I aren't doing much of anything right now."

Jack stopped and peered over his shoulder. "Dylan, please just call me Jack, okay? I feel like an old man when you formalize my name like that."

Matt elbowed Dylan in the ribs. "Way to go, loser!"

The lines on Jack's face softened as the idea of having company grew on him. "Sure, you're both welcome to ride along. I'll likely need some help anyway."

Chapter 3

Although the cargo in the rear of the Cessna was securely strapped in, pockets of turbulent air still managed to jostle things about; the resulting clamour causing both pilots to recoil as if someone was popping balloons behind their backs.

"This bumping around can't be good for that stuff," grimaced Dave, his head cranked towards the rear of the plane. "I'm wondering if we cinched everything down tight enough back there?"

Paul glimpsed over his shoulder. "Should be fine," he replied uneasily. "But the cameras are the least of my concerns right now." Paul nodded towards the front window. "It's what's going on out there that has my attention, not that it's a surprise given ATC's warning."

Dave swept his eyes across the narrow valley where lower chunks of mountains poked through heavyset clouds on both sides of the river. Paul's facial expression appeared anything but calm, not to mention his white-knuckled hands on the yoke struggling to control the bouncing airplane. Not one to skirt around an issue, Dave asked point-blank why his friend seemed uncharacteristically frazzled. "You doing okay, Ace?" he asked. "Because if you don't mind me saying, you look a bit . . . shell-shocked."

"I'm fine," Paul nodded unconvincingly. "Though I'm not appreciating the turbulence or these basement-dwelling clouds. I'm sure we're already scaring the wildlife half-to-death down there, and I'd rather not have to drop any lower if we don't have to."

Dave replied with a simple head nod. He knew how important this flight was to Paul, and though reluctant to tag along because of its hurried nature, he also understood that beggars can't be choosers when it comes to any measure of revenue. *Paul needs the income,* thought Dave. *And so do I.*

Adjusting for lower than normal cruise power, Paul reached for the throttle and eased it back until the manifold pressure dropped to twenty-three inches. In a similar fashion, he adjusted the propeller knob until the RPM gauge matched, the setting known as twenty-three squared.

Keeping an eye on the exhaust-gas temperature, Paul tweaked the engine mixture and waited for the big engine to adjust to the optimum air/fuel mixture being compressed and ignited inside each cylinder. The altimeter showed them at roughly 500 feet AGL over the Moose River as the rate of climb and descent indicator bounced erratically on either side of zero. He adjusted the trim as best he could and watched as the speed gauge dipped below 140 knots.

"Might as well try to enjoy the scenery," Paul suggested with a palpable air of uncertainty to voice. "At least it's a short trip, and we—"

A sudden jolt of wind hammered the Cessna, throwing pilot and co-pilot upwards against their straps, then back down. Paul's stomach was already unsettled, and the added turbulence wasn't helping. He tried to ignore the twinges of nausea and focus on flying the airplane, but seconds later another slap punched them hard to the right.

"For crying out loud!" Paul grumbled. "This is bloody ridiculous, and we can't turn around even if we wanted to."

"Maybe this was a bad idea after all," fretted Dave. "If I throw up on my coveralls, I'm billing you for the dry-cleaning!"

Paul snickered nervously to overshadow his snowballing doubts. "There's a barf bag under your seat, Dave. You know I'd buy you a real flight uniform if I thought you'd wear it, though I suspect orange coveralls are about all you have in your closet anyway."

Dave shook his head at the wisecrack. "Remind me again why I fly with you? Oh yeah, I remember now. It's because no one else will!"

As the Cessna passed through spirals of rough air, updrafts created short-lived positive G's that pressed Dave and Paul into their seats. Conversely, downdrafts raised them out of their seats, creating negative G's. So far, Paul's seatbelt held fast through all the jouncing around, but he worried about its integrity should the turbulence escalate.

As daylight waned throughout the river valley, Paul remained hopeful that visual flight rules, known as VFR, would apply for the balance of the trip. He could navigate visually as long as he stayed below the fluctuating cloud base, but with every passing second, their undersides seemed to dip lower and lower, and hug-the-deck river flying wasn't his preference in the least.

Paul banked the wings left and right in sync with the river's angular flow. Spruce trees lined the jagged slopes on both sides, their branches creating a carpet of green with lumps of cloud drifting over top. Paul wanted nothing more than to deliver his cargo to Jack as promised, with wheels back on deck at Owensville Municipal before utter darkness consumed everything.

Accustomed to the demands of bush flying, Paul's logbook registered thousands of hours of backcountry flight, but trips like this left him to ponder his reasons for continuing at all. It was a dangerous occupation, the money was so-so, and the hours were anything but nine-to-five. And while he had time after time questioned his competency since the Archer crash, the last thing he desired was to upset his family with doubts he thought best kept to himself . . . or Dave for that matter.

Paul obtained his private pilot's licence at the age of sixteen before he could even drive. Since then, flying became a near-daily ritual, a life necessity as important to him as water and air. And similar to an addiction, he needed a regular fix to satisfy those deep-rooted cravings for flight.

In the opening scene of the movie *Top Gun*, one of Paul's favourites, a fighter pilot turns in his wings to his commanding officer and says, "I've lost the edge." Paul always promised himself that if that day ever came for him, that he would do the same for his wife and daughter. No more hazardous flights or traipsing pell-mell into the unknown, and sadly to his way of thinking, no more fun.

"Let me know if you need a break, Paul," offered Dave. "I'd be happy to show you how a seasoned pilot flies in crummy weather."

Paul shot Dave a lopsided grin and glanced around the cabin with exaggerated head movements. "I'm good, but thanks. Besides, I don't see any other seasoned pilots around here besides myself." Paul hoped his taunting masked the trepidation he was feeling. "You just worry about not soiling those coveralls or—"

Wham! Another pocket of rough air smacked the plane, the downward force lifting everything inside the cargo hold upwards against their straps, and then roughly back down. The shift caused a horrible crash somewhere amidst the stored cargo. Once he found his stomach again, Dave cranked his head around. "Something's loosened up back there, Ace!" he noted. "Time for some new tie-downs, I'm thinking."

Stuffed into three custom-fit hard-shell cases was a trio of Panasonic P2HD digital video cameras, along with matching Vinten Vision 12 carbon-fibre tripods, three lighting kits and several bags of audio equipment. It was in Jack's words, "Everything we need to help facilitate the broadcast." And to twist Paul's finger, Jack added, "All proceeds support Cancer research, so you're backing a worthy cause, Paul. All the more reason to accept my offer."

The equipment was initially set to arrive at Spruce Creek earlier in the day, but due to the road closure, delivery by air was now the only viable option given time constraints. Tom Sullivan arranged for transport of the back-up gear to the airport, where Paul and Dave hurriedly loaded the plane and took flight.

Adding to the weather's instability, a now steady rain pelted the plane. Grateful the western sky still offered enough light to navigate, Paul allowed himself a few moments to try to relax. If conditions tanked any further, and they couldn't fly back out, they'd have no choice but to stay overnight. It wasn't his first choice, but not a big deal either. *Safety first*, thought Paul as his belly twitched nervously.

Paul glanced towards his friend. "Sorry, Dave, but we might have to bunk out tonight at the lodge if the weather doesn't cooperate. And chances are you'll have to forgo your taco soup and movie."

"No worries, mate," admitted Dave. "I figured that was a possibility, so I packed my toothbrush. Besides, taco soup I like, Dwayne Johnson I don't. I tolerate his mediocre acting because I know it's my husbandly duty to like what Tess likes."

Paul laughed. "I can relate, but for me its romance movies. I think I'd rather go shopping for clothes before watching another one of those predictable storylines. Girl leaves big city, moves to small town, hits boy with car, and they fall in love! They're all the same!"

"Bingo!" laughed Dave.

As a huge Dwayne Johnson fan, Dave's wife once joked to her husband, "If Mr. Johnson ever shows up at my front door, I love you, dear, but you'll need to find another place to live!"

Dave opened the air vent a notch. "Let's hope the guy doesn't start making romance movies, cause then we're both in for a world of hurt!"

Paul thought of his own wife. He had encouraged Diane to visit Tess for the evening, a girl's night out to offset her anxiety over the poor weather and his flight. Adding to her stress was the lack of cellphone coverage between Owensville and Spruce Creek, and unless they flew high enough, there was no way to reach them through conventional air traffic control. Paul knew Diane would spend the night at home worrying, so when she agreed to visit Tess, he felt the weight of guilt lift somewhat from his shoulders.

Never one to admit it, Dave knew that Tess also worried when he flew in poor conditions, so like Paul, he felt more at ease knowing she and Diane would take solace in each other's company. "Well, hopefully our wives are enjoying a relaxing evening of tea and gossip. Though, I'd guess most likely they're griping about us anyway."

"You're likely right," agreed Paul. "I know Diane wasn't impressed with my decision to fly tonight, not that I can blame her. She tried hard to talk me out of it, and I should probably have listened. I promised to call once we land at Spruce Creek and then another just before we leave." *If we leave tonight.*

Paul scanned the instruments to change his negative thinking. Engine temperature and oil pressure in the green; airspeed, RPM and manifold pressure, all tickety-boo. Paul anticipated a bumpy ride from the get-go, and he fully expected that even lousier weather-related dung was close to the fan, despite wishful thinking to the contrary. Until conditions degraded, he wedged his back into the seat, breathed deep and tried to loosen up his grip on the yoke. But no matter his best efforts, his body would not settle.

* * *

The three men slipped away from the gathering and headed out through the side door towards the lodge's old GMC Vandura passenger van. Jack shivered as wind and rain struck him on the face, whereas Dylan and Matt seemed oblivious to the elements, the two swapping stories of their most memorable bike crash while comparing notes on the newest light-weight bike frame to hit the retail market.

Minutes later, the van bucked around on the muddy washboard gravel road leading to Spruce Creek's airfield, its wipers struggling to clear away a now steady downpour. Jack was grateful not to be alone, but one nagging thought picked at his brain. *Inbound is an airplane stuffed with broadcast gear at my insistence, its crew risking their necks to satisfy my desire to succeed.* Jack reversed his initial thinking and decided that Mil would not have approved of the flight. And now with the weather deteriorating, his biggest concern was that even if he wanted to, he had no way to call it off.

As he drove, Jack felt strangely disconnected from reality and began to question his motives for expending so much energy into what felt like repetitive mundane routines. Negative thoughts quickly spewed their venom. *Jack, you fool! Why are you heading to meet a plane that shouldn't be flying in the first place? Your stubborn ambitions are putting lives at risk.*

Jack heard Dylan and Matt chattering, but their voices sounded muffled as though his ears were filled with cotton. He wanted to stop the van and run out into the night—anything to escape the devil on his shoulder. But he kept driving, steering the van through muddied tracks, grooved by years of erosion. As they passed by compact rows of birch trees, a jagged bolt of lightning flashed horizontally in the sky above the van, immediately followed by a booming crack of thunder.

Dylan and Matt stopped their kibitzing mid-sentence. The abrupt display caused Jack to cement his grip on the steering wheel. He forced himself to take deep breaths to calm his racing heart. Feeling suddenly devoid of energy and with the urgency of getting to the airfield now even more pressing, his face popped tiny beads of perspiration.

Just then another flash ripped through the clouds, the ensuing thunderclap causing Jack to slam on the brakes. The van slid to a stop, its front bumper narrowly missing a large boulder along the shoulder of the road. Not wearing his seat belt, Matt shot forward and caught himself before bashing into the front console. "Jack!" he yelled while regaining his balance. "Are you okay?"

"Yeah," Jack replied after a moment's pause. "I just need a second to regroup, that's all." He rested his head on the steering wheel. "I hate storms."

Dylan pressed his face to the window and turned to Matt. "Did you see that lightning bolt?" he asked excitedly. "It was straight down and then split off in all directions! There's no way that plane can land in this!"

Jack's temper flared. "Thanks, Dylan, for that positive statement!" he barked. "Just the affirming words I needed to hear right now."

Matt swatted Dylan on the arm. "Dude!"

"Quit doing that, Matt!" ordered Dylan while offering an apology to Jack. "I'm sorry, Mr. Ward . . . ah . . . Jack. I was just making conversation."

Jack sat back in his seat. "It's fine," he gloomily replied. "I just can't handle any more negativity right now. Things are bad enough as it is."

Glancing towards the sky and without saying another word, Jack reefed on the shift lever and slammed the transmission into drive. He stomped on the accelerator and the van jumped forward, kicking up a long trail of mud behind. Neither Dylan nor Matt said another word as they continued towards Spruce Creek's tiny airstrip.

* * *

"Do you honestly think they're all right?" Diane Jackson asked.

Before answering, Tess sipped her favourite beverage, a freshly made cup of iced tea, heavy on the ice. "Those two live to fly, Diane. They're probably on autopilot and are busy gabbing about airplanes!"

Diane chuckled nervously. "That does sound like a viable scenario."

Leisurely stationed at the island in Tess's kitchen, the two women sat on high-back steel chairs with a virtually untouched plate of cheese and crackers between them. Nestled on top of the cupboards, a small nineteen-inch flat-screen television flashed images from a travel magazine show, the volume not loud enough to compete with their conversation.

"I still can't believe they flew in this bad weather," complained Diane.

Tess grabbed the teapot and re-filled Diane's cup. Steam rose into the air and quickly evaporated. "There really isn't much they won't fly in short of a raging hurricane. And besides, that old plane has been through a lot, and it always keeps our guys safe." Dave often complained to his wife about the dilapidated condition of Paul's Cessna, but not wanting to stress her friend any further than she already was, Tess thought it wise to keep that info to herself.

Diane reached for her teacup and looked up at Tess. The hot beverage helped to settle her growing apprehensions. "I should be used to this by now, but lately when Paul flies, I become more and more restless. He's a good pilot and I trust his flying, so I'm not sure why I'm feeling this way."

Through the large kitchen window, Diane and Tess watched as blue jays faced-off over peanuts that Dave had set out on the patio table. As the wind pushed the treats around, it was almost comical the way the birds scrambled to snatch them up, their feet skidding on the wet surface as they briefly set down. Streams of rain rolled down the glass, each one racing the other and collecting in the sill below. Tess swung around in her chair, reached for the remote and began flipping through channels. "They'll be fine," she finally said. "Paul is an excellent pilot and Dave always says he'll watch his back."

Diane shrugged her shoulders. "They do make a good team, but I still need to worry. Besides, isn't that what bush pilots' wives do?"

Tess smiled. "If this delivery had been for anyone other than Jack, I bet the guys would have held off until tomorrow morning."

A sudden wind gust grabbed hold of two bicycles leaning against the outside deck wall. Both fell over with a loud thwack, causing Diane and Tess to jump. Some of Diane's tea spilled in the process. "Oh Tess, I'm so sorry!" she apologized. "My nerves are definitely on edge."

"All good," replied Tess. "Don't worry about it. I'll grab a paper towel to wipe the—" She never finished her sentence.

Launched from the wind's brute force, the plastic patio table lifted, its four slender legs drifting over the edge of the deck and flipping over, instantly scattering the remaining peanuts. Several chairs toppled in the process and the blue jays scurried into nearby trees—their instincts warning them of trouble brewing in the ugly skies above.

For Diane Jackson, her feelings of impending doom were now fully realized, and she hadn't the foggiest idea how to curtail the rancid premonitions flooding her mind: all of them involving her husband.

* * *

Jack Ward spoke with Paul on the phone prior to the Cessna's departure from Owensville, advising him that he'd be waiting at the grass airstrip with a cargo van. Spruce Creek's runway sat a kilometre south of the lodge, built into a cleared parcel of land that allowed for a shallow westerly approach off the lake.

Once the plane arrived, Jack planned to haul the television equipment back to the lodge and offer the flight crew food and a bed if necessary. Broadcast personnel drove into Spruce Creek Friday afternoon, expecting their gear to arrive by van the next morning. But as thunderstorms rolled through the valley during the overnight hours into Saturday morning, everyone's itinerary changed.

Tom and Dylan Sullivan delivered the satellite broadcast truck well ahead of time, arriving at Spruce Creek two nights earlier.

Tom's hope was to do a bit of fishing with his son before weekend crowds arrived, and all the available watercraft were spoken for. Many of the bike race participants trickled in on Thursday evening or during the day on Friday, while others planned for Saturday or Sunday morning in time for the show at 1 p.m.

Thanks to Matt Hawley's influence, several prominent bike manufacturers committed to setting up promotional booths near the finish line, eager to align themselves with anything charitable and soak up a bit of free television exposure in the process.

Puddles and potholes worked together to hinder the van's progress, so it took Jack longer than usual to cover the winding route leading to the airfield. The vehicle finally broke through a thick overhang of trees that created the illusion of a covered bridge. Jack stopped near a small decrepit wooden building, popped the transmission into park and left the engine running. "We're here, boys," he quipped.

Nearby, a few other buildings remained on site, one of them an old stucco storage shed, the other the size of a single-car garage, its exterior finished with siding and a metal roof. Back when the airstrip enjoyed more frequent use and the lodge was in its heyday, the buildings had once been used for equipment storage, housing the machinery and tools needed to maintain the stubbly runway and strip lighting.

Rather than traverse the narrow and often hazardous road leading from Owensville to Spruce Creek, more affluent people chose to fly in, so groundskeepers ensured the runway's surface was packed down and free of foreign objects. In addition, several families of ground squirrels had been disposed of and had their burrows filled in to ensure safer take-offs and landings.

Rarely used anymore and certainly not without forewarning of incoming flights, Jack occasionally inspected the landing area and the 400 feet of white runway lights installed along both sides, the lines running from the shoreline forward. Powered by a gasoline generator, the old bulbs were overdue for a swap-out, several dozen of which had either broken off or were not working at all.

"It's coming down in buckets now," said Jack. "So, I'm taking you boys up on your offer to help. I hope you don't mind getting wet."

Jack wished he could stay in the vehicle and let the young guns do the work. Unfortunately, his helpers had no idea how to fire up the generator inside the shed, and Jack knew there was no time to explain the procedure.

Despite the overall haggard condition of the largest building, Matt was surprised to see a light on through the small front window, its pale glow creating an eerie sense of warmth and offering a stark contrast to the chill of the evening. All three men exited the van and scurried to the front door, trying to escape the cloudburst.

"Knew I should have grabbed my cap," complained Jack.

"What's in here, anyway?" asked Matt, shielding his face from the rain. "And considering the power outage, what's with the light inside?"

"The generator's in here," Jack replied curtly. "There's a solar panel on the roof that powers the light twenty-four seven." Jack wasn't in the mood for idle chit-chat or any more questions. "Anything else you need answered?"

Dylan noticed a keyless entry system mounted into the door, which also seemed out of place given the structure's ramshackle appearance. He looked at Matt but said nothing. Jack keyed in the security code and the locking mechanism released. The men wasted little time ducking inside.

Rain thrashed the aluminum-clad roof and found its way through several open rivet holes on its surface. Fed by tiny streams of water, small puddles collected on the floor which Jack side-stepped around. Covered in a thin layer of dust and cobwebs, a generator occupied the only dry space on the cracked concrete floor. A few weeds had found their way through the foundation and were undeniably thriving, some as high as a foot.

"There she is, boys," pointed Jack. "And apparently none the worse for wear!"

Mounted into a metal-wheeled frame, the eleven-horsepower gas generator could be repositioned as required, but for now, its roosting place near the door was dry and free of weeds. Brandishing a 5,500 watt power plant, the beast was more than adequate for the task at hand, but to Jack, bigger was always better. He checked to make sure its muffler was properly vented outside through a hole in the wall, and with his stomach flipping somersaults, all he cared about now was powering up the lights for the plane he prayed was still coming.

* * *

Tess found the channel she had searched for and turned up the volume. On the screen, CFCB meteorologist Frederick Nguyen's upper torso was perfectly keyed over a mishmash of computer-generated numbers, trough lines, and coloured precipitation symbols. He spoke with self-inflating authority and just a hint of empathy, his tone almost apologetic as he delivered the dismal forecast: "Owensville can expect winds to pick up before midnight, with gusts between fifty and seventy kilometres per hour . . . "

Tess adjusted the volume. "Tell us something we don't know," she huffed.

"Rain will continue through the evening and overnight hours with amounts of fifteen to twenty millimetres expected. Our exclusive Doppler radar shows a band of thundershowers tracking in from the Bayshore Lake area and, with that, heavier localized precipitation through the district of Spruce Creek."

Frustrated, Diane slapped the countertop and a few crackers fell off the plate. "Oh, isn't that just a stellar forecast!" she snapped. "Just what our guys need, and they're flying straight into the belly of that mess." Diane scrounged in her purse, ripped out her cellphone and began punching in numbers from memory.

Tess lowered the volume on the television. "Who are you calling? If you don't mind me asking."

Diane stopped taping her phone. "I want them safely back on the ground, Tessa. Call it woman's intuition, but I don't feel right about any of this. Paul should never have flown tonight, and now with this awful weather, I'm even more worried." Diane inhaled deeply. "You know me Tess, always the optimist. But this time I . . . oh, Tess, I'm sorry . . . you asked me who I was calling, and I completely brushed off your question."

"All good," replied Tess. "No need to explain. It's not my business anyway and I—"

"Kim," interrupted Diane. "I need to get hold of Kim. And this whole thing is totally your business, Tess. Dave's up there too." Diane began to redial. "I know she has Jack's direct number at the lodge, and I need to speak with him. Maybe somehow it'll help calm my nerves."

Tess reached for a cupboard drawer. "Maybe. But right now, what we need is dark chocolate. I'm thinking a few squares at the least, or perhaps the entire bar!"

Diane smiled weakly and held the phone to her ear. "Okay, doctor, whatever you say."

* * *

At eighteen years of age, Kim Jackson grew up surrounded by airplanes. Flying shotgun with her dad before she could walk, Kim hoped to one day acquire her pilot's licence, a pursuit destined to fill her mother with more than a few anxious moments. For now, Paul and Diane's only child recently began her last year of high school and planned to attend college for an educational degree to complement her inherent gift of working with special needs children.

A virtual duplicate of her mother, Kim stood five feet three inches, a touch shorter than her mom, but every bit as feisty. Wavy shoulder-length blonde hair accentuated a slim, well-proportioned figure, prompting her dad to coin the expression "Boys are evil," a phrase he often expressed loudly in her presence. Kim attracted friends easily, her bubbly personality and inborn charm wreaking havoc with clusters of the male populous. "They're like sharks on the hunt!" her dad would complain, much to Kim's red-faced chagrin.

One day when Kim returned home from school, she noticed a large sign in the front window of her house. In bold red letters, the poster-sized billboard read, THIS HOUSE GUARDED BY SHOTGUN 3 NIGHTS PER WEEK. YOU GUESS WHICH THREE! Paul thought it a uniquely funny way to scare off potential suitors. Kim, on the other hand, failed to share her father's warped sense of humour, and the poster swiftly came down.

When Jack and Mildred Ward first acquired Spruce Creek Lodge, Jack hired Paul's charter service to fly in supplies and a carpenter for finishing work on several of the newly renovated suites. Paul loved to bring Kim along on these flights. She, like her dad, possessed a natural predisposition for flying. They logged many chatty hours together, which helped solidify a deeply rooted, father-daughter connection: one that Paul always cherished.

Over time, Kim also drew close to Jack and Mildred. They considered her family and she, in turn, happily and unofficially adopted them as aunt and uncle. After Mildred's passing, Jack gave Kim his private phone number, which connected to a non-business-related line in his office. He encouraged Kim to call him anytime if she needed future boy advice or just a word of comfort or encouragement.

* * *

Knowing that Kim would have just finished her job providing in-home evening respite care, Diane waited impatiently for her to pick up the phone. She counted six ring tones before the call transferred to voicemail. *"Hey, this is Kim, leave a message."* Frustrated, Diane jabbed the END button without leaving a voicemail.

"No response, I'm guessing?" asked Tess.

"Nope," Diane replied. "What's the point of these kids having cell phones if they never pick up. She's probably busy texting, which lord knows is far more important than a phone call from her mother."

"You could always check online for Jack's number. Or call the lodge and have them put you through to Jack's office. Tell them it's urgent."

"That would be the easiest solution," agreed Diane. "Guess I'm fixated on calling Jack directly and having him pick up right away. Truth is I think I just need to hear Kim's voice." Diane looked at her watch. "Jack's probably not in his office anyway, and speaking to him won't do anything to guarantee Paul and Dave's safety." Draining the last of her tea, she looked at Tess. "Who knows what sort of issues Jack's dealing with right now, especially if things are as bad as the weatherman says. I should probably leave him alone." Diane massaged her neck and reprimanded herself for not having better control of her emotions. "I'm sorry, Tess. I'm acting as though it was me in that stupid airplane. I'm being selfish."

Tess wasn't sure what else to say, so she replied with a simple "No worries, I get it. This is a tough scenario to deal with."

But Diane wasn't so sure her friend really understood. "There was something in Paul's eyes before he left for the airport," she recalled. "Like he needed to tell me something but couldn't. I wanted to ask, but he's proud and—"

Tess noticed the colour drain from Diane's face. "Hey, no crying at my table!" she ordered to offset growing tension in the room.

"I'm scared, Tess," admitted Diane. "I tried to talk him out of this flight, but he's stubborn and proud. I'm to the point that I want him to quit the business and find some other way to make money—not to quit flying but just to pack in the charter end of things. It never used to bother me, but now it's becoming more difficult for Kim and me when he flies through the mountains."

Tess rose from her chair, wrapped her long arms around her friend and squeezed. At that moment, a simultaneous flash of lightning and ear-splitting thunder echoed across the neighbourhood. Diane recoiled and Tess hugged a bit tighter. "Hang in there, kiddo," she offered encouragingly. "They'll be on the ground in no time, you'll see."

Tess let go and grabbed the kettle, her own stomach feeling squeamish. "I'll boil some more water. Maybe another cup of tea will do you some good."

Diane's face contorted. "We both know, Tess, there are two ways to land an airplane: controlled and uncontrolled. Right now, its door number two that freaks me out the most."

* * *

With Dylan and Matt wedged in behind him, Jack added fresh gas to the tank, switched on the generator's fuel valve and set the choke by pulling the knob all the way out. Because the machine was electric start, all he technically needed to do was flip the control switch as long as its battery still held enough of a charge. *Please God,* thought Jack.

Though his accomplices had little room to step aside, Jack still felt the need to bark a command. "Stand back, lads," he ordered. Dylan and Matt adjusted their feet as best they could without really moving. "As soon as this thing is up and running, there's a side lever on that panel behind Dylan's head. When I say so, I need one of you to yank it up. Got it?"

Jack rotated the start button and the machine sputtered but wouldn't catch. Straightaway furious, he disengaged the starter and kicked the side of the generator in frustration. "C'mon you blasted thing, don't fail me now!"

Trying once more with no luck, Jack worried that the battery had lost too much of its charge on the first couple of attempts. But on his third desperate try, the generator mercifully coughed to life, quickly filling the cramped quarters with an eardrum piercing roar. Jack elbowed his way past Dylan and Matt, poked his head out the door, and gazed towards the airfield. He knew the runway lights were out there, hundreds of tiny bulbs awaiting the necessary current to reveal their place in the grass.

"All right!" yelled Jack, his heart pounding with anticipation. "Throw the switch!"

Dylan reached up to the panel, grabbed the lever and drove it upwards. Unsure of what to expect, he and Matt both leaned out the doorway and turned their heads in the direction Jack was looking. Rain pelted their faces as the men stared into the twilight and waited for the airstrip to materialize.

With the generator howling behind them, Jack expected the lights to appear within seconds of the circuit being closed. He waited ten agonizing seconds, and when nothing happened, he decided the lever might need a reset. "One more time, Dylan!" grunted Jack without taking his eyes off the field. "Try it again, only this time slam it to the stop! It's sticky sometimes."

In one fluid motion, Dylan snapped the side lever back down and strong-armed it so hard that he thought for a moment he broke it.

"How long does it usually take for the lights to come on, Jack?" yelled Matt.

Ignoring the question, Jack's mind raced as his brain frantically tried to understand why the field in front of him remained dark. He inwardly scolded himself for not inspecting the lights earlier, and for presuming the system would work after sitting idle for several weeks.

This time it was Dylan shouting over the roar of the generator. "Should we be seeing something by now, Mr. Ward?" he asked.

Matt threw Dylan an icy stare, a reminder that he messed up Jack's name again. But that didn't matter to Jack, not this time. He neither looked at Dylan nor bothered to respond. With now heavier rain and fleeting daylight, Jack concluded that without the runway lights, any chance of the plane landing safely was next to impossible. With an awful feeling of dread in his gut, a chill ran the full length of Jack's body as panic grabbed hold.

Matt was about to ask Jack another question, but he never got the chance.

With no warning, Jack raced into the field towards his defunct lighting. With surprised looks on their faces, Dylan and Matt watched from the doorway stunned. Seemingly oblivious to the cat-and-dog weather, Jack halted his sprint fifty paces from the shed and stood motionless. He spun around, shrugged his shoulders in noticeable confusion, and then pointed up.

Turning their heads towards the top of a nearby pole and then to the field, Dylan and Matt watched as shafts of white light glided over the grass. It took Matt but a second to understand Jack's quandary. He turned to Dylan. "The beacon is on, but the runway lights aren't. Both are powered from this generator through the switch, and Jack can't figure out what's wrong!"

A large windsock, there to offer pilots a visual indicator of wind speed and direction, extended almost completely horizontal underneath the beacon. Jack promptly dropped to his knees; his head aimed towards what should have been a nicely lit airstrip. Instead, the grass remained void of the lighting needed to bring a small airplane to rest and his dream to fruition.

* * *

As he manoeuvred his airplane through the snug mountain pass, Paul Jackson thought of his wife. During their twenty-six years of marriage, she had always encouraged full disclosure between them. "Except at Christmas and my birthday," she would joke. For Diane, complete honesty included a healthy balance of friendship, support, mutual respect and good old-fashioned romance. Paul could hear her voice in his head: "Besides our faith, honesty between us is the glue that will hold things together when problems arise."

Paul's stomach knotted up. He rolled his head side to side to stretch his stiffening neck. He had meant to tell her but needed time to weigh his options as he often did when neck-deep in manure. Paul thought about his recent doctor's appointment. Had he been honest with himself and truthful with his wife from the start, this present situation could have been avoided.

Paul knew Diane had picked up on his sudden close-mouthed nature, and to this point, he felt extremely grateful she had not confronted his odd behaviour. But in his current frame of mind, he also realized that the cockpit wasn't a place where he should be right now—that for the first time in his flying career he had failed his flight medical, and on all accounts, should not be flying at all.

Chapter 4

Diane's cell phone suddenly chirped, and a picture of Kim appeared on the display. Diane scooped it up and tapped connect. "Kimmy!" she answered bluntly. "I was just trying to call you! How come you never answer your phone? Are you okay because I—"

"I'm fine, Mom!" interrupted Kim. "I couldn't pick up because I was—"

"Do you need a ride?" Diane cut in again. "I'm over at Tess's, so I could—"

"Mom, stop and listen!" pleaded Kim. "I'm home now. Everything's fine."

From the tone of her daughter's voice, Diane sensed the exact opposite. "It doesn't sound like you're fine. What's the matter?"

"Nothing with me," replied Kim. "Uncle Jack called for you, that's all. I missed it and just listened to his message. He was out of breath and wants you to phone him—"

Diane's mind raced. "Jack called?" she asked. "I was hoping to speak with him but didn't have his direct number. That's why I was trying to call you. But then I assumed Jack would be at the airfield by now and wouldn't be able to talk anyway. Did he mention what he wanted?"

Kim's awkward silence told Diane her daughter was growing impatient. "He was at the airfield, Mom, but said there's a problem. Something about the runway lighting, but I don't know for sure."

With that news, Diane struggled to find her voice.

"Mom, are you still there?" Kim asked.

"Yes, dear," Diane finally replied. "I'm here. You said there's a lighting problem? What kind of problem?"

Kim inhaled deeply. "Uncle Jack said he just came from the airfield and was trying to get the runway lights to work, but they won't turn on. He wants Dad to turn around and hoped you could help. That's all I know, Mom."

Another flash of lightning tore through the kitchen, which Diane courageously ignored. Tess jumped and nearly spilled her iced tea when the ensuing thunderclap vibrated the walls.

"What about the charity event tomorrow?" Diane asked. "Without the camera equipment in your dad's plane, they won't be able to broadcast—"

Kim interrupted a third time. "I don't know anything about that, Mom. Please, just listen! All I know is Uncle Jack asked if you could get hold of Dad. He said something too about the airport, that maybe someone in the control tower could tell him to come back."

Flush with anger, Diane wanted to blast her husband for leaving her in this predicament, but for now, she needed to collect herself and focus on one issue at a time. Kim's voice brought Diane back to the moment at hand. "And Uncle Jack said the wind and rain have gotten bad. He sounded really upset."

"Okay, thanks, dear," replied Diane calmly. "Just sit tight. I'll call you back if I hear anything about Dad."

"Will he be all right, Mom?" asked Kim, her voice noticeably shaky.

Diane tried to sound reassuring. "Don't worry, sweetie, I'll do my best to get them turned around. Your dad's a tough cookie. He'll be fine."

"When you call again, Mom, I promise I'll pick up," added Kim. "Love you."

Then, the line went dead.

Diane gawked at her phone and then at Tess. "Well, the good news keeps getting better and better," she announced bitterly.

Tess noticed Diane's trembling hands. "Talk to me," she urged. "What's the problem now?"

"For starters," explained Diane. "The runway lights at the lodge aren't working, and the weather's deteriorating." Diane brushed aside a strand of hair that flopped into her eyes. "So, unless the guys arrive before dark, they apparently won't be able to land. Jack wants them to turn around and thinks for some reason I can arrange that."

Tess scrunched her face. "And how are you supposed to do that?" she asked. "They're out of cell range, so unless you have a magic wand or call the airport and—"

"Way ahead of you, girlfriend." Diane scrolled through the browser on her phone. "I need a number for airport administration to try to get someone in the tower . . . if that's even possible."

"I'll help however I can," encouraged Tess.

"I know you will Tess. I'm not even sure how to help myself right now."

Several numbers were listed in the directory for Owensville Municipal Airport. Diane scrolled down the list and finally located the general information line. She waited for the call to connect, but it went straight to an automated reply. "Strike one," she cringed.

Childishly crossing two fingers on her other hand, Diane tried the flight-services number, the fourth down on the list. This time she hoped the call would be answered by a human being instead of a stupid machine. Dampening her mood even further was the lousy weather brewing outside Tess's kitchen window—its unpredictability fueling an already overactive imagination.

* * *

The curvy Moose River narrowed considerably as the small aircraft ventured closer towards Spruce Creek. As the clouds thickened,

Paul had little choice but to descend even lower beneath the water-filled blobs. The river, now only 300 feet under the airplane, raced along as its frothy current tore away anything not rooted or firmly anchored down. Winds continued to buffet the Cessna as though purposely trying to push Paul and Dave from the sky. Along both sides of the river, lower mountain slopes appeared as hazy silhouettes, their scraggy bases still reflecting enough daylight to safely avoid flying into them.

Paul attempted to squash his jitters with idle conversation. "Jack better have those lights fired up by the time we get there," he mentioned nervously. "In hindsight, I should have charged him triple for this run."

"You got that right!" agreed Dave with zero hesitation. "And you should have paid me double for being dimwitted enough to agree to this trip. As it is, we already abandoned our safety protocols for the sake of expediency."

You have no idea, thought Paul. "Well, as the saying goes," he added glumly. "Time is money. Sometimes we have to break the rules to earn the moolah."

"We didn't break the rules," reminded Dave. "We offed the rules. We didn't even bring a bottle of water for crying out loud!"

"We'll be fine, Dave," assured Paul. "You worry too much."

"Yes, I'm worrying," reported Dave cynically. "And with you flying and these damn clouds boxing us in, I'm extra, extra worried!"

"As always, you're a beacon of optimism," smirked Paul.

"Just keeping you humble," admitted Dave while monitoring the GPS mounted to the cockpit's instrument panel. The unit showed a top-down view with the airplane registering as a small white aircraft symbol. Blue was water, green the terrain. Dave tapped the minus symbol on the screen until it showed a large pool of water farther west. "Good news, Ace," he mentioned cheerfully. "I see Bayshore Lake. So as long as you don't fly us into a mountain, we'll be over open water before you know it. Though I'd feel safer if we could magically switch from wheels to floats."

"Like I said," badgered Paul. "You worry too much."

Inwardly, Paul Jackson was doing just that. If the weather did, in fact, deteriorate to the point of IMC, or instrument meteorological conditions, he would rely on the instruments and GPS to maintain their place over the water while avoiding mountain topography. It wasn't fancy or his first choice, but it was an effective way to transit the narrow valley in poor weather.

"It's doubtful we'll be flying back out tonight with the conditions as they are," Paul reasoned. "I think Jack owes us both a steak dinner once we set down."

"That's a fantastic idea!" agreed Dave. "I'll take mine medium rare with a huge baked potato and a tub of sour cream!"

"You know what, Dave? I'll buy you that steak dinner even if Jack doesn't give us a much-deserved freebie."

"Deal!" grinned Dave enthusiastically. "Dinner is the least you can do to ease my blossoming anxiety!"

Paul rolled his eyes. "I think it's time for a new co-pilot."

"Like I said before," heckled Dave. "No one else will fly with you!" Dave changed the subject. "The airstrip should be easy to spot with the beacon on, and once the field lights turn on, it's a walk in the park!"

Working the pedals hard to counter vicious yaw in both directions, Paul dabbed a thin film of sweat from his forehead. His plane felt unusually sluggish, almost as if the continuous barrage of wind and rain deliberately undermined the engine's ability to generate power. "Yeah, let's hope so," he said, nodding absently. "I don't know if it's just me or if there's something out of whack," he fretted. "But something doesn't feel right with the controls."

"I keep telling you, Ace," provoked Dave. "It's your flying! Airplanes know when their stick isn't being finessed by a pilot of upstanding laurels!"

Paul cringed but said nothing. He usually enjoyed melding with his plane, but tonight he wasn't enjoying the ride. Everything felt off, his usual dexterity of balancing roll, pitch and yaw, disconcertingly absent.

Bush flying required improvisation, where rapid-fire changes in weather forced a pilot to be creative if not completely spontaneous. Rarely did backcountry flight afford the luxury of a paved runway with edge lighting. As Paul scanned his instruments and tried to understand what his airplane needed from him, his level of confidence slipped another notch. He squeezed the column harder and hoped that in the fading light, Dave wouldn't notice his shaking hands.

At first, Paul convinced himself that his physician had made a mistake, that his heart was perfectly fine. Arrhythmia had never been a hindrance to maintaining his pilot's licence in the past. This time, however, his electrocardiogram registered several irregular heartbeats, flagging the need for further tests. Devastated when he failed his flight medical, Paul knew that his decision to fly this trip was nothing more than willful defiance, and in the end, very, very wrong.

As rain collided with the fuselage, another bump of heavy turbulence flung the crew upwards against their seat belts and back down, the repetitive cycle adding to Paul's misery. The onslaught caused him to ponder how one tick on a piece of paper could sideline everything he once thought of as important—how one wrong decision could potentially end his beloved career.

Bush flying was not without its challenges, and Paul knew that going in. Yet overcoming such obstacles was the very thing that attracted him to it in the first place. He enjoyed ferrying passengers and cargo to remote locations. For him, it was for him an elixir, a cure-all solution to life's pressing issues. Paul had hoped to fly for another twenty years, but now all that was in serious jeopardy. And not able to climb into an airplane each day was something he simply could not comprehend.

Diane knew of Paul's recent flight medical, and in the past, she had no cause for worry. This time she asked how it went as a way of showing interest. His canned reply was the same as always: "No problems, dear." Paul knew she rarely gave it a second thought, and he preferred it that way.

Another stab of pain hit Paul in the gut, a convicting reminder that not only did he fail his exam, he had also withheld the truth from his wife. The strikes against him were adding up, and so was his need to spill the beans to Dave. The problem was he couldn't bring himself to that point of disclosure, at least not yet. And he wasn't at all certain that Dave would understand.

* * *

Owensville Municipal Airport lay under a solid canopy of cloud, low and fast-moving west to east. The rotating beacon atop the control tower tried it's best to cut through the murky sky but could only penetrate the clouds so far before the beam faded to obscurity. Driving rain pounded the tower, and from his lofty perch, Air Traffic Controller Bruce Macbeth watched with interest as sheets of precipitation washed over the airfield below.

The airport was now under IFR, or instrument flight rules. This meant that any pilot wanting to land or take-off, required the training necessary to fly an airplane using instruments only. With conditions so poor, there was little for Bruce to do except refill his coffee, stare at his blank radar screen, and listen for calls. He expected the arrival of a Beechcraft turboprop shortly, a daily scheduled commuter flight. But aside from that, the only active traffic had been the departing Cessna 185, a flight that in his professional opinion should never have left the ground.

But knowing the crew as he did and the fearless mindset of bush pilots, Bruce decided to each their own. When his shift ended, his plan was to swing by the house and pick Marilyn up for dinner. Their twenty-second wedding anniversary was already overdue for celebration, and he needed to set things right or at least try.

Sipping a fresh coffee in his coveted de Havilland Beaver floatplane mug, a gift from a close friend and flight-simulator enthusiast, the image of the Cessna lifting from the tarmac was still fresh in his mind. He suspected they'd be compelled to hug the river all the way to Spruce Creek, and with the weather imploding at break-neck speed, he felt grateful that it wasn't his bottom strapped into Paul's airplane. Bruce wrapped both hands around his cup to warm his chilled fingers. *You can have it, buddy,* he decided.

Under normal flight parameters, Bruce would monitor on radar the progress of aircraft through each plane's transponder and a four-digit code issued to the pilot from ATC. Once entered, the transponder would send data from the aircraft to the tower, allowing him to see the aircraft's position and speed. But with the Cessna's ground-hugging low-altitude flight, the transponder proved useless and the radar screen remained blank.

Bruce always felt a deeply ingrained personal responsibility for the well-being of every plane, passenger and crew member under his control. On occasion, he flew in Paul's Cessna to better familiarize himself with checklists, procedures and the overall mindset of pilots. This he discovered worked both ways because aircrew seemed to appreciate knowing the person barking orders at them through their headsets, had also spent time in a cockpit.

Tonight, Bruce enjoyed the solitude of not having much to do. The interior lights were dimmed down, and for the first time in months, he allowed himself the luxury of propping his feet up on the radar console. Bruce tucked in a corner of his red Oakley polo shirt and adjusted the hem of his revered pair of slim-fit blue jeans. Once comfortable, his thoughts wandered back twelve years to when he plodded as an electrician. Though lucrative, the long hours and monotony of installing, repairing and maintaining electrical systems had become nothing more than a means by which to pay bills and feed his family.

In the recesses of his mind, Bruce had always been fascinated by people who spent their days controlling air space. Such a career for himself he never thought possible, until one day when push came to shove, he applied for and was surprisingly accepted for ATC schooling after passing an exam and interview. Sixteen months later, Bruce officially traded his electrician's belt for a headset, and eagerly accepted his first posting at Owensville Municipal Airport as a tower controller. Since then, he had rarely looked back.

Bruce scanned his console before focusing his eyes outside. Several lightweight sport aircraft were tied down at the ramp, their wings rocking in step with howling winds. Feeling sluggish, he extended his arms high over his head and stretched. It was then the phone next to the radar console began to ring, readily terminating his relaxed mood.

Staring at the device as though its shrill tone originated from a distant world, Bruce cleared his throat and answered with as much enthusiasm as he could muster. "ATC, Bruce Macbeth here."

"Bruce, its Diane Jackson, have you got a moment?"

Not overly surprised to hear the urgency in her voice, Bruce sat upright in his chair. "Oh, hey Diane," he replied. "How are you fairing on this stormy evening?" Bruce immediately regretted mentioning the weather.

"I'm sorry to call you at work, Bruce. I know you're busy. I called Marilyn and she said you were working tonight. She was kind enough to give me your direct number. So, if you have a moment, I need to ask you something?"

"Your timing is actually perfect, Diane," explained Bruce. "It's pretty quiet up here because of the conditions outside. Nobody's flying." *Except your crazy husband.*

Diane got right to the point. "Jack Ward up at Spruce Creek called. He said he couldn't get the lights powered up at the landing site and is worried about Paul trying to land."

Perplexed, Bruce scratched his head. "That's not good news, Diane, though without sounding insensitive, I'm not sure why you're telling me this—"

Diane interrupted out of sheer frustration. "The weather's taken a turn for the worst up there, Bruce. Power at the lodge is out and the road's closed. Needless to say, it's turning into a big headache for everyone, and Paul's heading straight into it. I need your help."

Bruce shook his head as he stared at his radar screen. "Sorry, Diane, but I'm still unclear about what it is that you want me to do."

Diane's voice raised a notch in pitch. "Jack wondered if there's any way to contact Paul and get him turned around. He thinks it's too dangerous for them to land without lighting unless they show up before it's too dark."

"I agree that would be very challenging," Bruce stated sympathetically.

The line went quiet and Bruce wondered if the connection had terminated.

Finally, Diane spoke. "Is there any way to contact Paul and let him know about the situation at the lodge and get him turned around?"

Bruce answered reluctantly. "It's ironic you called because I was just thinking about Paul and their departure. Just so you know, I tried to talk them out of it, Diane, but he was very insistent. In answer to your question, they're flying too low for any sort of radio communications, so I can't get hold of them."

Diane sighed audibly. "That's what I figured."

Bruce swallowed and continued. "I can't track them on radar either, and until they arrive at Spruce Creek or turn around on their own accord, there is nothing I can do from here. I'm truly sorry."

Diane quietly replied. "Okay, Bruce, thanks anyway for your time."

"Listen, Diane," added Bruce. "Once they discover there aren't any runway lights, I'm sure they'll head back if they can't land. What else can they do?"

"I hope you're right, Bruce," replied Diane. "I know my husband likes to challenge the odds sometimes. Please let me know if you hear from them. I think you have my cell number."

"Absolutely," Bruce affirmed. "He's a good pilot. Try not to worry."

"Too late for that," Diane remarked. "It's just that …" Bruce waited patiently through an uncomfortably long pause. "Paul was acting very unusual before he left," added Diane. "Like he was distracted or hiding something. I should have asked him if he was okay, but I didn't. Poor choice on my part, I guess."

Bruce wasn't sure how to respond to that admission. "Maybe he was just nervous about the flight. I'm sure he'll figure things out and take appropriate action to ensure their safety."

Diane wasn't as convinced. "I'll let you go, Bruce. Thanks."

Bruce was about to say goodbye, but the line was already dead. He hung up the phone and turned his attention to the western sky. Flashes of lightning lit up the distant hills long enough to expose a dense mass of clouds hovering on top. He picked up his coffee mug, stared at it briefly and set it back down. He reached for the phone and began to dial his home number. "Marilyn's going to kill me for this," he murmured out loud.

* * *

Unsure of what tormented his digestive system, Tom Sullivan finally sat up after sharing equal time with a bed and bathroom, and now that his stomach had fully purged itself of food, he felt better. The wood-burning fireplace in his room had died out to a few glowing embers, and the temperature was anything but cozy. He got up and chucked two pine logs into the fireplace along with strips of newspaper. One minute later the dry timber caught, and the resulting heat breathed new life into his chilled bones.

Tom wandered towards the doorway. He threw on his coat and moseyed out in search of Jack Ward. As his feet carried him through the corridors, he listened as rain impacted the roof, which he thought sounded like the roar of a waterfall. Tom felt strangely alone. The darkened halls were creepy enough, and his distorted shadow on the floor and walls from the emergency lighting caused an icy shiver down his spine.

Approaching the lobby, Tom finally heard muted chatter and felt an immediate sense of relief. He picked up the pace and discovered throngs of people milling around the central lobby fireplace. The scene reminded him of a company dinner party he once attended with clusters of people engaged in what he had considered entirely meaningless conversations.

Folding tables sat end to end, their tops adorned with floral tablecloths, sandwiches and pastries of all sorts. And from all appearances, the goodies were being snatched up faster than kitchen staff replenished their supply.

Tom's stomach growled, a reminder that he had not eaten for several hours since becoming ill. Glancing around the room, he spotted Jack Ward standing off to the side, chin-wagging into an old-style rotary-dial wall phone. Tom headed for the food, grabbed a paper plate and helped himself to several small triangular meat and cheese sandwiches, and a bottle of water. He could only hope that his stomach would mercifully accept the food.

Not wanting to bother Jack until his phone call ended, Tom spun towards the window. Lightning flashed through the tinted glass, followed seconds later by cracks of thunder, the force vibrating the panes like a toe-kick slapping into a base drum. Disappointed with the weather, he watched the rain as it plowed into the windows and rushed away. "What a lousy weekend for an outdoor television broadcast," he grumbled.

Jack found Tom in the crowd and held up two fingers indicating that he would still be a few more minutes. Despite the distance across the foyer, Tom saw that Jack's face was pale, and he could only speculate that things were not going well with whoever was on the other end of the line.

Tom walked back towards the fireplace, its heat and light providing a stark contrast to the foul weather outside and lack of power inside. The calming sensation offered a misleading sense of peacefulness amid the myriad of difficulties. As he nibbled a mustard-filled ham sandwich, Tom watched as Jack pitched the receiver into its cradle, then sauntered over. He did not look happy.

"Jack," smiled Tom casually. "You look like you've seen better days."

"I could say the same about you," Jack replied sourly. "How are you feeling? Dylan said you were sick?"

"Better now, thanks," acknowledged Tom. "But not a hundred percent yet. Food should help, though admittedly you look worse than I do."

Jack smiled weakly. "Well then, I'd say we make a fine pair in our own troubled ways, though my clothes are certainly wetter than yours."

Tom shoved the last bite into his mouth. "I'm guessing that everything is not going entirely to plan. Did the plane make it in?"

Jack plopped himself on an old wooden stool near the fireplace. "That would be the understatement of the year," he huffed as he lowered his voice. "And no, the plane isn't here, and it won't be."

"Why is that?" asked Tom quizzically.

"Simple," frowned Jack. "I just got back with Dylan and Matt, and I can't get the runway lights on. I'd try again if there was time, but I think I've single-handedly screwed things up for everybody, Tom."

Tom became serious. "I thought you were going to check the lights the other day to make sure they were working?"

Jack bypassed the comment. "There's no way the plane can land. The weather's closed in and now it's getting too dark. They don't stand a chance without the strip lighting, and since I—"

"Take it easy, Jack!" snapped Tom, as though scolding a child.

Jack stared at Tom open-mouthed like he'd just been backhanded.

"I can tell you're upset, Jack," Tom noted. "But you need to calm down so you can think. When's the last time you had the lights working?"

"Uhm, I, I'm not sure," replied Jack. "A month ago, perhaps. I just assumed they'd work. They always have in the past."

"And you've checked all the connections?" asked Tom.

"Of course," snapped Jack. "It's no use anyway."

Out of the corner of his eye, Tom noticed his son and Matt Hawley walking into the lobby. He waved to catch their attention before continuing with Jack. "You mentioned that you wanted to head back out to the field? Why don't I help you troubleshoot? It's probably something simple that you overlooked."

"I already said it's too late," fumed Jack.

Irritated with Jack's pessimism, Tom tried to keep his own anger in check. "It's not too late, Jack! We should at least try."

"You don't understand, Tom," added Jack despairingly.

Dylan and Matt wandered over and stood beside Tom, the two men giving the impression they had also showered with their clothes on. Tom acknowledged them before gripping Jack's arm. "Think about the guys in that plane, Jack, and the lousy time they're having up there on a night like this. You booked this flight, so we need to do everything in our power to help them land." Tom looked at his watch. "The clock's ticking, and if it doesn't work out, then nobody can say we didn't try."

Jack's blank stare appeared far-off like his body and mind were detached. "I know all that!" he finally squawked. "I did try already, or weren't you listening? The plane has to turn back."

"What are you rambling on about?" asked Tom, now completely bewildered.

"Paul and Dave," explained Jack. "I was just on the phone with Paul's wife when you walked in." Jack rubbed his eyes wearily. "And that call was anything but pleasant."

"What did she want?" asked Tom.

"At my request, she spoke to an air-traffic person at the airport," explained Jack. "Apparently there's no way to contact the plane. And if they can't land here or get back to the airport because of the weather"—he stared at Tom—"where are they going to land?"

Tom, Dylan and Matt all exchanged glances, but nobody tackled Jack's legitimate question.

"That's what I thought," grimaced Jack. "You boys don't know either. I had hoped that someone could get them turned around before it was too late." Jack stared at the floor. "Diane's upset, and rightly so. And though she never came right out with it, I know she's angry about my screw up with the lights." Jack sensed people watching him, but he didn't care. "All this planning and preparation, the sponsor involvement and all these good people here, now all for nothing."

Jack accepted the fact that he held no control over the weather but still felt as though Mother Nature had dealt him a poor hand of cards at the worst possible time. He slouched further, his body and soul ready to fold up for the evening. *I don't deserve this Mil*, he thought. *We don't deserve this.*

* * *

Dave saw that his friend was struggling. "Listen, Paul, why don't you chill for a few minutes. I'll fly us through what's left of the river, then you can set this bird down once we hit the lake and find the airstrip."

Knowing that he shouldn't be piloting an airplane, Paul's guilt-tripping thoughts appreciated Dave's offer. And under the circumstances, willfully jeopardizing his safety and that of his co-pilot was absolutely deplorable. That alone was reason enough to let Dave fly.

Paul glanced at Dave. "Okay," he conceded. "Sorry, partner. I don't know what's wrong with me," he lied. "Nerves are a bit frayed tonight. Must be the weather." *Keep lying to yourself, Ace. Brilliant plan.* "Yes, I could use the break if you don't mind."

Dave grabbed hold of the yoke with both hands. "I've got the plane, Ace."

Paul removed his hands from the control column. "You have control," he replied solemnly.

With that done, Paul leaned back in his seat and closed his eyes. His inner barometer was rising—an internal measurement of his inability to cope with his own deceit. His poor choices were beginning to catch up with him, and the gnawing in his stomach proved as much.

As the airplane thumped along towards Spruce Creek, Dave wrestled with the yoke to control roll and pitch but did little to correct the tail from slipping about. Hanging below a sinking cloud deck, the Cessna popped in and out of grey ribbons of moisture. Visual flight conditions were deteriorating, and Dave noticed how the mountains were blending in with the onset of dusk. He widened out the view on the GPS and looked at Paul, whose eyes were still closed. "Not much longer," he mentioned encouragingly. "We're still over the river and looking good."

Paul nodded but did not reply.

Dave performed a quick instrument scan and returned his eyes to the front window. It was then he saw it, a wall of descending cloud, swirling and twisting, its mammoth size spanning the entire width of the valley. He knew visibility would disappear the moment they broke through it. Dave fused his hands to the yoke and barely had enough time to speak the only three words that came to his mind. "Hang on, Ace!"

Paul's eyes shot open as the mass of churning cloud swallowed his Cessna whole, the plane's aluminum carcass devoured by an opaque wall of obscurity.

Chapter 5

Bruce thought about sending his wife a text, but in retrospect, that seemed dangerously impersonal within the context of their anniversary. The phone rang several times before voicemail finally picked up the call. *"You've reached the Macbeth residence, leave us a message."* Bruce waited for the beep.

"Hey, Marilyn, it's me. Can you give me a shout when you get in? A possible . . . situation has come up." He adjusted his inflection. "Sorry, I love you."

Bruce hung up and wondered if Marilyn had taken the kids out for a pizza. He sank back in his chair and peered outside. Thick grey clouds were visible over the foothills as jagged bolts of lightning flashed to the west. He knew his decision to stay in the tower might be overzealous, but with lives potentially at stake, he needed to see what help he could offer.

Marilyn usually understood and accepted the ups and downs of her husband's wonky schedule, but she'd still be disappointed at having to postpone their anniversary dinner. Bruce would make it up to her, as he often did, and Marilyn would hold him accountable, as she always had.

If Paul and Dave made it back to the airport tonight, Bruce would call Diane Jackson as promised. He wanted them safe like everyone else but could not stop his mind from swirling through a myriad of potential outcomes, some of which were not in any way pleasant. He reached again for the phone and

Deliveries

entered a number from memory then waited impatiently as the call connected through.

* * *

Owensville Municipal Airport, though small in stature, was richly diverse. The grounds displayed a vast array of retail and commercial businesses, the gamut ranging from fixed-wing and helicopter charter services to a Cessna flight school, coffee shops and a small, but well-adorned static aviation museum next to the terminal. There were several small-to-medium-sized hangars scattered about, some private and others leasing their floor space to anyone needing a haven to store their private or business aircraft.

With only one runway-oriented east to west, the 5,100 foot length of asphalt suffered from lengthy cracks, its weathered surface displaying ribbons of black patchwork crisscrossing end to end. It was, in all respects, functional and reasonably smooth considering its outward appearance. Scattered puddles of rainwater reflected the runway's edge lighting, creating the illusion of rippling lights across its surface.

Nestled into a small cluster of birch trees at the northwest corner of the airfield, there sat an obscure building about the size of a small bungalow. To all appearances, it seemed out-of-place. Its beige wood-slat siding needed fresh paint and the roof's shingles were curling from years of UV exposure. Facing towards the taxiway, two large rectangular windows adorned the walls on either side of the cherry-red entry door. To a casual observer, the building might have reminded them of an old military barrack dating back to the Second World War.

Alongside that building was a Quonset, its arched semicircular roof running fifty-eight feet end to end. A retracted metal bi-fold door revealed a compact high-wing airplane tucked inside, its lime green fuselage reflecting the ceiling's light fixtures. Running down the sides of the plane were yellow stripes in the shapes of lightning bolts, the kind of decals one might find on a classic hot rod. The design extended from the engine exhaust pipe all the way back to the edge of the horizontal stabilizer. Along both sides of the aircraft just behind its windows, a two-foot diameter reflective decal had temporarily been added to the skin, the design featuring the Owensville Search and Rescue logo, and emblazoned with bright orange lettering.

Small, lightweight and extremely agile, the forty-year-old single-engine Piper PA-18 Super Cub was well-known for its short take-off and landing, or STOL, capabilities. Under the cowling, a robust 150-horsepower Lycoming engine produced a cruise speed of 115 mph. The Cub had room for two with tandem style seating and was ideally suited for low-level search and rescue in the Owensville area. Cheap to run, the machine also offered excellent visibility and ease of handling for the pilot and passenger alike. The Piper's thirty-five-foot wingspan generated lift at a respectable 960 feet per minute, and its young jockey could not have loved it more.

Polishing the airplane was also quick and simple. A bottle of spray wax and a microfibre cloth was all he needed to bring the outer skin to life, and that's exactly what pilot Kevin Davies was joyfully engaged in. He spritzed a small section of the fuselage behind the door, and then gently wiped the liquid away in uniform circular motions. This was the third time in the past two weeks he had detailed the plane, but with time on his hands, the task was in no way menial. Behind him on a small folding table, an old AM/FM battery-operated radio played a soft-rock tune he didn't recognize, but he tried to whistle along anyway.

Above his head, rain pinged off the metal corrugated roof, its trajectory falling away from the entrance, so he didn't have to worry about the torrent of rain finding its way in. Kevin always enjoyed a good thunderstorm, and he couldn't bring himself to lower the hangar door and miss out on another free light show, the second in as many days. And tonight, he wasn't disappointed.

Currently enrolled in flight school, Kevin volunteered several evenings per week at the Search and Rescue base situated at the airport, the branch serving as a small but effective civilian offshoot of the local military. There wasn't much to do in the hangar except mop floors and keep the place tidy, but as long as he was close to anything with wings, particularly the Cub, he was more than content.

Inside the main building, Kevin had already set up folding tables and chairs in preparation for tomorrow morning's seven o'clock training session. He restocked the old vending machine with chips and candy bars, sanitized the bathroom not as carefully as he should, and if the phone rang, dutifully played the role of receptionist. He also served as a groundskeeper, cutting and trimming the weeds and grass around both buildings as required.

Overall, Kevin was happy to pay his dues if it meant logging flight hours and gaining experience as a mountain flier. He already held his private pilot's certificate and night endorsement and was currently receiving instruction for an instrument flight rating. In time, his ultimate goal was the airlines, but in the short-term, he dreamed of piloting the Martin Mars, a massive four-engine water-bomber used for fighting wildfires. So, the more time spent in a cockpit, any cockpit, the better.

As he worked, Kevin ignored the fact his jeans were damp from the crotch down because of a leaky spray nozzle attached to the hose. "Glad it's only water," he chuckled. *Could be embarrassing otherwise!* Setting down the cloth and wax, Kevin brushed his fingers through a mop of thick black hair. At twenty-two years of age, he spent most of his time smiling, watching soccer, and searching for any other way to have fun and secure a laugh at other people's expense.

Born and raised in Owensville, Kevin's parents had identified him a rascal early on because of his antics and propensity for gags. In grade school, he was a regular attendee in the principal's office for pranking teachers and fellow students, and despite ongoing reprimands and notes home to his mother, Kevin was widely loved by his peers. Now, as an adult, he still enjoyed good-natured tomfoolery when such opportunities fortuitously presented themselves.

Kevin peeked at his watch. It was almost time to pack up shop and head for home. He sprayed down the rear elevator with a few squirts of wax and then polished it dry. Admiring his handywork, he stepped back from the plane to see if he had missed any spots. It was then he heard the clang of the outdoor ringer connected to the phone in the main building next door.

Kevin sprinted from the hangar, and by the time he reached the Search and Rescue building, his clothing and hair were thoroughly wet. He tore open the front door and bolted for the desk phone. Out of breath, Kevin brushed aside the rain from his face, sucked in a lung full of air and snatched up the receiver.

* * *

After a dozen rings, Bruce was about to hang up when he heard, "Owensville Search and Rescue. You call, we haul! Kevin speaking."

"Kevin, its Bruce Macbeth in ATC. And for what it's worth, cute catchphrase. I'm guessing that was your idea?"

"Sure was. The old greeting sucked and needed a revamp, so I invented a new slogan. So, you like it?"

"Not too bad, actually. If you ever quit flying, maybe you can venture into some kind of tagline marketing."

"Yeah, maybe," laughed Kevin.

"I knew you liked spending Saturdays over there, and I wasn't sure if you'd still be around this late. So, how are things going?" asked Bruce sincerely.

"Can't complain. I was just shining up the Cub for something to do and was getting ready to go when I heard the phone. Wasn't expecting any calls tonight. What can I do you for?"

Bruce passed over Kevin's question for a moment. "How about the flying lessons? I'm guessing you're going through"—a blinding flash, followed by a slam-bang crack of thunder made Bruce jump—"Wow! This system is right on top of us. Are you okay over there?"

"Yup," answered Kevin. "Other than wetting myself just now, I'm fine! That was sure a loud one! In answer to your question, I'm part of the way into IFR training. It's stressful when I'm under the hood but I think I'm doing pretty well. I haven't had my instructor grab the controls away yet, so that's good!"

Flying under the hood involved the student pilot wearing a large visor that restricted vision to the flight instruments to prevent any visual reference outside the cockpit. It was a major component of IFR tutelage.

It was easy for Bruce to hear the enthusiasm in Kevin's voice. "That's good to hear, Kevin. Say, if you ever need a passenger when you're shooting non-IFR circuits to get your hours up, let me know. I still like getting out of the tower and into the air once in a while."

Another flash as bright as day lit up the inside of the tower. The ensuing thunder shook the building top to bottom.

"Another loud one!" Kevin remarked excitedly. "I hope the Cub's all right. The hangar door is up, so I shouldn't be away for too long."

"That was loud," agreed Bruce. "I won't keep you but a few more seconds. Though you might want to consider calling it a night and head for home."

"I'll leave pretty quick," replied Kevin. "And yes, it's always fun to have company when logging hours. Be happy to have you along anytime."

Bruce knew that his conversation with Kevin was premature, but when lives were possibly at stake, he'd rather leave nothing to chance. If the 185 failed to show up, then no one could fault him for due diligence. He got down to business. "Listen, Kevin," he explained. "I know I'm jumping the gun according to protocol, but I wanted to give you a heads-up that the possibility exists we'll need you folks tomorrow . . . and your Cub. I'd like you to pass along my nervous Nellie instincts to your coordinator."

"Roger that!" replied Kevin excitedly. "So, what's happening if I may ask?"

Bruce leaned back in his chair and glanced out the window. Tree branches twisted and bashed into one another from the storm's offensive. "You may," he cautiously stated. "Airflow Charters has their 185 enroute to Spruce Creek Lodge tonight."

"Tonight? In this weather?"

My sentiment exactly, thought Bruce. "From what I've been told, it doesn't appear they can land up there due to inoperative field lights, but I'm speculating they don't know that yet. Once they figure it out, I'm sure they'll flip around and try to make it back to the airport here. I thought it best to light a fire in case things do in fact go south."

"So, besides me making a phone call, anything else I can do?"

"Not really at this point. Like I said, I wanted to put a bug in Search and Rescue's ear. If the crew does have to set down somewhere because of the weather, there's but a few iffy places along the river that'll take an airplane. I've flown that route, and even under VFR, it seems to me that finding a spot to land would be extremely challenging. The plus is that these guys are experienced mountain fliers, but that doesn't always equate to a get-out-of-jail-free-card."

"Bruce, you sound like my flight instructor. He drills me with those little reality checks all the time. But, okay, sounds good. . . . I mean, the situation doesn't sound good but flying sounds good. I'm all trained up on the Cub and could use the real-world experience."

Bruce let Kevin off the hook. "I know what you mean, Kevin. If we need you, nothing will likely happen until sometime tomorrow once the weather clears out. If anything else comes up,

Deliveries

I'll let you know. Stay close to your cell and let the boss know. I would have called Rob directly but for whatever reason, I can't find his cell number."

"I'll keep my phone turned on," assured Kevin. "I'll let Rob know what's going on as soon as I hang up with you. The Cub is set to go if needed. Even got it shined up and bug-free."

"Thanks, Kevin," replied Bruce. "Nothing would make me happier than to see that plane on final approach tonight. No disrespect to the good work you people do, but I sure hope we don't need your services."

"None taken," Kevin quickly answered with pronounced enthusiasm in his voice.

Bruce's cellphone began to vibrate. He reached into the holster and grabbed his phone, the caller ID displaying his wife's name and picture. "Listen, Kevin, I have a call coming through on my cell. I'll phone you back if anything materializes between now and morning."

"Ten-four. Thanks for the information. Talk to ya later."

Bruce swallowed several times and tried to lubricate his dry throat before he answered his mobile. "Hi, Marilyn," he answered timidly.

"So, despite your 'possible situation,' are you heading home soon?" his wife asked hopefully. "I'm starving!"

Bruce instantaneously felt heat course through his body. "About that. We've got an issue developing here, and I'll be home later than expected. I'm sorry, but we may have to delay our dinner plans."

Bruce waited a moment for Marilyn to say something, but the dead air over the phone line was more than a bit demoralizing.

***

When the Cessna entered the cloud, Dave's eyes instinctively swept from the view outside to his instruments, the transition to IFR flight seamless. With both hands grasping the yoke, he pushed forward slightly to place the aircraft in a shallow descent with the hope of breaking through a hole in the bottom. But knowing there was precious little altitude to play with, he did his best to finesse the plane with gentle control input and trim.

Paul loathed gazing into nothing. No sky, no mountains, no visual reference of any kind. Essentially blind, his racing heart felt as though it might explode from his chest. "Where the devil are we?" he asked with eyes as big as saucers. Paul glanced at the GPS and took comfort knowing they were still positioned over the river.

"Welcome back to the land of the living, Ace," grunted Dave, his voice calm but louder than usual. "I can tell ya we ain't in Kansas, Toto! Don't worry, I'll get us out of this soup, so hang on to your gitchies."

"Altitude!" Paul shrieked as he eyed the altimeter. "Watch the altitude! The river's right under the wheels and—"

"Can it, Paul!" snapped Dave. "I said I've got this!"

Paul went suddenly quiet.

Dave understood Paul's alarm. The river canyon was extremely narrow and mountain slopes loomed unseen beyond both wingtips. Climbing wasn't an option because of dense cloud cover, and descending lower was out of the question. The only choice was to hope the cloud they were flying through quickly ran out of substance.

Concentrating on the artificial horizon, Dave made sure the wings stayed level, right-side-up and over the water. The vertical speed gauge showed the airplane pitched slightly downwards, and despite the incline, he worried that a sudden downdraft could smack them into the river. No wonder Paul was of the same mindset.

Struggling to interpret their flight attitude, Paul's sense of direction was not coinciding with reality. His head started to swim as he tried to make sense of flight instruments and the world around him. And because he closed his eyes before entering the cloud, his nervous system reacted almost immediately when he opened his eyes. His eyes told him one thing, but his brain reported the exact opposite. Paul wasn't sure if the wings were level, or the Cessna's nose pointed up or down, but he was coherent enough to recognize spatial disorientation when he felt it. "Just get us out over the lake, Dave," he moaned. "And away from these invisible mountains!"

Dave caught on that his friend wasn't well. "Aye, captain," he replied.

Paul loosened his shoulder strap and grappled under his seat for the air sickness bag. Through shallow breaths, he tried to quell the rapid onset of nausea as his inner ear wrestled to find its balance.

Dave flew the airplane to match the river's path, trying as much as possible to place gentle bank angles on the wing for Paul's sake. He dutifully monitored their altitude to keep the wheels out of the cold rushing water directly below.

"Hang in there, Paul," offered Dave reassuringly. "We'll be fine. I'm sure we'll break free of this soup in no time."

When Paul didn't answer, Dave turned to see him holding a sick bag, his hands fumbling to find the opening. "That thing's got a bottom and a top, Ace," joked Dave. "Make sure you find the end that opens!"

As Dave checked his engine mixture and power settings, it was obvious that Paul wasn't in the mood for wisecracks. He watched the man lean forward and rest his arms on the top edge of the cockpit's dash with his head tucked between his elbows. A few moments later, Paul started to heave as he fought to open the bag.

* * *

After his phone call with Bruce, Kevin Davies decided not to go home. He felt too wound up to even consider leaving the airport and wasn't thrilled about driving through heavy rain, bone-jarring thunder and blinding flashes of lightning. With junk food in the vending machine and a small cot in the infirmary to crash on, the decision was easy to make.

Kevin could not stop thinking about the Cessna. The very thought of flying a legitimate rescue sent chills down his spine. It's not that he wanted any harm to befall the crew. It was the exact opposite. He wanted them healthy and safe like everyone else, but he wanted to play a significant part in securing a positive outcome and to show his peers that he was more than capable of leading the charge.

Reaching into his left back pocket, Kevin grabbed his cell phone and checked the battery level. *Seventy percent.* He plugged the device into a nearby wall charger and made certain the ringer was on. To the best of his ability, Kevin wanted everything primed and ready: his phone, the Piper Cub, and more importantly, himself.

If called upon, the team would quickly mobilize, and the building would become a hub of activity and planning. Each person would have a job to do, and what thrilled Kevin the most was that his role would be pivotal to the group's success. He tried to curtail his thinking, and in doing so, remembered the hangar door was still open and the Cub needed to be tucked in for the night.

Kevin wandered back outside and hustled his five-foot-ten-inch frame back to the hangar. The fuelled and shined Piper reminded him of his first car, a tan 1999 Audi A4. The first day he drove it home, Kevin washed the sedan and applied three coats of wax to the dreary paint. Despite a multitude of scratches, dents and door dings, the buggy might well have been a Ferrari. It was his ticket to freedom and roads unknown, and Kevin felt that same exuberance for the Cub. The bird was built to fly and just like his Audi, he could hardly wait to climb aboard, turn the key and go.

Kevin shivered as another gust of wind rattled the hangar and caught the fuselage of the plane, rocking it gently. The wind had evidently changed direction as rain blew in through the open hangar door and settled on the engine cowling. Frowning, he walked to the door control panel and jabbed the down arrow button. As the bi-fold inched down, its hinges squealed from lack of grease—the sound similar to nails on a chalkboard. Inside of a minute, the door closed fully, sealing out the elements and calming the nerves of an increasingly jittery young pilot.

Hanging between higher panels of fluorescent lights, dual mercury-vapour ceiling lights created angular shadows under the fuselage, basking the entire airplane in a pale orange-yellow glow. Since deciding to remain at the airport, Kevin thought he'd kill some time by checking over the Cub yet again. He stood at the front of the Piper and ran his fingers along the edges of the propeller, his eyes scanning for any nicks or gouges. Strips of brass covered the leading edges at both ends, running a full twelve inches forward from the tips.

The shiny chrome spinner reflected a distorted image of Kevin's face and body. He leaned in close, made a goofy face and smirked at the warped likeness. Kevin squatted down to inspect the engine intake and then made sure the cotter pins were properly installed in the engine cowling. He checked the Cub top to bottom like so many times before. Kevin climbed aboard and just sat there, luxuriating in the moment and his surroundings. He couldn't help but smile. He was living the dream, his dream. *And how many guys my age can say that?* he pondered.

Scanning the instrument panel, Kevin briefly studied each display: airspeed, attitude and altimeter across the top; oil temperature and pressure, RPM, turn coordinator and the magnetic compass tucked underneath. Just above his knees were a small radio stack and transponder, plus a portable suction-mounted Garmin GPS.

Kevin placed both hands on the stick and jostled the control back and forth, side to side. This activated the horizontal stabilizer at the rear of the plane and the ailerons at opposite ends of the wings. He watched as the control surfaces worked together in perfect sync. Kevin wedged his feet into the pedals and checked the rudder. No impediments. "Perfect," he exclaimed happily. *Ready for engine start!*

Snapping on the master switch, Kevin turned the fuel valve to select the left tank, primed the engine and thumbed the mixture knob to full rich. A quick visual check confirmed carb heat was off. He cracked the throttle an eighth of an inch and set his feet into the toe brakes before retrieving the key from his hip pocket. Kevin inserted it into the ignition and rotated the switch two clicks to the right. Three clicks would have engaged the starter, but he thought better of it inside the closed building. "Time to log some shuteye," Kevin chatted to himself.

Returning everything in the cockpit to normal, Kevin sat motionless, his mind once again drifting to the Cessna 185 and its crew. Eyeing his cellphone on the nearby workbench, he wondered if the device might ring before morning. In truth, he wanted nothing more on earth.

* * *

The torturous few seconds of dead air over the phone felt like an eternity to Bruce Macbeth. He squirmed in his chair and waited for Marilyn to rescue him from the unnerving quiet. Lightning flashed, its vibrancy increasing as the storm passed over the field. The ceiling pot-lights inside the tower flickered momentarily as thunder reverberated through the building. Glancing up at the suspended ceiling, Bruce half expected something to shake loose and bean him on the head.

"Are you there, Marilyn?" Bruce finally asked.

"I'm here," she bluntly replied. "What is it this time?" she asked, her voice tinged with playful sarcasm. "Diane Jackson phoned me a while ago and asked for your direct number, but she never mentioned why. Is your *situation* pertaining to that?"

Bruce slipped into his own version of business mode. "Yes," he replied. "Might be nothing, but I've got Paul's Cessna 185 outbound to Spruce Creek. Diane just called me and said there's a chance they can't land up there and will need to return to the field here."

"I'm sorry, dear, but I don't see the problem. Besides, I thought your shift was about done. Why can't you come home and let somebody else handle this?"

Bruce wasn't sure how to respond. He decided not to candy-coat it. "The weather's tanking, Marilyn, and it's even worse at Spruce Creek. If they can't land at the lodge, then I'm hoping they can make it back here. For now, I'd like to remain on site until I know they're safe. I promised Diane I would call her as soon as I had anything to report."

Bruce heard Marilyn tapping her fingernails on the phone, but her voice remained quiet. She finally released a highly exaggerated sigh, no doubt for his benefit. "Well, if you must, you must. I'm disappointed, but I'll survive. I suppose I'll see if the kids left any pizza for me, which I highly doubt."

Bruce tried to place a positive spin on things. "I'm sure it'll just be for an hour or two. I'll call you as soon as I know what's going on. Maybe, we can still grab a late dinner."

Marilyn knew her husband better than he knew himself. "You know that isn't happening, Bruce. You invest too much of your heart into the planes you control. Go ahead and take care of your flock. You've always played the role of good shepherd when you're in that tower, so why stop now?"

"I'll make it up to you," replied Bruce apologetically. "I promise."

"Oh, you've got that right, buster! Now you owe me dinner, and a down payment on that double-linked curved necklace I've been wanting. You remember you said you'd replace the one I lost at the grocery store?"

Bruce chuckled. "We can talk about that blatant act of bribery later, though I don't recall making any such promise."

"Too late. I've already placed an order for it. I put fifty percent down . . . on your credit card. Thank you very much, dear!"

Bruce was about to deliver a counterargument when the tower lit up as bright as the midday sun, followed simultaneously by a booming crack of thunder. The lights flickered again, dimmed to half intensity, and fizzled out altogether. The control tower's emergency lighting snapped on immediately, basking the inside of the tower in a spooky red glow. Bruce spun in his chair and glanced out the tower windows towards the runway and taxiways. Everything was dark.

"I'm sorry, Marilyn, I'll have to call you—"

In that instant, the tower lights flicked again and came back on. The airport marker lighting along the runway and taxiway flickered to life, then as quickly returned to darkness. Bruce put the phone to his other ear and tried cradling the handset under his chin. As he reached for a pen and nearby logbook, he discovered he was talking into a phone that was no longer connected to his wife.

"Perfect," he blurted. "Just bloody perfect."

Chapter 6

Triggering unpleasant memories, the nausea Paul felt now from being jostled around in zilch visibility could not have come at a worse possible time. He had only been sick in an airplane once before, and that incident had occurred over two decades ago while piloting a cramped, fully loaded Cessna 172 over bright yellow canola fields for inspection and photography . . .

The repetitive circling at low altitude, choppy humid air, and most assuredly a coffee and stale honey-glazed donut one hour before taking off had caused the motion sickness of that flight. He never imagined he could throw up while piloting an airplane himself, so the event was not only hugely embarrassing, it also became a popular topic of conversation for his peers around the office water cooler.

Married at twenty-six, Paul's first job as a commercial pilot was for a local geographical air survey company operating a small squadron of salmon-coloured Cessna aircraft. The company also offered an aerial platform for pipeline inspection, photography or other services relating to the oil and gas industry.

Prior to his employment, Paul often noticed these brightly decorated planes from his car while driving around the city. Intrigued by their low altitude and incredibly steep bank angles, their unusual sight reminded him of a bird of prey stalking its next meal. Curious as to their origin, and not having seen them parked at Owensville Airport, Paul began to ask around.

Like many young and aspiring commercial pilots, Paul's hunt for anyone willing to offer employment to a rookie with minimal logbook hours became an all-encompassing pursuit. Most aviation companies insisted on seasoned pilots, so the prospect of securing a salaried flying gig felt to Paul like a hopeless impossibility.

As good fortune would have it, Paul met someone at the flying club who knew about the Cessna fleet and the rural business that operated them. Soon enough he found himself conversing with the company owner, only to discover that one of their senior pilots had just retired, thereby leaving a left seat open for immediate occupancy. Paul's timing could not have been better, and contrary to his greenhorn pilot status, he was recruited on the spot following a short interview and white-knuckle, but hugely successful check-ride.

Now all Paul could think about on this flight was how badly he wanted out of his airplane. Every dip of the wings escalated his nausea. He sucked in several large gulps of air to try to calm his system down, but nothing seemed to work. Adding to his misery, Paul's thoughts were ripe with indignation, and he wanted nothing more than to be home with his family and a clear conscience.

Opening his eyes, Paul tried to focus on the instrument panel, but the gauges appeared fuzzy and nondescript. He raised his head and peered through the front window. There was little to see but wisps of grey passing over the engine cowling and disappearing into the darkening sky. Rain on the windscreen intensified and just as quickly dissipated, the effect conjuring an image in Paul's mind of God turning on a huge shower head, switching it off and on, and repeating the action over and over.

"You with me, captain?" asked Dave. "You're not looking too well."

Paul rotated his head slowly towards his co-pilot. "That's stating the obvious, but yes, I'm here. Just barely, I think. I could really use a Gravol about now, or a whole box for that matter."

"I'd produce 'em if I had 'em," snickered Dave.

As Paul smiled at his friend, he noticed Dave had somehow unzipped his coveralls down to the waist and extracted both arms from the sleeves. Given the likelihood that Dave's eyes had never left the instruments or his hands from the controls, Paul couldn't understand how he had done it.

"We should be over the lake soon, Ace," added Dave. "I wish I knew where this split-pea soup bottoms out."

Dave double-checked the cowl flaps were closed and swept his eyes across the oil pressure and temperature gauges. Both were in the green. RPMs and manifold pressure were holding steady, and the attitude instrument confirmed the wings were more or less level.

Paul's right hand supported his head, while his left clutched a small white bag, no longer empty. "We, we have to punch through this pretty quick. It can't go on forever," he rasped.

Dave glanced at Paul. "One would certainly think so. And might I say again that you don't look so good."

Paul frowned. "I feel as bad as I look, so thanks for twice pointing that out. You good to keep flying, Dave? I know I'm not much help right now."

"Someone has too," Dave replied. "And you, my friend, are certainly in no shape to fly, let alone set this bird down when the time comes."

"Don't think I'd even try to argue that point," offered Paul weakly. "Just get us on the ground and quicker the better."

"That," assured Dave, "is absolutely my top priority."

* * *

Aside from wind coursing through the trees at Spruce Creek's airstrip, and rain spattering into a bevy of growing puddles, the only other sound emanated from the nearby generator. The beacon rotated inside its globe, its muddy white light sweeping the area at regular intervals. Had the unit been properly maintained, the colour combination would have been white and green, indicating a land-based airport. But the green side of the fixture broke last year when someone threw a rock into it and was now overdue for repair. It was yet another item on Jack Ward's lengthy fix-it list. Spruce Creek's airfield was technically nothing more than a cleared parcel of infrequently used grassland, so repairing the beacon wasn't a top-of-the-list priority.

As it spun, the beacon revealed four figures crouched in the grass, the shaft of light illuminating their place for a moment before returning them to ill-defined silhouettes. Despite Jack's arguments and lack of resolve, Tom convinced him to try to rectify the runway lighting issue while there was still time.

Dylan Sullivan and Matt Hawley again volunteered to come along, the two always happiest when at the forefront of any kind of mayhem. Each man donned a flimsy blue poncho, the cloaks doing little to protect them from the elements. With the clock ticking, Dylan and Matt both held flashlights, the duel beams aimed towards an open junction box buried in the grass.

"Matt," ordered Jack Ward, "run back to the shed and switch the main power off. You know where the lever is. But leave the generator running for now and close the shed door behind you. That racket is driving me crazy."

Matt hustled away without replying.

"The last thing I need is to electrocute myself," Jack huffed. "Although maybe that's what I deserve for this fiasco we're in."

Jack worried if the Cessna showed up in the next few minutes, the flight crew would be greeted by nothing more than an airstrip shrouded in fading shades of grey, assuming they could even find it. It was, in his opinion, simply too dangerous for them to attempt a landing without the runway lighting, especially with low-lying clouds diminishing visibility across the entire surface of the lake.

Around Jack's feet, rivulets of rainwater trickled through the grass, crisscrossing every which way and pooling around the soles of his shoes. Matt returned and redirected his flashlight to the task at hand. Keenly aware they were running out of time, Jack tore into the junction box and peered inside. "Bring those flashlights in closer guys. I can't see what the devil I'm doing."

Dylan and Matt complied.

Jack fumbled with clusters of white and black wiring, and then twisted off several wire nuts connecting the strands. "The problem must be in here somewhere," he growled while inspecting each line. Finding nothing out of the ordinary, Jack tried to wipe away the rain from his face with an already wet sleeve, but this did little to stifle the flow.

"All the current from the generator enters through this box and splits off to the rows of lights," explained Jack. "It's not a complicated setup, so I can't figure out what's wrong. Everything looks fine in here."

Watching over Jack's shoulder, Tom Sullivan stood up and glanced towards the eastern sky, half expecting the Cessna to pop through the low curtain of cloud. He knew they'd hear the engine long before the airplane actually revealed itself to the naked eye. He crouched back down to where Jack was fumbling with the wires, using his body to shield the box from moisture.

"It makes no sense," complained Jack. "The beacon lights' wiring runs through this same box and it works fine when the power is on. So why not the cursed runway lights?"

"Well, Jack," confessed Tom. "I'd be lying if I said I know anything about this setup. It looks like a hornet's nest in there."

"It's really not as bad as it looks," explained Jack. "It's as simple as white to white and black to black. I just don't get it. Everything looks fine. There must be another break farther down the line."

Rain fuelled by strong winds bit into the faces of all four men hunkered in the grass. Soaked for the second time that night and beginning to shiver, Dylan spoke to Matt through chattering teeth. "Imagine trying to bike through this rain?"

Matt looked up. "You'd need some pretty gnarly tires for sure," he replied. "Once the TV broadcast is over tomorrow, we should take our bikes up through the valley a few kilometres. Be muddy but fun!"

Both flashlight beams strayed off the target.

"Hey, guys!" scolded Tom. "Lights, please, if you don't mind!"

Dylan redirected his flashlight towards the wires. "Oops, sorry Dad."

Matt did the same. "My bad."

"Is mountain biking all you two ever yap about?" asked Tom, knowing full well the answer to such a rhetorical question.

The two young men exchanged glances. "What else is there?" they asked through cheeky grins.

Tom shook his head disgustedly. "Unbelievable how the two of you seem entirely oblivious to the situation here, not to mention that if that airplane doesn't land tonight, the show tomorrow won't air. No cameras equal no broadcast."

Matt was about to reply when Jack's voice interrupted their chitchat. "I don't see anything wrong with the connections in here," he declared. "I'm going to have a quick look at—"

Jack's ears suddenly detected the faint but unmistakable sound of a faraway aircraft, a low rumble echoing from somewhere across the lake. He craned his neck towards where he thought the sound was coming from, and it was then the truth clobbered him like a ton of bricks. As suspected, he was going to be too late.

* * *

Diane slammed her car door. "I'm just saying, Tess, that I feel extremely guilty doing this."

"There isn't anything we can do, Diane," replied Tess. "So, there's no point in sitting at home stewing about something we have no control over."

Tess shifted into reverse and backed her silver Nissan Pathfinder out of the driveway, narrowly missing a downside-up blue recycle bin on the curb.

"Yeah, I know," agreed Diane. "I hate this helpless feeling, and it drives me crazy that our guys are in that stupid airplane on a night like this, and for what? A new dishwasher?"

"We married pilots," declared Tess. "And bush pilots no less. It's a choice we live with each day." Tess looked at the sky and noticed the clouds tumbling into one another. The rain continued to fall, its path straight down.

The SUV accelerated and merged into light traffic a block from Tess's driveway. A pair of crows swooped in low across the front bumper and narrowly missed being clipped. "Stupid birds," she griped. "Not every flight will be perfect, Diane, but I'm glad they're together on this one. I bet you'll get a call anytime now from Paul that they made it safe and sound."

Diane wished she shared Tess's optimism, "I really hope you're right, Tessa. My anxiety levels have spiked with this flight and this crazy storm."

"Well, you know the old saying . . . When the going gets tough, the women go shopping!"

Diane reached into her purse and immediately thought of Paul. "Yup, I'm all too familiar with that phrase," she replied. Paul always thought it a mystery how his wife could pack so much paraphernalia into such a compact space. He liked to call her Mary Poppins from time to time. Diane smiled at the thought, grabbed her cellphone and called her home phone number.

Tess steered her vehicle in the general vicinity of their preferred shopping haunt, a busy second-hand thrift store called Value Village, or as they both liked to say using a French accent, *Valoo-Valauge*. Up scaling the name of the discount store added a measure of fun to each trip, and together they procured frugal bargains on everything from shoes, clothing and household knickknacks, to collectibles and books, many of the items still displaying manufacturer tags.

Diane felt relieved that Kim picked up the call on the second ring.

"Hi, Mom, any news?"

"Nothing yet, dear," Diane replied. "Tess and I will be there in a few minutes. You sure you still want to come along? I know thrift stores aren't typically your thing."

"I'll be ready," answered Kim. "And, yes, I want to come along. Better than being stuck here by myself. Don't worry, Mom, Dad will be fine. He always is."

Diane's voice lacked her daughter's conviction. "That's what everyone keeps telling me. Thanks for being so positive, dear. That really helps."

"You're welcome, Mom. I'll see you and Tess in a few."

Diane hung up and knew that shopping would be a welcome distraction, but her intuition left a usually composed woman feeling very unsure of herself and her future.

Minutes later, Tess and Diane arrived to pick up Kim. In short order, the teen emerged from the front door with her head down and her fingers busily typing. Unfazed by the rain and keeping her eyes glued to her phone, Kim safely navigated three concrete steps, dodged the corner of the garage and then breezed around several planters, all without missing a step or tripping up.

Amused, Tess shook her head and smiled. "Looks like Kim's internal radar is working just fine!" she chuckled.

"It remains one of life's great mysteries," agreed Diane. "I have no idea how she can type on that thing and not walk into something or someone."

Kim paused just long enough to look up while reaching for the door handle. She flicked the lever up, whipped open the door and launched herself into the back seat of Tess's SUV. "Hi-hi," she said happily. "Thanks for picking me up, Tess."

In the rearview mirror, Tess saw Kim's fingers dance across her phone's keypad quicker than what she thought humanly possible. "Not a problem," grinned Tess. "Glad you and your phone could join us."

The women drove in relative silence, and Diane wondered how Tess remained so calm in light of their exasperating situation. Diane craved information and needed to hear Paul's voice to know he was safe, but Tess seemed to take it all in stride as if she had expected things to go sideways and resolved early on to not get upset. *Or maybe*, thought Diane, *it isn't like that at all. Maybe Tess is as scared as I am but is better at concealing her emotions.*

As Tess drove, Diane's inner thoughts flowed audibly from her mouth. "Come on, girl. Get a grip," she berated herself quietly. *This isn't the first time your husband's been in a stew. He'll be fine. He's a good pilot and Dave has his back.*

Tess momentarily lifted her eyes from the road and looked in Diane's direction. "How're you doing?" she asked. "I'm thinking you talking to yourself is not a good thing."

Embarrassed, Diane replied, "Don't mind me, Tess. I'm admittedly bordering on the edge of crazy, that's all."

"You're entitled to a bit of insanity every now and then," Tess offered reassuringly. "It's called life."

Kim spoke up from the back seat. "Now you've got me worried, Mom. Aren't you supposed to be strong for your daughter's sake?"

Diane flipped her head around. "Sorry, Kimmy. And here you just told me a moment ago, not to worry. You're right, I should be stronger through this."

Kim's lips quivered as she continued texting, "Dad always taught me to put on a brave face, except that's not always as easy as it seems. I wish he hadn't gone flying tonight." She looked up at her mother. "I just don't get why men are always out to prove something."

Diane couldn't help but laugh at her daughter's youthful understanding of the male ego. "That makes two of us, dear."

"Nope," Tess interjected. "That makes three of us."

* * *

All four men cranked their heads towards the distant hum of an aircraft engine as the valley walls relayed the sound waves from across the lake. Jack Ward shot upright and froze. Tom also rose to his feet without saying a word. Matt and Dylan shuffled their stances, both twisting their heads towards the sound. No one moved, their faces a mask of both intrigue and foreboding. It was as though each man was listening to a piston engine for the first time and had no idea what it was.

In that surreal moment, it felt to Jack as if the rain froze mid-flight, each drop suspended and held in place by a now silent wind. Except for the drone of an approaching aircraft, everything became hushed. He glanced at Tom, Dylan and Matt, each apparently trying to process the scene before them, and each clueless about what to do next.

Apart from the glow of their flashlights, the airfield in which Jack stood remained void of runway lighting or beacon, its surface unable to welcome a plane he felt entirely responsible for. Nearby, something small and furry scurried through the stubby grass, the rodent causing Jack to shiver and promptly sidestep away in fear.

As quickly as the plane announced its presence, Jack returned to the moment and his troubled world started up again. He unlocked his mannequin posture and shouted over the noise of the wind. "Guys, get that beacon light back on! We've got to at least give them that!"

This time it was Dylan who raced back towards the shed. Matt still hadn't moved, his feet rooted to the field as if stuck in concrete.

"Well, Jack," announced Tom flatly. "They sure can't set down here, and I hope they're not foolish enough to try. It's getting too dark."

Low clouds hanging over the lake hid the Cessna from view, and Jack knew the landing light would be the first thing to appear, its haunting glow searching for runway lights that weren't there. Jack's fitful gaze remained transfixed on an area of the sky where he expected the plane to appear. "What in blazes is taking Dylan so long to throw a lever? I should've done it my—"

Just then the beacon flickered to life.

"It's about darn time," fumed Jack.

"At least that's functioning," Tom remarked while holding his stomach.

"What's the matter with you?" asked Jack harshly. "Still feeling sick?"

"I'm fine," assured Tom. "Too much coffee and mini sandwiches earlier."

Dylan sprinted back and stumbled along-side the trio, almost slipping on the wet grass. With all eyes skyward and ears tuned, no one was sure when the plane would first appear through the muck, or where exactly from.

Jack looked away bitterly. It seemed unfair that one man's day could so utterly backfire, that everything he worked to achieve this weekend was crumbling around him. The lodge without power. The road blocked. A televised charity event with no cameras. And now an airplane unable to land because he failed to inspect the field lights days ago. He stared at the ground through unfocused eyes, his thoughts muddled. At that moment a hand walloped him on the shoulder, causing him to lurch forward.

"Jack, look there!" shouted Tom. He raised his arm and pointed.

Re-setting his feet, Jack lifted his head and followed Tom's index finger to a small pinpoint of light low on the horizon. It appeared briefly and quickly faded from view behind a wall of cloud. Seconds later the sparkle returned, a piercing blip of light in the twilight sky, its brilliance distinctly out-of-place against a backdrop of shadowless tones. Tom thought it resembled an alien spacecraft emerging from a nebula, the sudden appearance of an eerie white light sending icy chills through his body.

Over their heads, clouds drifted by no more than 100 feet up. Jack gazed at the lake and wondered how the crew managed to travel through the narrow valley so quickly and under such lurid conditions. More alarming to Jack's nagging conscience was why they bothered to try. But Jack already knew the answer to that question, and he rebuked himself for pushing his agenda on others in the first place.

Chapter 7

Distant lightning cast a weak volley of light into the night sky farther east, the flashes reaching the Cessna as it temporarily broke free of low-lying clouds drifting over the eastern shore of Bayshore Lake. The rain had eased off, but a strong westerly flow of air continued to push hard against the plane as it flew towards Spruce Creek.

Had an eagle been flying above and behind the aircraft, its razor-sharp eyes would have observed an aerial beast slicing through waves of swirling mist, the frightening apparition appearing and then passing from sight in a repetitive cycle of hide-and-seek.

Powerful headwinds created moderate turbulence as Dave fought to control the plane. He looked briefly out his window. "Hey, Paul, we're finally punching through this soup! That's a good sign!"

Paul grunted but did not reply.

Easing up on the power, Dave noticed the choppy lake water below, its surface churning with waves from the steady fusillade of wind. The airplane settled just below the cloud deck, and Dave held it there as best he could. A glance at the altimeter showed them less than 200 feet above the water. Any lower and they might as well be a boat.

Out the front window, a small blip of white light appeared to the left of their current heading. Dave knew a beacon when he saw one. He blinked twice to moisten his eyes, and when he looked again it was gone. Aside from a few cottages and small log cabins randomly scattered around the lake's sizable perimeter, the secluded shoreline remained void of light or definition.

Paul leaned forward in his seat; his neck craned for a better view. "I saw it too," he confirmed groggily. "That was the beacon, Dave, no doubt about it."

"How are you feeling, partner?" asked Dave without looking over. "Thought I'd completely lost you there."

Paul twisted uncomfortably in his seat. "Me, too. I'm feeling a bit better now that I've lost half my lunch. I'm sorry, Dave."

"Sorry for what? You didn't ask to get sick."

"No, I didn't, but I should have called this trip off. I should have listened to you when you suggested we go tomorrow morning."

"No need to apologize. We're here now, and you don't control the weather or how you're feeling. Besides, your wife paid me a hundred bucks to keep tabs on you, so that's all I'm doing."

"I don't think I'd be surprised if that were true."

A smirk rolled over Dave's face. "Who says it isn't true?"

Paul chuckled. "I do appreciate the distracting small talk."

"Tell ya what, Ace. Let's get this bird on the ground, and we can talk about that steak you owe me and whatever else is troubling you."

Paul flinched. "That transparent, huh?"

Just thinking about food churned Paul's stomach, but the withholding of his secret really tore him apart. "Dave, I . . . there actually is something I need to mention, so I can unload my con—"

"Listen, Paul," interrupted Dave. "Can it wait 'til were back on deck? Right now, we both need to focus on getting this plane safely on the ground and my steak on the grill."

Understanding that Dave was right and that now wasn't the best time to confess his sins, Paul scratched a non-existent itch on his head and conceded. "You're right," he replied. "We can chat later over dinner. Sorry, mate."

"You certainly do apologize a lot!" Dave joked. But he knew Paul well enough to recognize the difference between lighthearted needling, and serious matters of the heart. Something of significance was bothering his friend but allowing him to spill the beans would have to wait.

Landing the airplane from the right seat wasn't a big deal but under the current arduous situation, Dave needed his full concentration. And the idea of a ragged, uneven grass runway with minimal lighting wasn't helping to quell his uneasiness. In his opinion, the tail end of this flight pointed towards a bad day as an aviator, and for him, the aforementioned was the last thing on earth he wanted or needed. "I can't get a fix on the beacon," rasped Dave. "You see it at all, Ace?"

"It was just off to the left, about eleven o'clock low."

Dave cussed as the Cessna popped back into the clouds. "Until we lose these clouds, I can't get a visual on anything."

Personal quandary aside, Paul recognized his need to focus and help Dave as much as he could. "Once we spot the runway lights, we'll be able to set up for a shallow approach over the lake. Full flaps and sixty-five knots should do it. The field is pretty short."

"Shallow approach? Ha!" complained Dave. "We're already about as shallow as we can get!" A breath later he saw the beacon. "Got it! Right where you said it was!" Dave corrected his heading and pointed the nose directly at the rotating white light. "Can you handle the landing prep? My hands are full here."

"That's one thing I can do," agreed Paul through lasting nausea. "Thanks for bringing us in. I actually do feel pretty crummy." Paul reached into the side window pocket and grabbed the checklist.

"Just remember to hold it right side up this time. And you're welcome. Like I said before, watch closely and you'll learn!"

Feeling less burdened, Paul deftly unfolded the checklist. "Don't you ever let up?"

"Not as long as I have to keep flying with you!" Dave chuckled. "Let's just hope your buddy Jack is ready for us and has our steaks thawed."

Seeing the beacon plainly now, Paul raised his index finger to point the way. "That's definitely Spruce Creek," he said. "We'll be over the field in no time, so let's dirty up." As the airplane buffeted between alternating updrafts and downdrafts, the bumps left Paul feeling more unsettled than ever. And like an insect at night flying towards a bright source of light, Paul only hoped the beacon ahead would be their safe-haven and not their demise.

* * *

Intently focused on the small cluster of lights tracking slowly towards Spruce Creek's airfield, all four men watched with keen interest. It would take several minutes for the plane to travel the remaining distance from its current place in the sky to the darkened grassy strip in front of them.

Matt Hawley stepped forward to escape from the soggy grass he stood in. "Will they still try to land without the runway lights?" he asked without waiting for an answer. "Why can't they just set down using the plane's landing light? It looks bright enough from here, and there's still a bit of daylight left to see the field."

"If it wasn't windy and raining, maybe they could," Jack tersely replied. "But without the lights on, it's just plain dangerous and, in my opinion, stupid to try. And if they miss the grass area, which is highly probable without the side lighting, they'll be dealing with all sorts of unpleasant obstacles outside the landing area."

Years ago, when the previous owners of Spruce Creek decided to build a short runway, they hired a company to purge the area of rocks, small bushes and trees. Since then, Jack had tried his best to make certain the field remained as airplane friendly as possible, while areas outside the landing zone remained covered with native vegetation. Tree stumps, fallen logs and uneven terrain were endemic throughout the small cluster of foothills and mountainous terrain around Spruce Creek, so an airplane trying to set down outside the clearing might encounter a crash-bang plethora of obstacles.

"Well, there's no doubt they've homed in on the beacon," stated Tom. "Looks as though they're heading straight for us now."

"Yup," Jack agreed. "And I'm sure they won't be happy campers once they discover they've got no runway lights. I assured Paul they'd be on."

Jack's heart banged in his chest, the moment miserably dreamlike. He wondered for a moment if he was standing alone in the middle of a field, wet and miserable, his eyes deceiving him as approaching lights grew larger in the dismal night sky. In the worst way, Jack wished it was a dream. He wanted to wake himself up, but the rain against his face was authentic, the wind not an illusion.

Jack fully anticipated the plane's crew would have no choice but to turn around and fly back into the mouth of a roaring lion. He also felt quite certain they were experiencing one of their worst days as aviators. Little did Jack know that his friend Paul Jackson had already been experiencing his worst day as a pilot before the wheels of the approaching aircraft had even left the ground at Owensville.

* * *

Easily seen from the cockpit, reflections from the Cessna's landing light shimmered across the choppy waters of Bayshore Lake. At such low altitude, the bright halogen beam exposed a ballet of watery peaks and valleys. Whitecaps frolicked on the crest of each wave, dissolved away and then were quickly replaced by a million others.

A flock of Canada geese crossed under the belly of the Cessna; their flight path violently altered from disrupted airflow over their wings. Not expecting company on such a stormy night, the startled waterfowl honked at the intruder as the monster passed overhead. The frightened birds re-grouped in a sloppy V-formation and flew on.

Paul Jackson watched as clouds rolled over the canopy of the airplane. He tried his best to call out the landing checklist despite shaky hands and bouts of dizziness. Thankfully, his cognitive skills were reasonably intact.

"Fuel selector, both on," Paul remarked with little enthusiasm.

"Both on," acknowledged Dave.

"Cowls closed," added Paul.

Dave answered before Paul visually checked the switch. "Cowls are closed," he replied. "That I do know."

Paul checked anyway. "Cowls are closed," he confirmed.

Dave glanced at his airspeed indicator. Eighty knots. He eased off on the power and dropped the flaps a notch to slow down. On final, he planned for sixty-five knots as Paul suggested. Last thing he needed while over the lake was a life-ending stall at low altitude.

Paul was about to slide the prop knob forward to the low-pitch, high RPM setting when Dave brushed his hand away. "Hold off, Ace, we're still too far out. Besides, you passed control to me, and I do things the right way! Prop stays back until just before landing. It's hard on the engine otherwise, and your airplane needs all the help it can get."

Paul was always of the mindset to advance the prop well before touching down. Dave's was not. Pushing the prop control forward flattened the angle of the blades and decreased drag, so if a sudden go-around was required, the engine could quickly spool back up to max RPMs when it was needed the most. The before landing task was standard operating procedure and was an ongoing topic of discussion between them. Paul knew this wasn't the time or place to re-open that debate, but even so, he felt a sudden rage course through his body. "Just following the checklist," Paul crowed.

Deliveries

"You asked me to read it off and help out, so that's what I'm doing. By the book!"

Dave scrunched his face. "You can't handle not being right, can you?" he said accusingly. "Fine." Dave reached for the prop knob and began to push it forward. "If you want to destroy the pistons, then be my guest."

Paul's attitude quickly reversed. He grabbed Dave's hand and tugged it back along with the control. "Sorry, Dave, I . . . it's not that I don't trust you," he admitted. "It's just that—"

"Baloney," Dave interrupted. "I don't know what's going on with you tonight, but we have to set it aside and focus on landing in one piece . . . us and your plane."

Paul rubbed his eyes and stared out the front window. He concentrated on the rotating beacon, its beam of light cutting through the growing darkness. Without looking away, he stated the obvious. "Last thing we need is a go-around . . . if that's even possible here. I'll help you as best I can."

"That's all I ask, Paul. Though I'm wounded you have so little confidence in me," Dave mused.

Paul gazed at his friend. "I know you're joking, but it's not you I'm worried about. It's me. A go-around would do me in, I think."

"I'm the one-take wonder," replied Dave reassuringly. "I got this!"

After a moment of awkward quiet, Paul tucked the checklist back into its slot, snugged up his seat belt and looked at Dave smugly. "Don't forget to flair."

Except for adding full flaps and trimming for final, Dave felt as ready as he could be. He'd made countless short-field approaches before, many along riverbanks or areas never meant for an airplane. But he had to admit that this nail-biter was different, and the thought of screwing up generated a rare pang of anxiety deep in his gut from one of his own less than stellar memories . . .

Years ago, while landing from the right seat at a remote hunting cabin, Dave wheelbarrowed the loaner Piper Tri-Pacer he and Paul were flying. An excessive nose-down attitude was necessary for the steep tree-covered approach, but Dave wasn't quick enough on the flair and the nose wheel struck the ground first—the impact causing minor damage to the front landing gear and a treasure trove of embarrassment. It wasn't a landing he was proud of, and now under similar circumstances, Dave felt more keyed up than usual when he factored in the trees, rain, wind and dismal lighting. He was grateful Paul rarely brought it up in conversation.

* * *

Nestled into the foothills near twin mountain ranges, the City of Owensville was home to slightly over 45,000 residents. Urban sprawl covered the hilly terrain along both sides of the Moose River, which essentially split the city in half. Groves of fruit trees dotted the landscape outside of city limits, with checkerboard farmland scattered as far as the eye could see. Each parcel of land showed off its jacket of late-season colours, some golden with wheat, others tall with corn stocks or blotted with pumpkins.

Strategically constructed between thoughtfully designed areas of commercial development, old and new subdivisions graced the area between stretches of stately elm trees and newly planted saplings. Flower baskets of every size and shape adorned each corner of the vibrant downtown core, while old colonial streetlamps stood proudly, the fixtures casting a normally appealing yellow glow to cobblestone streets below.

But for now, sections of downtown lay in darkness, the usual vibrancy absent. Sheets of rain rolled through the streets, leaving deep puddles and overflowing storm sewers. Flowers drooped in their pots under the relentless bashing of rain, their typical beauty lifeless and void of splendor.

Cars plodded through small lakes and rivers in the streets as tires pushed the water away, only to backfill a moment later. A few brave souls wandered the sidewalks, some with umbrellas tightly clenched as they tried to deflect the elements. Others defiantly went about their evening business, their clothing soaked. At the south edge of town where the storm's severity intensified, lightning blazed from the sky at irregular angles, with one such tentacle striking a power transformer in a blinding flash of pure white light. The resulting thunderclap blasted the municipality with a clamorous boom, its energy rattling windows and triggering car alarms. Momentarily paralyzed by the sudden flash-bang combination, people froze in place no matter where they were. The blast immediately spawned additional power outages, including further sections of the downtown core.

For years, the city had received electricity from an inefficient grid, its population suffering from recurring loss of power at high-demand intervals throughout the year, especially during the winter months when consumption was at its highest. Each time the grid failed, frustrated residents were asked to conserve electricity during peak hours, but households still incurred annual rate increases on their utility bills with minimal upgrades to show for it.

City Council's plan for two years running was to replace the grid, but the proposal was repeatedly squashed for lack of sufficient capital funding. There were always more pressing infrastructure projects on the City's wish list, and the regular impasse left citizens scratching their heads in displeasure at elected officials' decisions.

The electrical grid that supplied power to the city also supplied current to the airport six kilometres to the west, it too now cloaked in darkness. Owensville Municipal Airport was equipped with an auxiliary generator that should have kicked in when the power failure occurred. This would have allowed navigation systems and marker lighting to remain operational and for ATC to continue functioning. But as dumb luck would have it, the back-up generator was currently off-line and awaiting repairs due to an ongoing fuel-backflow issue. Ironically, it was the overuse of the generator in the first place that caused a problem with its fuel system, a headache stemming from Owensville's failing power grid and a heavy reliance on the airport's back-up electrical system.

With parts of the city in darkness, the control tower in which Bruce Macbeth sat, was again void of lighting, and this time the power never came back on. Blank radar screens were unsettling enough, but with navigational aid systems and marker lighting also dark, he was furious that back-up systems weren't already kicking in.

Radio communications and landline phones were non-operational as well, and Bruce thought it atrocious that airport maintenance staff had been so lax in repairing something as critical as a back-up generator. Undoubtedly, they weren't doing their jobs, and somehow, someway, he would see to it that heads rolled. But for the time being, his focus was on what was brewing outside: a dangerous combination of moisture, unstable air and lift. The cluster was generating a perfect storm and all Bruce could do was watch.

Walking to the south windows, Bruce gazed towards the maintenance garages at the far end of the airport grounds. Aside from an aircraft fuel truck with its hazard lights on, there was surprisingly little activity. He envisioned technicians scrambling to start a wayward generator that should have undergone repair weeks ago. Shaking his head in disgust, Bruce felt his cellphone vibrating. He extracted the unit and checked the caller ID. *Marilyn*. Bruce tapped the answer button, and before he could say hello, his wife's voice blared through the earpiece.

"So," teased Marilyn, "not only do you bail on our anniversary dinner plans, you hang up on me too?"

"Guilty of the first accusation," replied Bruce. "Innocent of the second. Power and landline phones are down here. Our call dropped, and for a second, I thought you'd hung up on me! Did you lose power at the house?"

"Nope," answered Marilyn. "We're good here. It's just me, the kids and our cold pizza. But when I drove past Fiore's, it still had power if you wanted to know. And to think we could be there right this minute sipping wine and enjoying a plate of cannelloni! But don't worry about me, dear. I'm fine," she pressured.

Though Bruce knew that Marilyn's clowning around about missing dinner was in jest, the underlying dig had not gone unnoticed. Had he gone home like he should have; he would have been able to take Marilyn to their go-to Italian restaurant. And with two other air traffic controllers now on duty, he pondered about leaving regardless. But, until he knew the status of the Cessna and crew, his instincts told him to stay put, and that decision was in his mind, final.

Bruce wasn't sure how to respond to his wife. "Well, that's good about the house not losing power. At least that's something. We're sitting here in the dark again. It's a good thing the airport is quiet with this storm raging."

When Marilyn didn't respond, Bruce continued. "Apparently, the backup generator still isn't fixed, so it's been a comedy of errors tonight. The airport's essentially blind. And to think this all could have been prevented with a little common sense and prioritizing."

"Well, dear," Marilyn finally replied. "You still have electrician's blood in your veins, so maybe you should go down and show them how it's done."

Bruce shrugged and walked over to a small shelf containing several document trays. "I would if I could, but I'd probably just get in the way. Besides, they've likely only got the money for a Band-Aid solution anyway." Bruce snatched up a partially crumpled piece of paper from the top of the pile. In bold red letters, FLIGHT ITINERARY was printed in the upper left corner.

Marilyn agreed. "Yes, electrical concerns at the airport have bothered you for some time. But you're right, it's inexcusable."

"Listen, Marilyn, I better go. I'm glad you guys are all right. I'll be home as quickly as I can."

"Trying now to get rid of me, eh?"

"Not at all, I just—"

"No need to explain, dear. I just wanted to make sure the tower was still upright and for that matter, you. I'll let you go. If you hear anything about Paul and Dave, text me or call if you can."

Bruce tried to read the itinerary under the dim emergency lighting. "Will do, Marilyn. Love you, and hi to the kids from their derelict dad."

"You said it, dear," chuckled Marilyn, "not me! I love you too. Bye."

Pilots had the option of filing either a flight plan or flight itinerary before departure. Filed with ATC, a flight plan included information such as fuel, expected altitude, and estimated times of departure and arrival. If a plane was overdue by more than an hour, a phone search would begin to track down its whereabouts. This would include calls to ATC, the pilot's home or any other place the airplane and crew might have ended up. If overdue by two hours, someone from flight services or air traffic control would inform the military of the delay. From there, Search and Rescue would be called into action, often with assistance from law enforcement and the public.

Bruce remembered Paul had chosen the flight itinerary route, as he had filed the document before departure. This standard form had information about the aircraft and the proposed route of travel. Different from a flight plan, a flight itinerary was left with a responsible person instead of flight services or ATC—this being a spouse or close friend. Paul, however, chose to leave the document with air traffic control, and in this case, the responsible person on duty was controller Bruce Macbeth.

Bruce skimmed the paper. It indicated Paul hoped to fly round trip this evening, but with the weather closing in, he reported they might spend the night at Spruce Creek if unable to return. Bruce checked his watch. He expected the Cessna would arrive at its destination shortly; then, hopefully, he'd have some good news to report to Diane Jackson.

Tilting his head, Bruce wondered if the events of the evening could get any worse? Thundershowers causing havoc at both landing sites were bad enough, but the real concern in his mind was if Paul Jackson's airplane was still flying at all. Wandering over to his friend and fellow controller Ken Hamill, an ATC veteran with a dozen years more seniority, Bruce handed him the flight itinerary. "Hey, Ken, if the lights ever come back on and you hear anything from this flight, would you please let me know?"

Ken read the document. "Sure," he replied as he ran his fingers through a tuft of short silvery-grey hair. "Shouldn't you already be home by now?"

"Yes, I should be, but my gut's telling me to stick around here until I learn the whereabouts of that 185. I promised the pilot's wife I'd call when I knew they were safe. As I understand it, they can't land at Spruce Creek, and she thought I had a way to make them turn around. Being a forward-thinker, I already placed a call to Search and Rescue, but hope it doesn't come to that."

"Let it go, man," advised Ken. "You're too vested in your job. Why waste your time stewing over a plane you no longer have control over?"

Bruce thought about that for a second, then shot Ken an amusing sidelong glance, "Because," he replied cynically, "some of us in this business actually care about the airplanes we have control over."

"Ouch!" whimpered Ken.

Bruce lightly cuffed Ken on the back of his head, "Truth's a bugger sometimes."

Chapter 8

By and large, Paul and Dave's business flights carried them over intricate river systems and pristine lakes, the emerald-green pools untouched by humans but teeming with fish and wildlife. The mountainous river valley lay carpeted with dense vegetation and thick forests, a landscape undeniably harsh yet astoundingly beautiful, especially when viewed from the air.

Notwithstanding the rundown appearance of Paul's airplane, his maintenance and care of the engine were utterly scrupulous. To his rationale, correct power settings meant lower operating costs, which according to the performance charts in the pages of his Cessna's operations manual, those numbers were to be meticulously followed. In past years, Paul flew with pilots who seriously disregarded "by-the-numbers" engine settings, and these disparities often resulted in heated debate after the engine shut down.

Aware of the delicate balance between investing in his business and being chintzy, Paul lovingly ensured his big Continental engine received proper funding. This included regular engine maintenance and overhaul as required in the manual; strict monitoring of manifold and RPM settings as documented in the checklists; and correct engine mixture settings to maximize fuel economy. And because Airflow Charters had only one airplane, he typically placed greater emphasis on preserving airworthiness than on the expedient delivery of goods.

Nevertheless, this delivery to Spruce Creek changed the rules, and when Paul heard the urgency in Jack Ward's voice, he also sensed an underlying plea for help from a man who sounded like his own personal demon needed slaying. So, while facing a moral dilemma of his own, Paul related to Jack. In Paul's mind, by fulfilling the man's request, it would in some way diminish or make right his decision to fly while under restriction.

In an effort to try to outrun abysmal incoming weather farther west of Spruce Creek, Dave and Paul settled on adjusting manifold pressure to twenty-five inches and RPMs to 2,500. This allowed for a cruise speed of roughly 155 knots with thirsty cylinders burning fuel at a rate of sixteen gallons per hour. It was faster than either man preferred, but in the interest of expediency, exceeding personal comfort levels and putting this trip behind them was the top priority.

Had Paul topped up the fuel tanks before departing Owensville, as was his custom, the engine would have drawn gas from an ample sixty-two-gallon supply, far more than needed for a return flight. But he began this trip with the tanks one-third full—easily enough to make the half-hour trek—but that assumed a trouble-free flight and landing on the first attempt. "Besides," Paul had said to Dave. "We can gas up when we arrive." Spruce Creek had a crude yet functional refilling station, the setup consisting of three forty-gallon drums topped with aviation fuel, an antiquated hose nozzle and a pump.

Posing less of a threat to forward visibility, clouds flowed over the airplane as it bled off the distance to the shoreline. Currently visible from the cockpit and lying directly ahead, the Spruce Creek beacon flashed low on the horizon. Sweating uncharacteristically, Dave was glad he had removed the top part of his coveralls. He reached down and pulled back the air vent knob. A cool blast of air flowed into the cockpit. "Hope you don't mind, Paul, I'm really dying in here."

"Don't think I've ever seen you stress this bad," noted Paul. "I'm fine with the air. I can use it too."

Aware of how forcefully his hands were gripping the yoke, Dave eased his fingers from the column and flexed them without actually letting go. With his eyes locked on the beacon, he had one thing in mind: *Get the airplane on the ground and end this miserable flight.*

Paul furrowed his brow. "I've flown in here at dusk only once before and found it tricky. The approach is shallow off the lake, and the moment the wheels hit the grass, you'll need heavy braking."

"You're a fountain of encouragement, aren't you?" scoffed Dave. "You should be flying this, not me."

Paul seemed oblivious to Dave's voice. "The runway lights run along both sides of the field, but only so far. They're not bright to begin with, and the rain will diminish their visibility, but we should see them well enough to line up for a decent short final. Low and slow, right to the threshold."

Dave snickered. "Easy for you to say because, I say again, you're not the one flying!"

"Point taken," Paul finally admitted. *Truly wish I was.*

As the Cessna rocked side to side in step with gusty winds, Dave wasn't at all optimistic he could pull the landing off without some sort of mishap, and his apprehensions were not what he wanted to convey to Paul. He tried to cover his nerves with jest. "And to think I could have been safely home tonight watching a movie and nursing my soup." Dave glanced at Paul. "I let you talk me into this trip because why?"

Feeling emotionally drained, Paul leaned forward with his head tilted down. One way or another he suspected this flight would be his last. "I don't recall holding a gun to your head for this trip. You came willingly as I recall."

Dave smiled and continued his rant. "Yes, on the grounds that I promised Diane I'd babysit you and save your bacon if required." Dave shook his head. "And now that's exactly what I'm doing. Some things in a co-pilot's life never change!"

"Well," Paul stated wearily. "You can't ever say that flying with me isn't an adventure."

"True enough," agreed Dave. "But in hindsight, this experience is fast becoming one I could have done without. If this chop keeps up, I'll be joining you in the barf club."

"I understand how you feel," Paul added glumly. "But there's only room in this plane for one airsick passenger. Got it?"

Dave sighed. "Whatever you say, boss."

Adequate daylight remained for visual separation between water, mountains and the approaching shoreline. In the next few minutes, Dave knew everything outside the cockpit would fuse into an ocean of dark grey shadow less tones, and for the first time in his piloting career, he truly wished he wasn't the one flying.

* * *

The navigational beacon at Spruce Creek completed one full rotation every five seconds, its beam indiscriminately striking trees, rocks, and men. Behind Jack Ward, headlights from the lodge van stretched far into the field, then trailed off into the growing darkness. Raindrops shimmered briefly as they passed through the beams and whacked into the muddy ground below.

Jack glanced at the vehicle and thought of his wife. He had always left the van running and the lights on when he and Mildred ventured into town with a long list of errands, all of which required immediate attention to Mil's jovial way of thinking.

"Jack," she'd declare emphatically, "I only have a few things to pick up at each stop, so keep the van running and the lights on. When I'm done, we'll run your errands. How's that sound, dear?" But things always took longer than expected, and Jack's chores usually waited for another day.

Jack was forever amazed at his wife's ability to complete multiple tasks in one shopping excursion. He'd watch Mildred flit from chore to chore faster than a butterfly—everything from banking and doctor appointments, to notions for the lodge, including flowers! Mil loved selecting arrangements of vines and blossoms with expert precision, each variety destined for that perfect spot in and around the lodge property.

"Mildred," Jack often teased. "I swear your eyes can spot flora and fauna from miles away."

And Mil's reply was always the same: "We all have our gifts, dear."

Jack relished her unique ability to turn bland into beautiful, sadness into joy and sickness into hope, not just for herself but for everyone she met.

During the dreary winter months, Mildred adorned each table in the lodge's dining room with a delightful bouquet of fresh flowers, while stunning freestanding baskets graced the hallways and corridors. Jack willingly accepted his role as chauffeur, and most often found himself smiling as his wife procured everything from soup to nuts, and a healthy dose of everything in between. In one form or another, Mildred's heart was on display around the lodge, and guests of Spruce Creek always seemed to genuinely appreciate her efforts.

Jack sadly tore his eyes away from the van, its engine idling rough and in need of a tune-up. Tom, Dylan and Matt had not moved, their gaze frozen, their bodies stock-still. Jack thought the men resembled wax figures as they stiffly watched the scene play out before them. No one spoke.

Without the runway lights, it was clear to Jack the airplane couldn't land in the growing darkness, and he thought they'd be foolish to try. He also assumed that in the next minute, Paul would discover the lights were off . . . if he hadn't already. And should he decide to hang around in the off chance they did fire up, Jack didn't want them burning more fuel than was necessary. In his mind, the only course of action was for the crew to head back home—the sooner the better. The question now was how to wave them off.

Deliveries

Somewhere over Jack's head, a massive crow cawed loudly, its shrill call scolding the men who dared to interrupt its evening roost. The jet-black bird jumped a few branches lower, surveyed the scene below and began to preen its tail feathers. A moment later the bird's funnel-shaped ears picked up the sound of something foreign. The animal cocked its neck side to side: the unwelcome sound triggering the bird's instinct to flee. Seconds later, its glossy wings bit into the evening air, carrying the bird aloft in a full retreat.

As the Cessna approached, its navigation lights were momentarily visible but disappeared as the airplane popped back into a cloud. Jack waited for a moment for the lights to reappear before shifting his eyes from the plane to the van. It was then his mind kicked into gear. Without saying a word, Jack hustled away with an urgent sense of purpose.

* * *

Blustery headwinds pushing against the Cessna impeded its forward movement as it approached the lodge. In the cockpit, it felt to Dave as if they were hovering instead of progressing forward. Foamy waves were visible along the shoreline as turbid concoctions of mud and water pounded ashore. Dave thought about raising the flaps a notch to help with sagging airspeed but decided against it. Instead, he added a bit of power and waited for the airspeed to stabilize. The beacon appeared brighter now, its tentacle of light reaching farther into the bleak night sky, the eerie sight invoking a shiver from deep inside Dave's core.

Being too ill to fly was already tough on Paul's ego, but it was more than that. No matter how he spun things in his head, he'd screwed up bad. Paul thought about where he sat. Once a defining place of character, and for him, pride, his nondescript captain's chair had become a seat of despondency and shame. Upset with himself, Paul shook his head and glanced out the front window. "I don't understand it," he stated nervously amidst ongoing nausea. "The runway lights should be visible by now."

"Did you say something?" asked Dave distractedly.

Paul looked across at his friend. "I said we should see the runway lights by now, just north of the beacon."

"Yup, I would have thought the same. I don't see anything and it's getting blacker than molasses out there."

Struggling with growing turbulence, Dave jostled the yoke side to side to keep the wings level. He noticed the airspeed dipping again, so he added a touch more power. With the beacon directly ahead, he gripped the column firmly and configured the plane as best he could for a straight in, short-field approach. Dave squinted out the window and beyond the engine cowling. "Where in the heck are the lights, Ace?"

Paul Jackson never heard Dave's question. He was too busy filling his sick bag for a second time.

* * *

"Where'd Jack go?" asked Matt, suddenly realizing the man had vanished.

Tom gawked over his shoulder and noticed movement by the van. He watched Jack yank open the rear door and climb inside. A moment later he emerged clutching a small object of some kind. *What are you up to, Jack?* Tom wondered.

Dylan swung his head around towards the van. "What's he doing, Dad?"

"Wish I knew, son," replied Tom, turning his attention back to the sky. "But whatever it is, I bet it's something to do with that airplane."

Jack returned without saying a word, his hands fingering something resembling a gun. He made no attempt to explain himself or his intentions.

Matt walked over. "What's that, Jack?" he asked while the others gazed curiously at Jack's hand with puzzled expressions.

"What's everyone staring at?" barked Jack. "You guys never see a flare gun before?" Jack inspected the device and smiled. "Been in the van for years. I knew it would come in handy one day, and today is that day."

Jack had purchased the gun five summers earlier at the Owensville flea market. Though he never specifically had a use for one, it seemed like a good deal at the time. The storage shed behind the lodge already contained items most would regard as junk, but Jack loved his trinkets and determined that one day everything stored away would become useful.

"I'm not sure it'll even fire. But I'm about to find out. It might blow up when I pull the trigger," he joked, "so, you boys might want to stand back."

Tom's raised both eyebrows. "Pull the trigger, Jack? Why exactly would you want to do that?"

Unsure as to Jack's intentions, Dylan and Matt backed up several paces.

"Oh, for heaven's sake," scoffed Jack, "You're all looking at me like I've lost my mind. Well, maybe I have. Lord knows it's been a heck of a day, so I'd appreciate if you'd all give me the benefit of the doubt."

"So, I'll ask again, Jack," repeated Tom. "What are you—"

"What do you think I'm doing? I need to warn those boys that we're royally pooched down here. I don't want them circling all night thinking we'll get the lights working when evidently that isn't happening. The sooner they go back home, the better."

Tom stared at the flare gun like it was a live nuclear weapon. "They'll figure it out on their own, Jack. You think this is necessary?"

Jack wasn't listening.

"What about the charity ride tomorrow?" asked Matt. "We can't do anything without the camera gear on that plane." Matt looked at Tom for moral support.

"Isn't going to be a broadcast tomorrow," Jack coarsely replied. "It's done and over. We'll try again another time. People can still ride if they want, and we'll make the best of it, but there won't be a fundraiser. If the road was open, we'd have had the cameras here by now. But it's not"—Jack pointed towards the Cessna— "and our only means of getting them here is right there in front of us, which evidently can't happen. So, they need to hightail it back home, and I'm simply offering a gentle push, that's all."

"Maybe they'll have the road open by morning, Mr. Ward," offered Dylan optimistically. "Then we could still get the cameras here by car."

"Sure, Dylan, and maybe I'll win the lottery by morning too," Jack countered harshly. "It's not going to happen. Realistically, I expect it'll be a day or two before the road re-opens, so let's just drop it, shall we?"

Dylan looked down at his feet but never replied.

Jack immediately felt bad and apologized. He shuffled his stance and looked Dylan straight in the eyes. "And Dylan?"

Dylan looked at his dad and then nervously at Jack.

Jack's voice softened. "I thought I told you to call me Jack."

"Yes, sir, you did," admitted Dylan. "Sorry."

"Apology accepted," smiled Jack. "Now can we get back to business?"

Moulded in black plastic, the flare gun's trigger was designed to blast a twelve-gauge parachute flare through a one-inch bore, assuming it didn't misfire. Surprisingly nervous to pull the trigger, Jack swallowed hard before hoisting the gun skyward out over the lake. "This sucker should get their attention," he stated explicitly.

Jack slipped his index finger around the trigger and glanced left and right. It was then he discovered that Dylan, Tom and Matt were no longer standing beside him, the men not even close.

Deliveries

* * *

Paul's stomach felt better, but his inner ear was drastically out of whack. He cracked open the window and waited for fresh air to flood the cabin. "Sorry about the smell," he apologized.

"No problem," admitted Dave. "I'm sorry you're feeling so lousy."

Paul brushed off Dave's concern. "Where are the runway lights?" he asked. "Jack said they'd be on."

"No idea. But it goes without saying that there's something wrong down there. It's a lot darker outside than I thought it would be, so I'm not at all thrilled about this approach without side markers. I can't land on what I can't see."

"Jack promised he'd have things lit up for us," Paul repeated. "And we're relatively on time for when I said we'd be here, though, by the looks of it, I seriously misjudged the light levels out there."

Aside from scattered lightning around the area, there was little in the way of ground definition. Dave glanced briefly towards Paul and then back out the front window. "Let's keep on the approach. We can spin around and shoot another quick pass if needed. Maybe Jack needs a few more minutes. He knows we're here, that's a given." Dave glanced at the fuel gauges. "We can't hang around for long, Ace. We'll have to go back before we run out of—"

The sky directly in front of the airplane suddenly erupted in a bright red flash of light, a mini sun rising vertically to match the altitude of the aircraft. The phosphorous charge arced towards the plane as the wind carried it aloft. Seconds later a small chute deployed, slowing the descent rate as it burned through its fuel and floated back to Earth.

Reacting impulsively, Dave kicked in hard right rudder and cranked the yoke in the same direction even though the airplane was in no immediate danger. The Cessna snapped to the right, tossing both men the opposite way against their straps. "What the devil?" he shouted angrily.

"Someone's popping flares!"

"Must you always state the obvious, Sherlock?" needled Dave.

"I bet it's Jack!" declared Paul. "Be like him to fire a warning shot."

"A warning shot? A warning shot for what?" asked Dave incredulously. "It's not like we're a Spitfire inbound to strafe the lodge!"

"He must be having trouble with the lights," added Paul. "Jack isn't one to sit back and waste time . . . his or anyone else's. My guess is he's trying to wave us off because he can't get them on."

Dave killed the flaps, added power and began a gentle circle back out over the lake and then in towards the lodge for another look. "Well, Jack needs to get his fool head examined! I'm seeing a big streaky red spot before my eyes that I can't shake."

"We're definitely not landing here tonight," Paul admitted. "I know Jack means well, so don't be too hard on him."

Dave kept an eye on the vertical speed indicator throughout the turn. "And just where do you propose we land this thing, Ace? We were going to fuel up here, remember?" Dave tapped the fuel gauges as pilots often did in old war movies. "You know that making it home with the fuel we have left is dicey at best. Just pointing that out."

Paul smirked. "We have plenty of gas to get back if we conserve what we have. Or worst-case scenario we go back as far as we can."

Dave's frustration was beginning to rear its head. "Go as far as we can to where? There aren't any places between here and Owensville to land, especially along this mountain corridor in the dark. Give your head a shake, Paul!"

Peering out his side window, Paul tried to focus his eyes. An unearthly blood-red glow lingered over the shoreline. The flare was almost to the water, barely visible behind and to the left of the plane. Paul watched it peter out as it contacted the lake. "Let's work our way back towards the river. Depending on the weather, we can try for Owensville. Otherwise, we find a place to set down before the tanks dry up, which they won't."

Surprised by the sudden resolve in Paul's voice, Dave lashed out. "Set down? Don't you mean tear off the gear and cartwheel into the trees? There's no place to land, Paul! It's all slopes, mountains and trees—unless you know something I don't, which I strongly doubt."

Paul reached up to the visor over his head, flipped it down and allowed the sectional map to flop out. He unfolded the page and squinted to get his bearings in the dimly lit cockpit.

Dave was growing impatient. "Unless you can abracadabra us a flat new runway somewhere and it magically appears on the map, you're wasting your time. Why in heaven's name did I allow us to leave without the tanks full? Spruce Creek gas or not."

Paul thought for a moment before speaking. "I'm sorry I got you into this mess, Dave, and I'll accept full responsibility for our fuel status. I messed that up, plain and simple. I anticipated landing here without incident. We'd fuel up and fly home."

Dave settled a bit. "You had no way of knowing we couldn't land, Paul. Like you, I viewed it as a short flight and that we'd be filling the tanks here. Let's just say we both screwed that one up. Deal?"

"I appreciate your attempt to shift blame," Paul acknowledged. "But this is one of those, 'Look, everybody, I'm an idiot' moments. You keep us flying and I'll see if I can find a place to land if our fuel situation becomes an issue."

"Time for another reality check," taunted Dave. "There's no way we'll not run out of gas before Owensville. Look at the gauges. This whole scenario's looking more and more like it's not going to have a happy ending." Dave levelled the wings at 300 feet and flew parallel to the shoreline while dodging expanses of clouds. He glanced over his shoulder. "Still no runway lights visible. Big surprise."

Paul continued to stare at the map. "Slow up and steer us to a heading of zero-nine-zero, back the way we came."

Dave began to laugh in a tone oozing with sarcasm.

Without lifting his head, Paul nonchalantly asked. "Something funny?"

"Besides the fact its dark out, we're low on fuel and surrounded by mountains? No, nothing at all funny here."

* * *

Tom pointed at the flare gun. "Good lord, Jack, you just about hit them with that thing. And with the sudden turn they made, I bet you scared them half to death. What's the matter with you?"

"Had to let them know we've got trouble down here," admitted Jack defensively. "And for your information, the flare wasn't even close to them. Besides, God only knows how long they'd stay up there waiting for the lights to come on if I didn't do anything. I know they're low on fuel, and if they can't land here, they can't gas up. Sooner they head back home the better."

"They did turn away pretty quick," Matt concluded.

"Wouldn't you?" replied Dylan. "If someone shot a flare at me, I'd be bugging out too!"

Jack wasn't appreciating the finger-pointing. "I didn't fire it at them!" he retorted. "They were . . . oh what's the use of trying to justify my—"

"Low on fuel, Jack? How'd you know they're low on fuel?" gasped Tom. "Wouldn't they have had the forethought to depart with full tanks, especially through the mountains?"

"Normally, yes," agreed Jack. "But not this trip because Paul was going to refuel here. Because of time constraints, he didn't want to take the time to gas up. He asked me before they left if the drums were full. I told him they were." Jack looked everyone in the eyes. "Anything else any of you needs clarification on?"

Tom probed again. "You mean to tell me they don't have enough gas to make it back to Owensville? How is that possible with two experienced pilots?"

"I just told you," snarled Jack. "And I'm not repeating myself! Now if you gentlemen will excuse me, I'm burned out, cold and soaking wet. The show is over here anyway." Jack turned abruptly and shuffled towards the sanctuary of his old van. "You three want to keep standing out here in the rain, be my guest. I've screwed things up enough for one day, so I'm going home to nurse my bottle of scotch."

For the first time that night, Tom Sullivan experienced genuine fear. Not for his own safety, but for the two men inside the plane.

Dylan and Matt turned away and began to walk towards the van when Tom called out, "Guys, wait a minute."

Both men stopped and spun around.

"Let's give Jack a few minutes to himself," added Tom. "I think he might need it."

Not wanting anyone to see him, Jack stood alone on the opposite side of the van. He gazed skyward and closed his eyes. Tears trickled down his cheeks and blended with a steady stream of rain. Jack lowered his head and stared at his feet. His heart raced inside his chest, his soul reeling from a deep-set loneliness engulfing every molecule of his body. With everything around him gone wrong, all Jack Ward could do was hope that by some magical stroke of luck, tomorrow would be a better day.

Chapter 9

Diane Jackson was scarcely in the mood for shopping but tried hard to shelve her apprehensions for her daughter's sake. She found it impossible to let go of the fact that her husband was flying through mountainous terrain in the worst of conditions. Diane rarely complained or stood in the way of his business dealings, but Paul so easily desensitizing himself to the expressed misgivings of his family was downright infuriating, especially when both his girls asked him not to go.

Eyeballing rows of footwear, Diane reached for a pair of silver low-heel pumps. Holding them up, she examined the shoes with mild interest. The leather felt soft in her hands, yet her eyes looked past them. She glanced sideways and noticed Kim one row over, happily engaged in her own bargain hunt. The sight made Diane feel better, but only somewhat.

Store shelves lay stocked with all variety of essentials, anything a thrifty shopper could want or need. Despite the selection and through no fault of the staff, it was clear that neat and tidy merchandising wasn't possible as shoppers rummaged for bargains. Diane glanced back down at the pumps in her hands. They were cute and brand-new, just how she liked them, but then Paul's voice found its way into her head. "Do you really need another pair of shoes?" he would ask semi-jokingly. "You could open a thrift store of your own with all your footwear!"

Reluctantly, Diane set the shoes down and backed away as a much-needed smile played across her lips. *Even when you're not here, Paul, you're here.* Seconds later a cute pair of champagne sandals caught her eye, and she headed in that direction with her husband's words still echoing inside her head. "Darn you," she mumbled.

Kim sat nearby on a small stool, the area around her feet strewn with shoes and topped with a pair of fuzzy bear-paw slippers. Rising from the chair, she spun on her heels and ogled a nearly new pair of blue open-toed flats for the mirror. Kim noticed her mother approach. "Hey, Mom, what do you think of these?"

"Those are adorable," Diane replied enthusiastically. "How do they feel?"

Kim walked a few steps away and turned around. "They pinch a little in the toes, but once they're broken in, I bet they'd be good for school. They're brand new!"

Kim's cheerful personality and carefree outlook on life reminded Diane of herself when she was that age. "Well then," Diane replied. "I suppose you best give them a home."

"Really, Mom?" asked Kim excitedly. "But I've already found two other pairs. You know that Dad will complain when he finds even more shoes stacked by the front door."

"Oh well, he'll get over it," chuckled Diane. "And besides, he isn't here now to offer his opinion, is he?"

Kim's facial expression changed. "No, he isn't," she sadly replied. "I can't stop thinking about him, Mom. Shouldn't he be at Uncle Jacks by now?"

"I would certainly expect so," nodded Diane. "He said he'd call as soon as he arrived at the lodge. Try not to worry." *Like me.*

Tess wandered over protectively gripping a small hand-carved turtle, her face beaming. "This was actually made in Hawaii!" she announced proudly. "Almost everything on the islands is either made in China or Central America." The painted turtle was intricately decorated with tiny seashells, forming the shape of another small turtle. "See," Tess explained. "It's a baby riding on its mother's back!"

Diane leaned in for a closer look. "How on earth is someone able to carve like that with such precision?" she asked. "I'd never have the patience for it."

"Well, it's authentic Hawaii and it's mine now!" Tess heartily stated.

Dave and Tess spent as much time in the Hawaiian Islands as possible, and with Tess's passion for turtles, real or otherwise, Diane couldn't help but smile at her friend's excitement and new-found treasure.

Tess placed the turtle in her cart. "You okay, Diane?" she asked.

"I suppose so," Diane replied. "It's upsetting to me that I worry so much when the guys fly. It's not like I've never been down this road, but as I said before, I feel very edgy and can't explain it."

"Well, tonight's flight is certainly different from their usual routine. The weather's awful and it was a spur of the moment decision, so I think you're justified in being worried."

Diane sighed heavily. "I know, Tessa, but you seem fine with it, so what's wrong with me? I feel like such a china doll. I wish Paul had declined Jack, just this once. If not for my sake, then for Kim's. But that's my husband for you. He can't say no when money's involved, and he's a people-pleaser."

"True enough," admitted Tess. "He's in business to make money after all. The flying part won't always be risk-free for them or stress-free for us, but that's their livelihood. Sometimes, all we can do is pray and leave things in God's hands."

Diane thought for a moment. "I know, Tess. Come to think of it, Paul mentioned something silly about reaching superhero status once he delivered the TV equipment to Jack. The man sounded pretty desperate from what Paul told me."

"Hero status?" laughed Tess. "Then I suppose that brands my husband as his trusty side-kick."

Diane snickered. "The flying dynamic duo. Heaven help us all!"

Tess laughed. "The world isn't safe with those two at large."

Diane looked around the store. "Well, I better keep myself occupied until my super-fly-guy checks in. Maybe I'll see if I can find a pair of black leggings, not that I need another pair."

"Clothes, shoes and jewelry!" replied Tess. "A girl can't have enough!"

* * *

Kevin Davies rolled to his side to evade a pokey couch spring digging into his back. The vintage sofa offered little support because the cushions had lost any measure of firmness eons ago. Every couple of minutes, intensely bright flashes of lightning tore into the planning room of the Search and Rescue building, followed by sharp cracks of thunder that rattled the windows as the brunt of the storm passed through. Rain falling against the roof caused a roar as billions of droplets bashed into the shingles. A steady trickle of water coursed its way through a tiny crack in the ceiling and then dribbled haphazardly into a plastic wastebasket, which Kevin had already emptied twice.

A porcelain table lamp cast a faint yellow glow on the wall, its shade split and curled up at the bottom. The bulb flickered from a loose connection somewhere inside the socket, and rather than fuss with it, Kevin decided to leave the fixture on. He tossed and turned a while longer, then dismissed the idea of sleep for the time being.

Stretching once, Kevin got up, walked to the front window and peered into the turbulent night sky. There were usually white and blue lights running along the length of the taxiway and runway, but they were out. He knew of the airport's electrical woes, so he wasn't overly surprised by the cloak of darkness given the ferocious thunderstorm outside. What he did find puzzling was why the building he stood in had power, when the bulk of the airport was dark.

Kevin watched a deluge of rain slam into the window, sounding more like pea-size hail than water. A huge cat spider sought shelter in the upper left corner of the windowpane, its legs holding fast to a tattered web as rain pelted the poor creature's body. Kevin tapped the window near the spider, but it never budged.

Sauntering back to the couch, he grabbed the television remote off the coffee table and aimed it straight ahead. Six feet away, two plastic milk crates supported an old nineteen-inch RCA colour television, a heavy relic that predated the flat screen era. The machine flashed twice, then winked on with a picture sadly lacking in definition. Kevin scrolled through the channels until he found an old episode of Star Trek. The volume button on the remote wasn't working, so instead of getting up, he left it as it was—low and nearly inaudible. For Kevin, the near-silent pictures on the screen were good enough to provide him company.

A weather alert caught Kevin's attention as it scrolled across the bottom of the screen. Owensville residents were being advised to take necessary precautions as heavy rain, large hail and damaging winds were possible tonight and throughout the overnight hours.

Kevin hoisted his feet to the coffee table. "No kidding!" he grunted.

Wearily viewing the screen, Kevin thought of the Piper Cub and hoped it was staying dry. Excessive damp weather commonly resulted in a myriad of new leaks in the hangar, which not surprisingly were infrequently repaired. He decided that when the storm eased up, he'd scoot back out to check on the plane and make certain all was well.

Except for the occasional blink, Kevin sat un-moving. Reaching up, he tugged down the brim of his cap over weary eyes. He craved rest, but his overactive mind would not settle. Memories of his training soon yielded to disjointed thoughts of checklists and procedures, steps to be followed, and routes to fly. Abstract depictions of his day and possible outcomes for tomorrow clouded his thinking, entangling one another as he teetered between consciousness and sleep. As dreams began to take root, Kevin's body jerked involuntarily as he broke into a sweat . . .

From his vantage point, Kevin stood frozen in place, his feet locked into sludgy mud lining the slope, and his eyes fixated on the scene unfolding across the river. Wreckage hovered menacingly over unworldly terrain: twisted sections of airframe, deformed doors and struts, wheels gashed and torn open. Piece by piece, the disfigured aircraft rose slightly as if trying to fly one last time. Giving way to gravity, each mangled section clattered to the ground. Kevin wanted to turn his eyes away and run, but his feet would not move. He watched as two figures fell from high above, their limbs flailing about like rag dolls. They flopped into the river and were immediately swept downstream by the raging current . . .

Kevin heard himself scream as he jolted awake. Disoriented and reluctant to move, he froze until his heart rate slowed and reality overpowered the grogginess of sleep. Not ordinarily prone to nightmares, he stared long and hard at the television to re-anchor his thoughts, reluctant to close his eyes again for fear of the same dream or one even worse. Lightning and thunder continued to ravish the world outside, and Kevin suspected the hours leading to sunrise would be anything but restful.

* * *

From inside her purse, a familiar ringtone reached Diane Jackson's ears, the noise stopping her in her tracks. She hung a skirt back on the rack and fidgeted with the purse's zipper. Once open, she dug for the phone in a bottomless pit of doodads. "You've got to be kidding me!" she grumbled. "Where is it?"

After a frantic search, Diane found the device and ripped it clear from receipts and tissues. Several crinkled papers spilled to the floor. As she bent to pick them up, a frumpy woman scowled while trying to squeeze through the narrow aisle to pass by. "Pardon me!" she snorted. Ignoring her, Diane flipped the phone around to look at the display. She hoped it was Paul's name on the caller ID, but it was not. "Applewood Medical Centre?" she questioned. "That's odd."

Diane's letdown gave way to idle curiosity, and then to genuine alarm. She had learned years ago to trust her intuition, and something about this call sparked legions of red flags. Willing to bet the conversation would somehow revolve around her husband, Diane nervously tapped the answer key. "Hello?"

For several seconds, all Diane heard through the receiver was papers being shuffled and background chatter. She was about to hang up when a stern female voice began to speak, the woman's tone undeniably void of personality. "Ah yes, is this Mrs. Jackson? Diane Jackson?"

"Yes, this is Diane. Who's calling please?"

"My name is Hilary Filmor from the Applewood Medicentre. I'm Dr. Alan's secretary."

"Yes, Hilary," replied Diane. "Is there something I can help you with?"

"I'm trying to reach your husband, Paul, on his cell to be exact," Hilary robotically explained.

"Yes, I'm well aware of who my husband is," Diane candidly replied.

"Well," explained Hilary. "I keep getting a digitized message saying he's unavailable, and he doesn't seem to have voice mail set up."

"It's very perceptive of you Hilary to notice that he doesn't have voicemail," countered Diane. "For your information, he has a new phone and his voice mail hasn't been set up yet. Is there anything else you need clarified?"

"I see," added Hilary. "Well, for whatever reason the clinic doesn't have your home number on file. So as per our policy, we call cell phones next."

This call was not off to a good start, and in her current frame of mind, Diane was more than prepped for a round of verbal jousting. "Our home number is unlisted," replied Diane in a quick-tempered manner. "We prefer it kept that way."

Hilary sounded as though she was reading from a script. "Well then, Dr. Alan asked me to book a follow-up appointment for your husband as soon as possible. Mr. Jackson needs to call the office right away."

I was right, thought Diane. *This is about Paul.* "May I ask what this follow-up appointment is about?"

"Well, Mrs. Jackson," continued Hilary. "I'm not at liberty to discuss exact details with you, but what I can tell you is that it pertains to his recent medical."

"His flight medical?" asked Diane with trepidation. "He never said a thing to me with regards to his medical. He's always passed that. Was there something wrong?"

"Non-disclosure is his prerogative," stated Hilary. "As I'm sure you know, we stress confidentiality and privacy of information with all our patients."

"Don't go there with me," cautioned Diane. "I've worked in the medical profession and know all about its privacy policy. And for the record, my husband and I are in the habit of discussing everything together!"

"Be that as it may," acknowledged Hilary. "I'm not at liberty to discuss the details of your husband's medical with you, Mrs. Jackson, or its results. That is entirely up to him."

"You've mentioned that twice to me now, Hilary," replied Diane. "I get it."

"Yes, well, if you would please have him call the clinic, Dr. Alan can proceed with follow-up tests."

Chills ran the full length of Diane's body as her brain processed what she heard. "What did you just say? Tests for what?"

The receptionist stammered, her hesitation a clear indicator that she already said too much. "Um-nothing really, your husband just needs to arrange a follow-up appointment. That's all I can tell you, Mrs. Jackson."

Though visibly trembling, Diane kept the tone of her voice composed. "Well, Hilary, he's flying now. I'll have him call you when he's back in town."

There was a long unsettling pause. "He's flying?" sputtered Hilary.

"Of course," explained Diane. "That is his job."

Dead air over the phone line told Diane all she needed to know.

"Uhm, thanks for your time, Mrs. Jackson," babbled Hilary. "I'm sorry, but I have other calls to make and need to go." The line went dead.

Diane repelled the urge to call the woman back and blast her for lack of common courtesy, but that would have to wait for another time. Instead, she leaned into a nearby rack of clothes for support, her head swimming. It took barely a few seconds for emotions to bubble up. "Oh Paul, what haven't you told me?"

Kim had noticed her mom on the phone and wandered over. "Was that Dad?" she asked excitedly.

Gawking absently at her daughter, Diane couldn't find the words to reply.

"Mom, what's wrong?" asked Kim. "Is Dad okay?"

Diane's eyes became misty with tears.

"What is it, Mom?" pleaded Kim again. "What's happened?"

It was now crystal clear that her husband was flying while under a medical restriction, and whatever specific issue he was hiding, Diane felt cheated that he chose not to share it with her. His dishonesty was like a full-force open-palm slap in the face. *How did I miss this?* she wondered. Paul always embraced full disclosure in their marriage, traits Diane admired from the start in their relationship.

With conflicted, tormenting thoughts, Diane's vision narrowed. She reached out for Kim and felt her balance wane. Kim grabbed hold of her mother and locked her footing to keep them both from toppling over. "Mom!" she cried out. "What's wrong?"

Diane found her voice. "We, we need to go home, Kim. Now!"

Kim's emotions were now on high alert. "What's going on, Mom?"

Regaining her balance, Diane answered her daughter's question. "I don't think your dad is supposed to be flying. We just need to go."

"Isn't supposed to be flying?" repeated Kim. "I don't understand."

"Kim," pleaded Diane a second time. "Can we please just go?"

Bowled over by the news and without fully understanding the ramifications, Kim glanced around the store for Tess. She was nowhere at hand.

* * *

Since turning away from Spruce Creek, the mood inside the cockpit turned dismal. Neither man said anything as the airplane followed a reverse course across the lake towards the eastern shore. Dave adjusted back the manifold pressure and RPMs to minimum cruise power to conserve fuel. With such ominously low clouds hanging in perpendicular layers, it felt like being squeezed into a long gloomy tunnel, with no idea what greeted them at the other end.

The cramped river valley leading towards Owensville widened out in places, and then quickly closed back in. And with the Moose River twisting left and right the entire distance, the trick was to ensure they stayed over the water at all times, especially in degrading light and visibility. Straying beyond the banks could prove fatal because of uprooted pines, their limbs tipped towards the water, but not completely fallen over.

Dave clenched his teeth out of sheer frustration and wondered if they shouldn't have circled the lake once or twice in the off chance the lights came on. Or that by retreating so hastily, they had already sealed their fate to running out of gas in the middle of nowhere. Dave glanced at Paul whose face was buried in the sectional map. "You gonna stare at that thing all night, Ace?"

Several miles ahead, lightning turned the dreary valley walls into surreal postcard-like images, scenes that would have made any photographer proud if lucky enough to trip the shutter at the right moment. Paul raised his head to take in the view and then re-focused his attention on the map without responding to Dave's sarcasm.

Dave sighed loudly for Paul's benefit. "I could really use your eyes on the GPS. And if you hadn't noticed, we're about to fly down the throat of that pretty light show up ahead. So, if it's just the same to you, Ace, I'd rather not smack into a mountain tonight."

Paul spoke quietly without taking his eyes from the map. "Just give me another minute," he ordered defensively.

"Another minute for what? I'm serious, Paul! Once we hit the river, we start playing Russian roulette with your airplane, and maybe our lives." Dave eyed the fuel gauges as if by glaring at them long enough the indicator needles would magically swing to the right where he desperately wanted them to be. "And I'm having serious doubts that your gas gauges are showing us the true picture here."

The Cessna's fuel lines carried gas equally from both wing tanks to the six cylinders, ejecting hot gases through each of six exhaust valves. The cycle would continue until they reached Owensville or, God forbid, until they ran out of gas. And Dave wanted no part in the latter outcome. "Are you hearing me?" he fumed.

Paul glanced at the GPS and back to the map. He pressed his index finger to a spot on the paper that could be construed as the middle of nowhere by a casual observer. "I know a place we can land if the weather prevents us from reaching Owensville, or we approach bingo fuel."

"You can't be serious, Paul!" Dave protested. "There's only one way out of this valley, and we have no choice but to follow the river. Aside from Spruce Creek and Owensville, there is no place to land. I think it's time you focused your attention on—"

"Are you done your lecture? Because we really don't have time for it. I'm aware of our less than ideal situation and I'm trying to find a solution. So, please can it and just trust me!"

Dave stared at Paul wide-eyed, his mouth slanted open.

Despite feeling physically lousy and emotionally spent, Paul resolved to dig deep if this flight was to have a survivable ending. With a renewed sense of purpose, he vowed to accept responsibility for not only his deluding conduct inside and outside the cockpit but also for their current fuel-related condition. Still, it was undeniably fun for Paul to witness a tongue-tied Dave McMurray. "I never thought I'd see the day you were speechless," he teased. "And you can close your mouth now."

Dave finally spoke. "I was only trying to get your head back in the game. You snooping at that map is pointless unless you're keeping secrets, which now I fearfully suspect you are."

Paul cringed at Dave's unsuspecting comment about keeping secrets. It was yet another blunt reminder of his dishonesty. "It's okay, Dave," he said. "I know our fuel is low. We both know the ramifications of that. I've got a place in mind to set down if it comes to that, and with the engine running. Better a spot of our choosing than a forced approach with no gas in the tanks, not that I think it will come to that."

"You're preaching to the choir again," refuted Dave. "I get all that. But you know as well as me that there's not a place on that map we can get to before the motor quits. And because I don't trust your fuel gauges, I think it will come to exactly that."

A smile formed on Paul's face. "Oh, ye of little faith. Who said anything about landing within the borders of this map?"

For the second time in as many minutes, Dave McMurray was at a complete loss for words.

Chapter 10

Regardless of their wet attire upon returning from the airfield, Dylan Sullivan and Matt Hawley beelined it straight for the sandwich table to appease their ravenous appetites. Tom Sullivan offered to hang out with Jack, but his offer was respectfully declined. More than anything now, Jack craved solitude and wished to brood alone without having to engage in well-intentioned conversation.

Sitting alone in his bleak office, Jack fidgeted with an oil lamp on the corner of his desk, its small flame providing the only source of light. Directly behind him, faint shadows flickered on the wall and moved lazily in sync with Jack as he stretched weary arms above his head.

After changing into dry clothes, Jack poured himself an ounce of scotch to help to soothe his glum state. Holding the crystal glass loosely between his fingers, he spun the cup in circles and watched as the golden liquid swirled inside, almost to the point of spilling over the rim. Lifting it to his lips, he enjoyed a healthy sip and shivered as he swallowed.

Setting down the liquor, Jack reached for his pullover sweater on the back of his chair. Frayed at the sleeves, the black-and-beige striped V-neck was still his most cherished, a treasured gift from Mildred the year she was diagnosed with cancer.

In his current frame of mind, Jack was sure he could not have felt worse. The evening had been a complete train wreck, and without the television cameras and support gear, the broadcast was not going to happen. Stalling the inevitable, Jack's reluctance to pass the news to his guests created further anxiety. With a lodge full of young people, whispers and conjecture were sure to abound. The truth was that Jack decided he would rather sit through a screechy opera than address the masses with any form of bad news.

At the moment, Jack's primary concern was for Dave and Paul's well-being. Plus, the anger he charged himself with for not checking the runway lights sooner also added to his misery. Jack angled his neck back and downed the remaining scotch in one gulp. A guilty conscience was the last thing he wanted or needed, but until this sinking ship righted itself—if it did—he knew he'd be stuck in a state of perpetual self-loathing.

With electrical power still out, the stuffy air inside Jack's office felt clammy against his skin, the sensation on equal footing with his already bummed mood. Through his window, Jack watched as faraway lightning lashed out, the residual flashes illuminating his room like a weak floodlight being turned on and off in quick succession.

Jack visualized the Cessna and its crew trying to piecemeal their way through stormy unforgiving skies. There was no doubt in his mind that the airplane would be flying dangerously low beneath the cloud deck, and if they ran out of gas, Jack agonized over how long before rescuers found them and what sort of shape would they be in. His stomach twisted into a knot and the scotch wasn't helping.

Staring open-mouthed at his empty glass, Jack felt blameworthy for the entire mess, and even in some warped way, the weather. He wondered how it might feel to face a judge over charges of negligence and manslaughter. Not that it would come to that of course, but in his current frame of mind, self-condemnation was eating away at his resolve to press on no matter what—as Mil would have expected of him.

Against his better judgment, Jack reached for the bottle and poured another shot. As the beverage trickled into the glass, his desk phone rang unexpectedly, the unnerving intrusion causing him to spill some liquor on his desk. "Son of a gun!" he grumbled.

Reaching with one hand for the phone and the other snatching a handful of tissues to soak up the spill, Jack wasn't at all pleased by the fresh stain on his Day-Timer or the squandering of his eighteen-year-old single-malt whiskey.

"Hello," he gruffly answered, not wanting to talk with anyone.

"Jack, is that you?" asked the noticeably strained female voice. "It's Diane Jackson again."

Grimacing—this was the last person Jack wanted to speak with—he collected himself and faked a cheery tone into his voice. "Diane," he answered. "How are you this stormy evening?" Jack immediately regretted the hypocrisy of his question.

"That's twice tonight I've been asked that question, Jack," Diane retorted. "How do you think I'm doing?"

Jack apologized and immediately felt the need to unburden his conscience. "I'm sorry, Diane. That was an insensitive question. It's been a challenging evening here as well, and I admit I'm a bundle of nerves." *As no doubt you are.*

Jack heard Diane sigh, but when she didn't reply he continued. "We've still got no power and its damn cold inside the lodge. I've got no cameras for the show tomorrow because Paul couldn't land. It's been a real mess and—" Jack knew he was word-vomiting and cut himself off.

Diane's voice softened. "So, with that being said, Jack, I take it my husband is still airborne?"

Jack swallowed hard. "Yes, I'm afraid that's exactly what it means. I messed up with the runway lights. They're out and I have no idea why. I tried to get them working, but I was too late. It's my fault they couldn't—"

"Jack, it's all right," Diane interrupted. "It's not your fault."

Jack rested his head against his other free hand. "I should have checked the lights sooner. I just assumed they'd fire up and the guys would land, refuel and take off again. It should've been nice and simple."

Jack wouldn't have been surprised if Diane blasted him for his lack of preparedness, but deep down he knew she didn't operate that way, even if he felt he deserved it.

"Jack," plead Diane. "Tell me what happened. Whereabouts are Paul and Dave now? Did they even try to land?"

Gathering his courage, Jack tried his best to answer her rapid-fire questions. "They couldn't, Diane. It was too dark by the time they got here. I mean they could probably have tried, but only the field beacon was on. And with such strong winds, the plane just hung there below the clouds like it wasn't even moving."

Jack knew he was rambling but couldn't stop himself. "My immediate concern was that if they kept circling around waiting for runway lights to come on, they'd waste fuel they didn't have. So, I shot a warning flare at them to go back to Owensville while they had the chance."

"You, you shot a flare at my husband?" asked Diane completely mortified.

"No, not at them! I fired it straight up and the wind carried it out towards them. They got the message because the plane banked away pretty quickly. They headed back down the lake and I'm guessing out through the river valley towards Owensville."

"Oh, dear God," blurted Diane. "So, they're heading back here? Is that what you're telling me, Jack?"

"That's it as far as I can guess," Jack admitted. "But the problem isn't so much the storm system as it is, they're low on fuel." Jack tried to sound positive. "But if Paul can navigate the river and stay low, they could easily make it back to the airport. He's a good pilot, Diane."

"Did you say they were low on fuel, Jack?" asked Diane. "Please tell me that's not what I heard."

Jack cringed. "Your ears are working fine, Diane. As I'm sure you know, Paul flew here in a hurry at my request and didn't fill up before they left. He knew I had gas at the airfield, so he planned on topping up once he landed. He assured me it was a short flight and not a big deal."

Diane's voice quivered as she replied. "So, my husband is flying through the mountains at dusk, in this storm, and he doesn't have enough fuel to make it home? Are you kidding me, Jack?"

Jack felt a lump form in his throat. "It wasn't supposed to happen this way, Diane. It's my fault they aren't on the ground now. I should've checked the lights several days ago. I just imagined they would—"

"Jack!" Diane chimed in. "I'm not in the mood for self-pity or excuses, so enough with the sob story. It's not you up in that airplane, it's my husband! And now you tell me about their fuel situation! You don't know the half of what's going on here, Jack, so quit blaming yourself. Paul's the one at fault. He never should have flown tonight, and this entire fiasco could have been avoided if he was honest with himself and everyone else. His plane should never have left the ground, at least not with him on board. And I'll tell you something else, Jack …"

Jack heard Diane suck in a gulp of air, and he cringed. It was beyond question that she was about to disclose something he would rather not hear. In Jack's view, the less he knew about private matters, the better.

"My husband shouldn't be flying, Jack. I think he failed his flight medical or something of the sort. He lied to himself, to me and to you. I don't know what he's trying to prove, Jack, but his stupid decision might cost him his flying career and from what you've told me, now maybe his life."

"Shouldn't be flying?" Jack repeated. "I don't understand. He failed his medical and he's flying?"

Frustrated, Diane spewed an angry reply. "That is what I just said, Jack! Why isn't anyone listening to me tonight? I have to go, Jack, and I . . ."

With closed eyes, Jack leaned back in his chair and listened to Diane spout off. Suddenly, he wanted nothing more to do with any of it. The lodge, the broadcast, the airplane. He'd played his part and failed miserably at it. With events beyond his control, Jack had little choice but to sit back and watch things further unravel. Diane's words blended into the background as his bitterness overpowered the voice streaming through the receiver.

With the phone cupped under his chin, Jack guzzled the remaining scotch. Crestfallen, he chucked the glass forwards and watched as the cornflower crystal shattered into pieces against the far wall. He promptly regretted his tantrum because the glass was part of a larger set, a collection passed down from Mildred's side of the family. He began to tremble because he knew she'd be horribly disappointed with his childish attitude.

In his "poor me" stupor, Jack suddenly clued in that Diane's voice was no longer there, that at some point she had hung up. He set down the handset and walked away to collect the broken crystal fragments. If she said goodbye, he never heard it. Jack concluded it was of little consequence either way because in his heart he believed that he'd received exactly the treatment he deserved.

* * *

The fire alarms chirped briefly, followed by the unexpected resurgence of electrical systems, computers and overhead lighting. As radar panels winked back to life, Bruce Macbeth stared out the control tower windows with intrigue. Seconds later, runway and taxi lights flickered on, their white and blue lights breathing new life into the sleeping airfield. Bruce figured that either city crews had restored power to the grid or an on-the-ball technician had restarted the airport's back-up generator. In either case, power was back on. Stepping away from the windows, Bruce headed for the coffee pot. The numbers on the machine's display flashed as a result of the outage. He stabbed a few buttons to reset the time and proceeded to brew a fresh pot.

Veteran controller Ken Hamill noticed Bruce fussing with the machine.

"It's about time you did something useful around here. And if you stick around long enough tonight, you might learn a few new things now that we're back up and running!"

Accustomed to the ridicule, Bruce offered his own smart-aleck reply. "Very funny. But seeing as your knowledge base is poor for an air traffic controller, learning anything from you is next to impossible. And for what it's worth, I'm only making enough coffee for myself."

Ken shook his head repulsively. "You're a solid team player, Macbeth. Don't forget I do your performance appraisals."

Bruce saluted sloppily. "Every man for himself. Besides, every time I come to you with an issue, all I ever hear is, 'I know, Bruce, I know.'"

Ken yielded with a chuckle. "Well, I do what I can."

Bar none, Bruce made the best tasting coffee in the tower, and everyone knew it. Regardless of the chiding, he already intended to brew a full pot as he watched heavy rain smack into the tower's slanted windows. Lightning flashed from varying altitudes, the pulses revealing a thick cover of cloud drifting across the waterlogged airport.

The magnitude of the storm caused Bruce to reflect on the incredible power of nature. Over the years he'd seen his share of harsh weather from the tower and the bevy of complications it created around the airport and for air traffic in general. As another blast of thunder vibrated the tower, a chill ran along his spine. Bruce thought again about the Cessna 185, its crew caught somewhere in the middle of that raging mishmash. *If only you guys had waited like I suggested.*

Deliveries

Bruce added a filter into the basket and measured out eight precisely rounded tablespoons of Costa-Rica dark roast coffee. He closed the lid, filled the reservoir with ice-cold water and turned the machine on. Sauntering to his workstation in no particular hurry, and hoping to shake a sense of gloomy intuition, he plunked himself down at the computer beside Ken. "I'll check the weather," he announced. "Because I know you don't know how."

Ken shrugged his shoulders. "That menial task is below my pay grade. Besides, you're the one who needs the practice, not me."

Bruce smirked. "You need to learn to suppress your pride, Mr. Hamill. It's most unbecoming of a professional, and I'm using that word lightly."

Not waiting for a reply, Bruce changed the subject as he clicked open a series of weather radar maps. "I'd bet you anything our raging storm is multi-cell to be packing this kind of wallop," he stated emphatically. Bruce selected another window and gasped in surprise. "Steering winds alone are upwards of fifteen grand!"

Ken pulled his eyes from the radar scope and turned his head towards Bruce, his eyebrows slanting upwards. "Sheesh," he admitted. "You sound like a bona fide weatherman. Someone paid attention during meteorology classes."

"Quit with the eyebrow thing. You look like Spock when you do that!"

"Except I'm more logical than Spock ever was," added Ken, followed by two thumbs up.

"Don't flatter yourself."

"Tell me more about the multi-cell, oh wise one," taunted Ken.

Bruce always enjoyed studying weather and being gifted with the power of recall; certain paragraphs from his textbook were forever etched into his memory. He knowingly smiled at Ken. "While some thunderstorms are stationary, others clip along at speeds up to fifty miles per hour. Between 10,000 and 20,000 feet, steering winds determine the storm's speed and direction. While it dissipates, a new storm can rise from the outflow of the dying one. This creates a squall line capable of wind speeds up to 100 miles per hour."

Ken shook his head. "Unbelievable that you have that monologue committed to memory. You really need to get a life, buddy, and a good glass of wine. Or maybe in your case, the whole darn bottle!"

Bruce politely bowed before re-gluing his eyes to the weather radar. Their good-natured ribbing kept the work atmosphere light in an otherwise stressful environment. "I'm good with the whole bottle," agreed Bruce. "As long as you're supplying."

"Ha, fat chance. I just spent a small fortune on a dozen bottles from a winery tour my wife and I recently took. And there's not a hope in all creation that Colette will give one up." Ken changed the subject. "So, what's the forecast, oh learned one? Is this mess ending soon?"

"Storm warning's continued for Owensville," replied Bruce without looking up. "But it's been removed for areas due west, including Bayshore Lake." Bruce glanced at the flight itinerary for Paul's Cessna. The document sat in a nearby tray which he reached for and picked up. "Just wish I knew where they were. Drives me nuts that we can't get hold of them."

"Seriously, man," teased Ken. "Those guys are competent pilots, so quit worrying so much." The smell of fresh-brewed coffee filled the tower. "While you're at it, grab me a java will ya? With lots of cream." Ken handed over his mug. "I don't know why you insist on staying up here. Your wife's going to file a complaint against you for gross negligence. It's your anniversary for crying out loud!"

Bruce was surprised that she hadn't done so already. "Point taken," he admitted. "And I'll even agree that you're right, but just this once."

"Besides," added Ken. "There's nothing you can do for that plane, and you know it. They either show up or they don't. If we don't hear from them soon, and they're not at Spruce Creek, then we'll mobilize the troops." Ken snatched the 185's flight itinerary from Bruce's hand and looked it over. "Your airplane is most likely on the ground by now, nicely tied down and abandoned for the night."

"Maybe," replied Bruce. "But I don't think so. The people at the lodge were having trouble with their field lights. Last time I spoke to Paul's wife, she said that landing at Spruce Creek was a definite no go."

Ken spoke through a wide yawn. "If the Cessna wasn't able to land up there, they'll have no choice but to head back this way."

"Agreed," admitted Bruce.

"So, what's the issue that has your knickers in a knot?" asked Ken.

"I want to know they're safe before I head for home," explained Bruce. "I know I won't relax otherwise, anniversary or not."

Ken turned towards his friend. "Tell ya what. How about you hightail it out of here and take your wife to supper. I promise I'll call you if we hear anything. I bet the crew is enjoying steak and lobster at the lodge this very minute, and here you are stressing yourself out for nothing."

Bruce sighed heavily. "If they turned around, the plane will be hugging the river all the way back. You've got to admit, Ken, their chances aren't the greatest given this storm and low cloud cover through the mountains."

Ken pointed his index finger towards his co-worker. "I'm the senior controller here, Bruce, so go home! That's an order."

Bruce snickered. "Someone needs to be the voice of reason around here, and it's not you!" He handed Ken his empty coffee mug. "And for what it's worth, you can fetch your own coffee. I'll barf if I have to add cream to a perfectly healthy cup of high antioxidant black coffee."

"I can't," replied Ken. "I'm on shift, and unlike you, I won't leave my post. Be a gentleman and help me out. In fact, I think there's even a bottle of raspberry flavouring in the fridge. You could always use that instead of—"

Ken's headset crackled to life. "Owensville tower, Beechcraft Charlie, Lima, Kilo, Mike, how copy?"

The inbound turboprop finally showed up.

Ken spun in his chair. "Beechcraft Charlie, Lima, Kilo, Mike, Owensville tower, we read you five by five."

Given the recent plague of adversities, Bruce wasn't overly surprised to learn the plane suffered from a gremlin of its own. As he listened to the problematic conversation through his headset, Ken asked the pilot to squawk an ident code using the onboard transponder. But as reported, the device wasn't transmitting properly, which meant both intermittent and improper altitude data on Ken's radar screen.

Following several failed attempts to correct the issue, the pilot finally gave up and relayed their altitude verbally through the turbulent descent and approach. Within five minutes of the initial call, the Beech was safely on the ground after a noticeably rough landing as observed from the tower.

Bruce shook his head as he considered the events of the evening. "How is it that so many things can go wrong so quickly?" he asked Ken. "It's like the world conspired against us all at once."

"You're doing it again," observed Ken. "You're thinking too much. Poop happens, and tonight is one of those nights. And speaking of things gone wrong, you still haven't fetched me my coffee."

Reaching for the field binoculars, Bruce focused on the Beechcraft as it taxied towards the tower and nearby parking ramp. The pilot carefully steered the plane to a marked spot on the asphalt and stopped with a lurch. Bruce watched until the engines shut down. "No doubt those passengers are glad they're on the ground," he stated. "I bet that was an unsettling ride."

"No doubt," agreed Ken.

Sheets of rain smacked into the windows from what seemed impossible angles. Rising from his swivel chair, Bruce set down the binoculars and grabbed the mug from Ken's workstation. "I'll get your coffee, oh lofty one, but no cream. That stuff will kill you. You just sit and lord over your kingdom."

As he walked away, Bruce's cell phone broke into song with a jazzed-up rendition of Beethoven's Fifth Symphony. He set the mug down and wrangled the phone from its holster. Certain it was Marilyn, he clicked connect without bothering to check the caller ID. "Hello gorgeous, miss me already?"

Following a moment of awkward silence, a male voice replied with humorous undertones, "You ATC guys are sure a touchy-feely bunch. I'm touched that you care!"

Bruce immediately recognized Kevin Davies' jovial voice and felt relieved the young man couldn't see his red face. "Ah, sorry buddy," he stammered. "Thought you were the Mrs."

"That's a big negative," snickered Kevin. "But I'm feeling loved just the same!"

Bruce wanted to change the subject as quickly as possible. "So, what's up?" he asked.

"I can't stop thinking about the Cessna you told me about," admitted Kevin. "I was wondering if you've heard anything from them?"

Bruce tucked the cellphone under his chin, grabbed up Ken's mug and aimed for the coffee pot. "Great minds think alike. We were just discussing them up here." Bruce filled the mug and grabbed a cup for himself.

"So, any idea where they are?" asked Kevin again.

"Wish I knew," replied Bruce. "My guess is they've done a U-turn and are heading back to Owensville."

"That won't be an easy flight in this storm," admitted Kevin.

Bruce handed a steaming cup of jet-black coffee to Ken, who upon noticing the lack of cream, immediately frowned in displeasure. Bruce overlooked the man's sour face, sipped his own and promptly burned the tip of his tongue. "That's what has me so jittery," he painfully agreed. "The cloud base through the river valley is at best a few hundred feet, so they'll have to fly low and slow to make it back. Plus, at that altitude, we have no way to contact them. All we can do is hurry up and wait."

"That's what I expected," acknowledged Kevin. "I couldn't sleep anyway, and this stupid roof is leaking like a sieve. This old building should likely be bulldozed."

Bruce knew Kevin's whereabouts without even asking. "Kevin, please tell me you're not still here at the airport?"

"Okay, I won't tell you," laughed Kevin. "I wanted to stay close by, so I decided to bunk it out here. Plus, I can keep a closer eye on the Cub. The hangar leaks worse than this place."

Bruce admired the young man's dedication. "Well, try to get some sleep. As soon as I hear anything, I'll let you know. You won't be of help to anyone if you're dog tired in the morning. I'm thinking I'll head home myself. Ken said he'd let me know when the 185 checks in." *If, it checks in.*

"Roger that," replied Kevin. "I better let you go, Bruce. Thanks for chatting and—"

For a moment, Bruce thought he'd been disconnected because the phone line crackled and all audible sound died away. "Kevin? Hello?"

Silence.

"Are you there, Kevin?" asked Bruce.

Kevin quietly replied. "Yeah, I'm here. Hang on a second—"

More silence.

"Kevin, what is it?" asked Bruce. "What's going on?"

"Sounded like something outside just crashed into something else," Kevin reported. "Like metal on metal. I better go, Bruce. The wind's really howling now and the noise came from the direction of the hangar. I'll call you back."

"Okay," Bruce replied. "Let me know what's happening and I'll—" Bruce stopped talking when he clued in that Kevin already disconnected the line.

Setting down his coffee after only a few sips, Bruce unconsciously re-holstered his phone. He snatched his windbreaker from the back of his chair and headed for the exit leading to the tower's stairwell.

Ken noticed a blur of movement behind him, followed by a rush of air.

"Holy smokes, where's the fire?" he challenged. "You heading home or what?"

Bruce called back over his shoulder. "I'll go with the *or what*."

"So, what then?" asked Ken. "You running from the cops again?"

Bruce grabbed hold of the door and jerked it open. "I'm heading over to Search and Rescue. I think our evening may have gone from bad to worse."

"Why is that?" asked Ken. "Wait, I really don't want to know. Just stay away from me. You're bad luck!" But instead of receiving an answer, he ended up staring at a closing door. "You suck, Macbeth!"

Bruce descended the stairs two at a time until he reached the front doors of the tower. As he hopscotched the waterlogged asphalt towards his car, he checked for his phone, not because he needed to make a call, but simply out of habit. When his fingers discovered nothing but an empty holster, a sudden wave of panic stabbed his gut. He froze, spun around and scanned the area between the tower and his car. Except for widespread puddles, Bruce saw nothing out of the ordinary. Assuming he had left his cellphone at or near his workstation, he thought about going back inside for it but decided to check in with Kevin first.

The phone would have to wait.

The Search and Rescue building wasn't hard to get too, but the windshield wipers' inability to clear the rain away fast enough made the drive unmercifully slow. Nonetheless, Bruce tromped on the gas and navigated the soggy roadway as quickly as he dared.

At the base of the control tower, crickets chirped from the sanctuary of a small bush near the walkway, their song barely audible over the noisy pounding of raindrops striking the ground.

A short distance away, an object foreign to their turf sat motionless in the wet grass. The insects stopped their chorus when they detected a weird new vibration reverberating across the ground and adding to the stormy ambiance.

Only a few bars into the musical interlude, rainwater worked its way deep into the device, instantly sizzling micro-electrical parts and frying the circuitry. Bruce Macbeth's cellphone died within seconds, it's now lifeless shell drowning in a rapidly expanding puddle of water.

Chapter 11

Cruising 100 feet over the river to avoid punching through disorderly clouds, Dave found it easier to control the airplane at a lower speed while navigating the reverse course through the valley towards Owensville.

At present, the narrow river curved gently left and right which allowed for shallow bank angles on the wings, but Dave knew that would change. With gentle precision, he guided the Cessna through slow flight, doing his best to stay over the water. Because of pitchy air currents, the needle inside the vertical speed gauge fluctuated up and down on both sides of the zero marker. Dave adjusted the elevator trim to combat the ongoing differentials, but this had little effect.

Notwithstanding the engine already leaned out for maximum fuel economy, Dave worried that any less gas being fed to the cylinders would result in an engine out. He nervously eyed the fuel gauges and felt certain the distance yet to travel would exceed the amount left in the tanks—which according to the needles and Paul's opinion, would be enough. Dave thought not.

The landscape below appeared grey and lifeless, void of any specific detail. Hidden from view by cloud were sloping ridges dotted with towering spruce trees and outcrops, all rising vertically toward mountain peaks, and all perfectly capable of terminating flight if the plane wandered too close. The GPS's screen added the only real colour to the dimly lit cockpit, faithfully displaying the

Cessna's position above the river. Dave's eyes drifted from the GPS to key flight instruments, then back to the GPS.

For the time being, the heavy rain eased to a drizzle, but Dave guessed the reprieve would not last long. If the brunt of the storm was lying farther ahead, he knew the real fun had yet to begin. Beside him, the beam of Paul's flashlight created small circles of light on the sectional map. A sudden updraft impacted the fuselage and hiked the Cessna towards the cloud base. Dave edged the yoke down and adjusted the trim. "Talk to me, Ace. What's the game plan here?" he asked nervously. "I feel like we're about to enter the Bermuda Triangle."

Paul remained quiet as though he never heard the question.

Rather than prod for an answer, Dave allowed Paul to collect whatever thoughts were rattling around in his head. His friend was noticeably out of sorts, and Dave could only guess the reason beyond low fuel and bad weather. But he also fervidly believed that skeletons in one's personal closet had no place in the cockpit, especially now with their situation so dicey.

Two minutes later, Dave's patience maxed out. "Okay, Ace, enough with the silent treatment. You said you have a contingency plan so let's hear—"

"Keep following the river, Dave, I'll let you know well in advance when it's time to change our heading . . . if it even comes to that."

Dave exhaled loudly as his impatience brewed to anger. He sternly pointed to the fuel gauges. "That gives me nothing to go on, Paul! If we do cook the cylinders from fuel starvation, which I'm sure in this boat we will, then we drop into no-man's-land."

Paul raised his head. "I'm aware of our fuel status!" he snapped. "Listen, Dave, I know we're in hot water here. I get it. The weather sucks, and we never should have left without full tanks. But we did, I'm sorry. Just keep us in the air until I figure out where to land. Then, we can hopefully avoid dropping into no-man's-land, as you so bleakly called it. Does that work for you?"

The already cramped cockpit suddenly felt even more constrained and stuffy. Not wanting to escalate the tension, Dave made a conscious effort to control his rising temper over Paul's complacency. "I could slap you right now," he calmly stated. "But I know you cry easily, so I'll refrain."

Lightning tore into the sky northeast of the Cessna's nose, the brilliant pulse capturing the attention of both men. Paul and Dave raised their heads in unison, but the sky had already returned to darkness. Paul rubbed his face and neck with both hands as he continued to study the map. "This nausea makes it hard to concentrate," he admitted. "I am truly sorry, Dave. I saw only dollar signs and a quick turnaround with this trip, and I didn't think things through from a margin of error standpoint."

When Dave remained quiet, Paul began to laugh. "You know, I've never been a target for a search and rescue. I wonder how many more thousands it would cost than what I stand to earn on this trip?"

"It's okay, Ace," replied Dave. "Search and rescue only come into play if we run dry, or we're forced down by the weather and potentially destroy your plane. Listen, I forgive you for lashing out. But right now, you need to forgive yourself, for whatever *it* is."

Paul muscled a weak smile and sucked in a deep breath. "Dave, I, uhm, I really do need to tell you something. I know it's not the best time, but I, oh wow, this is harder than I thought."

"Listen, Paul," acknowledged Dave. "I don't mean to sound insensitive, but your focus right now should be on finding us a place to land. Can the outpouring of your soul wait until we're safely on the ground?" Dave noticed a pained expression on the man's face. "Ah, nuts," he yielded. "You look like Tess did when she told me about cracking up the Vette. Okay, Ace, what's on your mind? Spill it." Dave turned back to eye the GPS. "And just because I'm not laying eyes on you, doesn't mean I'm not listening."

Paul's stomach churned. He swallowed aggressively to combat a toxic mix of nausea, fear, and guilt. He wasn't sure where to start or if he should even try. "You're doing a great job, Dave, and I appreciate you taking over and—"

"No offence, Paul," interrupted Dave. "But a trailer version of whatever it is you're about to say would be appreciated. Once we're on the ground, you can unleash the full-length movie."

Paul decided he should say nothing at all. "Always subtle, aren't you?" he joked. *But Dave's right,* thought Paul. *I've got no business adding my baggage to an already poor situation. What's done, is done. The ball and chain should be my own.* The emotion left Paul's voice. "It's just a personal situation I'm dealing with, so you know what, Dave? Never mind. And you're right, let's get this thing on the ground, preferably at Owensville. We'll talk later."

Dave was now more curious than ever. "For crying out loud, Paul, now you've left me hanging. I want to hear about it, really, I do. But more than anything I'd like to know your plan come flame-out time."

Paul gazed out his side-door window, not that he could see much. "If we can't make it to Owensville with the fuel we have left, or the weather forces us down, I've got a place in mind we can land in one piece."

"One piece would be good," agreed Dave. "And that part you've mentioned already. But as I keep saying, we're surrounded by mountains, and the terrain doesn't level out until we reach the foothills."

Paul screwed up his face and attempted to elaborate. "True enough, but we don't have to go that far. I know a spot just outside the borders of this map that we can reach, but I need to be sure which corridor to fly down." With his index finger, Paul tapped the GPS. "I'm cross-referencing the GPS with the map. A little farther ahead, the river forks south. We'll turn there away from the main branch."

"Track south to where exactly?" objected Dave. "It's not like there's a paved runway out there for us. It's all trees and bush."

Paul held the map closer to his eyes, trying to focus on the markings. "For reasons only a geologist would understand, there's a small lake tucked into a plateau several miles downstream where the valley walls flatten out. On the east side of that lake, there's enough room for a short approach and landing. The downside is that it's bloody narrow, and to find it, I need to be certain which passage to fly down away from the river."

Dave remained skeptical, yet knew their options were few. "So, you're proposing we find a slew that's not on the map, and land in a field that we can't see until we're right on top of it? How do you even know it exists?"

Paul didn't back down from Dave's cynicism. "My dad and I explored the area shortly after I got my licence. We found it by accident. I guess you could call it a slew, but it's deep and full of lake trout. The open space beside it will take a 185 but just barely. Of course, it was VFR each time I flew in there, and it was a relatively easy approach. This won't be the same."

"That's comforting, Ace," chided Dave. "I'm starting to think we should have taken our chances at Spruce Creek. Maybe they've got the lights on by now, and we should turn back. And how come I never knew about this little sanctuary of yours? Friends tell friends everything!"

Paul clicked off the flashlight and folded his map. "Fine. It's your choice, Dave. You're pilot-in-command. If you think it's better to go back, we go back. We probably have enough fuel to make it. But if the lights aren't on, and we can't land, then we're for sure ditching into the lake. It's as simple as that. We can try for Owensville now, or if you're concerned about fuel, we play it safe and set down while the engine's still running. We activate the ELT and wait for somebody with a gas can. I'll support your decision either way."

Dave sighed. "No beating around the bush with you, huh?"

"Just stating the facts. I've got your back too, you know."

With low fuel already against them, Dave thought for a moment. He factored in the effects of wind, engine-power settings and a loaded airplane, but nothing seemed to compute in his brain. Heading back to Spruce Creek held a high probability of failure, and he knew it. And yet continuing towards Owensville was risky too. According to the fuel gauges, they had enough fuel to make it home, but that was based on pristine flight parameters—not a storm from the depths of hell.

"Okay, Paul, you win," conceded Dave. "How far before we turn this buggy south? I'll agree to this because I don't trust the fuel gauges, and I'm not one to tempt fate. And I'm partial to landing with the prop spinning."

Paul zoomed out the view on the GPS. "I'd guess another five minutes. At our current speed and altitude, it'll be easy to change our heading." He pointed to the screen. "At this junction, we head south and follow that branch of the river until we turn off towards the lake. As I said, I just need to aim us down the right corridor."

"I hope you know what you're doing, Ace," added Dave. "And I hope your ELT's working. It could take days for them to find us if we're upside down in a field and the thing's not sending out a distress call."

Designed to broadcast an emergency signal in the event of a crash, the ELT, or emergency locator transmitter relayed an aircraft's position via a satellite to emergency rescue personnel. It also transmitted a homing signal on the VHF emergency frequency, allowing searchers to find the downed airplane quickly and co-ordinate ground assets for rescue.

"It'll work," Paul affirmed. "Now you're the one worrying too much."

Dave reached into the lower right pocket of his coveralls and extracted a small Swiss Army knife. "I hope you're right, but I'd rather not take any chances." He handed the knife to Paul who stared at him suspiciously.

"Open the blade and grab the sleeves of my coveralls," ordered Dave.

"What?"

"Listen carefully to me, Paul. I want you to cut the sleeves off. The full length. But for goodness' sake be careful. I know how you are around knives and I don't want you stabbing either of us."

Despite the dig, Dave's voice was deadly serious. Paul wrinkled his nose. "You want me to do what?"

"The sleeves, Paul. I need you to slice them off, then cut them open into a big rectangle."

"What on earth for?"

With both hands gripping the control yoke, Dave turned his head to the left and looked Paul in the eyes. "Insurance, Ace. Just a bit of insurance."

* * *

Kevin Davies' clothes had soaked through by the time he reached the rear of the hangar. Unsure of where the sound had come from, he walked along the side of the building and stopped when he heard creaking metal. Duel motion sensor lights blinked to life, one mounted under the eaves where he stood, the other towards the front corner.

Rounding the edge of the hangar, Kevin's breath vacated his lungs. One glimpse at the pummeled folding door told him he wasn't entering that way. Ignoring the carnage before him, he sprinted to the side entry door and tried the doorknob. Locked. It was then he realized he'd forgotten his keys inside the main building. No key meant no entry—and the door before him was the only other way inside. Kevin felt the rapid onset of panic.

As he ran back towards the search and rescue building, he called Bruce Macbeth's number on his cell. The call transferred straight to his voice mail. Kevin waited for the beep. "Bruce, it's Kevin," he spoke breathlessly. "There's a huge tree branch across the front part of the hangar. That was the crash I heard earlier while we were talking. I'm going inside to check on the Cub. Call me when you get this!"

Kevin slipped the phone back into his pocket. Inside of a minute, he retrieved the key ring and scampered back to the hangar. Kevin glanced up towards the massive oak tree towering over the building. Halfway up and protruding outwards from the main trunk, a jagged stump was all that remained of the enormous branch that only minutes ago was attached. Smaller branches and clumps of oak leaves littered the ground at Kevin's feet. Acorns were strewn everywhere. Torn away from the trunk's massive girth, the huge branch lay diagonally across the front section of the hangar, its weight and size too much for the flimsy, light-weight structure.

Other than survey the destruction, Kevin knew that without proper equipment and help, there was nothing he could do but go inside and check on the Cub. The entire left side of the hangar door lay buckled like tissue paper, its frame having been torn violently from the standing track. Sections of the roof had collapsed, and though still holding the branch's weight, Kevin guessed the entire mess was on the verge of collapse. With the Cub trapped inside, and the structural integrity of the hangar in serious question, Kevin looked again at the oak tree and worried it might shed another limb.

Subsequent flashes of lightning created a freakish scene of light and shadow across the battered hangar. Equally disturbing was the loud series of thunderclaps only milliseconds later, the shock waves leaving Kevin with the feeling that the airport was under bombardment. He staggered back while trying to assess the damage. The middle portion of the fallen limb held firm against the crushed bi-fold door and the frame, its branches swaying violently as strong winds ripped through its timbers.

Fumbling with the keys, Kevin scrambled to the side door and tried to find the proper key—a daunting task at the best of times—but even more imposing with cold wet fingers and several keys of similar size and shape. He scolded himself for not marking the proper key with some sort of easy to identify label. With trembling hands, he willed himself to calm down. As Kevin tried feverishly to insert different keys into the lock, he noticed headlights appear in the distance, their beams moving at a high rate of speed towards him. The car reached Kevin's location in less than a minute, and it wasn't a vehicle he was familiar with.

Kevin found the proper key. He rammed it into the lock and twisted until the mechanism released. At that same instant, the car door popped opened and his heart leapt to his throat. With everything starkly backlit from pole lights behind the car, not to mention rain and dismal shades of grey, a lone occupant emerging from a car was enough to fire adrenaline through Kevin's body. The unexpected sight caused his already overtaxed nervous system to spike. He dashed inside the hangar and was about to slam the door when someone called out.

"Yo, Kevin, wait up!"

Recognizing the voice and straight off relieved, Kevin leaned through the door and peeked outside. "Jeez, Bruce," he croaked. "You scared the tar out of me. I had no idea who you were with that hurried Nascar approach."

From the parking lot, Bruce was unable to see the carnage at the front of the hangar, so he had no idea what had taken place. "A bit restless, are we?" he asked, the concern in his voice genuine.

"Yeah, you might say that," admitted Kevin, now completely embarrassed. "I just left you a message on your cell. You sure got here fast!"

"Message?" asked Bruce. "I've misplaced my phone somewhere, so never got it. In the meantime, I thought it best to pop over and see what the commotion was during our call. And also, because I'm inherently snoopy!"

"No worries," replied Kevin. "With the racket I heard, I knew something wasn't right, so I needed to check it out. And I was right."

"So, what's got you so riled up now?" asked Bruce.

Kevin pointed at the hangar. "Go around front and look for yourself," he directed. "It's not pretty. I'm heading inside to check on the plane."

"Roger that," nodded Bruce. "I'll be right there."

Shielding his face from the constant salvo of wind and rain, Bruce walked purposefully towards the front of the building. Rounding the corner, he stopped dead, his jaw falling open as he gazed upon the twisted mass of wreckage under one of the largest detached branches he had ever seen. The thickest part of the branch held rock-solid; its bulk wedged securely into the smashed roof and door frame. The upper portion of the limb containing off-shoots and leaves whipped back and forth as it succumbed to the wind. Jagged sections of soffit, fascia and eaves-trough protruded at irregular angles. The complete upper left section of the roof and hangar door had been torn open and crushed from the weight of the branch.

The tree branch reminded Bruce of a massive sprig of broccoli. Tilting his head, he noticed the point of separation where the bough had ripped away. He stood transfixed; surprised the entire hangar hadn't collapsed entirely.

"Bruce, you better get in here!" shouted Kevin from somewhere inside.

"On my way," Bruce hollered back, struggling to pull his eyes away from the damage. "I can't believe what I'm seeing out—"

Another knock-down gust of wind grabbed the branch and wrenched it violently sideways. The tangled hangar door with its large surface area caught the full brunt of the wind and blew farther in by several feet. The sheer weight of the branch toppled the outer right-side frame of the hangar and drove it downward in a devastating blow, ripping the large door completely from its track on both sides. The entire assembly folded in upon itself and thudded to the ground.

Bruce thought he heard Kevin scream, but he couldn't be sure over the sound of grinding metal. The front of the hangar

Deliveries

crumpled further, exposing its interior and the Piper Cub to the elements. The heavy branch came to rest atop the entire mass, leaning haphazardly against the debris. Unable to see Kevin through the wreckage, Bruce scooted around to the side door, which sat far enough back to have remained intact. He mindfully stepped inside, but only by a few feet.

"Talk to me Kevin. Where are you?"

After an anxious scan of the interior, Bruce noticed Kevin crouched down near the tail of the airplane, and he breathed a huge sigh of relief. Fortunately, the Piper Cub rested near the back of the hangar and away from any rubble. Except for small branches, twigs and acorns scattered on the fuselage and the wing, it appeared unscathed.

Kevin launched himself upright and raised the tail section a few feet off the ground, "Give me a hand," he shouted. "I want to back it up as far as it'll go. Keep an eye on the wingtips for me."

On the hangar floor, rain trickled into large puddles as lightning ripped through the turbulent sky, followed by waves of intensely sharp thunder. Bruce hadn't moved from his spot inside the door. "This building isn't safe, Kevin! Forget the Cub! It's not worth risking your neck for!"

Of the four lighting fixtures mounted to the ceiling, only two remained on. The two light clusters nearest to the hangar door, one fluorescent, the other mercury vapour, had ripped away when the front section of the roof fell in. The two farther back cast a bizarre top-down glow on Kevin, his face showing grave concern as would a parent whose child was trapped in a car wreck. Kevin inched the airplane back. "We've got to find a way to get it out of here, Bruce! Like you said, we might need it in the morning."

"There's nothing we can do right now," declared Bruce. "Not without help."

The Cub's front landing gear rolled slowly as Kevin guided the airplane backward by several feet. When he could back up no more, he lowered the tail and gently set it down. "I'll just be a second," Kevin added. "I want to quickly look it over before I come out."

"That's a bad idea!" cautioned Bruce as he watched Kevin scurry around the plane. Bruce wasn't sure he could get his feet to move beyond their current position. "Let's go back to S and R and make a few calls," he pleaded. "If we get some bodies and machinery to help clear away the debris, maybe we can create a space big enough to roll the Cub out. I know there's a backhoe inside the maintenance shed. That should be enough to lift away the branch."

"I'm not losing this airplane, Bruce!" pledged Kevin.

"I understand that," replied Bruce. "But don't be stupid! This hangar's integrity is seriously compromised, and I'd prefer you come out, so I can breathe easier."

Ignoring Bruce's plea, Kevin snatched up several small branches off the wing and engine cowling then checked the left strut and left side aileron by moving the airfoil up and down. The right aileron moved properly in the opposite direction with no impediment. "No obstructions here," announced Kevin. "I'll check the rudder and elevator."

Bruce fixed his eyes on the torn open hangar roof. "And if the rest of this building collapses on you, there won't be an airplane to fly or a pilot to fly it. Please, for heaven's sake, get your butt out of there!"

"Yeah," grumbled Kevin, "one more minute!"

Kevin grabbed hold of the horizontal and vertical stabilizer control surfaces. He jockeyed them up and down, side to side. Satisfied, he performed a cursory check of the Cub's skin for puncture marks. "All good, I think," he remarked. "Okay, I'm coming out!"

Closing the side door behind them, both men ran for the search and rescue building. Once inside, Bruce stripped off his wet jacket and stood shivering near the window. Kevin wasted no time in placing a phone call to his superiors, explaining the situation and all but demanding immediate action to save the Cub.

Bruce leaned in towards the window and watched the wind howl with renewed intensity. He placed his hands against the glass and felt the building shake. The surrounding walls creaked noisily, and from his vantage point, the only part of the hangar visible was the back end. Bruce had never experienced a tornado, but with such violent winds and all the debris flying around, he half expected the building to lift away and take the Piper Cub with it.

Hanging up the phone, Kevin walked over to the window and stood beside Bruce. "Should have some people here in a half-hour or so," he announced. "Then we can try to get the Cub out."

"That's good news. Listen, Kevin, I should head back to the tower and look for my phone. Besides, there's nothing you can do until your buddies show up, and I'd just be in the way. So, warm-up and take a breather. They'll get your baby out, so try not to worry."

Kevin thumped Bruce on the shoulder. "That baby could save the day if your missing plane doesn't check-in." Kevin slipped past Bruce and headed towards the front door.

"Now where are you going?" asked Bruce.

Kevin grabbed the doorknob and twisted. Before stepping outside, he turned his head around to look at Bruce. "To keep my baby company. And don't worry, Dad, I'll be careful."

"You pilot folks are an oddball lot."

Kevin smiled and threw up his arms. "You ATC boys wouldn't understand."

* * *

The massive bulk of the white oak withstood the wind with relative ease, its stately presence providing shelter and shade for almost 200 years. From a tiny acorn, the sapling initially began its life unhindered, its growth unobstructed by man or anything else foreign to nature.

Owensville Airport grew and expanded around the now mature behemoth, no one group or person wanting to accept the wrath of tree-huggers by chopping it down. Its palm-sized leaves grew each spring from thousands of branches, their bark appearing distinctly white when viewed from a distance. But as with all living things, there comes a time of disease, sickness and eventual death.

The limb that dropped on the hangar wasn't so much from the effects of the wind, but from what arborists call oak wilt, a lethal fungus that works its way beneath the bark and causes the tree to die one branch at a time. As a result, the leaves fade and droop, offering a visual clue that nobody ever noticed from ground level. Strong winds served as the catalyst, easily tearing away the diseased limb from its place in the tree's proud lineage.

Unknown to Kevin as he approached the hangar, a second branch had weakened to the point where it too, if given just the right push, would snap and fall. Bigger than its predecessor, this section of timber hung directly over the rear part of the hangar and directly over the Cub. Kevin glanced at the tree for a brief moment, shook his head in wonder, and then scrambled inside.

Chapter 12

"What is that, your third plate of sandwiches?" asked Matt Hawley grinning from ear to ear.

Juggling a flimsy paper plate stacked high with wedge-shaped sandwiches, Dylan Sullivan's cheeks were stuffed full. Reaching for a ham and cheese on rye, his plate buckled under the weight and appeared dangerously close to folding in. A pea-size blob of white salad dressing stuck precariously to the corner of his mouth as he chomped another bite.

"So what?" he stated matter-of-factly. "Just because you're full after three sandwiches, doesn't mean I am. I'm starving. Besides, I missed lunch."

"You always get this defensive?" inquired Matt jokingly.

Dylan hoisted two sandwiches at once. "When it comes to food, darn right!"

Both he and Matt stood near tables spread high with a vast array of finger-sized sandwiches, vegetable trays and pastries. Numerous bodies filled the cavernous room, some lounging in easy chairs while others stood, each voice combining to create a symphony of incoherent gibberish. To combat chilly temperatures inside the lodge, everyone wore a jacket or sweater, some even donning light gloves and the occasional toque. Burning logs snapped in the fireplace as yellowish-orange flames danced about, the blaze providing coveted heat and light to anyone close by.

Matt leaned in close to Dylan. "Just a suggestion, but you might want to consider leaving a few sandwiches for someone else."

Dylan tucked a turkey sandwich into his mouth. "Dude, I don't tell you how to ride, so don't tell me how to eat! There's lot's here for everybody."

Matt shook his head and laughed. "At least I know how to ride."

Dylan coughed out loud and captured the attention of two women nearby, both of whom flinched and turned their backs. "All good here, ladies," he reassured. "Carry on!"

With mild displeasure, the women shook their heads and resumed whatever discussions they were engrossed in. Matt held a cup of coffee in his hands which had cooled to the point of no longer being palatable. He wasn't sure what to do with it, so he continued to carry it around. "Guess we should think about throwing on some dry clothes," he said. "I'm starting to feel like a fish out of water."

"Yup," agreed Dylan. "It feels like I'm wearing a wet bathing suit, but all over!"

The two men strolled towards the fireplace and stopped near a row of windows facing the beachfront. Rain trickled down the glass as droplets raced each other to the bottom of the water-logged sill. Despite growing darkness, Matt watched as waves pounded into the shoreline and clouds lingered freakishly low over the lake. A wooden dock bobbed from the continuous battery of waves, their impact kicking up large volumes of spray into the air. A handful of nearby gulls attempted flight, but when their instincts told them it was futile against the blustery wind, they settled back onto the dock and gave up.

Matt wondered about the Cessna and its crew. If the birds were having this much trouble, how much more so that small airplane? A sudden chill coursed through his body and he shivered. Dylan finished off his last few sandwiches, briefly considered going back for more, then thought he'd be a gentleman and quit. "Okay," he finally said to Matt. "You're turning blue from hypothermia, and

Deliveries

I'm only half full. So, let's go change and I'll meet you back here in fifteen. I could really use a hot chocolate once we're back."

As both men turned towards the corridor, fire alarms chirped a quick note and overhead lighting flickered a moment, then popped on. A collective gasp erupted, followed by cheering from all points in the room. A few people shielded their eyes from the sudden onset of light, and baseboard heaters along the south wall creaked as electricity began to flow.

"Finally!" exclaimed Dylan. "Let there be light! I was beginning to think we'd be in blackout mode all night. See, Matt, things are shaping up!" Suddenly rejuvenated, Dylan eyed the hot chocolate carafe and forgot about his wet clothing. "I think I'll celebrate now with a hot chocolate before I change!"

"Oh, good grief," groaned Matt. "You're such a foodie. Fine, you go on and keep stuffing your face. It's too painful to watch!" Matt walked away and disappeared into the now lit hallway. As he sauntered along, his thoughts again shifted to the Cessna and its crew, his concern for their well-being now set firm in his mind.

* * *

Jack Ward returned to his desk with shards of crystal cupped in his hand. He dropped the loose fragments into the trash can, but a few pieces missed and ricocheted off the hardwood floor. Too disgruntled to care, Jack swung his chair 180 degrees and flopped down, stretching his weary legs under the desk. He wanted to kick off his shoes, but the room was too cold for his thin polyester socks. A heartbeat later, the walnut chandelier on the ceiling sprang to life as did his driftwood desk lamp, a rustic antique resting dangerously close to the edge.

Taken aback by the unexpected intrusion of light, Jack raised his head and gawked at the fixture, half expecting the thing to willfully return him to darkness as some sort of cruel hoax. Remarkably it stayed on. He reached forward and slid the lamp in and away from the edge. Jack placed his chilled fingers near the bulb and enjoyed its radiated heat. "Thank God," he stated wearily.

For the first time that evening, Jack breathed a sigh of relief. Of the many burdens he was carrying, power had now been lifted from his shoulders: a small glimmer of hope that maybe, just maybe things were changing for the better. Jack leaned back in his chair, basking himself in light. Restored electricity meant that work crews somewhere had been hard at work, no doubt feverishly struggling against the elements to splice lines and breathe life back into people's lives. And of all the souls holed up inside Spruce Creek Lodge, Jack Ward felt he had just benefitted the most.

Eyeing the scotch, Jack questioned if the road leading to Spruce Creek might also be cleared or, at the least, was being worked on. He reached over and grabbed the bottle, unscrewed the lid and almost had it to his lips when someone rapped hard on his office door.

"Jack, you in there?" asked the muffled voice from behind the door.

Peeved, Jack set down the liquor, boosted himself from the chair and stood there, silently hoping that whoever it was would go away.

BANG, BANG, BANG. "Let's go, Jack, open up!"

Jack recognized Tom Sullivan's baritone voice when he heard it. "Hold your horses. I'm coming!"

Jack shuffled along without the slightest hint of urgency; his preference having been to enjoy a few minutes more of solitude. But then nothing this evening had gone his way, so why should things start now? Jack released the deadbolt and reached for the doorknob. With a gentle tug, the heavy pine door swung open and there was Tom, a grin on his face that Jack straightaway found annoying. "Geez, Tom," he snickered. "You look like a Cheshire cat for crying out loud. Go away."

"Well, it's good to see you too," replied Tom. "Looks like the gods of fate are finally working some magic around here. We've got light and heat!"

"My you're an observant one," Jack stated glumly.

Tom marched into Jack's room uninvited. "Come on, Jack, we should get a move on. Power's back on, and we've got places to go."

In no mood for frivolity, Jack turned and sauntered back towards his desk, leaving Tom alone inside the doorway. True the lights were on, but the Cessna was still out there, flying in the opposite direction and filled with equipment he needed. Jack stopped on his heels, spun around and stared his old friend down. "Get a move on to where?" he asked combatively. "There's nothing to do but wait. The airplane's gone and there won't be a broadcast. The show's over." Jack turned away.

For a few peaceful moments, Jack had felt rejuvenated, but now as reality gushed back in, his mindset once again regressed to attitudes of defeat, fear, and self-pity. Sensing the evening's events were far from over, Jack walked back to the door and tried to usher Tom out. But Tom anticipated the move and wedged his foot into the door frame at the same moment Jack tried to close it.

"Darn it, Tom," complained Jack. "I just want to be alone. It's peachy the juice is back on, but as I said, the races aren't going to happen, or at least the broadcast part of them. You of all people should get that in *light* of things. No pun intended."

Tom eyed his friend with a hint of genuine compassion. "Are you done, Jack?"

Jack's eyes slinked to the floor. He grudgingly lifted his head back up and met Tom's gaze. "Yes, I suppose I am."

A placid look appeared on Tom's face.

Jack spoke quietly. "Now that you've interrupted my 'poor me' time, what is it exactly that you want me to do?"

Tom leaned against the door frame. "I'm worried about the pilots too, Jack. But right here and now, we need to be proactive."

"So, what's your point?" asked Jack impatiently.

"You weren't listening, were you?" accused Tom.

"Listening to what? Quit playing games with me, Tom. I'm clearly not in the mood."

A picture of Ebenezer Scrooge flashed through Tom's mind, but he cast it off. "Grab your jacket and umbrella if you've got one," ordered Tom. "If the electricity's restored, then there's a good chance they're working on the road. Let's take a drive and see if we can't find out what's going on. Maybe, we can hustle them along. And besides, it'll be good for you to have a change of scenery to improve your . . . disposition."

"Doesn't that seem rather pointless? They're either working on the road or they're not. They said I'd get a phone call when the road is open, so why drive up there for nothing? That stretch will be dangerous with all the rain we've had."

"Because," explained Tom. "I intend to phone back to the station and order our techs to load another van. Cameras, tripods, microphones, you name it. Everything onboard the Cessna I'll duplicate for ground transport. We just need the road to re-open before morning, and then if things arrive early enough, the show is back on."

Jack re-positioned his feet while Tom continued his jaw flapping. "I'll be darned if I'm going to sit back and do-nothing, Jack. You're not the only one who has a vested interest in all of this. I had to pull some programming strings to make this happen."

Both of Jack's eyebrows slanted upwards, and Tom knew he had the man's attention. "We could still pull this off, Jack."

Jack was about to respond, but sensing that Tom wasn't finished, he held his tongue and remained quiet.

"It's times like this we don't curl up in a ball and play dead," ranted Tom. "I've known you a long time, Jack, and it's not like you to ever give up. I hope you don't mind me saying this, but I think Mildred deserves your best effort now."

When Jack heard his wife's name, he cringed and knew that Tom was right.

His mind-set softened when he thought of her and what she would expect from him when things went sideways. She'd be thrilled the lodge was filled with spectators and mountain bikers, even if all the planning, sponsors, airtime and weeks of publicity fell by the wayside. Jack wondered how he had gotten to this point of despair, but he knew that Mildred would never want him to quit or give up on something he started in her name.

Expecting Jack to buck up against him, Tom patiently stood his ground, his stature decisive and his eyes focused.

Jack finally spoke. "Must you TV guys always be right?" he asked.

Tom smiled.

"Wait here," added Jack. "I'll get my coat."

"Atta-boy! You've got nothing to lose at this point, Jack."

Jack walked back to his desk, grabbed his jacket and stopped. "Tom," he mindfully asked. "If I'm going insane, will you be honest and tell me?"

"What?" replied Tom, unsure he had heard Jack correctly.

Jack repeated his question. "If I'm really just imagining this whole mess I've created, and I'm actually standing alone in a field wearing only my underwear, drooling and talking to myself, would you tell me?"

"What in heaven's name are you talking about, Jack?" asked Tom wide-eyed.

Slipping his arms into the sleeves, Jack zipped up his coat and walked through the door before Tom even lifted his feet.

"Never mind," explained Jack. "C'mon, Sullivan, I haven't got all night."

*　*　*

Having sliced through the fabric belonging to Dave's coveralls, Paul gripped the orange sleeves rigidly in his left hand, the open knife in the other. "All right," he asked curiously. "Now what?"

"Well for starters," appealed Dave. "You can fold up that knife and hand it back to me before you hurt yourself."

"Very funny," stated Paul. "I told you the ELT will work, so this little scheme of yours seems a bit screwball, don't you think? This is hardly necessary."

"Noted," replied Dave. "But *should* the ELT fail, what you're holding in your hands might just save our bacon if spotted by anyone searching for us. Now be an obedient student and roll them up tightly, but separately."

Paul shook his head and complied. He rolled each sleeve into a snug sausage roll. "Seeing as you're the boss now, I have no choice but to defer to your wisdom. I just can't—" Paul coughed and clenched his chest.

"Jeez, Paul, you okay?" asked Dave.

Taking a moment to respond, Paul tried to de-clog his throat. "Just more heart palpitations," he explained. "Darn things take my breath away sometimes. And for what it's worth, don't let that earlier compliment go to your head."

"What compliment?" asked Dave. "You simply verbalized a factual statement. I am the boss now, and yes it's about time you validated my superior wisdom."

"Sorry I said anything," grunted Paul.

Despite the severity of their situation, Dave found their joshing around comforting. There was between them an unwritten pact, a pilot's code with each willing to go the extra mile for the other or, when necessary, to keep the mood as light as possible no matter their circumstances. In keeping with that tradition, Dave tried to further elicit a snide response from Paul. "But, are you absolutely certain the window won't rip away once you open it?" he teased. "Or the whole door for that matter?"

Paul responded with his own question. "You really have no faith whatsoever in my airplane, do you? I'm hurt deeply, not that I'd expect you to care."

To validate his point, Paul flipped up the latch and pushed it out from the bottom. The window sprung open and held fast by its upper hinges. Though not large enough to produce lift, the open pane created a sudden blast of air through the cabin, stinging Paul's hand as he grappled with the latch.

Satisfied, he wrestled the window back into place and fastened it securely. "Well, Mr. Skeptic, any other questions?" he asked.

Not wanting to concede defeat, Dave rapped his fingers on the side of his headset before pulling them off. "You say something, Ace? Because all I hear is static and all the other racket this plane makes." He slipped the unit back on and smiled broadly.

In truth, Paul knew Dave was right. Old and weathered from countless flights and years of ultra-violet exposure, the cockpit reverberated from a myriad of different sounds. Giving in, Paul hoisted the sleeves and switched back to serious mode. "When do you want these deep-sixed, MacGyver?"

"As soon as we swing south," Dave replied. "No one's expecting us to not make it back to Owensville, except maybe for Jack. The sleeves might give search and rescue a better chance of locating us from the air, or at least offer clues as to our last heading."

"Chances are they'll end up in the river," Paul cautioned.

"That's a risk we take," said Dave. "I know it's a long shot, but the way I see it, what harm can it do? I'd rather trust old-fashioned Dave McMurray ingenuity than a hunk of questionable electronic hardware, especially in this airplane. And no, I'm not trying to hurt your feelings."

Ignoring the dig, Paul unfolded his map and clicked on the flashlight. A glance at the GPS confirmed their position. "Okay, we're approaching our waypoint. At this speed, maybe two more minutes."

Flying mostly on instruments and referencing the GPS, Dave's grip on the yoke loosened, his confidence bolstered by the knowledge they'd soon be on the ground where foul weather and low fuel could threaten him no more. With gusty headwinds and little to see but cloud, Dave worried about crosswinds once they turned south. He kicked in a healthy dose of left rudder, then right, allowing the airplane to yaw in both directions before evening out. Relieved the vertical stabilizer functioned properly, Dave tried to relax his tensed-up muscles.

Far ahead of the airplane, brilliant flashes of lightning continued to illuminate the river valley. Dave hoped they'd avoid that ugly mass of weather once they turned south, and though not initially thrilled with Paul's alternate ending for this trip, he knew in his gut it was their best and safest course of action.

Paul suddenly slumped forward like he had been knocked hard from behind.

"I'll ask it, again," stated Dave. "Are you okay, Ace? You're really starting to freak me out with that move."

Hunched over the map with both arms wrapped around his abdomen, Paul gently rocked back and forth. The map lay partly across his lap with the flashlight tucked into one of its folds. Paul raised his head and tried to point his finger at the GPS. "Here, Dave, right . . . here," he murmured. "It's coming up. You'll need to zoom in the view a bit, but that's the—"

Without finishing his sentence, Paul flicked open his window.

Thinking Paul was about to launch one of the sleeves, Dave yelled. "Not yet, Ace! Only after we turn!"

"I know, Dave," moaned Paul. "I just—"

Dave watched as Paul vomited into the slipstream, his hair recklessly thrown about by the wind. Paul heaved a few more times until there was nothing left. Unable to aid his co-pilot, Dave zoomed in the view on the GPS. "Hang in there, partner. We'll be wheels down in no time, and we'll get you out of this tin can."

Paul brought his head back into the airplane, his chin wet and hair dishevelled. He offered nothing in the way of reply. The GPS showed the main branch of the river and exactly where it forked south, its path weaving left and right before disappearing outside the GPS's field of view.

Deliveries

"I see the spot, Paul," reassured Dave. "You try to relax."

Dave watched Paul twist sideways and lean his head against the door. The air temperature inside the cabin dropped considerably because of the open window. Though not a direct hazard to the safety of the airplane, Dave wanted it sealed. "Hey, chief, I know you're feeling lousy, but can you find the strength to close that thing?"

No reply.

On his own, Dave had no idea how far it was to the landing zone, and even if he did, he'd never find it without Paul's help. "C'mon, Ace, I need you right now," he pleaded. "I can't find this spot by myself."

Recognizing his friend's miserable state, there wasn't a thing he could do to help. Dave kept his left hand on the yoke and reached over with his right, gently squeezing Paul's shoulder to show his support. He returned both hands to the column and tried to focus on the task of keeping them alive. Collapsed against the door panel, Paul flopped back into his seat, still holding his stomach. "Talk to me partner," encouraged Dave. "You with me?"

Paul's head dipped low into his chest and then fell to the side.

"I need you to close the window, Paul. Think you can do that for me? I can't reach it."

Without warning, the plane's nose pitched up sharply and the left-wing dropped as a powerful blast of wind collided with the fuselage. Dave handled the jolt with little fanfare. Paul not so well. He leaned back into the open window and promptly threw up again. This time Dave ignored his friend and kept his eyes glued to the shifting horizon line.

Directly below them, an active low-pressure system voraciously sucked in large volumes of air from the surrounding valley, promptly re-directing the flow towards the centre. With nowhere else to go, the resulting air column shot upwards, the unstable mass rising vertically and straight into the underbelly of the tiny Cessna. The upheaval slapped hard into the fuselage, oddly striking the starboard side. In a matter of seconds, the right-wing rose twenty degrees, this time catching Dave completely off guard. Pitching up violently, the 185's nose lifted again, quickly eroding what little forward airspeed the aircraft had.

Both men were tossed against their seatbacks, especially Paul, whose arms and head thrashed about like a marionette. Falling from his lap, the flashlight struck the top edge of the rudder pedals and blinked out. The wind rushing through the cockpit from the open window picked up stray papers and flung them about like tissues in a hurricane.

Paul yelled something indistinguishable, a good indicator to Dave that his friend was conscious and breathing. The Cessna's abrupt deviation from controlled flight sent Dave's eyes to the attitude indicator. The airplane showed ten degrees nose up and a significant bank on the wings. On the verge of correcting the imbalance, Dave shifted focus to his airspeed but did so a few heartbeats too late.

The stall warning buzzer began to squeal, an audible warning that things had gone from bad to worse. "Oh, dear God, please no!" rasped Dave.

Flying just a few clicks above stall speed, Dave knew the right-wing would stall first, its surface generating more lift than on the opposite side. If allowed to continue, the plane would depart from its left turn and spin to the right. At such low altitude and if not immediately corrected, death was imminent.

"Hang on, Ace!" yelled Dave despite knowing Paul was incapable of doing so.

The stall warning sounded again.

Irate at himself for failing to notice their decreasing airspeed, Dave shoved the control column forward in a desperate attempt to avert the stall and subsequent spin. Paul's head tipped back against his seat, his arms lifting slightly from the quick onset of negative G's. Just when he thought he'd lost control, Dave advanced the prop and throttle knob fully in, kicking the engine to life. The

Deliveries

power plant surged while the propeller roared to full RPMs, a move critical to recovering the aircraft. Dave gripped the yoke forcefully. "C'mon you pig!" he shouted.

The 185's airspeed began to creep upwards as the river threatened to consume the tottering airplane. Easing off forward pressure on the column, Dave shouted at Paul. "I think I got it, Ace! Just a bit more speed!"

Paul tried to speak, but he ripped off his headset and his garbled words fell on deaf ears. Adrenaline coursed through Dave's veins, leaving his body vibrating and his heart pounding like a jackhammer. Unsure if the airplane had deviated too far left or right from its relative course, he twisted his head towards the GPS. Fortunately, it confirmed their place in the sky remained unchanged.

Dave felt the airplane respond as the effects of lift took hold. The nose angled up a few degrees and the Cessna began to recover. Once established in a gentle climb, Dave left the prop knob forward while easing off slightly on the manifold pressure. If another jolt hit them from underneath, he resolved not to be caught unawares a second time.

The roar of wind through the cockpit suddenly ended—the rush of turbulent air gone. Risking a glance to his left, Dave noticed Paul had closed the window, his hands dropping back into his lap after securing the latch. Attempting to lean forward, Paul fumbled to pick up the flashlight, but his seat belt locked up and prevented any forward movement.

"Easy, Paul," ordered Dave. "Just stay calm until we're out of this mess."

With Dave's grip on the yoke unflinching, he nursed the airplane through ribbons of low-hanging clouds. Aware of how lucky they were to avert disaster, Dave sucked in deep breaths of air to calm himself. He also knew they were using fuel at an alarming rate. "We'll be turning south pretty quick," shouted Dave for Paul's benefit. "Then let's try to park this thing! I know you just closed the window, but we'll need to toss the sleeves. You up to that task?"

Paul negotiated a weak chin nod as he clutched the swatches of fabric like a frightened child squeezing a teddy bear. Dave admired Paul's determination despite knowing what the man was going through. Airsickness was a miserable can of worms inside a cramped bouncing cockpit.

"Okay, good job, partner," affirmed Dave. "I'll let you know when."

Dave thought about squashing the sleeve idea, but his instincts had always played a huge part in his daily regimen, and he wasn't about to push aside the prodding in his gut. He learned years ago to never ignore such physical promptings and that such discomforts were there for a reason if a person had the God-given sense to pay attention.

As the Cessna weaved zigzag patterns through the valley to coincide with the river's flow, light rain pelting the windscreen reduced visibility to near minimums. Dave cussed under his breath at the growing darkness and the stark reality that the outside navigation lights were fast becoming the only source of light penetrating the sky.

Moments later the plane turned south, its fuel tanks far closer to empty than either man realized. At Dave's request, Paul fumbled to re-open his window, and then sluggishly dropped one of the sleeves into the abyss, followed ten seconds later by the other.

The first swatch of fabric floated along at the mercy of turbulent air currents, eventually finding the top edge of an eighty-foot pine tree, its trunk leaning out towards the river along the west bank. Quickly absorbing rainwater like a sponge, the sleeve grew in weight and the thin branch it rested upon began to droop. Another gust of wind ripped the fabric loose, hurling it away from the tip and into the darkness below.

Staying aloft longer than its predecessor, the second caught an updraft which caused the fabric to open like a sail and drift several hundred feet east of the river. It finally came to rest, wedging itself between clusters of jagged rocks and poplar saplings, but exposed enough to be seen by anyone wandering by or from the air at low altitude.

Had there been hikers on the ground as the Cessna transitioned through the valley, their ears would have easily detected the drone from the 185's engine as it slipped away to the south, the unique sound mixed with wind, rain and widespread rumbles of thunder. What they may not have detected was the sound of an aircraft engine beginning to sputter, its thirsty cylinders no longer receiving sufficient fuel to keep the plane aloft, and the two souls on board safe.

Chapter 13

Bruce Macbeth's front tires displaced most of the muddy rainwater pooling in the cracks and sagging concrete of his reserved parking stall. Re-surfacing the parking lot was also down the list of airport revitalization, so tower personnel regularly suffered the aggravation. Rolling to a hurried stop, the radials brushed aside rippling puddles of water, then quickly backfilled against the tread.

Bruce fingered the shifter into park and unlatched his seat belt. In one fluid motion, he snatched his keys from the ignition and popped the door handle. As was often the case, the door opened part way and caught. Bruce leaned against the panel and pushed hard with his shoulder. The door suddenly sprang open, and he lost his balance, almost launching himself to the pavement.

Scurrying the short distance from his vehicle to the control tower's main doors, Bruce scanned the ground as he looked for his cellphone. He slid his key-pass through the reader and the door lock released. Certain his phone was upstairs, Bruce conquered the steps two at a time, preferring the exercise over the tower's slow-as-molasses elevator. At this point, there was little to do except to find his cellphone and go home. He knew that when search and rescue personnel arrived to salvage the Piper Cub, assuming they even could, his help would not be required anyway.

Reaching the upper floor of the tower, Bruce staggered into the control room completely out of breath. The area was dimly lit with overhead pot lights and reeked of burnt coffee. Hunched over the coffee pot was Ken Hamill, his hands fidgeting with the filter basket. He turned his head when he noticed Bruce enter, and then promptly hoisted the empty carafe. "The prodigal son returns!" he teased. "And just in time! Hey, be a pal and take this over for me. I'm falling asleep up here."

Bruce grunted something unintelligible and whitewashed the request. Instead, he walked briskly from console to console searching for his phone.

"Macbeth! You hear me?" hollered Ken. "I'm outta java!"

Bruce halted his search just long enough to respond. "You know Ken, it's difficult for me to believe that someone with your IQ actually made it beyond elementary school."

Ken held up a tin of coffee, then slapped it on the countertop. "Yeah well, I still pull rank and the pot's empty. Admittedly my coffee sucks. But that's all I'm prepared to admit."

"I'll see what I can do," replied Bruce distractedly. "Seeing as you conceded defeat at something."

Ken walked away from the coffee pot. "Conceding to anything goes against my moral compass, so I hope you enjoyed it as a one-off."

Nodding distractedly, Bruce turned and resumed his search.

* * *

Winding through clusters of paper birch and Colorado blue spruce, the narrow gravel road leading towards Spruce Creek Lodge provided tourists with an unprecedented array of scenery. Much of the route lay covered under towering branches, their limbs rising high and melding together overhead. On sunny days, beams of light penetrated the canopy, creating stunning abstract shadows across the roadway. Alongside the road, tiny unseen streams trickled through the underbrush for miles before branching off in countless directions.

Slanting in towards the edge of the road, smooth layers of rock lined the shoulder—each nook stuffed with partially wilted wildflowers and fading vegetation. Tree covered foothills rose vertically, then tapered off near the base of higher mountains. Though visually spectacular, poor weather often proved hazardous to the narrow road below, and today was no exception.

As Friday evening thunderstorms developed, a deluge of rain pounded the slopes for several hours with nowhere to go but down. Rainwater picked up sediment and organic material as it flowed downhill. Mud, soil and forest debris slid unhindered, cutting deeply into the soft earth, the mass eventually stalling across the roadway and blocking passage to and from Spruce Creek through Saturday and into the evening.

Powered by large industrial generators, several work lights provided the necessary illumination for crews to tackle the mess. Leaning against their spades, workers stood nearby while a front-end loader cleared away piles of timber and mud. The rain continued to fall, a fine mist replacing the large heavy droplets. Once the loader punched a hole through the debris, men trudged in and used their shovels to push away leftover piles of rubbish. Mud encrusted work boots crisscrossed the roadway as a flurry of human activity scrambled towards a common goal. Re-open the road and go home.

Rather than picking up the debris with his seven-foot bucket, a rusted scoop large enough to carry off a compact car, the operator of the loader simply swept its contents over an embankment along the road. As he backed up, it was then he caught sight of approaching headlights from the direction of Spruce Creek. He watched as shafts of white light created linear patterns through the trees. Moving his head disgustedly side to side, the crotchety driver grumbled out aloud. "Haven't got the dang road open yet, an' sum fool's already tryin' ta get through."

Peering back over his shoulder towards the mudslide, the man knew from experience they'd be another hour before the road finally re-opened. As the headlights grew larger, he drove forward and parked the giant loader across the middle of the road to prevent passage. He then hoisted his considerable bulk out of the seat, and slowly negotiated his way to the sludgy road below. Not prepared to give an inch, and with arms folded, he stood his ground and waited impatiently for the vehicle to pull up. He decided that tearing a strip off whoever was stupid enough to attempt to get through on such a miserable night would actually be the most fun he'd had all evening.

* * *

Bruce shuffled through stacks of papers near the console, then walked towards Ken. Shifting side to side, his eyes scanned everything at once.

"What'd ya come back for anyway?" asked Ken. "I thought you were checking things out at Search and Rescue and then going home to your more-than-tolerant wife. If I was her, I'd kick your behind but good."

"That was my plan. And I'm extremely grateful you aren't her." Bruce eyed the radar console. "I've misplaced my cellphone and thought maybe it was up here somewhere. You haven't seen it, I'm guessing?"

"That's a negative. It's a wonder you remember how to get to work every day, and now you lose your cell on top of everything else."

Bruce grabbed the coffee tin off the counter. "In my current frame of mind, just be glad I agreed to make coffee for you."

"Well, you are the resident coffee-boy around here," teased Ken. "And in case you're wondering, we haven't heard hide or hair from your waylaid 185."

Rinsing out the coffee-stained carafe in the sink, Bruce answered without looking up. "That comes as no surprise, and I'm not certain we will." He noticed out of the corner of his eye that Ken was pulling a face at him. "Quit glaring at me and do something useful for a—"

A chime interrupted their ribbing, an audible alert that someone outside the tower's main doors wished access. Clenching his jaw, Ken's attention transferred from Bruce over to the two-way speaker system. "Now who'd be crazy enough besides you to be out there on a night like this?"

As Bruce continued to make coffee, Ken wandered over to the speaker keypad near the door. The chime sounded again. "For crying out loud, I'm coming!" he huffed impatiently. Pushing the button, Ken answered coldly. "ATC." No reply. "ATC, who's there please?"

"Hello?" answered a female voice. "It's Diane Jackson, Paul's wife. Is Bruce Macbeth up there? I need to speak with him if possible. It's urgent!"

Ken met Diane only once before at an airport open house and remembered her bubbly personality as she entertained guests with lively tunes from an electronic keyboard. But from the distressed sound of her voice, he knew this wasn't a friendly chew-the-fat social visit. He keyed the button again, "Diane, its Ken Hamill. Yes, Bruce is up here. I'll buzz you into the lobby. I'll send him down."

"Thank you, Ken."

Bruce overheard the two-way conversation, finished making coffee and headed to the stairwell.

"You caught all that, I take it?" Ken called out.

"That's affirmative," Bruce replied as he sprinted for the doors. When he reached them, he yelled over his shoulder, "And the coffee's on, Your Royal Highness!"

"About darn time!" Ken hollered back. But his reply fell on deaf ears. Bruce was already gone.

* * *

Deliveries

Livid the wing tanks were running dry; Dave tapped the fuel gauges again. "We should have several gallons remaining according to the needles," he griped. Paul tried to respond, but through his nausea, he floundered to form words. He felt like a hapless passenger instead of a contributing crew member, his ailing body strapped into a flying tin can to which he held no control. His only hope was that soon they'd be on the ground one way or another, as disturbing as that reality was. Realizing his life was in Dave's hands, Paul tightened his seat belt and braced as best he could.

Raw anger grabbed hold of Dave. "I was right!" he fumed. "Even the fuel gauges don't work properly, Ace! How is it this plane passes a safety inspection every year?"

Paul glanced briefly at Dave, tried to apologize, but looked away.

Dave's temperament cauldron reached a boiling point as thoughts of his own mortality brewed up from deep within. Unbelievably, they were on the verge of a forced approach at 200 feet above the ground and in a fully loaded glider no less. In all Dave's years of flying, he had never anticipated a situation like this, and one that could have so easily been prevented had common sense prevailed. According to Dave's mindset, such blatant stupidity would always stem from some other poor schmuck.

To make an already bad situation worse, they were in a sky void of any real detail, and over a landscape bristling with an overabundance of rocks, trees and lord knows what else, all nearly invisible until the last second. It was now up to Dave to guide the plane into whatever lay below, a responsibility he loathed. "Buckle up, Ace!" he hollered. "I'm betting this won't be fun!"

The Continental continued to produce thrust but coughed as fuel began to dissipate through the cylinders. Dave checked their speed, eighty-five MPH. With insufficient altitude and poor visibility, there was no opportunity to select a place to land, not that anything suitable existed this far back from Paul's proposed lakeside retreat. For the second time tonight, adrenaline flooded his system. Dave began to tremble, and his senses peaked. He couldn't decide if he enjoyed the sensation or despised it, but either way, his life now hung by a very thin thread.

Aware of Paul's physical struggle beside him, Dave all but neglected his friend. It wasn't intentional, but it was a necessity. There was simply no time to check on him, let alone properly brace for whatever freefall was about to take place. Dave listened as the engine sputtered several more times, desperately fighting to stay alive as it burned through the last drops of gas.

As Dave checked to make sure the landing light was on, the engine coughed one last time and fell eerily silent. Except for the wind slicing through the airplane's outer shell, the sudden quiet created a peculiar sense of calm amidst a surreal moment of sheer bedlam. Dave coddled the plane away from the river towards slightly more hospitable wheel capable terrain.

"We're going down, Ace!" he yelled. "Brace yourself!"

Paul eked out a weak reply. "Roger."

Watching the airspeed closely, Dave allowed the Cessna's nose to edge down, trading precious altitude for airspeed. "Eighty and dropping," he called out. A glance at the GPS showed the airplane slightly right of the narrow river below. On a normal approach, wing flaps would slow the plane down, but not wanting to bleed off airspeed too quickly, Dave left the flaps up. Raindrops glistened as they passed through the landing light's beam, each sparkling briefly like a diamond under showroom lighting.

Remembering the emergency locator transmitter, Dave checked the unit was in the ARM position, a setting that activates the transmitter when the "G" switch receives an impact of five G's or more. He hoped that such a hard landing could be avoided, but his gut told him otherwise. As the Cessna buffeted against the wind, Dave's wishful thinking goal was to land the plane intact with the wings right side up and preferably attached.

Like a warrior facing his gravest battle and fearing the outcome, Dave's mind churned through a sudden influx of memories. He had always questioned stories of people's lives flashing before their eyes when faced with life-threatening circumstances, and here he was experiencing a deluge of vivid imagery of his past. Dave allowed the sensation to carry him away, a sliver of peace overriding their precarious situation. Visions of his two boys appeared, and then Tess, their voices unified in urging him forward to a safe place of refuge.

* * *

Pulling down the brim of his frayed Blue Jays cap, the front-end loader driver cussed the rain as it fell, his face already wet and cold. As the car rolled to a stop a few car lengths in front of the loader, he watched as both the driver and passenger doors opened, one after the other. Two bodies emerged and began walking towards the now pugnacious operator.

"I beg your pardon, sir," Tom Sullivan called out. "May I have a moment of your time? We have a quick question about the road repairs." Receiving nothing more than an icy glare from the driver, Tom wasted little time in getting to the point. "Just wondering how long before the road opens, which incidentally we're happy to see is being worked on."

"And you are?" grumbled the operator.

Wishing that he'd stayed in the van where it was warm and dry, Jack Ward sauntered up behind Tom. "Told you this was a bad idea," he whined.

Tom ignored Jack and held out his right hand. "I'm Tom Sullivan, and this is Jack Ward, owner and operator of Spruce Creek Lodge."

The driver glared at Tom's hand and made no attempt to shake it. "And I'd care about that because why?" asked the gruff-faced man.

Tom dropped his hand and tried to sound upbeat. "Looks as though you folks are doing a first-rate job here." Tom thought the man standing before him seemed on par with a dead fish. "We've been without power most of the evening, and the washed-out road hasn't helped our situation. We decided to cruise up this way and see if anything was happening."

"Well it is," affirmed the loader jockey. "Ya can't get yer van through here yet, so ya best head back to where ya come from. When the road opens, it opens."

Jack leaned over Tom's shoulder and whispered in his ear. "What cave did they drag this guy out of?"

"Be nice, Jack," whispered Tom while trying to suppress a chuckle. But Jack was right, the man also reminded Tom of a Neanderthal. "We don't want to get through, sir," clarified Tom. "We simply want to know how long before traffic can use the road again. We have television equipment that needs to be brought in from Owensville."

"Bout another hour," barked the man as he rudely turned away. "Now, I got work ta do and you two standin' here's helpin' nuthin'." He waddled up the steps and proceeded to climb back into the cab and slammed the door, apparently not a simple task considering his girth.

Jack turned and walked back to the sanctuary of the van. "Well you have a good evening too, you tub-of-lard," he yelled.

Tom spun on his heels and caught up. "Well, old boy, looks like we might be back in business after all. I'll call the station as soon as we get back."

"Yeah, you do that," grumbled Jack. "I hope that doofus gets stuck in his seat for a month."

Tom laughed. "Now aren't you glad I dragged you out of your comfy office?"

Feeling slightly encouraged, Jack opened his door and climbed in. "Now please take me home, so I can change. I'm sick of the rain and sick of being cold and wet. I just want to go to bed."

"You know, Jack," observed Tom. "Sometimes you're a real stick-in-the-mud. Pun absolutely intended!"

Tom settled into the driver's seat and fastened his seat belt. "Buckle up, pops," he ordered. "I'll take you back to the seniors' lodge. I'm sure the men in the white coats will be hunting for you."

* * *

Neither man reacted as something scraped against the underside of the imperiled Cessna, not that evasive action would have helped anyway. Out of nowhere, jagged terrain rushed up to meet them, the high-intensity landing light picking up flashes of brush, pine trees and rocks. Churning river water glinted somewhere to the left, blurred tree limbs and foliage to the right.

Whatever else lay below frightened Dave the most, and he despised having to relinquish control of a perfectly good airplane to fuel starvation and gravity, not to mention the folly of human error—the "woulda-coulda-shoulda" mindset ravishing his thinking. Holding the wings level and the airspeed slightly above stall, Dave maintained control as best he could, his hands and feet jostling yoke and rudder in what seemed a fool's errand. The plus, if one existed, was that his defiant personality refused to concede defeat to an airplane that was no longer capable of powered flight.

* * *

"So that's it, Bruce," sniffed Diane Jackson as she dabbed her eyes with a tissue. "I had nowhere else to turn, and because I'm not one to sit back and do nothing, I thought I'd come here. Tess is worried also, but she stayed home with my daughter to keep her company."

Sitting opposite one another inside the control tower's board room, Diane and Bruce chatted for several minutes. Bruce slid a box of tissues closer to where she could reach them. "Well," he replied consolingly, "the important thing is that Paul and Dave are safe no matter where they are. And from what you've told me, chances are they won't be landing here if their fuel is low, which incidentally I still don't completely understand—but that's a moot point. Paul's failed medical is another whole issue, and a troubling one at that."

Bruce offered Diane a bottle of water, but she declined. "So, if they don't show up soon, I think it's likely we'll be mobilizing search and rescue in the morning. What upsets me is from what I know about the area, there are few if any places to land an airplane, especially in the dark. It's pretty rough terrain all the way to Spruce Creek along both sides of the river."

"That's not terribly comforting, Bruce," replied Diane. She grabbed a handful of tissues and stuffed them into her purse. "Yes, the fuel thing is hard to understand, but more than that, I can't believe he'd fly when his doctor told him not too. From what I know of Paul, it's not like him to take such a foolish risk. Why would he jeopardize his flying career like this?"

Bruce leaned forward and folded his hands on the table. "As I mentioned before, I was on shift when they departed and tried to talk them out of going, but Paul was insistent. And you know better than anyone, Diane, that it's not uncommon for bush pilots to head out in poor weather. I personally wished they had stayed on the ground, but all I could do was wish them a safe flight."

Diane stood and walked over to the window. The tarmac glistened from rainwater, each puddle reflecting rows of blue taxiway lights. "I'm not blaming you, Bruce. As you said, there's nothing you could have done. Sometimes, Paul focuses on dollar signs only. He stood to make a fast buck on this trip, so I suppose I can't blame him for that. His revenue stream is really hit-and-miss."

Bruce squirmed in his chair. "My guess would be he figured it wasn't that big a deal. Guys are funny that way. We sometimes think of ourselves as invincible, that the rules don't apply to us."

Diane chuckled at Bruce's declaration. "Sometimes?" she asked.

"I suppose I could rephrase that statement," Bruce offered in surrender. "But there's no point in denying the truth about the male ego. Even I'll admit to that."

Diane tried to smile. "You're a smart man, Bruce."

Red in the face, Bruce continued to offer a rationale for Paul's violation. "No doubt Paul thought that one more flight couldn't hurt anything. I don't believe for a minute he meant to cause you or anyone else any harm. In this life, we all make good decisions and bad. Ultimately, it's how we grow up and become wiser, or, so I teach my kids."

Diane walked back to her chair but did not sit down. "No disrespect intended, Bruce, but I don't need an ethics lesson."

Not sure how to respond, Bruce listened until Diane finished talking.

"I'm scared he's not going to come back," Diane admitted. "Or be ready to face the consequences of flying when he shouldn't." Diane surprisingly changed the subject, catching Bruce completely off guard. "How's Marilyn doing?" she asked pensively.

"Ah . . . well," stammered Bruce with a mechanical laugh. "Seeing as it's our anniversary today and I'm not spending it with her, one could assume I'll be occupying the couch tonight."

"Oh, Bruce," Diane apologized. "I'm so sorry; I forgot, and now I'm keeping you here."

"It's not your fault I'm staying late, Diane. I didn't want to go home until I knew the guys were safe. I'm really glad I was here when you stopped by. It's important to talk these things out, though admittedly I'm no shrink."

Diane smiled through glassy eyes. "You're doing just fine, Bruce. So, what now?" she asked candidly. "What's your gut telling you about all this?"

Bruce scratched his head thoughtfully. "They'll have no choice but to set down if the tanks run dry, or better yet, because of poor weather and visibility with the engine still running. Either scenario is most likely a given. If that happens, we'll pinpoint their location when the ELT activates. The only problem now is that the search and rescue plane is stuck in the hangar. The front end of the building collapsed from a fallen branch because of strong winds. But don't worry, they'll get the plane out before morning." *I hope.*

Diane sighed heavily. "Well, that news certainly rounds out a thoroughly messed up evening. Dare I ask what else can go wrong tonight?"

"Listen, Diane," added Bruce. "The best thing you can do is go home, keep your phone close by and wait for a call. As soon as we hear anything up here, I promise I'll call you. At this stage, there's nothing any of us can do but wait."

Gathering up her purse, Diane stood and began to fasten the buttons on her coat. "That's what frustrates me right now more than anything, Bruce. It's the not knowing where they are that I have such trouble dealing with."

Bruce got up and walked Diane to the stairs. "I hear you loud and clear."

"Thanks for your time, Bruce," said Diane. "You better go home yourself and spend some time with your dear wife. I hope the kids are well. And Happy Anniversary by the way. Though under your absentee circumstances, I offer that with some hesitation."

"Kids are fine," Bruce replied. "And thanks for the good wishes. Though admittedly it's the scorn of a neglected wife that I fear the most!"

Diane smiled knowingly.

"I'll see you down to your car," offered Bruce.

Chapter 14

"What took you guys so long?" asked Kevin Davies, his voice an octave higher out of frenzied concern. Kevin extended his arms towards the hangar, his feet already moving in that direction. "It's like I'm the only person around here who cares about that airplane."

Behind him stood a half-dozen people belonging to the Owensville Area Search and Rescue Association. With others climbing out of their vehicles, Kevin hollered from his spot near the hangar. "Can you guys move any slower? If this building comes down, then we're all out of business! So, can we please hustle and get my plane out?"

"What's this, *my plane,* baloney Davies?" asked Search Coordinator Rob Smith as he sauntered in behind Kevin. "You're being awfully possessive over something that doesn't belong to you. Relax your britches, we'll handle it. So, just how bad is this all-points bulletin disaster of yours?"

Kevin led Rob around to the front of the hangar and pointed. "Well, you better handle it quickly because this could all come down in a heartbeat if this storm doesn't settle and that tree sheds another branch!"

"Oh, crap!" was all Rob said as he surveyed the damage.

When the others caught up, each person's mouth hung open to varying degrees. Rob wasted no time in barking out commands. "Craig, get the backhoe fired up. I know you drive one at the garden centre, so you're the man at the controls. We need to get this branch moved away and hope the remainder of this building doesn't collapse in the process."

Glancing upwards at the massive oak, Rob noticed the spot where the limb detached. As winds continued to hammer the tree, its branches were swaying wildly back and forth as each massive leaf acted like a small sail, collectively working together to place incredible strain on the aged timbers.

Search and Rescue was all about finding downed aircraft and missing people, not rescuing the airplane used in those searches. Rob shook his head at the irony and addressed his troops. "Listen up people. I have no idea as to the trustworthiness of the hangar, so we need to work smart and work carefully. For now, let's clear the smaller branches and debris away from the door structure, but only the loose ones. Under no circumstances does anyone pull on anything that's wedged. We'll bring the tractor in and see if we can get this branch safely removed. If we can do that and the hangar doesn't collapse first, then and only then will we go in and open up a path to pull the Cub out. Everyone crystal clear on that?"

There were nods all around and more than a few spooked wide eyes.

"And nobody goes inside that building without my consent," directed Rob. "Last thing I need tonight is for someone to get hurt. We might be needed in the morning, so it's crucial we get this plane out as quickly as possible. Then, we can all hopefully get some rest."

Kevin spoke up proudly. "I've already checked the Cub over, and it seems fine. Just some leaves and small branches on it."

"You've already been inside the hangar, Kevin?" asked Rob accusingly.

"Well, yeah," Kevin admitted. "As soon as I discovered the branch, I had to go in and see if the Cub was okay. I grabbed the door key and went in through the side door. I even pulled the plane back several feet." Kevin expected a tongue lashing, but in his

Deliveries

mind, he had reacted to the situation like anyone else, possessive pilot or not. And he would defend that stance if necessary.

"Not the wisest move," objected Rob. "If that building collapsed with you inside, then none of us would have found you until morning. And besides, an airplane isn't worth risking your neck for."

Kevin shuffled his feet. "Yup, that's what Bruce said too. But I made a snap decision, and I don't regret it. In fact, I volunteer to go in and pull the Cub out when it's time."

"I repeat," bellowed Rob while making eye contact with everyone, especially Kevin. "Until I'm sure what's left of this building is stable, no one goes inside! Capiche?"

There were nods all around.

Kevin felt all eyes on him, but he couldn't have cared less. He simply wanted to rescue the Piper and fly a mission, a real one. "What are you all staring at?" he asked. "You heard the boss, mush!"

Steady rain and gusty winds dictated that each person dress in appropriate rain gear, a somewhat futile attempt to thwart the elements. As they cleared away debris, everyone heard the backhoe sluggishly fire up, its engine screaming in protest from lack of use. Rob glanced over his shoulder and saw a massive plumb of acrid black exhaust pouring from its stack. He leaned in closer to Kevin's ear and shouted over the noise of the engine. "You mentioned Bruce a minute ago. Was that Bruce Macbeth from ATC?"

Kevin replied with a head nod.

"What was he doing over here?" asked Rob curiously.

Kevin raised his voice. "He was off shift. Called to tell me about the 185. That's when I heard the crash and ended the call. He popped over to see what was going on. Like you, he said I should have stayed out of the hangar."

"You'd have been wise to listen to him," agreed Rob. "But for what it's worth, I would probably have done the same thing. For now though, we stay out. If we lose the Cub and still have to hunt for the Cessna in the morning, we'll try our best to beg, borrow or steal another plane from somewhere."

Minutes later, the tractor stopped a few feet from the hangar's torn apart door and stopped, its muddied wheels leaving a long trail behind. Craig extended the boom arm and tipped the bucket slightly forward before jumping out. He walked over to Rob and Kevin.

"Craig!" shouted Rob. "Shut it off for a few minutes. I can't hear myself think! We'll fire it back up in a minute."

Craig walked back to the machine, climbed in and powered down the engine. The abrupt silence caused everyone to stop what they were doing. Rob spun around and used the opportunity to bark further instructions. "Keep pulling away what you can. In a few moments, we'll use the bucket and attempt to pull the branch away. Everything's intertwined, so stay sharp people. Keep working, and we'll do what we can to save the plane." Rob winked at Kevin. "I should say, Kevin's airplane."

* * *

Following Tom and Jack's return to the lodge and their encounter with Mr. Caveman, Jack headed straight for his cabin. Exhausted and in desperate need of a shower and a catnap, he headed for his bathroom.

Tom aimed his sights on the guest services phone in the front lobby and placed a call to Master Control, the technical hub of CFCB Television in Owensville. "Yup, that's what I said Brian, but I'll repeat it again. The HD cameras are on board the Air Charters Cessna which we believe is heading back to the airport because of bad weather. We'll have to use the spare cameras in the Community Producer lockup cupboards. You built them, so I know you have the spare keys. Grab three tripods, spare batteries, chargers, AC power cords, the works. Get the techs to load one of the news vans. We'll also need extension cords, triax cables, mics and anything else they can think of. Is that understood?"

Deliveries

Craving a hot coffee more than anything, Tom waited patiently for the Master Control operator to write out the list of equipment needed. "I'll call back in the morning," he added. "But I'm hoping the road to the lodge will be open in the next few hours. I'd like the gear brought in at the crack of dawn, so we can hopefully still attempt this broadcast."

Tom fielded one last question and rolled his eyes. "Listen, Brian, I don't care who drives the van up here. I'll pay them overtime, or they can take time off in lieu. That's irrelevant right now. The road will be slick, so for goodness' sake, tell whoever it is to go slow and drive carefully."

Frustrated, Tom ran his fingers through a wet mop of hair. "It'll take a few hours to set up and test everything once it arrives, but with any luck, we'll go as scheduled at 1 p.m. Make sure that all the auction items are nicely displayed in the studio, lit up and ready for showcasing during the bike races. We'll be switching live between the mobile here and the studio."

Just then, Tom noticed his son and Matt Hawley wheeling their mountain bikes into the lobby. The room had thinned out considerably as people had turned in for the night. Those continuing to mill about began to laugh and point as both riders mounted their steeds and began riding around the foyer.

"Listen, Brian, I need to go," declared Tom. "Oh, one last thing. Make certain the techs double-check the studio phone lines. Last thing we need is people calling in to make a bid and not being able to connect them through." Tom hung up a second later.

Truthfully, Tom was doubtful the broadcast would even air. And with all the commotion tonight, there was simply too much yet that could go wrong. He had to remind himself to tackle things one at a time, and for the time being, no cameras at Spruce Creek meant no show.

Tom watched as Dylan and Matt rode circles around the couches and tables scattered about. He knew Jack wouldn't approve, but hopefully, he was sound asleep and oblivious to the noise. Unable to contain a smile, Tom enjoyed the carefree silliness in front of him. Someone grabbed pillows from a couch and tried to swat the riders as they cruised by.

Before heading off for some shuteye, Tom walked over to join the playful shenanigans. It was good to see young people laughing and having a good time. As he looked on, his mind drifted to the Cessna. Hopefully, the crew were safe no matter their whereabouts.

As Dylan lapped the makeshift obstacle course, he failed to notice his dad standing close by, nor did he see the glass of water in his hands. In a moment of complete spontaneity, Tom made eye contact with several other people and winked mischievously. From a nearby refreshment table, glasses of water were quickly snatched up, and a moment later Dylan and Matt howled as cold water splashed them head to toe. Laughter ensued, and Tom Sullivan allowed himself the luxury of momentarily believing that everything was going to fall into place.

* * *

Nearly ten minutes had elapsed since Diane Jackson had climbed into her car and drove home. Bruce was still at the airport, searching the grounds for his cellphone. He was having no luck. Puddles flooded the narrow sidewalk and grass, making it tricky to keep his shoes dry. And with steady rain continuing to pound the Owensville area, he expected conditions to not improve anytime soon, both at ground level and in the sky above.

Deciding he'd check in once more with Ken Hamill and wish him a good shift, Bruce gave up and headed for the tower's front door. He toyed with the notion of still trying for dinner with Marilyn, but he felt completely exhausted and wanted nothing more than to crash, watch some TV and go to bed.

Reaching for the door handle, Bruce cast one last look over his shoulder. It was then his eyes detected a brief flash of light from somewhere on the lawn near the sidewalk. He stopped, spun around and angled his head side to side to re-trigger the event. Then he saw it again. Not bright by any means, but unmistakably a shiny surface reflecting light from one of several pole lights scattered throughout the parking lot. Disappointed, Bruce knew he'd found his phone.

Tiptoeing mindfully across the spongy grass, Bruce retrieved the device and holstered it without inspection. This was the second phone in three months he had lost to water damage, the first ending up in the toilet at home after bumping it off the counter with his elbow.

Once inside the tower, Bruce discovered Ken Hamill near the coffee maker with an empty carafe in his hand. "Big surprise," grunted Bruce. Incredibly, the man single-handedly consumed an entire pot. Bruce glared at the empty decanter in disbelief and gawked at Ken.

"What?" grunted Ken. "There's nothing else to do tonight but drink coffee. Everything's grounded. If I'd known it would be this quiet, I'd have brought in my 3D puzzle of the Millennium Falcon. I've been dying to start it!"

An ardent fan of the Star Wars movie franchise, Ken collected anything and everything even remotely related. And with a surname matching that of Mark Hamill, the actor who played Luke Skywalker, his appetite for trinkets rarely let up. Ken shrugged his shoulders, placed the empty coffee pot back into its slot and walked to his radar console. "So, tell me, what's up with Diane Jackson, as if I couldn't already guess?"

Before answering, Bruce grabbed his water-logged phone and held it up for Ken to see. "Found my deader-than-a-door-nail cellphone, not that you'd care unless it was a defunct lightsaber. I would have totally missed it had it not been screen side up in the grass."

Ken couldn't help but chuckle. "Well, at least now you know where it is."

"Yup," agreed, Bruce. "Wish I could say the same for our Cessna." He pointed at Ken's empty coffee mug. "Hope you enjoyed your last sip because I'm not making anymore."

"Why?" asked Ken. "I added coffee prep to your job description, so you don't have a choice."

Bruce changed the subject. "The chat I had with Diane wasn't a social call. Her hubby left here without enough gas to make the round trip. They apparently hoped to fuel up at Spruce Creek, but since they couldn't land there, I'm guessing they'll try to make it back here despite the weather."

"Awful night to be flying," stated Ken as he snatched the Cessna's flight itinerary off the console. "Do we know how much fuel was on board? It doesn't say here like it should." Ken scratched his head and handed the paper to Bruce. "Odd they didn't log that, but who knows, maybe if they conserved, they'll be able to limp back here."

Bruce scanned the document. "Unlikely," he countered. "But you're right. I can't believe I didn't notice the fuel omission. Paul always logs that." He set the sheet back down. "They'll likely be forced to set down somewhere, activate their ELT and wait for pick up. Problem is we can't initiate a search until morning, and that's questionable with the rescue bird trapped in the hangar."

"Say what?" sputtered Ken.

"Never had the chance to tell you," Bruce replied. "The big oak over the hangar shed a limb. The sucker dropped on the front hangar door, pretty much destroying it. I'm guessing by now the guys are trying to get the Cub out, but if they can't we're pooched for searching with that plane."

"The good news never ends around here," added Ken sarcastically. "If that's the case, then we shouldn't wait too long to call our military friends. It sounds to me like we might be hunting for an airplane in the morning."

"That'd be my guess too," agreed Bruce. "And like I said, if the Cub can't fly, they'll have to scrounge up another set of wings from somewhere."

Bruce walked over to the landline phone to call Marilyn and to reluctantly tell her his cellphone was toast. "I'd call S and R directly," he said to Ken. "But we better go through the proper channels. Would you mind calling the brass? Tell them what's going on, and they can rattle the saber as needed. I need to go home. I'm shifted again at noon tomorrow, but I'm sure I'll be in sooner than that."

"Yeah, I got it," replied Ken. "Get outta here and I'll call you if I hear anything. I'll pop in later tomorrow too. I confess I won't rest easy until I know where that plane is and how the crew is doing."

"Is that a touch of genuine compassion in your voice?" Bruce asked jokingly.

"Nah, Colette says I need to better connect with my emotional side, seeing as everyone around here thinks my heart is made of stone."

Bruce placed a call to his home number and then looked in Ken's direction. "You mean it's not?"

"Talk to the hand, Macbeth," sassed Ken as he raised his palm. "The force is not with you!"

"My point exactly," quipped Bruce.

* * *

"All right, guys, that should do it for the small stuff. Let's see if we can get this huge bugger dislodged." Rob glanced towards the operator. "Mount up, Craig. It's your time to shine!"

Aside from leaves and small branches, most of the loose debris in front of the wrecked door had been cleared away. With its bulk entwined in the hangar door panels, the massive branch hardly budged. Everyone watched as the tractor's engine started up, and Craig drove it carefully forward. The boom arm extended out, followed by the bucket slowly reaching for the widest part of the limb's radius.

Rob motioned with his arms for everyone to step back. "When Craig starts pulling, the entire mess could come down, so I want you all far back!"

Kevin stood to Rob's left, yelling over the noise of the engine. "I hope we can clear an opening big enough to get the Cub out."

"That's the plan, but we'll find out soon enough," affirmed Rob. "If not, then we'll all be going for drinks tonight because there won't be a thing we can do until we get more help. This is beyond my experience level. I rescue people, not bogged down airplanes."

Kevin nodded as he watched the bucket's teeth hook under the branch. Craig tugged upwards with gentle nudges as a way of testing the structural integrity of the rear section of the hangar. *So far so good*, thought Kevin.

Inch by inch, the huge limb began to pull away from the hangar door, now a shapeless mass of metal, wood, springs, and hinges. Several small branches dragged along broken sections of the door with it, but so far, the back part of the building held fast.

Those standing behind and to both sides of the tractor saw the Piper Cub inside, its fuselage dangerously close to several collapsed metal beams. Kevin overcame the urge to race in and try jockeying the airplane a touch more, but its tail was already against the back wall. All he could do was watch helplessly like everyone else, and that passivity drove him crazy.

As wind thrashed the giant oak tree above, its upper section was nearly invisible against the dark evening sky and downpour. The broken limb wedged into the hangar lifted slowly and then slightly backward as the backhoe nudged it along. Shrieking sounds of metal grinding on metal pierced the air, reminding Kevin of fingernails on a chalkboard. He covered his ears with the palms of his hands. For a moment, the entire front section of the hangar bucked forward as offshoots from the main branch remained snagged in the tangled mess.

"Whoa!" ordered Rob, his arms waving frantically. "Hold there, Craig!"

Thankfully, Craig noticed Rob out of the corner of his eye and stopped retracting the boom arm just in time. Kevin's heart hammered in his chest, and he felt certain the rest of the building was on the verge of collapse. Incredibly everything remained upright.

Rob stepped forward; a move that prompted everyone else to do the same. He motioned for the backhoe to power down by making a slashing motion across his throat. Frowning at the fallen timber, Rob knew that pulling back on it any more would prove dangerous because of interwoven branches caught up in the battered door and frame. He shook his head in frustration and pointed. "We'll have to cut away these branches before the main trunk will come free. It's too tangled up."

Glancing around, Rob tried to find Kevin, but his intrepid pilot was nowhere in sight. "Where's Davies?" he asked. "I need him to grab the chainsaw."

"He was here just a second ago," replied someone over Rob's left shoulder.

"So, help me," scowled Rob. "If he's gone into that hangar, I'll ground him from flying for a month!"

As heads spun about searching for Kevin, a chainsaw suddenly roared to life from somewhere behind, the blare scaring everyone half to death. People turned and noticed Kevin near the maintenance shed, his feet pinned to the ground and the chainsaw slightly raised. What everyone could not see was the cheek-to-cheek grin behind the old welding helmet covering his face. The unusual sight elicited both nervous screams and laughter, while a few stepped back as they kept a wary eye on him.

Startled, Rob Smith held his ground and recognized the gag and Kevin's portrayal of the villain from the movie *Texas Chainsaw Massacre*. Rob smiled and rolled his eyes.

Kevin shut off the chainsaw and pulled up his mask, revealing a corny grin. He noticed both angry faces and stunned expressions staring back. "Just a bit of fun to lighten the mood," he offered sheepishly.

"Davies!" shouted Rob. "Are you out of your mind? Quit clowning around and cut those branches out, now!" Rob began to walk away. "Thanks to you I need to change my underwear and find the others, assuming they haven't already quit because of your warped sense of humour."

Twenty minutes passed before the dismembered branch finally came free and clear, albeit in pieces. Sections of timber lay everywhere. Foliage and sawdust littered the ground, trampled underfoot as work continued to untangle and remove remaining sections of the hangar's mutilated entrance.

Despite the gaping hole and damage to the front half of the structure, the aft section remained intact. Twisted lengths of angle iron required careful dismantling, but overall, it seemed to Kevin as if there might be enough room to roll the Cub out with just inches to spare.

Persistent rain soaked everything inside the hangar, including the Cub. Gusts of wind swirled about, creating spirals of dirt, leaves and loose papers. The airplane rocked back and forth as turbulent air lambasted the plane's lightweight fuselage.

"Okay," said Rob. "Now comes the moment of truth. Only Kevin and I go inside. Everyone else stands by to help guide the wingtips through. Call out immediately at the first sign of trouble. I don't care if a mouse scampers across the floor, call it." Rob looked at the backhoe driver. "Craig, move the bucket into place to support the upper roofline. Edge it under what's left of the frame. I'll feel better with the extra support."

"Yup, no problem," replied Craig as he scurried away.

"Let's move as quickly and as safely as we can," added Rob. "Hopefully the wind doesn't get any stronger before we get the Cub out."

The tractor started up and the bucket swung into place. Craig gently tucked the outer curved edge of the scoop under sections of the roof to hold things in place.

"You ready, Kevin?" asked Rob. "I don't want to spend a minute longer in there than we have to, so let's—"

Kevin sprinted into the hangar, not waiting for Rob to finish. Rob shrugged his shoulders and scampered inside. He caught up with Kevin at the rear of the Piper Cub. Together, they lifted the tail off the ground and inched the plane forward, carefully eyeing the wingtips for unwanted contact against anything potentially damaging. Only once did they need to swing the airplane hard to the right to avoid a section of twisted iron.

Kevin hurried forward to the left-wing strut. "We're almost there, Rob!" he shouted. "Another twenty feet before the spinner's out. I feel like I'm delivering a baby," he grinned. "First the prop, then the wings, fuselage and finally the tail!"

Rob glanced at Kevin, shook his head and motioned to keep going. "Are you sure you're even qualified to fly this thing, Dr. Davies?"

Directly above the hangar, the wind howled through the lofty oak, its crown yanked violently back and forth. Forty feet above the ground, another huge branch hung precariously, its wood decayed and weak. Each blast of wind caused an even greater fracture to the connection point between the main trunk and the foot-thick branch. Hundreds of pounds of leaves and secondary branches added to the strain, not to mention the force of gravity threatening to once again have its way.

A sudden gust walloped the leeward side of the tree, acting as a battering ram before moving on. The resulting force of the impact elevated the huge branch up and to the right, then back to neutral; but the joint could no longer support the limb's weight. With an ear-splitting crack, the massive branch tore away, its leaves acting like a partially deployed parachute and slowing down the rate of descent, but only slightly.

Clusters of lower branches, thicker and stronger than their sibling above, absorbed the weight and velocity of the falling timber, temporarily snagging the limb and depleting its kinetic energy. Caught up over the hangar's rear roofline, the branch waited only for the proper gust of wind to deliver a second crushing blow. And unbeknownst to those working directly below, stronger gales were less than two minutes away.

Inside the hangar, wind and rain added to already high levels of ambient noise, and the distinctive sound of splintering wood over their heads grabbed the attention of both Rob and Kevin. One of the Search and Rescue members hustled inside to help with the airplane's removal. "You guys better hurry because another massive branch just came off! It's snagged for now, but it's right on top of us!"

Rob noticed Kevin's wide-eyed expression. "We're better than halfway, so keep going," he ordered. Rob twisted around to face the demolished opening. "And everyone outside, keep an eye on that branch. If it shifts even a foot, we drop the plane and come out!" Rob glared at Kevin. "And that's an order!"

The Cub's nose cone was less than five feet to freedom, its propeller just seconds from emerging under the bucket of the backhoe. Rob feared the wings and upper fuselage wouldn't fit through the opening, but he kept that concern to himself. "Easy now!" he directed. "Kevin, you move back to the tail. Cory and I will guide the wings through. Hopefully there's enough room at either end for them to clear the opening." Rob glanced ahead. "From this angle, it looks like they'll fit."

Kevin scurried back to the tail. "Yup, looks good from back here," he agreed from his unobstructed vantage point of both wingtips.

Deliveries

In quick order, they rolled the Cub forward, careful to avoid jagged pieces of debris hanging at irregular angles. Both wingtips slipped past the mass of twisted metal and wood by inches. Rob ducked under the wing as the plane emerged from the hangar. "Wings are through, Kevin!" he yelled. "Now for the back half. Keep coming!"

As others rushed in offering assistance, Rob glanced up at the oak tree and noticed the second branch, its mass caught vertically within clusters of other branches. He shivered at the sight. "We'll grab the struts and guide you out the rest of the way, Kevin." Rob looked at the rear of the plane. "We did it! We're almost clear!"

But Kevin Davies was no longer there.

Just then an explosive blast of wind assaulted the airfield, its sudden arrival catching everyone by surprise. Striking the oak tree broadside, the brute force ripped away smaller branches and clusters of leaves. Everyone froze in place as if in a trance, their eyes locked to the tree above.

Like an open sail, the Piper Cub received the full brunt of the wind, lifting and skewing it sideways. All available hands grabbed for the plane to hold it down. At that moment, the massive branch fell from its perch, slamming with crushing force into the rear section of the hangar in the exact spot where the aircraft only seconds ago had been. Someone screamed while others jumped away in fear.

With the Cub safely free of its cage, the same could not be said for its pilot, who at the last moment ran back into the hangar to retrieve the plane's logbook. As the structure collapsed, Kevin frantically dove under a nearby workbench when he realized his world was coming down around him. In doing so, he cracked his head against the wall and snagged his thigh on something sharp amidst the clashing of metal. He also heard his name being called out from somewhere outside, a frantic cry of someone bordering on full-blown panic.

Then, everything became deathly quiet.

Rain and wind found their way into Kevin's cramped domain, causing him to shiver uncontrollably. Reaching for his right hip, the pain reminded him that he was alive and coherent, a definitive plus given his circumstances. Without checking, he knew the wound was bleeding because of warmth on his skin. He pressed his hand against the injury and felt relieved that nothing foreign protruded from the entry point. Kevin flinched as he added more pressure.

Despite his injuries and the magnitude of what just happened, Kevin's thoughts drifted to the Cub and to whether he'd still be allowed to fly if a search was initiated. With his view hindered by debris and his limbs unable to stretch more than a foot in any direction, Kevin forced himself to remain calm. Pinned beneath the bench, he waited until hearing his name called out, not just from one person, but from several. He tried to shout and let them know he was alive, but his windpipe had constricted from too much phlegm. Trying to cough it out, Kevin struggled to will his vocal cords to respond, but as hard as he tried, barely a sound emerged from his lips.

Chapter 15

EARLY SUNDAY MORNING

Tall pines reached up into the early morning sky, their boughs competing for light as the sun's rays began to crest over the eastern slopes. As the dank coolness of the previous evening succumbed to rising temperatures, downy woodpeckers bore into small fractures of decayed trees, while chickadees scurried from branch to branch in search of breakfast. High above, a bald eagle caught gentle thermals, its razor-sharp eyes scanning the ground below for unwary prey. Through the river valley, ground squirrels chirped heated warnings to one another, yet playfully found time to chase each other from burrow to burrow, ever aware of the dangers lurking above.

Along both sides of the narrow fast-moving tributary, clusters of long-suffering white daisies graced the craggy riverbanks, in some places giving the appearance of snow when viewed from a distance. Mountains hid behind a thin shroud of purple haze, each peak framing the valley in unsurpassed beauty. Nearby, a small meandering stream wound its way through a thick mass of fallen logs, rocks and lime-green moss, the sound of gurgling water the perfect complement to the start of a new day.

Receiving huge quantities of rain through the overnight hours, the entire area glistened with stationary droplets and standing pools of water. Vibrant rays of sunlight flooded the waking terrain as the sun rose, its warming light striking leaves and foliage, basking the river valley in rich tones of green, amber, and orange.

Downstream, a young mule deer stood rock still, its ears finely tuned for sounds unbecoming to the intrinsic landscape. Bending down to nibble a morsel of wild blackberries, the animal's eyes were at just the right angle to catch a glint of sunlight reflecting off a potential predator the deer had never seen before.

Frozen in guarded fear, the animal brought its ears forward, actively processing the sights and sounds that belonged in the valley, while analyzing those that did not. The strange intruder lay quietly, yet its size and shape prompted the curious beast to move a few steps closer and not flee. The deer lifted each hoof, careful not to disturb the brush underneath. Taking refuge behind a large stump, it froze again—watching, listening, unsure—yet not afraid. Minutes passed before the deer accepted the shiny foreign object as a non-threat, and then once again prowled for berries while its sharp eyes focused intermittently on the motionless newcomer.

As the deer meandered, the mouth of the metallic beast suddenly opened, creating an unfamiliar screech through the valley corridor. Alarmed and now on high alert, the deer bolted and then stopped a short distance away, its curiosity overriding its instinct to run away. The animal watched in fascination as a peculiar new creature slowly appeared, its head moving slow, nonthreatening, the eyes wide and searching, but locking on nothing.

Backing up, the animal stood motionless, its front hooves sinking into the soft ground. Mosquitoes buzzed near its head but were hardly noticed as the overpowering desire to watch overruled the necessity for breakfast.

Paul Jackson had no idea how long he'd been unconscious. The rising sun's blinding light stung his eyes as it streamed through the fractured Plexiglas of the Cessna's front windscreen. The left side of his head throbbed near his temple. Reaching up, he gently placed his hand to the upper corner of his hairline and could feel the wound, a squishy sensation that caused him to feel queasy all over again. Plucking a tissue from his pants pocket, Paul gently dabbed the area and was relieved to discover there was little in the way of fresh blood. Regardless, the partly clotted injury ached fiercely and the ensuing pain quickly led to the awareness of a throbbing headache.

Dazed and confused, Paul attempted to focus his blurry eyes on the surrounding landscape. Twisting sideways towards his skewed open door, he discovered his seat belt still loosely held him in place. He grabbed the buckle's clasp and yanked it roughly, but it wouldn't release. "Now you decide to lock up, you bloody thing!" he fumed. Feeling captive and becoming more anxious the harder he tried, it was then he clued into the vacant seat beside him. "Dave!" he shouted out. "Where are you?"

Paul understood the need to settle himself down in order to gain control of his emotions. Licking dry lips, he suddenly became aware of how thirsty he was. "Breathe first," he reminded himself. "Tackle things one at a time." After several deep breaths, Paul's head began to clear and the thumping in his chest eased. At least now he was able to collect his thoughts. "Okay, Ace, take stock of your situation. Where else are you hurt? And more importantly, where's your co-pilot?"

Now entirely convinced his flying days were over, Paul sat still for a moment. He speculated that with all that happened, he'd be grounded for life, if not by aviation authorities, then most certainly by his wife. An image of Diane flashed through his mind. By now she and Kim would be frantic with worry, and unless someone like Jack Ward tipped her off about their low fuel state and not being able to land at Spruce Creek, they'd not have a clue where he was. Paul knew how resourceful his wife could be; how at the first sign of a plan gone awry, she'd take action on her terms. He allowed himself the luxury of a smile.

Swallowing what little saliva he had in his mouth, Paul shouted again while fumbling with his seat belt. "Dave! Where are you?" Craning his head about, Paul also tried to take stock of his airplane's condition. Incredibly, Dave had managed to crash-land with the gear, wings, and fuselage intact, an astounding feat given all the vegetation scattered around them.

Gazing out the front window, Paul noticed the aircraft listing sharply to the right and slightly nose down. He speculated a blown tire or uneven ground but couldn't be sure until he climbed out. Thick groves of pine trees and clusters of rocks decorated the terrain in every direction, and Paul sat in awe at how they hadn't flipped over on impact or sheared the wings off in the process.

Bent out of shape in several places, the engine cowling was stuffed with pine branches, weeds, mud and even a few wildflowers. Twisted and bent in towards the tip, one of three propeller blades protruded at a bizarre angle. It was self-explanatory; the Cessna's nose had trenched into the earth and the fuselage fell hard back onto its tail.

With one more desperate attempt, Paul tried to unlatch his belt through bothersome waves of nausea. "Come on, you stupid thing!" he pleaded. With several rapid-fire tugs, it finally came free, but not before snagging his thumbnail and tearing it slightly back. He cussed and pressure-gripped the nail. *Breathe, Ace, breathe!*

Now that he was free of his seat belt, Paul could search for Dave. He rotated his body to the left, swung his legs around and tried to further push open the door with his feet. Fiery pain ripped through his lower back.

Wincing, and suddenly nervous to move in any direction, he froze in place. Situated partway out the door, Paul tried to not twist his spine any more than was necessary. He wiggled each joint to find out if anything was broken, but in doing so, also became aware of a burning sensation in his left upper leg. Glancing down he noticed his torn jeans and a red patch stained into the denim. He tried to find what might have caused the injury, but his bleary eyes wouldn't focus on any one thing for longer than a few seconds.

Paul blinked aggressively to eradicate the fog in his eyes and to try to make sense of his jumbled thoughts. The pain was one thing, but his mind attempting to sort out tangled memories from the crash was another. He tried to shake it off, to shelve the imagery for another time. But the harder he tried, the more his brain spewed out snippets of the landing, a horrifying replay he was unable to stifle . . .

He recalled the aircraft in a shallow left turn . . . Dave struggling for control, trying feverishly to dodge obstacles he could see and bracing for those he wouldn't have time to react to. Low clouds flashing over the airplane with no way to dog-leg around them . . . Then, wham! Something unseen slapping into the right-wing, snapping the fuselage sideways as it dropped the remaining distance to the tundra below . . . The ground rising hard and unforgiving, its surface tearing away the forces that just seconds earlier had kept the Cessna aloft . . . Dave yelling and fighting to control an airplane that was no longer responsive to his commands . . . His hands locked to the control column . . . his feet pushing hard on the pedals . . . both men being yanked up and down, side to side as if saddled to a bucking bronc . . . The tail wheel striking the ground first, followed by the mains . . . tires smacking into the dirt with a sickening thud . . . the airplane plowing ahead as small trees and rocks scraped noisily along the fuselage . . . Then as quickly as it began, the Cessna jolting to a violent stop, wildly pitching them forward and then zig-zagging right and left . . . Paul's head slamming into the window or door panel, and Dave shrieking painfully from his own unspecified injury . . . and then absolute silence . . . and Paul's world going dark.

Despite the vividly short flashbacks, they did not seem real. Paul shut his eyes and tried to focus on the present moment. Alive and breathing, he was coherent enough to know where he was and that his co-pilot was not beside him as he expected. "Dave!" Paul shouted again.

Careful not to move his body, Paul rotated his head side to side to relax stiff neck muscles. His clothing felt tacky against his skin and miserably damp. The sensation caused him to shiver as cool morning air wafted through the cockpit. He needed to push everything aside and find his friend.

Glancing skyward, Paul's ears picked up the far away, yet unmistakable sound of an aircraft engine, an encouraging sign that someone might already be probing for them. He tilted his head and tried to hone-in on the noise. But moments later, the engine faded away, leaving behind the sounds of gurgling water and birds chirping. *Was it even there in the first place?* he wondered.

Though alarming, Paul determined Dave's absence from the cockpit was a good sign. It meant he left the plane under his own power, and perhaps even now was scoping out the terrain for a way to fast-track their recovery. Knowing Dave the way he did, Paul knew he would always try to better the odds, no matter how bleak things appeared. That was Dave bar none.

Paul glanced over to the ELT. The device's gravity switch would have automatically triggered the beacon once it sensed a crash occurred, and since updating the transmitter, he knew its emergency signal would then faithfully transmit upon impact. Breathing a sigh of relief, this meant that search and rescue units should already know the precise location of the Cessna and its two embarrassed pilots.

This, however, was not at all the case. Unbeknownst to Paul, the existing problem wasn't with the ELT itself, but with the externally mounted antenna responsible for broadcasting the signal. As the airplane plowed through trees and brush on impact, a stubby, needleless pine branch sheared off the antenna at the base, much like a hammer to the side of a thin nail. In other words, although the ELT transmitted as it should, the outbound signal was going nowhere fast.

Paul tried again to exit the plane—slowly—inch by inch. As he rotated his head to the far left ahead of the rest of his body, he caught sight of something orange, a small patch of colour concealed behind a tangle of bushes fifty feet clear of the wingtip. An icy chill coursed through his body, and Paul knew immediately that he was looking at Dave's coveralls. "Dave!" he screamed. "Dave, can you hear me?"

Squinting, Paul wiped his eyes to try to focus. It was then he picked out more slivers of orange fabric, small splotches extending lengthwise through twisted branches and leaves. "Oh, dear God, please no!" he cried out. "Dave! Answer me . . . please!"

To Paul's growing horror, there was no response, not even a twitch. He rotated sideways and painfully guided his legs out the door, desperate now to exit the aircraft and get to his co-pilot. He called out again: a cry that went undetected except for the ears of a frightened mule deer, its legs bounding away in the opposite direction as fast as they could run.

* * *

It was just after sunrise when paramedics tended to the wound in Kevin Davies' hip. A cute EMS technician spoke to Kevin as she worked the tape dispenser, her gloved hands securing gauze into place over the affected area. "Given the hangar was destroyed, you're very lucky, Kevin, that you weren't hurt any worse than this. It's also a good thing that whatever sliced into your hip didn't cut deeper towards an artery."

Kevin rotated on his stool and then timidly smiled back in what he knew was a lopsided boyish grin. "Yup, I was lucky," he mumbled in a low voice.

"So, tell me," asked the paramedic. "How long were you stuck in there before we arrived?"

Kevin tried to make eye contact, but her piercing blue eyes disarmed his resolve, and he looked away. To make things worse, her shoulder-length blonde hair and shapely figure, all neatly tucked into a short-sleeved navy-blue jumpsuit unnerved him even further. A stethoscope hung around her neck, the diaphragm settling mid-chest. Abashed and now evidently love-struck, Kevin was grateful she wasn't currently listening to his heart's rapid-fire beating. He noticed her small hands perfectly fit inside a pair of light blue latex gloves. *Easy boy!* screamed his subconscious mind.

Suddenly aware of his headache, Kevin tried to focus on her name tag. *Carla.* Her last name started with an "F," but he couldn't pronounce the rest. *Maybe Italian,* he thought. He found her eyes again and timidly forgot her question. "Uhm . . . what did you just ask? Oh yeah . . . I think I know," he blathered with accelerated speech. "Well, I thought I'd be there all night . . . in the hangar I mean. That was your question . . . right?"

"More or less," laughed Carla.

Kevin tried to think. "I don't actually know how long I was in—" Kevin raised his hands to his head and massaged his temples.

Carla retrieved a small flashlight from her pocket and noticed Kevin's glazed and partly dilated pupils. "Do you have a headache, Kevin?" she asked while shining the light into his eyes.

"Yeah," he replied. "It just kinda' started, but I'm fine . . . really. I need to get to my airplane and—"

"You know, Kevin," admitted Carla. "I'd have lost my mind being stuck in that cramped space, even for a short while. In my opinion, you handled that trauma very well, but now I need you to relax. Can you do that for me?"

Kevin nodded bashfully as Carla's intense gaze all but destroyed his eye contact. She finished dressing the injury to his hip by adding one more piece of tape, then ran her index fingers over all four edges to ensure the bandage's adhesion. Her touch caused him to shiver and his face turned fire-engine red. Kevin buried his face in his hands and was certain she had already detected his sudden infatuation.

Finding it already tricky to concentrate, he blundered his words. "Well, I . . . you know. I just figured they'd eventually get me out, so I tried ta chill and . . . say, you got anything for this headache?"

When she leaned back, Kevin found a bit more courage to speak, the words trickling from his mind to his tongue, but out of order. "And besides, my rescue n' search training's helped. I learned ta stay calm when the fan hits the crap . . . I mean, no wait . . . it's the other way 'round!"

Kevin looked up and found several of his peers studying him, all with grins on their faces, but also etched with concern that something wasn't quite right with their intrepid pilot. Kevin ignored them and looked back towards Carla; her eyes boring deep into his with genuine compassion.

"Uhm . . . so," he looked at her name tag again. "Carla," he said quietly. "If you ever wanna go flying . . . I mean, if ya even like flying . . . I'd, well . . . be happy to take ya out . . . *I MEAN UP! UP! NOT OUT!* Sometime . . . maybe . . . aw dang!"

Kevin watched her eyes widen, and he immediately wanted to crawl into a hole. Now at a complete loss for words, his scrambled brain pondered a way out of his tongue-tied gobbledygook. Obviously used to being flirted with, Carla hadn't deviated from her crouched position, nor did she appear the least bit phased by her patient's chatter. A smile played across her lips as she reached into her bag. "Let's give you something for that headache, shall we?"

"Kay—good," he jabbered coolly, "My head really doesn't feel too good."

Carla handed him two white tablets and a bottle of water. "Here," she said. "You'll need to nurse that hip for a few days, and it might still require stitches. Let's get you to a hospital, so they—"

"A few days!" interrupted Kevin. "I'm supposed ta fly today and—"

Carla placed her hand over his mouth without making contact. "As I was saying, Kevin, let's transport you to the hospital because that's my job. You'll be checked over by a physician, and because of your headache and dilated pupils, I suspect you might be suffering from a concussion." Carla jumped up. "So, I'm sorry, but you won't be flying until you're authorized to do so. Do you have someone here that can pick you up?"

Before Kevin could answer, Rob Smith walked over holding an umbrella. "I'll bring our young Casanova home," he smiled. "Assuming of course that you can get him out of your ambulance." Rob saw by the look on Kevin's face that he was enjoying the paramedic's attention, so naturally decided this was the perfect time to have a bit of fun, at Kevin's expense of course. *Touché!*

"Listen, Carla," added Rob. "If I may call you that? I know you folks are busy, so if you'd like I can drive Kevin to the hospital. That way you're available for other calls." Rob glanced at Kevin mischievously. "Besides, I happen to know that Kevin hates ambulances and doctors, and especially long pointy needles."

"No!" Kevin suddenly shouted. "I'm good to go with her!"

Rob discounted Kevin's plea and continued his chat with the paramedic. "It's the least I can do for Kevin. You folks have already spent enough time here waiting for us to extract him from the hangar."

Kevin's rescue from the building had been slow and tedious, a process lasting almost two hours. And with so much debris packed in and around his place under the workbench, each piece required careful removal so nothing else caved in to make things worse. There were also concerns that yet another branch might come down while trying to get Kevin out, but regardless of the dangers inside the hangar or from above, Rob's pride for his team swelled. Their field training produced results, even for the well-being of one of their own in a critical time of need.

Carla handed her med kit over to her partner, who without speaking stuffed the supplies into a larger kit bag and walked towards the ambulance. Carla looked at Rob. "I appreciate the offer, but it's protocol we transport our patients to hospital after treatment. He'll be checked over as a precaution, but I'm suspecting a mild concussion. He's not repeating himself or asking the same questions over and over, so that's a good thing, but his pupils are dilated, and he's mincing his words. My guess is they'll release him in a few hours, so he'll need a ride home and then some rest."

Wobbly on his feet, Kevin stood up with help from two of his cohorts. When Carla stepped in offering help, Kevin spun around and shouted, "Hey Guys! Kudos fer digging me out, so ah . . . thanks!" Kevin focused on Rob. "Who'd a thought it'd be me you'd end up rescuing, eh chief? Sorry I screwed up and went back for—"

"Chief?" countered Rob. "You know, Kevin, I think you getting stuck tonight was the universe's way of paying you back for scaring us all with the mask and chainsaw."

"If that's true," grunted Kevin. "Then the universe has a lousy sense of humour."

Rob shook hands with both paramedics and turned back to face Kevin. "Okay, flyboy, you go with these nice people here, and I'll be right behind you. The rest of you head home and get some shuteye. We'll deal with the hangar later, or what's left of it. We may still have an airplane to find before this day ends. Make sure the Cub is tied down, and everyone stay close to your phones."

With Carla supporting his right side and the other paramedic on the left, Kevin hobbled towards the ambulance. As his head dipped towards Carla, it was then his nose picked up the scent of perfume, a flowery aroma he had not detected earlier. Leaning in towards Carla's ear, he whispered. "I hope it's you that smells so nice and not yer talkative partner here."

Unable to suppress a smile, Carla winked at Gerry whose facial expression was anything but amused. "Yes, Kevin," she replied. "That's me and not my talkative partner."

Aware his tongue had again run amuck, Kevin changed gears. "Thanks, fer patch in' me up. Ya did great! But I should 'pologize for my slip up . . . you know, the part 'bout taking ya out."

When Carla didn't answer, Kevin blabbed on. "I really meant the flying part though. Some people never fly in a small plane, an' I thought you might like to try it sometime and—"

"I'm glad we could be of service," Carla interrupted. "I know you'll be fine, Kevin. I am as you say, one of those people who has never flown in a small plane. They've always scared me a bit, to be honest."

Reaching the ambulance, Carla grabbed the door latch and opened the right side. Her co-worker opened the left door, stuffed the med kit into a hatch and sauntered to the driver's seat without saying a word.

Kevin sat on the edge of the ambulance tailgate. "That guy doesn't say much does he?" he snickered. "Hey, maybe I should just go home. I feel fine and don't wanna waste your time." Kevin tried to get up but promptly lost his balance.

Carla grabbed his shoulder. "Oh no you don't," she ordered.

Kevin grinned. "But if ya do want to fly sometime, I can take you."

Carla looked towards the demolished hangar and the small green airplane a short distance away. "Is that the plane you'd take me up in?" she asked. "It's pretty small."

Kevin raised his head and his eyes met her gaze. "Yup, I think I could get permission to take you in the Cub." Kevin blushed immediately. "I mean take you up in the Cub, up! It's called a Piper Cub!" he meekly back-tracked. "Or I'll find something bigger if you prefer."

Carla noticed Kevin's pale complexion. "Well, first things first. Let's get you to a doctor. Once you're cleared to fly, then and only then will I consider risking my life in that airplane. I'll give you my number if you accept my terms?"

Unsure his ears heard correctly, Kevin's composure tanked rock bottom. "I, ah . . . wow! That's really great! I mean, you'll really like me . . . It, I meant . . . the flying part. I guarantee you'll like that! I . . . " Realizing his mouth's never-ending delirious state, he promptly shut himself down.

Patient bribery wasn't typically one of Carla's professional strategies, but she needed Kevin's full cooperation for transport to the hospital. She prided herself on being an astute judge of character and could not deny he was cute, undoubtedly single, and his personality seemed sweet enough. *No risk in life,* she thought with observant spontaneity, *no romance.*

"Okay, then. That's settled so climb in. But if you fuss in any way, the deal's off. Got it?"

"Yes, ma'am," was all Kevin trusted himself to say as he floundered aboard.

After that, Kevin remembered little of his ambulance ride to Owensville Regional Hospital. Yet despite his mental confusion, he was acutely aware that his heart had fluttered wildly like a smitten teenager.

* * *

Trepidation took hold as Paul tried to exit the airplane. He forced open the door with his right leg. "Dave!" he yelled again; his voice hoarse. "I'll be right there so—" Fresh waves of pain tore into Paul's back, and he again froze in place.

The sun rose high enough to throw intensely bright light into Paul's eyes. As he blinked to moisten them, a sudden flurry of motion distracted his attention away from Dave. He gazed to his left and noticed a deer retreating into the woods, its black tail now just a blur.

For added leverage, Paul grabbed the door frame on both sides and slowly hoisted his butt off the seat. Wincing in pain and nervous to place weight on his legs, he mindfully lowered his feet to the uneven ground below. Still angry at himself for not taking the time to pack water, food and other supplies as was always the norm, Paul shook his head disgustedly. *No time to worry about that now.*

Standing outside with both hands gripping the wing strut for support, Paul noticed jagged branches interwoven with the landing gear. Watching his step, he staggered forward to the front leading edge of the wing. It looked as though someone with a baseball bat swung it vertically at random intervals, striking the surface all the way across. His eyes took in the scene, but his brain refused to comprehend the full scope of what had actually happened. He suddenly remembered the television gear and angled himself around to look inside the rear part of the cabin.

The camera cases had unquestioningly shot upwards and then ahead, but their restraints still held them reasonably in place. One of the tripods lay on the floor behind Dave's seat, two of its legs snapped in half. Another went into the roof, the head and camera mounting plate punching a large dent in the ceiling. A duffel bag had also broken open, the impact tossing several microphones, cables and 9-volt batteries all over the cargo hold. Paul thought it miraculous that neither he nor Dave was struck by anything projectile-like.

With little idea of where they were, or how far south of the main river the plane went down, Paul let go of the strut and quickly gave up when the pain in his back returned. Frustrated, he yelled again. "Dave! Can you hear me? I'm trying to get to you, so just hang on!"

Feeling altogether helpless and unable to reach his co-pilot, Paul stood rock solid and pondered the events which had culminated in his second crash. *Only difference being*, he thought, *this one I could have prevented.*

Birds chirped from the trees as if nothing unusual was taking place in their world. Squirrels scurried from branch to branch as clusters of pesky blood-thirsty mosquitoes arrived on the scene, their annoying buzz meshing together with nearby bumblebees and the sound of white water nearby. Thankfully for Paul, insect repellent was one item he knew he had, but without his mobility, there would be little hope of retrieving it from the cargo hold, if he could even find it.

The arrival of the morning sun offered little in the way of physical comfort. Shutting his eyes, Paul never felt so alone, and now the man who'd saved his life was lying a stone's throw away, and Paul couldn't move a muscle to get to him.

Chapter 16

Jack Ward awoke with another brutal headache. Sunlight streamed through his bedroom window, nailing him directly in the face. Its warmth felt soothing on his skin, but at the same time, the bright light caused his head to throb when he attempted to pry his eyes open wide.

Not entirely sure he even wanted to face the day, especially after all that had transpired the night before, Jack buried his head into the pillow. But notably, the sun was shining this morning, and maybe, just maybe, he thought he would be greeted with some good news once he got up and ventured over to the lodge.

Tucked in behind the main guest building, Jack's modestly cozy log cabin sat near a smattering of statuesque spruce trees, the entire perimeter surrounded by wildflowers that Mildred had planted years ago. Having been pelted from rain and wind, the already beaten flora hung limp and waterlogged, and even as the morning sun cascaded over them, it was unlikely they would be standing tall any time soon as Jack's wife always intended during the growing season.

The living quarters were small at 760 square feet. But then Mil always insisted they didn't require much in the way of creature comforts. She thought it better to invest their renovation dollars into making their guests more comfortable, instead of bestowing themselves with unnecessary luxuries. Though outdated, the interior decor displayed a woman's touch and had remained unchanged since Mil passed away.

Bouquets of dried flowers, oil lamps, doilies and candles were just a few of the items scattered about the living room and kitchen. There was no dishwasher and only a half-size fridge, and two of four burners on the old Westinghouse stove didn't work. The dulled hardwood floor throughout the cabin needed a broom and dustpan, but Jack hated cleaning and never permitted lodge cleaning staff into his living quarters for fear they would disturb his preserved memories.

Jack promised himself that one day he'd move things around, update the curtains over the bay window and buy some new furniture, but so far, he couldn't bring himself to make changes. Everything about his home reminded him of Mildred, and for now, he was perfectly fine with that. She, of course, would have wanted him to move on, always reminding him that change could be a positive thing and not to wallow in self-pity should something ever happen to her.

Aside from Jack's bedroom, kitchen, a small den and an 'L' shaped living room, the only other living space was a three-piece bathroom, and even that needed caulking and a scrub brush. But at this point in Jack's widowed life, he had let things go, not to the point of a dorm student bachelor pad, but to a level of functionality. If it worked and served a purpose, he was fine with it. Other than to sleep, change clothes and periodically escape the never-ending demands on his time, he spent little of each day in the cabin anyway.

Jack's stomach growled as he lay under his down-filled comforter, the corners torn and in need of a few stitches. He begrudgingly threw back the bed covering and swung his legs over the side, his feet landing expertly into a pair of moccasins. Transitioning from horizontal to vertical only served to increase the pounding in his head, but he did his best to push aside the discomfort. First and foremost, he needed to shower and dress. Then, he would head over to the lodge as soon as he felt semi put together.

Placing the palms of his hands to his face, Jack massaged his temples with his thumbs as he mulled things over. With electrical power restored, the baseboard heater along the south wall of the cabin kept things warm and comfortable. Rising, his knees creaked as he straightened his body. Jack sauntered to the window. A small flock of waxwings sat hunkered down inside a nearby mountain ash tree, the birds flapping their wings at one another in a feathery quarrel. He flipped up the curtains for a better view and the birds scattered.

Turning from the window, Jack wandered back towards the bed where an antique cedar chest rested near the footboard. On its scratched and weathered surface sat an old twenty-seven-inch tube television and rabbit ears, a spontaneous purchase he and Mil made years before. It too worked fine, and Jack saw no need to replace it. Together they would cuddle under a blanket on a frosty winter's night and watch TV. But during the last few months of her life, Mil found it increasingly uncomfortable to move and opted to stay in bed for longer intervals to help decrease her pain levels.

Reaching for the remote, Jack hit the power button and the screen flashed to life. With only a few channels coming through with any degree of clarity, he left the set tuned to CFCB, Owensville. Already in progress, the "Rise-and-Shine" breakfast program showed a tall balding man in an ugly plaid jacket, his jaw yapping about the health risks of too much sugar in our diets. Jack hoped to catch the forecast for the Spruce Creek area but finally gave up when the station went to a commercial break. "Aw ta heck with it," he huffed angrily before walking towards the bathroom.

Grateful his headache was letting up, Jack grabbed a bath towel from the closet near the door, and for the first time that morning, his thoughts unwittingly turned towards the airplane and its crew. *Did they make it to the airport?* he wondered. He hoped Tom could shed some light on that, and also tell him if the replacement broadcast gear was on its way.

With every lousy thing that had transpired last evening, Jack was reluctant to face the day. Above all, he wanted this one to be perfect, but from experience and the long list of recent failures, he knew that one's desires don't always pan out as one hopes.

Jack splashed cold water on his face and patted dry. He glanced towards the television; its screen visible through the partly opened bathroom door. The on-air personality was busy showcasing a display of pop cans and bottles.

"Mildred," Jack sneered. "Why don't these TV people ever say anything that's even remotely interesting? And around here, that's the weather!"

More often than he cared to admit, Jack talked to his wife as if she was physically in the room. But the air remained quiet, a dismal reminder that going through each day unaccompanied by his life partner was the miserable norm.

Swallowing down his emotions, Jack turned away from the TV and aimed for the shower, his eyes failing to notice the red headline banner rolling across the bottom of the screen. As he turned on the showerhead, the phone on his nightstand began to ring.

"Seriously!" he snapped, livid that his day was already being interrupted. Jack let the phone ring several times before deciding to move his feet. He reluctantly wandered back into the bedroom, and it was then he caught sight of the news banner. This time his eyes riveted to the screen as he reluctantly picked up the receiver and answered without formality. "What is it?"

"That you, Jack?" yapped a voice Jack didn't immediately recognize. "Glad you're up an' at' em."

"Who in the blazes is this?" demanded Jack. "Of course, it's me! I'm busy and—"

"What do you mean who is this?" interrupted the male voice. "It's Tom! Who else do you know that'd be calling you at this hour of the morning?"

"I should have known," grunted Jack coldly. "It's always you. I was about to jump in the shower and you're bothering me! So, if you don't . . . just hold a second."

The news banner started again from the beginning and Jack didn't want to miss it: "SEARCH TO BEGIN FOR TWO LOCAL AREA PILOTS NEAR SPRUCE CREEK, THEIR CESSNA REPORTED MISSING BY LOCAL AUTHORITIES. MORE DETAILS AS THEY BECOME AVAILABLE."

Jack's spirit crumbled. He lowered the phone and stared at the TV while Tom continued talking. Jack read the headline again and pressed the receiver back to his ear. Tom's voice sounded muffled like his words were being transmitted along a string and a pair of tin cans.

"Listen, Jack, I hate to start your day with bad news," apologized Tom. "But the Cessna and its crew are miss—"

"I said hold on, Tom!" ordered Jack. "Your channel's showing something about the plane, and I'm trying to read the thingy at the bottom of the screen."

"Yeah, Jack, I know," explained Tom. "That's what I'm calling about. The plane never made it back to Owensville, and now Search and Rescue's been notified. The media's all over it, and since learning the plane was flying TV gear to Spruce Creek, you might be getting more phone calls today than just mine."

Jack didn't know what to say. In his current frame of mind, he again assumed that somehow he'd be held responsible for the two missing pilots, despite the fact that Paul Jackson willingly agreed to the flight in the first place. His decision to fly against medical authority was in his backpack of trouble, and his alone.

"You still there?" asked Tom.

"Yup. Though I'm thinking I'd rather be elsewhere about now. I've only been up for ten minutes, and this day already stinks."

"I hear you, Jack," agreed Tom. "But listen, there's another issue besides the missing plane. The alternate gear hasn't shown up yet, and I'm worried they might have had car trouble of their own and won't be—"

"I'm sure they'll be along," grunted Jack, who upon hitting his first low of the day, held little faith his broadcast would even air. And with his mind fixated on the missing airplane and its crew, Jack couldn't have cared less about the missing van or its equipment, at least for the time being.

"Did you hear me, Jack? That's twice you've cut me off in the same conversation. Are you sure you're okay?"

At the moment, Jack struggled to hear much of anything. He tried to articulate his words through a myriad of strangling thoughts. "You don't know the half of it, Tom," he quipped.

"What are you talking about, Jack? The half of what?"

Jack nervously tugged at his pajama collar. "The pilot, Paul Jackson, he—"

"What about him? Did you get any sleep last night, Jack, because you're not making any sense."

Jack sighed heavily. "Paul Jackson wasn't supposed to fly, Tom. His wife called me last night."

"I don't understand, Jack. Paul shouldn't be flying? Why?"

"If those two pilots are upside down in a field somewhere, or worse yet . . . dead," stammered Jack. "It's because of me. They wouldn't have been flying last night had I not asked them too."

"You can't be seriously thinking that, Jack. I mean it's ludicrous to think that you're in any way responsible for someone else's decision. You need to come to your senses before—"

Unable to say another word, Jack sighed, offered a less than sincere goodbye, and hung up the phone. For the first time in months, everything previously important to him paled in comparison to the words at the bottom of his television. His desire to succeed—to build the lodge into something bigger and better—and for what? None of that seemed to matter now with lives at stake.

Feeling ashamed for placing more value on personal gain than on human life, or the risks taken by others on his behalf,

Jack stood still, his eyes fixated on the television screen. Suddenly exhausted all over again, Jack wanted nothing more than to go back to bed and sleep, but that option was most assuredly not on today's agenda.

Dumbfounded he'd been hung up on, Tom placed the phone back into its cradle. Whatever it was that Jack said would likely add serious complications to the day. But for the moment, as if a wayward airplane wasn't bad enough, Tom had another problem on his hands. His relief broadcast gear and driver were now also missing in action.

* * *

Awake since 5 a.m. and unable to settle her mind through the night, Diane Jackson hardly slept. She found herself repeatedly drifting off, only to awaken after a series of graphic dreams, each involving her husband to some troubling extent. At one point she yelled out, searching frantically for Paul amidst a forest of twisted trees, their roots above ground, reaching out for her like an octopus's tentacles in search of prey. At that point, her panicked voice breached the conscious world and Kim jolted awake from her room next door. A moment later she tucked herself into her dad's side of the bed where she tried to console her emotionally distraught mother.

Pulling the sheets under her chin, Kim chatted away. "Where do you think Dad is, Mom? I mean, if they couldn't get back to the airport, then they could be anywhere, right? Shouldn't people already be out trying to find them?"

Lost in her thoughts, Diane heard only a smidge of what her daughter just said. "What Kim?" she asked distractedly. "What are you asking about?"

Not wanting to repeat herself, Kim changed her line of questioning. "When are we going to hear something, Mom, and why hasn't anyone called? We should turn on the TV."

Since heading to bed shortly after midnight, Diane desperately hoped the phone would ring, but so far, nothing. Typically, a woman of action when life tilted sideways, sitting idly at home was not in her playbook. It was fear of the unknown that produced a toxic mix of anxiety and rising discontent, and every emotion she felt seemed over the top and grossly exaggerated. At this juncture, she wasn't sure who to call and could only assume that Paul and Dave had set the plane down somewhere because of poor weather and/or low fuel.

"I wish I knew, dear," Diane finally replied. "I'm sure we'll hear from somebody soon enough. Bruce promised he'd call the moment he heard something. I thought about calling Uncle Jack at the lodge, but he's wallowing in self-pity, and I'm not in the mood to hear any more of it."

Kim remained quiet, but after a couple of seconds she spoke up. "I need to shower, Mom. It's too stressful just lying around, and I want to be ready to go when the phone rings."

"And just where do you plan to go?" asked Diane curiously.

Kim glared at her mother. "If Dad's plane has crashed, then I'll be first in line to help look for it. I want my daddy home, and between us girls, I don't ever want him to fly again."

Diane sighed. *You just might get your wish.*

* * *

In the outer recesses of his mind, Dave McMurray heard his name being called, but for the life of him couldn't figure out where it originated from. Unsure of his surroundings or how he got there, Dave slowly opened his eyes and immediately squinted from the brightness of the morning sun.

As his conscious mind chased away the fog, Dave became aware of his body position, his senses slowly waking up to the musty smell of moss and dirt. Prickly branches poked into his face and torso as he lay prostrate in a mass of brush. There was a salty taste in his mouth, which he already knew was blood. Trying to move, Dave willed his joints to respond as desperate survival-mode commands raced from his brain.

"Dave!" called the voice again, a shrill violation of his strangely over-sensitive hearing. Unable to find his voice and nervous to move, Dave remained still, his ears processing the myriad of sounds around him; rustling leaves, birds, insects and flowing water all harmonized in genial accord.

When he attempted to pull his left leg in, knife-edge pain exploded from deep inside his ankle. Feeling suddenly dizzy, Dave locked his body in place. It was then his memory kicked in, and he knew exactly where he was. Carefully turning his head to the right, he pried his eyes wide open. He could see the Cessna, its wings resting at an odd angle, but intact. "Dave!" he heard again, the desperate sound of Paul's voice enough to ease the pain and lift his spirits.

Feeling as though he should man up and extract himself from what he considered an embarrassing position, Dave tried to roll slightly left. This prompted his legs and feet to move as well, again causing his ankle to catch fire and promptly firing the signal straight to his brain's pain receptors. Through buzzing ears and fading vision, the last thing Dave saw before he lost consciousness was Paul standing under the wing, frantically waving his arms and calling out his name.

Horrified at the sight of his co-pilot lying in a cluster of bushes, a feeling of relief swept over Paul when he noticed the coveralls move, a positive sign that Dave was alive and breathing. Calling out, Paul noticed Dave's eyes were open, their whites peeking through branches cloaked in drab green and sepia-coloured red

Deliveries

foliage. They locked onto Paul's for the briefest moment and then faded from view.

"Dave!" yelled Paul over and over.

With no idea as to Dave's condition, Paul's urgency to reach him escalated through growing waves of anxiety. He needed to push his legs forward regardless of his own pain and fear. Holding the wing strut for support, Paul wedged his feet into the ground and let go despite the injury to his leg. Moving his feet one in front of the other, he shifted his stance to the right, and mercifully the pain in his back eased off. He was on his way, even if it was as slow as a turtle.

To Paul's left, a pair of crows shuffled through the grass, their beaks snatching insects from their resting places. A steady breeze helped keep mosquitoes at bay, but a few found their way to his neck and face. Paul swatted them away as best he could while setting his eyes on Dave. A surge of adrenaline flooded his system when he noticed the coveralls not moving again.

Already on wobbly legs, Paul anchored his body for extra stability, then with determined resolve, ordered his feet to plod ahead unsupported. "I'm coming, partner!" he yelled. "Just hold on!" Paul tried injecting humour into his words for Dave's sake. "It's a good thing you're wearing those stupid coveralls because I'd never have spotted you sleeping on the job! But of course, for you, that's completely normal!"

Parallel to the trailing edge of the Cessna's wing and making progress, Paul's confidence grew. He widened his step, but in doing so, he snagged his left foot on an exposed root and almost toppled over. Wincing, he fortunately landed his other foot into the soil just prior to his balance drifting beyond his ability to control.

"Dang it," Paul growled. *Slow the pace, Ace.*

Straightening up and remaining still to collect himself, Paul waited for the pain to subside. He caught his breath before making any further attempt to move forward, then glanced towards Dave with renewed purpose. "C'mon, Dave, wake up!" he shouted.

"If you're not moving by the time I reach you, you're buying me breakfast for the next month! Are you hearing me?"

Regaining consciousness, Dave's eyes fluttered opened. He tried to focus on the view before him and on Paul's distant voice. He vaguely remembered hearing something about breakfast but had no idea as to the context. Despite the predicament and pain he found himself in, Dave's stomach growled, the irony he considered laughable. *What a time to be hungry*, he gloomily thought.

Acutely aware of his kinked body position, Dave felt the circulation in his right arm being cut off. He tried to release it from under his chest but found it too challenging to roll over without adding more pain to his system. Through the woody undergrowth, he saw Paul hobbling towards him, carefully traversing a path along the uneven ground while mindfully trying to dodge rocks and small bushes. The sight reminded Dave of an old man he had recently seen—the poor fellow taking nearly two minutes to trek through a crosswalk and totally oblivious to the long line of impatient drivers waiting to get through.

Paul babbled like an auctioneer as he progressed, and Dave knew the chatter was for his benefit. Paul was merely trying to offer encouragement. Dave found it difficult not to chuckle as he tried to understand whatever nonsense Paul was spewing out.

With Paul busy evaluating his steps, Dave angled his upper body ever so slightly while attempting to shift his arm into a more comfortable position. As it began to thaw, the entire limb filled with tingly pins and needles, the odd sensation a welcome distraction from the fire in his ankle.

Approaching from straight on, Paul toddled along in what Dave thought of as perfect slow motion, his head aimed down, and his steps calculated yet deliberate. Paul's jaw continued to flap. "So help me, Dave," he badgered. "I suggest you wake yourself up before I reach you, or I'll find me a new business partner!"

Dave figured it the perfect time to exercise his vocal cords because Paul likely hadn't the foggiest idea that he was conscious.

"I'm almost there, Dave," Paul went on. "This is your last chance to haul your butt out of those bushes and—"

"For crying out loud, Ace!" barked Dave in the loudest voice he could muster. "Would you shut your yap? I can't hear myself think down here!"

For the second time during his trek from the aircraft, Paul Jackson stumbled, his head lifting towards Dave's voice, a look of surprise plastered across his pained face! What Paul couldn't see was the widening grin on Dave's mug, or more importantly, the tears welling up in his eyes—a by-product of the gift of being alive, and the blessing of seeing his friend limping towards him to offer help.

Chapter 17

By the time he reached the top floor of the control tower, Bruce Macbeth's chest heaved as he gasped for air. Arriving for his shift a touch later than planned, he'd forgone taking the elevator and, per usual, chose the stairs instead. In hindsight, he wished he'd gone the easier route because this morning his legs felt like Jell-O.

Before entering ATC's main hub, Bruce blinked several times to force open heavy eyelids beyond the paper-thin slits he knew they were. As usual, the aroma of coffee was absent from the control room, and until he initiated brewing the first pot, the menial task would never get done. But today of all days he deplored being the appointed coffee boy.

Ken Hamill phoned Bruce at home an hour earlier to give an update on Airflow Charter's missing Cessna. Ken's message was simple: "The plane hasn't shown up yet and that's that." As Bruce guessed, the day's events would revolve around its whereabouts, and he couldn't bring himself to phone Diane Jackson as promised until he had solid answers. Paul's wife would also expect a decisive course of action to find her husband. But until he had more details from Search and Rescue, his chess moves were limited like everyone else.

Tossing his jacket on a nearby wall hook, Bruce headed straight for the coffee maker. He rubbed his eyes and tried desperately to eradicate whatever glue held them shut. To make matters worse, his dead cellphone meant he would need to buy a new one, and that financial hardship was not welcome in the least. As Bruce made coffee, Ken Hamill emerged from a nearby office and sauntered over. Without saying a word, he plopped himself down on a stool to Bruce's left. Bruce glanced over. "Holy smokes," he articulated. "You look way worse than I feel. And you pulled an all-nighter, and without coffee?"

"That was my shift," answered Ken grimly. "I hate nights and my coffee sucks. Not worth the effort if I won't even drink it."

"What are you still doing here?" asked Bruce. "I thought you were going home after we spoke on the phone."

"Well, at the moment I'm waiting for you to hurry up and make a pot of good coffee," sassed Ken. "But to answer your question, I could not in good conscience leave, not with the buzz of concern over the missing 185. I'll scoot home in a bit for some sleep." Ken rubbed his face and neck. "I'm not due back on shift until tomorrow night, so I've got some time yet to bark orders at you and fill you in."

"Oh, lucky me," snickered Bruce. "Fill me in on what?" he asked. "What's happened in the last hour that you haven't already told me, which was basically nothing?"

Ken grabbed the itinerary for the waylaid Cessna. "Nothing regarding the airplane, but an airborne search today may be out of the question."

"How come? I heard they got the Cub out of the hangar and it's fine."

"Cub's not the problem," explained Ken. "It's flight-ready. What I didn't tell you on the phone was that another branch dropped on the rear half of the hangar right after they got the plane out. And you'll never guess who was inside."

Bruce switched on the coffee pot and turned towards Ken. "Enlighten me because I'm not awake enough to offer guesses at the moment."

"It was your pilot buddy Kevin Davies. He apparently went back inside to grab the logbook, and that's when the branch took out the rest of the building. I can't believe no one has ever inspected that old tree. It should've been cut down or pruned back years ago."

"Was he hurt?" asked Bruce. "I told him to stay out of the hangar when the front caved in, though it seemed to me he was more than ready to give his life for that stupid plane."

Ken dragged himself off the stool and reached for his mug. "Yeah well, these youngsters never want to listen to us old farts. He got banged up a little, but I don't know to what extent. There's something to be said though for youthful reflexes because he dove under a workbench as the roof collapsed around him."

"So, what's the problem then if the Piper's okay?" asked Bruce. "Why can't they fly it for the search if there is one?"

"I was just on the phone with Rob Smith," explained Ken. "He's the head honcho for the S and R unit."

Bruce nodded. "I know who he is. We've met."

"Well, he told me it was dawn before they finally got Kevin out. Paramedics took him to the hospital for a check over, and from what I've been told, he's got a concussion. I haven't heard anything since."

"Ah, the poor kid. He'll be upset if he's not cleared to fly today. But S and R has access to more than one pilot, so I still don't get why they can't launch if required. In my opinion, that plane should be searching as we speak."

Ken walked over to the tower windows, the wraparound slanted glass offering an unobstructed 360-degree view of Owensville Municipal. Despite the sunshine and five-knot winds, not much on the ramps or taxiways moved. To his right, a young woman performed a walk-around on a flight school Piper Tomahawk while an instructor looked on, but that was it for activity.

Ken turned from the windows. "You should know by now, Bruce, that things seldom go off without a hitch. If Kevin can't fly today, then the plane's not going up. The other pilot's out of town for a wedding, and according to Rob, he and Kevin were the only guys checked out on the Cub. It's a small S and R group here

Deliveries

at the field. Between you and me, they're seriously ill-equipped to look for anything larger than a butterfly, let alone an airplane in a haystack. The way I see it, the Cessna crew could be in serious trouble, or they're hunkered under the wing playing cards as they wait for an airlift of fuel and a sixer of vodka coolers. Either way, the sooner we find out, the better."

"You do realize that an airplane in a haystack makes no sense, right?" asked Bruce smiling. "The correct expression is a needle in a haystack."

"Yeah, yeah," shrugged Ken. "It's an analogy simpleton, and it's a huge haystack. At least I didn't hit you with a pun. But I still could!"

"No thanks. I've been forced to listen to your cheesy puns for years now." Bruce changed the subject. "Has the Cessna's ELT been picked up by anyone?"

"There haven't been any reports of a signal. Absolute radio silence. So, there's a possibility it's malfunctioning, and now with the plane officially missing, S and R are trying to rally up with little to go on."

Civil air search and rescue units typically operated using a four-seat aircraft like a Cessna 182, a plane with room for a pilot, navigator and two spotters in the rear seats. Funded by the Defense Department, search and rescue airplanes were often times privately owned and volunteered to local search and rescue detachments. But at Owensville Municipal, there weren't any such aircraft available within the private sector, so the Piper Cub was the only machine up for grabs, donated for use by a retired airline pilot who spent all his time in the deep south and rarely flew the thing.

Bruce pondered the dilemma of a search aircraft and the lack of a pilot.

Personally," he remarked. "I also think the Cub a poor choice for S and R, but I realize it's all we've got. What I don't understand is why arrangements can't be made to bring in a different airplane and pilot? We've got other squads in nearby cities. Doesn't Bakersfield have an aircraft available to them?"

"To answer your question," replied Ken, "another airplane is improbable for today given the fact that Bakersfield is three hours away by plane. They'd need time to mobilize—time we don't have. Even if we find another pilot for the Cub, it'll take twice as long to fly a typical search pattern with only one spotter."

Bruce agreed but decided to play devil's advocate. "Why?"

Ken took the bait. "Because, oh unlearned one, in a tandem seat airplane like the Cub, the pilot has to modify his search pattern and fly the same track twice, once in one direction and then in reverse. One spotter means only one side of the track is searched at a time. It's inefficient, but as the saying goes, 'It's better than nothing.'"

A smile formed on Bruce's lips. "Wow!" he chuckled. "It would seem you're not as daft as you look." Bruce turned away without waiting for Ken to reply. "I hate not knowing what's going on, and I need to call Diane Jackson. Problem is I don't have a thing to tell her yet."

"Tell her the truth," advised Ken. "This whole thing is out of our hands now. It's up to the S and R guys to find the plane, not us. All we can do from here is our job. We grant clearance to whichever plane eventually goes out looking for them." Ken grabbed his mug and tipped it side to side. "And we drink coffee . . . if it ever finishes brewing."

Not the type of person to sit back and wait for crucial information to come to him, Bruce smirked at Ken's complacency, grabbed the portable landline phone and punched buttons at breakneck speed.

Ken noticed the determination on Bruce's face. "Oh, I've seen that look before," he declared. "Now who on earth are you calling? Search and Rescue's already been notified, and now the media's got hold of the scoop. Our job's done, Bruce, so time to let it go."

"Things are moving too slowly and time's wasting," pondered Bruce as he walked toward the west-facing window. "We've got a missing airplane and two pilots out there. I need to light a fire under someone's back end. I also want solid intel before I update Paul's wife."

Ken shook his head. "You sound like an air force general who can't sit still. And you never answered my question. Who ya calling?"

Bruce held his hand up to shush Ken, not because he didn't want to answer, but because his phone conversation already started, and he couldn't reply.

Within seconds of very intentional eavesdropping, Ken got his answer and walked away. He shook his head and commented loudly enough so Bruce could hear. "Macbeth, you're slipping to the dark side."

* * *

"Well, that was something completely different," scowled Rob Smith as he sternly hung up the phone. "So, what is it with air traffic controllers? And since when do they find it acceptable to bark orders outside their menial jurisdiction?"

Rob grabbed a cherry cheese pastry from a nearby tray and marched to the sofa where Kevin Davies lay half asleep. He bopped underneath Kevin's runners. "How are you feeling fly-boy?"

Kevin repositioned himself and looked at Rob through glazed eyes. "What'd you say, boss? And who was on the phone?" asked Kevin, his voice flat and without its usual jovial undertones.

"You heard that call, did you?" asked Rob. "It was nothing that pertains to you, so go back to sleep. Besides, you're sitting this party out anyway."

"Yeah, but I feel—" Kevin sat up too fast and the blood rushed from his head. Feeling suddenly dizzy, he returned to the horizontal. "Oh man," he groaned, "this really sucks!"

Chuckles erupted around the room from several of Kevin's cohorts.

"You're lucky, Kevin, that I agreed to bring you back here," acknowledged Rob. "You should be home on your couch."

Rob walked to the east window. Sunlight streamed through the Venetian blinds, a welcome break in the weather compared to steady rain overnight. He stretched his arms high over his head and stifled a yawn. Pushing fifty-nine, the retired dentist usually exuded more energy than people half his age, but this morning he felt entirely worn out and scarcely in the mood for taking flak from anyone, especially ATC. With his face still an angry shade of red, he wasn't pleased with being told how to do his job.

Tossing the last bite of turnover into his mouth, Rob spun on his heels and began to speak in a moderately sarcastic voice. "All right people, listen up. The high and mighty tower gods are wondering when we're, and I quote: 'Getting our fingers out of our behinds to start searching for the missing Cessna.'"

A few people exchanged amused glances but said nothing.

Rob continued. "To which I replied, perhaps you should mind your own business and stick to playing with your radar knobs."

Laughter erupted around the room, but at the same time, Rob couldn't disagree with Bruce Macbeth and his crankiness. Things were moving too slowly, especially with lives at stake. It didn't help that he'd been up half the night trying to rescue Kevin, but the early morning wake-up added pressure to an already less than ideal situation.

Rob glanced around the room. "Of all days for a perfectly good airplane to be stuck on the ground without a pilot, it's today. No offence to Mr. Davies over there." Rob made eye contact with everyone in the room and asked jokingly. "Is anyone else hoarding a pilot's licence they've not told me about, and specifically with a Piper Cub rating?"

No one spoke.

Walking back to the window, Rob placed his hands on the pane and looked out towards the runway. "I know I don't have to state the obvious, but I will anyway. We can't get airborne without a pilot, so for now, we're in a holding pattern. And if we don't find a pilot, our military friends will step in and send us whatever plane they have available, and we know what kind of financial hardship that creates for our missing pilot. As you all know, he'll get the fuel bill. If that happens, then let's hope for his sake it's not a four-engine C-130."

Rob craned his neck around the edge of the window frame when an aircraft engine started up from somewhere on the parking apron. When he couldn't see anything, he spun around and purposely walked towards an old wine rack that someone had mounted to the wall years ago. But instead of wine bottles, the slots contained rolled-up maps, each one wrapped in a plastic sleeve.

Grabbing from the top left slot, Rob unravelled a sectional map on a small table. Without being asked, everyone crowded around as he pointed in the general vicinity of Spruce Creek. "This is where they were going to land last night, right here at Spruce Creek Lodge. They were planning to offload TV gear for a charity broadcast that's happening today. After making their delivery, they were to head straight back here to the airport." Rob looked at his people. "Everybody with me so far?"

Nods all around.

"But," Rob continued. "Here's the puzzler in all of this, and the reason this airplane is missing and presumed crashed. We've been told by authorities that the pilot left without a full tank of gas, and with not being able to land at Spruce Creek to fuel up, the crew tried to make it back here to Owensville, which we now know did not happen."

Someone to Rob's left spoke up. "So why couldn't they land at Spruce Creek?"

Rob twisted his head around. "According to ATC, the runway lights weren't operational at the airfield and it was too dark for them to land without field markers. Whatever possessed the pilot to fly into the mountains without proper fuel is beyond me, but the fact remains he did."

To everyone's surprise, Kevin shimmied up to the table and spoke with surprising clarity given his groggy disposition just moments ago. "What about the ELT?" he asked. "Any signal picked up yet?" Kevin noticed people staring at him with blank expressions. "What?" he asked. "I'm young and I heal fast!"

Not overly surprised by Kevin's sudden physical reversal, Rob smiled and addressed everyone on mass. "We've had no reports of an ELT signal, so without that, we've got no idea where the 185 is, except for somewhere along the Moose River between here and Spruce Creek. And that's a mighty long stretch. So, the sooner we get a plane into the air, the quicker we can eliminate quadrants of land, find our pilots and get them home. And us for that matter."

Rob eyed Kevin warily. "Hopefully the crew is safe, and they've lit a fire by now. Smoke signals would sure make our job easier. So, for now, I want everyone ready to move when the time comes."

Nervous excitement coursed through Kevin's body, followed by another hit of adrenaline. The gnawing pain in his leg eased, along with his groggy head. He glanced outside towards the Piper Cub. The bird needed a pilot, and he was the only one in the present company qualified to fly it. Fearing that his rebound was purely temporal, Kevin stood motionless and sucked in several rapid-fire breaths to calm down and slow his excited heart.

Rob noticed Kevin's sudden rapid breathing. "You okay there, hot-shot?"

Kevin's mind was already cascading through pre-flight checks, his fingertips tingling as he imagined them gliding across the fuselage, the aircraft's skin already warming under the early morning sun.

"Kevin!" shouted Rob, the sudden outburst rousing the pilot from whatever delusion he was in. Rob's face contorted as Kevin stared at him blankly. "When I said I want everyone ready to move, that didn't include you. You're not going anywhere this hop. You're injured with a concussion, in case you forgot."

"No! I'm fine," insisted Kevin as he spun on his heels and bound for the door. "I can do this!"

"Davies!" yelled Rob again. "Just where do you think you're going?"

Everyone in the room turned, all eyes falling on the eager pilot.

Kevin stopped and turned around. "I'll be doing a pre-flight on the Cub," he calmly explained. "As you said, the sooner we get into the air, the better!"

"What's this 'we' stuff?" asked Rob. "'We' does not include you, Kevin! You're grounded for twenty-four hours. Remember my orders? I'll find another pilot to fly the Cub. Your ability to fly safely is seriously compromised."

"I know you don't believe me, but I feel better!" boasted Kevin, and all too convincingly. "Besides, the doc said it was a mild concussion, remember? And we don't have twenty-four hours. So, you guys figure out what track you want me to fly and who's spotting. In the meantime, I'll have the Cub ready to go."

Rob stood there with his mouth open, but no words came out.

Kevin smiled a boldfaced grin, wishing he had a camera to capture the dumbstruck expression on Rob's face. "Might I suggest re-creating the Cessna's original flight path, and then backtrack from Spruce Creek? But seeing as my mental faculties are *compromised*, that's only my lamebrain suggestion. You guys figure it out and I'll abide by your wishes." Kevin glanced at his watch and tapped the dial. "Time's wasting."

With that being said, Kevin muscled the door open and left the building.

Rob Smith eventually found his voice and began yelling vulgar expletives at Kevin. But his words never made it to the pilot's ears. Instead, they echoed off the closing door and through a room filled with stupefied people.

* * *

Jack handed the keys to Tom Sullivan. "Don't crack it up," he niggled.

Snatching the keyring from Jack's fingers, Tom spun around and walked away. "I wouldn't think of it, Jack. And besides, you'd never even know with all the dents it has already."

Jack forced an unconvincing smile. "I mean it, Tom! That van is special to me."

Climbing into the driver's seat, Tom asked one more time. "You sure you don't want to come along again, Jack? I could use the extra pair of eyes."

"No thanks," grunted Jack. "I've got enough fires to put out around here. You be careful on the back roads. They'll still be slippery and washed out in places. Personally, I think it's a harebrained idea."

"Don't worry, Jack," assured Tom. "I'll take it easy. You go make yourself some oatmeal and a nice cup of prune juice, and I'll willingly risk life and limb looking for the TV gear we need for *your* charity broadcast."

Feeling instantly defensive, Jack walked several steps closer to the van and pointed his finger. "That's your choice, Tom, so don't put this on me. I never asked you to bring in more camera stuff. That was your decision. I was prepared to scrub the auction, and I don't need anything else on my already guilty conscience."

Tom started the engine which sounded like several of the spark plugs were misfiring. "I'm trying to be proactive here, Jack, because it seems like the universe is doing all it can to squash this event today. And might I say your defeatist attitude isn't helping."

Tom waited for Jack to reply, and when none came, he popped the van into drive. "I better get going. I'm worried my guys might have hit the ditch trying to get up here this morning. Come to think of it, we've not had any new cars arrive at all for that matter. Something's screwy, Jack. I'll be back as quick as I can."

Jack stepped back a few paces and offered Tom an uninspired shoulder height wave. Moments later the van drove out of sight through the canopy of trees leading to the main road, its wheels splashing mud and water to the sides. Glancing back towards the tall pines, Jack tilted his head and noticed a large whiskey jack peering down at him from above, its head twisting one way and then the other as if able to read his thoughts.

"What are you glaring at?" asked Jack. "You never see a man lose his mind before?" The bird never budged. "I'm guessing not." Jack waved his arms over his head. "Shoo! Go stare down somebody else."

The bird swiftly sprang from its perch and flew to a nearby tree.

Shafts of sunlight streamed through the trees and the cool morning air caused Jack to shiver. He turned and walked back towards the lodge, his head rotating side to side as he rambled. "I wish you'd never told me about mountain biking, Tom, and I should never have listened." Jack looked skyward as if he could see his wife in the heavens. "Mildred, you, on the other hand, I should've listened to when you tried to talk me out of buying this place from the start. Now you can say, 'I told you so.'"

Jack stopped at the rear door; his mind fixated on having to once again tell his guests the video coverage was in all likelihood a bust. One last glance over his shoulder confirmed the feathered onlooker still gawking. Yanking the door open, Jack lumbered into the lodge. "Dumb bird."

Seconds later, the bird defecated and flew away.

Chapter 18

Finally reaching Dave, the fire in Paul's back returned with a vengeance. He bent down as low as his aching body allowed. "I'm here now, partner," he grimaced. "I made it!"

Paul's heart jumped to his throat when he saw Dave lying face down and not moving. He placed one hand on his friend's back and prayed silently he still had breath in his lungs. With his other hand, he flicked off a small cluster of ants closing in on his neck. As he tried to lift Dave's upper body, it was then Dave suddenly flipped his head around. "Holy smokes, Ace, slowdown! I don't need the rest of my body messed up too!"

Startled by Dave's sudden rebuke, Paul fell back on his tailbone. His entire body erupted in pain from the harsh movement. For a moment he sat in the dirt completely tongue-tied, but then broke into a wide grin seconds later. "Quit your bellyaching," he rasped. "If it wasn't for me, you'd be lying in these bushes forever with every red ant in the valley trying to colonize on those stupid orange coveralls!"

Dave snickered. "I was beginning to fancy my little hovel until you stumbled by." Dave noticed the dried blood on Paul's head. "What happened to your melon? Cut yourself shaving again?"

"Always the jokester," mused Paul.

"That's me. But seeing you hobble over here like a ninety-year-old man was worth the pain in my ankle, which incidentally I can't move without blacking out. I'm pretty sure it's broken."

"Let me take a look. Once I can move that is."

"Look, but don't touch," ordered Dave.

As Paul examined Dave's swollen ankle, it seemed that every mosquito in the area suddenly found the two men hunkered down on the forest floor. Paul nodded his head. "Yup," he confirmed. "You messed it up good, so try not to move. Looks pretty swollen."

"You should have been a doctor," teased Dave. "I would never have thought of not moving it."

Paul deflected the wisecrack through his shallow breathing. "I'll go back to the plane . . . and get the bug spray, and the first aid kit. At least we have that. Then, I'll find . . . some wood to . . . splint it."

"Quit breathing so heavy, Ace," croaked Dave. "You're expelling enough carbon dioxide to attract every blood-sucking insect on the planet!"

Paul altered his body position, trying to ease the pressure on his spine. "Wh . . . What?" he asked. "What's carbon dioxide . . . got to do with mosquitoes?"

Another grin appeared on Dave's face. "Just stop breathing so hard and help me sit up, but for heaven's sake slower this time! I'll explain the mosquito thing over our make-believe bacon and eggs pancake breakfast."

Paul wasn't much help, but after a few minutes of painful struggle, Dave repositioned to his side and leaned his back partway against a tree. He watched as Paul began the arduous trek back to the Cessna. "And I like my eggs over easy, bacon crisp, brown toast, coffee with one cream, one sugar."

With a lump forming in his throat, Paul reflected on their situation and his reckless abandon for trying to earn a few extra dollars with undue care and attention. And now he and his best friend were hurt, his airplane badly damaged, and his flying career most assuredly over. Paul swatted at another cloud of mosquitoes; his face downcast. "I'll go light up the Coleman," he stated glumly, wishing to God he had one.

* * *

Like Diane Jackson, Tess McMurray wasn't taking kindly to the fact that not a shard of information had been offered in regard to finding their husbands. After a brief phone call with Diane, Tess showered, ate a light breakfast, and in the next few minutes planned to drive to the Jackson homestead. Mutually deciding they would head for Owensville Municipal, she hoped that in doing so, they might get answers from someone with half a brain and a decisive strategy to begin a search.

Tess checked the weather on her phone, and what she read did little to alleviate her growing concerns. Though currently bright and sunny, the late afternoon forecast again called for showers and the risk of thunderstorms, with higher probability in the mountains, including the district of Spruce Creek. "Oh, isn't that just splendid," she grumbled.

Snatching her car keys from a nearby ledge, Tess slipped into a pair of shoes, grabbed her jacket and hurried through the front door. One minute later, the wheels on her SUV were travelling far quicker than they should, its driver far angrier than she wished to be.

* * *

Growing more impatient by the second, Kim shouted from the front door. "C'mon, Mom, hurry up! Tessa will be here any minute, and we should be ready!"

Not at all surprised that her daughter just pulled a "Mom" thing, Diane leaned partway out the bathroom door as she spritzed her hair with spray, or as Paul knee-slap called it, "glue!"

"I'm hurrying!" she replied in an exasperated voice. "Why is it that when I need to go somewhere you doddle. But when you need to be somewhere, it becomes an all-points bulletin!"

"What'd you say, Mom?" Kim called out. "I missed that."

Not bothering to repeat herself, Diane cast a final glance into the three-way mirror. Hair and make-up weren't to her usual standard, but she decided both would do given the hurried circumstances. A quick fluff of her hair, jeans, a long-sleeve pullover hoodie and sneakers were fine for the task of fact-finding.

Turning away from the mirror, Diane reached for the bathroom light switch. It was then she noticed one of Paul's shirts hanging behind the door. This was nothing unusual as he often hung up his work shirts before they went into the laundry hamper. But what caught her eye was a folded white paper tucked into the left breast pocket, the crumpled corner barely visible.

"Mom!" boomed Kim again, her voice higher pitched than before. "Are you coming? I think I just heard Tess pull up!"

"On my way!" shouted Diane, her voice matching the intensity of her daughter's.

Feeling similar to a kid raiding the cookie jar, Diane's innate sense of curiosity suddenly overpowered her wifely virtue. She wasn't normally one to snoop, but this time her gut told her otherwise. Rarely did Paul stuff his pockets with anything other than a Chapstick and a lens cleaning cloth for his glasses, so the paper seemed out of place. She presumed it could be something as simple as a to-do list or even a business invoice, but as Diane thought of Paul's flight medical and her chat with the medical receptionist, she wondered about a possible connection.

There were only two people who knew that her husband wasn't medically cleared to fly, and yet Diane understood how the lure of gossip may have escalated that number beyond her control. Deeply hurt that Paul did not share the results of his medical with her, Diane had already infringed on her husband's right to privacy by telling Jack Ward and Bruce Macbeth. She broke her own rules with a loose tongue and felt horrendously guilty because of it.

What bothered her even more was that similar to her husband not being honest with her, Diane also withheld mentioning anything to Tess about Paul's medical or the clinic's phone call. Undoubtedly, Tess knew something was wrong when they left Value Village in such a hurry and vowing to spill the beans once Tess arrived, Diane hoped her friend would forgive her for not doing so earlier.

Lifting the document from the pocket of Paul's shirt, Diane knew professional stationery when she saw it. Unfolding the paper, her heart pounded as if her husband might suddenly materialize and confront her. In an instant, Diane's eyes keyed in on the top of the document: "FAA Denial of Medical Certification." Other prominent words in the context of the letter stood out like a sore thumb. Her breath caught in her chest. "Cardiovascular Evaluation," "Moderate High-Grade Murmur," "Mitral Valve Prolapse." Her eyes skimmed the rest of the letter, its contents short and to the point.

So, there it was . . . proof positive that her husband should never have left the ground last evening. And pending the outcome of this letter, he may never do so again. Feeling a wellspring of emotion, Diane re-folded the letter and reluctantly brought it with her.

* * *

The speedometer registered fifteen clicks per hour more than the posted speed limit, but Tess couldn't have cared less. Scarcely in the mood for abiding by the rules, she wheeled her vehicle around the final corner leading to Diane Jackson's house. With the stereo blaring a song from Nickelback, Tess navigated the remaining few blocks in record time, her front wheels leaping over the concrete lip that separated the road from Diane's driveway. She popped the transmission into park and was about to climb out when the front door of the house opened. Out walked Kim with her fingers busy on her phone's keypad.

"Some things never change," smirked Tess.

Diane followed behind within seconds; her eyes aimed down. In both hands, she clutched a white piece of paper, and from the expression on her face, Tess knew something was very wrong. Kim reached the rear passenger side door, flipped up the handle and climbed in. "Hi, Tessa," she said. "Thanks for picking us up."

"Not a problem, Kim. How are you both coping with all this?" asked Tess.

Kim fidgeted uncomfortably in the seat. "Up until two minutes ago, not too bad I guess."

Almost to the SUV, Diane's eyes were still on the paper. Tess thought her face looked pale but thought it wise to keep that observation to herself. She spun her head around and quickly asked Kim. "Why, what happened?"

Kim watched as her mom rounded the front corner of the vehicle. "I'm not sure exactly, but Mom went from annoyed to super annoyed when she found that paper she's holding, whatever it is. She wouldn't tell me."

Unable to shake a sudden feeling of dread, Tess expected her already soured mood to nose-dive. She watched as Diane reached the door, pulled the latch with noticeable hesitation and climbed in. She offered nothing more than a nod and no explanation for the paper in her hands.

For what seemed an eternity, Diane sat a few long seconds gazing blankly out her side window. For Tess, her silence spoke volumes while she waited for both shoes to drop. Until then, she thought the best course of action was to simply drive and not attempt any small talk. Prior to backing out of the driveway, Tess gazed in her rearview mirror and noticed Kim staring back, her eyes wide. With Diane's head turned towards the window, Tess was about to back up when Diane finally spoke. "Hold on, Tess . . . please."

Tess complied.

"There's something I"—Diane struggled with her words— "Something that I need to share with you."

"Okay," replied Tess suspiciously, "shoot."

Diane passed across the half-folded sheet of paper. As Tess grabbed it, she noticed her friend's moist eyes. "I'm always here for you," added Tess. "You know that, right?"

"I know, Tessa," admitted Diane. "But this is something I should have told you about sooner than this. I just found this paper in one of Paul's shirts, and it confirmed my suspicions. I didn't want to say anything until I was sure. Now I am."

As Tess's eyes skimmed the document, her eyebrows raised and her facial expression changed, the reaction causing Diane to feel even worse. Tess handed back the paper, threw her vehicle into reverse and spoke only three words. "Buckle up, girls!"

* * *

"I'm not sure this stuff could smell any worse," Dave bitterly complained.

Paul held the spray button down a few long seconds, thoroughly coating his arms and neck, then Dave's. "It'll keep the bugs off, so suck it up."

"Listen, Ace," grumbled Dave. "I don't mean to sound ungrateful. Bug spray is great, but I'd trade that stuff in a heartbeat for some water and something to eat."

"Me too," was all Paul could muster.

"But hey," smiled Dave. "The plus is you seem to be moving faster now."

"Yay me," Paul replied in a flat voice. "I'll go find a hunk of wood that we can use to splint your ankle. Don't go away."

"Wouldn't think of it. Besides, you haven't paid this much attention to me in years! I kinda like it!"

Hunched down beside Dave and fighting a lump in his throat, Paul turned his head away from his friend and stood up. "I'll be right back."

As he limped towards a cluster of fallen timber, Paul wondered how it had come to this. He had allowed the hurried request from Jack Ward to throw off his usual by-the-book, rational thinking. Normally he would never dream of leaving the ground without water and provisions. Even a lighter or box of matches was standard fare before venturing into the mountains. And the issue of flying while under a medical restriction? Well, that was an altogether different level of stupidity.

While hunting for a small piece of wood to use as an ankle splint, Paul replayed in his mind the events leading up to his decision to fly, and he wished more than anything that he could wind back the hands of time and make it all go away . . .

Early yesterday morning, Dave had flown a pair of brash fishermen to a remote mountain lake not far from the Owensville airport. Because of the short flight, Paul chose to stay behind and catch up on paperwork instead of tag along. In addition to fishing gear, the anglers packed a cooler topped with ice and beer, along with cooking essentials, including a frying pan and some sort of odd-smelling batter to fry their fish in. Dave openly questioned the men about how much fishing they'd actually get done, which immediately generated an uproarious amount of laughter in response.

When Dave finally picked up the tipsy anglers later that afternoon and brought them back to Owensville, Paul thought it high time to purge the inside of his filthy airplane, a long-overdue task. And because Dave had scheduled an early load of cattle to haul by truck the next morning, Paul sent him home to get some well-deserved rest, a plan Dave happily complied with.

Paul thought it both ironic and humorous that his business partner had no aversion to pressure spraying the inside of a filthy manure-encrusted cattle trailer, yet despised cleaning out the cabin of the Cessna, which now reeked of fish, sweaty fishermen and spilled beer.

Upon closer inspection of his plane, Paul elected to gut nearly everything, even those essentials he usually kept on board, like water, energy bars and camping supplies. For Paul, sterilizing the interior of his Cessna reminded him of cleaning out the car after a long family vacation. A thorough decluttering became a necessary evil if the vehicle was to be used again in a safe, comfortable manner.

Tackling the accumulated mess, Paul eventually stuffed a trash bag with everything from empty water bottles and candy bar wrappers, to half-eaten sandwiches and loose fishing tackle. He also removed a storage bag filled with freeze-dried food that he kept for unexpected emergencies. In the cargo hold was another small duffel bag, its contents ranging from a change of clothes and rain ponchos to boots, hats, and extra sunscreen. An hour later and well into the task of trying to reclaim the space inside the Cessna, his cell phone rang.

"Airflow Charters, Paul speaking," he answered distractedly.

"Paul is that you?" squawked a male voice that Paul didn't recognize.

Furrowing his brow, Paul replied sarcastically. "I do believe I just said it was. Who's calling please?"

"Paul, it's Jack Ward up at Spruce Creek. Sorry, I know my voice is a bit raspy, but have you got a second? It's been a rough day up here."

"Hey, Jack," answered Paul, not really wanting to talk. "How are things going up—"

"Well, I just mentioned it's been a rough day," interrupted Jack, "So I'm not sure who's not listening to whom. Anyway, that's beside the point. I'm up to my neck in trouble here, Paul. We've been swamped by rain, the power's out and the road to the lodge is closed. To make matters worse, I've got a big mountain biking event scheduled for tomorrow which we're broadcasting as a charity auction for Mildred's old cancer support clinic."

Clearly distraught, Paul wondered if Jack would pause long enough to breathe, but he somehow kept going and his voice rose in pitch.

"So, here's my dilemma," Jack continued. "We can't get the broadcast gear in by car, so I'm wondering if you'd consider flying it in tonight. I'll pay double your rate. Someone from CFCB television will bring the gear to you, so it's as simple as that. You drop it here tonight before dark and then fly home, quick, and easy. What'd ya say? I'll even make sure the runway is lit up nice and pretty for you!"

Taken aback by the sudden request, Paul wasn't sure how to answer in light of his recent flight medical. He wasn't ready to share that with anyone just yet, not even his wife. But from a financial standpoint, he needed this flight, especially if double the dollars were on the table.

"Well, Jack," explained Paul. "The airplane just came back. It needs fuel and I've gutted the cockpit and cargo bay for cleaning. It's actually not ready for such a quick turnaround and I—"

Jack broke in. "Sorry for my rudeness, Paul, but you are operating a business, aren't you? And I'm offering your business my business, right here and now. Listen, you'd be a lifesaver, a real hero to a good many people up here. It's a short flight, so how hard can it be? Truthfully, I'm out of options, and without the TV gear, we aren't broadcasting so much as a bike wheel. And here's the guilt trip part. No auction would be a real shame for Mildred's sake, and for a good many other folks up here, including me."

"You're laying it on pretty thick, Jack."

"Well, it's all the truth, Paul. So, what's your answer?"

Paul's brain was already busy converting a wallet full of cash into repairs on his airplane and a dishwasher for Diane. And though Dave already went home, he seldom passed up a chance to fly, and Paul was certain he would agree to a quick evening trip if asked.

Paul's way of justifying the unjustifiable was simple. *My heart feels perfectly fine, so why not one final trip? Who would know if I don't tell anyone?* Convinced that grounding him was completely unnecessary with bills to pay and a family to feed, Paul even tried urging the doctor to grant temporary medical certification, contingent on follow-up appointments and tests. But his request fell on deaf ears and was vehemently denied.

"Jack, how soon can you have the cargo here at the airport?" asked Paul decidedly. "The forecast isn't good here either, so the sooner we leave the better. I think we can get in an' out before things really close in."

"You're the man!" sang Jack happily. "I owe you, Paul. You give me a price and I'll cut a cheque when you get here." There was a long pause before Jack spoke again. "And I hope you don't mind my assertiveness, but the gear's already heading your way. I was pretty sure you'd say yes, so took a chance and had Tom Sullivan send it over. He's up here now with his son."

Shocked by the admission, Paul stammered. "It's . . . already being delivered here, Jack?"

"That's affirmative. No time to waste, I always say."

"But . . . what if I had said no?"

"Well, you didn't, did you? And that's all that matters."

Before saying another word, Paul rubbed his temple and sucked in a deep breath. "Let me give Dave a call and see if I can swindle him into riding shotgun. I've already sent him home, but I'll see what I can do. I'm not flying this alone and need a co—"

A car horn suddenly blared from near the parking lot next to Paul's Cessna. "Hang on a second, Jack," stuttered Paul while looking towards the noise. To his surprise, a CFCB Television van rolled to a stop by the access gate in the fence, and the driver's side door flew open.

"You Paul Jackson?" asked a hunched shouldered man sporting a fedora and dreadlocks.

Astounded the gear had shown up already, it took Paul a moment to collect his thoughts. "Ah . . . yes," he finally admitted. "That's me."

Sliding open the side door of the van, the driver gawked at Paul and spoke without much interest. "Where'd ya want all this stuff?" he asked.

With his head not in the game, Paul attempted to arrange his thoughts into something that made sense. "Uhm . . . " he pointed his finger. Load it here by the plane. I'll let you through the gate."

In the next moment, Dave McMurray's car jerked to a stop, leaving Paul even more befuddled. "Listen, Jack," he finally mumbled. "Both your television gear and Dave showed up at the same time, and I've got no idea how Dave knew to come back, but I—"

"Guilty again," Jack confessed. "I took the liberty of calling him before I called you. Like you just said, the weather isn't great and time is of the essence here."

Blindsided again into silence, Paul watched as Dave strolled over, a knowing grin plastered on his face. "Close your mouth, Ace," he laughed. "We've got work to do, so dump the call and let's haul!"

Paul shook his head. "See you shortly, Jack. And yes, we'd appreciate the field lights. Been a while since I've flown in there."

"Fly safe," Jack implored. "I'll have the lights on. Thanks again, Paul."

With that, the line disconnected, and Paul was left staring vacantly at the phone like it was a foreign object. He watched as Dave assisted the CFCB driver with the TV equipment. Utterly dazed, Paul wandered over. "Let me help you."

"I'm good for that," replied Dave as he looked towards the Cessna. "I see you're doing some housekeeping. Are we loading all that junk back in or do we tempt fate like we're always so good at?"

Paul thought for a moment. "It'll be a quick flight there and back, so let's just secure Jack's gear and go. Besides, I want to vacuum out the plane later anyway. I'll do that once we're back.

Hopefully, we'll stay ahead of the weather and then can gas up at the lodge to save a bit of time."

"Roger that," Dave remarked. "I'll load the camera gear. You're the pilot in command this hop, so you do the pre-flight."

Paul nodded his head and walked to the front of the airplane to begin his checks. His heart beat uncharacteristically fast as he began to question his principles. "What are you doing, Paul?" he mouthed to himself. "None of this is a good idea, and you know it."

Gambling on personal safety wasn't the norm for Paul Jackson, but for this particular trip, he couldn't figure out why he was so willing to turn a blind eye to safety protocol and medical authority, and then leave behind the essentials that are always on board his plane for unexpected emergencies.

As Paul checked the prop, he made up his mind that the benefits of this flight outweighed the risks. He knew full well that money, rebellious pride and his refusal to believe his heart was actually flawed all factored into his willful decision to proceed.

As Paul ran his fingers across the engine cowling, he broke into a defiant smile. He peaked around the side of the airplane and said to Dave. "Wheels up in ten."

Tall grasses as high as four feet fluttered gently as morning breezes drifted across the river valley. A large jet-black dragonfly, appearing more like a tiny helicopter, hovered nearby, its transparent wings reflecting the bright sunshine as it darted through the brush. Under different circumstances, the entire scene would have been tremendously appealing, but for Paul Jackson and Dave McMurray, the unblemished beauty of their surroundings had gone pretty much unnoticed.

"Well," jested Dave. "This is one fine situation you've got me into, Ace. So, we left home with no water, nothing to start a fire with and nothing to eat. What kind of employer are you? But hey, I will admit you did a fine job of splinting my ankle, so I owe you something."

Berating himself for their predicament, Paul in no way appreciated Dave driving the point home. And since his flight medical, a guilty conscience seemed a recurring theme that he desperately wanted to shed. "I'm sorry, Dave," Paul stated glumly. "The plane was such a mess inside and when I took everything out, I thought we'd be fine for a quick turnaround. Admittedly I felt rushed with Jack and just wanted to get into the air and go." Paul looked skyward, then towards his feet. "We'd land and unload, fuel up, eat quick and head back. Simple right? It figures the one time we don't pack the supplies, that's when we need them. Lesson learned the hard way."

As unproductive as it seemed, Dave adjusted his body to get more comfortable. He too had chosen to compromise their safety, so he felt he needed to accept half the blame. "Leaving without enough gas was bad enough," he admitted, "but now we both deserve the dummy pilot award."

Another pang of guilt tore at what little self-respect Paul retained. He couldn't disagree. "Listen, Dave, seeing as were ground-dwellers now, this might be the best time to admit something I should have told you before we took this gig." Paul tried to smile. "Now that you're injured and can't come after me with a tree branch, I'm actually not sure where to begin."

"Try at the beginning," Dave suggested. "I'm all ears. But just so you know, I can still throw rocks if I don't like what I'm hearing."

Tiny beads of sweat formed on Paul's face which he made no attempt to wipe away. "Quite frankly, my actions may well mark the end of my flying career."

"Now you're scaring me, Ace," worried Dave. "I know we've experienced a lot of mischief together over the years, but what sort of mayhem did you single-handedly get yourself into this time? Or do I even want to know?"

Paul swallowed his pride and knew there was little point in sugar-coating his indiscretions. Besides, Dave would want the news straight up—no bull—no fluff. Paul brushed away a mosquito on his nose, the momentary distraction welcome. Paul met Dave's gaze. "I . . . I failed my flight medical."

Dave's forehead lifted. "You know, Ace" he cringed. "For a second there it sounded like you said, and I quote, 'I failed my flight medical.' But I'm sure I must have heard that wrong?"

Paul spoke in a quiet, child-like voice. The words agonizing to repeat. "You heard me right. I failed my medical, and I shouldn't be flying."

After what seemed an eternity, Dave blinked several times and let out a huge sigh. "Well, I'm no expert, but I'm guessing you've just re-written all the chapters in the newly revised, *When-Not-to-Fly, Journal of Aviation*."

Running shaky fingers through his greying hair, Paul exhaled much of the tension he'd kept locked inside. Admittedly, confession felt empowering. "Well," he admitted. "I've always wanted to author a chapter in a flying publication, though this is one story I'd rather wasn't printed."

"My lips are sealed, Ace," offered Dave convincingly. "It's not my business to spill the beans to anyone, but I'm guessing the cow dung has already hit the fan somewhere. Maybe it's a good thing we're missing in action now."

"It's not you that needs to be worried, Dave," added Paul. "I can't believe I've acted so foolishly since my medical. I don't know where my head's been at. What kind of moron flies when he's been grounded, then doesn't tell his wife or business partner? I feel like a kid rebelling against his parents, and as crazy as this may sound, I've actually been enjoying it."

Dave shook his head. "That's twice now I'm sure my ears deceived me. Did you say you kept the results of your medical from Diane too?" Paul's silence provided Dave with the answer to his question.

Rising slowly to his feet, Paul found it heart-wrenching to watch Dave scrunch his eyes in bold-faced stun mode. It was hard to tell if the look was one of condemnation or sympathy. Either way, Paul began to hobble away.

"Where are you going, Ace?" asked Dave. "You can't escape from this, even out here in the middle of nowhere."

Paul stopped and turned. "I always told Diane that if I ever did something really dumb, she had permission to take me out into the back field and shoot me. But since I don't have a gun and she's not here, I think I'll go find a grizzly bear and steal his berries. Because after what I've done, a bear mauling is far more appealing than being shot by an angry wife."

Dave watched solemnly as Paul walked away. "Seeing as you're offering to pick berries for breakfast, I prefer raspberries to gooseberries, Ace."

Paul ignored the suggestion and kept walking.

"And try not to mush them up," ordered Dave. "I don't want jam!"

Paul turned around and smiled at his friend, his head skewed. "I'll see what I can do."

Chapter 19

Rob Smith wasn't having the best of luck with phone calls this morning, and despite the good fortune of saving both the Piper Cub and Kevin Davies from serious harm, things weren't as rosy in regard to search and rescue. Being chewed out by ATC for a sluggish start was one thing, but now in light of Kevin's recent trauma, his best efforts were coming up short in finding someone else to pilot the Cub.

"Listen," he ranted into the phone. "I'd fly the thing myself if I knew how. But I'm not a pilot, and the only one I've got thinks he's still fit to fly despite a blow to the head."

Rob twisted around to where several blank faces stared back at him. With his free arm raised slightly and fingers splayed, he quietly mouthed, "I can't believe this is happening," accompanied by an exaggerated rolling of the eyes. As he continued listening to the unsympathetic voice in the phone earpiece, he reinforced his grip on the device and his face began to tint red. "So, what you're telling me is that we're on our own, is that it?" he asked disgustedly. "Well thanks for nothing! What's the point of neighbouring civil air search and rescue units if we don't help each other in times of crisis?"

Rob listened for a moment longer and then hammered home his final point. "Let me remind you again that I've got a downed Cessna in the mountains and no ELT. I need a plane in the air and don't have a pilot. So, thanks for nothing!"

Rob threw the handset into its cradle but missed. It ricocheted and hit the floor with a loud crash. Someone scooted in, picked it up and gently placed the device into its resting place.

"You know," growled Rob to nobody in particular. "I shouldn't have to deal with this BS. I'm a volunteer like everyone else around here, and I don't understand why it's like pulling teeth to get a little help when it's asked for."

Rob enjoyed drawing from a subconscious list of dental puns as warranted. This often resulted in a chorus of groans from anyone close enough to hear, but this time the room stayed eerily quiet. "Don't everyone laugh at once," he sneered.

A search coordinator's job was to develop a strategy and work to implement that plan, all the while ensuring the search and rescue effort was handled as efficiently as possible. Rob wasn't even remotely convinced that Kevin Davies was fit to pilot the Cub, even when he appeared coherent and in charge of his faculties. He even considered sending him back to the hospital for another assessment, but with time being of the essence and his options few, his gut told him to let the kid fly, while his brain screamed, "Nothing doing."

His attempt to secure another pilot for the Cub failed, as did bringing in a different airplane and someone qualified to fly it. Now it was crunch time, and Rob needed to get the ball rolling by either calling the military or allowing Kevin to fly. Both options equally stunk in his opinion.

The only other operational squad of civilian air search and rescue was at Bakersfield Airport, a small aerodrome southwest of Owensville. Separated by a spiky range of mountains, the two municipalities were connected by a twisty two-lane highway, its asphalt having seen better days and its share of nasty accidents. And because of narrow valleys and erratic air currents, air travel between cities was lengthy and often extremely hazardous.

To Rob's dismay, that unit was already engaged in an active search for missing hikers, a husband and wife duo last seen crisscrossing a ridge of cliffs over two hours ago. Part of his job was coordinating with other agencies, and he couldn't believe the unfortunate timing during the one instance he so desperately required assistance.

Wanting eyes in the sky as quickly as possible, Rob knew it would be only a matter of time before the media sniffed blood and arrived on sight, the hungry mob prowling like sharks for a juicy lead story. He was also surprised that family members of the two missing pilots hadn't shown up yet, which typically occurred under these types of unsettling circumstances.

For now, Rob's immediate goal was getting the Piper Cub aloft, and with Kevin bouncing back so quickly, he reluctantly decided to let him fly against his better judgement. Initial signs of a concussion were inconclusive, and though the ER physician suggested to Kevin to get some rest, he surprisingly placed no restrictions on his activities or flying status.

Observing the tone in the room, Rob saw that his people were eager to move, but at the same time, they understood their duties were minimal until the missing plane was found. It was now a waiting game that nobody liked, but everyone accepted. Proud of his group, Rob wanted nothing more than for them to succeed today, especially given the previous night's unexpected activities relating to Kevin. He knew that teamwork was paramount, that his group of volunteers were now looking to him for direction; direction he, unfortunately, could not provide with so little to go on.

Prior to becoming a search coordinator, Rob trained in each one of the volunteer positions his team now occupied. Everything from ground crew and aircraft spotter, which he excelled at, to navigation and radio operations. But now his responsibility was to get a bird into the air the sooner the better. To expedite the process, he thought briefly about occupying the backseat of the Cub himself to better direct the search from the air but then opted against it.

Kevin's advice about flying to Spruce Creek and back-tracking was bang on, and Rob would leave Kevin and Susan McCutcheon to it. He walked back to the sectional map, spun around and pointed. "We'll assume the Cessna set down somewhere along the banks of the river here, east of Spruce Creek. The pilot and co-pilot are experienced mountain pilots, so we can also assume they have enough provisions to last until we find them."

Rob glanced around the room. "Hopefully they've lit a fire which'll make them easier to spot from the air. But we also can't rule out the possibility that both men have injuries and can't help themselves or each other. Does anyone have any questions at this point?"

The room remained quiet, so Rob continued. "We have no way of knowing what they encountered on the way down or what sort of control the pilot had or may not have had. The terrain isn't airplane friendly, and since this crew either flamed out or tried to set down before the engine quit, we don't know what we're dealing with until we find them. But the fact remains they're overdue and haven't checked in, so that's why we're here."

Someone coughed loudly to Rob's left, but nobody spoke.

"And contrary to popular opinion," added Rob. "I'm not a fan of hearing my own voice all the time, so feel free to step in with suggestions or comments. We work as a team people, and just because I'm SC, doesn't mean I have all the answers." *And right now, I have no answers.*

It suddenly dawned on Rob that Kevin had yet to return from his pre-flight of the Cub. And because he was the one person who specifically needed to attend this briefing, Rob promptly excused himself. "I'll be right back. It seems we're missing our jockey and I—"

Kevin bounded through the front door, short-winded and visibly sweating. "Houston, we've got a problem!" he announced through heavy breathing.

"What's wrong?" asked Rob nervously. "I was just on my way out to get you."

Kevin stopped his advance a few feet from Rob's position. "I never noticed until I did the complete walk-around . . . but there's a small gash on top of the . . . wing, just forward of the left aileron. Something . . . struck it hard and I—"

"Whoa Kevin!" exclaimed Rob. "Slow down and catch your breath. You said a gash, like as in a hole, a tear or what?"

Kevin blurted out. "I don't know what caused it, but whatever it was might still be stuck inside the wing. We can't fly the Cub, not like that."

Scratching his head, Rob spewed out the next obvious question. "So, did you look inside the hole, or gash, or whatever it is?"

"I'll need a ladder and a flashlight," stated Kevin emphatically. "That's why I came back. The ailerons are moving okay, but if we can't fix the hole, we don't fly." Kevin's face sank. "We're effectively grounded."

Several people groaned.

Satisfied that his peers were taking him seriously for once, Kevin added a final retort. "We can't fly it like that. It'll rip open further if we do. Or if a pulley comes loose or a control cable breaks in flight, then you'll be searching for another airplane."

Kevin thought for a moment, pausing for dramatic effect. A sly smile played across his lips. "Anyone got any duct tape?" he asked seriously.

The sudden, off the wall question, prompted blank stares from everyone.

Everyone but Rob Smith.

* * *

Now that Paul's missteps were on the table, Diane Jackson couldn't remember the last time she'd seen her friend so upset. On the drive to the airport, Diane chose to sit quietly despite a storm of emotion brewing under her skin. Kim too remained placid, grateful for noise-cancelling earbuds and the music coursing through them.

As Tess rounded the final corner to the airport's main entrance, she nearly side-swiped a small four-door sedan as the driver cut to the outside to attempt to pass. Furious, Tess laid on the horn. "You idiot!" she bellowed. "Learn how to drive!" The car shot ahead and disappeared.

The sudden altercation frightened Diane further into her shell. Tess nevertheless ran off at the mouth, "What a jerk!" she roared. "If I ever see that guy face to face, I'm gonna tear him a new—" Tess stopped, her voice silenced when she saw Kim's ashen face in the rearview mirror.

"Sorry, Kim," Tess apologized. "I hate egocentric drivers like that, and I also realize I need to better control my temper."

"That's okay," replied Kim. "It was justified from what I could see."

Tess spun her head to the right. For a moment, she thought Diane resembled a mannequin, her body completely still. "You okay, lady?" she asked.

Diane inhaled deeply, her head rotating sideways towards her friend. "I . . . I don't know, Tess. I honestly don't know what I'm supposed to feel right now. This has been a lot to process."

Tess sighed loudly, her attention now focused on a peculiar blue utility van that suddenly appeared in the rearview mirror, its front end far too close for her liking. "What's with people today?" she complained. "What am I, a magnet for everyone that doesn't deserve a driver's licence?" Tess tapped her brakes twice and waved her arm for the vehicle to back off. It stayed in place.

When she was certain Tess had calmed down, Diane spoke through forming tears. "We don't know where our husbands are"—Diane grabbed a tissue from her purse—"or even if they're alive. Paul's been dishonest with me, Tess, and I've been dishonest with you."

"That's why we're doing this," assured Tess. "And seeing as we've not heard anything from anyone, advocating for ourselves is all we can do. Hopefully, we get some answers from somebody here. Don't worry, I'll find out what's going on. That I can guarantee."

Tess wheeled her SUV into the visitor parking lot and wasn't impressed when the tailgating vehicle shot past, its side panels covered in CFCB Television decals. "It would seem the media are after the same answers we are," observed Tess. "Might be a coincidence, and they're here for something else, but I'm guessing not. Unfortunately, the word's out."

Diane dabbed her eyes with a tissue. "News travels fast," she agreed.

Tess eyed up a parking stall four down from where the TV van had stopped. "Listen, Diane, I'm not angry with you. I needed time to process all this too. Did Paul act irresponsibly? Yes. Did both our guys make a poor choice to fly last night? Apparently, yes." Tess adjusted her rearview mirror. "Now we focus our attention on getting them back. That's all that matters."

"Agreed," uttered Diane. "I appreciate your understanding, Tessa."

Tess slipped the wheels of her SUV neatly between the stall lines and jerked to a stop. She waited for Kim and Diane to unbuckle before reaching for her door handle. As she exited the van, Tess's mood darkened again as she glanced at the television van and the diminutive driver just climbing out.

Tess also noticed a meticulously groomed, tall black man exiting the passenger side. Wearing a navy-blue suit over a noticeably trim physique, he carried a microphone in one hand and a small note pad in the other. His broad face and short buzz-cut hair accented the whitest teeth she had ever seen. The man glanced her way, smiled and waved as if he knew exactly who Tess was.

Tess looked away and casually pointed her finger for Diane and Kim's benefit. "If Dwayne Johnston has a twin, that guy certainly fits the bill!"

Tess noticed the van's driver making a point of not looking in her direction, his body language indicative of a puppy on the verge of receiving a tongue lashing. His cowardly stature seemed enough to temporarily appease Tess's anger for being tailgated. "Okay girls"—Tess pointed— "from what I remember, that's the search and rescue building over there. Let's see who's in charge and what they're doing to bring our guys back."

Already walking away, Tess's long stride proved difficult for Diane and Kim to match. After a few extra sprints to catch up, they finally reached Tess's left flank. Side by side, the trio appeared more like gunslingers on the hunt than women in distress, their long shadows distinctly crisp and moving with purpose across the shortcut grass. Not far from the rear of the building, Diane was the first to notice another shadow appearing in their formation, the hulking shape coming up fast on the right side.

"Excuse me, ladies," came a deep voice from behind. "Might I have a moment of your time?"

Tess, Diane and Kim all slowed up, their heads turning in unison. As the man approached, all three women stopped, the move perfectly synchronized as if rehearsed. With pearly whites gleaming, the Mr. Dwayne Johnston look-a-like stood before them, his broad shoulders accentuating his handsome face, while his hairline reflected the sun with perfectly rimmed backlight.

"I'm Dwaine Ennis. A reporter for CFCB Television. I was wondering if any of you might be willing to answer a few—"

Tess coughed out loud, the man's first name snagging her funny-bone completely out of the blue, but at the same time adding a much-needed reprieve from her ill-tempered mood.

"Are you okay, ma'am?" asked the reporter.

"Yes," replied Tess while forcing down a laugh. "I'm fine. It's just that you remind me of someone famous, that's all."

"I get that a lot," laughed Dwaine. "But I assure you, I'm no actor."

Kim and Diane hadn't moved, yet both correctly guessed where this man's line of questioning was headed. The cameraman stayed several paces behind the reporter, his head pointed timidly at his feet. Tess knew the arrival of the media wasn't a coincidence. The sharks were prowling.

Dwaine pressed on. "As you may have heard, there's an airplane missing, and we're here to pick up the story." He angled his head towards the search and rescue building. "Might any of you at all be related to this incident? It seems a coincidence that we're all heading in the same direction."

This time, Tess established solid eye contact with the reporter. "No offence, Mr. Ennis, but we'd appreciate it if you and your camera minion would back off and clear our personal space. For this story, you'll have to take a number and get in line."

* * *

Rob Smith was about to say something when someone raised their arm and pointed out the rear window facing the parking lot. "We've got company, gang!"

All heads turned in that direction. Rob walked to the window and sighed loudly. "What a laughable coincidence," he muttered. "So now we have local media and what could only be the distraught wives of our missing airmen. And one of them is flailing her arms in what looks like a heated exchange with the television crew. Just what I need right now."

Rob scurried to the front door and latched the deadbolt. He spun on his heels. "No one unlocks this door until I say so." He grabbed the phone and began to punch numbers from memory.

"Who are you calling?" asked Kevin while trying to contain his excitement.

Stealing another glance out the back window, Rob answered Kevin's question in two concise words: "Airport Security."

* * *

Tom Sullivan wasn't sure how long he had been driving, but at thirty kilometres per hour, his progress seemed unmercifully slow. Torrential rain from the night before had created huge water-filled potholes, while in several places small rivers had carved mini grand canyons into the narrow gravel road. Wishing he had brought a coffee, Tom rubbed his bleary eyes and listened to his stomach growl, an aggravating reminder that he'd skipped breakfast once again.

Butterflies flew erratically in front of the van, while frogs croaked from marshy trenches along either side of the road. Aside from insects, amphibians and birds; the only signs of human activity were the odd beer and pop can along the ditch. Tom again found it peculiar that with the broadcast slated for this afternoon and the road now apparently open from last night's repairs, there weren't any vehicles heading towards Spruce Creek. He suddenly felt less optimistic about finding his missing equipment and driver. Squeezing the wheel out of frustration, Tom steered the van through a plethora of mini lakes and mud-filled crevasses.

Under normal conditions, when the road was dry and in good shape, there was easily enough room for two vehicles to pass in opposite directions. But this morning, Tom kept the van aimed down the middle to avoid dangerously soft shoulders. And with all the money Jack had sunk into restoring the lodge, including the construction of a bike park, Tom was at a loss to figure out why his friend hadn't pushed the township for improvements to the road. He toyed with the idea of turning around, but the question was where?

Committed to plodding ahead, Tom could only guess the whereabouts of the CFCB vehicle. As he rounded a blind corner, the driver's side front tire caught a mound of small rocks, jostling the front end of the van sideways. His heart raced as he aimed the buggy away from sloping terrain he wanted no part of.

"C'mon you piece of junk!" he stammered. Hammering on the brakes, the van slid diagonally several feet. Tom cranked the wheel hard right as the left front tire slid another foot before finally biting into heavier gravel close to the road's embankment.

Frozen in place, and fully aware of just how close he'd come to sliding down the hill, Tom rolled down his window to let the cool breeze brush over his skin. Enjoying the sensation, he couldn't help but wonder about the pilots of the missing Cessna. *Where did they end up and are they okay?* he wondered. Tom had trouble imagining what it would be like to fly in fading light through mountainous terrain, not to mention bad weather and low fuel. *No thanks.*

Releasing the brakes, Tom straightened the wheels and rolled the van forward, this time vowing to keep his foot off the gas. *Idle is fast enough.* Having already past the area where the mudslide had previously closed the road, Tom painstakingly nursed the vehicle another few kilometres with no sign of oncoming traffic.

As the road curved, trees and shrubs hindered visibility, their branches extending outwards like claws reaching out for the van. Keeping to the left to avoid a cluster of potholes, Tom's eyes scanned for more trouble spots. It was then he saw blue and red lights, the pulsating strobes reflecting off trees and bushes, but their source remaining out of view. Now more alert than ever, Tom eased forward towards the police cruiser now just coming into view. It was parked diagonally to block passage in either direction. As he approached, a young female officer appeared suddenly near his front bumper, her arms up and palms facing outwards.

Tom jumped in his seat. "Where did you come from?" he asked while rolling down his window.

"Hold up, sir!" the woman ordered.

Tom stuck his head out the window and immediately deduced her uniform was one size too small for her body type. "What's happening, officer?" he asked curiously, while at the same instance noticing a missing chunk of road.

Her snooty voice matched her persona. "As I'm sure you can see between my car and your van, another part of the road washed out earlier this morning. For your own safety, you can't get through, sir."

"Yes, I can see that," Tom replied sarcastically. He looked past the officer and noticed dozens of vehicles stacked up in a long line farther up the road, all apparently heading towards Spruce Creek and all at a dead stop. People milled about and several cars had bikes secured to roof racks, tailgates and small trailers.

The strait-laced policewoman waddled to within a foot of Tom's open window. "It'll be a few hours until we can get you through, sir. Repair crews are on their way, but until then, you're better off to spin around and go back."

"Spin around?" asked Tom incredulously. "It was all I could do to get here by going forward. I've hardly the room to flip around."

Ignoring the comment, the officer asked. "Where were you heading, sir?"

Tom sounded flustered and he knew it. "I came from Spruce Creek. I was expecting a van filled with TV gear to arrive hours ago, so thought I'd venture out to find them. I thought the road had re-opened after the earlier mudslide."

"Well, sir, until we get this new trouble spot patched up, there won't be movement in either direction. So, the choice is yours. You can stay put, or you can head back. I can help you turn around if you'd like."

Jack's marathon would now be a complete bust, and Tom dreaded passing on the bad news to his friend. He accepted the reality that people already at Spruce Creek could still ride, but proper fundraising would be negligible without live television coverage or the masses of people lined up behind the police car.

Sighing loudly, Tom looked at the officer. "Spot for me, if you please?"

Chapter 20

"So, that's the lowdown folks," reported Jack Ward. "If the cameras and support gear don't show up, then you're all still welcome to ride for the afternoon and compete if you want. Broadcasting the races may have to wait for another day."

Jack's voice sounded completely deflated, his resolve weakened along with the belief he could invoke positive change within his circle of influence. With little more to say, Jack felt compelled to add a few more words. "There is plenty of food, drinks and giveaways, so I encourage you all to enjoy your time here at Spruce Creek and try your best to have an enjoyable day. And please, for my sake, don't break any bones! I don't need any lawsuits."

In truth, all Jack wanted to do was return to bed and further sleep off the crummy memories of the past twenty-four hours. He knew that Mildred had never been one to quit or bow to defeat, but he also knew he wasn't cut from the same cloth. Notwithstanding his recent plague of misfortunes, he'd tried time and again to adopt his wife's stick-with-it attitude, but it wasn't as easy as she always made it appear.

Loitering around the front steps of the lodge, several dozen people who had gathered to hear what Spruce Creek's owner had to say, slowly began to move off. Nearby, canvas from white event tents flapped in the morning breeze, some filled with sponsor swag, others with tables piled high with cases of water, boxes of energy bars, sandwiches and sweets of all sorts. Chilly, despite the rising sun in the eastern sky, the air felt crisp and clean, a musty-sweet aroma filling the grounds in and around the property.

Every conceivable design and colour of mountain bike leaned against fence posts and trees, while others roosted along the lodge's exterior walls. Jack had never seen so many two-wheelers. Some riders sat on their bikes in full-face helmets; others stood beside their bikes, their gloved hands holding onto the knobby hand grips. Many riders wore head-to-toe protective gear, everything from full body armour to knee and elbow protection. A few brave souls, or in Jack's opinion, *stupid fools*, wore nothing but t-shirts and jeans, the regard for their own personal safety apparently of little or no concern.

Individuals scheduled to race flaunted numbered pinnies, their riding garb plastered with sponsorship patches and logos. Casual riders appeared less opulent; many wearing clothes badly in need of laundering—not that devout mountain bikers paid any heed to the concept of tidiness.

The sight brought a smile to Jack's lips, a short-lived moment of joy amidst a bevy of disappointment. It was more the sudden personal awareness of his need to trust God and take things one day at a time, as Mil had learned during her illness. He recalled one of her favourite bible verses from Proverbs: "Trust in the Lord with all your heart, and do not lean on your own understanding. In all your ways acknowledge Him, and He will direct your path."

She would have expected him to develop an "attitude of gratitude" following her death, to squash any pressure he placed on himself from allowing negative circumstances to outweigh the positives. In Jack's soul, light and hope began to flood compartments he long ago forgot existed, a simple epiphany lifting away a string of emotional baggage and self-loathing. The happy faces around him reminded Jack that perhaps he'd been on the right path all along, and since Mildred's death, he had allowed himself precious little time to reflect on the good things in his widowed life.

Jack theorized that most people here today were following their passion for life and riding. Did any of them really care if the day's broadcast was a flop? Jack thought not. Most never knew Mildred personally, or even about the charitable foundation she created to aid families of loved ones in palliative care. Riders wanted to ride, and if raising a buck or two for her legacy was still the end result, then even better for everyone involved. The more he thought about it, the more Jack felt the weight of expectation lift from his shoulders.

People would enjoy their day regardless, the majority oblivious to Jack's personal agenda. He took comfort in knowing he had fulfilled his initial mandate. He had constructed the bike park, and now for the first time in months, he took pride in knowing that Mil would have been pleased with his efforts, no matter today's outcome.

"You okay, Mr. Ward? You look . . . lost."

Jack spun around to see Dylan Sullivan watching him intently. "Yes, I'm fine Dylan," replied Jack. "I was just deep in thought. It's what old people do."

"You're not that old, Mr. Ward," observed Dylan.

"That didn't sound too convincing. And for the umpteenth time, it's Jack. Please, Dylan, call me Jack or I'll ban you from my park!"

Matt Hawley walked up and stood beside Dylan, the young rider's appearance more like he'd prepped for a magazine cover photoshoot than a day of downhill racing. With gloved hands casually gripping the sleek aluminum frame of his custom-built from-the-ground-up mountain bike, Matt chuckled. "Still not getting it right, eh dude?"

Dylan shrugged his shoulders and eyed Matt dubiously. "What's it to you pretty boy?"

Jack put his hand on Dylan's shoulder and continued. "You know what Dylan? Call me whatever you want. In the grand scheme of things, it really doesn't matter. What does is that your dad is out trying to find the camera gear. I expect him back soon with what I trust will be good news."

Jack felt better by the second. "And whether he's successful or not, the day will go ahead. We may not raise the dollars I'd hoped for, but that shouldn't stop us from making the best of things."

Still concerned for the crew of the Cessna, Jack understood and accepted that the situation was now entirely out of his hands. With thoughts turning to Diane and Kim Jackson, the pressing need to contact them crept into his mind. His last conversation with Diane had ended on a bad note, and Jack needed to set things right. He vowed to call her the moment things wrapped up at the park and offer whatever support he could.

"Listen, guys," Jack said with new-found conviction. "Once Tom gets back, and whether he's got the TV gear or not, I'm heading back out to the airstrip. It's been bugging me to no end why those runway lights wouldn't come on, and I need to fix the problem."

Not understanding the urgency, Dylan and Matt exchanged glances and asked together, "How come?"

Jack evaded the question and looked away, his focus on shafts of sunlight streaming through a vast cornucopia of pine and poplar trees. Nearby, a blue jay belted out a raucous litany of calls, the noise competing with a chorus of tree frogs somewhere high above. People were everywhere; not as many as Jack hoped for, but enough to make the day count for something.

High and to his right, Jack saw the top upper section of the chairlift, the rig already ferrying passengers to the mountain peak. Near the summit, a small cabin could be seen, its front bay window at the perfect angle to reflect sunlight into his eyes. Jack had affectionately named the shack "Mil's Café," a gathering place for coffee and fellowship, and a place where riders and non-riders alike could relax and enjoy the incredible panorama of Spruce Creek.

Jack laughed when he noticed Dylan and Matt gazing fixedly at him with puzzled expressions. "Sorry fella's, my thoughts like to drift. I seem to catch myself doing that more and more the older I get."

"That's okay, Jack," stated Matt as he nudged Dylan. "We understand."

"I doubt that. But thanks for trying to make me feel better. Anyway, as I was saying, I intend to repair those lights so what happened last night doesn't happen again."

Matt looked a bit apprehensive but asked anyway. "As a matter of curiosity, Jack, why the rush now? It's not like the airstrip's going to be used again anytime soon."

Dylan tilted his head. "Is it?"

Jack smiled. "When you get to be my age boys, you learn not to neglect the feelings in your gut, and mine's telling me this can't be overlooked. I can't explain it beyond that. I've always believed that when the Lord puts an idea into your head, you pursue it, so that's what I'm going with."

Jack turned away and headed towards the parking lot. "Anyone who wants to join me is welcome to tag along. Wink-wink, nudge-nudge."

* * *

"So, I'm curious," asked Paul Jackson. "How in the dickens did you end up in the bushes and so far away from the plane?"

Adjusting his legs, Dave McMurray fielded Paul's question despite the fire raging in his ankle. "The real question, Ace, is what are we doing out here with no food or water and a busted-up airplane?"

Paul sighed. "You're not going to let that indelible fact go, are you?"

"It is forefront in my mind. But in answer to your question, I needed to relieve my bladder in the worst way, so I limped out of the plane while you were napping. And yes, I made sure you were breathing first."

"How neighbourly of you," mocked Paul.

"I try. Anyway, I couldn't put any weight on my ankle, so I hopped around our newly acquired campsite for a bush to pee on and the prospect of berries for breakfast. Pee was successful, berries were not."

Paul smiled but did not reply.

"And seeing as we brought nothing to eat this trip . . . Or did I mention that already?" Dave noticed the pained expression on Paul's face, so he eased off with the candour. "Sorry, Ace, I share equal responsibility for that fail. I know I sound like a broken record, but I simply can't believe we just climbed aboard without packing the usual rations. That's not like either of us."

Not sure what to say, Paul stared at the ground. He picked up a twig and began stripping off the bark to keep his hands busy. Paul could not disagree. Dave was bang on. Their lack of common sense was costing them dearly.

"Where you found me was where I fell," Dave went on to say. "The pain in my ankle was bearable until I caught some brush and tripped. Last thing I remember is my world turning black and passing out. I woke up dazed a few times and tried to move, but the pain was too strong to even try."

"Well," Paul finally said. "If anything, I guess this makes us even."

Dave cocked his head. "And how exactly do you figure that?"

"Easy," Paul replied. "You saved my bacon last night and I rescued you this morning from legions of bloodthirsty mosquitoes and ants."

"True," Dave nodded. "And now we both need rescue. Let's hope they've picked up the ELT so we can get the heck out of here." Looking towards the Cessna, Dave shook his head. "And for what it's worth, Ace, sorry about your plane. I know that'll be an expensive repair."

Paul thought for a moment. "That's what insurance is for. Besides, at this point, I really don't care about the plane. I'm in enough cow dung already to last me the next decade, and that's assuming my wife doesn't have my head on a platter before the FAA does."

"Another true point," agreed Dave. "I'll tell them we've never met if they ask me about you."

"Always a pal," Paul announced ruefully.

"Always!" affirmed Dave.

With little to do now except lie in wait for the sound of a rescue aircraft, Paul's thirst reared its ugly head. He wasn't a fan of drinking from the river unless out of absolute necessity, mountain water or not. "How's your thirst level?" he asked Dave.

Dave licked his lips. "I wish I had a cold beer in the worst way, but I'm fine for now. I'd rather a shooter of morphine at this very moment."

Using each other for support, both men limped their way back to the Cessna and hunkered down under the port-side wing. Dave half-lay, half-sat against the wheel. It was painfully uncomfortable, but the angle allowed him to keep weight off his ankle. Paul stood above, his arms and torso supported by the wing strut. For the time being, his back pain had eased off, but the same couldn't be said for a stomach-turning headache and the throbbing cut to his leg.

Several minutes passed without either man speaking and though left unsaid, both Paul Jackson and Dave McMurray knew they were lucky to have survived the previous night's escapades. And in the grand scheme of things, nothing else at that moment really mattered.

* * *

The small building that housed Owensville's civilian air search and rescue was abuzz with more activity than Search Co-ordinator Rob Smith preferred. It wasn't that he didn't believe more hands

Deliveries

made light work, but in his opinion, the current hub of activity was anything but useful.

No sooner had Rob picked up the phone to call airport security than, as if on cue, a small mob of people arrived at the front door, none of whom seemed overly happy to find it locked. At the front of the pack was the CFCB cameraman, his lens aimed towards a large black man heatedly talking into a microphone while trying to gain entry.

Everyone inside the Search and Rescue building watched as the camera panned over to three women standing nearby, the tallest on her cellphone and most certainly not happy. Seemingly out of nowhere, other people began to show up, the clusters of humanity not entirely sure what was going on, but curious enough to deviate from whatever business brought them to the airport in the first place.

Rob wasn't surprised by the influx. With his younger brother also a videographer, he knew the presence of a television camera and reporter inevitably attracted crowds. He sucked in some air and then warily changed his mind about the door. The last thing he needed was negative publicity in light of an already bad situation. Rob ordered the door to be unlocked, and then he stood back and waited for the influx.

As expected, the television crew was among the first to barge in. Seconds later a dazzling white light flared to life atop the camera as its operator began to collect his footage, the man apparently oblivious to the concept of discreet or tact. The reporter caught Rob's eye and aimed straight for him. Rob looked away but knew he was too late to ward off the encounter.

Inside of five minutes, Rob briefed the media about the missing Cessna and crew and then offered a simplified plan of how his team would find them. The reporter, Mr. Dwaine Ennis, as he identified himself, wasted little time in pursuing an interview with anybody willing to talk, including the pilot's wives. Rob overheard the taller blonde woman's response. "I told you once already that we've got nothing to say to the media, and for the last time, get your cameraman to lower that thing before I lower it for him!"

Not waiting to be asked again, the cameraman immediately complied. The reporter spun his head around with a scowl on his face. "What do you think you're doing? Keep shooting! I'll tell you when to stop recording! We need all the B-roll we can get."

Rob chuckled and walked away.

The cameraman nervously returned the camera to his shoulder and when he caught Tess's icy glare, he backed off again, befuddled about what to do.

"Oh, for goodness' sake," barked Dwaine. "If you're not going to do your job, then give me the darn thing and I'll shoot this myself. You go wait in—"

Diane interrupted their bickering. "Instead of trying to dredge up a story based on guesswork, why not use that camera to help to get our husbands back." Diane glanced around the room. "It seems to me these rescue people could use any assistance they can get because this whole charade is already behind schedule."

Not saying a word, Tess and Kim smiled as they watched the exchange.

In a different corner of the room, Kevin Davies held a roll of silver duct tape. Standing to his left was Rob Smith and several members of his team, including Susan McCutcheon, a fifty-eight-year-old retired elementary school teacher and busy grandmother of nine rambunctious grandchildren. Her clothing choice for today was dark blue jeans, a long-sleeve woolen lumberjack shirt and a puffy white vest, its pockets stuffed with lord knew what. She seemed ready for business, and that's exactly what she wanted to happen.

Susan's keen eyesight and love of airplanes seemed a natural fit for her involvement in search and rescue, a place where she could divvy up her time between family, church work and contributing to the general well-being of others. Her long-time friendship with Rob Smith eventually resulted in becoming an active member over a year ago. In Rob's opinion, Susan had become one of the most gifted spotters he ever worked with, only this time she wasn't impressed with the flying arrangements or the pilot, and she made no bones about her displeasure.

"Talk some sense into him, Rob!" Susan pleaded; her glare directed at Kevin. "I'm not flying in that plane if there's a hole in the wing. And if you think patching it with tape is going to make it any safer, you're crazy. Both of you!"

To Susan's absolute horror, Kevin suggested applying duct tape to cover the gash in the wing, a short-term fix that would get the Cub airborne and start the search ball rolling. And Kevin's assurance that control cables and pulleys remained undamaged did little to appease her skepticism.

"You don't have to worry, Susan," Kevin emphasized. "Duct tape is carried by lots of pilots as an emergency tool. It's joked about as being the 100 mile per hour tape!" He glanced at Rob for support. "We've got no choice and we're running out of time by arguing."

Rob listened patiently as his people debated, but Kevin was right. Time was of the essence, and with the late-afternoon forecast calling for rain, he knew his window was closing. The least desired outcome would be to maroon the downed pilots for another night, and for Rob, that scenario was neither acceptable nor an option.

The chaotic ambiance inside the search and rescue building would indicate to anyone watching as a casual observer, that all forms of leadership had vaporized. Aside from those originally on-site, the addition of media, family members and curious onlookers added to the sense of confusion. As the decibel level rose, Rob needed to gain control and fast. So, instead of addressing Kevin and Susan's argument directly, he broke away and positioned himself near the door. "Everyone, may I please have your attention?"

With his words going unheard, Rob placed two fingers in his mouth and blasted out a piercing whistle that even he surprised himself with.

Voices subsided immediately, the resulting silence causing him to break a light sweat. With all eyes on him, he suddenly wished he were elsewhere, away from the lunacy of a situation he held little control over.

Rob's mind transported him to a winding road . . . his body strapped in behind the steering wheel of his teal blue 1973 MG convertible. Gliding under a canopy of green, he envisioned perfect synchronization between the clutch and stick, his hands and feet working together in harmony as the wheels devoured the pavement. But as quickly as his brain conjured the heavenly image, it vanished.

Collecting his thoughts, Rob spoke loudly for everyone's benefit. "First off, I'll address the media again, and what I've got to say is off the record until I instruct you otherwise." He eyed the CFCB reporter. "Is that understood?"

Dwaine Ennis began to protest. "I've got a story to cover here and I—"

"Mr. Ennis," countered Rob. "I've got no time for this, so unless you're willing to comply by the rules—my rules—you can leave this premise and not come back."

Dwaine was smart enough to know when not to push it, so he nodded and remained quiet.

Rob continued while intently focused on the reporter. "You can capture video to your heart's content once you're outside this building. In fact, with what I just overheard"—Rob glanced at Diane Jackson—"and I believe her to be correct . . . Perhaps you'd consider helping us find our missing pilots with a, 'Yes, I genuinely care,' mindset. That means instead of pushing your way around, you work with us, not against us. Mutual cooperation earns mutual respect, and we can all benefit from each other if we work together."

Dwaine nodded his head a second time. "Fair enough."

"Good." Rob shifted his focus. "For everyone else's benefit, including the family of the missing airmen, I'm letting you know

Deliveries

we'll be launching our search aircraft in the next half hour. We've not picked up an emergency beacon, so our plan is to fly a general search pattern from Spruce Creek, back-tracking towards Owensville. Our ground assets will head out as well, and since there's only one road in and out of Spruce Creek, we'll rendezvous at Moger's Point and wait for a confirmed visual on the 185. I will update the media and family members as information becomes available. For now, you people are welcome to stay here, or you can leave with us. It's up to you."

At that moment, the door swung open and in walked Bruce Macbeth, followed closely behind by a stocky man wearing a grey short sleeve shirt, loose necktie and biceps as thick as bowling balls. Shoulder patches identified him as airport security, and his gruff voice matched his physical stature. "Somebody here call for airport security?" he asked.

"That was me," acknowledged Rob, surprised the guy actually showed up. "Sir, if you don't mind waiting around a few minutes, I'll chat with you shortly."

The man looked around at everyone and shrugged his shoulders. "Fine by me, I'm paid by the hour."

Rob had met Bruce Macbeth a few months earlier at an airport fundraiser. Despite his hazy memory, Rob recognized him straight away, and the last thing he wanted was another tongue lashing in front of his team. If that were to happen again, Rob wasn't sure he'd be able to control his temper in a face-to-face verbal skirmish. Thankfully, Bruce kept his distance, at least for the time being.

"I want air and ground crews together for a joint briefing in ten minutes," ordered Rob. "Anyone here not actively involved in this operation but still wanting to help, we'd graciously accept sandwiches, coffee, water, or anything you can provide to get us through this to help ensure a successful outcome for everyone involved."

Kevin Davies and Susan McCutcheon stood side by side, the two impatiently awaiting a resolution to their debate over the flight status of the Cub. Rob walked over and leaned in close to avoid being heard by the media. "Patch the wing, Kevin. Do your pre-flight and make darn sure that plane is safe to fly. And for heaven's sake, take a minute before you go wheels up to do a flight orientation with each other. You two need to work together, and I want zero animosity between my pilot and spotter. Check your radios with the ground teams and be ready to go wheels up as soon as possible."

Smirking at Susan, a conquering grin appeared on Kevin's face which she defiantly chose to ignore.

"Go!" barked Rob as quietly as he could.

Kevin offered a sloppy salute. "Aye, sir!"

With the tape in hand, Kevin blazed a path for the door, followed on his heels by the television crew and other interested bystanders.

Susan tried again to express her point about the duct tape, but Rob cut her off after only a few words. "Listen, Susan, you've got the sharpest eyes of anyone here. Right now, you and Kevin are the best chance we have of finding that plane before bad weather settles back in, and believe me, it's coming. I know you and Kevin haven't flown together before, so if you're not comfortable going up, then I will. But we need to go now. You can stay back as part of ground ops if you want, but the more time wasted discussing this, the less chance we have of finding them today. So, let me—"

"All right!" yielded Susan, followed by a twisted smile. "I'll go. You know as well as I do that we'll never find that plane if you go. . . . No offence."

"None taken," conceded Rob, the muscles in his face relaxing. "I think."

Susan poked Rob's chest with her index finger. "But if the wing comes off because of that patch job, I'm going to smack Kevin sideways and then I'll come after you!"

"Deal," agreed Rob through a plastic smile. He knew Susan well-enough to know that she'd have gone up regardless of the wing issue and was in all regards a consummate team player. If anyone could find the missing Cessna, it was her. And though

Kevin was young and inexperienced, he was without argument a very competent pilot.

Without saying another word, Susan spun about, grabbed her backpack and headed for the door.

"Hey, Susan?" Rob called after her.

Stopping mid-stride, Susan looked over her shoulder. "What now?"

"Good hunting out there. Make us proud."

Nodding, Susan locked eyes with Rob. "Don't I always?"

* * *

Still early in the day, Paul noticed clouds beginning to build in the western sky, a tell-tale sign that another round of weather pandemonium was at some point in the cards. Shifting his gaze upwards, Paul commented to Dave, "S and R better get to us before those clouds do. I'm not in the mood to hang around here for another chilly night, regardless of the consequences I face at home."

Dave followed Paul's gaze, the task a bit challenging considering his body angle under the wing and the fact he faced east. "Yup, I'm with you on both accounts," he agreed. "Tess might disown me too for lack of brain function on this trip."

As Paul's eyes meandered across the inclement sky, his heart suddenly skipped a beat, and then another. Staggering back, he dragged both hands to his chest and felt the organ's pitter-patter go wildly out of sequence. Beginning to cough as the irregular rhythms sucked the breath from his lungs, his blood pressure dropped, and all strength vacated his muscles.

Dave looked up in time to see the colour drain from Paul's face and then watched in horror as his friend's body collapsed to the dirt like a tumbling deck of stacked playing cards.

Chapter 21

Already weary, Jack Ward returned to his office with the hope of resting his eyes for a few minutes before the day really got going. He had not yet heard from Tom Sullivan and wasn't sure when or even if his friend would return. For all Jack knew, Tom had slid off the road and was in need of rescue himself.

Lounging back in an old recliner, Jack flipped his head towards the window. The stark contrast in conditions from last evening to this morning left a bitter taste in his mouth. "Stupid weather," he huffed. But now with blue sky and sunshine currently dominating the outdoor habitat, the reprieve felt like a heavenly recharge to his soul. Visible was Bayshore Lake, its now calm water framed perfectly between two distant flat-top mountains.

Knowing that others were dealing with far more pressing issues than exhaustion, Jack felt guilty for basking in a few quiet moments to himself. He needed to get hold of Diane Jackson, or at the least make a concerted effort to do so. Turning away from the window, he stared at the phone on his desk, loathing that his last phone call on the device had been hugely unpleasant. The last thing he wanted or needed was another.

Closing his eyes, Jack felt the onset of sleep within minutes. His last conscious thought before drifting off was of his wife, her face's image close to his, the sound of her voice encroaching into his murky subconscious. Jack fell asleep with a smile on his face and an abnormal sense of peace in his heart that today might be a good day.

*　*　*

When Paul Jackson's vision returned, he hadn't the foggiest idea of what had happened or why he was lying on the ground. His body felt detached from the neck down, and he felt scared to try to flex any part of it. With squinty eyes and blurred sight, Paul tried to speak. Dave appeared overhead, his face at most a foot from Paul's. "Easy does it, Ace. Welcome back."

"Wha-what the heck happened?" asked Paul, his voice groggy.

"You blacked out. Spooked the crap out of me when I saw you fold. I thought you kicked the bucket. You were standing there one second and then hit the ground. How you feeling, old boy?"

Paul's senses were slowly returning. "A little dicey, but I think okay. I remember my heart banging hard and . . . how long was I out for?" he asked.

"Not long," replied Dave. "A minute, tops. I tried to wake you but honestly didn't know what to do other than elevate your legs."

"My doctor never mentioned a thing about blacking out," recalled Paul. "I'd never have flown, Dave, if I knew this could happen."

Dave looked at Paul as if reading his mind. "Ace, you should have grounded yourself for this flight, period. But I'm sure you've figured that out by now. I'm just glad your eyes are open, and you aren't still lying in the dirt unconscious. But now I'm completely freaked out, so please don't do that again!"

Paul tried to sit up. He tasted dirt in his mouth and felt as though a brick wrapped in sandpaper had swiped the side of his face.

Dave grabbed Paul's shoulder. "Maybe you should stay down. Like I said, I really don't want to see you go through that again. Seeing you crumple even once is plenty enough for me. Stay put and take it easy for your sake and mine."

Paul settled back to the ground and wavered as he supported himself. "You're probably right," he agreed uncomfortably. "I think I'll rest here and"—a jolt of pain stabbed him in the back along his spine. He grimaced and froze—"we seriously need to . . . get out of here . . . Dave. I need a doctor and so do you." Paul licked his lips. "Man, I'm thirsty."

Dave looked skyward. "Me too, Ace. We just need to chill and tough it out until the cavalry shows up."

"And if they don't find us? Then what?"

Dave looked at Paul. "We need to stay positive, so let's agree to that, shall we?"

Paul thought for a second and shrugged his shoulders. "I suppose, but in light of the fact I just passed out, I think I'm justified in being nervous."

"That you are," assured Dave. "But try not to worry. I bet we're back before nightfall. There's only one way into Spruce Creek and one way out, so it's only a matter of time before somebody spots us down here."

Paul shook his head in anger. "What you're forgetting is that we're not along the main river. We split away, remember? We're likely a good thirty–forty clicks south of where we should be. They won't have a clue where to look for us. We can't even light a fire for crying out loud."

"And what you're forgetting, Ace," reminded Dave. "Is that you tossed my sleeves out the window, remember? Any good spotter should easily pick those out from up top. I've spent time with the search and rescue guys. They're trained to look for anything, especially something as straightforward as orange fabric in the middle of nowhere. You gotta have some faith in the system, amigo, and in your business partner's ingenuity!"

"Well, right this minute my faith is waning. And you're assuming the sleeves landed where they're visible. Even then, there's no guarantee that if they see the first one, that they'll fly

Deliveries

far enough in this direction to see the second. You're basing the hopes of our being found on pretty slim odds."

Dave remained silent, the wheels in his head-turning. He understood Paul's bone of contention, but pessimism wasn't helping his frame of mind. "Let's just hope for the best, Ace," he urged. "Patience is a virtue."

"Yeah," answered Paul. "If I had either."

A sudden wind gust rolled across the ground, its unexpected arrival lifting soil, twigs and leaves into the air. Both Dave and Paul struggled to place their backs to the onslaught, not an easy task given their joint lack of mobility. Thankfully, most of the mosquitoes blew off for a moment's reprieve, though a few stragglers hung about and were quickly whacked when they tried to light upon exposed skin.

Dave tried to blink away the grit from his eyes, and when he looked up, he noticed Paul doing the same thing. "Let's just hope that whoever's flying the rescue bird has a top-notch spotter with hawk eyes."

"I'd drink to that," admitted Paul quietly. "If I had one."

* * *

"No sign of your dad yet?" asked Matt Hawley. "I sure hope he's okay."

Dylan found the donuts and was on his last bite of a Boston Cream. "Not yet," he replied. "I'm not even sure when he left, but I bet he'll be along soon enough."

Matt shook his head as Dylan rummaged through the donut box. "You know you should really cut back on those things. One day, they might catch up with you, and not in a good way."

"Oh man!" exclaimed Dylan excitedly. "There's a double-chocolate buried in here!" He snatched it up and smiled. "If it's donuts that eventually kill me, then so be it. At least I'll go out full and content, not like you all mangled like a pretzel around a tree."

"Pros like me don't hit trees! In fact, there's not a tree out there that doesn't bow as I streak by!"

"Oh please!" groaned Dylan. "It's great to see you're keeping your ego in check. I think I need another donut to calm the sudden nausea I'm feeling!"

Matt laughed as he often did around his friend. The two men squabbled back and forth a few more minutes; their conversation turned serious when Dylan noticed a white van emerge from the far end of the road. Pointing over Matt's shoulder, Dylan began to step away. "Look who just showed up," he announced.

When Matt turned around, his eyes immediately picked out the vehicle. It was obvious that Tom spotted them because he flashed the van's headlights on and off. Matt noticed there were no other vehicles in tow. "Looks like your dad struck out," he observed. "I don't see a TV truck with him or anybody else for that matter."

Dylan was already heading off to intercept the vehicle.

"Hey, wait up!" hollered Matt.

Dylan watched as his dad grabbed the first empty parking spot he could find. The van jolted to a stop and the engine died. No sooner had Tom opened the door and got out, when Dylan approached. "Hey, Dad! Any luck?" he asked.

But the look on his dad's face told Dylan everything he wanted to know.

Tom stepped up to his son and gave him a hug. "Good to see you too, buddy! And no, I didn't have any luck. The road's closed again several miles east. Part of it washed away and the police aren't letting traffic through. People are trying to get into Spruce Creek, but for now, they're all stuck behind the police car. That road needs a serious redo and some paving."

"No sign of the TV truck in the line-up?" asked Dylan.

"Not that I could see," replied Tom. "But it's not to say it wasn't there, only farther back. The officer helped me get turned around and said they'll let people through when the road's fixed. Heaven knows when that will be."

Matt stood close by but remained quiet. Tom was speaking fast, and he decided not to butt in.

"So, what do we do now?" asked Dylan. "No show I guess then?"

Tom looked around in the hope of spotting Jack Ward amidst the people gathered near the outdoor food tables. "Not a thing we can do about that son. And unless the road miraculously opens and the camera gear shows up, there won't be a show today. So, where is Jack anyway? I need to give the old fart an update, not that he wants one or if he even cares for that matter."

Dylan pointed to the lodge. "He went inside a while ago. Said he wants to go back out to the airstrip and try to repair the landing lights. Haven't seen him since."

"What on earth for?" asked Tom curiously.

Matt spoke up. "That's what we were wondering. He said it was just something he needed to do."

Tom walked away with Dylan and Matt close behind. "I'll talk some sense into him, assuming I can find him."

A short distance from the lodge's front door, Tom stopped suddenly and flipped around. Dylan and Matt nearly trampled his heels. "Any word on the Cessna and crew?"

"Nope, nothing," answered Dylan. "We haven't heard a thing."

"Too bad. I should probably call the station and see if they've got any updates."

As quickly as he stopped, Tom dashed away leaving Dylan and Matt alone to exchange glances before they hustled to catch up. Tom entered the lodge's front door and was barely through when he unabashedly yelled out, "Jack! Where you at?"

Anyone within shouting distance heard Tom's voice. That also included a slumbering Jack Ward, his office halfway down the left-wing, its door slightly ajar. Jack woke up, wearily tuning into the fact that someone was calling his name from beyond the confines of his office. He wasn't impressed.

"Jack!" called the voice again, only louder this time.

Angered by the intrusion, Jack placed both hands over his ears and got up to close the door. But he was too late to stop Tom Sullivan from bounding through and nearly knocking Jack ass over teakettle.

* * *

Growing tired of Paul's negative line of questioning, Dave allowed him to vent anyway. He tried to re-position his ankle but gave up when the pain increased.

"Unless they bring in a chopper, there isn't enough room to land a fixed-wing," grumbled Paul. "Even quads would have trouble getting through this brush."

Dave motioned to the left and pointed. "You worry too much, Paul, because just beyond those trees there's a patch of land that'll take a plane or helicopter no prob—"

"And how would you know that?" interrupted Paul. "You can hardly move your foot without passing out, and that's a fair distance away."

"Yes, it is," affirmed Dave, his patience waning. "Before I really messed up my ankle, I found a walking stick and scoped it out at first light while you were napping." Dave let that sink in. "It's possible a chopper or STOL capable aircraft could set down if the right pilot was flying it. We climb aboard and away we go."

Paul gazed west. "If your theory proves correct, then let's hope it happens before those clouds roll in. By the looks of it, we're in for another round of two-faced weather."

Dave glanced at the sky when a sudden urge to re-check the ELT washed over him. Without saying another word, he positioned himself to a place where he could better see into the cockpit. The ELT switch was on the upper right quadrant of the panel, while the actual internally mounted unit was affixed to the upper right side of the tail section, behind the cargo bay. From the ELT, a cable connected to an external roof antenna that then linked to a remote switch on the dash.

"Where are you hobbling off too now?" asked Paul curiously.

"Not that I don't trust your airplane's emergency features, and I don't. I need to double-check the ELT switch for my peace of mind."

Dave grabbed the leading edge of the wing for support and guardedly inched towards the pilot's side door. The movement awoke the fire in his ankle, and not wanting to agitate the beast more than it was, he froze. Dave looked down at Paul who sat directly below the wing strut. "Can you creep over just a bit, Ace? I can't quite see the panel from here and I need to move in a bit closer."

Paul complied as best he could, which allowed Dave to shuffle over and hang on the strut for support. Dave leaned in and pressed his head against the door window. "The ELT appears fine and it's transmitting." Dave glanced towards the top of the fuselage, and it was then his blood ran cold. "Oh, that's unfortunate."

Paul looked up. "What's the matter? What are you looking at?"

Dave's jaw hung partly open; his eyes fixated to the spot where the ELT transmit antenna should have been. "You better get comfortable, Ace," he finally said. "Because we might be here awhile."

*　*　*

Susan McCutcheon was visibly nervous. She kept glancing upwards, her eyes scanning the joints between the wing and fuselage. Every bump of turbulence sent her heart into her throat. She envisioned the gash in the wing ripping open further, the duct tape peeling away as lethal winds efficiently shredded apart the wing and sent them plummeting to the ground. Susan knew her mind had entered a dark place and it was time to snap out of it and focus on the job she had been entrusted to do.

The Piper Cub's less than adequate seat cushions provided as much shock absorption as a car with bad struts. Susan's tail bone ached and the muscles along her spine grew increasingly sore. For her, the back seat of the tiny plane was anything but comfortable, and though she knew she was best suited to the task, she wondered if it might have been better to stay behind and take Rob up on his offer. Truthfully, she wanted credit for finding the missing Cessna herself, vile ride or not. And find it, she would.

Knowing they would be aloft for several hours, Susan tried to massage her neck and shoulders. She rubbed her eyes and shut them tight. Once she and Kevin located the Cessna, the plan was to remain on station until ground teams arrived or until their fuel status forced them back. Also playing a factor would be the weather, but Susan tried hard not to focus on that.

As if the wind sensed Susan's trepidation, a sudden gust clobbered the Piper Cub and flung it hard left. The right-wing shot upwards by several feet while the nose plunged down. Kevin reacted with opposite stick and rudder, but it was more than required to bring them back to level flight. The plane rolled the other way, its left-wingtip dipping sharply. Kevin swore, his over-correction duly noted as he brought the airplane under control. "Sorry!" he yelled apologetically. "Wasn't expecting that." The Cub levelled out. "I've got it now, so we're all good."

Thankful for chewing anti-nausea tablets before climbing in, the sudden upheaval still churned Susan's stomach. "You sure you can fly this thing?" she asked half-seriously. "Because I'm truly second-guessing your knowledge of flight."

Inwardly, Kevin was happy that his passenger could see the back of his head only, because of a thin cover of sweat on his face. And though he'd never admit it, his hyperactive nerves had gotten the better of him. Kevin tried to add an air of confidence to his voice. "That last round of turbulence snuck up on me, but it won't happen again."

"Yeah, whatever. Just try to keep the wings level. That's all my stomach asks."

Kevin wiggled in his seat. "Make sure you're buckled up because you can bet that bump won't be the last. I'll be ready next time."

Knowing that Kevin had no control over the elements, Susan couldn't resist a final shot. "So, you keep saying. I'd like to see my grandchildren again."

By not bothering to respond, Kevin ended the distracting chit-chat. He tried to hold the Cub straight and reasonably level at 1,000 feet AGL. Beside his left knee was a small rotating handle mounted to the panel, along with a red ball indicating nose up or nose down trim attitude. He adjusted the lever, trying to relieve back pressure on the control stick so the airplane would settle, but strong headwinds made that task extremely fatiguing.

Kevin knew that conserving fuel was paramount to staying aloft for as long as possible. He glanced at the airspeed indicator. Seventy knots, well below the Cub's top cruise speed of 115.

A cursory check of oil pressure and temperature assured him the engine was operating as advertised. *So far, so good*, he thought.

On the left side of the instrument panel, a small GPS occupied the space just above the radio stack. Kevin reached up and touched the zoom-out button until the field of view grew to show more of the surrounding valley on both sides of the river. Even with outside visibility near perfect, Kevin felt safer with the wider GPS view.

Straddling his ears was an older model Bose headset. Something prickly kept poking his right ear lobe, the irritation becoming seriously painful. In the back seat, Susan wore a matching device, the two units allowing hands-free communication between the pilot and passenger. Removing his headset, Kevin eyed the padding and noticed the cracked outer casing had split and come apart. With his headset off, he tore off the offending piece of plastic and threw it away. It was precisely at that moment he failed to hear the call from Rob Smith.

But Susan McCutcheon did. Leaning forward, she tapped Kevin's shoulder. "Put your headset back on!"

Kevin spun his head around when he felt the poke. Susan pointed at her headset. "Your headset!" she yelled again loudly. "Put it on!"

Kevin immediately complied. As he fumbled to secure it over his ears, another jolt of turbulence swatted the underside of the Cub as if they'd just been walloped by a huge fly swatter. Susan's voice-activated mouthpiece carried her panicked shriek straight to Kevin's ears.

Careful this time not to over-correct the sensitive controls, Kevin expertly manipulated the ailerons, elevator and vertical stabilizer to place the aircraft back under his control in quick fashion. "You okay back there?" he asked Susan. "Conditions are likely to get worse the farther we go."

Susan tried to stifle her escalating fear. "Yeah, I'm top-notch and thanks for the positive vibes," she replied sarcastically. "Headquarters was just calling for you! It was Rob. Why on earth did you take your headset off? What's up with you anyway?"

Kevin ignored the question. He double-checked his Com 2 channel and made certain it was tuned to the discrete frequency used between air and ground.

He keyed the button to transmit. "Owensville Rescue, Piper Romeo One, how copy?" Except for the low hum of electrical interference through his headset, there was no reply. Kevin tried again. "Owensville Rescue, this is Piper Romeo One, anyone by the channel?"

Typically, there wasn't much chatter between the search plane and base, except for the customary "Ops Normal" check-in by the search aircraft. This was usually conducted via radio or text message, but due to lack of coverage in the areas between Owensville and Spruce Creek, texting and cellular use were impossible. Kevin thought it unusual for Rob to check in with the plane before everyone else arrived on station, and assuming ground teams hadn't left yet, he was all the more concerned for the premature call. Kevin tried the radio one last time, but the airwaves remained silent.

Not wanting to interfere with Kevin's radio call, Susan suffered quietly through a series of moderate wind gusts, each of which left her more and more uneasy. She had hoped to rest her eyes but found it stressful to keep them closed given the choppy ride. Following another minute of trying to relax, Kevin's voice interrupted the silence between them.

"I have no idea what Rob wanted Susan. So, until we hear otherwise, let's continue as planned. Once ground teams are in place at Moger's Point, we can try to call them again and—"

Another upheaval of dense air violently lifted the airplane from its already not so stable flight attitude. The rising blast socked the fuselage so hard that Kevin thought for sure the wings had come off. As he scrambled for control, another scream from the backseat bit into his ears.

Susan McCutcheon had enough before the flight barely got started. "I'm done, Kevin! Turn this thing around, and I mean like right now!"

Too busy to answer, Kevin battled the Cub for directional control with everything he had in him, not only to save his beloved airplane but their lives as well.

Chapter 22

"So, it's a no-go, Jack," sighed Tom Sullivan. "The road's blocked by police and traffic isn't moving in or out, so I had no choice but to come back. There's a load of cars trying to get in here, but so far nobody's able to move."

Sitting at his desk bleary-eyed, Jack eyed the bottle of scotch near his table lamp. Disheartened with worse news, it was all he could do not to pour a shot, but he successfully threw off the craving. After a moment, he met Tom's gaze. "Thanks for the effort, Tom, I appreciate it. And might I say how much I hate that road. But no one can say we didn't try to pull this off. The races can go as planned today, and we'll have to make the best of it. I'm sure everyone will have a good time regardless of TV coverage."

Tom noticed Jack eyeing the scotch, and at the same time was pleasantly surprised by his friend's mood reversal. Expecting a gloomier response, he questioned if Jack already partook and was bordering on tipsy.

"You feel all right, Jack? Sorry for being blunt, but you don't sound yourself and that bottle appears close to empty."

Jack couldn't suppress a smirk. "First of all, don't judge me. Secondly, you always said I was full of surprises. And, no Tom, I'm not drunk as I know you're suspecting, although I think I have every right to be. Besides, overdoing it has never been my thing."

Tom shifted uncomfortably. "I'm sorry, Jack, I—"

"No need for apology," interrupted Jack, his hand raised. "I've simply decided to bow to defeat gracefully. I can't change what's happened. We'll try the charity gig another time. Maybe next year we can extend it over a whole weekend if the weather cooperates." Jack enjoyed the deadpan look on Tom's face. "I'm not all doom and gloom, Tom. I do have my moments of PMA."

"PMA?" asked Tom curiously.

"Positive mental attitude. But you better enjoy it because it may not last. The day is still young."

Standing since entering Jack's office, Tom stepped back and plopped down into a nearby wicker chair. He wished Dylan and Matt would have followed him into Jack's room, but the boys performed a conveniently slick about-face just outside the door, announcing the sudden need to check on the mechanical condition of Matt's bike.

"Well then," said Tom, his voice less strained. "That's that. Sounds like you've made amends with the universe. I'll contact the station and let them know the situation here. We've still got several hours before we'd have gone to air, so they'll have plenty of time to schedule something else into that slot. Sorry it's all worked out this way, Jack, but if by some freak chance the road opens and the camera gear shows up, we can maybe pull things off."

Jack exhaled. "It really doesn't matter at this point, Tom. What's important is that we're open for business, and those people lucky enough to be here can bike until the sun goes down or until the last bone's broken, broadcast or not. I'm honestly more worried about where that plane ended up and how the crew is. Speaking of which, I want to go back out to the airstrip and see if I can figure out the problem with the lights. Be easier to troubleshoot in the daylight."

Not having taken the time to shave that morning, Tom ran his fingers over the stubble on his face. "The boys mentioned you wanted to do that. May I ask why?"

"You can ask," Jack replied. "But I don't have a concrete answer for you. Last night was unquestioningly one of the worst nights of my life, and I need to right that wrong. It's just something I have to do, a bit of personal closure if we can we leave it at that?"

"Fair enough, Jack," replied Tom, not pressing the issue further.

Tom's eyes locked to the near-empty bottle of scotch. "You plan on hogging the last of that stuff, or might you be a gentleman and share with your best friend?"

"I'll split the last of it with you on one condition…"

Tom's face contorted ever so slightly, but he didn't say anything.

Jack reached for the bottle, then reached into his desk drawer for another shot glass. "You keep me company when I go back out to fix the landing lights, and next time you're in town, you replace this bottle with a full one."

"That's two conditions, Jack."

Jack was already tipping the bottle towards the second glass. "Yeah, well, Mil said I never could count very well. Do we have a deal or not?"

* * *

"I'm serious, Kevin," argued Susan. "I don't think I can handle this bumping around, and I don't trust this stupid airplane. It feels like it's going to break apart any second!"

As Susan continued her plea to return to the airport, Kevin pitched the nose down to descend to where he hoped they'd find smoother air. "Just hang on," he urged. "It's only turbulence, the Cub's fine. We can't go back now, Susan. Everyone's depending on us to find the Cessna. If we don't keep going, we may not get another chance today and those guys are stuck out there for another night. Is that what you really want?"

"Why can't you stabilize us better?" asked Susan. "And no, I don't want them left out there any more than you do."

"I know we've never flown together," added Kevin. "And I didn't make the time to go through any kind of flight orientation with you like Rob ordered. That was my responsibility and I failed you on that. Things were rushed and I'm sorry. But I'd like you to humour me for a moment. I'm holding the stick and I want you to put your hands on the one in front of you and place your feet on the rudder pedals too. I want you to feel what I'm feeling on the controls. Can you do that for me?"

Not appreciating the unexpected air currents that unnerved her to the point of near panic, Susan breathed deep and grasped what Kevin was up too. Feeling calmer, she replied, "For what it's worth, I think I can do that."

"Okay," said Kevin. "Wrap both hands around the top of the stick and gently place your feet onto the pedals. I've still got control of the plane, but you'll be able to feel the forces acting on the airplane's control surfaces. This will give you a better idea of what I'm facing and why it's easier said than done to hold steady."

Closing her eyes, Susan uttered a short prayer and pushed hard to cast aside her fear. "Okay, Kevin," she replied while taking the controls. "I've got them."

"Excellent," responded Kevin. "Now gently move the stick left and then right. You'll feel the airplane turn in both directions."

Susan complied and was amazed at how much effort it took to move the control. "Oh wow," she blurted. "It's harder than I thought! It feels like someone is countering what I'm trying to do!"

"That's the wind's brute force against the ailerons on the wings and the elevator on the tail," explained Kevin. "Now push your left foot into the rudder pedal, followed by the right. You'll feel the tail slide out in both directions."

With her left foot, Susan worked the pedal forward and felt the Cub's tail yaw in the opposite direction. She then did the same thing on the right. "That takes real effort too!" she surprisingly observed. "My joints would be sore from that in no time." Susan removed her hands and feet from the controls. "Okay, Kevin, lesson learned."

"I just thought it would be helpful for you to understand what it takes to maintain control in these conditions," declared Kevin. "Plus, I have to monitor the engine instruments and—"

"I get it," quipped Susan. "I'll try to curtail my comments about your flying but no promises. Okay, we'll keep on this flight for as long as we can, or selfishly speaking, as long as I can. Let's find the plane, get hold of ground ops and wait until they arrive. Then, we go home. Agreed?"

Kevin grinned ear to ear. "That's a huge roger!" he exclaimed. "Once we start our track, don't be scared to call me around if you see anything that doesn't look like a rock or tree. Your scan range won't be huge because they followed the river to Spruce Creek and presumably back out."

Susan knew that open communication between pilot and spotter was critical and that everyone on the team depended on the chemistry inside the airplane. But in her current frame of mind, she felt that Kevin was too busy preaching to the choir when he should be flying the plane. "This isn't my first rodeo, Kevin. I know all that already. How about we simply trust each other? You fly and I spot. If and when I see something, I'll let you know. But seeing as you felt the need to tutor me, you should know what I need from you. This works both ways."

"That's fair," agreed Kevin as the Cub's nose fell sharply. "I'm taking us to 500 feet. We'll hug the left side of the river and steer clear of the slopes to the right. We'll stay low until we get closer to Spruce Creek. So, how can I help your effort?"

Susan leaned to her left and looked over Kevin's shoulder, trying to catch a glimpse of higher clouds farther ahead. "First off, please give me a bit of warning before those sudden fighter pilot moves," she demanded. "I'm already edgy and I'm sure you don't want me upchucking down the back of your neck."

"Sorry about that," Kevin lied. "I tend to forget I'm not alone in this thing. I promise I'll keep my aerobatics to a minimum."

"That's appreciated," remarked Susan. "And secondly, now that I better understand what it takes to fly this thing, I can really use your eyes on the ground too. I'll be scanning both sides, but if you see anything, please let me know, so I can get the same visual for target confirmation. In my experience, we need to work as a team to be successful. Even if we're not sitting side by side, two sets of eyes are still better than one."

Kevin's attitude softened. "I know you're worried about the weather and the safety of this airplane, but I assure you on both accounts that we'll be fine. And I'll do my best to lend my eyes to your cause."

The more Susan thought about it, the more she determined the actual source of her trepidation. It wasn't so much the bouncy ride, building clouds, or even the taped hole on the wing. It was the simple fact that Kevin Davies was young, inexperienced and horribly impulsive, and the idea of her life resting on his shoulders did not sit well. Susan had to remind herself that Kevin was a fully qualified pilot and had gone through all the necessary hoops to get where he is. But that notion did little to ease her jitters.

When Susan didn't respond, Kevin spun his head around. "You still with me back there?" he asked out of genuine concern.

"Yup, still here," assured Susan. "Just lost in thought for a moment."

Choosing to set her emotions aside, Susan grabbed the sectional map from a small bag near her feet, the distraction welcome. She unfolded it and used her index finger to track where she thought they were. "Where does the GPS show us at?" she asked. "I'm trying to cross-reference our position."

Rather than try to explain, Kevin unlatched the device and passed it back. It took only a moment for Susan to pinpoint their place on the map. She handed the GPS back to Kevin. "Since we have no idea how far from Spruce Creek the plane went down,

I'm not waiting much longer to start scanning. I know we talked about backtracking from where the lodge is, but I think it's wise to start looking earlier. We might just get lucky."

Kevin couldn't disagree with Susan's logic. "Sounds like a good plan to me. Sooner we spot these guys, the sooner we can get you back on the ground. We should be able to check-in with ground ops once they're in range. I would think they'd be on the move by now."

"One would certainly think so," agreed Susan.

Kevin levelled the Cub at 500 feet above the river, then adjusted his mouthpiece. "Once they set up their command post at Moger's Point, they'll have to wait it out until we get a visual on the plane. Not much for them to do until we give them a target."

Susan felt pleased that she and Kevin were roughly on the same page now. Up to this point, they'd been locking horns, and it seemed foolish to allow her insecurities to derail the search effort. Susan leaned her head back. "I'm going to rest my eyes for a bit, Kevin."

"Copy that," he replied.

"Talk to me if you need to," added Susan. "I won't be sleeping, especially with you flying."

"Gee, thanks . . . I appreciate the vote of confidence."

"Anytime," chuckled Susan.

The Piper followed the Moose River, its wings dipping left and right as Kevin made repeated corrections to counter headwinds. Regardless of the turbulence, the sun's warmth created a blissful sense of well-being. Kevin felt he was in the right place at the right time. He was living the dream and doing what he loved the most. For him, the ultimate prize for the day would be to find the missing Cessna and rescue its crew, and to prove to Rob and everyone on the ground that he was more than just the class clown.

A cursory check of the instrument panel showed everything as it should. The cabin temperature began to cool off, so Kevin pulled out the heater knob, wedged his feet into the rudder pedals and enjoyed a brief lull from the wind. Loosening his grip on the stick to flex stiff fingers, the Cub felt as though it were floating on rails, albeit temporarily, he knew.

His to command, the airplane became an extension of his arms and legs, everything linked together by a simple thought. It was a feeling he couldn't put into words, one that only a pilot would understand. Kevin glanced at the GPS, more out of habit than from needing to know their location. The Cessna 185 could be on either side of the river, but the question in his mind was how far east of Spruce Creek they would have flown before setting down or running the tanks dry. "Shall we give it another ten minutes?" asked Kevin. "Then show-time?"

"Sure," replied Susan. "I think that's a good—"

The calm air suddenly ended. From the left, another bump sent the airplane sideways, then sharply down. Kevin wrestled again with the stick, pulling it back too hard. "Ah nuts!" he boomed angrily. "Sorry, Susan! These gusts are hard to anticipate."

When she didn't respond, Kevin asked half-jokingly. "What're ya doing back there? Sleeping?"

"No," Susan replied emphatically. "I'm praying."

* * *

All told, Rob guessed there were twenty to twenty-five vehicles forming the convoy. He couldn't take his nervous eyes off the road long enough to be sure, but his passenger-side mirror showed enough of the entourage to tell him the gong-show was mobile. The first five cars belonged to Owensville Search and Rescue, the rest to relatives of the missing pilots, media and wannabe rescue rangers, some of whom were just snoopy, others genuinely keen to help out. There was little Rob could have done to stifle the masses from tagging along, so he had focused his attention on those he was responsible for, leaving the rest to fend for themselves with minimal intervention.

With ever-increasing media coverage, anyone with a working television or radio would by now have heard reports of the efforts to find the missing crew and their airplane. The pushy TV crew from Owensville sat ten cars back, and though Rob wasn't happy they had tagged along, he understood the futility of trying to keep reporters at bay. They'd eventually abandon ship to file their story, so until then, Rob would tolerate their presence and do his best to spin things to his advantage.

Situated about halfway between Owensville and Spruce Creek, Moger's Point remained a popular tourist spot despite heavy recent rains and several small but troublesome landslides flanking the boxy parking lot. An old trestle bridge just off the highway carried vehicles north across the Moose River, where sightseers would navigate a gravel road to a picturesque view of the river valley. Park rangers allowed access to the stairs and observation gazebo during daylight hours, but the area closed up from dusk until dawn.

Rob hoped the lot wasn't already stuffed with RVs and sightseers, because it was the only practical spot he knew of for staging a mobile command post. And if the missing Cessna was anywhere along the east/west corridor of mountains spanning both sides of the river, Rob's team would be centrally located and could deploy in short order, assuming, of course, the surrounding terrain allowed access to the plane's location.

Unable to reach Kevin on the radio, Rob's dismay over not receiving a reply was unsettling, but communication in the area was sketchy at best. He wanted to remind Kevin not to take any chances with the weather and to head back if things got nasty. Rob also feared his over-exuberant pilot might stay aloft for longer than necessary if only to prove a point. He remembered the forecast of thunderstorms by early evening for Owensville and areas west. That meant fewer hours to locate the Cessna, and the last thing he needed today was even less time on the clock to operate.

Straying left of the imaginary centre dividing line, the lead vehicle in which Rob was a passenger rounded a sharp corner, narrowly missing a car travelling the opposite direction with a roof rack loaded with bikes. A shiver went clean through Rob's body, the kind you get when your brain runs a scenario of a collision that could have just happened.

"Do you need me to take over, Laura?" Rob asked directly. "Because you're driving is starting to raise the hairs on my neck, and I'd rather not die today."

"Sorry," replied Laura Hastings as she corrected to their side of the road. "I'm not entirely used to these narrow mountain roads."

"What do you mean you aren't used to them? You spent ten years in the Yukon and you're not used to narrow roads? How is that even possible?"

"That's true, but I rarely drove up there because I was government employed. I was a chauffeured technical writer, never the chauffeur."

Rob bowed his head slightly as might a commoner to a royal. "Oh, well pardon me, Your Majesty! Do carry on!"

Laura snickered. "It's about time you show me a little respect. I'll get us to Moger's Point safely; I promise. I've got this."

"That's what I'm worried about," confessed Rob with a measure of half-truth. "You look far too relaxed behind the wheel for a rookie mountain driver."

"Would you rather I was a trembling, nervous lunatic?" asked Laura jokingly. "I can switch to that persona if you'd prefer!"

Wearing pyjama style blue jeans, a thick plaid wool shirt and padded vest with a dozen cubby-holes stuffed with flashlights, notepads, pens and other survival-related trinkets, Laura appeared to Rob as if she had not a care in the world. Her wispy jet-black hair rested lazily atop her shoulders, but her easy-going demeanour did little to curtail his growing mistrust. To him, it seemed the newest member of Owensville Search and Rescue was highly adept at concealing her behind-the-wheel jitters.

Rob snugged his seatbelt and glanced over to Laura. "Nah," he replied. "I'll take the calm, cool and collected version. Just keep your eyes on the road so everyone in this brigade doesn't follow us over a cliff like a herd of buffalo!"

Laura ran her left hand through her hair and focused her view straight ahead. "So much for trust and respect," she snickered.

As a former freelance video producer, a job at which she excelled, Laura added one more anecdote to the conversation. "Just so you know, I remember I once worked with a cameraman who trusted me implicitly. He never doubted the accuracy of my scripts and storyboards, and never once brought into question my driving. In fact, we did a series of science excursion videos together, and he always told me how much he trusted my—"

"Just drive Laura," ordered Rob with a twisted smile on his face.

* * *

Clouds building to the west amassed quicker than Dave McMurray expected. White towering cumulus were already forming, their tops stretching skyward above rugged peaks of tree-covered mountains. From his place in the dirt, Dave watched in fascination as their shapes changed, the masses forming into majestic displays of sculptured white cotton. Despite the chilly morning air, his clothes felt sticky against his skin, and he longed for a shower. Finding shade would become the order of the day and a proactive step to hinder dehydration.

When in a tough spot, Dave typically wasn't one to remain idle. He endeavoured to be part of the solution and not a contributor to the problem. Yet here he was, stranded because of incompetence in the middle of nowhere with nothing but the clothes on his back and a broken ankle. No water, no emergency kit, and worst of all, no chance of shifting the odds to his favour. He was as good as stuck, and it was this undeniable truth that bothered him the most.

Still upset with Paul for placing financial gain over safety, the more he mulled things over, the more Dave came to realize how annoyed he was with himself. *Just climb in, fly off without supplies and don't listen to your conscience.* It was true Paul agreed to this transaction for a quick buck, and Dave could not fault him for that. But flying when he shouldn't? Dave understood the first, but not the second. He closed his eyes and shook his head side to side. "Real smart," he verbalized louder than he intended.

Sitting under the wing with his back against the wheel, Paul stretched out within the narrow band of shade the airfoil created. "I hear you conversing with yourself again," he smirked. "Who's real smart?"

"Guilty," Dave confessed without pointing a finger. "I absolutely can't believe we're in this predicament. What else could go wrong? Now the antennas busted off; the very thing we needed to get us out of here. The irony is laughable. No food or water. Nothing to light a fire with and the ELT is toast. I mean what's not to laugh at. We asked for it and got exactly what two idiots deserve."

Unable to disagree with Dave's assessment, Paul glanced skyward and pointed to the clouds. "You forgot about that," he reminded.

Dave followed Paul's gaze and nodded. "Yeah, I see them, but it's good of you to point them out just the same. More salt to an already open wound."

"We can jump back into the plane when it begins to storm," decided Paul. "Better a couple of dry idiots than two soggy ones."

Dave smirked. "Does it matter at all to you that we'd be sitting ducks for lightning strikes? If you want to sit inside a lightning rod, be my guest! I think I'll take my chances under those shorter pines over there."

Paul began to chuckle. "Maybe if we're zapped by lightning, we'll turn into superheroes like in the movies. Then, all we have to do is ignite the jet-packs and fly out of here!"

"Yeah, right," smirked Dave. "You with a wrecked back and bad ticker. Me with a busted ankle. That'd be a sight for adoring fans. They'd call us Limpy and Gimpy, the Dynamic Dorks!"

Paul laughed and Dave found himself helplessly chiming in. Soon both men were laughing hysterically, a much-needed release of emotion that carried on for several minutes despite the pain in their bodies.

A flock of black-billed magpies roosting in nearby trees suddenly took off, their otherwise peaceful morning suddenly interrupted by human exuberance. Dave and Paul raised their heads in unison when they noticed the movement above. Squawking loudly, the trailing bird relieved itself in what seemed an endless stream of white. The comical sight added more humour to their situation, and with cheeks wet with tears, Paul Jackson couldn't figure out if he was laughing or crying. But it really didn't matter. He'd never felt so alive.

Chapter 23

Diane Jackson wasn't convinced that driving to Moger's Point was a good idea, but as part of the wagon train, she couldn't suggest turning around without Kim as an ally. "Maybe, Tess, we should have stayed back at the airport. They did say they'd let us know the moment they located the plane. We might just get in the way up here."

"Nothing doing," countered Tess determinedly. "Besides, we're in my car so my rules apply."

Diane smiled weakly. "Oh, so it's like that is it?"

"Darn right," smiled Tess. "Someone needs to keep an eye on these people, so we stick together and offer whatever support we can. It's our men out there. This whole entourage is in motion for them, and I'll be darned if I'm not going to make us part of it. Even if we just stand around and watch, so be it. Here we'll get information first-hand which is better than waiting for someone to contact us had we stayed back at the airport or gone home."

"I suppose you're right," replied Diane with a huge sigh. She looked into the backseat where Kim stayed busy playing on her phone. "You okay doing this, Kimmy?"

Kim raised her eyes from the screen. "Dad would be disappointed if we didn't do this, Mom. He'd do the same for us. He'd want us involved."

Diane laughed. "Must you two always be in cahoots? I guess I just don't like being at the centre of all this media attention. I wish they'd leave us alone."

Tess widened the gap between her front bumper and the vehicle in front. "I'll keep them at bay, Diane. Don't you worry about that! We can head back home if we decide too. But for now, let's see what happens. Kim's right. This is the best place for us, and Dave and Paul would expect no less."

Remaining quiet, Diane stared out the window at the undeniably beautiful scenery. It had been a long time since she'd paid attention to the different shades of green and brown packed into the trees and surrounding landscape. Nestled into clumps of long grass, wildflowers dotted the area, and it was excruciating to imagine her husband out there amid this beautiful scenery, and not knowing if he was dead, alive, or badly injured.

Diane thought about the contrast in her emotions. One moment happy, enjoying reasonably calm waters, the next a bevy of churning swells with a gruesome undertow ripping away any semblance of peace. She knew trials were part of life, but for her, Paul had always been her bedrock when life pressed in. It was never about the size of a paycheque or the square footage of the house he provided. It was about a partnership, a deeply ingrained trust that no matter what, he'd defend and uphold her integrity. He always stood unwavering in his commitment and to the vows they exchanged so many years ago.

With that institution in jeopardy, Diane couldn't imagine life without her husband. The idea of Kim without a dad made her stomach churn, and as angry as she was at Paul for placing her in this situation, she just wanted him back. Unable to quell the influx of emotion, tears clouded her vision, followed by gentle sobs which she tried unsuccessfully to dampen.

Tess looked over, and at the same time, Kim's hand reached forward, resting on her mom's shoulder. "It'll be okay, Mom. You'll see. We'll have Dad back in no time."

Diane squeezed Kim's hand and wondered how her daughter could be so sure. There were no words to express an uncertain future, and a future without Paul was more than her anguished thoughts could bear.

* * *

The growling in Paul's stomach equalled the pain in his back. Thirst was another issue, but for now that beast was manageable. With a steady breeze rolling over their hovel in the dirt, Paul looked up and watched with interest as branches and leaves swayed back and forth. Unexpectedly, a rogue gust of wind kicked grit into his eyes. Closing them tight, Paul felt the tiny pieces of gravel between his eyes and eyelids, the irritation invoking an immediate sense of rage. Spitting out a gob of dirt, Paul slugged his fist into the airplane's underbelly and swore.

Wanting to stand, but scared to place more strain on his spine than was necessary, Paul remained where he was, his darkening mood shifting away from the laughter of just moments ago. Amazed at how quickly his emotions flipped between hope and despair, he saw the chink in his armour—a wounded ego that he wasn't at all sure he appreciated or understood. And it seemed that Dave wasn't faring any better with his own vacillating temperament.

Since their laughing jag, Dave had lumbered back into the cockpit where he could, "stew in comfort," as he so frankly announced. Upset over the broken antenna, it was for him another slap in the face. Also feeling the need to dissipate his anger, Dave grabbed the control column and jinked it left and right, slamming the ailerons hard against their stops. The fuselage shuddered as control cables inside slid along their pulleys. Dave forced the column forward and drew it back, forcing the elevator violently down and back up.

Paul jumped where he sat from the sudden noise and movement. "Are you having fun up there or are you purposely trying to further render my plane incapable of flight?"

Dave leaned out the door and glared down. "It's already incapable of flight. And you're Mr. Righteous?" he asked. "You cuss and pound dents into your plane. I slam the controls around. We're both cursed, so what's the difference? Besides, a few more broken parts on this clunker won't matter now anyway once your insurance kicks in." Dave sighed and instantly regretted snapping at his friend. "Sorry, Ace, but you have to admit that we're as helpless out here as two newborns with over-loaded diapers."

Paul swiped a mosquito off his chin and tried to stifle his funny bone for the sake of his bodily aches. "Would you quit it with the wisecracks?" he begged. "My heart's already racing, and I'm scared spitless I'll pass out again if I start laughing."

Dave withdrew his hands from the yoke. "I'd really prefer if you'd save that stunt for the hospital, Ace. I'd rather not spend another night out here with you, 'bromance' and all."

Paul tried to blink the sand from his eyes. "Believe me," he stated glumly. "I want out of here as badly as you do, but like you said, all we can do is bide our time, conserve our energy and try to curb our poor attitude."

Dave painfully kicked the rudder pedals with his good foot, and the airplane shook. "You know you're preaching to the choir, right?"

"Will you please stop abusing my airplane? At best, it's a long shot I'll be able to pay my insurance deductible and fix what's already broken, so I don't need extra battle damage."

The ailerons flipped up and down once more, then became still. "Sorry," Dave replied again. "But seriously, Paul, how much dumb luck in one day can two guys have? Wait, don't answer that!"

Overhead, the sun slid behind one of many rapidly ballooning clouds. Another gale kicked up, its force whipping up a dust devil in front of Paul's feet. Scrunching his eyes again, he felt the sting of tiny pebbles against his face. Then as quickly as it appeared, the micro tornado fizzled out. Paul swayed as he tried to stand. He arched his head to look at Dave. "That's it," he bitterly announced. "Move over, I'm coming aboard."

Enjoying his friend's plight, Dave couldn't help but dole out another barbed comment. "With how slow you're moving, Gramps, it'll be Christmas before you get yourself in here!"

* * *

Forty-five miles southeast of the defunct Cessna 185, a small off-white coloured airplane broke free into calm air, its two front wheels spinning after bouncing along a patch of very irregular mud-packed ground. As it climbed, the pilot initiated a steep thirty-degree right turn, positioning his craft parallel to an obscure, murky green oval-shaped lake. Though full of weeds and algae, it also contained an abundance of pole snapping pike, several of which had recently been plucked from their home by the venturous angler.

To the right, huge poplar trees whipped past the wingtip, some branches precariously close to making contact. The leading edge of the wing, elevator and vertical stabilizer were all pitted with nicks, bug guts, and pea-sized dents from years of unconventional flight, not only by him but from several previous operators. But to the pilot, those unsightly issues in no way hindered his schedule or ability to fish and fly.

As the airplane ascended through 200 feet, throngs of tiny insects smacked into the fuselage and windshield, a few larger ones creating long yellow splatter marks along the pilots' eye line. "Rotten stinking bugs!" he grumbled. "Why ya fly in' up this high anyway?"

As a self-appointed expert in hair-raising arrivals and departures, unconventional flight was nothing new to sixty-five-year-old Gary Nordhavn. He revelled in the challenge of stuffing his airplane into the most inhospitable of places, and though occasionally ferrying passengers, his wayward method of flying was one of the reasons he typically flew alone. Except for his wife, there were precious few who would tolerate his backcountry high jinks or frequent bone-chilling near-aerobatic manoeuvres.

For Gary, his theory on life was simple. If you wanted to catch big fish, there was no better place than an unspoiled and unfished body of water. And his airplane was the perfect vehicle and only practical mode of transportation for delivering a brazen explorer like himself to snippets of unexplored angling paradise.

Occupying the floor area, rear seat and cargo hold were several fishing poles, two oversized tackle boxes and a badly dented Styrofoam cooler. Inside the cooler and wrapped in foil were a dozen large pike fillets, the stack packed around a sealed bag of nearly melted ice. The cockpit reeked of fish but to Gary such an aroma equated to peace and relaxation. Every man needed his crutch. Flying and fishing were his.

Gary's airplane, a 1967 model, single-engine Maule M-4 wasn't just a mode of transportation, it was his man cave, or as he jokingly called it, "My Maule cave." Wedging his six-foot-four-inch frame into the cockpit was never easy, but once inside, he felt as though he belonged. Whatever he required the old bird to do, it responded in droves and always asked for more. It didn't matter the weather, the terrain or even if a suitable landing pad existed. Gary and his high-wing fabric-covered monoplane were up for any challenge as long as making money and jigging lures were on the books.

The Maule was not equipped with floats as one might expect from a backwoods pilot and fisherman, nor was Gary even floatplane qualified. In fact, for this type of aircraft, he never received a check-ride or any formal instruction. From the start, it was climb in and go, learn the ropes and fly or die. The machine was his to pilot, a tool of the trade so to speak; on loan for as long as he stayed in the business. And he wasn't the first.

On the whole, Gary enjoyed dropping his ride into areas not meant for wheeled airplanes. With two main wheels forward and one on the tail, Gary relished the idea of setting down along a sandy shoreline or cramped area using full flaps and just the right finesse of the throttle against whatever winds prevailed. He could roost his plane in less than 300 feet, the semi-erect landing more like a helicopter than a fixed-wing aircraft.

Levelling off at 700 feet AGL, Gary trimmed the plane and adjusted power to ninety-five knots. Heading north through the valley canyon, stronger than normal crosswinds warranted the application of hard left rudder to stay on course and overtop the twisty south extension of the Moose River. Even with the Maule yawed sideways, his manipulation of the controls kept him flying more or less in the direction he wanted to go.

Gary knew this rugged terrain like the back of his hands—every nook and cranny, every slice of mountain topography committed to memory. He had no need for a GPS. It was all in his head, an internal synaptic map allowing him to accurately shift from point A to point B and everywhere in between.

Despite an underlying and well-justified pang of anxiety, Gary let out a whoop of contentment. This was his backyard, a vast playground dotted with a glut of fish-rich lakes and all fed from a bevy of river systems that branched out in every conceivable direction like bolts of lightning.

The plan was to head north, intersect with the Moose River, then swing east towards Owensville to wrap up a pressing business transaction. From there, he'd maybe jaunt back to Spruce Creek and see if the Lodge's airstrip was still in operation. In Gary's opinion, their cookhouse had the best triple-decker clubhouse in the land, and with the wheels in his head always spinning, Gary wondered if the camp cook might swap him a free lunch for a handful of fresh pike fillets. *Ask not, receive not,* he thought contentedly.

As the ground rushed by underneath his airplane, Gary knew the valley walls would close in the farther north he flew. Unimpressed with the ugly clouds amassing off the nose of the

Maule, he chose not to fret about what he couldn't change. As a pilot, he learned that weather patterns were meant to be cautiously respected, avoided if possible, and yet still enjoyed for their beauty. If worse came to worst, Gary would initiate the same hide-saving strategy he had used for years; find a place to set down and wait for conditions to improve. It was simple but oftentimes life-saving.

Always packed for the unexpected, Gary knew he wouldn't go hungry if he terminated the flight. Cans of cooking fuel, a frying pan, chocolate bars and a huge bag of trail mix were standard fare. Additionally, a sleeping bag lay tucked near a few dozen bottles of water scattered about the rear seat. A small rolled-up pup tent rested on the seat beside him, the flimsy shelter not long enough to completely house his long legs. But it belonged to his kids when they were small, and Gary couldn't bring himself to part with it.

If he had to seek refuge on the ground, Gary had his dinner planned out; a feast of deep-fried pike nuggets, roasted almonds and a cross-section of chocolate bars. Also, tucked into the cooler was a small jar containing his special fish batter, a one-of-a-kind concoction that transformed smelly pike meat into the taste and texture of popcorn chicken.

Gary thought of his wife Cindy. After twenty-nine years of marriage, she had learned not to worry if her husband failed to return by nightfall. She knew he'd be along the day after or the day after that; and if not, then and only then would she contact the authorities. But he did always return, a man covered head to toe in horseshoes as Cindy liked to believe. Gary knew she fretted that one day his luck would run out, but sharing those thoughts was an unmentionable taboo he rarely liked to discuss.

After this trip, Gary planned to retire, not from flying or fishing, but from the pursuit of dollar signs. It was time to enjoy the fruits of his labour and spend more time with Cindy. *Maybe,* thought Gary, *she'd fly more with me if I bought my own plane and settled a bit.* Gary tweaked his manifold pressure and RPMs, then added a bit more down-trim. The airplane engine purred nicely, and he couldn't help but smile. "Soon," he drawled. "The sooner I deliver, the sooner I git out!"

* * *

Paul Jackson's climb into his broken Cessna wasn't easy, but now that he was inside, the effort had been worth it. Sick of lounging on the dusty, uneven ground, the old cushioned seat he now perched upon was nothing short of heavenly. Beside him, Dave looked as if he was asleep, his head tilted back, his eyes closed. Paul knew he wasn't sleeping because there wasn't a hint of snoring, as was usually the case when Dave drifted off. His growling stomach, on the other hand, was loud and very clear. Paul slapped his friend's leg. "Shall we call out for beer and pizza?" he asked. "My treat."

"There's nothing I'd like more," replied Dave sombrely. "Fire up the radio and let's see if we can't reach Pizza Hut. They deliver everywhere."

Without replying, Paul snapped on the master switch, toggled the avionics and watched the radio stack spring to life.

"What are you doing, Ace?" asked Dave with only partial curiosity.

Paul caught Dave's quizzical look. "You said to call out for pizza, so that's what I'm doing . . . sort of. Besides, you gave me an idea just now. With the ELT not working, we should have tried this a while ago."

"Should have tried what, oh delirious one?" scoffed Dave. "You are aware that we're surrounded by mountains, not to mention that we haven't seen or heard any other airplanes within—"

"Shush!" Paul interrupted. "Seeing as we can't start a fire or do anything else to signal our position, we should try broadcasting on the Unicom channel. Maybe we'll get lucky and someone will hear us."

Dave threw his arms into the air. "Did you hear what I said? Mountains? No airplanes?" Dave shrugged his shoulders. "Well, you are the captain of this ship, so as second mate I'll defer to your command."

Paul shook his head disgustedly. "Yes, and look where my brilliant plan got us. I have a feeling that when all is said and done, I'll have little choice but to hand in my wings. Either Diane strips them off my shoulders or the Department of Transport does. I'm toast either way."

Dave had nothing to add, so he remained quiet.

"Your silence speaks volumes," Paul remarked bitterly.

"Sorry, I'm not sure what more to say. I feel bad for you and for whatever comes your way."

"It'll be okay, Dave," admitted Paul. "You can plead innocent in this. But for now, maybe the radio will help. It's the only proactive thing I can think of doing."

Paul rotated the knob on the Com 1 channel to 126.7 megahertz, a channel used for reporting one's position and weather updates. Though not an official emergency channel, it was not written in stone that a pilot had to use it, or even monitor the frequency. Most kept the frequency tuned while away from an airport. It was at best a mustard seed of hope, and Paul needed whatever measure of optimism he could conjure up.

"Guess it's worth a shot," agreed Dave. "At this point, we've got nothing to lose, though I think our odds are better that a sasquatch strolls by in the next few minutes, waves hello and brings us a basket of fruit."

Paul unlatched the microphone, unplugged his headset, and keyed the button. Before he got a word out, a blast of feedback ripped through the overhead speaker. "Oh, for the love of pearl!" he shouted angrily. "Maybe it's best this airplane is written off after all."

Dave reached for the squelch knob, beating Paul's hand by a half-second. "Here," he offered. "Let me get that for you, captain. At least then I'm doing something around here to earn my danger pay."

Ignoring the comment, Paul began his broadcast. Minutes later, Dave fell asleep and began snoring loudly.

* * *

Since departing his remote log cabin at the crack of dawn, Gary's airplane had burned through ten gallons of fuel. Checking the fuel gauges, he knew there was enough in the long-range tanks for another five to six hours if he regulated his gas consumption.

Content, Gary performed another cursory check of his instrument panel, then lounged back in his seat despite having to fight gusty winds. The cabin temperature was on the cool side, just the way he liked it. With a bit of finagling and both hands momentarily off the control column, he reached to the back seat for a bottle of water. In the process, his knee brushed the corner of the yoke, flipping it to the right. Because of the airplane's touchy controls and excellent roll rate, the wings dipped abruptly. Gary dropped the bottle he had just grabbed, spun around and quickly ended the roll. "Easy girl," he admonished. "Why so temperamental? I just needed a bottle of water."

At that moment, the rising sun passed behind a sinister-looking cloud, the sudden change in light levels playing havoc with Gary's eyes. The terrain below became flat and lifeless, it's vibrant colours dismal and entirely void of the textured detail it displayed just moments ago. From the air the effect was astounding. Gary blinked several times, impatient for his eyes to adapt, and angry that his airspace was shrinking due to degrading weather. Glancing out the window to where the sun had just retired, he shook his head. "Don't leave me now," he griped. "The day only just started and yer already play in' hide' n seek."

For the next five minutes, the Maule weaved about, twisting and turning through a darkened corridor of mountains framing the usually picturesque valley. With the sun still at bay, Gary thought he would try again for a bottle of water. Carefully ensuring his knee was clear of the yoke, he reached back with his right arm and fumbled to grasp the cap of the closest one. "Oh, for crying out loud," he barked. "How hard is it fer a man ta git a drink 'round here?"

In that instant, the band of clouds blocking the sun separated. Beams of sunlight flooded the cockpit, the sudden influx causing Gary to squint. Forgetting the water for a second time, he spun his head back around, his pupils constricting to compensate. "Dang it!" he scowled.

As the sun intensified, Gary shielded his eyes from the onslaught by tipping his head down. It was then he completely missed the obscure glint of light off the left corner of the Maule's nose. The distant ground level flash was there for a heartbeat, then gone. Gary never saw a thing.

Giving up on the water, he fought to keep the plane's nose level against strengthening winds. Pockets of cloud swirled at a higher altitude, their masses drifting across the upper slopes of nearby peaks. Knowing that mountain flying could shift from glorious to dismal in a heartbeat, Gary wasn't surprised that flight conditions were deteriorating so fast.

Remaining calm, he waited as the aircraft slanted down following a strong gust, then corrected with trim and countered its tail slide with opposite rudder. The nose satisfyingly slipped back to the right. With gentle persuasion, a good pilot knew how to manipulate the headstrong nature of his stallion, and Gary considered himself among the best.

What Gary could not anticipate was the Maule settling towards the perfect angle of incidence to repeat the reflection he just missed. And this time his focus was out the front window as another downdraft punched the airplane. As he corrected from the sudden jolt, the blossoming aura again appeared off the nose, its intensity not something easily missed the second time around.

Understanding that ground-based reflections could result from small hidden lakes, rivers, puddles or even hand-held mirrors used by hikers and campers, Gary could not recall another time seeing a glare from this particular place in the sky. So, given the unexpected brilliance of this newcomer, he was surprised by its sudden appearance. As he squinted to sharpen his view, the sun disappeared, and the glint vanished without a trace.

After a moment's thought, Gary dismissed the phenomena as insignificant. At his current altitude, he knew the ground displayed all sorts of subtle nuances: an ever-changing palate of light, shadow and atmospheric mumbo-jumbo, all conspiring to confuse an aviator's mind. Despite his inquisitive nature, Gary believed he had just fallen victim to such trickery.

With the weather crumbling, Gary toyed with the idea of retreating home, but the idea of surrendering to the elements was in direct opposition to his usual bulletproof mindset. Besides, with business to take care of, he needed to stay the course and continue north through the valley. *Debate over.*

Humming a made-up tune, Gary took pride in maintaining a steady compass heading despite blustery winds and roller-coaster fluctuations in altitude. The lanky pilot loosened his hands on the yoke and stretched as best he could in his seat.

As of late, Gary had pushed himself hard to achieve his goals, so the idea of mixing business with pleasure was often a delicate task. Just then his stomach flipped at one horribly repetitive thought. With grappling fingers and sudden waves of justified panic, he nervously reached under his seat as though his stash might have mysteriously vaporized. When his fingertips brushed against both items, relief flooded his body. Gary leaned back and resolved to play this dangerous game no more. He would complete this last delivery and business transaction and be done.

Chapter 24

For the last few hours, moist air lifted skyward and condensed, which allowed the formation of cumulus clouds in the western sky. As warm air continued to rise and the clouds grew in size and volume, they held the potential to morph into cumulonimbus clouds, a heavy and full of water evil twin. Fortified with cool dry air from above, meteorologically speaking it was the perfect recipe for severe weather and a huge concern to anyone caught in the open, including Dave McMurray and Paul Jackson, occupants of an aluminum Cessna: a perfect conductor for lightning.

Even with both doors open, the cockpit became too stuffy for its increasingly ornery passengers. Every so often a breeze kicked up and wafted through the cabin, but its cooling effect on the skin proved less and less effective. For now, the sun was out, its heating properties intensified through the windows. Wishing the fireball would make up its mind—either in or out, Dave closed his eyes as the repetitive sun-shade mix wore down his already hypertense nerves.

As if transfixed by the swinging watch of a hypnotist, Paul sat with his body leaned forward and his neck craned towards the sky. Stone-faced and with fatigued red eyes, he watched as white and grey clouds drifted through areas of rapidly shrinking blue. With nature's drama unfolding, he reached over and nudged Dave's shoulder. "Are you seeing this, Dave?" he asked nervously.

Ticked off at being poked, Dave reluctantly opened his eyes. "See what? What I *was* seeing, Ace, was that beer and pizza you promised to call out for. You just torpedoed that mental image, so thanks."

Paul ignored Dave's comment and pointed to the sky.

Dave's eyes locked on the massive clouds above, their shapes multiplying into what could only be described as fearfully majestic. The spectacle reminded him of weather documentaries he watched years ago, where through time-lapse photography, the sky transforms from pristine to tumultuous in a matter of seconds. The only difference was that these clouds had not been sped up.

In addition to their towering beauty, neither pilot appreciated seeing another cloud type, their structure resembling groups of tennis balls hanging from underneath the cloud base. Paul knew trouble when he saw it, the dual cloud formations historically capable of producing very memorable thunderstorms and pea to golf-ball-sized hail.

"Tell me if I'm wrong, Ace," asked Dave alarmingly. "And I rarely am. But aren't those shenanigans up there happening far too early in the day? And those few mammatus clouds I see are not a welcome addition to the already screwy mess over our heads."

Paul's neck began to ache. "It does seem a bit premature. But then we shouldn't be surprised. We are in the mountains after all, where the normal laws of nature don't seem to apply."

"Tell me about it," replied Dave irritably.

A swarm of mosquitoes suddenly invaded the cockpit, several of which flew straight for the front window and feverishly tried to push their way through the glass to freedom. Without forethought, Paul and Dave reached forward, their right hands swatting in perfect sync. The men stared at each other and shared a laugh.

"We've been hanging around each other for way too long," noted Dave. "Not only do we crash perfectly good airplanes together, we kill bugs in unison."

Dave frowned. "There's a winning team if I ever saw one."

Ignoring Dave's cynicism, Paul continued to broadcast his distress call. "This is Cessna one-eight-five, Golf, Foxtrot, Charlie, Sierra, broadcasting a Mayday to anyone monitoring 126.7 megahertz. We have two souls on board, both with"—Paul thought for a second—"non-life-threatening injuries. Requesting help and rescue as soon as—"

Dave interrupted with a sarcastic ramble of his own. "And seeing as we don't know where we are because our GPS is broken, good luck trying to find us, whoever you are."

Paul released the transmit button. "That wasn't helpful. Wasn't it you that just told me to stop worrying and to stay positive? I'm doing the only thing I can think of to help us out of this situation, so unless you have something positive to say, please can the negative backseat commentary."

Dave pointed defensively at his chest. "First off, I'm in the front seat, and secondly if you'd care to recollect, I'm not the one who flew with a restricted licence."

Paul slammed the microphone back into its cradle and shut off the master. "Do we need to go down that road again?" he challenged. "I think I've already come clean on that little admission, so why do you insist on nailing me to the cross with it?"

"Because, Ace," replied Dave. "We wouldn't be in this spot if you had been true to yourself and honest with me. I'll share the heat for our fuel status and lack of preparedness for this mess we're in. I should've asked questions and I didn't. But you know as well as I do that this trip never should have happened. We're just lucky the vultures aren't circling to pick our bones clean."

"Are you done?" fumed Paul. "Because I really don't need this. Your frustration with me is duly noted, but it's not helping! I'd appreciate your support right now, not a lecture! That I'll save for my wife."

Like two preschoolers caught arguing over the same toy in a sandbox, Paul and Dave angled away from each other, neither willing to budge in the way of an apology, but both knowing full well they should. Without saying another word, Dave spun his body further sideways and began to jockey his way out of the airplane.

"Now where are you limping off to?" asked Paul guardedly.

"Like I told you before," replied Dave, his voice less combative. "I'm going to find a tree to pee on, then I'm going back to where you found me in the bushes. When the lightning starts up, I figure it'll be safer over there with the ants. Better a drenched rat than a crispy fried one."

Paul sighed; his thoughts increasingly tormented. *Maybe the crispy rat scenario wouldn't be such a bad outcome*, he pensively decided. *At least I won't be court-martialed, and Diane gets my life insurance. A win/win for everybody.*

Tears formed in Paul's eyes. He wondered if laughing one minute and crying the next was anything close to the whacked-out emotions his wife experienced once a month. He watched Dave struggle painfully to exit the Cessna. "Dave, hold up a sec."

Dave stopped but never turned around. "What?" he panted.

"I'm sorry for spouting off. It seems like all I'm doing this trip is apologizing. Stay in the cockpit. You'll be dry in here and—"

"Close it, Ace!" barked Dave, his palm out flat.

Paul squawked in disbelief. "What? I'm trying to apologize here, and don't think I deserve—"

"Can it, Paul. Do you hear that?"

"Hear what?" asked Paul, notably upset at Dave's insensitivity.

Dave froze in place. "I thought I heard an aircraft engine. It was distant, but I'd bet my good foot it was there!"

A surge of hope flooded through Paul's core. "Are you sure? Maybe someone heard my broadcast. I told you it might—"

"Would you quit yapping!" ordered Dave. "I need to listen for a second."

Paul cocked his head sideways to better position his ears. Except for gusty winds rustling through the trees, a few birds and the flow of nearby water, he heard nothing unusual. He watched as Dave balanced against the wing strut, his head rotating like a satellite dish.

"I know I heard an engine, Paul. It's gotta be a search and rescue bird. I bet they're on—" Dave stopped talking as his ears picked up the sound again.

"What? You hear it again? I don't hear a thing."

But an instant later, Paul's ears detected the same unmistakable sound of an engine. He shared a goofy grin with Dave, and together they broke into raucous whoops of delight, their cackle also perfectly synced.

* * *

Gary Nordhavn knew without a doubt the reflection had mushroomed from a large metallic surface. Normally he wouldn't bother with such a trivial thing, but because of its size and intensity, and since his flight path already carried him in that direction, he felt obligated to snafu a closer look.

His analogy was simple. Big fish came to those willing to cast a line when others would say it's fruitless. In like fashion, Gary believed a curious mind led to prosperity and self-fulfillment, and not knowing would drive him nuts for weeks. He could not allow that to happen. *Could be something, could be nuth in',* Gary aptly decided.

Easing the throttle back a touch, Gary added a notch of flaps and slowed his airplane to eighty knots. Ideally, he wanted low and slow before moving into a favourable position to spin circles if the need arose. He allowed the nose to drop, added trim and descended to 400 feet above the rugged landscape.

Where the blinding sun was just moments ago, thick clouds blanketed what little blue sky remained. Increasing wind gusts made controlling the aircraft even more challenging, and with visual flight deteriorating faster than he expected, Gary wasn't

Deliveries

planning to snoop for long. He would do a quick flyover to appease his curiosity and then retreat. Or, if the conditions forced him to land and hunker down, then so be it.

Usually unfazed by whirlwind changes in the weather, the rapid transformation in the sky now had Gary's full attention. His immediate concern wasn't if he could land, but where? The terrain lay thick with trees and dense vegetation, rocks and fallen timber. Aside from narrow shorelines along both sides of the river, there wasn't yet visible a suitable place to rotate the tires.

Gary's instincts told him to throttle up, forget the anomaly and hightail it through the degrading weather as fast as his plane would allow. His lifestyle already bore significant risk without adding more, but despite that gnawing reality, he simply could not bring himself to carry on through without a sneak-peek flyby. "One quick look and that's it," decided Gary as the Maule speedily closed the distance to where he last witnessed the flash.

Leaning towards his side window, Gary's sharp eyes scanned the ground in large chunks. Aside from trees, vegetation, and normal topography for the area, he saw nothing out of the ordinary.

Whatever it was, it has ta be close, he thought. *Otherwise, I'm gone.*

* * *

Suddenly forgotten, their desire for food and water bowed to the prevailing notion that someone had found them or was about too. Bravely trying to ignore the fire raging in his back, Paul carefully guided his body sideways and swung both legs out the door. Placing his one foot on the strut and the other to the ground, he made it out of the plane in remarkably quick fashion.

Without taking his eyes off the sky, Dave balanced on one foot and used the wing for support. He noticed Paul shuffling around the Cessna's nose towards him. "See, Ace, I told you," he boasted. "If you hear it too, then I know I'm not going crazy!"

Paul rotated to the left. "I hear it all right, but I can't tell where it's coming from. One thing's for certain, it seems to be getting louder which means it's coming this way."

"You got that right!" agreed Dave excitedly.

It was then both men felt the first few drops of rain on their faces.

"Well now," quipped Dave. "Isn't that just perfect timing? We're on the verge of being found and the sky is about to crash in." Within seconds, it felt as if someone switched on a sprinkler and air conditioner, both at the same time. The rain and sudden drop in temperature caused Dave to shiver. "Too hot one minute, wet and chilled the next," he remarked. "Gotta love mountain weather."

Paul stepped away; his head aimed skyward. Random gusts of wind whipped up clouds of dirt and fallen leaves directly into his face and eyes. "For crying out loud," he sighed. "If there's one thing I hate more than anything, it's the wind."

"I'll second that," declared Dave while pointing to the sky. "But imagine the sketchy ride for the pilot up there."

With the wind blocking its true point of origin, the engine's hum seemed to radiate from all directions. Jagged mountain ranges to the north and south blocked a clear line of sight along both sides of the river valley, and Paul figured it unlikely an aircraft would approach from the east or west given higher elevations. Whatever type of plane it was, the pilot had throttled back as the distinct sound of a constant speed propeller echoed throughout the valley. It was sweet music to the ears of both men.

Dave turned his head side to side. "He's gotta be darn near on top of us!" he grimaced in frustration. "Why can't we see the blasted thing?"

"Beats me. Everything imaginable echoes between these—"

It was then they both saw it, low and slow from the south. A small white airplane appearing atop a ridge of pine trees and heading directly towards them. From their vantage point, it looked as though the pilot had already spotted them because he made no attempt to veer away. Paul's heart pounded, the sight before him overwhelmingly beautiful, yet surreal as though staring at a mirage—an oasis offering hope and deliverance. His only hope was that this image would not eerily fade away as all mirages do.

Paul's mouth hung open. "You seeing this, Dave? Tell me I'm not hallucinating."

"Nope, it's real! What an awesome sight!"

Recognizing the airplane's shape as a Maule, Dave had always aspired to fly one but was never presented with the opportunity. *Today,* he thought, *might just be that day.* "You ever see that plane before in your travels?" asked Dave. "I don't remember seeing it before. It's completely white by the looks of it. No livery at all."

"Nope. I don't think it's from Owensville. I have no idea where's he's from. Maybe from Bakersfield?"

"Well, I don't give a rat's butt where he's from," smiled Dave. "All I care is that he sees us down here, and we blow this pop stand."

Feeling a touch queasy, adrenaline flowed liberally through Paul's body, causing his legs to shake. He grabbed hold of the wing strut for stability and lowered his head to counter the seasick feeling.

"You okay?" Dave asked nervously. "Please tell me you're not going to pass out again."

"Okay, I won't tell you," sputtered Paul, his head down. "I'm fine. Legs are off-balance, and I feel a little nauseous." Paul raised his head. "Is he still heading this way?"

"Would appear so," replied Dave. "But it might be nothing more than a coincidence that he's on this heading. If he sees us, you'd think he'd approach from either side of centre to better see out his side window. He's taking a beating up there with how much his wings are rocking."

Less than a mile away, the Maule closed the gap in seconds, its pilot making no attempt to rock his wings or flash landing lights as one might expect. With arms waving frantically, two sets of weary eyes stared in absolute disbelief as the aircraft flew overtop and continued north up through the valley.

Adding misery to Paul's dampened hopes, the clouds opened their taps and let loose a deluge of rain. It seemed the perfect self-imposed stab in the back by a world heck bent on teaching him a lesson about personal ethics.

Dave glanced at Paul who wore the same dumbfounded expression on his face. "C'mon, Gramps," he stated glumly. "I'll help you back into your easy chair, and we can cry in our mashed potatoes together."

* * *

Gary Nordhavn's hands were trembling. In the last thirty seconds, he felt like he was trapped inside a large ping-pong ball as paddles of wind unmercifully spanked his plane back and forth. If that wasn't enough, thin sheets of rain began to cascade over the front window, eroding visibility and momentarily forcing his attention back into the cockpit. Whatever it was he'd been searching for would have to wait as the instinct of safeguarding his life took precedence.

Gary mulled over three plausible options: retreat, find somewhere to land and seek refuge, or the unmentionable third and least desired—crash. He needed to take decisive action now to avoid that grim scenario.

As increasing turbulence buffeted the plane, Gary felt the surprising onset of panic, a foreign sensation he wasn't at all impressed with. It created in him a sudden awareness of his own mortality, that if he failed to properly execute his skill as a pilot, he could, in fact, end his life. He ran a quick mental diagnostic and, in doing so, realized he needed to force his body to fly the plane while convincing his brain to ignore the uncommon fear bubbling up from under his skin.

Deliveries

Each time Gary worked the pedals to correct for a jolt of crosswind, he seemed a step behind for the next gust. As he struggled to keep the plane level, the steady bumping around felt like a wind tunnel, but instead of blowing from straight on, the barrage hit from every conceivable angle.

Without the luxury of time to rationalize strategy or weigh options, Gary raised the flaps and added full power. The surging engine provided comforting reassurance, but it wasn't a question of whether his airplane would come through for him, it was more would he come through for his airplane.

Rain slamming into the fuselage made the task of flying nearly impossible. Gary's hands and feet jostled the controls, his limbs struggling to obey the myriad of commands they received from their master. Directly ahead, obscure clouds swirled menacingly, and in no way did he wish to take them on. There was nothing at all heroic in challenging the elements with an ego out to prove something. Enough was enough. "Alrighty then," he grunted while glancing left and right. "Let's see if we can't git you spun 'round the other way, shall we?"

Following a quick scan of the terrain, Gary determined there was enough room to flip around but not without a measure of precision flying. Where he didn't want to end up was anywhere near the sloping mountains along both sides, where rising terrain could easily outclimb the capabilities of his plane.

Acutely aware he'd have to cut it tight; it was now or never to implement Plan A, a box canyon turn. This retreat procedure worked best in confined spaces, and because of unpredictable weather ahead, the only way out of this muck was from the point of entry. Gary would have rather continued north, but that wasn't in the cards, pending business or not.

The textbook procedure for a box canyon turn was in theory simple enough: slow the plane, roll wings thirty degrees, apply full power to avoid a stall, and then set flaps no more than half. But what concerned Gary the most was the uncertainty of the wind and of maintaining altitude during the turn.

Gary checked his altimeter. *Three hundred fifty feet. Too low.* Nervously adding power, he pulled the yoke back and climbed another hundred feet for added insurance. Slowing to sixty-five knots, he sucked in a deep breath, raised the Maule's nose ten degrees and rolled the yoke to the right. Adding a notch of flaps, Gary watched the compass needle rapidly swing towards his initial goal of ninety degrees or due east.

As the airplane bounced through the turn, Gary eyed the vertical speed indicator, a key instrument for maintaining altitude while banking. Sweat stung his eyes, but there was no time to wipe it away. Shouting over the roar of the engine, Gary's confidence spiked. "C'mon girl, this ain't so bad. We've been through a butt load more than this and—"

Just then, a shrill buzzing sound interrupted his retreat, the unwelcome intrusion throwing off his concentration while sending chills down his spine. The airplane began to shudder, and the nose slipped downward. Gary suddenly understood that in his haste to evacuate, he'd forgotten to add full power in the turn. "Stall!" he screamed as if a verbal outburst would somehow offset his negligence.

Gary jammed the throttle forward and fiercely tried to recover as the ground slid towards him. Believing for certain that he was about to die, the only words to leave his mouth were, "Too little, too late, you dang fool!"

* * *

Paul and Dave still hadn't moved, the astonishment of the Maule passing them by invoking waves of shock and, for Dave, absolute rage. Shaking his head in disbelief, he shot his arm skyward while a string of not-so-nice words spewed from his mouth. "And besides that, if I ever find out who you are, I'll first slap you silly, then I'll willfully commit first-degree murder!"

"Wow! You truckers sure know how to express yourselves. You know you can get help for that, right, Dave? I hear the old time-tested remedy of a bar of soap in your mouth works well."

"Not funny, Ace. How could he not have seen us? I mean he was right on top of us for crying out loud!"

Though out of sight, the Maule's engine remained audible but fading. A moment later, both men heard the sound of an engine throttling back followed by the unmistakable growl of a full-power throttle up.

"What in heaven's name is that idiot doing?" asked Dave, his voice oozing with anger and sarcasm.

"Maybe engine trouble? That could be the reason he just flew by." Paul sneezed when a fluff tickled his nose. "No doubt this lovely weather is giving that guy a run for his money."

"Be real, Paul! He didn't see us, plain and simple. I bet he'd have missed us even if we had a bonfire licking the underside of his stupid airplane! Maule's are built for this kind of weather, and no, he wasn't experiencing engine trouble. Those airplanes are nearly bulletproof."

Soaked and shivering, Paul glanced towards the perilous northern sky and sighed. "Well, either way our only immediate chance of getting out of here just flew by. He's got to have a pretty big pair to fly off into that mess."

In that instant, the Maule suddenly reappeared, slightly above the tree line with its wings rolling out from an absurdly steep angle. The wobbling airplane grew larger by the second as it closed the distance.

"He's coming back!" shouted Paul. "But why's he so low?"

"Lord only knows. But one thing's for certain . . . he's not coming back for us because he doesn't know we're here. From the sound of his engine and angle on the wings, I'm guessing he chickened out of his flight plan and performed a canyon turn. Now he's in full retreat back to wherever he came from."

"He'll be on us in less than a minute!"

"We need to do something!" insisted Dave as he ducked into the cockpit.

"Where are you going?"

"It's 'the something' I'm doing!" bellowed Dave. "We've got light's, Ace, so let's use 'em!"

Before Paul could respond, Dave flipped on the master. In rapid-fire succession, he toggled the beacon and strobe switches, then the landing and navigation lights. The Cessna lit up like a Christmas tree.

"Should have done this before," hollered Dave. "If he doesn't spot us this time, then he's flying with two glass eyes!"

* * *

Feeling lucky to still have his life and airplane intact, Gary struggled to regulate his breathing and heart rate. Due to quick reflexes, he rallied back from the partial stall less than fifty feet from splattering himself into the tree line. Never had he come so close to crashing his plane, the demoralizing experience more sobering than he thought possible. Suddenly nothing else mattered but his survival and to get back to Cindy. He would somehow deal with a missed delivery when the time came.

At full throttle, Gary began a shallow climb out through the valley he had just passed through. Winds continued to push hard, but this time more of a kick-in-the-pants-from-behind tailwind. As he steered towards what little blue sky remained, it was then he saw it, the sudden and very distinct appearance of airplane running lights at ground level, just off the left corner of the nose. Astounded by the spectacle, Gary instinctively yanked back on the throttle, then brought the nose down. "Well, mystery solved," he remarked indifferently.

An airplane plopped into a scruffy patch of land was the last thing Gary expected to see, its fuselage surrounded by trees, brush and a whole gamut of unfriendly aircraft destroying vegetation. But even more bizarre than the sight before him was the impending notion that his business-slash-pleasure trip was about to undergo another radical shift sideways. Whoever it was down there needed help, and though Gary wanted to flee and deal with his own mess, the ugly sky and tortuous winds dictated a sudden alternative game plan.

Gary dropped a notch of flaps, eyed the surrounding terrain, and brought the power off a touch more. He reached for his landing light switch and spluttered to those below. "Hope y' all got room fer one more down there, cause ready or not, here I come!"

* * *

The Maule unexpectedly changed course, and from his vantage point, Paul Jackson knew they'd been found. Already an emotional wreck, instant tears mixed with a steady flow of rain dribbling down his cheeks. He watched as the aircraft banked left and reduced power, a clear-cut attempt by the pilot to obtain a better view. Adding to the euphoric moment, the landing light snapped on, flashed several times and then remained on.

Paul's arms were already waving long before his brain commanded them to do so. In the blink of an eye, his perspective changed. The poor choices that lead him to this spot paled in comparison to the hope of going home and facing whatever discipline came his way.

They'd been found and, for Paul, not a moment too soon.

Chapter 25

Prior to initiating the search pattern, pilot Kevin Davies chatted briefly with his spotter, Susan McCutcheon. Following normal search procedure, Susan would select a landmark on either side of the plane. These visual references allowed for a specific scanning range so Susan's eyes wouldn't drift too far from the target area or grow tired too quickly.

Except for short random areas of scraggy grass and sand dunes along the banks of the Moose River, there was little in the way of what could be construed as a suitable landing zone. That being said, Susan decided her scanning range would be relatively narrow, the search points along both banks of the river her main area of focus. It was anyone's guess where the plane had set down, but odds were nil the crew had time to select anywhere safe for a landing, mandatory or otherwise.

Ordinarily, airborne search and rescue involved more than one spotter to allow for greater efficiency. That required a four-seat airplane, and Owensville S and R weren't equipped with that luxury. With Kevin flying the plane, and Susan's eyes focused on the ground, they would have to improvise and make do with less than ideal.

The target in question was a silver-skinned Cessna 185 with red detailing along the fuselage and engine cowling and along the leading edge of the wing. Susan hoped it would be easy to pick it out from ground clutter, but that assumption was based on the crew not smacking themselves into a hillside, and the plane not scattered in pieces among the trees.

With her neck kinked at an uncomfortable angle, Susan pressed her forehead to the window. "I see nothing that really stands out," she announced. "If that plane went down in the trees, it'll be tough to spot."

"We may not be far enough west," replied Kevin, his voice failing to hide frazzled nerves. "And by the looks of the sky up ahead, I'm not sure how much farther we can go today anyway."

Turbulent winds higher up demanded the Cub fly at a lower search altitude than was Kevin's preference, but at least Susan hadn't made any further demands to return to base. But even he had his limits, and the degrading conditions weren't helping to offset his jitters. For a moment Kevin's mind shifted to Carla, the cute paramedic who treated his injuries and apparently stole his heart. Perhaps it was boyish infatuation and nothing more, but he convinced himself he needed to see her again. He thought she had seemed genuinely interested, unless that too was his overactive imagination playing inhumane tricks.

Susan's voice interrupted his thoughts. "Go as far as you feel is safe, Kevin. I don't want to become a statistic any more than you do, and now with the sun hidden from view, it's hard to see any real definition down there."

Kevin glanced at the GPS and zoomed out the screen. "The river forks up ahead where another branch swings south. Let's go as far as that, and we'll reassess our situation there."

"Sounds like a plan," agreed Susan, trying herself to stay calm.

The Piper Cub followed the river for another five minutes, zigzagging to match the water's twisting path. So far, there was no sign of the Cessna, and Susan's discouragement was taking its toll. "There's nothing down there, Kevin. No airplane or even a piece of one. It's all just rocks, trees and dirt. This is pointless."

"Keep looking," urged Kevin. "In the meantime, I'll see if I can reach our ground teams on the radio. If we can't go any farther now, maybe we can try again later if this soup blows off. Who knows, it could be bright and sunny in an hour. I know Rob won't be happy if we pull the plug, but it's getting too risky. Besides, it's us risking our necks up here, and I'm willing to stretch mine only so far."

"Ditto."

A light rain began to strike the Cub, its arrival perfectly on cue as if scripted in a movie scene for dramatic effect. Gentle at first, the cloudburst soon hampered Kevin's view out the front and Susan's scan to the side. Gusty headwinds also kicked up from the west and tossed the airplane about, the turbulence further swaying Kevin's decision to retreat.

Below the Cub, valley walls widened out as the Moose River forked, the main artery continuing west, the smaller tributary meandering to the south. Recognizing a good place to flip around, and without announcing his intentions, he swiftly rolled the cub into a steep left turn, the hasty manoeuvre more a response to his disappointment than to any form of impending doom. After a few harrowing seconds, he levelled the wings and flew the plane partway down the south fork where the landscape semi-plateaued for what he decided would offer a safer completion of his 180 back towards Owensville.

Susan spoke up, her voice tense from the unexpected move. "I take it we're done for today, Kevin?"

"Yup, that's affirmative."

"You know, Kevin, my stomach really doesn't handle those sudden moves. You said you'd discuss your intentions with me before I feel like I'm about to die."

"Sorry, but the weather's only going to get worse the farther west we fly," explained Kevin defensively. "So yes, I'm pulling the plug. Looks like you get your way after all."

Though relieved they were turning around, Susan in no way appreciated Kevin's snarky remark. But she vowed to hold her tongue and keep her eyes on the ground just the same. Underlying shades of dark-green and copper blended together, and the absence of sunshine resulted in a muddy wash of undertones that stretched for miles. And with rain now in the mix, finding anything abnormal seemed less likely than ever.

"Okay," she replied. "You're the captain, but you better let Rob in on what we're up to. I have little doubt he's worried about us."

"I'm turning again now," announced Kevin sarcastically. "I'll try to reach him once we're safely spun around towards home."

As the plane tipped to the left, decidedly more gently this time, Susan's view of the south river began to improve. Not nearly as wide as the Moose River, the smaller fork claimed its own majestic beauty and twisty curves as far as she could see. Strangely enough, the curtain of rain between the two river junctions suddenly dissipated as though a dividing wall fell into place. Susan felt her stomach twitch as the aircraft lost altitude. "You do realize that we're descending, right?" she asked nervously.

"As you've learned, it's tough in this wind to maintain altitude. Especially in a turn. So, yes, I'm taking us lower."

Scanning rows of pine trees along the riverbanks, Susan's eyes travelled from the edges of the river to higher up towards the tree line. It was then her level of engagement rocketed from low to off the scale. "Kevin!" she screamed into her microphone. "Circle back the other way! South! Keep going south! I just saw something!"

Kevin jumped in his seat at the unexpected outburst. "Where?" he asked excitedly, already reefing on the stick. "What'd you see?"

Susan felt squeamish from the sudden reversal in direction but somehow managed to swallow the bile rising in her throat. "There's something there, down the south fork!" she replied. "It's in the trees on the right side! Might be a piece of clothing or fabric, but I can't tell until we swing back around. Whatever it is, it's small and unmistakably orange. Plus, it's too high up for anyone to have put it there from ground level."

The target in question rested on the outer edge of a large tree branch about half-way down the trunk, the pine skewed at an odd angle and out-of-place among its smaller freestanding neighbours. The item's fluorescent orange colour offered Susan a stark contrast against the flat green tones of the surrounding landscape.

"A piece of clothing?" asked Kevin skeptically. "You're calling me around for that! What makes you think that's got anything to do with the Cessna we're searching for? It could have come from anywhere!"

"My point exactly!" countered Susan, her focus now entirely on this presumably insignificant object. But her instincts screamed otherwise and ignoring them directly opposed her clinical way of aerial assessment. She squinted, which oddly enough helped her obtain a sharper view.

"Are you hearing me?" asked Kevin again, his patience wearing thin. "I think it's time to get the heck out of here and return to base!"

"You told me to call you around for anything," reminded Susan. "So, indulge me for a minute. Fly along this river for a few minutes. I know it's a gamble, but at this point, it's the only abnormal thing I've seen. Besides, the rain's eased off in this direction."

Already straightening the wings, Kevin focused his eyes directly ahead. "You do realize the weather looks much worse to the south, and in the off chance you're directionally challenged, that's the way we're heading!" Kevin trimmed the nose level as best he could. "And what makes you think the crew would have flown in this direction anyway? It's completely off the beaten path."

"Woman's intuition maybe," replied Susan. "But since you're still single, I'm guessing you haven't experienced much of that yet."

Kevin grunted but said nothing.

Not long after, Susan McCutcheon nearly lost her voice. "Another one!" she called out, her pitch an octave higher. "There's another one on the other side!"

Stunned at finding two near-identical objects a short distance apart, Kevin wasted no time in picking up the mic and reporting the sighting of both targets to an increasingly worried Rob Smith.

* * *

When he wasn't piloting his airplane, Gary Nordhavn sold portable sawmills to local contractors or anyone else who sought to become a weekend lumberjack. At this unpleasant juncture of the flight, he decided he would rather be standing in a spruce forest splitting logs, than trying to land in a mini typhoon. He also convinced himself that his course of action was on par with what any smart pilot would do, especially with fellow aviators in trouble. *Besides*, thought Gary, *I stumbled upon them, and I expect full kudos for fishing them out.*

Flying over top of what appeared to be a visibly damaged late-model Cessna, Gary noticed two men by the fuselage, both standing with their arms flailing about. "Well, their alive," he noted calmly. "That's always a dang good thing." For now, Gary set aside his burning curiosity about what led to the crash. He needed to figure out how to set his own plane down in one piece, and then, opportunity permitting, focus on becoming the man of the hour. And with weather conditions imploding ridiculously fast around him, he knew he needed to be quick.

Figuring out his strategy, Gary noticed a snug tract of land near the downed plane, an area shorter than a football field and about half as wide. The patch of earth ran north-south, so he would benefit from headwinds on final, followed by an imperative short landing roll and quick stop. The topography also appeared to slope upwards, which for short field landings was his preference. Gary wondered if this crew tried for the same plot but missed. *Poor buggers,* he thought.

Not fond of a second near-death experience inside of ten minutes, Gary swung the plane around for the approach, only this time he performed the steep move correctly and at full power. Despite the sudden escalation of rain and wind, he kept his eyes riveted to the landing zone, while his brain calculated the odds of a missed approach, or if he'd even risk a second attempt. He fizzled on both accounts. Glancing at his airspeed, the needle showed fifty-four MPH, a cushion of sixteen over stall speed. *So far so good.*

A final check of power settings alleviated the incubating knot in Gary's belly. Satisfied with what he saw, his attention turned to the channels of rainwater scurrying up the windshield. He angled his head left and right to dodge the streams, but the effort became useless despite the prop-wash. He couldn't see squat.

Given the ruggedness of the terrain, the fact an open patch of dirt existed in the first place was a timely marvel. Pine trees covered everything, their bases rimmed by parcels of thick vegetation, fallen logs and rocks. Gary knew if he veered off the target, his chances of a go-around were slim to none. He toyed with skipping out altogether, reporting the Cessna and its occupants as soon as he was able, then focusing solely on his shipment when conditions improved. Remaining firm in his choice to stay the course, Gary tagged the right side of his face with an open palm as a reality check.

"And no mistakes this time," Gary reminded himself. "A quick flair, three wheels down, kill the throttle and flaps up fast." *Easy-peasy like a thousand times before. Last thing I need is ta maroon myself out here like them two.*

As prevailing winds flung him up and down in a sickening vertical dance, Gary discovered he needed little in the way of the rudder. Struggling to see over the front cowling of the Maule, each gust created a new control issue that required immediate correction. Setting engine mixture to rich and the prop to low pitch, high rpm, Gary eased off on the power and allowed gravity to work its magic. "C'mon you confounded thing," he pleaded. "Settle down before ya kill us both!"

Deliveries

As Gary stretched in his seat to offset ballooning tension in his body, his seatbelt buckle slipped under his shirt and pinched a fold of skin. He hollered out in pain and cussed, the sudden distraction happening at the worst possible time. And it wasn't letting go.

Needing relief and fast, Gary's right-hand came off the throttle to grab the clasp. As he struggled to loosen the belt, the airplane lifted sharply upwards just as his fingers contacted the latch. The buckle separated—the resulting click a horrifying confirmation of what he had just done. No longer secured to his seat, and with no chance to remove his other hand from the yoke and re-fasten the belt, he decidedly wedged his back into the seat and fortified his body position as best he could.

Closing in on his touchdown point, Gary thought of slamming the throttle forward and climbing back out, but poor visibility and now heavier rain dictated otherwise. Rocking side to side, the wingtips passed dangerously close to nearby pines. As he settled the Maule towards the ground, Gary's intense concentration caused his hands to shake. And with no possibility of retreat, he braced for what he knew would be a horribly rough landing.

* * *

Paul Jackson swept back his wet hair and then asked. "He can't be seriously trying to land here, can he? There's not enough room. He'll kill himself!"

"Remember I told you, Ace," Dave excitedly replied. "There's a patch of open land behind that treeline. Wish I had seen it last night because maybe I wouldn't have trashed your airplane as much. But if this guy's any good, it should be easy for him to set down there." Dave eyed the plane through the trees, its landing light popping in and out behind rows of timber. "And by the looks of it he's already on short final!"

Dave grabbed his crudely fashioned walking stick and hobbled in that direction through fresh waves of pain. Several feet away from the Cessna, he stopped and spun at the waist. "You coming?" he asked Paul.

Paul shook his head. "You go ahead. I'd never make it before he sets down, so I'll stay and guard the fort. And so should you with your ankle all messed up. He knows we're here, so I'm sure he'll come to us if he doesn't break every bone in his body first."

"Suit yourself," winced Dave. "With the weather tanking, I'd bet he doesn't have any choice but to land, and we've become a happenstance sideshow." Dave grinned. "Maybe I'll get to fly a Maule after all!"

"Just don't be flying off without me!" shouted Paul. "Or you don't get paid."

"So much for that plan!" smirked Dave. With that, Dave shuffled away toward the trees in remarkably quick fashion.

With his clothing soaked and stomach growling, Paul stayed under the airplane's wing. Despite waves of pain rippling through his body, his spirit filled with renewed hope that this nightmare might soon be over. Settling into the door frame for support, he gazed towards the trees, but could not see the Maule.

Then, he heard the unmistakable sound of an aircraft engine throttling to idle, the snapping of branches, followed by the slamming of landing gear into hard earth littered with vegetation and debris. The harmony of sound normally associated with a controlled bush plane touchdown was absent, and Paul figured that the pilot just experienced one of the worst landings of his flying career.

Not yet to the trees, Dave stopped and spun around. From his facial expression and the hand on his head, it was clear as mud to Paul that his co-pilot thought the same.

* * *

There were two screened-in tent awnings set up at Moger's Point, one to house folding tables, maps and mobile communications, the other to serve as a rest station and muster point or to grab food and a beverage as needed. Except for a bit of shielding from the rain, the structures did little to curb the brisk west wind transiting through the area.

Rob Smith planned for his briefing to take less than five minutes, quick and simple. But when he found himself staring into blank faces, not only of his rescue team, but also of those belonging to Diane and Kim Jackson, and a less than impressed Tess McMurray, he realized the error in his thinking. All three women huddled under a red-and-white-striped golf umbrella with coffees in hand.

To his right, Rob noticed the television camera pointed directly at him, the sun gun turned on at what he assumed was full intensity. Reporter Dwaine Ennis stood next to his videographer and extended a long-slender microphone forward to better record Rob's comments. Those smart enough to have packed umbrellas already had them deployed. The rest manoeuvred for a spot under nearby trees or their neighbour's canopies.

Only moments ago, Rob had ended his radio conversation with Kevin Davies. He still held the mobile receiver in his hands as he addressed the gathering. Thankfully, his back was to the wind. "I've got good news and bad news people. First off, thanks for setting up shop so quickly. I know the weather sucks, but we'll grin and bear it as we're trained to do."

"What's the good news?" someone shouted without letting Rob finish. Rob scanned faces but couldn't tell who had spoken. He adjusted the brim of his newly donned MG Car Club cap and spoke. "As I was about to say, the good news is that our search plane found two targets of interest where the Moose River splits and runs south. One object right near that junction, and the second not much farther downstream."

Laura Hastings repositioned her umbrella over Rob's head when a gust of wind skewed it sideways. "Was it airplane wreckage?" she asked.

Rob momentarily dismissed the question. "Can someone please bring me a coffee?" he asked. "And to think I don't even like coffee." He zipped up his raincoat to the top and flipped its less than adequate hood over his head. "We don't know yet what it is Laura," replied Rob. "Our crew topside is trying to get a closer look."

"What pray tell are we talking about then?" snapped Tess McMurray, her tone noticeably impatient. "Something big or small, a wing or tail? What exactly?"

Bolstered by Tess's direct question, Kim mustered her courage and asked in a surprisingly strong voice. "When will we know if it's from my dad's plane?"

Rob eyed the women and tried to choose his response carefully. He preferred to withhold details until certain of what they were dealing with, but then decided full disclosure was the best avenue to follow. "We're not sure at this point," he explained. "Both objects are the same colour and are apparently of similar size, which incidentally is quite small. What doesn't add up is that there aren't any hiking trails through that area, and the fact that one is resting in the lower branches of a tree on one side, and the other is farther south along the river's opposite bank, is well . . . very peculiar."

Frustrated, now it was Diane's turn to speak up. "That's it?" she asked. "No offence or pun intended, but I think we're barking up the wrong tree."

Someone chuckled.

Diane ignored their reaction. "I thought we were searching for a big shiny airplane, and more importantly, our husbands?"

"We are indeed searching for both," assured Rob patiently. "But we also scan for other clues that might relate to our main target, in this case, your husband's big shiny airplane as you described it. Our spotter reports anything out of the ordinary, so we need to keep an open mind to anything we stumble upon, especially when they're bright orange."

Tess staggered back slightly, her heart suddenly in her throat. "Did you say orange?" she asked, the shock in her voice catching everyone's attention.

"Yes," replied Rob. "That's what they told me. If you have anything you'd like to share, I'm all ears. Our success here depends on everyone's input."

Tess stared blankly at Rob, his face a mix of curiosity and interest.

"My husband," added Tess, her voice shaky. "He wears orange coveralls when he flies or drives his truck. It's sort of his fashion trademark."

"Coveralls?" asked Rob, his brain trying to fit the pieces together. "You're suggesting what our spotter found is related to his coveralls?"

"Not related to," corrected Tess. "But part of, like a sleeve or some part of the coverall itself. It's something Dave would have thought of doing. I know him. He's always thinking ahead if his neck is on the line." Tess glanced at Diane. "Or anyone else's neck for that matter. That's how he is." Tess felt all eyes on her, including the camera. She offered the cameraman an icy stare but did nothing to shoo him away.

"I know it sounds crazy," added Tess. "But I'm telling you Dave would have cut up his coveralls and thrown the pieces out the window, especially if he was in trouble or needed to leave a trail. Whenever someone razed him about the colour, he'd joke about using the fabric as marker beacons if he ever needed a rescue. Seems he was right all along."

Rob and those around him stood expressionless a few long seconds, each person's brain processing what their ears just heard. "Unbelievable," Rob finally said. "It would seem your husband is a very astute thinker, Mrs. McMurray. I'm amazed he had the time and forethought to leave behind a clue like that, especially in what I can only assume were very trying circumstances."

A smile formed on Tess's lips. "Well, he did his part, didn't he? Thanks to his ingenuity we know they headed south, so now I"—Tess looked at Kim and Diane—"we'd like to know your plan of action to get them back."

Rob seemed deep in thought, and when he failed to reply, Tess continued to offer her assessment. "If the clothing does belong to my husband, which is highly probable, then I hope your search plane is heading in that direction."

Rain dribbled off Rob's cap. "That's actually the bad news," he answered pensively. "My pilot says that poor visibility and strong winds are preventing them from venturing any farther down the south fork. He's—"

"So that's it?" Diane cut in angrily. "We just leave them out there? What if they're badly injured or even—" Diane couldn't bring herself to say what was really on her mind. Tears filled her eyes and she had to look away.

Anticipating this reaction, Rob walked over and placed his hand on Diane Jackson's shoulder. He spoke with as much compassion as he could muster. "We aren't walking away, Diane. May I call you that?"

Diane met Rob's eyes. "Yes, that's fine," she replied. "I'm sorry, but as you can imagine this whole ordeal has been a nightmare, and"—Diane couldn't help herself—"you still don't know the half of it."

Rob looked a bit surprised at the giveaway but chose not to push. "Okay, let me be clear," he stated reassuringly. "I personally assure you that we are staying right here. So as soon as the weather improves, we'll get the search plane back up. For now, we have no idea how far south your husband's plane is, or what side of the river they might be on, so we can't mobilize a ground team until we have more exact co-ordinates. According to our maps, there's an old logging road that runs alongside that south extension of the river and a bridge farther down that allows access to the other side. So, that's a big plus as long as the road is passable. Does that make sense?"

Diane nodded.

"Okay, good," added Rob. "We'll stick around and be ready. We've got thermoses full of soup and coffee, and I believe someone brought donuts and muffins with more on the way." Rob redirected his focus. "Everyone doublecheck your gear and radios. Make sure the quads are full of gas and ready to go. If possible, I want those pilots out of this bush by nightfall!"

Someone handed Rob a cup of coffee, which he gratefully accepted. He strolled towards the map table. Several of them were open and held down by a large rock on each corner. There was little to do now but wait for the search plane to check back in. Rob glanced over his shoulder at everyone who followed, the group consisting of media, pilots' wives and civilian help. Rolling his eyes, he regrettably felt like the pied piper, but without the benefit of a flute.

Chapter 26

Gary Nordhavn realized he had just upset a perfectly good record. Never before had he broken a bone. Frozen in place with his numbed body pressed sideways against the door, he glanced at his lap. He knew his unfastened seat belt had led to injuries, but now the question was to what extent and where. At present, he felt reasonably pain-free despite several hard body slams, but he also sensed his adrenaline-laced system was doing a fine job of concealing any physical trauma.

Trying to shift back to centre, Gary froze when his entire left shoulder region caught fire, the area nauseatingly looser than it should be. He tried to lift his arm and rotate his shoulder forward, but a sickening bone-on-bone grinding sensation escalated the sudden pain. Without inspecting any further, Gary knew he had broken something. Locking his body into place, he gently began at his toes and carefully flexed other extremities for wounds. Everything else seemed reasonably intact, a good thing considering the inharmonious landing.

Glancing out the front window, Gary noticed the prop no longer spinning. For the life of him, he could not remember shutting the engine down, but the fuel mixture knob was already out, and there was no one besides him in the cockpit. Foggy in the head, the grim knowledge that he just stranded himself began to settle in. *Be no rescuing today or fly in' back out,* he thought miserably. *Not in this condition.*

Gary snorted and craned his head skyward but far too quickly. He grimaced from the pain and again froze in place. Scared now to move, he tried to slow down his rapid breathing by watching the clouds drift overhead, the waterlogged blobs pinging steady rain off the fuselage. Usually calming to listen too, the wind buried most of the sound, its relentless blast rocking the airplane side to side as it howled through the airframe.

Gary's sobering mood suddenly reversed to laughter, the emotional shift snapping his brain to attention like a massive injection of espresso. He chuckled. "Ya made it down Nordhavn! You were stupid fer undoin' yer belt, but ya made it down." *Now, be a good pilot and power down the avionics and electronics.*

Reaching over very slowly with his right hand, Gary raised the flaps to neutral. He shut off the fuel and running lights, killed the master switch and ignition, and then leaned back in his seat with closed eyes. The whole dismal escapade flashed through his mind in vivid detail. He recalled the sudden downward jolt just before touchdown. It felt as if he'd been smitten from the sky by the hand of God himself. One second with the field lined up in a sloppy, haphazard descent, then a few heart-stopping seconds of free-fall as the effects of lift terminated.

Gary remembered lifting out of his seat, his head and shoulders slamming into the ceiling, and a snapping sound from somewhere in his upper body as unseen forces shoved him painfully back down and threw his untethered frame into the door. Glancing out his window, Gary noticed the left-wing entwined with an array of foliage. He could still hear the thwacking sound as the wing's leading edge sheared off rows of saplings.

Thankful the wheels settled after the first hard bounce; aggressive braking resulted in another body slam, this time forward into the dash. A heartbeat later, the airplane ground to a halt and everything fell eerily silent. Gary thought he'd seen a man dressed in orange emerge through the treeline before impact, but that image was hazy in his mind.

Gary recalled his wife's face and her troubled expression before his departure. Though Cindy rarely let on, he knew how much she fretted over his flying escapades, and that if he failed to arrive home by sundown, she vowed as always to contact local authorities, which he adamantly opposed.

"I'll always come back," Gary would argue. "No need to involve the police. What I do with my time is none of their business anyhow."

Cindy often questioned Gary's way of thinking and his refusal to validate her concerns did nothing to breed trust between them. But her husband always did come back, and she once again found herself conceding to his wishes while having to stuff down her apprehensions. And when asked about his reasons for such frequent trips, or the issue of excessive money in their savings account despite his modest salary and occasional sales commissions, Gary as always strategically circumvented the questions.

Notwithstanding a happy marriage, Gary knew his recent flying exploits resulted in red flags for his wife. But to this point, it remained imperative he let sleeping dogs lie. He believed the less she knew the better, and yet in light of the fact that he nearly killed himself just now, the nagging question in his mind was *How much longer can I stall the inevitable?*

Distant rumbles of thunder roused Gary back to the present. He craved a bottle of water more than anything, but how to retrieve one from the back seat was another challenge. Trying not to move his collarbone, he gently twisted at the waist and rotated his head. The cabin lay in shambles with fish fillets strewn about, and the cooler torn open like a paper bag. Ice, water bottles, his food stores—all of it scattered from the violent impact, then slammed back down.

One of the tackle boxes had also been ripped open. Fishing lures hung precariously at odd angles as their barbed hooks snagged seat fabric. "What a dang mess!" croaked Gary as he painfully grappled for a water bottle. "It's a wonder I don't have any hooks clawed into my hide!" *Though Lord knows I probably deserve it.*

When it proved too unbearable to move, Gary gave up on the water and gingerly rotated back around to face the front. In that moment he nearly jumped from his skin, the sudden jolt sending shots of white-hot fire from his collarbone to the receptors in his brain. He screamed once from the pain and a second time when he noticed someone peering through his side-door window; a big man soaked to the bone and wrapped head to toe in orange sleeveless coveralls. The stranger's face contorted into a smart-alecky wide grin; his mouth flapping words that Gary found impossible to understand through the closed cockpit door.

Taken aback, Gary watched as the man's hand reached for the latch and the door popped open. "You all right in there?" he yelled over the wind howling through the exposed cockpit. "Heck of a landing bud! Never seen anything like it!"

Dave spotted the mess inside the plane, and ogled the scrambled water bottles and chocolate bars. He decided to temporarily forgo his cravings. "Name's Dave, Dave McMurray! And you are?"

Rendered speechless by the man's sudden appearance, Gary completely lost his train of thought. The door whipped open farther, followed by the insertion of a beefy right hand. Nervous to move, Gary stared at it but purposely slighted the gesture.

Dave dropped his hand. "Boy, are we ever glad you stumbled upon us!" he gabbed excitedly. "We were thinking the Calvary was never going to arrive, though you weren't exactly who we expected. Took guts for you to land here, but I'm guessing in addition to your rousing curiosity over us, the weather forced you down? Am I right?"

Gary nodded. "Yeah," he responded guardedly; his eyes wide. "I saw yer plane and decided I better land before the weather got any—"

"Say," interrupted Dave. "Would you mind sharing your provisions? And might I say your cockpit looks like my cattle liner's interior, except my rig doesn't reek of fish, if you catch my drift!"

Gary was not warming up to this man's cheeky behavior. "I'm aware of how my plane smells," he answered coldly. "I'm a fisherman and"—Gary stopped with the realization that he owed this fellow nothing in the way of an explanation. He suddenly shivered and shrank back in his seat—"I think my collarbone's busted, and I'd prefer not to move right now if it's all the same ta you."

Rain blowing in through the open door stung Gary in the face. He tried to wipe it aside but gave up. "I'm Gary . . . Nordhavn," he announced with some hesitation. "I'd hoped ta pick you fellas up and"—another jolt stabbed his upper shoulder—"how 'bout ya close my door and climb in the other side. I'm gettin' chilled. While you're at it, grab us both water and a candy bar."

Dave did not need to be asked twice. He forcibly closed Gary's door, painfully moved to the other side and tore open the passenger door. "Appreciate the offer!"

Dave's splinted ankle and walking stick did not go unnoticed by Gary. "Your landing must've been pretty rough too by the looks of it."

Being careful not to bump his ankle as he side-saddled his way in, Dave reached into the back of the plane for water and candy bars. "Yup," he replied. "We hit pretty hard. Royally messed up my ankle. Pretty sure it's broken too with how much it's swelled up. The pain's been off the charts."

"That I can relate too," grunted Gary. "Seems this here patch of ground is bad luck fer airplanes and pilots. But we're alive, so that's sumthin'."

"That we are. And I'm not typically one to sit idly by waiting for the cavalry to show up, so I try to get stuff done through the pain. But I did too much and tripped up. Passed out like a boxer in a first-round knockout."

Dave handed Gary a bottle of water and a Mr. Big chocolate bar. In an instant, Dave guzzled his entire bottle and all but inhaled his candy bar like it was a tiny breath mint.

A twisted smile appeared on Gary's lips. "Enjoyed that did ya?" he asked while sipping from his own bottle. "I saw you when I first flew over. So, where's the other guy you were with? He hurt too?"

Dave licked chocolate off his fingers. "He stayed back at the Cessna. And yes, he's got a few battle scars. Can't move very fast either, but I'm thinking he'd give both legs for some water and a chocolate bar. We've been stuck here since last night and"—Dave tried to sugarcoat the truth—"It was a rushed trip, and we didn't pack our usual mountain provisions."

"What happened?" asked Gary with lop-sided eyebrows. "Engine trouble?"

Dave's face turned a shade red. "Yup, guess you could say that. We were on a cargo run to Spruce Creek. We planned to gas up there and head right back to Owensville. But we arrived later than planned and couldn't set down because the field lights never came on. Then, we flamed out before I could set us down with the engine running." Dave pointed back towards the Cessna. "That airplane is cursed!"

"What's yer cargo?" asked Gary. "Isn't there a bike park there now?"

"Yup," Dave replied. "We were hauling a load of television gear for a charity broadcast. It should have been a cakewalk, but Murphy's Law intervened and stung us on the hindquarters like we deserved."

Gary jerked a bit and started to feel more comfortable with the man in his airplane. "So, how'd ya end up way down here? Owensville's east, not south. Your ELT turned on?"

"ELT's on, but it's not transmitting. It's a long story. Maybe hang back and I'll go check on the third member of our wounded pilots' club. I know he'll appreciate the food and water." Dave glanced at the sky. "With the looks of the weather, we might be stuck out here for a while yet, so there'll be ample time to share our grievous tale of senselessness."

"So, nobody but me knows you guys are here?" asked Gary cautiously.

Dave eased himself out of the plane. "Nope, you're it as far as I know. The hilarious irony of all this is that your airplane seems perfectly fine, but with you injured too, none of us are in any shape to fly it back out once conditions improve."

Dave grabbed another water bottle and two more candy bars. "I'll see if I can find something to sling your arm and shoulder. What'd you slam into if you don't mind me asking?"

"The roof, then the door," explained Gary. "My seatbelt come undone right before I landed. Dang thing was pinching so bad that when I tried loosening it off, it let go altogether and I couldn't fasten it back up. Was a stupid mistake on my part."

"Well, you're in good company then," affirmed Dave. "I'll be back shortly if I don't fall again and pass out first."

Gary watched Dave exit the plane and eventually work his way through a small opening in the trees. With his heart racing, he fumbled under his seat for the pouch he installed when he first took delivery of the airplane. "There ya are," he drawled. Gary's right index finger traced a path across a checkered grip, then along the cold steel slide and barrel, and finally to the trigger. He inhaled deeply, his body shivering. The tactile sensation provided a peculiar sense of relief that no matter how things played out from this point on, he retained a few aces in the deck. But the relic Colt 45 calibre pistol wasn't specifically what he was searching for.

Leaning forwards a bit more, Gary recovered a tiny fabric tote bag about half the size of a pop can. He untied the strings with his teeth as a layer of sweat appeared on his face. Reaching inside, his fingers brushed across the serrated lid of a prescription-sized plastic bottle, its contents rattling inside as he shook it gently. Satisfied, he nervously closed the bag and re-stashed it as pain erupted from his now swollen collarbone. With turtle-like speed, Gary sat back in his seat and tried to ignore the discomfort. *Last delivery, Nordhavn. . . . Last delivery.*

* * *

Jack Ward stood at the end of a wooden dock, the floating platform bobbing up and down in the choppy surf. Despite the growing warmth of the morning sun, a chilly breeze off the lake caused him to shiver. Farther out, a thin blanket of fog floated across the top of the water. Behind him, waves lapped into the shoreline in close succession, the soothing noise creating a peaceful ambiance when mixed with squeaky chairlift pulleys, hoots and hollers from early morning riders, and nearby waterfowl. The atmosphere lulled Jack into a reflective mood.

Glancing left, Jack focused on a shallow cove tucked in behind a grove of birch trees. In what seemed a past life, Tranquility Bay, as he named it years ago, was a favourite place to paddle his yellow fibreglass canoe. Mildred always sat on a cushion, low to the hull with her body facing towards Jack. He loved to chauffeur her around the bay, its shallow waters loaded with fallen logs and old root systems. He couldn't help but smile at the memory of those special times together.

Biting his lip, Jack felt ashamed at how he'd allowed many of the enjoyable pursuits in his life to get cast aside by things he once considered more important. A ball of emotion welled in his throat as he thought about life's unpredictability and the notion that if he didn't look after himself, he could end up in a senior home sooner than later, or worse yet, six feet under. *Time you start smelling the roses, old boy, and thank the good Lord above for your blessings.*

To his right, cheering erupted near the bottom of the main downhill course. Turning towards the sound, Jack watched with interest as Matt Hawley roared across the finish line, performed an expert wheelie and locked his wheels. Huge clouds of dust kicked up, causing some spectators to turn away, while others held fast until the dirt settled, then swarmed in congratulating their hero and, maybe if lucky enough, scarf an autograph.

Grateful the rain held off, Jack looked at the sky and frowned. If stormy conditions returned, the chair lift would be shut down for safety's sake, and so would the cash flow to his operating account. He snickered at his ongoing bad luck but quickly shrugged off the notion as inconsequential in the grand scheme of things. *Of all the weekends to plan a live TV show, it had to be this one.* "What did I do to deserve this, Mil?" he asked himself grudgingly.

"What did you do to deserve what?" asked Tom Sullivan from behind.

Jack recoiled from the unexpected voice. "Sheesh, Tom! You purposely trying to give me a heart attack? What's the big idea sneaking up like that on an old man?"

"Sorry *old* boy. We saw you standing out here all alone and thought you could use some company."

"Who's we?" grumbled Jack. "And who says I need rescuing?"

Tom pointed over his shoulder towards the van. "I've got Dylan in the jump seat. Wondered if you might want to tackle the landing light issue before we get clobbered by rain and whatever else is festering up there."

Jack glanced to the right. The lodge van sat under a nearby canopy of trees, the passenger door open with Dylan's legs dangling over the side. He waved enthusiastically, then dropped his arm when Jack didn't respond.

Jack reluctantly waved back. "Can't believe I never heard you pull up. Mildred always said I was going deaf, and you apparently just proved it."

"Well, Jack, since you were talking to yourself, we decided it was time to help deliver you from the apparent demons within."

"Gee, thanks," replied Jack, who then promptly changed the subject. "Any word on the airplane and crew? I haven't been near

Deliveries

a television or made any attempt to get hold of Diane Jackson. Some family friend I am."

Tom rested his hand on Jack's shoulder. "You're still being too hard on yourself. Might I remind you it wasn't your fault? The pilot didn't have enough fuel, end of story. And you don't control the weather either. As far as the landing lights go, it was simply bad luck. You never anticipated them not turning on. If you had, I know you'd have been out there days ago to fix them. I know you, Jack. That's how you roll."

Appreciating Tom's attempt at shifting blame, Jack wasn't entirely convinced. Sure, Tom's points were valid, and Jack needed to keep reminding himself he wasn't to blame for the poor choices of others. *Easier said than done.* "You're skirting around my question, Tom. What about the plane? And any word on your missing TV truck?"

Tom's eyes followed a flock of gulls, the streamlined birds drifting over the lake just inches above the surface. "Funny you should ask," he replied. "I just called back to the station. So far it doesn't sound like the plane has been found. There is a news crew covering the rescue efforts at Moger's Point, and yes, our waylaid news truck just returned to the station. They gave up with the road being closed."

Jack spun around and headed towards the van. "Any good news," he asked.

"That last bit was the good news," added Tom. "One mystery solved. And it won't do you any good to call Diane Jackson."

"Why not?" asked Jack.

"I found out that both pilots' wives are with the search and rescue teams at Moger's Point, including Diane's daughter."

Jack thought of Kim. "Poor kid must be scared spitless over her dad."

Tom climbed into the driver's seat. "You're close to her, Jack, aren't you? I remember you telling me she was like an adopted granddaughter to you and Mildred."

Jack reached for the passenger door latch, popped it open and climbed in.

"Yup," he replied. "Though after this fiasco, she may not want anything to do with me once she finds out about my part in her dad going missing, if she hasn't already."

Ignoring Jack's self-condemnation, Tom fastened his seat belt. "Let's go fix up those lights, Jack. I think we both could use the diversion."

"Humph," snorted Jack. "I wish I had some way to go back and reverse this whole bloody mess."

Tom started the van and roughly shifted the transmission from park to drive. "Let's start with the lights, shall we? Then we can focus on inventing you a way to time travel."

* * *

Matt Hawley had just autographed an 8x10 glossy photo of himself careening down a pebbly near-vertical incline when he noticed the lodge van parked near the lakeshore. He passed the print to a pimply-faced teenager. "Here you go, kid," he rattled off distractedly. "Thanks for coming to watch."

Several more fans assembled around Matt like he was a movie star, which technically in the world of mountain biking, he was. Perched on his bike for an impromptu autograph session and photo op, Matt understood that personal marketing was everything. He always made time for people, whether he felt like it or not. Someone to his left thrust a bike helmet into his face and a sharpie marker. "Hey, would you please sign this helmet?" asked an attractive middle-aged woman. "It's for my grandson, Hayden."

But this time Matt Hawley's focus turned elsewhere. Politely ignoring the request, he noticed the white van starting to pull away. Without offering any kind of warning to those around him, he broke from the pack and peddled away as if he'd been propelled from a slingshot. "Sorry everyone," he yelled over his shoulder. "I'll be back in a bit! Duty calls!"

"How rude!" he heard the woman catcall behind him.

Peddling as though his life depended on it, Matt bounced furiously along the uneven ground and was immediately grateful for the recent upgrade to his suspension. "Hey, wait up!" he shouted while shifting gears as he recklessly gained on the slower moving vehicle.

Through the open side door of the van, Dylan had been watching as Matt Hawley signed autographs for his entourage. But he was unaware that his celebrity biker friend had also been watching him, especially when the van drove away. Bouncing along on the road leading to the airstrip, Dylan casually glanced out the back windows. It was then he noticed Matt racing towards them as fast as his legs would go, his right arm waving frantically. At first, Dylan thought his friend was simply goofing around, but then realized that Matt was actually in hot pursuit and trying feverishly to flag them down.

Dylan suddenly whipped the side door open. "Stop the van, Dad!" he yelled. "We've got company!"

Matt was less than a stone's throw from the rear of the vehicle when it ground to a sudden halt. Not expecting the move, and being a touch slow with his reflexes, he nearly ploughed into the back doors. He squeezed the brakes in time to avoid the impact, but his rear tire slid out to the side and Matt's kinetic energy threw him partly over the top of the frame in the opposite direction. He expertly hoisted his right foot off the pedal and planted his shoe into the dirt to counter his roll rate. Several small rocks impacted the rear of the van, followed a moment later by a splattering of loose muddy soil.

Matt climbed off his bike and watched as Dylan exited the van and walked over. "Emergency braking lesson is over!" Matt boasted triumphantly. "I hope you were all paying attention!"

"Are you insane?" asked Dylan. "You could have broken your neck!"

Matt smiled broadly. "Why yes, my young Padawan, I believe I am insane!"

"What the blazes is going on back there?" hollered Jack while trying to undo his seat belt. "No wonder my blood pressure spikes every time I'm around you people!"

Amused by Jack's temperament, Tom casually glanced over in Jack's direction. "Try to relax, Jack, and go with the flow."

"Well, the flow came to a sudden stop and I dang near wet my pants," objected Jack. "What's up with these darn kids anyway?"

"They're spontaneous, Jack," reflected Tom. "You should know that by now, given that your bike park is full of them!"

Jack continued to grumble as he leaned back in his seat. "Yeah, what was I ever thinking?" he griped.

Dylan and Matt walked to the open side door, the two once again sparring with biking related jargon that Jack didn't understand.

"If you guys had told me the plan," squabbled Matt. "I wouldn't have had to chase you down! And what's with the sudden stop? I nearly ruptured my spleen just now!"

"I thought you were racing for a while longer," added Dylan. "I saw you signing autographs, so figured your legion of fans came first anyway."

"I am still racing," replied Matt. "But I'm not scheduled again for another two hours, so I've got time to help you guys with the lights. And besides, some fans tend to get a bit demanding. So, when I saw you guys drive away for the airfield, it was the perfect excuse for me to escape."

Dylan's facial expression registered surprise. "How'd you know that's what we were going to do?"

"Are you kidding me?" replied Matt. "I watched you all climb into the van and I knew right away. There's only one road leading to the airstrip, and you guys were on it." Matt made eye contact with Jack and smiled. When the gesture wasn't returned, he continued bellyaching to Dylan. "After the adventure we endured last night, I can't believe you'd even consider shutting me out for round two."

Dylan seized the opportunity and scrunched his face. "Truth is, Dad and Jack needed someone along this time who could actually be of some help."

Matt rolled his eyes and hoisted his bike with one arm. "Well, here I am!"

Dylan snickered. "Ha, very funny!"

"Besides," assured Matt as he lifted the bike into the van. "You guys won't have any luck fixing those lights without me because I'm your good luck charm!"

Dylan groaned. "See, Dad," he cringed. "We should have left sooner like I said. Now we're doomed to failure by Mr. Ego here."

Jack sounded off with something unintelligible as Matt climbed aboard. Moments later, the van rounded a sharp corner and disappeared through rows of pine and poplars, its shocks and struts squeaking noisily.

Jack Ward sighed loudly. "One for all, and all for one," he chanted pessimistically. "The biker boys' gang is at it again."

Beside him, Tom nodded in agreement and couldn't suppress another smile.

* * *

Kevin Davies spoke slowly into his microphone so there would be no misconstruing his intentions. "We're at the end of our rope, Susan. We need to bail now if we want to get back to Owensville in one piece."

Regardless of abnormally calm winds and a spattering of rain, thick grey clouds drooped low all around the Piper Cub. Kevin's main bone of contention was the rapid decrease in visibility, and whether they could escape while there was still a chance. As a result, he'd descended to 300 feet where hazy VFR conditions remained. To the south, gradient curtains of rain filled the sky, the unearthly sight appearing to Kevin as more like a portal to another dimension than a mountain shower.

Convinced the missing Cessna was along this smaller valley corridor, Susan felt reluctant to call off the search but knew better than to argue. "All right," she finally conceded. "Can you store our co-ordinates into the GPS? That way, we'll know where to resume when we come back later."

Kevin increased the throttle and began a breakneck right turn. "Already done," he replied. "There's not much room to flip around here, so hang on." Kevin glanced to the north as the Cub's nose came around. What he saw sent chills down his spine. Layers of rain and dense cloud slid down mountain slopes towards them like they were drawn in by a huge vacuum. He searched for an opening and a way to escape, but there wasn't one.

Kevin levelled the wings and kicked in opposite rudder to counter a sudden kick-in-the-behind crosswind. "We've got hells gate to the south and Niagara Falls to the north Susan. And north is where I had hoped to go."

"You're not very good at sugar-coating doomsday scenarios for the sake of your passenger, are you, Kevin? Now what?"

Kevin knew strong winds preceded an approaching front, and with no easy retreat, the only option on the table was to stay below the clouds, hug the river low and slow, then punch holes through whatever cloud got in the way.

"Snug up your seat belt," ordered Kevin. "And because I know you're a praying woman, we could use some of that too. Things are about to get bumpy!"

* * *

Paul Jackson popped the last bite of chocolate bar into his mouth, followed by a half bottle chaser of water. It might well have been filet mignon and the finest of wine because the taste was exquisite. "I never thought I'd see the day when you actually stripped off your coveralls," he admitted to Dave. "I'm relieved you have clothes on under there!"

"Well, enjoy it," replied Dave. "Because offing my coveralls only happens in emergency situations."

In one hand Dave held his pocketknife; in the other, his sopping wet coveralls. "Give me a hand here will ya?" he asked. "I need to make a sling for our new roomie. That guy isn't flying out of here any time soon, which means neither are we. His plane is fine from what I can see. A few tree scuffs and small dents on the leading edges of the wing but otherwise intact. He's lucky to have survived that landing because the crazy fool wasn't strapped in! Darn near cartwheeled his plane, and he has a broken collarbone to prove it."

Paul held the coveralls by the neck with his body leaned against the engine cowling for stability. "Wasn't wearing his seat belt?" he asked.

"Nope," replied Dave. "He said he accidentally unlatched it right before landing and didn't have time to refasten it. Something about the buckle pinching his skin. And we thought our luck was bad. I'm starting to think this valley has strong ties to the Bermuda Triangle."

In one fluid motion, Dave sliced the fabric open along the seams. A few quick slashes of the blade left a relatively symmetrical square of cloth. "There," he proudly announced. "Just like filleting a trout! This should work for a sling just fine."

"Pretty impressive," agreed Paul. "Though when have you ever filleted a trout? I know you don't fish, and I'm nervous when I see a knife in your hand. What scares me even more is that you have no idea you almost stabbed me just now."

"Baloney," argued Dave. "I'm an expert with a knife, especially when I'm carving a slab of tenderloin!"

Paul chugged the last of the water from his bottle and smacked his lips.

"I could sure use one more of these. Remind me to buy that guy a steak dinner once we get out of here."

"Yup," agreed Dave. "Though he can get in line behind me. I get first dibs on that, remember? But you're right, it's lucky he found us and is willing to share his rations."

Dave wrung out the fabric and loosely folded it. "I'll head back to the Maule and get his arm patched. You want to try walking over?"

Paul slipped back under the wing to escape from the rain. "If we're stuck here for another night, then I might as well be social. So yeah, I'll try to shuffle over." Paul sneezed twice in a row. "You sure seem like you're moving faster now," he observed. "I take it your ankle isn't as painful thanks to my superbly crafted splint?"

"Hurts like the dickens. I'm just trying to ignore the pain. Figure that since it's already swollen the size of a grapefruit, how can I make it any worse?" Dave paused. "Wait, don't answer that, Ace."

"I just wish this stupid rain would stop. I feel like a drenched rat and I've got the chills. Not what my body needs."

"Be careful what you wish for. If the rain quits, then the bugs come out. Personally, I'll stick with the rain and a few body shakes for now." Dave glanced at the sky. "I just hope it stays as rain and that we don't get a full-on hail-producing thunderstorm."

Paul thought for a moment. "Though I don't like to admit it, I suppose you do have a point about the bugs."

Dave began to walk away. "Don't I always? This guy claims he's a weekend fisherman, but he seems awfully nervous for a guy who lives that kind of life. But on the plus side, he's got several fillets in and around what's left of his cooler. He'll for sure have matches or a lighter, so maybe we can start a fire and have ourselves a fish fry."

"There likely isn't a dry piece of wood around here," observed Paul. "But seeing as our ELT is toast, a fire would be ideal to signal our whereabouts and help dry us out at the same time. If we could just get one—"

Dave stopped in his tracks. "What did you just say?"

"About what? I said there's no dry wood to—"

"No . . . no!" blurted Dave. "I mean about the ELT and a great way to signal."

"That's what I was trying to say," explained Paul. "We have no ELT, but a fire would be—"

Dave clapped the side of his head. "Stupid! Stupid! Stupid!"

Paul seemed even more confused. "Are you, okay?"

"You're a genius, Ace! I was so focused on food and drink that my brain locked up. Something so completely obvious, and we missed it!"

"What on earth are you talking about?"

"The Maule. It's got an ELT! We can activate its transmitter if the thing didn't trigger itself already with that rough landing."

Before Paul responded, Dave was already on the move as fast as his good foot could carry him. Paul couldn't believe his agility, especially with a bad ankle. "Do you realize how insane you are? If you fall on that again, I'm not coming to rescue you this time."

"No pain, no gain," countered Dave without looking back.

Under Paul's feet, the ground lay clotted with globs of mud and expanding puddles. He turned up his collar, not that it helped. Stepping out from under the Cessna's wing, Paul yelled at Dave. "Hey, wait for me!"

Dave wasn't slowing his pace to the Maule. In no time flat, he left a befuddled Paul Jackson standing in a mound of slop but with a hopeful smile on his face, nonetheless.

Chapter 27

"Is that tape on the wing going to hold?" asked an antsy Susan McCutcheon. "All this rain can't be good for the sticky side holding it down."

"It'll be fine," replied Kevin tersely. "Even if it rips away, it's not like the wing will come off. Quit worrying about it. You just need to make sure your seat belt is snug."

"You already said that multiple times," Susan snapped back. Nonetheless, she reached for the latch and drew it tight for the umpteenth time. "It's snug, but my heart's in my throat! What's our game plan again?"

To survive, Kevin wanted to say. Instead, he offered a pat answer: "To get us back in one piece for starters. We'll head back up the valley the way we came in. Once we hit the main river and assuming the weather doesn't get any worse, we'll head east to Owensville and get this thing on the ground. We might be hugging the river, just to give you a heads-up."

Susan tilted her head, her eyes settling on the quagmire of ugly weather directly ahead. The Cub really bumped around now, and she knew the turbulence would increase the farther they flew towards it. "And if it does get worse?" she asked nervously. "Then what?"

"Then, we go to Plan B," assured Kevin, his voice edgy. *If, in fact, I had a Plan B.* "Let's try not to think about it. We'll stay below the cloud deck as much as possible. I'll get us home, Susan. You can trust me."

Susan appreciated Kevin's air of confidence but sensed her pilot was as anxious about their safety as she was. "I'm sorry I insisted that we keep on searching. We should have left the valley like you suggested right after reporting the ground targets."

"What's done, is done. Yes, we should have left before the weather closed in, but we were just doing what we trained to do. Listen, Susan, I've got my hands pretty full up here, so I might go quiet for a bit. Just breathe deep and try to relax."

"Not like I can do much else. You're the pilot. I'm just along for the ride."

Kevin backed off a bit on the throttle. "Once the rain picks up, we'll likely get tossed around even more. Hopefully it's short-lived, and we'll break into clearer conditions on the other side."

Inhaling deeply, Susan closed her eyes. "Unless I'm throwing up down the back of your shirt, I'll be quiet. I'll just say one more thing and it's a desperate bribe on my part. You get us out of here, and I'll buy you a gift card for anywhere you like."

"I'll take that bribe!" agreed Kevin enthusiastically. "How much cash we talking about? There's a vintage Omega aviator's watch I've been eyeing at Ostrander's Jewelry that's less than 200—"

"Just fly, Kevin," ordered Susan. "Before I change my mind."

Kevin reefed on the stick and the plane tilted down sharply. "Yes, Ma'am."

* * *

From inside the Maule, Gary watched as Dave slowly made his way back. In his hands was a scrap of orange fabric, and Gary could tell from the look on his face that the big man was in a great deal of pain. Stopping every few moments to rest, Dave glanced towards the plane, raised his makeshift sling so Gary could see it, and then kept moving forward.

Sitting motionless in his seat, Gary pondered his dilemma. *Bad weather and an unscheduled, no-choice landing. The Maule in the middle of nowhere and a broken collarbone. Plus, an unsuccessful delivery.* The more he thought about it, the more he rationalized that his circumstances were forcing his hand. It was decision time.

Gary watched as Dave approached. He'd be at the plane in less than two minutes, so he decided to use that short window to ponder his options. Four thousand bucks every month, and a generous fuel allowance for the plane was not easy to pass up. He loved providing Cindy with a life he couldn't otherwise afford. Plus, he'd been promised his involvement would be kept hush-hush by those responsible when the operation eventually changed venues, and it would.

Considering himself as nothing more than a coerced aerial pawn, the idea of ratting these people out wasn't on Gary's to-do list. He was smart enough to know that if he talked, he'd be just as quickly implicated and arrested. Missing today's drop within the appointed time could result in threats against his personal safety. This had happened on one previous occasion by way of a scathing telephone call but was never followed through because Gary quickly rectified his delivery roadblock within an extended grace period. He hoped to do the same this time, but in light of his hapless physical state, he hadn't a clue how.

With the clock ticking, a boatload of manure would soon pass through the fan if he didn't figure things out, and fast. And now because of escalating worries that his business dealings could come to light with these outsiders, he felt a sudden rage boil up from deep under his skin. It felt like hundreds of mini volcanoes oozing from his pores. Sweat popped on his face as though he'd been sprayed with a fine mist.

In a heartbeat, Gary's mood soured. He openly berated himself for trying to help these men in the first place. "Too bad ya screwed up a good thing, Nordhavn!" he bellowed. "You should've kept goin' and made the deposit. No fuss, no muss!" Incensed, Gary kicked his feet against the rudder pedals and his broken bone caught fire from the jolt. Locked in place, he inwardly struggled to control his emotions before his company arrived. He placed his fingers against his injury and felt the bulge along his collar, the sensation nauseating.

Now only steps from the plane, Dave again hoisted the swatch of fabric, his face etched with both pain and determination. Unsure of how to act and scared of being found out, Gary watched Dave round the front corner of the Maule. It was then he reached under his seat with his hands shaking. *Could this man be trusted?* he wondered. "Time ta find out."

The turf underneath the Maule resembled a mini marshland as exposed grass became less and less. All around, the valley lay concealed under chunky low-lying clouds, the imposing formations drifting by lazily. Wet, exhausted, and in more pain than he cared to admit, Dave McMurray inched his way around to the passenger side of the Maule. He ducked under the wing where the sudden absence of rain felt like a ray of sunshine. Splatters of mud covered his clothing and work boots, some dollops reaching up to his chest.

Bracing his shoulder against the wing strut, Dave reached for the door latch and kept his eyes aimed towards his feet. He popped the door open and side saddled his way into the cockpit without paying attention to Gary. "I brought you a little something to sling your arm," he announced proudly. "This should help to keep your shoulder from being jolted around." Dave erupted into a full-face smile. "Everyone teases me about my coveralls, but in fact, they're like a Swiss army knife and have all kinds of uses if—"

What little colour remaining in Dave's face suddenly drained away. Peering straight ahead, Gary made no attempt to look over at Dave or acknowledge his presence. Stone-faced and sweaty, the man just sat there with his left hand flipping a transparent plastic container topsy-turvy as its contents slid end to end. In his other hand Dave saw the handgun, its barrel pointed away, but hugely disturbing, nonetheless.

Dave's first instinct was to flee, but he wondered how far he'd get before a bullet drilled him in the back, if that was even Gary's intent. Despite a sudden flood of adrenaline rushing through his system, something told him to hold fast, that this man wasn't an immediate threat. Dave found his voice without taking his eyes off the gun. "Are those, diamonds?" he slowly asked while trying to hide his fear. "Because that sure is what they look like from my perspective."

Figuring he'd be dead already if Gary meant him harm, Dave watched as Gary's fingers patted the gun like it was a cat. His ashen facial features showed no hint of movement. Dave stared at the weapon and his curiosity suddenly overruled his loose tongue, "And what's with your little black friend there?" he asked nervously. "I can't imagine you use that for fishing?"

The bottle flipped end over end one more time and stopped dead. Gary continued to stare straight ahead, his body rigid. Several intolerable seconds ticked by and Dave feared his lippy attitude would get him shot. He decided his best move was to back out of the plane as discreetly as possible while Gary lingered in whatever sort of freaky trance he was in.

As he began to swing his legs back out the door, Dave noticed Gary's sweat covered head twist mechanically in his direction. *Busted.* Gary's dilated pupils sent heebie-jeebies through Dave's body. Shuddering, Dave found himself remarkably calm on the inside. "You, you okay man?" he asked. "Look, I have no idea what's going on here, and I'm not sure I even want to know. But can we lose the gun? Those things make me really, really nervous."

Without saying a word, Gary slowly passed the bottle to Dave who reluctantly accepted the disturbing hand-off. His eyes wandered between the gun and the container he now possessed. Gary placed the firearm on the dash and rested both his hands on the control yoke, his casual mannerisms indifferent to the seriousness of the real-world scenario playing out around him.

Gary pointed to the bottle. "That there," he blandly explained, "is the object of my confession. And now that I got yer attention, you'll hear me out." Gary's hands began to shake as though frostbite was settling in.

Dave's mind raced. *I've had two grown men confess their sins to me in the past day. Tess was right; I should've become a pastor instead of a trucker.* Trying to conceal his intent, Dave scanned the instrument panel, his eyes searching for the ELT. "I'm all ears," he stammered. "Though like I said, I'd listen better if you put that gun somewhere else."

Gary pulled his right hand from the yoke and grabbed the pistol by its grip, careful not to place a finger near the trigger. "Sorry," he nervously replied. "I've never even fired the thing. They just gave it ta me and said it was fer protecting what's in your hands there. Told 'em I didn't want it, but they insisted." Gary painfully tucked the firearm back under his seat. His hand came up to his very tender collarbone and stayed there.

Dave's fingers gently cradled the bottle of diamonds like it was a small and very sensitive explosive device. "They?" he asked hesitantly. "Who's they, if you don't mind me asking?"

Gary looked down, his hand rising to meet his face. He had no idea where to start. "Don't know," he admitted. "All I know is that I pick up that bottle once a month from an old hunting cabin at Morris Landing. It's a tiny lake not far from where I live and hangar my plane." Cringing, Gary realized he was saying too much, but now it was too late to stop. *Damage done.*

"Can't say I've heard of it," stated Dave, his eyes drifting from the instrument panel to Gary and back to the panel. *Where's the ELT in this thing?* "How come I've never seen your plane before at Owensville Airport? Your bird needs fuel and maintenance like anybody else."

Gary looked at him briefly, ignored the question and continued. "They always leave an envelope of cash as a deposit 'til the delivery's done."

Gary couldn't stifle the vomit of words. "I fly the bottle to a vacated farm airstrip east of Owensville. There's always a car in the barn with keys under the grill. I drive into town to the post office . . ."

As Dave listened, he realized he was caught up in a yarn he wanted no part of. *Paul's going to croak when hears about this.* Dave just wanted to go home, back to his wife and to something normal. Even his smelly, manure encrusted cattle liner would be a better place than here. He scanned the tree line for Paul. Thankfully no sign of him yet. Dave turned his attention back to the outwardly troubled man beside him.

"… and from there," Gary explained, "the bottle goes into a post office box which I have a key for. That's it. That's what I know. Pretty crazy, huh?"

Dave wasn't sure how to respond. This was something off a movie screen, not from real life, and certainly not something normally divulged to a stranger smack dab in the middle of nowhere. For Dave, the events of the past day were surreal enough, and now this. *I'm talking to a real diamond smuggler, or at least the delivery boy.* Dave shook his head while trying to make sense of his ongoing misfortunes. *Maybe time to get back to church,* he resolutely decided. *The Lord indeed works in mysterious ways to get one's attention.*

"Ya don't believe me, do you?" asked Gary. "That's okay. I don't believe it myself sometimes, but it's dang true. All of it. Now I'm stuck here, and that there bottle's gonna be late for delivery." Gary scrunched his face from another shot of pain. "This'll sound crazy," he grimaced. "But I've been lookin' fer a way out, something ta force my hand. Maybe finding you guys is the push I needed."

Realizing his mouth hung open, Dave closed it but said nothing.

"Twas easy money. I was on the verge of losing my business." Gary's eyes moistened. "These people are very convincing, and I couldn't say no. Don't reckon you'd understand none."

Dave was about to respond when he noticed movement through the trees.

Gary suddenly lashed out, "I'm as good as dead!"

Dave jumped at the man's sudden outburst. To his horror, he noticed Paul sluggishly working his way towards the plane, completely unaware that anything was remiss. Paul waved briefly in Dave's direction and then turned his attention back to his shuffling feet.

No, Ace! Go back! Dave wanted to shout.

As Gary kept talking, Dave's mind wandered. His ears picked up only snippets—something now about being hunted down if he went to the police. Dave tried to empathize, but he failed in any way to relate to the man's absurd dilemma.

Dave stealthily continued to scan for the ELT. The instrument panel layout was old school. One glimpse of the tarnished knobs, splotchy dials and oval-shaped control yokes, and anyone could tell the airplane had incurred a butt load of tumultuous log-book hours. Even with a few chipped steam gauges and its general over-the-hill condition, Dave thought the aircraft a beautiful piece of craftsmanship for its time.

"Yer trying ta find the ELT aren't ya?" asked Gary stone-faced. "It's what I'd be doing if I was in yer shoes."

Taken by surprise, Dave sat back. "I, ah . . . was curious if it triggered when you hit the ground so hard. That could be our ticket out of here. Then maybe you can go to the police and tell them everything you just told—"

"There"—Gary pointed—"the hole beside the transponder. That's where the ELT was."

Dave's blood ran cold. He reached up and traced his fingers along the edge of the small rectangular gap. "Was?" he asked dumbfounded. "You can't fly into controlled airspace without one, so where's yours?" he boldly asked.

Dave kept his eyes on Paul who was now less than fifty paces from the plane. He continued to plod along, baby-stepping the cluttered terrain under his feet. Dave nervously smiled and thought he looked like Tim Conway's "old man" character from the classic Carol Burnett Show.

Dave suddenly clued in as to why he had never seen this plane before. He locked eyes with Gary. "You don't want to be found, do you? Even if you crash or shoot a forced approach like you did here, you want to stay off the grid." Dave's wheels were spinning. "You're ordered to be invisible. Is that it?"

Gary closed his eyes. "It's delivery day," he announced through clenched teeth. "It's not that I don't have an ELT. But on delivery day it comes out." Unable to find a body position where he wasn't in considerable pain, Gary wriggled in his seat. "Ya guessed right. Their orders, not mine."

Flabbergasted, Dave knew his mouth had dropped open again. He stared at Gary for a few long seconds before passing the diamonds back. Gary accepted the handoff, gingerly placed both hands over his face and began to moan like a cooped-up animal.

* * *

As dreadful a situation as Susan McCutcheon found herself in, there was little she could do from the backseat except to hold on and trust her pilot. Not unaccustomed to harsh flight conditions, this search ranked at the top of her list for all-out misery.

Up front, Kevin shifted left and right, his shoulders rising and falling as he battled with the plane. The Cub's lightweight construction was no match for the menacing conditions outside. Feeling the full effects of roll, pitch and yaw, Susan felt her stomach churn as Kevin countered the onslaught with quick aggressive movements of stick and rudder.

As the Cub slipped between masses of ugly grey clouds, Susan tried to focus her eyes on something at ground level, anything that might help squash her nausea. But it seemed their visual reference to the ground eroded exponentially the farther up the valley they flew. As quickly as she locked her eyes to a solid object, it disappeared from view. A sudden bump caused Susan to cry out, the scream tripping her voice-activated microphone and filtering straight to Kevin's ears.

"You okay, Susan?" asked Kevin distractedly.

Gathering her composure, Susan chose her response carefully. "I trust you, Kevin, and I'm fine. Just fly like I know you can."

Like a child being told they could accomplish anything in life if they worked hard and believed in themselves, Susan's vote of confidence boosted Kevin's inner resolve. Despite his own escalating fear, he found himself smiling. Gripping the stick hard with his right hand, Kevin swung his left arm over his shoulder, his fingers stretched out. Susan's fingers found Kevin's hand, and she squeezed for a moment, then let go.

"Thanks, Susan," Kevin replied. "Appreciate it."

Kevin checked the GPS. They were almost to the Moose River. *East or West?* Kevin leaned forward, his eyes searching for the path of least resistance in a sky ballooning with anger and discord. To the right, a slightly clearer patch of sky beckoned towards Owensville. Left towards Spruce Creek appeared as a wall of murky sludge, and in Kevin's opinion, no place for a featherweight Piper Cub and rookie mountain pilot. Whichever way they chose to go, Kevin hoped it wouldn't be any worse than the broiling mess surrounding them now.

* * *

When Paul got closer to the Maule, Dave hobbled out, closed the door and waited. Unsure how to tell his friend what he just learned; his mind raced. This whole botched mess had compounded into a zany escapade of human-induced hogwash, and in Dave's mind, an absolute disregard for common sense. Paul ground to a halt ten feet short of the Maule, his breathing shallow.

He bent over and placed his hands on his knees, then with great hardship, raised his chin to look at Dave. "So, what's the . . . word?" he panted. "You get his arm in a sling? Or did you both just sit around and eat chocolate bars without me?"

"I wish everything were that simple, Ace," whispered Dave.

"What about the ELT?" Paul asked hopefully. "Is it broadcasting?"

Dave wagged his head, looked towards Gary whose face stayed buried in his hands, then back to Paul. "He doesn't have it installed. Apparently, it's"—Dave's face contorted—"delivery day."

Paul's face warped into a dopey grimace at what he just heard. "It's what? What on earth are you talking about?"

Dave leaned in and placed his hand on Paul's shoulder for emphasis. "I'd tell you to sit down for this, Ace, but seeing as we're short on recliners around here, I'll lay it out straight."

Paul tilted his head sideways like a puppy trying to understand. "Lay what out straight? I don't under—"

"Zip it and listen up. The guy sitting in that plane is hauling diamonds! He's packing a handgun, and he's supposedly in a heap of trouble if he doesn't deliver them today. He says he wants to quit but doesn't know if he—"

Paul swiped Dave's hand away. "I'm not in the mood, Dave, for one of your bull stories, so you can knock it off right now and tell me the—"

Dave stood his ground and stared Paul down, his eyes wide open and intently focused.

Paul tilted his head and felt his legs weaken. "Oh, dear God," he gasped. "You're telling the truth, aren't you? He's actually hauling diamonds, as in bootleg black-market?" Paul's body sagged a few inches like he was on the verge of collapse, not to mention unbridled shock.

Dave reached out offering support, but Paul waved him off. "I'm okay," he lied.

"I'm telling the truth and nothing but the truth," assured Dave. "And yes, he's packing diamonds. Well, technically he's the delivery system. But the good news is I don't think he means us any harm. He, for whatever reason, told me his story and showed me the stones. Without a doubt, the guy's messed up in his thinking but said he wants to come clean. He put away the gun when I told him it wigged me out."

"And he's confessing this all because why?" Paul asked sarcastically. "So, let me get this straight. You're telling me we've been rescued by a gun-toting diamond smuggler?" Paul glanced at the Maule. "This cannot be happening! I must be in an alternate universe because what you just told me is nothing short of absurd!"

Wiping rain off his face with both hands, Paul turned around and shuffled forward, his feet slopping through a small river of mud and tall grass. Dave made no attempt to stop him, nor did he know what else to say. He watched as Paul approached the Maule, half expecting his friend to collapse from the sheer folly of all that occurred since leaving Owensville the night before.

"What's the plan here, Ace?" asked Dave.

Paul stopped suddenly and turned around. "Ever watch tag-team wrestling when you were a kid?"

Not sure he heard right, Dave simply replied, "Pardon me?"

Paul knew they were being closely watched by the man seated inside the Maule. "Wrestling," he replied. "There's always two guys. One in the ring, one ready to spell him off behind the ropes. Sometimes both are on the mat at the same time, working together to win the match."

Dave thought Paul had snapped. "You feeling all right, Ace? What's tag-team wrestling got to do with anything here?"

"You said you always wanted to fly a Maule," Paul out-and-out stated. "Am I right?"

Dave nodded in confusion.

"Like you," explained Paul. "I'm sick of being stuck here. With both ELTs not working, my guess is that no one else is coming for us any time soon, so if the guy in that perfectly good airplane can't fly us back out, then we will!" Paul allowed a moment for that sink in before he continued. "I don't care what this guy is involved in or what his transgressions are. Lord only knows I'm on a similar playing field as him. With that said, I think we all deserve a second chance, don't you think?"

Dave gnawed on the inside of his cheek, the wheels in his head spinning.

Paul looked at the sky before heading towards the pilot's side door. "I'll go introduce myself to our diamond smuggler. And as soon as this ungodly weather clears out, we tag team. You're on the stick, I'm on the rudder. Our new friend here can coach us from the backseat if he doesn't shoot us first."

Dumbstruck by Paul's impromptu speech and game plan, Dave noticed a crazy smile play across Paul's lips. *He really has lost his mind!*

"I'll go tell him the good news," Paul announced. "I'm sure he'll be ecstatic and will be happy to lend his airplane to our insanely noble cause."

From inside his plane, Gary Nordhavn watched the verbal exchange between the two men. Except for garbled voices meshed with rain and wind, he had no idea what their conversation entailed. He wanted out of his plane to stretch his legs but was scared to try because of his collarbone.

Realizing now how foolish he was to spill the beans; Gary felt a resounding sense of dread well up. The diamonds required delivery—not tomorrow, but today. And his window of time was closing. Gary knew he couldn't fly himself out of this mess and with these men now aware of his secret, he had no choice but to accept whatever came next. Deciding they needed him as much as he needed them, Gary hoped they wouldn't rat him out. Only time would tell if he needed to convince them otherwise.

As Gary watched the other man approach his door, he stuffed the diamonds back under his seat and pondered how to play this out. With his thoughts in turmoil, and a battle raging between his good-guy, bad-guy conscience, he intentionally improvised a smile as his door popped open a moment later.

"My name's Paul Jackson, and I hear we have a lot in common."

Chapter 28

Standing outside on either side of the doorway, Dylan Sullivan and Matt Hawley peered into the generator shack, their faces a mask of anticipation.

Waiting for the racket he knew would come, Dylan wedged both index finger into his ears. Matt wasted little time in calling him a wimp, but his slight went unheard. From the previous night's rain, the grass under their shoes remained wet and spongy, and both men tried to shift to a dryer spot but gave up.

Tom Sullivan stood at the ready beside the power lever. Puddles of muddy rainwater blotted the concrete floor from a mass of small leaks dripping from pooled water on the roof's topside corrugated surface.

Nobody was more surprised than Jack Ward when the generator started up on the first attempt, its engine piercing the stillness and startling a family of partridges nearby. Pleasantly surprised, Jack allowed himself to bask in this small personal victory, a definitive plus amid the endless pit of big, fat negatives.

Though generally considering himself a handyman, electrical issues weren't Jack's specialty, and he wasn't overly familiar with this lighting configuration. Updated years ago by a friend, and though not complicated, the fact remained that somewhere along the line, electricity wasn't getting through. Jack realized the odds of finding the problem were slim to none, but for the time being, he had nothing better to occupy his time.

This time Tom came prepared. He brought a small toolbox from the storage shed behind the lodge, the badly dented container full of screwdrivers, a pen-sized voltage tester, electrical tape, a wire cutter and several small spools of insulated wire. A bag of loose connectors lay strewn in the bottom.

While the generator clattered away, Jack grabbed the toolbox off a nearby table and headed for the open door, nearly colliding with Dylan and Matt on the way out. A few feet past the door frame, he stopped suddenly, spun and issued the order. "Let's give it a go, Tom! No time like the present!"

Snapping up the lever, Tom wanted nothing more than for the lights to miraculously appear, that whatever gremlin plagued their circuitry last evening would magically repair itself, saving them a heap of aggravation now. Stepping towards the door, Tom looked out across the airfield. *Figures. No lights. Just the beacon.*

Jack shrugged his head and shoulders in disappointment before shuffling towards the junction box for further inspection. Tom and his two cohorts followed closely behind. "Do you think he'll find the problem, Dad?" asked Dylan in a raised voice. Tom squeezed his son's shoulder. "I hope he does because that man deserves a break in more ways than one."

* * *

Rob Smith released the transmit button on the portable-base-station radio. For the last few minutes, he'd been trying to reach the Piper Cub, but all he received back was hissing. Beginning to worry, he knew the real challenge would be keeping his face from showing it. As search co-ordinator, the last thing he wanted to do was dump his own insecurities on people who were already restless and looking to him for decisive leadership.

Almost everyone at Moger's Point sought refuge in their cars to escape from the rain, warm up, and wait for something definitive to happen. This included the missing pilots' wives and the increasingly tenacious television crew. Increasingly fed up, Rob finally asked reporter Dwaine Ennis to quit harassing people for off-the-cuff interviews and to direct all future questions only to him. So, with no added footage or interviews for his story, the newshound and his videographer also abandoned ship and retreated to their news cruiser.

Directly behind him, Rob heard twigs snapping under approaching feet. Instead of turning around, he kept his eyes down and his index finger pinned to an open terrain map splayed on a wobbly folding-table. Someone brushed against his left shoulder.

"Did you need a fresh refill on your coffee?" asked Laura Hastings.

Rob turned and handed over his paper cup. "Sure," he replied appreciatively. "That'd be great, thanks."

Laura tipped the cup and dumped out its now cold contents.

"Just black," added Rob. "And a few ounces of Baileys."

Laura clicked her heels and spun, "Aye, aye, chief," she answered. "Now I just have to hunt down a thermos of hot coffee, if there's any left. And the Baileys, which I'd venture to say that someone here actually has."

Rob snickered. "I wouldn't doubt that. Seems like coffee is about all we're hunting for now. Without a positive ID on the Cessna, we're nothing more than a troop of boy scouts and girl guides camping in the woods."

Laura walked back towards her mentor and kept her voice quiet. "I take it there's no word from the Cub?"

Rocking on his heels, Rob rolled up the map and tucked it into a plastic sleeve. "In all likelihood, they're trying to get back to Owensville until the weather improves. Moger's Point is along their flight path, so that should put them right on top of us and back within communication range. Hopefully, then we can find out what's going on up there." Rob looked at Laura and frowned. "Knowing how unpredictable the weather is through here, I never should have let them go. I assumed they'd be in and out, that we'd have a fix on the Cessna by now and be on our way. Between you and me, Laura, I just want this one over with, but with a positive outcome for everyone involved."

"There's always a catch with these searches," noted Laura. "That was your advice to me when I first signed up. You also told me I needed to prepare for anything. You've drilled that into all of our heads, so that's exactly what we're doing. Sometimes all we can do is standby mode."

Laura pointed at the base radio when she saw Rob staring at it. "I bet that thing crackles to life soon enough and you're back in touch with them."

Though not as certain, Rob put on his best game face. "Hope you're right."

Laura nodded. "I'm always right! We're exactly where we should be, and everyone is ready to go, thanks to you."

Rob smiled. "Is this one of those times when the student lectures the teacher?"

"I just don't want you coming down on yourself for a situation that's beyond your control," explained Laura. "I'm sure Susan and Kevin are fine."

"What eats away at me," confessed Rob, "is that we've got a downed plane out there somewhere and can't search for it because of the weather."

"The weather changes quickly in the mountains," reminded Laura. "We just need to be patient and wait for a break. Then, we're back in the game."

Rain trickled off Rob's brim. He removed his cap and shook off the excess water. "Yes, it can. I just hope it changes to our advantage before it's too late for today."

Not sure what else to say, Laura spotted someone nearby clutching a thermos possessively. "I'll get you that coffee, boss. Listen, Rob," she added, "I know it's easier said than done but try not to worry. My mom always told me that worrying won't add a single day to your life."

Rob grabbed another map and unrolled it on the table. "Thanks for the wisdom, Laura, but it's not my life I'm worried about."

* * *

Of the twenty cars in the parking lot at Moger's Point, most were occupied, their inhabitants enjoying the comforts of warmth and cushioned seats over the ongoing wrath of the currently less than ideal wilderness setting. From Tess McMurray's vantage point over the dash of her SUV, the tops of awnings set up as part of the S and R base of operations were barely visible from the lower elevation parking lot. Diane Jackson occupied the front passenger seat, while Kim stewed in the back, miffed that her cell phone was utterly useless from lack of signal.

With the engine running, Tess adjusted the heater control to provide a steady trickle of warmth through the vents, but the inside windows were fogging up. "Sorry girls," she apologized. "But we need to switch to defrost for a minute." Tess rotated the control knob and the glass began to clear.

Diane drew a face on her side window and pressed her thumb to the glass to form a nose. "I hate sitting around like this, Tessa," she remarked. "And what drives me around the bend is that everyone here is acting like this is nothing more than a practice exercise. Do these people care that lives are at stake?"

Tess looked across to her friend. "I'm not taking sides, Diane, but in their defence, the weather's the bad guy here. If it wasn't for that, then I'm guessing they'd already have a fix on the guys and be underway. Like everyone else, I'm hoping it improves enough for the search to continue."

"So, what do *we* do? I honestly don't think my nerves can take much more of this. It's the uncertainty of not knowing that Dave and Paul are okay that makes this so horrible. And with Paul's heart issue, I'm even more worried now." Diane clenched her fist and smeared over her window art. "This messy ordeal should not be happening, Tess!"

Tess could not disagree with Diane's thinking. With a little common sense, this whole situation may have been prevented. Now everyone here at Moger's Point was nothing more than a string puppet, all bowing to the whims of unpredictable mountain weather and circumstances beyond their control. Like her friend, Tess felt entirely helpless and sitting around doing nothing did little to bolster an already low sense of moral.

"Well," replied Tess, "the way I see it we can do one of two things. We can stay and wait around, or we leave for a while. Maybe go back home, grab some food and come back. I don't know about you two, but I'm going to need a decent bathroom pretty soon that doesn't have a splintered wood seat."

Kim chuckled, but then decided a bathroom was a very good idea. "I'm kinda with Tess, Mom. Besides, I'm getting hungry and my phone doesn't work here."

Diane flipped her head around. "This from the girl who told me she wanted to be on the front lines for finding her dad."

"I do, Mom," assured Kim. "But it seems pretty obvious that nothing's going to happen until the weather clears. We might as well do what Tess said and come back when—"

A sudden "tap-tap-tap" on the driver's side window startled the three women and rudely ended their conversation. Crouched low and with a hilariously small umbrella perched over his massive head and shoulders, reporter Dwaine Ennis peered in through Tess's window. Tess recoiled, straightaway despising the man's pompous grin. Once her heart found its rhythm again, she dropped the window an inch. That's all she was giving him. "What?"

"I'm sorry to disturb you ladies," Dwaine apologized. "And I didn't mean to frighten you, but—"

"But what?" barked Tess from behind the glass. "Do you always go around rapping your knuckles on car windows? You nearly gave us a heart attack! What's the deal with you anyway?"

Tess looked around for the cameraman, certain the weasel was close by trying to grab candid camera footage.

"I'm really sorry," admitted Dwaine. "I just wanted to tell you that we're going back into Owensville to file our story, or what we have so far. It's more an update really, seeing as there isn't much happening here."

"You got that right," agreed Tess. "So why are you telling us?" she asked. "You're a big boy, or do you still need permission for everything you do?"

"I was trying to be courteous," clarified Dwaine. "We'll come back later and see what's happening. But in the meantime, I wondered if you needed anything? Perhaps food, drinks, or maybe fresh coffees?"

The window dropped a few inches as Tess's defensive attitude softened. "We appreciate the offer, but we're fine. As a matter of fact, we toyed with the idea of leaving here ourselves. And you're right about nothing happening. It seems the weather's shut down any hope of finding our husbands any time soon."

Dwaine took a step back. "Okay then, drive safely. But if there's anything I can do to help move things along here, don't hesitate to ask." The big man reached into his jacket, procured a business card and passed it through the window. "I know I come across as overbearing, but it's typically how I roll to get the story told. I don't mean any disrespect."

Tess, Diane and Kim all watched as the reporter turned away. It was the first time Tess had seen him without a microphone cemented to his hand. She glanced sideways at Diane, then at Kim through the rearview mirror. Tess rolled her window down the rest of the way. "Mr. Ennis," she yelled, "wait for a moment, if you don't mind."

Dwaine stopped, planted his feet and spun at the waist. "Yes?" he replied curiously, the blank look on his face as deadpan as they come.

"Before you go, there is actually one little thing."

"And . . . what might that be?"

A resolute look appeared on Tess's face as she leaned out her window. "I'm ready now for that interview."

Unsure he heard correctly, Dwaine asked for clarification. "You, you want to be interviewed? As in right now? In the rain? What about might I ask? And why the sudden change of heart?"

Tess smiled. "Just round up your camera minion and I'll give you a talking head for your story before you go. You did say you were light on content, did you not?"

Stumbling over his feet, Dwaine nodded and scurried away to retrieve his cameraman. "I'll be back in a flash!"

"Tessa!" objected Diane. "What on earth are you doing?"

"It's fine," Tess offered reassuringly. "The rescue people here need some motivation. They've found Dave's sleeves and yet won't go out to look, even by ground. They've got quads, but don't use them. So, I think it's high time we light a fire and apply some public pressure."

Diane sat back in her seat. "I don't know if that's a good idea, Tess. He reminds me of a greasy used car salesman and—"

Tess put her hand on Diane's arm. "It'll be fine girlfriend, you'll see. If we want our men found before dark, we need to get the ball rolling. If we don't advocate for them and ourselves, who will?"

"But how?" asked Diane. "I don't see how an interview with that man is going to accomplish anything."

Tess smiled. "I bet there are a thousand people in Owensville who own quads or dirt bikes," she answered decisively. "And I bet that each one of them would be willing to help three women in distress. I'm giving them a reason to get off the couch and do something meaningful with their otherwise mundane lives."

Diane's face softened. "You are truly unequalled Tess, and the more time I spend with you, the more I value our friendship. Admittedly, it's how you get things done that really scares me sometimes."

Deliveries

* * *

In its heyday, the Spruce Creek airstrip helped transport guests back and forth from Owensville and outlying areas. Smaller bush planes proved the perfect size for navigating the 1,100-foot grass runway, usually with enough room to spare if a pilot misjudged his takeoff or landing roll.

When the rugged landscape was first cleared for an airstrip, runway lights were unnecessary because all incoming and outgoing flights occurred during daylight hours. As customer demand grew, and charter pilots wanted to expand their hours of operation, the lodge owner thought it beneficial to add modest strip lighting along both sides of the field to aid with identification.

To decrease costs, eight 100-foot lengths of green socket line were acquired, the cables similar to what might be used for a perimeter or Christmas lights around personal property. Each socket held a clear-white seven-watt bulb, each row of lights staked into the ground with tent pegs and lengthened as straight as possible. Connected with heavy gauge extension cords, the snug rows of lights created a crude, yet effective way of visually assisting pilots with initial side to side runway orientation. Some pilots referred to the arrangement as a poor man's localizer.

On his knees and bent uncomfortably at the waist, Jack Ward checked the male-female plug ends between strands of lights to make sure connections were solid. The entire set-up was routed through a three-pole safety switch and then looped into the generator bellowing over his shoulder from inside the shed. So far, diagnosing the issue was non-productive.

Tom Sullivan walked up from behind. "Any luck, Jack? I've checked every connection point on the other side, and things are good. There are several sockets where bulbs are missing or broken. But other than that, it all looks okay to my untrained eye."

"I haven't found anything here either," replied Jack irritably. "It's just a repeat of last night. I don't have the foggiest idea what's wrong."

Jack hoisted himself up and walked towards the next connection point. "I'll check these last few plugs. Then I'll inspect the main cables from the generator to where the lighting begins."

Tom followed behind Jack and stopped suddenly. "Let me take a look at that for you, Jack. Maybe there's an exposed or broken wire somewhere along the main cable."

Jack turned his head side to side. "Where on earth are those boys? I thought they were here to help out."

Tom pointed towards the van. "They're inspecting Matt's bike. Funny how when there's work to do, they conveniently find somewhere else to be."

"Humph. Must be nice to not have a care in the world."

"Boys will be boys. I'll be back in a few minutes. Yell if you find anything."

"I'm sure you'd be the first to find out. I don't think those kids would hear me yelling if a pack of wild boars was on my tail."

Tom chuckled and walked away. He glanced up and watched as puffy white clouds swirled about, their growing mass not yet enough to block out the sun. *Not yet anyway,* he thought. From the west, haphazard wind gusts ripped across the open field from Bayshore Lake. The water's surface gurgled with sudsy waves that grew in size farther out.

The extension cables running from the shed to the runway lights appeared relatively new, or so Jack said. Tom didn't expect to find any issues, and the last thing he wanted to do was crawl through the wet grass. He chose to start his inspection at the lights and then backtrack to the generator. As he walked the length of the cable, he glanced at the van and observed Dylan and Matt heading back towards the shed. He waved to get their attention, but his gesture went unnoticed. "You're right, Jack. It must be nice to not have a care in the world."

***

Precariously low to the south branch of the river, the Piper Cub flitted about like a moth struggling for control in a pestilent wind. Rolling side to side, the plane trudged ahead, its occupants desperate to plant their feet on solid ground. Strewn with rows of angry-looking clouds, the narrow valley rose on both sides of the river, the ragged slopes kissing the tree line and disappearing from view as the elevation increased. With little choice but to stay below the cloud deck, Kevin Davies worried that a sudden blast of wind could smack them into the water. Now at 100 feet, he struggled to neutralize the oscillating fluctuations in altitude.

Accustomed to flying with one hand on the stick and the other nursing the throttle, Kevin wrapped both hands around the control for added peace of mind. His calf muscles were beginning to cramp from dogged use of the rudder, and the injury to his thigh burned something fierce. He tried to ignore the physical discomforts and fog lingering in his head from his so-called concussion, the latter concern he would not be admitting to any time soon. "How are you holding up back there, Susan?" he asked.

Trying hard to overlook how close they were to the water, Susan McCutcheon held on to the edges of her seat for dear life. She thought Kevin's ability to stay over the river and away from rows of pines along the riverbanks was admirable, and she tried to sound upbeat. "I'm trying to remind myself why I signed up for search and rescue in the first place."

Beginning to question his own sanity and the reasons he wanted this flight so badly, Kevin related to Susan's plight. He wished that Susan held a pilot's licence, so she could spell him off and allow his aching body to rest. But clearly this wasn't the time to give her another flying lesson.

In back, Susan noticed the stick jostling about as Kevin stubbornly refused to turn over control of the plane to the elements. "You're doing a good job up there," she offered encouragingly. "Glad it's not me flying this little—"

The Cub suddenly jolted to the left. Susan's right knee drifted towards the top edge of the stick, and when Kevin jerked it the opposite direction, it whacked her painfully. "Ouch!" she screamed.

"Sorry!" yelled Kevin. "I felt that bump. That was your leg?"

"My fault," countered Susan. "I'm struggling to keep my knees clear with all this bumping around. I feel like a rag doll."

Kevin apologized again. "I'm so sorry, but don't worry. You can't hurt anything back there. I'm more concerned about hurting you."

"I'm fine, Kevin," lied Susan. "Just get us home."

In the next few minutes, a sliver of calmer air offered a merciful reprieve from the turbulent air battering the Cub. In stark contrast, proliferate nooses of cloud soldered their grip, further boxing them in. Feeling helpless, Susan again took solace in the comfort of a simple prayer. Inexplicably, she felt protected and wanted to tell Kevin that they'd be okay. But to avoid any further pilot distraction, she held her tongue.

Kevin glanced at the GPS where the screen showed the Moose River just coming into view. At the T-intersection, a decision would have to be made. Either east to Owensville or carve a path west to Spruce Creek—a place Kevin had neither been to nor landed at. Door number one aligned them with Moger's Point and communications with ground ops, plus a paved runway at Owensville. Door number two would be a gamble pure and simple. Kevin hated basing his decisions on a knee-jerk reaction, but it seemed he had little choice.

Early in his flight training, Kevin knew that one day he'd be thrust into a situation like this, but he always hoped it wouldn't be so soon in his career. *Trial by fire, amigo*, he reminded himself. *The best way to learn.*

"We're almost back to the main river," announced Kevin. "Let's take a look both ways, and we can decide together which road to take. I'm partial to Owensville because I've never actually landed at Spruce Creek."

"Owensville is my preference too. But I'll take anything as long as we can land. I just want out of this thing, and I keep fighting off twinges of nausea. I'm not sure how much more my stomach can take."

"Barf bag is under your seat. And if this turbulence doesn't soon let up, I might need one too."

Reaching down beside his left knee, Kevin tried to adjust the trim to counter the extreme pitching of the Cub's nose, but his efforts made little difference. And due to stronger headwinds, he needed to push the engine hard at ninety percent power as opposed to the usual cruise setting of seventy-five. The airplane offered no complaint, so Kevin left things as is to hasten their retreat.

Susan watched the clouds whip past the wingtips. At such a low altitude, the ground sped by disturbingly fast. Fighting the urge to close her eyes, she instead leaned forward and tipped her head to the side to look out the front window. Forward visibility was negligible, and with steady rain, she wondered if any direction on the compass would allow them safe passage.

As they approached the Moose River junction, Kevin peeked to the west and down into the main valley. The river blended into a wall of cloudy mush about a mile away, the blobs rising vertically from the river's surface before towering out of sight. He glanced east towards Owensville, and though less obstructed, the sight caused equal trepidation. In that instant, Kevin made up his mind. "I vote east. I think Owensville is our best option." A second look down the west valley solidified his decision.

Susan wasn't about to offer a counterargument, not this time. "Fine by me," she concurred. "Go for it."

"I'll try checking in with home base once were closer to Moger's Point," added Kevin. But this time he never received a reply; Susan was too busy reaching for the air sickness bag under her seat.

* * *

About to step away from the generator shed and offer their help to Jack, Dylan stopped a moment to cup his hand under a steady drip from the ceiling.

For a bit of sport, he began flicking water in Matt's direction, and in doing so, he stumbled on a chunk of uplifted concrete, lost his balance and slipped towards the generator. His right foot caught an extension cable and snapped the plug from one of the generator's sockets, which in actuality was the plug for the runway lights, a slightly cracked plug end that harboured a loose wire inside and resulted in a short that nobody knew about.

"Way to go, klutz," kidded Matt. "That's what you get for trying to get me wet. Instant justice!"

Dylan pulled himself upright, reached for the extension cable plug and hollered back. "Did you see which outlet this went into, or does it matter?"

Matt raised both arms. "I think the middle, but I'm not sure. You better pop it back into one of them quickly before Jack realizes you just cut the power."

"The lights aren't on anyway," replied Dylan. "So, he wouldn't even know."

"Well, genius," needled Matt. "They can't troubleshoot the runway lights with a dead line. Jack says he needs a live current, so he can test each socket. Just pick a spot and plug it back in."

"Yeah, yeah," sassed Dylan while taking note of the available sockets. "I don't think it matters either. They all look the same."

"Shake a leg!" scolded Matt. "It's time we made ourselves useful out there."

On the front side of the generator, there were three vertical panels, each containing a pair of dual outlets. Of the six spots available, the left panel was already filled with plugs from the beacon and a rusty drill on the floor nearby. The others were empty. Glancing at Matt, Dylan subconsciously wiggled the end of the plug and opted for the right side. He rammed the prongs into the bottom receptacle and stood back up. "There," he shouted over the noise of the generator. "All fixed and no harm done. And no thanks to you."

But Matt wasn't paying Dylan an iota of attention. Instead, he stood transfixed in the doorway, frozen in place as if hypnotized.

"What's wrong with you?" asked Dylan condescendingly.

Matt offered Dylan an over the shoulder glance. "Dang!" was all he said in way of a reply.

"You look like you've just seen a ghost," mocked Dylan. "But then you always look like that!"

Not saying a word, Matt pointed outside.

Dylan angled himself closer to the door, his eyes following Matt's hand towards the airfield. "Double-dang!" he spit out. "Please tell me I just did that."

* * *

At that same time, Jack Ward crouched on his knees by one of several unlit bulbs. He twisted the lamp to check its connectivity when suddenly the entire row of lights flickered to life. Jack fell backwards into the grass from the unexpected shock. Not believing what his eyes confirmed, he blinked several times to ward off the idea he might be dreaming. "They're on!" he gasped. *But how?*

Jack glanced down the row, then he watched as the lights on the opposite side of the field blinked to life a second later. Dumbfounded, he noticed Tom nearby and couldn't suppress a chuckle as the man stood with his arms raised in what could be construed as a victory pose.

Rising to his feet, and with a smile reaching both ears, Jack turned around to find Dylan Sullivan and Matt Hawley a few steps behind, both wearing equally silly grins. Jack eyed them both warily, and from their smug expressions, he suspected they had something to do with the now lit-up field. He backed up and fist-bumped them both on the shoulders. "Talk to me boys," he happily ordered, "because I'm all ears!"

Chapter 29

Sitting in the rear seat of his airplane felt extremely odd to Gary Nordhavn. He'd slept in the back on occasion but never occupied the space as an ill-fated passenger. Gary relished being alone in the cockpit with no dependency on others to get him to where he needed to go. He viewed the Maule as both a source of revenue and a place of sanctuary—the win-win combination allowing him the freedom to pick and choose his fishing exploits. But since deciding to ferry diamonds, he knowingly relinquished a sizable chunk of that privilege. And now as a result of his own poor decisions, his life rested in the hands of the men he so naively tried to help.

Personally, Gary thought their scheme bordered on reckless, a half-baked plan based solely on desperation to escape their circumstances. The thought of two injured pilots trying to finesse an unfamiliar aircraft out of a tiny clearing was, in Gary's opinion, madness. He realized, however, that by not lowering his pride and accepting help, his troubles would escalate. And even if he felt he deserved it, the last thing Gary wanted was ridicule and finger-pointing.

What surprised him though, was how a simple confession could ease his burden of guilt, and yet, could these men be trusted with his secret? Gary thought not. Whether genuine in their intent to help, or playing him for a fool, Gary wouldn't know until this scenario played itself out. Now simply a matter of when and where, he knew the police would eventually enter the picture once his business dealings came to light.

Feeling suddenly angry, Gary's mood darkened, and his chest felt heavy. He envisioned himself being grilled by the local authorities, and when Cindy learned of his misdeeds, he believed she would be inclined to shoot first and ask questions later. Gary wouldn't blame her. He wondered if letting these men fly off without him might be a safer bet, and yet the idea of being left alone was even less appealing. Gary tried to calm himself back down before his rage intensified beyond his ability to control it.

Up front, Dave McMurray busied himself from the left seat. With one hand on the yoke and the other holding the checklist, he ran through the start-up procedures. Except for switches and knobs in different places, Dave thought it pretty straight forward. Even so, in regard to the intricacies of the Maule's engine and power management, he would rely on Gary for advice.

A bone-chilling whine suddenly erupted from the backseat. Dave jumped and swung his head around. "You okay, man?" he asked. "Listen, I know you're hurting, but you can't be doing that when we take off. I'm already on edge with this cockamamie plan."

Gary sat stone-faced with his head rolling side to side. He made no attempt to respond, which left Dave feeling extremely ill at ease.

Continuing to work through the checklist, Dave watched as the yoke shifted back and forth, causing the plane to shudder. He pulled his hand away to not interfere with the control's movement. The column moved again and then stopped. Dave peeked over his shoulder and noticed Paul at the rear of the plane, carefully inspecting the tail as part of the preflight check. He watched as Paul checked the vertical stabilizer, no doubt making certain the connection points were secure by moving the rudder side to side.

What Dave required now was accurate information on weight and fuel, critical details he could not get without Gary's input. "What's the empty weight of this bird?" he asked despite the man's strange behaviour.

Gary replied immediately. "By the book, 'bout twelve-fifty empty. Why you askin'?"

Surprised by Gary's question, especially from a pilot, Dave tapped the fuel gauges. "And how much gas is in the tanks with the dials at three-quarters?"

Frustrated with not being answered, Gary huffed before slapping the side of his head. "Thirty gallons, give or take. Enough questions. I got a killer migraine."

Dave missed Gary's head slap. "That's about 200 pounds. I'd ballpark our combined weight at 475. We've not much room to get off the ground here, and I'm concerned about clearing the trees at the end of the field. I know Maule's have exceptional STOL performance, but how'll she handle with three cripples trying to flee a mini cyclone?" joked Dave.

Gary suddenly loathed this man's dry sense of humour but attempted to focus his rapidly clouding mind to recall the take-off specs on his airplane. "Take-off roll is . . . 380. Obstacles over 50 feet need 600 ta clear." Gary snapped his neck sideways to release a pesky kink. It didn't work. "Them trees, they look higher 'n fifty."

Twice that, thought Dave pensively. "Your power of recall is impressive, despite your headache. We've got strong headwinds in our court, so depending on flaps and horses under the hood, we should clear them." *Just barely.*

"One-eighty," answered Gary quickly. "It's a smaller engine. Stalls at thirty-five. I've measured the take-off roll. Winds were twenty with a DA of 3,500 feet. Had twenty-six in the tanks and lifted them wheels at the 350 mark and twenty on the flaps. Was by myself. But now we got three, and the MSL elevation here is four grand and change." Gary surprised himself with a chuckle. "Best be sure we can make it, or I'm stayin' here. I seen videos of dumb fool pilots not calculating the DA right. Want no part of that, no I don't."

Me either, thought Dave. But Gary was right. As temperature and altitude increased, decreased air density could result in poor lift and a longer distance needed for the takeoff or landing. So, Dave knew that if the DA, or density altitude, wasn't properly calculated, the plane might in a sense feel it's flying at a different altitude than it really is. Such a slip up can result in a bad day, something Dave wanted to avoid at all costs. "I don't think it's a problem for us," he assured. "But you're right. We need to be sure. You landed this thing on a dime today, so I'd expect similar performance for take-off," Dave shrugged. "I'd rather we not have to pluck pine needles from our hides if we end up in the trees."

"That's a dang nasty visual," cringed Gary.

"Indeed, it is," Dave agreed as he flipped a few pages ahead in the Pilot's Operating Handbook. He found the section he wanted: *BEFORE STARTING and STARTING CHECKLIST.*

Low cloud and gusty winds dominated the airspace around the Maule. The rain eased to what Dave considered a less troublesome mist, and as he turned his head, he noticed Paul hobbling towards the right-side door, his friend appearing as though he just emerged from the shower. In Dave's view, the man's determination was admittedly contagious, and despite nagging doubts about this knee-jerk plan, Dave would never consider it with anyone else in the seat beside him.

The passenger door whipped open. "All good out here, Dave," he confirmed. "Let's crank this sucker and get outta here!" Paul shot a nervous glance in Gary's direction but kept his inklings to himself.

"You don't have to ask me twice!" agreed Dave. "Climb in, Ace, and let's end this self-perpetuating nightmare." Dave repositioned himself, checked his seat belt and made sure the flaps were up.

As Dave watched Paul carefully side-saddle his way into the plane, his friend grimaced and froze. "You okay?" Dave asked.

For a moment Paul stayed perfectly still. He felt his heart racing, its beat stumbling to find its natural rhythm. Avoiding Dave's inquiry, Paul nodded awkwardly as he closed the door. "You've got taco soup waiting for you at home, Dave. Let's just go. I'm fine."

Dave nodded while he checked the circuit breakers. "You're not a very good liar, Ace. Buckle up, boys. This train is leaving the station."

"Taco soup?" asked Gary in a raspy voice. "What's that 'bout?"

Dave shunned the question. "Brakes, Paul," he ordered. "Lock 'em up."

Paul rested his feet into the pedals and fixedly set the brakes. His back protested the strain, but he disregarded the physical warnings that his body required medical attention.

"What in tarnation is taco soup?" asked Gary in confusion.

Dave continued to run his finger along the pre-start checklist. He shot a glance in Gary's direction and watched as Paul snugged his belt. "Assuming we survive the take-off," snickered Dave. "I'll tell you about it."

* * *

With the Piper Cub heading east over the Moose River towards Owensville, Kevin felt less burdened about splattering themselves into the side of a mountain. "Is that enough vent air?" he asked Susan. "We'll be on the ground in no time, so just hang on."

"Yes," replied Susan. "And soon would be good, but I don't believe you."

"Just trying to stay positive," replied Kevin earnestly.

The Cub's wings continued their teeter-totter motion and had it been that alone, Susan figured she'd have been able to stomach the ride. But it was the knockabout combination of up and down that twisted her guts into a knot. After dry heaving a few times, Susan discovered that tipping her head back and breathing deeply helped, but only momentarily. Her mindset had flipped from search and rescue mode to one of personal survival. "I just want out of this airplane, Kevin. I'm feeling really awful."

"Yes, I know," acknowledged Kevin flatly. "You've mentioned that several times. I'd set us down if I could, but there isn't anywhere between here and Owensville to land. We just have to tough it out."

"It feels like we're barely moving. Can we throttle up a bit more, or is this it?"

Kevin smirked. "We have a good tailwind, so that helps. I could add more power, but I want to conserve fuel. We'll keep following the river and stay low. Moger's Point isn't much farther, so I'll try the radio shortly."

"I need to open the window for a second. I feel really nauseous and need cold air."

"Got for it, but make it quick.

A sudden icy blast of air mixed with rain roared through the cockpit. Susan barely had the window open when Kevin's frantic voice bellowed through her headset. "Hang on, Susan!"

Seconds later, the Piper entered another thick wall of cloud, rendering its already haggard occupants full-on blind as a bat.

* * *

"Engine's still warm," informed Gary. "If you prime, it'll flood. She's finicky that way."

"Copy that," Dave replied as he edged the throttle in by a quarter inch.

"And full lean on the mixture," barked Gary. "When the engine catches, kill the throttle and go full rich, but not too dang fast. She don't like fast either."

Dave scrunched his nose. "Sheesh. I feel like I'm on a check ride with my old flight instructor, except I don't remember my airplane smelling as bad as this one!"

Paul chimed in. "I hope that's the fish and not us."

"Likely a bit of both, Ace," acknowledged Dave.

"The smell grows on ya," scowled Gary. "This engine's quirky. I'm tryin' ta save us all some grief. If ya don't want my help, just—"

"I appreciate it, Gary," interrupted Dave. "You know your plane best, so with your advice and the smell of fish to keep our senses sharp, it's all but assured I won't turn us into a tree ornament."

Gary blathered something unintelligible before slamming his fist into the back of Paul's seat. "I don't want ta hear that!" he roared.

Paul shared a nervous sideways glance with Dave and shook his head. "Not funny, Dave," he objected. "So, for Gary's sake, let's not dwell on that scenario, shall we? We'll clear the trees just fine and be on our way."

"You know I like to joke when I'm stressed," reminded Dave. "Okay then, enough with the humour. You're my feet, Ace, so be sharp. Steer us straight and true once you let the brakes off. I'll do the rest."

"Don't worry about me," ordered Paul. "You fly. I've got the steering."

Continuing through the checklist, Dave noticed the fuel tanks contained equal amounts of gas, so he set the fuel valve to both and the mixture to idle cutoff. "Anti-collision lights," he read out loud.

It took a moment for Paul to find the switch. "On," he confirmed.

"Battery and alternator switches," recited Dave to himself. "Check."

"And no primer!" shouted Gary, his voice steeped with fear. Paul and Dave both jumped at the sudden outburst.

Dave held his tongue. "We'll skip the primer so says the man in the back seat. Heaven knows we need to keep our persnickety engine happy, don't we?"

Paul was growing impatient. "Let's can the chatter and just start this—"

"We do it right, Ace!" interrupted Dave. "By the book, no fast-tracking." Dave lowered his voice and his mouth twisted into a

Deliveries

crooked smile. "We do it step-by-step to keep our passenger stable. He's really getting on my nerves."

Paul knew Dave was right, and that Gary's erratic conduct was peculiar. He was about to reply when Gary suddenly leaned forward, his voice even toned like it was a completely different person. "Ignition's sticky too, so force the key hard right. It'll catch a bit on the way through."

"Lucky me," joked Dave. "My second demanding airplane in as many days." Dave suddenly remembered the gun under his seat but chose to dismiss that concern for now. He thought about tossing it out the window, but then decided he'd be tampering with evidence in any subsequent police investigation. *As long as it stays there, we'll be fine.*

Paul grabbed the checklist from Dave's hands and looked it over. "Okay," he said. "We're good to go, so let's fire it up."

Twisting the starter full right, Dave's pulse raced uncharacteristically fast as the Lycoming engine tried to catch. The propeller rotated briefly and stopped. He backtracked the key so he could try again.

Paul scanned the instrument panel. "What's wrong?" he asked impatiently.

Dave raised his arms. "No idea. I'll crank it—"

"Wait!" Paul ordered while reaching for the prop lever. "Not that this should affect anything, but we're still high pitch on the blades." He pushed the control all the way in. "We aren't focused, Dave. We both missed that. Maybe the engine needs a prime after all."

"No primer!" ordered Gary. "Try it again!"

"Someone's eager to get home and face the jury," added Dave while he rotated the key through both mag positions, then to "START." The airplane shuddered as the drive shaft engaged the propeller. It still didn't catch.

"Punch it now fer dang sake!" roared Gary. "Mixture!"

Dave was already on it. In one fluid motion, he advanced the engine mixture to full rich, which flooded the cylinders with fuel.

The engine coughed loudly as though it had received a dose of fouled gas. A few anxious moments later it roared to life.

"Yeah, baby!" hooted Dave as the RPMs became active.

"Now let's finish this and go home," ordered Paul.

Dave burned through the last few procedures as the engine warmed up. He leaned the mixture to not foul the plugs and watched as the EGT needle rose and fell slightly. It felt extremely odd to not have his feet on the pedals when he was the one flying, but he needed to trust that Paul could handle the brakes and steering on the ground, and the rudder in the air. Their lives depended upon it.

"Let's get the brakes off a bit," ordered Dave. "We should test them."

"Affirmative," Paul replied while trying to ignore the misery in his back. Easing off on the brakes, he allowed the wheels to roll forward a short distance, but it was at that exact moment that an explosive blast of wind grabbed the plane, followed by sheets of rain cascading across the fuselage. Paul locked the brakes and howled from the jolt.

"Perfect timing as always," complained Dave.

The prop wash helped to disperse the rain off the front window, but the degrading weather did little to ease Dave's growing apprehensions. "I vote for waiting until things improve a bit," he stated. "Anybody second—"

Paul cut in. "If we don't go now, chances are we don't get out at all today."

"Where have I heard that before?" murmured Dave.

Paul shot Dave an angry look. "I'm not spending another night out here. Once we're off, we stay low and follow the river up the valley. We've flown in worse, Dave. Besides, this airplane was built for crummy weather and low-level flying. Where's your backbone?"

Dave glanced out his side window and over to Paul. "This airplane is also filled with three wounded guys, each with a recent history of making bad decisions, Ace. I don't want this flight to be our last. Besides," he added. "I haven't got a clue how to turn the wipers on!"

Paul let out an audible sigh. "I vote we go now. The sooner we get back to civilization, the sooner we all can seek medical attention. Gary?"

Dave backward glanced in Gary's direction. The man's contorted face lay covered in a sheen of sweat. "You all right back there?" he asked.

"Just go," scowled Gary. "I'm already dead."

"Alrighty then," surrendered Dave. "You both win. Help me with the run-up checklist, Paul, and then we go wheels up." *Or torn off,* thought Dave.

Unbeknownst to the men up front, Gary had snatched the gun and diamonds before he climbed into the backseat. With a growing sense of dread, he thought about tossing both once airborne, sacrificing them to the wilderness, and himself to a life of dodging vengeful bad guys. Panic gripped Gary's body, sending icy chills through his spine. He knew they would eventually find him and deal with his willful insubordination. That scared him the most. Tensing, waves of red-hot pain erupted from his collar, and he screeched in agony.

Paul glanced over his shoulder. "We can hold off if—".

"Go!" scowled Gary. "Just git on with it!"

Dave and Paul exchanged ill-at-ease looks and raised their eyebrows in unison.

"I'll set the flaps and trim for take-off," Paul calmly announced.

Dave checked the elevator and ailerons for freedom of movement. "Free and clear," he stated firmly. "How's the stabilizer?"

Paul cautiously finessed the rudder pedals back and forth. "No restrictions," he grimaced.

Scanning the engine instruments one last time, Dave sucked air deep into his lungs. "Tally ho. Steering and brakes are all yours, Ace. I've got the power. It's tag-team time!"

Gary's voice cracked. "What?" he asked nervously. "It's what?"

Dave slowly nursed the throttle. Sluggish at first, the wheels finally unglued from the muddy ground and began to roll. He expected considerable crosswind from the northwest, and Paul would have to deal with it for the taxi back to the south end of the field.

Keeping his back as straight as possible, Paul steered the plane to the short brush-covered meadow in perfect sync with Dave on the throttle. As the Maule turned into the wind, he wedged his feet painfully into the toe brakes. Everyone lurched forward. "We're locked," winced Paul with his body rigid. "And right now, with the pain in my back, my feet are about all I can move."

"Hang in there," encouraged Dave. "We got this."

With its propeller slicing through vaporous air and wing rocking in step with gusty winds, the aircraft sat in place for a few long moments. Like his Cessna, it seemed to Paul as if the machine was alive, examining its resolve to fly under such harsh conditions. He looked over at his long-time friend. "Time to go partner."

Dave nodded his head. "Define 'Time to go.'"

* * *

The grey beast had literally dropped out of nowhere, its mass swallowing everything like a black hole, including Kevin Davies and Susan McCutcheon. Susan's anxiety barometer had already exceeded its limit and had it not been for Kevin's assurance that they'd be okay, her nerves may have completely unwound to the point of no return.

Kevin wasn't yet IFR qualified, nor was his airplane IFR capable. However, it did house the gauges required to maintain temporary control while inside the cloud, but not for long. He checked his compass and attitude indicator, making sure to keep the wings level while holding their altitude steady. Even if visibility permitted it, there wasn't enough room within the confines of the valley to reverse direction or steer around, so thankfully the GPS helped to keep their place over the river and away from lurking mountain slopes on either side. After what seemed an eternity of white-knuckle flying, the cloud mercifully spit them out into a relatively open sky.

"Oh, thank God!" Susan gratefully announced.

"Piece of cake," added Kevin stoically, his eyes shifting automatically from instruments back to visual flight. Glad that Susan couldn't see his widening smile, Kevin found himself beginning to revel in the challenge they faced. *The Cub's still flying, and thanks to me, we're still alive.*

"Sorry, Kevin," added Susan. "But I'm not sharing your confidence here. This is anything but a piece of cake."

"Well, now it's just a matter of threading our way through the muck and getting the Cub's wheels back on deck. Lucky for you I'm a good pilot!" joked Kevin with self-gratifying undertones.

"Sorry, I don't begrudge that you're a good pilot. It's the reckless ego part that has me so uncomfortable."

* * *

"Hard on the brakes, Paul," ordered Dave. "We'll go full power, let the RPMs and manifold come to full, and then it's all you for keeping us straight 'til I raise the nose." Dave went full rich on the mixture.

No pressure there, thought Paul miserably. Miffed, he turned towards Dave. "That all goes without saying. Quit worrying about me. You just be ready on the yoke and get us over those pine trees!"

With the Maule configured for take-off, Gary forced his lungs to breathe. Bordering on panic, waiting for the throttle to advance was sheer misery. He understood they'd either make it or they wouldn't, that his life could end in a matter of seconds. The men in the front seat of his airplane seemed genuine enough in offering him unbiased support, but Gary's pounding heart and lack of trust provided him with a stern warning in his gut. He thought about demanding they let him out, but just then the engine began to rev up. *Too late Nordhavn. Now yer committed.*

With Paul's feet welded to the top of the pedals, Dave goosed the throttle all the way to the stop. The engine eagerly responded as the RPMs rose through 2,500 and the airplane shuddered under the strain of being held in place. The front wheels began to slip on the spongy turf as wind rocked the fuselage back and forth. With only one notch of flaps selected on the wings, Dave gripped the yoke hard. "Now, Paul! Let'er go!"

Paul hesitated briefly as his doubts picked away at his concentration. "Copy," he finally replied as he released the brakes. "Straight and true."

As the brakes let go, the Maule staggered forward. Nuggets of semi-dried mud uprooted from the field and sprayed every which way as the prop bit into the air. The plane skewed sloppily to the left, catching Paul completely by surprise.

"Steer!" shouted Dave.

Paul drove his foot into the right pedal and the track corrected. "Yeah!" he replied. "I got it!" His back protested the savage physical movement while the airplane bounced along as if on railway ties. He felt certain the landing gear would tear away, but it held fast. Paul glanced at the airspeed indicator. "Speed's coming alive, Dave, but not fast enough!"

Rimming the back perimeter of the clearing, pine trees loomed, their tall slender boughs growing in size at an alarming rate. From his view in the back seat, Gary's eyes grew wide. "We're runnin' outta field!" he shouted.

"No kidding, Sherlock!" yelled Dave while he tried to ram the throttle beyond its limit. "C'mon girl!" he pleaded. "We should abort this, Ace!"

As Paul fought to keep the wheels on track, the Maule shook and rattled as it slid to the right from gusty crosswinds. The left-wing started to lift. "No!" he shouted. "We'll make it! Ailerons, Dave! I need full left!"

"Sorry!" Dave gasped. "Forgot that!" Dave slammed the yoke over, forcing the left aileron up and the right down. This helped to offset heavy crosswinds by holding the affected wing down until the plane reached rotation speed, the point at which lift took hold.

As the plane devoured the haphazard landscape, the tail wheel suddenly broke free of the ground. "Tail's up!" cheered Gary excitedly.

Dave slowly eased off on the ailerons and returned them to neutral.

"Almost there!" announced Paul. "Just a bit more speed!"

Pushing through fifty MPH, the plane felt like it wanted to fly, but the mains held fast to the diminishing turf. Paul sensed Dave was right, that they should abort while there was still time. But his gut told him to keep going, that they would make it despite the overwhelming odds against them. In a final act of reckless abandon, Paul reached for the flap lever between the seats and adjusted it to the next notch, or twenty degrees.

"What are you doing?" screamed Dave. "You'll stall us!"

"More lift!" Paul coolly explained as if he was teaching a flying lesson. "We need a bigger push, and we've got the speed now!"

Dave's voice left his throat. He clasped his fingers around the yoke as he frantically calculated their odds. Coming up with a gigantic zero, he reached for the flap handle, but Paul quickly swatted his hand away. "This'll work!" he barked. "Leave it alone!"

Fighting the urge to close his eyes, Dave convinced himself to play out this laughable scenario. They were now guaranteed one of two outcomes—aerodynamic lift and avoid the trees, or the pull of gravity slamming them into the trees. Either way, the forest of green rushing up to meet them spelled bad news. As it was, Dave half expected the airplane to nose over from the rugged terrain beneath the wheels.

In the next instant, the mud-clogged tires lifted. Dave glanced at the airspeed which showed fifty-five and climbing. A sudden wind gust kicked the plane sharply left and up. Airspeed fell slightly, but not enough to affect lift.

Paul dropkicked as much right rudder as his aching body allowed. "Get us up, Dave!" he boomed while reaching for the yoke himself.

This time Dave swept Paul's hand aside. "No, I've got this!" he roared.

Dave eased the column towards his chest. The Maule's nose pitched up sharper than he expected, and he feared a stall would as quickly drop them like a stone. Mercifully the buzzer stayed quiet as the wings chewed into the air and the trees sped towards them.

"More elevator!" ordered Paul. "You've got enough airspeed, Dave, so bloody well use it!"

"Who's flying this thing?" snapped Dave as he pulled the yoke back to add ten degrees nose up. The plane rocketed an extra forty feet in barely a second, just enough to dodge the boughs. Tips of needle-sharp pine trees scraped the underbelly as it passed over, its wheels shearing off several sprigs of pine cones.

"We're clear!" screamed Dave hysterically.

Distraught with unbridled fear, Gary suddenly realized he had stopped breathing. He gulped a breath of air. "Git them flaps up!" he gasped. "Let the speed come up!"

Dave allowed the nose to drop a few degrees. "Yeah, yeah, we got it!"

Paul raised the flaps and added quick bursts of rudder to keep the nose as straight as possible and away from taller nearby trees. He brushed away a layer of perspiration from his face and tried to disregard the pressure in his chest and the searing fire raging throughout his body.

As the flaps retracted, Dave reached over and slapped Paul on the shoulder, but it wasn't his smartest move. White as a ghost, Paul yelped but said nothing. Dave recognized the look of a man who just beat the odds. "Sorry for the slap, but good call on the extra flaps, Ace! I thought for sure you'd completely lost your mind, again!"

Tiny curls formed at the edges of Paul's lips, and Dave found it next to impossible to refrain from smiling himself. They had dodged yet another bullet and could now go home. Paul backed his feet off the pedals to ease the strain on his back and legs. He flipped his head around and chuckled at Gary's wide-eyed expression. Then, he turned back to Dave. "Maybe I have, Dave. Maybe I have."

With low slung clouds throughout the narrow valley, a short climb brought the Maule to within 100 feet of the cloud base. Dave evened out the angle on the wings and adjusted the power and trim. Paul added a touch of rudder here and there, but the plane held relatively stable in the bumpy air. A few moments later, three men began to hoot and holler like school kids on the doorstep of summer vacation. As they flew north towards the Moose River, the raucous silliness continued for several minutes as the idea of civilization took hold.

***

Kevin's legs shook uncontrollably. He squeezed his knees to get them to stop, but it didn't help. As a pilot, he accepted the risks of flying in unpredictable conditions, and though cocksure in his ability, he knew Susan wasn't as ironclad in her thinking. This enduring fact proved true a moment later.

"Tell me again we'll be fine, Kevin!" pleaded Susan nervously. "If we enter another one of those clouds, I'll lose it for sure. I signed up to find missing people, not risk my neck in a cauldron of goop."

"Susan, listen to me!" implored Kevin. "I know you're scared, but we'll make it, I promise. What I need you to do for me is to stay calm, so I can focus on getting us home safely. Unless I know you're okay and have my back, I can't do that. Do you understand what I'm saying?"

Kevin's gentle slap in the face was exactly what Susan needed. She realized that allowing her nerves to go unchecked wasn't helping their situation. But holding things in wasn't healthy either. "I'm usually stronger than this when I'm scared, Kevin. I'm sorry, I'll be fine. You fly and I'll shut up."

When Kevin didn't reply, Susan wondered if he was too upset with her to say more, but that wasn't at all the case. His focus lay beyond the front window and on the entire width of the eastern valley. Indistinct cloud formations hung menacingly low, their grey tentacles reaching into the river as if drawing life and breath from the fast-moving rapids. Kevin's brain warned him away and to take immediate evasive action. He knew Susan wouldn't be pleased, but a cushy landing at Owensville Municipal wasn't in their cards. "We're turning around, Susan," he sternly remarked.

As Kevin banked into a steep thirty-degree left-hand turn, his headset snapped to life. The untimely intrusion was not at all welcome. This time the anxious voice wasn't coming from his spotter.

"Piper Romeo One, this is Owensville rescue, please respond!"

"It's base!" yelled Susan under the strain of the turn. "That's Rob!"

Kevin thought about telling Susan to zip it but refrained. "Owensville rescue, Piper Romeo One has you, but you're weak," he grunted. "I was beginning to think you'd all gone out for drinks without us."

The stress in Rob's voice was noticeable. "I've been trying to reach you guys. What's your status?"

As Kevin continued the turn away from approaching clouds, bile rose in Susan's throat from the steepness of their retreat. She grabbed her airsick bag and kept it close to her mouth just in case.

"The weather's forcing our hand, Rob," stated Kevin. "We're keeping low to the river and I'm turning back to Spruce Creek. Owensville's a no go."

That announcement generated silence. Kevin pictured Rob's face as he processed what he'd just been told. But decisions in the cockpit were Kevin's to make, especially in regard to personal safety.

"Listen, Kevin," replied Rob. "Do what you have to do to stay safe. Spruce Creek will take a Cub no problem during daylight hours. They've got fuel, and if the weather improves you can get back into the air and resume the search. We're blind—out you—there. We'll remain on station—dusk, then head back to O—sville to—some rest."

"We're losing you, Rob," said Kevin. He waited for a split second and tried the radio again. "Owensville rescue, Piper Romeo One. Do you copy?" His headset remained quiet. Kevin allowed the Cub to gain a bit of altitude in the turn. Clouds to the west appeared less intimidating, and it felt better not to be so close to the river. At 300 feet, he eased off on the throttle to conserve fuel and rolled the wings level. Selecting the path of least resistance, Kevin aimed the nose back towards Spruce Creek and to a tiny grass runway, he honestly wanted no part of.

At the same time, Susan McCutcheon vowed to quit Owensville Search and Rescue and never fly again in a small rickety airplane, assuming this flight didn't end her life first.

Chapter 30

Frustrated, Rob Smith half threw the handheld radio back into its charging cradle. "What good are these blasted radios if they don't even work properly? It's not like we're on the moon for crying out loud!"

Several volunteers gathered around the base-station radio following the conversation between Rob and Kevin. But when the discussion abruptly ended, any long-standing hope of finally being dispatched to find the missing Cessna and its crew all but evaporated.

"Sorry, people. As you all just heard, the weather sucks up top, and they've called off the search. They were trying to get to Owensville but are now heading to Spruce Creek until conditions improve."

Behind Rob stood an increasingly embittered Diane and Kim Jackson. Tess McMurray stood to the side chatting with Laura Hastings. Rather than return to Owensville with the television crew, they decided to stay a while longer at Moger's Point. But now that the search for Paul and Dave was temporarily off the table, the women couldn't have been any less pleased.

Rob spun on his heels and nearly bumped into Diane. "Oh, I'm sorry," he apologized sincerely. "I didn't see you there. I, ah"—Rob sideways glanced at Tess—"I noticed your friend conducting an interview with the reporter a while ago, and then I saw you drive away with them. I assumed you all went back home, but I see that wasn't the case."

"No, that obviously wasn't the case," replied Diane. "We collectively decided to turn around and come back, but I'm thinking that all we've done is waste more of our time. I also get the sense that by us being here, you feel that we're wasting yours as well?"

Facts were facts, and Rob was never one to blow sunshine where it didn't belong. "Actually, that's not at the case at all, but as I'm sure you just heard, the search plane is unable to continue. For the safety of my pilot and spotter, they've wisely decided to land at Spruce Creek and wait out this weather system. As soon as it's safe to do so, we'll continue our search."

Out of the corner of her eye, Laura Hastings watched curiously as her boss further explained the situation to the undeniably disappointed mother and daughter. She wanted to step in and offer Rob her support but knew there was nothing she could say or do that would change anything. She ended her conversation with Tess, turned and walked towards a trail leading to another scenic view of Moger's Point. Facing the wind and rain head-on, Laura zipped her vest to the top and hiked through the trees.

Diane wanted to lash out at Rob but knew such an outburst would accomplish nothing. Instead, she simply bit her lip and walked away. Tess watched her friend leave and then stepped up to Rob. "It's frustrating for us to watch you just standing around. You've got quads and dirt bikes, and lord knows what else at your disposal, and yet you won't allow your people to head out. Isn't being proactive better than doing nothing?"

Rob looked Tess in the eyes. "Please understand I won't jeopardize the safety of—as you call them—*my people*. Not without a definitive sighting on the Cessna. That's why we need to wait for the search plane to resume its pattern. Without the resources to effectively cover such a wide area, the last thing I need is everyone running helter-skelter in pursuit of a needle in a haystack. Two missing people are challenging enough; no disrespect to your husbands."

Tess stood her ground. "Well, if it's more people and resources you need, perhaps your wish will come true."

Rob's eyebrows lifted curiously. "And why would that be might I ask?"

"Because once Mr. Ennis broadcasts my interview, I'm sure you'll have all the extra help you'll need."

"So, let me guess. You pleaded your case to the good people of Owensville to amass and bring their hiking boots and binoculars to Moger's Point?"

Tess nodded. "Yup, something like that. I figure the more eyes and ears on the ground, the better. And you said it yourself that you don't have the people or resources to cover the area. Well, now maybe you will, and then this long-overdue search can actually take place."

Rob cocked his head sideways as his brain processed what he just heard. "Well, as we tentatively await the arrival of our new recruits, I've decided to drive up to Spruce Creek to check on my pilot and spotter once they land. I'll be back in time to offer up a poignant call to arms for those joining our merry ranks." Rob edged his voice with sarcasm. "The more of us just sitting around here, the better I suppose. And I repeat, sitting around is all anyone is going to do until my search plane is back in the air. Now, if you'll excuse me, I've got a plane to catch."

Tess huffed once before adding a parting shot. "No offence, but it's too bad it's the wrong plane you're trying to catch!"

* * *

Plunked on the corner of Inspector Stan Fenwick's desk, a small legal-sized folder stamped "Case File 201, Diamonds" lay open. The four-year-old investigation stalled early on from lack of evidence, and with more pressing matters occupying his time, Stan had not torn into the file for some time. He glanced at the loose papers but never bothered to pick them up. Instead, he leaned back in his antique swivel chair and sighed. "Soon buddy, soon."

Needing to slug out another six months to secure full pension, Stan thought himself entirely deserving of a golden handshake, a handsome severance, and then finally retirement. He'd been at this policing gig long enough and felt entirely ready to partake of the proverbial "good life."

Recruited directly by the Owensville Police Department during a high school career fair, the young cadet learned early on the value of keeping his eyes and ears open and his mouth shut. Stan latched himself to some of the best in the business, the end result being rapid acceleration through the ranks, and then finally to chief inspector, the spot he always strove for. Finally, content, his career ambitions never proceeded beyond that point on the corporate totem pole.

At five-foot-nine, Stan was never the burliest man on the force, but his sinewy build served him well in less hospitable areas such as skanky downtown back alleys. But that was then. At sixty-four, the relentless curse of ageing showed every aspect of itself with each passing day, and Stan wanted out before the "old man" persona really grabbed hold.

Rising from his chair, Stan wandered over to a small mirror tacked to the wall. He despised his sagging jowls, grey hair and wrinkles. But figuring he was luckier than many other men his age, he tried to overlook the inevitable with as much grace as his weary bones could muster.

At this stage of life, Stan believed that slowing down was nothing more than a balancing act between the blending of work and recreation. With retirement beckoning, his pattern of thought leaned more to golf, fishing, and wine. Never married, he intended to spend his golden years as an active senior as opposed to, as society often described it: "a weathered prune in a rocking chair."

Stan glanced around the inside of his office and couldn't help but smile. Like him, the space had seen better days, but the familiar surroundings felt comfortable like his old pair of moth-eaten slippers. He sauntered over to one of two corner windows and peered outside.

Built in the early seventies, the OPD occupied an old red brick three-story building just a few blocks south of City Hall. The interior mid-modern decor was long overdue for a makeover, and its patchwork halls and drab office spaces showed their age. Stan had always been thankful for his third-floor west-facing office because it stayed cooler during the summer months. And with less than adequate air conditioning throughout the building, the added benefit of a cool breeze drifting through the open windows was a bonus. For Stan, this small blessing eliminated the need for an office fan, which for the stuffy cubicles downstairs, was an absolute necessity.

With its branches flush to the window, a granddaddy oak tree graced the front lawn, its limbs inhabited by squirrels and blue jays. Stan watched with interest as they scrambled for the rights to several branches clotted with acorns. Beyond the tree, heavily congested Marie Avenue could be seen in all its over-crowded glory.

On a per-capita basis, the City of Owensville had its share of bad guys and trouble spots, with most police investigations dealing with the usual cases of missing people, hit and runs, homicides and several caught-on-camera videos that required viewing and analysis. Stan never saw the work as glamorous, but it was for the most part, rewarding. Each day offered new challenges, and just enough variety to keep him engaged and happy throughout the bulk of his career.

When asked by aspiring recruits how he liked his job, Stan always used a food analogy to describe his work and career: "Some days a guy eats hotdogs, while other days allow for steak and potatoes." Some investigations were ho-hum and some involved extensive manpower and department resources, the effort taking months or even years to flesh out, solve, or in some instances, like the diamonds case, never officially put to rest.

Monday to Friday, Stan typically wore a collared shirt, khaki pants and a sport jacket. But today was Sunday, a coveted day off. This meant sweats, a t-shirt, and breaking in a shiny new pair of Asics court sneakers which he'd been dying to wear. But at breakfast, his lounging came to a sudden end following an unexpected call to his cellphone, its nature warranting an unplanned trip to the office, casual garb and all.

For Stan, a juicy spin-off from years of pounding the pavement was a repertoire of informants, a mottled group ranging from petty thieves and street people to citizens willing to place themselves in harm's way if it meant eliminating scruff from the streets. This morning's call hailed from a bedraggled middle-age peddler who, oddly enough, called himself "Rebellion."

Stan met the titan only once, the encounter happening last year in a dingy back alley littered with grease vats and garbage bins from several Asian restaurants dotting the area. Despite the quick introduction and passing of semi-useful information, the fellow more recently seemed in-the-know with regard to inner-city gossip and foreknowledge of crimes yet to happen. Subsequent calls proved Rebellion a reliable snitch. This time, his phone message was short and surprisingly simple. "Fenwick, stones inbound today by air. Post office drop. Rebellion." Then, the line went dead.

Outside his window, Stan watched a highly modified pick-up truck gun its engine and blow through a stop sign, prompting several nearby motorists to blast their horns in protest. "Idiot," Stan remarked angrily. In his opinion, Owensville traffic had evolved to include far too many redneck pick-up trucks, and despite heavy citations levied against this demographic, the numbers of self-absorbed brainless drivers continued to grow.

Stan walked back to his desk and picked up the case folder. He leafed through the pages, scanning vague reports of loose diamonds filtering in or through Owensville. But with so little physical evidence, the case never proceeded beyond a few phone calls and the scribbled notes he held in his hands. Initial smuggling reports were deemed bogus, and since nothing was ever found or pawned locally, not even so much as a cubic zirconia, the investigation was shelved as implausible. That was until now.

Stan always wondered about the small factions of transient biker gangs drifting through town and any connection to Mr. Rebellion's fresh lead. If dealing hot stones was in fact their gig, then it warranted a closer look. Stan scratched his head. To him, delivery by air was the biggest puzzler. If the gems were being flown in, then by whom and to where? Several farms in the area had small grass runways for light sport aircraft, all capable of being used as a platform for illicit activity. Only one main airport existed, and that was Owensville Municipal. Stan felt certain the bad guys would never be foolish enough to be so out in the open, but then criminals of late seemed more and more brazen in their comings and goings to help offset suspicion by the police or nosy do-good citizens.

The more he thought about it, the more Stan believed those responsible would be as stealthy as possible, so how his informant caught wind of this scheme, he hadn't the foggiest idea. *Unless,* thought Stan, *he was somehow involved?* Such a tip-off demanded a higher degree of scrutiny, bogus or not.

Having already chugged two cups of coffee at home, Stan decided that a third couldn't hurt, but not here, and not dressed like this. Grabbing his jacket, he flicked a spider off the window's ledge and headed for the locker room in the basement. *Uniform first, old boy, coffee second, and then to your least popular back alley for hopefully an enlightening chat.*

* * *

Five miles south of the confluence between the Moose River and the smaller south tributary, the Maule wound its way through layers of cloud and rain, its occupants more subdued than when the plane first left the ground.

Turbulent air meant for strenuous pitch corrections, and with visibility floundering, Dave McMurray had no choice but to venture lower than he had hoped. The fast-moving river seemed close enough to dip the wheels into, and had it not been for his vigilance, they might already have found themselves in very wet company with the river's thriving brook trout population.

Paul's use of the rudder pedals had, for his back's sake, mercifully eased off. Winds from the north abated the need for nonstop yaw input, but he knew as soon as they turned east towards Owensville, his legs and feet would resume their workout. On the plus side, Paul felt an absolute sense of relief to be going home instead of staying with the Cessna and waiting for a rescue that may never come. Despite locking its doors and what he assumed was a near-zero populous transiting through the area, he worried about security and the cargo inside. But recovery would have to take place another day, if heaven forbid, there was anything left to recover.

Under such ridiculous circumstances, seeing Dave at the controls made Paul smile. He knew his friend could have balked at going along with the absurd idea to fly out themselves, especially with injuries, but Paul had banked on Dave's lust for flight, especially when the chips were down. Dave wasn't one to sit back and take the easy way out or let someone else have all the fun, especially when flying was involved. Simply put, the man thrived on flight.

Gary Nordhavn was another issue. He was an inarguably troubled man who had backed himself into a shrinking corner with his lawless career path. Paul wondered if the police would slap Dave and himself with a lame charge of aiding and abetting a smuggler. But the fact remained, he saved their bacon by providing a way out of the bush and, in a sense, turning himself in. Paul reasoned that such an effort deserved accolades of some sort, if even minor.

Paul thought of Diane and of his own misgivings. She had always demanded honesty in their marriage, and he had broken that trust. But if push came to shove with the police, he'd speak the truth no matter the outcome or charges laid against Mr. Nordhavn, or even himself for that matter.

Trying to offer some encouragement, Paul spun his head around and found Gary inspecting the bottle of diamonds resting in his lap. Paul had not realized that Gary had them, and for whatever reason, the sight caused him to shiver. He immediately scanned for the gun. "How are you doing back there?" he asked nervously. "You've gone pretty quiet."

Gary looked up; his face expressionless. He met Paul's gaze, then lowered his head. "Sorry I involved ya in my troubles," he gruffly stated.

Paul thought he looked anything but sorry.

Gary angled the bottle up close to his face and inspected the contents. "I'll tell 'em you weren't involved . . . that I"—Gary stopped mid-sentence—"The cops. They'll ask questions when they catch me, and—"

"Hey, man," interrupted Paul. "Don't worry about that right now. If it wasn't for you, we'd still be rotting away in the forest, dehydrated and starving to death. We're grateful you agreed to let us fly your plane out of here. We all need medical attention, and once we take care of that, you and I can worry about dealing with our lapses in moral judgement."

Paul eyed the diamonds. "What are you planning to do with those? No doubt you're aware that your friends won't be happy when they find out they aren't getting their delivery today or that you're retiring from—"

"They're not my friends!" exploded Gary.

"I'm sorry," cringed Paul. "I didn't mean anything by that. I was just—"

Another chill ripped through Paul's body as he watched Gary's face change. Veins popped out in his neck and dark lines formed around his eyes as if a makeup artist just applied grotesque accents for Hallowe'en. Not blinking, the man looked straight ahead with a furrowed brow, the colour drained from his face.

The sight caused Paul to shudder, so much so that his feet came off the pedals. Dave felt the airplane slip to the left. "Hey, Ace. We need yaw correction in these cross-winds. Stay on it if you can."

Paul re-positioned his feet but kept his head turned and his eyes on Gary. "Sorry, Dave, I—" Then to Paul's astonishment, Gary's face softened, and the lines flattened out like they were never there. Even creepier was that he chuckled before continuing from where he'd left off only moments ago.

"And when I'm caught," yammered Gary, "I'll use my one phone call ta get hold of my wife. Pretty sure she'll tell me not ta come home." Gary sighed and rapped the side of his head. He shrieked from the jolt. "Can't believe I let myself get caught up in this." Gary punched himself again, only harder.

Watching Gary reminded Paul of a toddler dealing with shame over a poor choice. "We all screw up, Gary," assured Paul nervously. "It's like I told you before. I flew against doctors' orders, and I'll pay the piper when the time comes." The Maule slid sideways again, and Paul corrected with opposite rudder. "If they take away my licence, I might have to drive a truck and haul cattle like poor Dave here." Paul laughed to ease the tension. "Maybe I'll even get myself a pair of ugly orange coveralls too!"

Dave glanced in Paul's direction but missed the up-sloped eyebrows and subtle head nod towards the back seat. "Tell ya what, boys," Dave suggested. "You can hold hands and face the judge together once we're on the ground. But for now, Paul, I need your focus up here and on those pedals. Tag team, remember?"

Paul tried again to let his friend know that something weird had just happened to Gary, but Dave wasn't cluing in. He decided to let it go and turn his attention back to the task of helping fly the plane.

Up ahead, the Moose River slowly came into view, its east-west flow barely visible under a snug cloud deck. Dave watched their undersides drift over the airplane at most an arm's length above. "We're about to take a hard left at the lights, Ace, and we'll likely need heavy rudder in the corner. The wind's gonna really hammer us once we turn east towards Owensville. Think you can handle that?"

"I told you not to worry about me," Paul replied defensively. "You do your part, and I'll do mine." Paul pressed his back into the seat to minimize any upper body movement. His spine protested and he cringed in pain. "Think *you* can handle that?"

"You know," joked Dave. "You're getting a touch ornery in your old age. I've heard that B6 vitamins aren't just for PMS anymore." Dave motioned towards the back seat with a slight head nod. "And you might consider picking up a bottle as well for you know who."

It consistently amazed Paul how Dave's witty comebacks always defused his temperament. Smiling, he knew the mocking was all part of Dave's coping mechanism while under duress, and he felt extremely grateful for the man beside him, verbal quips and all.

Ahead, ribbons of cloud hung below a thick opaque mass, and as Dave banked the Maule to go around, a small, yet robust vortex of air from above spiraled downwards and took the plane with it. Reacting immediately, Dave pulled back on the yoke, but it was too much too fast. The sudden reversal elevated them into the sagging clouds, swiftly terminating visual flight. Dave checked the wings were level, eased off on the throttle and waited for the nose to drop. Seconds later, the clouds spit them back out and the gnarly winds eased off.

"If we're forced down any lower by these clouds," Paul noted, "we'll wish we had floats on this thing!"

Deliveries

Dave glanced out his window and replied nervously. "We've still got a hundred feet to play with, give or take. But I share that concern."

Beyond the Maule's nose, tree-covered mountains loomed, their bases jagged and angled towards the river. Adjoining outcrops of rock poked through shrinking holes in the clouds, and when Dave glanced up, several mountain summits sat completely obscured. With turbulent skies closing them in, he knew their odds of reaching Owensville airport also shrank. Dave clamped his hands to the yoke. "We've got killer mountains ahead boys, no foreshadowing intended. And because I'd rather we don't plow into them, it's time for a compass change."

Paul secured his feet to the pedals and kept his eyes forward. "Roger that," he replied. "You ready back there, Gary? This'll be a steep turn."

No reply came, and Paul didn't concern himself as too why.

Dave began with a gentle ten-degree bank angle on the wings, followed by twenty, rolling to thirty. Paul kept his eyes on the bank and turn coordinator and added enough rudder to keep the ball close to the centre. The airplane began to shudder from gusty west winds as though a huge wind machine suddenly turned on and slowly rotated towards the airplane.

Dave held altitude throughout the turn, managing to keep them a safe distance over the river and away from mountain slopes. "Walk in the park, Ace," he expressed confidently. "Unlike you, this is easy for a good pilot like me."

Paul shrugged his shoulders. "Whatever you say, Dave. Just keep us flying."

For an increasingly befuddled Gary Nordhavn, it all became too much. With his mental faculties decaying, he felt entirely powerless. It was that feeling of absolute defeatism that made him realize he needed to regain some measure of control. Problem is, he struggled with how to make that happen as his fingers stroked the gun wedged behind his back.

Chapter 31

At 100 feet above the Moose River, the Piper Cub sliced through an increasingly tumultuous sky, popping in and out of perpendicular wisps of cloud with spindly legs that touched the ground in places. For the time being, the rain had tapered off to a light smattering, but one glimpse up the valley and Kevin Davies knew the reprieve would be short-lived. And with impending heavy rain came an even more radical decline in visibility.

Blustery headwinds seemed intent on obstructing the forward progression of the plane. Kevin slid the throttle in a quarter inch to counter the effects of reduced speed and floundering directional control. The stick felt increasingly sluggish in his hands, while his feet on the pedals struggled to correct a notable yaw in both directions.

As promised, Susan remained quiet despite the wild flight conditions. Admittedly, Kevin enjoyed the solitude, but at the same time was grateful he wasn't alone. For the most part, he enjoyed solo flights. Yet at times like this, he welcomed the company inside the plane. Kevin broke his silence. "You okay back there, Susan?"

"Yup. No place would I rather be."

Kevin smiled to himself. "That's good to hear because I—"

"When do we land, Kevin?" interrupted Susan, her voice flat.

"I'd say we're less than twenty minutes to Spruce Creek. Fuels good, so before you know it, we'll—"

A sudden wind gust drove the nose sharply down. "Good grief!" said Kevin bluntly. He pulled the stick back and quickly recovered. "Sorry about that, Susan. Why is it every time I try optimism, we get pounded?"

"Maybe you should refrain from trying to polish a turd," Susan curtly replied. "I need straight-up answers, Kevin, especially when my life's at stake. I can see the gas gauge from here, and it seems low. So, how is that good?"

Kevin suddenly wished he'd remained quiet.

"And another thing," Susan went on to say. "According to my eyes, the clouds straight ahead look thicker than what we just turned away from towards Owensville. And I know we aren't IFR capable, nor are you. So, this mess is hardly a 'piece of cake' as you call it."

Kevin decided to let the dust settle before answering. "Polish a turd! Where'd you come up with that? That's one expression I'll store in my memory banks!"

Susan inhaled deeply to quell her anxiety and growing anger. "Please, Kevin, for the love of God just fly, and get us *safely* on the ground!"

* * *

Prone to passive-aggressive mood swings, the apparent hopelessness of his situation served as the catalyst, a tipping point that warped Gary's face into despair, chasing away his brain's ability to reason. Baffled by sudden thoughts of aggression, he shuddered as his brain toyed with ideas of trying to crash the plane; a quick and permanent fix to end his miserable plight.

Gary's eyes swept the forward cockpit and the two men at the controls. He felt increasingly captive with no way to escape his dire circumstances. As his muddled thinking grew more unstable, the bottle of diamonds on his lap caught his attention. They were the source of his angst, the poison fueling his desire for someone to pay for his mess. Anyone.

Reaching behind his back, Gary's fingers probed for his negotiating asset. Padding an already ugly mood swing, the pistol felt good in his hand, its raw power peeling away his insecurity—that he and no one else would control his destiny. Holding it nervously against his chest with his right hand, Gary painfully racked the slide once which he knew inserted a round into the chamber, and then he cocked the hammer. He pointed the Colt forward and aimed it loosely about the cabin. The sensation felt delicious, and though his collarbone spewed fresh waves of misery from the jolt, he found himself relishing it.

Coherent enough to decide the police could never find out about his business, Gary gave his head a shake and convinced himself he'd been hoodwinked by these self-serving bastards. That just like the scum who first strong-armed him into running diamonds, he was again being used as a puppet on someone else's string. And now the two men flying his airplane were taking him to where he didn't want to go.

Enraged, each new thought triggered waves of desperation. Gary looked again at the diamonds. *They need ta be delivered, and then it'll end*, he thought. Images of Cindy popped into his head. *We kin disappear into a foxhole, and they'll never find us. I'll make this all go away Cindy, you'll see.*

"We're turning around!" barked Gary decisively. "Back ta yer plane."

Paul Jackson kept hard on the rudder as the airplane rolled out of its bouncy turn towards home. "What'd you say back there?" he asked. "Sounded like you said you wanted to turn around." It was then Paul felt a hard tap on his shoulder. When he looked back, the air promptly vacated his lungs as if punched in the stomach. Pointed at his head was a black handgun, most of its bluing visibly worn away, but imposing nonetheless. Paul's feet unintentionally left the pedals and the Maule's tail slid out.

"Ace!" yelled Dave. "We're not out of the turn yet! What are you—"

Dave's peripheral vision picked up the weapon. He spun his head around and his eyes locked to its handler's sweaty face. "What's going on back there?"

"I said were turning around!" roared Gary as he swung the weapon in Dave's direction. "We're goin' back to yer plane and yer both getin' off!"

Gary's hand shook so badly that Dave thought he might drop the firearm. He watched him aim the pistol towards the roof and wave it about like it was a party favour.

"Have you lost your mind?" shouted Paul. "If this is some sort of joke, then it's not very—"

Gary squeezed the trigger. The gun fired one round into the roof, punching a jagged hole clean through and allowing a tiny ray of daylight to shine in. The smoking hot brass casing ejected from the right side of the weapon and pinged off the side window and onto the floor. Gary painfully lowered the heavy weapon and reissued his demands. "Back," he ordered, his lips throwing out strands of spittle. "Take us back. Now!"

Dave's ears buzzed from the ear-splitting concussion. "Are you crazy, man?" he screamed. "We just turned towards Owensville. Put that bloody thing away before you kill somebody, or yourself!"

Dave glanced at Paul and saw the raw fear in his friend's eyes. It was then he realized the gun's discharge was no accident. Gary Nordhavn had come unhinged and wanted his airplane back. Even more horrific for Dave was that in complete contrast to his problem-solving character, he hadn't a clue how to defuse the situation he and Paul found themselves in. And to make matters worse, he had always loathed the smell of gun powder.

* * *

"Kevin!" screamed Susan McCutcheon as she instinctively grabbed for the stick without being sure of what to do. "Pull up!"

Running a quick instrument scan, Kevin's eyes were aimed down and not out the front window. When he glanced up, his brain took a moment to process the rapidly burgeoning mass, while his eyes told him it wasn't possible. He struggled to make sense of what exactly he was seeing, but there was no time to process the visceral scene. They were about to die. That he totally understood.

The oncoming plane was right there, a white streak and spinning prop racing towards them dead on like a guided missile. In an act of desperation, Kevin heeded Susan's advice and yanked the stick to his chest. As the Cub launched skyward, he prayed the other pilot would see him and split off in any direction other than his. Kevin thought he heard Susan scream, but as the distance between the two planes eroded, he realized it wasn't her panicked voice. It was his.

**

Paul Jackson saw it first, followed a millisecond second later by Dave McMurray. Completely unexpected, the sudden appearance of another aircraft at their altitude seemed unbelievable, and yet there it was, a green blur directly in front and closing fast. Dave knew they'd be dead in a matter of seconds without immediate evasive action. The question was, which way to go? His first instinct was to pitch the nose up to avoid the collision, but he hesitated, and that split-second of indecision saved their lives.

The oncoming plane angled up steeply.

"He's climbing!" yelled Paul.

There was no hesitation now. Dave drove the yoke forward, plunging them wildly towards the Moose River. The Cub shot overhead, its main wheels missing the top of the Maule's fuselage by a paltry ten feet. The sudden disruption of airflow between the two opposing aircraft created pounding turbulence. Dave tussled with the plane and finally levelled off a mere thirty feet above the

Deliveries

river. His hands shook uncontrollably as he looked over at Paul. His co-pilot's palms lay flat against his chest.

"Ace, you okay?" shouted Dave, his voice stuttering.

Paul felt his heart, the organ hammering in his chest so hard that he thought for certain it might explode. "That was—"

"Take it easy!" interrupted Dave as he tried feverishly to regain control. "Save your breath!"

Paul's throat felt thick and dry. He tried to swallow. "Search and Rescue . . ." he grunted with his eyes closed. "That . . . was the . . . Cub out of Owensville."

"How'd you have time to see that?" asked Dave skeptically. "All I saw was a green blur and imminent death." Dave eased back on the yoke to regain lost altitude.

"Doesn't matter," Paul stammered. "Point is they were looking for us after all. Maybe we . . . should have stayed with the Cessna."

Dave smirked. "Too late for that now."

For a moment, neither Dave nor Paul gave any thought to their obstinate passenger, but that may have been just as well because Gary Nordhavn was utterly bewildered by the savage departure from level flight. Furious, his wild eyes tried desperately to absorb the scene in front of him. "What's goin' on?" he spewed. "Yer not gonna scare me with fancy flyin'. I said turn around!" Gary waved the gun about, the end of the barrel coming to rest at the crook of Dave's neck.

Horrified, Paul watched but couldn't find the words to speak.

Dave felt cold steel press against his skin and knew from Paul's expression exactly what it was. He closed his eyes a moment as a wellspring of emotion rose from the pit of his stomach. Certain his life would end in a matter of seconds, he quietly spoke the words, "Been a pleasure, Ace."

* * *

Susan McCutcheon's body shook so badly that she felt light-headed from the horror of what they had just survived. Frozen in fear, she teetered on the precipice of hysteria. Despite their near-death experience, one thing was certain; her warning to Kevin had very likely saved their lives. That, along with Kevin's quick reflexes. Now she needed to calm herself down. Susan reached up, squeezed her shoulders and neck at the same time, then thanked the good Lord above for saving their necks.

Like Susan, Kevin's adrenal had spiked, so much so that he found it difficult to keep his quivering feet on the pedals. Once he levelled the Cub off, he tried to regulate his breathing. He had read plenty of accident reports about midair collisions but never thought he would come so close to one this early in his career. Especially a near-miss over a mountain river in the middle of nowhere. "Where did that guy come from?" asked Kevin as he wiped the sweat from his neck. "I owe you big time, Susan! You saved us!"

"No, Kevin," Susan replied earnestly. "God saved us."

* * *

The shot never came.

Dave opened his eyes when he felt the gun's barrel leave his neck. He turned his head around and saw Gary Nordhavn grinning, the pistol back in his lap. From the crooked smile on the man's face, Dave knew they were in a heap of trouble as long as this lunatic held a weapon. In hindsight, Dave wished he had grabbed it away from Gary while they were still on the ground. Now he couldn't help but lash out. "You crazy son of a—"

"Enough!" rebuked Gary. "No more tricky stuff. If you don't do what I say, yer gonna die. We all will." Gary brandished the gun for emphasis. "I'm not scared to use this no more. I'm not scared of nobody no more!"

"What are you talking about, man?" barked Dave. "We nearly hit another plane just now! That's why we dove for the deck! Are you insane?"

Completely unnerved, Paul watched the exchange but never spoke. He tried to catch Dave's attention with his eyes, motioning for him to look towards the radio stack, but in his anger, Dave missed the cue.

"Maybe I am," barked Gary. "Don't matter now. Nothing matters now 'cept to deliver my diamonds and go away. I need you two off my plane, so turn around. Now!"

"All right," Dave conceded. "You win. But aim that bloody thing somewhere else, or so help me I'll—" Dave cut himself off. He wanted to lash out further but worried the gun would again come to bear. He glanced at Paul.

This time, Dave noticed Paul's eyes. He followed Paul's eye line to the radio panel. Shrugging his shoulders, he mouthed the word, "What?"

Paul hoped their freshly minted hijacker wouldn't notice the subtle exchange between himself and Dave. He brought his right hand slightly upwards, his index finger pointed towards the Com 1 radio. Dave noticed the frequency at 123.45 megahertz, a channel used for pilots to talk to each other between aircraft. Paul tipped his head towards his hand. Dave's eyes followed, and he saw Paul's finger holding down the button on the microphone.

Suddenly, Dave got it.

Paul was broadcasting their on-board chatter to anyone tuned to the same frequency, or more specifically to the Search and Rescue aircraft they nearly crashed into moments ago. *Assuming, of course, they were even listening?* thought Dave.

Dave nodded enough to let Paul know he understood. For Gary's sake, he made an exaggerated show of deliberately gripping the yoke with both hands. "We're turning around Gary, just like you asked. We'll go back to our Cessna, and you'll never have to deal with us or see us again."

"Smart choice," spouted Gary. "That's good."

Dave rolled the wings into a snug 180 degree turn away from Owensville and back towards the river valley they just flew out of. Paul tried to keep up on the rudder but had trouble coordinating the turn.

"But," added Dave, "on the condition you put the damn gun away. You have the control here, not us. Calm down, and we'll do what you ask."

With Paul's finger still on the button, it now became a question of whether the pilot of the Cub had his radio tuned to the same frequency. *If not*, thought Dave, *then this is the part where we fly off into the sunset and are never heard from again.*

Chapter 32

Kevin Davies wasn't sure what to make of the chatter coming through his radio, but he knew for certain it stemmed from the airplane they almost met head-on. "You hearing this, Susan?" he asked completely struck dumb. "They said something about turning back to their Cessna! That's gotta be the bird we're after!"

"Yup," Susan replied. "And something about a gun and diamonds? What on earth is going on inside that plane, and what does it have to do with our missing airplane and crew?"

The radio blared to life again, only this time it was a different voice. "Have you completely lost your mind, Gary? What's wrong with you? You rescue us, and then in the next breath you're threatening us by waving that gun around?"

"I think you just got your answer," announced Kevin. "This is incredible! It sounds like our missing pilots have already been rescued, if you can call it that. I can't believe I'm even saying this, but now we're also dealing with a possible hijacking? Whoever it is must have landed and picked them up, then gone off the deep end. At least we know the pilots are alive!"

"You can bet this broadcast is intentional, Kevin," added Susan. "And most likely for our benefit or anybody else who's listening on this frequency. Those guys are smart to do that. We need to notify base, and they can get hold of the authorities."

"One can assume they were heading to Owensville when we passed them," stated Kevin unquestioningly. "That's a given. But like us, they'll find out pretty quick that route isn't going to work. And if they are in fact going back to the Cessna, they'll also be forced to turn around, and that won't be easy in this weather. Maybe they'll head to Spruce Creek like us and—"

Another bit of radio chatter interrupted Kevin. "If we go back to our plane and get out, how are you going to fly with a broken collarbone? Let's think this through Gary. Just put the gun away, and we can work this out."

Kevin had heard enough. "Eastbound aircraft over the Moose River. This is Owensville Airborne Search and Rescue Piper Cub Romeo One, on Unicom channel one-two-three decimal four-five. I understand you have a weapon-related"—Kevin wanted to say hijacking, but switched his thinking—"situation? Do you copy?"

No reply.

"Do you think that was wise, Kevin? If there's a bad guy on that plane, then we can only assume he just heard you ask for a status check. I don't think he'd be happy that we're on to him. You may have just put our pilots at risk."

"Either way, we've got a job to do," replied Kevin. "We nearly died a moment ago, and I need to find out what's going on. So, the sooner we figure that out, the sooner we get ourselves back on the ground and those men to safety—and their gun-toting passenger into custody."

Kevin tried the radio again but received nothing but unsettling static.

* * *

More than surprised when he heard the radio call, but still levelheaded enough to understand the ramifications, Gary Nordhavn flew into another rage. "Don't be answering that," he roared. "Let it be. We keep goin' back, just like I said."

As Dave rolled out of their turn and aimed the Maule's nose back towards the south fork of the river, he wasn't at all pleased with the view out the front window, or in any direction for that matter. A sudden wind gust chucked the plane sideways and then viciously upwards. Coming to blows with the yoke as if it had a mind of its own, Dave battled the control as it jerked opposite to where he needed it to go. "I hate to burst your bubble, Gary, but the road you want us to take isn't one I'm flying through. We're surrounded by pumpkin soup. So, I hope you've got a Plan B because there's no way we'll get back to our plane. In fact, I'm not sure we can land anywhere just now. Open your eyes, man! The weather has us completely—" The end of the gun's barrel pressed in on Dave's neck, lingered a few tortuous seconds, then pulled slightly away.

Paul flipped his head towards Dave, noticed the pistol, and felt a huge sense of relief when Gary withdrew it all the way to his lap. "Dave's right," he added watchfully. "The valley is completely closed in. It's suicide to fly through that wall of cloud. We'd never even find our plane, let alone be able to land. Is that what you want, Gary?"

Gary craned his neck forward to look for himself. As his eyes processed the dismal scene, large raindrops began to pelt the fuselage as if someone turned on a fire hose from high above. Panicked, the sudden realization that his plan backfired sent waves of dread into his already tormented system. Gary eyed the gun warily, then as quickly raised it back up, but this time he aimed it loosely towards Paul. "This plane'll land on a dime, so find another place. I still got a job ta do, and I want you's both off." Gary winced painfully without letting go of his trump card. His collarbone felt red-hot, as though a smelting poker rammed through the joint.

Paul tempered his voice despite his growing urge to lash out in anger himself. "If we get off, Gary," he patiently explained, "you can't fly this airplane without us, and you know it. Look at you. You can barely hold that gun and—"

"Shut up!" screamed Gary. "Just land somewhere and get off!"

Paul's focus went from the distraught man's face to the gun. He couldn't bring himself to believe that Gary would actually have the nerve to use it on them, but then he wasn't at all willing to test that theory. He turned to Dave. "Let's maintain this heading. I think Spruce Creek is our only bet if the weather cooperates. There isn't anywhere safe that I know of to set us down along the river."

Dave nodded miserably.

Paul noticed the gloss of perspiration on Dave's face. He tried feverishly to keep the Maule's tail from sliding about in the wind, but with every bump of turbulence came stabs of pain through the entire length of his spine. He pulled his feet from the pedals and froze.

"You okay there, Ace?" asked Dave nervously.

Paul rotated his head side to side. "I need to rest my back, Dave. We'll need rudder when we land this thing. I'm not sure if—" Paul achingly scrunched his face—"I'll be much use to you when the time comes."

Dave tried adjusting the trim to offset a persistent nose-down attitude, but his efforts did little to counter the problem. The Maule thrashed up and down in the turbulence as he finagled the nose towards Spruce Creek.

Gary fussed but made no attempt to protest their new heading.

"Don't worry about the landing," assured Dave. He keyed the microphone for the benefit of his audience hopefully listening in the Cub. "We need to keep our backseater happy and ourselves alive. The air to Spruce Creek could become a lot bumpier than we're experiencing now. And I don't want that gun going off again, by accident or otherwise."

Paul tried to recover his stomach from the extreme oscillations in pitch. "If it gets any worse than this," he cringed, "then I think I'd rather be shot than have to endure this turbulence and nausea."

"Be careful what you wish for, Ace," cautioned Dave. "Sometimes wishes come true."

Deliveries

* * *

"They've turned around, Susan!" shouted Kevin. "They'll be on our six in no time!" Kevin eased off on the throttle. "With any luck, we'll get a visual if they go by and I can see what kind of plane it is. Yell if you see them. I don't want to become a hood ornament."

Susan wasn't sharing Kevin's enthusiasm or his attempt at being smart-alecky. "Not funny, Kevin," she complained. "I wish we could get hold of somebody on the ground and let them know we've found our pilots, not to mention what's going on inside that plane."

"It's okay," replied Kevin. "At least Rob knows we're heading to Spruce Creek. And knowing him, I bet he's heading there too."

Susan swallowed hard. "The clouds are thick through here, and there's barely enough room for us over the river, let alone two airplanes trying to squeeze through."

Kevin chuckled. "Our missing pilots are in that plane with a lunatic and a gun. We can't contact Rob, and we're flying half-blind. Plus, I've never landed at Spruce Creek. And all you worry about is another mid-air?"

"Well, the first near-miss wasn't overly pleasant!" snapped Susan. "And by my count, we're out of options to help anyone besides ourselves. We're low on gas and I feel like I could throw up again if we don't—"

An undercut of wind forcefully lambasted the Cub, lofting it twenty feet up in a matter of seconds. Kevin reacted immediately by pushing forward on the stick and kicked in hard left rudder to counter the sudden tailslide. Susan screamed as the plane levelled back out and Kevin regained control. "You okay?" he asked.

"Peachy," replied Susan quietly. "And quit asking me that. We need to get our wheels on the ground, so how about you just focus on that!"

"I couldn't agree more. How about I get on the Com channel and ask our friends behind us to watch they don't end up chewing our tail off with their prop as the go by."

This time, Susan couldn't have agreed more.

* * *

Back alleys were not one of Stan Fenwick's happy places, but unbecoming locations came with the job. He had spent enough time conducting creepy investigations in their dank confines to last a lifetime, but this one had him on edge. He inhaled deeply as he reluctantly crossed over the invisible line from civility to depravity. At times like this, his holstered 9 mm Beretta service pistol and uniform provided a welcome sense of security.

Because of heavy rain the day before, puddles littered the cracked pavement in and around rows of dented garbage bins and heaps of litter. As Stan circumvented the debris field, a hideously ragged cat pounced from behind a trash bag and spooked him half to death.

"Easy Fenwick," he said aloud. "Last thing you need now is a heart attack this close to retirement."

Amazed at how existing daylight diminished the farther down the alley he walked, Stan glanced up at the weathered multistory buildings along both sides. Rusted metal frame stairwells hung below several doors and window frames, and it wasn't long before a pungent aroma filled his nostrils. He wondered how long it had been since the city's sanitation department had collected the trash here. Stan figured they purposely shied away from servicing alleys when they could get away with it, which by all indications happened frequently. He filed away a mental note to contact City Hall and kick somebody's butt over that.

Whether his informant was in this particular alley on this particular day was more a guess than anything else. Stan learned that his stool pigeon friend often hung out near the rear door of an

Italian bakery, snagging expired baked goods when made available by the head baker.

Void of any distinguishable detail, the alley presented itself in bland tones of grey and black. With everything surrounding him damp and splattered in muddy rainwater, Stan shuffled along tardily. He half expected to trip up on a sleeping hobo hidden by garbage and clutter. As he approached the area where he thought Rebellion might be, he paused a moment to listen. Water dripped from downspouts and a pathetic sounding dog yapped somewhere far off, the poor creature assuredly distressed. Muffled voices bled out from the inside of several unkempt brick and mortar walls. Stan mustered the courage to take a few more steps forward when suddenly a gravelly male voice echoed from the shadows.

"You a cop?" spewed a hidden man in a highly combative tone.

An icy shiver crawled up Stan's spine. He backed up several paces and instinctively placed his hand on the grip of his gun. For a moment, Stan found himself unable to answer. He half expected a razor-sharp blade to flash past his eyes and slam into his gut—then lights out.

"Yes," Stan finally answered. "So the uniform would suggest. Inspector Fenwick is my name from OPD. I'm looking for a man who calls himself Rebellion. Do you know him or where he might be today? It's important I speak with him, sooner than later."

"Pretty nervy to show yourself in here," rasped the voice. "You got a death wish, Inspector?"

"No," replied Stan. "No, I assure you that I don't. I'm simply here following up on a case and a recent lead. Do you know where Rebellion is? I'm fine with one-word answers if that's all you can offer, so yes or no is fine. Then, I'll leave you be."

Stan froze for several bone-chilling seconds when out of the shadows emerged a hulk of a man rimmed in silhouette from a pole light directly behind him. "I'm Rebellion."

Stan retreated several more steps to reclaim his personal space while fingering his 9 mm. "You're certainly a stealthy one, aren't you? I didn't hear you or see you at all for that matter."

"Gotta be 'round here," the man growled. "It's how I survive."

Stan tried to control his noticeably shaky voice. "I'm sorry to interrupt your day, but I'm following up on the message you left for me this morning on my cell phone, and I'm trying to figure out how legitimate this is?"

Rebellion leaned in, the crown of his head seven inches above Stan's. "You questioning my information?" he snapped. "My sources are good, and that's all you need to know."

Dark shadows playing across Rebellion's face made it nearly impossible for Stan to recognize any detail or see his eyes. "Well," he replied. "I believe what you said has merit, but I need more than what you gave me to proceed with this investigation. Do you know anything else? Anything at all?"

Rebellion turned away. "Can't tell you no more. I gotta protect myself."

Protect yourself from what? wondered Stan. "May I at least ask how you know about the stones, which I imagine are diamonds, and their method of transport into the city?"

Rebellion kept his back towards Stan. "You won't find these bloody people Inspector, cause they're like ghosts. What I told you is true. End of story."

"And how exactly do you know this?" Stan carefully probed.

"Because," growled Rebellion as he quickly spun around.

Stan pulled his 9 mm from its holster but kept it near his hip.

"I used to run goods for them myself," announced Rebellion with obvious reservations.

That news rendered Stan speechless. Before he could respond, the man in front of him spoke again. "But I messed up and missed a bunch of drops. They started to threaten me, so I stole from their inventory. That's why I'm in here living like a dog because they don't give up looking to hurt people who screw them over. I had to disappear." Rebellion walked away.

Stan holstered his gun and watched the figure slide back into the shadows. He called out one last time. "One final thing if I may? You said you used to run goods for them. Any chance of you elaborating on that?"

Stan waited for a moment. When no answer came, he turned and headed back towards the lit comfort of the street. Just then, the bowels of the alley once again called out his name.

"Fenwick."

It was Rebellion, his voice softer this time.

Stan stopped in his tracks and spun around, but he saw no one. "Yes?" he asked quietly. "Was there something else you—"

"You gotta promise me you'll not come after me when I tell you this," insisted Rebellion. "I know I did wrong and living like this is punishment enough. I can't do jail time. I'll trade you info for clemency. We have a deal?"

Stan thought for a moment. He needed whatever information this man was about to share and only hoped that silence on his part was worth the forthcoming admission. "Fine," he agreed. "You have my word."

"Okay then," confided Rebellion. "I flew diamonds in just like the poor stooge doing it now. I know their system. All of it."

Awestruck by what he heard; Stan dragged his feet back into the darkness towards the voice. "You're a . . . pilot?" he asked incredulously. "But how did—"

"Was a pilot," interrupted Rebellion. "Don't fly no more. But the last thing I'll say is the plane I flew is likely the same one that's bringin' diamonds in now. It's an old Maule M-4 they give to whatever schlep they coerce into flying the stones. Now, I'm done my piece and you need to go."

Stan lingered a moment longer to see if any other information might be offered. When none came, he shivered and promptly left the alley. Pondering the notion of grabbing another much-needed coffee to mull over his options, the underlying problem was that he hadn't the foggiest idea what those options would be. What he did know for certain was the uniform had to come off, a tool of the trade he seldom enjoyed wearing.

* * *

"So, it was just a bad plug connection to the generator all along?" marvelled Jack Ward. "Something so simple and I completely missed it. I guess troubleshooting electrical issues is not my forte."

Tom slapped Jack on the shoulder. "It's always like that," he laughed. "The easiest way to solve a problem is often the thing most overlooked. But what's important now is the field lights are on, and we can lay that mystery to rest."

"Amen to that," agreed Jack. "Thanks to the tomfoolery of those boys out there. Otherwise, we'd likely still be chasing a wild goose. I was so sure the problem was in the junction box or the connections between the cables that I would have bet money on it."

Tom smiled and eyed the two young men. "See, Jack, slaking pays off, and I should have taken that bet!"

Matt Hawley and Dylan Sullivan walked along the rows of lights replacing burnt-out bulbs. Dylan carried a box containing dozens of the little white lights, while Matt held a bag with broken or dead ones.

"I need to be sure this doesn't happen again, Tom," Jack remarked. "It haunts me to think that airplane could have landed here safely last night had I checked things beforehand."

"Still berating yourself for that, eh amigo?" asked Tom. "What's done is done, Jack."

Jack shrugged his shoulders. "Easy for you to say. But now that we've dealt with this mess, I should probably get back to the lodge and see how things are going. Hopefully nobody's burned the place down."

Tom started to walk towards Dylan and Matt, both of whom were crouched down swapping out bulbs. He turned and spoke to Jack. "You coming or are you planning to stay there and reminisce about all that could have been in the past twenty-four hours?"

Jack offered a cranky look in Tom's direction before stepping forward through wet clumps of grass. "Hold your horses, will you? I'm just trying to soak up a rare moment of bliss, and there you go ruining it again."

Tom waited for Jack to catch up. "Let's give the boys enough time to finish with the lights, and then we'll get something to eat. I need a coffee in the worst way and should make a few calls."

"I'll second that motion," responded Jack with genuine enthusiasm.

Even in broad daylight, the rows of lit bulbs stood out dramatically in the grass. As his eyes took in the scene, Jack conjured in his mind an image of fireflies spreading out in a long line. He decided at that moment to keep the lights on until dusk to make certain there were no further issues.

As Dylan and Matt continued the repairs, Tom picked up a flat stone and tried his best to skip it across the inner shoreline of the lake. The disc caught the edge of a wave and promptly sank.

A bold-faced smile played across Jack's face. "You're not too good at that are you, Tom? Perhaps you'd allow me to demonstrate?"

"Do I have a choice? Though come to think of it, you rarely give me one."

Jack selected what he thought was the perfect skipping stone. "No, my friend, you don't have a choice! Some things, runway lighting excluded, is best left in the hands of a master."

Tom bowed and motioned with his hands for Jack to continue. "The lake belongs to you, master stone skipper."

Jack positioned the rock in his fingers with the care and precision of a baseball pitcher prepping a fastball. He leaned to the side and jettisoned the stone in one fluid motion. The projectile hit the water flat between two waves and glanced off. The process repeated itself so many times that Tom lost count. Jack stood upright and selected another stone. "Care to watch that again, old boy?" he asked in a sassy tone.

Tom shook his head. "Nah, I know when I've been beaten, Jack. But I have a feeling you'll skip another just to solidify your point."

Jack grabbed another stone. "You know me too well."

Tom glanced towards the lake. "Then skip away, and I shall again bear witness to your mastery of—"

Tom stopped mid-sentence, immediately catching Jack's attention. "What is it?" he asked. "Cat got your tongue amid my superior skill?"

"Quiet!" ordered Tom. "Do you hear that, Jack?"

Jack cocked his head. "Hear what? All I hear is wind and birds, and you ordering me to shut my yap."

Tom walked to the edge of the shoreline as if a few extra feet would improve his hearing. "For a second, I thought I heard an airplane engine. It was faint, but I'd swear it was there."

Jack listened for a moment but heard nothing beyond the natural sounds around him. "I think your ears are playing tricks on you."

Tom cupped his hands in behind his ears. "You may be right," he agreed. "But then my hearing has always been a strong point for me." He inclined his ears a moment longer and then gave up. "Guess you're right."

Suddenly Dylan yelled from mid-field. "You hear that, Dad?" he asked excitedly.

Tom spun around to face his son. "Hear what exactly?" he asked without revealing his suspicion.

"An airplane," replied Dylan. "Pretty sure."

Doubting no more, Jack flung another stone. "Like father, like son."

Chapter 33

Infuriated that outsiders knew of his escapades, Gary Nordhavn's rage ballooned. In his mind, only three things mattered: survival, delivery of his package, and skedaddling. But he couldn't accomplish those tasks with others flying his plane. He needed these men off and the sooner the better. Gary flashed the gun between Dave and Paul. "How'd them guys know 'bout me?" he demanded. "Only one way as I figure."

"Does that really matter now?" argued Paul. "You've got the upper hand anyway, Gary. The people in that Cub are just doing their job, so don't worry about them. We'll set down at Spruce Creek and then you can—"

"Won't be no Spruce Creek," bellowed Gary. "Land sooner and get off." Gary held the bottle of diamonds aloft. "I got business, and then I vanish." A razor-sharp stab of pain erupted in his collarbone. He yelped and fell back. As he did so, the bottle left his fingers and tumbled off the top corner of Dave's seat, ending up in Paul's lap.

It took but a moment for Paul to realize what had happened. He snatched the diamonds from his lap and opened his side-door window. In one swift movement, Paul undid the lid, discreetly emptied the contents into his shirt pocket for leverage, screwed the lid back down and ejected the bottle into the Maule's slipstream with exaggerated movements. The container vanished into the raging current of the Moose River.

Despite searing pain, Gary was coherent enough to know what just happened to his precious cargo. His delivery was no more, as could soon be his life. "What've you done?" he wailed. "Them diamonds keeps me alive!"

"It's for your own good!" Paul yelled back. "I did you a big favour!"

The gun flashed and came to bear at the back of Paul's head. "What ya did was just condemn me! Without them diamonds, I'm a dead man and so are you!"

With distractions beside him and from behind, Dave unwittingly allowed the Maule to dip too close to the river. He frantically reefed back on the yoke, recovered the aircraft and turned to Gary. "For God's sake, if you're going to use that bloody gun on us, then make it quick! I've had it with you waving that thing around like a kid's squirt gun!"

Paul looked at Dave with a horrified expression. "Not the best choice of words to defuse things."

"Sorry, Ace," added Dave. "But I say it like it is!"

"Enough!" barked Gary as he pulled the gun away. "Yer lucky for now, but you'll pay for what ya done to my diamonds. Both of ya!"

For Paul, this whole absurd fiasco was like something from the pages of a movie script and having a loaded handgun pointed at his noggin wasn't helping his cardiac anomalies in the least. Skipping beats was nothing new but fading vision and shortness of breath were. Paul massaged his chest and lowered his head which helped to alleviate the symptoms. His fingers brushed against the loose diamonds in his shirt pocket, and he wasn't sure if Dave saw him pocket the stones before tossing the bottle. For now, they simply needed to get off this airplane.

"Put us down now!" growled Gary. "Just find somewhere ta land."

"We can't!" Paul retorted. "We already told you there isn't anywhere to land. By the sound of it, you fly this route all the time, so you know I'm telling the truth. Spruce Creek is our only option. You can drop us off there and go."

In Gary's delusional state, every shard of rational thought collapsed into a horrid mental debate. It felt like an angel on one shoulder and the devil on another, and no matter how hard Gary battled the demon within, he could not stifle his downward spiral. At this moment, his situation felt hopeless, so much so that Gary struck the side of his temple with the gun, which instantly drew a trickle of blood. The resulting sting of pain added to his quandary.

"I told ya"—Gary leaned against his right-side window and moaned. Holding the gun in his right hand with his index finger wound around the trigger, he tried unsuccessfully with his slung arm to dab blood as it rolled down his cheek. "I don't wanna go to Spruce Creek. Land now, so I—"

The Colt discharged again, only this time the slug passed through the left side of the fuselage behind Dave's shoulders. Disoriented and unable to comprehend where the deafening concussion stemmed from, Gary began to shake as a horrified expression played across his face. His wild eyes darted about the cockpit, then to the smoking gun. It was at that moment he realized what he had done. Panicked, he hurled the weapon to the floor and placed both hands on his head like a child who realized they just did something terribly wrong.

Paul wasn't immediately sure if he'd been shot, or worse yet, Dave. His adrenaline spiked body and ringing ears needed to settle before that could be determined. Following a quick self-assessment, he glanced at Dave, who except for displaying a look of horror on his face, appeared unscathed and fortunately still had the plane under his control. "You okay?" he asked through taxed breathing.

Too shaken to verbally reply, Dave nodded and offered a barely discernible thumb' up. If they had any hope of landing safely at Spruce Creek, he understood the necessity of settling his pulse and somehow neutralizing their troubled passenger. More than anything now, Dave sensed their odds of surviving this debacle grew smaller with each expended bullet. He wanted out of the airplane as much as Gary did.

Paul spun his head towards the back seat. Gary sat quietly with his face buried in both palms. No sigh of the gun. Fresh blood stained the side of his face from an ugly gash behind his eye, and Paul could not help but wonder if he might be somehow returning to his pre-meltdown senses. He felt again for the diamonds in his shirt pocket and would use them as collateral if the gun came into play again. Paul toyed with the idea of letting Gary know he had them but changed his mind.

Dave glanced at the GPS and zoomed out the display. The western shore of Bayshore Lake came into view and Dave knew they'd soon be on the ground one way or another. He grabbed the POH and handed it to Paul without saying a word about the gunshot. He wasn't hit and neither was Paul, so that's all that mattered. "Flip to the landing checklist, Ace," he ordered. "We should get ready for whatever type of wheels-meet-earth touchdown is coming."

"It's the whatever part I'm stressed about," added Paul. "And right now, I'm worried we won't even make it that far." Paul used his thumb to point towards Gary. "As you said before, I get the feeling he doesn't mean us any real harm, but that gun has to go."

Dave keyed the radio transmit button again. "Are you kidding me, Paul?" he angrily rebuked. "This guy's as unstable as a bottle of nitroglycerin in a paint shaker. Two bullet holes in this airplane are harmful enough for me. And since you offed the goods, Mr. Happy Pants isn't too happy. How do we know the next two shots aren't directed at us? Boom-Boom we're dead. The fact remains that as long as the gun's back there, and we're up here, the ball's not in our court."

Paul reached into his shirt pocket and grabbed a handful of diamonds. He discreetly opened his palm in front of his chest to prevent Gary from seeing them. "Things aren't always as they seem."

Dave shook his head in disbelief. "Yup, apparently not," he acknowledged.

*　*　*

Except for the SUV tucked in closely behind, the twisty road to Spruce Creek remained void of traffic. Rob Smith wasn't pleased he had company but knew better than to try to control the willful actions of others, especially three determined women who wanted the rescue party to start. He turned up the radio and wished his MG surrounded him instead of the bucket he sat in. A song by the rock band Trooper filtered through the speakers. "*We're here for a good time, not a long time. So, have a good time, the sun can't shine every day.*" Rob snickered at the irony.

In the driver's seat sat Laura Hastings. She glanced at Rob briefly and then into the rearview mirror. "They sure like to follow close, don't they?" she complained.

"I'd have preferred they stay at Moger's Point," Rob added. "There isn't a thing they can do anyway once we get to Spruce Creek. I told them we'd be back once I checked on the Cub, but these women are very determined."

"Guess you really can't blame them given what they've been going through," replied Laura. "I'm sure I'd behave the same way if my husband went missing . . . if I had one that is."

Rob turned the radio off when the song ended. "Yup, I suppose you're right. This whole ordeal has been a first-class screw-up right from the get-go. We've had everything against us, and we're still no closer to finding these guys. It's frustrating, to say the least."

Laura nodded without taking her eyes off the road. "Well, boss, we can only do what we can do. Can't get water out of a stone unless you're Moses."

Rob smirked. "And what pray-tell do you mean by that?"

Laura tapped the brakes as the van swung around a sharp corner. "Just that," she explained. "No sense in getting worked up about things you have little control over. We can only handle the problems one at a time as they come up. That's all anyone can do in these situations."

Rob shook his head. "You know," he stated respectfully. "For a writer with little mountain driving experience, you're about as wise as Moses."

This time Laura chuckled. "Just trying to keep you grounded, boss. Don't want you beating yourself up when none of this is your fault to begin with. When I produced videos for a living, I learned early on that no matter how much I prepared for the shoot, once on location, things often went south, and it was rarely because of my lack of preparedness. Things sometimes happen that are totally beyond our control, and sometimes it's those surprises that result in the best outcome."

Rob nodded in agreement and patted his stomach when it began to growl. "Oh great," he remarked disgustedly. "Just what I need right now."

Laura smiled but didn't say anything further. She reached into one of her vest pockets, grabbed a granola bar, and passed it to Rob. Then she flicked on the windshield wipers to offset a sudden sprinkle of rain from a plethora of thick, dreary clouds directly above.

"Thanks, Mom," added Rob as he watched the wiper blades swish back and forth. What little blue sky remained was shrinking as stormy weather slithered in from the west. He knew mountain-based systems could roll through quickly or last for hours, and any chance of resuming an aerial search today would be entirely dependent on the whims of nature. Quite certain his pilot and spotter would spend the night at Spruce Creek, Rob beat the top of the dash with his fist. *Not a good weekend for being a search and rescue coordinator,* he thought angrily.

Laura flinched but kept driving.

Despite his disappointment, Rob decided that driving away from the endless pelting of questions and suggestions from well-intentioned people wasn't a bad thing. As the van rounded another hairpin corner, Laura balanced her braking and acceleration to make sure the wheels stayed centre along the narrow road. Rob leaned forward and glanced into the sky. He wondered about the Piper Cub and hoped his crew had already landed safely at Spruce Creek.

Rob picked up the hand-held radio from the seat beside him, turned it on, and as quickly killed the power. Given their location and presumed distance from the Cub, he realized that any attempt to contact the plane would be in vain. He brought it along more as a security blanket than anything else.

Checking his side-view mirror and not seeing any cars behind, Rob wondered if his tiny entourage had given up. But to his disappointment, the SUV reappeared over the crest of a steep hill and quickly caught up. Sighing loudly, he gripped both his shoulders and tried to squeeze out the tension he felt building up in his muscles.

* * *

"Do we need to follow him so closely," asked Diane nervously. "I hate mountain roads, Tess, and I'm scared we'll slip over the edge."

Tess eased off the gas to allow further separation between the front of her SUV and the bumper of Rob Smith's vehicle. "Sorry, Diane. I just want to get there already, and they're driving like a pair of old women." Tess shifted uncomfortably in her seat. "Besides the fact I'm starving and really need a bathroom, it'll be good for you and Kim to visit with Jack too. No doubt he feels bad for what happened and could use a touch of forgiveness."

Diane shrugged her shoulders. "I don't feel too forgiving right now, Tessa, but I know this mess isn't Jack's fault. He did his best, and that's all I could have asked from him. I know I sound like a broken record, but this is all on Paul's shoulders. He never should have flown and"—Diane's voice caught—"if he's still alive, he may never fly again."

Kim reached forward consolingly and gently massaged her mom's shoulders. "Tess is right, Mom. It'll be nice to see Uncle Jack again. I bet he cheers up when we all give him a big hug. And yes, food and a bathroom would be really great about now. And as far as Dad and Dave go, I bet they're both just fine."

"Always the optimist, aren't you Kimmy?" acknowledged Diane. "And I love you for it. Maybe I'll feel better once we get to Spruce Creek. It would be good to see Jack again. I wasn't the kindest I could have been to him on the phone, and I feel bad for that."

Tess looked over at her friend. "Stress levels were pretty high at that moment, Diane. I think you had every right to be curt with Jack. He did, after all, play a part in all of this."

Diane stared thoughtfully out her side window at the passing scenery. It felt void of any real beauty, and she wondered if life from here on would ever have meaning if Paul failed to come home.

"You okay?" asked Tess.

Diane shook her head side to side. "I'm not even sure what okay feels like anymore, and it's been less than a day since this all started. I just want my husband back, Tess, and it's the not knowing if he's dead or alive that's ripping at my heart. Why are you not pulling your hair out? Dave's in this mess too."

"I can't explain it. I just have this feeling that our guys are fine."

"How can you be so sure?" asked Diane. "And don't tell me women's intuition."

"No," Tess answered consolingly. "This is Paul and Dave we're talking about here. Those two don't know the meaning of the word quit. Somehow, someway, I know that whatever trouble they've found themselves in, they'll find a way out. They always do no matter their battle scars."

Diane smiled. "I hope you're right, Tess." *I truly hope you're right.*

* * *

Dumbfounded by the realization that the men they'd been searching for had somehow ended up in the plane behind them, Susan McCutcheon wasn't sure what to think. The very notion they were being held at gunpoint seemed outlandish. And from what she and Kevin heard on the radio about shots being fired? Well, that iced the cake for unbelievable. Susan could not help but wonder if the whole charade was nothing more than a fabrication of someone's ill-advised attempts at trying to be funny. But whether true or false, she wasn't about ignoring the chills coursing up and down her spine.

With the missing airmen apparently heading to Spruce Creek, the situation would play itself out one way or another. At this point, Susan worried more about having their tail sliced off than anything else. When she twisted her head around, it was then her heart went into her throat. The white-skinned aircraft suddenly appeared through a mass of cloud, hanging in the sky like a bird of prey waiting for the right moment to strike. It quickly closed the gap and tucked in on the left side of the Cub, lower and slightly behind.

Susan's mouth had never felt so dry. She tried to speak. "I, I see them Kevin!" she reported. "Left side. They just came out of nowhere like a ghost! I see the pilots, but don't see any movement from the backseat. I don't see anyone back there. Maybe things have settled down, and they're okay."

Busy steering the Cub around a menacing wall of cloud, Kevin gazed out his window and saw what he recognized as a Maule, the plane flying in loose formation a few hundred feet away. He watched in fascination as the aircraft tucked in alongside, far too close for his liking. Fighting the urge to wave them off, Kevin decided they must have a good reason for moving in so close. He focused on keeping the Cub as steady as possible. The last thing he needed was a high-five with the wingtips of both birds.

"I wouldn't count on it," Kevin replied distractedly. "According to the crew, it sounds like the dude in the backseat isn't firing on all cylinders. I can't see him either, but if he's desperate enough to have already fired the gun inside the cabin, then I have little doubt he'll use it again to get what he wants. Whatever that is."

Susan tried with no success to re-position her stiffening limbs. She promptly gave up and refocused her eyes on the Maule's cockpit. Both pilots stared back, and the one in the closest seat was trying to articulate something with his hands. "Is there any way we can get closer to them?" asked Susan.

Kevin laughed. "You're kidding, right? We're already close enough to spit at them. With the winds through this valley tossing us around, I don't want to be any closer than this. Besides, I doubt they'll stay with us for long. I'm betting those guys want to land ASAP."

"How close are we to Spruce Creek?" asked Susan.

Kevin glanced at the GPS. "The western edge of Bayshore Lake is just coming into view, so not much longer."

"That's good," replied Susan. "Because the guy in the backseat just sat up and opened the window. And now he's waving something small and black around."

Kevin glanced in the Maule's direction and it was then he noticed the distinct shape of a gun in the man's hands, its barrel pointed right at them. "Oh, not good!" he shouted. "Hang on, Susan!"

Susan instinctively leaned away, but there was nowhere to go. "Oh my God!"

Kevin yanked the throttle back and added a notch of flaps. The Cub lifted and fell behind the Maule. "That's one crazy son-of-a-gun in that plane, no pun intended!"

Susan's voice shook. "It's not every day you have a gun pointed at you! The farther we stay away from that plane, the better. Let them go, Kevin, and we'll catch up at Spruce Creek."

But Kevin wasn't listening as he applied full throttle to close the widening gap.

* * *

Gary Nordhavn struggled to close his window, and that simple task alone added to his fury. He ditched the gun on the seat beside him and tried feverishly against the rushing wind engulfing the cabin. He cussed several times and inadvertently rammed his knees into the back of the front seat.

The sudden jolt startled Dave, causing him to accidentally push forward on the yoke. The nose slipped down a few degrees, but he quickly recovered. Dave glanced at Paul whose contorted face displayed the obvious pain in his body. "You okay, Ace," he asked. "Sorry, I know I keep asking you that."

Paul held up his hand, palm out to indicate he needed a moment to recover. "Yup," he finally answered. "My spine doesn't react well to sudden bumps like that." Paul leaned back into his seat. "I'm fine except for a few slipped discs, but the same can't be said for our friend back there. This really has to end."

"Won't disagree with you there," said Dave.

Paul watched Gary fussing with the window. It wasn't a difficult task for someone of sound mind, but this man was wobbling on a very dangerous precipice and clearly needed a healthy dose of crisis intervention. But until they landed, there wasn't a thing he or Dave could do. Paul noticed the handgun on the seat, but any attempt to grab it could result in bullets flying, and he wasn't at all willing to take the chance.

Dave piped up. "He needs to get that window closed, Ace. I've seriously had it with this guy."

"Me too. But from up here and with us both injured, there isn't much we can—"

The rushing wind through the cockpit abruptly ended. Paul turned to see Gary flashing the gun about in quick, unpredictable movements. He began to laugh hysterically, followed by a litany of verbal nonsense.

"What's he yammering about," asked Dave. "He sounds like a damn Klingon!"

Paul brushed aside Dave's reference to Star Trek, as twisted and ill-timed as it was. He thought again about trying to rip the pistol from Gary's hand, but the risk of it going off was far too great. He watched Gary a moment longer and noticed, curiously enough, his unlatched seatbelt. Whether undone by choice or by negligence, it didn't matter. Paul's brain suddenly conjured up a preposterous idea.

Chapter 34

The puzzle pieces were starting to fit together for Stan Fenwick, but after his bizarre meeting with Rebellion, he still had no idea when or even where the diamond toting airplane and its pilot would show up. Figuring it too risky and out in the open, he dismissed Owensville Municipal as the likely staging ground. He theorized the plane would land somewhere outside of town on one of many rural private airstrips. There was also no shortage of remote county roads with enough room to serve as a runway. As Stan understood it, the diamonds would be brought into town, stashed at the post office and later retrieved. The Maule and its pilot would then hypothetically vanish until the next delivery date.

For Stan, cases like this one proved more frustrating than anything else. It wasn't uncommon to come up empty-handed after months or even years of investigation. Leads were often scarce or resulted in dead ends. Stan scratched his chin and thought about the plane in question. *It needs fuel and maintenance just like a car, and somebody somewhere must see the darn thing once in a while? How hard can it be to track an airplane?*

For lack of anything else to go on, Stan decided to drive to Owensville airport. He wondered if perhaps anyone there knew something about the Maule and might be able to shed light on its registration and ownership. Buckling his seatbelt, he cranked the ignition and waited for the engine to recover from what felt like a faster than normal idle. "Always something needing attention," he complained. "And to deplete my meagre retirement fund."

The route to the airport was reasonably direct from the downtown core. A few quick turns to connect with the freeway, and inside of ten minutes, Stan found himself parked near the control tower. He jumped out and watched a small low-wing plane taxi past the front of his vehicle on the adjoining taxiway. He didn't know much about airplanes, and in fact, had no idea what a Maule M-4 even looked like. *Some investigator I am,* he thought. *Don't even know what I'm looking for. All the more reason to retire, Fenwick.*

At that moment, a vehicle pulled up a few stalls down and screeched to a stop. The driver door opened with apparent difficulty, and out jumped a middle-aged man wearing blue jeans and a sky-blue polo shirt. In his left hand was a small file folder of some sort, while his right clutched a massive travel mug which Stan assumed was coffee. Stan watched as the man stopped near the front of his car, preened his moustache and then glanced up at the tower with express purpose. After a few long seconds, he walked towards the control tower's front doors.

That was Stan's cue. In a flash, he exited his car and sprinted towards his objective. "My apologies, sir!" he shouted through shallow breaths. "Might I steal a moment of your time?"

The man stopped and turned. "And you are?" he asked guardedly.

Stan closed the distance and flashed his badge. "I'm inspector Stan Fenwick with the Owensville Police Department. I'm sorry to bother you sir, but it seems to me you might be someone who could perhaps help me with an investigation I'm conducting."

"Well, Inspector," the man replied without introducing himself. "That's a rather presumptuous statement given you have no idea who I am. And what investigation might that be, if you don't mind me asking?"

Stan cocked his head sideways. "Are you in any way involved in the workings of this airport?" he asked probingly. "In particular, the operations of this control tower? If not, then I won't waste your time any further."

Bruce smiled. "As a matter of fact, I am. My name is Bruce Macbeth, and I'm an air traffic controller here. How may I be of service to the good people of Owensville, and to you for that matter?"

Stan beamed at his good fortune. "I'm sure you're very busy Mr. Macbeth, so if you'll indulge me, I won't take but a moment to explain."

"Your timing is impeccable," replied Bruce as he adjusted his glasses. "I'm not on duty for an hour, so why don't you come upstairs, and we can chat. My coffee's gone cold anyway and seeing as I'm the only one up there who knows how to make a decent cup, I'll brew us a fresh pot."

"That, sir, is the best news I've had all day!" grinned Stan. "Please lead the way. I assume I don't need any special clearance?"

"I'm the only clearance you need," assured Bruce as he headed for the doors with Stan close behind. He flashed his entry ID over the sensor panel and the latch clicked. Seconds later, the two men stepped inside. "I hope you're fine with the stairs," asked Bruce. "Doctor says I need to get more steps in, and so does my wife for that matter."

Truthfully preferring the elevator, Stan lied. "No, that's fine. I'll try to keep up. Lord knows I could use the exercise too at my age."

Bruce headed for the stairwell, but then stopped suddenly. "As a matter of curiosity," he inquired. "Would you being here have anything to do with an older model white aircraft? It's called a Maule M-4."

Stan's jaw dropped. "Why yes! But how could you possibly know that?"

"Well," smiled Bruce wittingly, "interesting story. The senior controller here in ATC noticed something odd a week ago when that particular airplane, the one in question, tried to land. He hadn't seen it before, which wasn't anything unusual since non-resident airplanes fly in and out of here all the time. But the pilot seemed disoriented. Radio communications were not of standard procedure, and he tried to land several times but was ordered to go around on each attempt."

"Why is that a red flag?" asked Stan, not understanding the significance.

"Because the guy sounded pretty desperate to land but never declared any sort of emergency. He'd overshoot the runway one time and then undershoot on the next approach. It was like he'd never flown before or was under the influence of something. Perhaps medicinal or banned, we have no way of knowing. But he was certainly confused and said he had a delivery to make."

"So, what finally happened?" asked Stan with genuine interest and raised eyebrows.

"The pilot, a male, became rather ill-tempered with Ken on the last failed attempt to land. So, instead of staying in the pattern and trying again, he simply did a straight-out departure and never returned. We tried to get him back on the radio, but he never returned our calls."

As the two men began to climb the stairs, Stan asked another question. "You wouldn't happen to know the aircraft's registration, would you?"

"That's the curious part inspector," retorted Bruce. "It's registered to a Cessna Skylane, not a Maule. Ken wrote it up right away and sent it to the Feds. If they catch that guy, he'll be in a heap of trouble. That's a given."

Stan shook his head in disbelief. "Therein lies the problem, Mr. Macbeth. As I've been led to believe from a reliable source, catching up with this guy might be the hard part."

Deliveries

* * *

Dave McMurray glanced out the window where his visual reference was hampered by low slung cloud and mist. Squinting at the GPS, both indicators confirmed they were over Bayshore Lake. It seemed unbelievable to think they tried this approach the night before in the 185. And now here they were again, only this time in a different airplane, and at the hands of a very troubled man with a gun no less. *Another one for the logbook*, Dave reflected.

At 300 feet altitude, Dave adjusted the trim and watched the clouds drift over the windscreen at most a healthy spitting distance away. Typically priding himself at remaining cool under pressure, he felt anything but calm and collected. Ground-level visibility improved once over the lake, and this would mark the first time Dave attempted to land on an off-kilter grass field with someone else on the pedals. "Be ready on the steering, Ace," he ordered. "As soon as the wheels hit, keep us straight and true. Then, hammer on the brakes. Last thing we need is to wheelbarrow or end up in the trees, so be careful that—"

Gary suddenly leaned forward as the Colt's barrel poked into Dave's right shoulder. "We ain't landing here! Told ya already I need you off my plane!"

Dave leaned away and toyed with the idea of slamming his fist into Gary's jaw. But while his brain calculated the odds of a successful outcome, the gun came to bear once again and discharged with an ear-splitting crack.

The upper left corner of the front window fractured where the bullet tore through. Paul watched in horror as Dave lurched forward and the plane pitched sharply down. Paul reached for his friend with one hand, and the controls with the other. "Dave!" he shouted while trying desperately to raise the nose.

Gary clipped the left side of Paul's head with the butt of the gun. "No ya don't," he ordered. "Your friend's fine."

Ducking away, Paul let go of Dave and flung his hand to the re-opened gash that was already there. He felt the warmth of his blood ooze through his fingers, the gross sensation causing both instant nausea and rage.

Dave sat back up clutching his right shoulder, yet incredibly he recovered the plane to level flight despite the fresh wound. "I got it, Paul!" he spat through clenched teeth. "I think I'm okay."

"See," barked Gary. "The bullet only nicked his shoulder like I planned. Now you know I'm serious! We ain't landing at Spruce Creek! Put us down along the shoreline. There's 'nough room. Then, you both get off and I leave!"

Dave's shirt absorbed most of the blood from the graze, and though presently more numb than painful, he applied pressure to the wound to stifle the bleeding. Too stunned to react to being shot, Dave held his tongue and focused solely on flying the plane. Revenge would come later if given the chance, and Dave satisfyingly imaged driving his fist into Gary's collarbone.

Paul's head felt as though he'd been hit with a baseball bat full force. Enraged, he twisted around as searing pain roared along his spine. His vision narrowed, and for a moment he thought he might blackout. "You're insane," he stammered to Gary. "You could've killed, Dave!"

"But I didn't," taunted Gary. "I aimed exactly where I wanted and the next shot's in your direction. I know this gun has seven rounds. Three I used, and I'm not scared ta use 'em all to get my way."

Paul angled his neck back and glanced at Dave's shoulder. "Maybe I should try to land, and we'll get off this bloody airplane. You should rest until the bleeding stops."

Dave tried to ignore the sudden shockwave-like throbbing radiating from his wound, but he managed to snicker at Paul's unintentional wordplay just the same. "I've got the *bloody* plane, Ace, which it officially is with both of us bleeding. This'll sound cliché, but it's just a flesh wound . . . yours too by the looks of it. Let's just do what he says before he forgets how to aim."

Paul bitterly objected. "But there isn't enough open shoreline anywhere around the perimeter of this lake to set down. It's impossible!"

Dave nodded. "I know that, and you know that, but try to convince Mr. Phyco of that fact. He's done listening to reason. We'll find a spot. It's a big lake and there's a smattering of beachfront we can *shoot* for, pun absolutely intended."

"Quit yer talkin' and put my airplane down. Now!" shouted Gary.

Dave asked Paul to add a notch of flaps. "Let's slow up and do what he says. We might kill ourselves, but I'd rather kick the bucket trying to land than take another bullet full force."

Dave reached for the throttle to pull off power when Paul quickly pushed his hand away. "Hold for a second," he directed.

"Why?" Dave asked. "This guy's not fooling around, Ace. I think there might be a stretch along the north shore. We passed over it a few minutes ago. I'll turn us around and—"

Paul held up his palm just high enough for Dave to see it, but not Gary. "No wait," he mouthed.

Dave shrugged his shoulders and directly regretted the decision. "Ouch!" he cringed. "Feels like I've been branded. Now I know what a cow feels like. Take a look at it, will you? I can't see it and would probably faint if I could."

Paul leaned back, but he couldn't see the full extent of the wound through Dave's shirt. Fresh blood dribbled down Dave's arm. "I don't have anything to patch you up with unless there's a first aid kit in here," he remarked. "Which I highly doubt."

Paul glanced around the cabin. In doing so, he noticed Gary's mood had evidently shifted again. The man's lips moved as he rocked his head in his hands. All ten fingers cradled the gun and his seatbelt remained unlatched. Paul turned back to face Dave. "If you've got your pocketknife handy, I can cut a piece out of your coveralls and use that as gauze."

"Left leg pocket," replied Dave. "What's left of them are rolled up behind my feet."

Before retrieving the coveralls and knife, Paul grabbed a notepad from the door panel beside him and the pen stuffed into its coils. He scribbled on a sheet of paper and showed it to Dave, whose eyes bulged when he read the words: *Land at Spruce Creek. Have plan to disarm Gary.*

"Whatever it is," replied Dave, lay it on me. Better an ill-advised scheme of yours that ends my life, than a bullet to the head."

Paul scratched out another note: *Circle and climb, gently.*

Without asking another question, Dave started an almost imperceptible left-hand climbing turn. Paul leaned down and grabbed the damp coveralls. He found the pocketknife and cut a swatch, folded it into a square and pressed it firmly to Dave's shoulder as gently as he could.

As Dave painfully screwed up his face, Paul noticed movement over his shoulder and found himself once again staring down the barrel of the pistol. Gary's face contorted into what Paul thought looked like a grisly disguise.

"Next bullet's yours, threatened Gary. "Land now!"

* * *

"From here it looks like they're turning and climbing," observed Kevin excitedly. "What's he doing?"

"No idea," replied Susan. "But whatever it is, it can't be good."

The Piper Cub's altitude closely matched the Maule they were chasing. Kevin added power and began a slow climb through layers of cloud floating listlessly over top the lake. The view reminded him of an obstacle course or video game, a stick and rudder challenge to avoid being swallowed by ghostly airplane-eating clouds. It wouldn't be long before the Maule disappeared if they climbed any higher, and instrument conditions were something Kevin wanted no part of.

With Spruce Creek just minutes ahead, it made little sense to Kevin why they turned away. "Well keep an eye on him for a minute or two, Susan, and then we're done. The landing will be bumpy, so reef on your belt. It's just a cleared-out field at Spruce Creek, assuming I find it."

"That's comforting," added Susan dryly. "With you flying, I've made sure my belt has been cinched tight since we left Owensville."

"Gee, thanks. Does that mean no gift card then?"

"I'm a woman of my word. Right now, though, I'd appreciate it if you made sure we don't hit that other airplane."

Kevin focused his eyes on the Maule. "Yes, Ma'am, I have a visual."

There had been no further radio chatter from the Maule, another possible indicator that something else had gone awry. Kevin could only imagine what might be going on inside that plane, but now he had to focus on his own flying. His primary responsibility was for the Cub and that of his spotter, so all that mattered in these next few minutes was a landing they could walk away from.

As Kevin watched the Maule swing back towards them in a shallow climbing turn, what had up until now been a gentle rain began to intensify. Pockets of turbulence belted the Cub, forcing a stranglehold grip on the stick.

"I can't do this anymore, Kevin," fretted Susan. "Please land this thing now before I lose what's left in my stomach."

"I want to see where they're going," replied Kevin. "Their landing light is on, which doesn't make sense if they aren't actually landing. Let's wait another minute, and then I promise we'll set down."

"You've got sixty seconds," agreed Susan. "And the clock is ticking."

While gusty winds buffeted the Cub's fuselage, Kevin watched the Maule turn away from them again and continue to climb.

Levelling off to stay out of the clouds himself, he triggered his radio mic. "This is Owensville Airborne Search and Rescue, Piper Cub Romeo One on Unicom channel one-two-three decimal four-five. Maule circling over Bayshore Lake, do you copy?"

After several tries and no reply, Kevin watched the Maule a few more seconds, checked his compass heading and steered the Cub towards Spruce Creek. There was nothing more they could do but land, report to Rob Smith what they had seen and heard, and contact the police. "Okay, we're done," announced Kevin dejectedly.

"Oh, thank God!" blurted Susan. "That was two minutes by the way."

"Whatever," replied Kevin.

The challenge now was identifying the lodge and landing area. Other than being at the west end of the lake and stuffed in between a quagmire of spruce trees, Kevin wasn't sure of its precise location. From what he recalled during a recent conversation with Rob, the airfield sat in a small clearing not far from the main lodge. Supposedly equipped with a beacon and frontal edge lighting, the latter of which he did not expect would be on, low clouds covered most of the western shoreline, so spotting the beacon could also prove interesting.

Kevin set the altimeter for Spruce Creek's elevation, applied carb heat and left the engine mixture leaned out for the time being. He wanted the Cub prepped for landing well-ahead of time. "One approach, no go-around," Kevin pep-talked to himself.

"What was that?" asked Susan nervously.

"Nothing," assured Kevin. "Just pilot talk."

"Well let's *pilot talk* our way to the ground," prompted Susan.

"I'll need your eyes, Susan. Once we spot the beacon, the landing zone will be to its left. It's running east-west, so with any dumb luck the sidelights are working now."

"Already scanning," Susan remarked candidly. "There's too much cloud blocking the western shore, and the rain isn't helping visibility. I've lost sight of the Maule, which scares me I might add."

They're higher than us, but we'll head for the water to be safe," added Kevin. "Be better visibility closer to the deck, and we'll be out of the Maule's way."

Kevin made a customary radio call to announce his landing intentions should the Maule attempt to land at the same time. "Piper Cub Romeo One, descending through 400 feet, bearing two-seven-zero degrees, about five clicks back, inbound for Spruce Creek . . . and God willing, a full stop."

"Super encouraging," protested Susan.

Kevin eased off on the throttle and waited for the nose to drop. The Cub settled in at fifty knots and began a shallow cruise descent towards the choppy waters of Bayshore Lake. As he trimmed the plane, a pounding gust of wind bashed into the fuselage and lifted the left-wing sharply up. Susan let out another blood-curdling shriek, and as Kevin regained control, the radio came to life. "Rescue Cub Romeo One, we're the Maule circling Bayshore Lake at your six-o'clock, holding at 700."

Startled from the unexpected radio call, Kevin was about to reply when another transmission blared through his headset. "Either get your behinds on the ground pronto or get out of the way. We're coming in hot, and I guarantee it won't be pretty."

Chapter 35

Work crews eventually cleared away most of the debris responsible for the earlier road closure. A few remained on site, urging people to drive carefully through the area while they finished up. Tess manoeuvred around two burly workers, and then once through the slowdown, she hit the gas.

The wiper blades lumbered to swish away a sudden heavy shower. Trying to find the cloud responsible, Tess craned her neck and glanced up. There were numerous patches of blue sky stuffed between tracts of low hanging cloud, but there didn't seem to be any explanation for the deluge. She flicked the wipers to their high position, and when the rain just as quickly ended, she turned them completely off.

For Kim, the remaining distance to Spruce Creek seemed to take forever. She was about to start another game on her phone when she bolted forward in her seat and pointed out the front window. "I see the sign to the lodge! Bathroom and food, here I come!"

"Yes, thank God," agreed Diane. "I really need out of your van, Tessa, no offence."

"None taken. I'm actually pretty sick of following these slowpokes anyway, and I'm with you guys. I need a bathroom and an iced tea in the worst way."

Tess gently braked as the vehicle ahead slowed to make the turn into the resort. She wondered if Rob Smith truly understood his role in all of this. He was too indecisive for her liking, and now that he'd decided to drive up to the lodge rather than stay at Moger's Point, she questioned his resolve even more. Also, grating on Tess's nerves was his refusal to get people into the area to begin a search. She wanted to blast him a second time but also understood the need to curb her tongue. In the grand scheme of things, all that mattered now was Dave and Paul's safe return.

From the main road, the drive into the lodge parking lot took less than five minutes. Tess impatiently parked her vehicle three stalls down from that of Rob's van and watched a moment as he and a woman climbed out. She thought Rob's face appeared weary and drawn out and then wondered about her own. Diane and Kim exited before Tess even killed the ignition. Inside of thirty seconds, the three headstrong women made tracks for the lodge's front door.

Rob Smith tried to make pleasantries as he followed a cautious distance behind but gave up when he realized he was being shrugged off. He stopped and waited for a moment for Laura to catch up. "You coming, slowpoke?"

Laura took several long strides to close the gap. "You were really motoring there," she huffed while trying to regain her breath. "How you doing, boss?"

Rob shook his head. "Quite frankly, I'd rather be tipped back in a chair getting a root canal done by a first-year dental student."

"That good, huh?" chuckled Laura.

"At least I'd be frozen from the pain of the situation. This mess we're in feels like a tooth abscess where the dentist just ran out of Novocain."

"It's certainly easy to tell you were a dentist in your former life," observed Laura.

"Why is that?"

"Because your descriptors are always slanted in that direction," Laura replied. "And I'm not sure you even realize you're doing it."

Rob shrugged his shoulders, "I should have stayed a dentist," he admitted sourly while stepping away. "Let's catch up to our . . . friends."

When the small entourage reached the lodge's front steps, the women stopped unexpectedly as though an imaginary traffic light suddenly flashed red above their heads. Rob and Laura nearly plowed into them from behind but managed to skirt around opposite sides without collision. Rob climbed the staircase, held the door for Laura and waited for the others to follow. When they didn't budge, he shook his head, sighed, and disappeared inside.

As Diane watched Kim snap pictures of a huge rain barrel stuffed with weary but still pretty mixed petunias, she could not help but appreciate the rustic decor of the lodge's architecture. From what she remembered of its former dilapidated condition, the transformation Jack and his late wife had done was truly incredible and a remarkable testament to the power of structural rehabilitation.

Several patrons milled about, some enjoying a cigarette while others sat on their mountain bikes engaged in biking chatter, none of which Diane understood. She watched them with mild interest and tried without success to understand their infatuation with two-wheelers. Kim was never big on riding, preferring instead to hang with her dad at the airport and talk airplanes. Diane smiled at her daughter and those special memories she held so dearly.

Kim suddenly turned away from the flowers, cocked her head and got up. "Mom," she asked, "I swear I can hear an airplane engine. Do you hear that?"

Diane listened briefly, looked over in Tess's direction and back to Kim. "Yes, as a matter of fact, I do," she replied. "It's faint but there."

"So do I," agreed Tess. "It's probably the search plane. We should let Mr. Search Coordinator know, so he can get busy coordinating something."

Tess climbed the stairs with Kim and Diane close on her heels. She tore open the heavy door like it was made of Styrofoam, and they all paraded inside. Tess immediately caught sight of Rob who seemed pre-occupied looking for someone or something. "Mr. Smith," she called out. Several heads turned, including his.

For the time being, Rob had hoped to avoid any further confrontation with the pilots' wives. "Yes," he answered reluctantly. "What is it?"

"You searching for the restrooms too?" asked Tess. "You look like a man on a mission."

"In a bit," replied Rob distractedly. "First I need to find Jack Ward and get to the airfield before my search plane gets here. . . . Assuming they haven't landed already which may well be the case."

"Speaking of that," announced Tess. "Before we came inside, we all heard a distant airplane engine."

Without excusing himself, Rob dashed outside and returned in a matter of seconds. "Yup, you're right," he affirmed. "It's likely my people inbound." The alluring scent of coffee filled his nostrils, and Rob shunned his desire to find its source as a matter of priority. "I'm not sure how we beat them here, but I need to get to that airfield right away."

Diane stepped up. "I know where it is. There's a dirt road that heads south off the main parking lot where we came in. You take that road and it's only a short drive through the trees to the airport, or airfield as you call it."

"Excuse me," heralded a deep voice from behind Rob. "I couldn't help but overhear your conversation and that you're trying to find Jack Ward?"

Rob spun around and was greeted by a tall young man wearing a charcoal grey suit, white shirt and a very loud tie emblazoned with the word, "Google" in various font sizes and colours. He also sported the shiniest pair of black patent dress shoes Rob had ever seen. In his right hand was a smartphone of some sort, while his left clutched a thick and clearly outdated electronic tablet. If the word *efficient* needed a visual illustration, Rob thought this handsome lad certainly fit the bill. "Yes, that's right," Rob finally answered. "And you are?"

"My name's Darien Sheffield," he proudly announced. "I'm a weekend porter here at the lodge, and as they say in this business, "I'm at your service."

Kim slipped past her mother and immediately liked what she saw. Without saying a word, she soaked in the view with genuine interest. Rob shook Darien's hand and was impressed with his firm grip. "Good to meet you, Darien. Would you happen to know where Jack is at this moment?"

Darien smiled and lifted his broad shoulders. His eyes floated briefly towards Kim then back to Rob. "Indeed, I do," he knowingly replied. "He's already at the airstrip working on replacing and repairing the runway lights. There was a plane supposed to come in last evening with television gear for our inaugural charity auction broadcast. But the runway lights wouldn't come on and the airplane, a Cessna I believe, was unable to land. Since then, it's been reported missing and there is currently a search—"

"You're a wealth of information, Darien," interrupted Rob. "You certainly seem in-the-know about all that's going on here. Good for you."

Darien's eyes met Kim's, and he felt suddenly flushed. "Well, it is part of my job to know these things," he spluttered.

Rob deliberately rolled his eyes before spinning around to face Diane and Tess. "I'll bring my pilot and spotter back here for food and rest. I promise you both that we'll resume our search as soon as the weather allows and the Cub's checked over and topped up with gas. Now, if you'll both forgive me. I really have to go."

Rob cocked his head towards the east-facing windows. Small waves bristled over the lake's surface, each one toppling over with equally small white caps on top. He frowned while scanning the foyer for Laura, who had evidently wandered off. After a hurried

Deliveries

search, he found her in a nearby hallway peeking at photographs depicting the lodge from years gone by. "Time to go," he ordered. "We've got our plane inbound. And I'll drive."

With Laura in tow, Diane watched them exit the building in what could be described as a full-on sprint. Through the windows, her eyes followed them as they headed straight to their van, climbed in and sped off towards the airstrip.

Somewhat befuddled at being cut off, Darien tinkered with his hair to regain his composure. His eyes met Kim's for a second time, which sparked in him a sudden jolt of nervous energy. He noticed the other two women eyeballing him with knowing expressions, and he awkwardly blushed. "Well, uhm, he's certainly a spirited one, isn't he?"

Kim found it hard to wipe the smile from her face, a fact that also did not go unnoticed by her mother and Tess. "He's the search and rescue coordinator for the airplane you were just talking about," explained Kim. "My dad and his friend were the ones flying it, and now they're missing. That's why we're here."

Darien glanced once at his phone as if he were expecting the device to tell him what to say next. He skirted his feet to the left to angle himself closer to Kim, coughed nervously and turned. "Perhaps you'd all care for some refreshments and a few moments of rest by our fireplace?"

Kim chuckled. "That sounds good, Darien, but first we need a ladies' room before we all explode. We'll be back, and yes, food and a fireplace would be appreciated."

As Darien watched the women stroll away, he swallowed nervously when Kim peaked back at him over her shoulder and smiled. For the first time in his short stint as a porter, or in his life for that matter, Darien nodded and astoundingly forgot how to breathe, speak or swallow.

***

Waves curled ashore in front of the landing strip in quick succession, and despite a splash of rain and an increase in the wind's strength, a thick towering pine tree served as an umbrella while four men hunkered underneath.

The runway lights were on, as was the beacon. Or at least the white side of it. Jack scanned the eastern sky over Bayshore Lake but could not see any sign of an airplane despite its engine growing unmistakably louder.

"This stupid low cloud makes it tough to see anything," complained Dylan. "Though it sounds like it's heading this way."

Matt sneered. "That's a given, bright boy!"

Dylan raised his hand to swat his friend, but Tom budged his way between them. "Would you two knock it off for a second? It's hard to hear anything with you guys always squabbling like an old married couple!"

"Agreed," stated Jack. "You both give me a headache!"

Tom positioned himself beside Jack. "I wonder if that plane is landing here or just passing through?"

Jack stepped out from under the tree and walked towards the shoreline. He stopped and spun around. "Either way, thanks for all your help, guys. This whole mess with the lighting is one nightmare I can put to rest."

"No problem, Jack," replied Tom. "I told you we'd get them working."

"That you did," acknowledged Jack thoughtfully. "I'd say I'm sorry I got you guys involved in all this, but I'm really not. I'm grateful you stuck with me. Best thing now would be to know the crew of our waylaid Cessna is all right." Jack squeegeed away small rivulets of moisture from his scalp and turned towards the lodge. "I should get back and see if there's any further update. Hopefully somebody there's watching the news. But first I need to be sure the plane out there isn't landing here."

Tom leaned into Jack and patted him on the shoulder. "We got your back," he affirmed. "But with the clouds drooping so close to the water, whoever is in that plane better hurry and land if that's their intent."

A fast-moving vehicle suddenly appeared through the overhang of trees leading back towards the lodge, its driver in no way adhering to a "drive for the conditions" mindset. The passenger van braked hard and fishtailed around the last sharp corner leading to the generator shed, where it ground to a rock-throwing halt beside the lodge van. A male figure launched out of the driver's seat, followed by a female passenger on the opposite side. Both occupants spotted the four men near the runway lights and headed towards them like charging grizzly bears.

"What in blazes is up with them?" asked Jack, the anger in his voice unmistakable. "Crazy fools are going to kill somebody driving like that! Any of you recognize that vehicle because I sure don't." Already on the move, Jack did not wait for an answer.

Tom, Dylan and Matt all watched with interest as Jack rushed to head off the newcomers, no doubt to give them a piece of his mind. But to their surprise, Jack shook hands with both parties a moment later. The male passenger had something in his hands that Tom thought resembled a large walkie-talkie.

As they walked back, Jack pointed towards the lake for Tom, Dylan and Matt's benefit. "Let's all move back!" he shouted. "That's a rescue plane out there, and they need to land." Jack made quick introductions. "This is Rob Smith and Laura . . . Ah nuts, I forgot your last name. I'm sorry."

"Hastings. Laura Hastings and no apology necessary."

Jack tried to catch his breath. "Rob's the search coordinator for the team looking for my . . . our missing Cessna. These folks drove up from Moger's Point and need to get that plane and crew on the ground, pronto! They've called the search off for now because of the weather."

Jack watched as Rob and Laura shook hands with the other men and then added nervously, "And Paul Jackson's wife and daughter are apparently here too, along with Tess McMurray.

They're over at the lodge." Jack swallowed hard. "And no doubt they're all ready to unleash a tongue lashing on me once they find out where I am."

Rob walked to the row of lights that marked the north side of the field. "I'm not sure what kind of landing this'll be," he admitted. "So, for everyone's safety, I suggest we all step back towards the shed over there."

"Darn good thing we got the lights fixed when we did," added Tom. "Good call, Jack, on coming back out here to fix them."

"Must be Mildred's influence on me," replied Jack. "She always told me that if something's broken, don't delay in fixing it. I just don't always heed her advice as quickly as I should."

Tom repositioned his feet to bypass a splotch of wet grass. "A wise woman," he agreed.

As the group walked towards the shed, Jack tried to listen to the approaching airplane, but the generator overpowered everything, including conversation. "I can't hear a confounded thing or even myself talk," he bellowed. "Let's move back under the pine tree. We'll still have a good view and be out of the way at the same time. Plus, we'll be sheltered from the rain."

With diminished visibility and a now steady downpour coating everything in a fresh layer of moisture, remaining pockets of blue sky between the clouds became fewer and fewer. Dylan and Matt took the lead and began to walk away towards the tree when suddenly Matt turned and pointed. "There!" he shouted. "Low over the water and heading straight at us. I just saw a white light!"

All heads spun to where Matt pointed. Rob lifted the portable radio, checked it was on the proper frequency and clicked the button to transmit. "Piper Romeo One, this is Owensville Rescue, please respond!" He listened a few seconds and tried again. "Piper Cub Romeo One, Kevin, this is Rob, how copy?" Frustrated, Rob adjusted the volume and made sure the squelch wasn't set too high. He lifted the radio to his mouth to try again when the speaker blared.

"Rob? Is that you?" asked an excited voice. "Man, am I glad to hear your voice!"

Rob breathed a huge sigh of relief as Laura sidestepped in to better hear the conversation. "Good to hear from you too, Kevin," he acknowledged. The others tiptoed in as well without trying to appear nosy.

"Where are you?" asked Kevin. "And how did you manage to connect through to us from Moger's Point?"

Rob smiled to himself. "I'm not at Moger's Point. You're heading right for me. I'm here at Spruce Creek. You should have the runway lights in sight any moment now."

"You mean they're actually on?" asked Kevin, the surprise in his voice obvious. "I don't see them yet, but it's thick as soup up here. I'd be standing well-clear of the runway if I was you. And no, that's not a slam against my piloting ability. We're getting thrown around pretty good and it could be a rough go."

"Just be careful up there, Kevin," ordered Rob. "No heroics."

"Won't be any of that," replied Kevin. "Besides, Susan would have my head if I tried any funny business. We just both want out of this thing."

Rob turned around when the others leaned in.

Jack shrugged his shoulders and smiled. "We're a curious lot," he said. "When your radio started squawking, we wanted to hear the banter. Hope you don't mind."

Rob smirked. "Well, it's your land and your airfield, so I can't say no. But we all need to stay well back when the plane touches down. My pilot has never landed here before and isn't familiar with the terrain."

"Well, the wind's sure picked up," acknowledged Jack. "That could really make things dicey for them."

Rob ignored Jack's negative observation and lifted the radio to his mouth. "Let's get you guys safely on deck, Kevin. We'll get you some food, fuel, and rest. I'd like to send you back up if the weather permits, but unfortunately our missing airmen might be stuck out there until tomorrow morning."

The radio stayed quiet for several seconds, and just when Rob feared it might be malfunctioning, Kevin's voice crackled through the speaker. "Ah, about that, Rob …"

Rob shared a questioning glance with Laura and the other men before all eyes went back to the radio like it was some sort of otherworldly device about to divulge a universal secret.

A moment later, Kevin's voice broke through. "You might want to make sure you're sitting down for this, but we aren't the only airplane right now inbound to Spruce Creek."

* * *

The Piper Cub descended through 200 feet and danced around like popcorn in a hot pan. Kevin had both hands wrapped around the stick, while his feet negotiated the pedals in a redundant back and forth motion. He wondered how on earth he was going to land on a tiny patch of grass when it was all he could do to keep the wings level and the plane in the air. He decided to keep that tidbit of paranoia to himself.

With the Cub aimed roughly towards Spruce Creek, low wisps of cloud restricted Kevin's view. He tried repeatedly to locate the shoreline, and more specifically the lodge and beacon. But, with rain also hampering visibility, Kevin started to fear a ghastly rip-off-the-gear type of landing.

"Listen, Rob," Kevin explained slowly. "The two pilots we've been searching for are aboard an old white Maule aircraft. Somehow, they got picked up, and for whatever reason they're in a climbing turn way behind us. We just went by them over the east end of the lake, but—"

Susan shouted excitedly! "I see the lights, Kevin! The beacon just came into view. Turn left a bit. It's at our eleven o'clock."

Deliveries

Kevin complied immediately. He double-checked the engine's mixture and made sure the carb heat was still on. "I see it!" he replied. "Buckle up nice and snug."

"Seriously, Kevin," answered Susan coldly. "How many times are you going to tell me that? I'm fine. Just land this blasted thing!"

With no reply coming from the ground, Kevin keyed the mic. "Cat got your tongue down there, chief?" he asked. "And by the way, we've got the airfield in sight. Make sure you're well-clear and have the crash trucks ready to roll." When neither Rob nor Susan replied, Kevin realized his stress-relieving attempt at dry comedy was likely ill-timed.

When Rob finally did respond, he sounded a trite perplexed. "You're sure about that, Kevin? About the pilots? How on earth could you know that for certain?"

Kevin smiled to himself. "One hundred percent sure. It's a long story, but I've only given you half of it. I assume you've not been monitoring the Unicom channel?" Kevin paused for added dramatic effect. "Whoever owns that Maule has a gun on board, and from what we heard on the radio, you better get the police up here asap. And to let you know, there have been shots fired in the cabin."

From the ensuing radio silence, Kevin knew he'd struck a chord with his boss. He lowered the Cub's nose towards Spruce Creek. At that exact moment the duct tape on the top of the wing ripped away into the slipstream. The horrible sound of wind rushing into the open wing cavity sent chills down Kevin's spine.

"Kevin?" asked Susan in a deeply troubled voice. "What was that? Exactly?"

* * *

There were few times in Rob's career as a dentist, or even now as a search coordinator that he found himself utterly speechless. This was one of those times. Never would he have expected to hear what

Kevin had just announced over the radio. He tried to compose himself before answering.

"That's . . . unbelievable, Kevin. We'll ah, we'll contact the authorities, and . . . I don't even know what else to say. Just be safe. See you on deck."

"Well, how do you like them apples," declared Jack. "Looks as though all the chips are falling right here and now. A grand finale at Spruce Creek Lodge. Who would have thought?"

Rob smirked at Jack's off-handed comment. He cast a glance in Laura's direction. Her face also displayed total surprise. Rob wondered if he had looked like that just seconds ago while hearing Kevin's news. He turned to face Jack. "Yes, it would sure seem that way," he agreed.

Jack continued. "If what your pilot says is true, then we could have a real situation on our hands here." He turned to face Dylan and Matt. "I suggest one or both of you scoot back to the lodge and phone the police. Then, round-up Diane and Kim Jackson, and Tess McMurray. Something tells me they'll want to be here as this drama unfolds."

Dylan and Matt shared a pained look in as much to say, "We're staying here and don't want to miss this!"

Tom sensed their hesitation. "Nothing doing, you two. Age pulls rank here. Get to the lodge and do as Jack says. And let the police know it's a Maule aircraft our missing pilots are hitching a ride in."

Dylan protested. "But Dad, we want to stay here and—"

"Go!" barked Tom. "That's an order! We don't have time to screw around here, son. If the Maule's inbound as well and there's indeed a gun on board, then the clock's ticking. We need to notify the police pronto. Lives are at stake here for real. This isn't a video game."

Jack threw Dylan the keys. "Make it fast!" he barked. "And for goodness' sake, don't smack up my van! I don't need any more trouble today."

The two young men shared an exasperated shrug and, without saying another word, rocketed towards the van like two jets in full afterburner. Thirty seconds later the vehicle hotfooted through the trees kicking up huge blobs of mud.

Jack turned and faced Tom. "I don't think I've ever seen those two hustle away so fast when the conversation didn't revolve around mountain biking or food."

"That's an understatement," agreed Tom. "And I bet they're back before the Cub's wheels even hit the ground."

Rob Smith was on the radio again. "We have a good visual on you now, Kevin. Just take it easy. The field is lit on both sides, but it's narrow and short. Low and slow on the approach."

Instead of verbally responding, Rob heard two clicks of Kevin's transmit button as a way of letting him know he understood the transmission but was too busy to reply. The Cub grew quickly in size, and though still several kilometres away, the wings could easily be seen rocking back and forth from blustery winds.

Rob spun towards Tom and Jack. "I think it's time we back up gentleman because I actually have no idea what to expect here."

Jack cocked his head funny. "You make this sound like your pilot has never landed a plane before."

"Oh, he's a good pilot," assured Rob. "He's just one to tackle life and flying, how shall I say . . . unconventionally."

Chapter 36

Kevin knew in a heartbeat that his tape repair job had let go. The flight controls still felt normal, but for how long he had no idea. The other more pressing concern was whether the brute force of the wind might shred open the wing's fabric and plunge them to their deaths. *Nothing I can do about it anyway,* he bleakly decided. *The wing stays together, or it doesn't.* Kevin swallowed hard and tried to focus on nothing more than his touch down point directly ahead.

Grateful for the added benefit of field lighting, Kevin heartily preferred not to be in this situation at all. This landing scenario was not at all what he expected for today, but he knew that piloting an airplane would at times be full of surprises. "Brace yourself," ordered Kevin.

"On what?" grunted Susan. "We're sitting in a tiny plane made of tissue paper and toothpicks! And now there's an exposed-to-the-elements hole in the wing, no thanks to you. I warned you about—"

Just then another gust of wind plowed the Cub from the left side. The airplane slid sideways, and the nose sunk sharply. Kevin swiftly corrected the imbalance and pulled the stick back towards his chest while jamming his foot into the left pedal. The plane responded, but alarmingly more sluggish than usual, or so Kevin thought.

"Are you sure you can do this, Kevin?" asked Susan with the uncertainty in her voice all too apparent.

Kevin scrambled to level the wings and get the nose to settle. "Always one to bestow me with confidence, eh Susan? It's not like we have a choice. Assume crash position," he taunted out of sheer frustration.

"That's not funny, Kevin! Tell you what. While you figure things out up there, I'm praying back here. God knows we can use it."

"You do that, because we'll be on the ground in two minutes." *Hopefully right side up and with breath still in our lungs.*

* * *

Dave McMurray's shoulder throbbed like someone had paddled it with a meat tenderizer. He knew if there was any hope of surviving the screwy plan his co-pilot showed him on another slip of paper, then a firm grip on the yoke was necessary despite any personal discomforts.

The topside of the Maule slid through the sky only slightly under the cloud base, and it was time to level out and unload the wings from the gentle turn they were in. Dave backed off on the throttle and added a touch of forward pressure on the yoke. After a modest trim adjustment, the airplane settled on a westerly heading directly towards Spruce Creek.

Paul successfully convinced an already dubious Gary Nordhavn that climbing and circling were necessary to find a safe shoreline upon which to land, and so far, he'd bought the ruse. But Dave wasn't at all convinced their passenger wouldn't blow another gasket when he discovered the truth.

With Gary's mood fluctuating between moments of civility and bouts of gun-waving rage, Paul and Dave realized the weapon as well as the man needed to be brought under control. Undoubtedly suffering from some sort of passive-aggressive weirdness and now a full-on emotional collapse, for this situation to end with any sort of positive outcome, Gary's warped agenda needed over-throwing.

Paul snuck a glance at Dave and then pointed out the front window.

"There," he muttered. "Aim for there."

At 700 feet above the lake, the distant shoreline lay obscured in fog. Bands of heavy cloud hung like giant hands groping for the water. Thankfully the airfield's beacon remained visible, and as they zeroed in on its white light, a sudden outburst from the backseat caused Dave and Paul to jump simultaneously.

"Enough stalling!" barked Gary. "Why we up this high anyways?" He glared at Paul while loosely pointing the gun towards the man's head. "You said we was looking fer a place ta land, but I don't even see the shoreline."

Paul stared briefly at Dave and then turned towards Gary. The man's seatbelt remained unfastened and Paul hoped it would stay that way. "We are looking for a place to land," he explained earnestly, hoping his fib lay hidden. "We're heading towards the western shore. Then we'll circle the lake at this altitude until we find a spot. We land and get off like you want."

Gary wasn't buying it. Paul watched in horror as the man's face contorted into a grimace worse than before, the transformation so sudden that Paul thought for certain his life would end with a chunk of lead. But instead of the gun discharging, Gary slid over to the right side of his seat and stared out his window. His head rotated back and forth several times as his brain processed the scene. It reminded Paul of when as a child, his West Highland White terrier would flip his head about as he tried to understand human language; especially the words "walk" and "treat."

"Where are we?" shouted Gary. "I can't see no shoreline. Just cloud and water!" Flailing the weighty gun about as he distressingly absorbed the view, Gary slid back to the middle. Sweat covered his face.

Dave wrestled the Maule around a band of clouds. It was then he decided that if he got out of this alive, the first thing he'd do is take Tess to Maui, rent an ocean view condo and spend day after day on Big Beach at Makena State Park. Or Kauai, with mornings savouring coffee at the Kauai Coffee Company, and afternoons at Salt Pond Beach. He wondered how she was handling his disappearance. But knowing his wife as he did, she'd be in the thick of the mess he and Paul created for themselves and everyone else involved in the search effort.

"Now might be a good time, Ace," suggested Dave. "Let's just get this over with before I change my mind."

Paul eyed the gun in Gary's hands. With two fingers extended, he motioned for Dave to hold their heading for another two harrowing minutes.

Gary leaned forward and flaunted the pistol. "Ya, let's get this over with b'fore I use my little friend here again. Land my plane, now!"

"Listen, Gary," reasoned Paul with as much diplomacy as he could muster. "We're not setting down until you quit waving that thing around. If you kill one of us, which you nearly did, you're up on murder charges. As it is, you'll be charged with attempted murder and kidnapping, not to mention weapon offences and hijacking." Paul was on a roll. "Then you've got your diamond smuggling situation on top of everything else. So, tell me this? Once we land, just how far do you think you'll get? You can't fly this plane in your condition, and you know it." *Or do you?* Paul wondered.

Gary stared curiously at Paul with dark foreboding eyes but never spoke. He lowered the gun to his lap. Paul swallowed hard. "Dave and I are your best chance at helping you through this. You're obviously dealing with something you can't control, so let's work together and see if we can't resolve things before—"

The gun came up quickly and fired twice, one bullet punching a clean hole through the radio stack and destroying the tuning knobs, the other shattering the Nav One dial just to the left, the impact sending tiny shards of glass in all directions. The smoking-hot brass ejected one after the other into the roof and back into

Gary's lap. He flung the casings away in a panicked rage and kept the gun aimed forward.

Thunderstruck by the rapid-fire concussions of two more expended bullets, a horrified Dave McMurray watched the gun come to bear at the back of Paul's neck. Unable to find words to speak, Dave sideways glanced at his friend. When he caught Paul's wide-eyed expression, the two men exchanged a nearly imperceptible nod that it was now or never.

* * *

From the shoreline, it appeared to Rob and everyone watching that the Piper Cub would simply flip over and nosedive into the lake. Gusty winds seemed to counter any forward progress, hindering the plane's light-weight construction and pushing it backwards. But it was all an illusion. Rob couldn't help but wonder how Kevin maintained any control at all. He watched helplessly as the airplane approached the shoreline, its wings rocking up and down like an out of control teeter-totter. Jack stood beside him with Tom stationed a few steps to the left. Large droplets of rain plopped heavily into the choppy waters of Bayshore Lake as increasingly bulky waves crashed ashore.

If not for the drama unfolding in the sky above, Rob would have otherwise enjoyed the relaxing ambiance of waves rolling into shore, and the rain striking the lake and foliage of nearby trees. But such pleasantries he quickly tossed aside. He knew his young pilot would need to draw upon every ounce of his skill to avoid a roughshod landing or heaven forbid a full-blown crash.

* * *

Upon their hasty return to the lodge, it took but a moment for Matt Hawley and Dylan Sullivan to find who they were nosing around for. After a few fruitless inquiries, Dylan began calling out the names. The frantic effort garnished a multitude of puzzled faces in the lodge foyer, but it also resulted in discovering the women milling about near the fireplace. Matt headed that way with Dylan hot on his heels.

"Excuse me, ladies. I'm Matt Hawley, and this is Dylan Sullivan. We are here to—"

"And we would care who you are because why?" asked Diane without reserve. Tess and Kim shared a surprised look in response to Diane's blunt reply, but in the grand scheme of things, they understood.

"Uhm, Jack Ward sent us!" boasted Dylan quickly. "He's at the airstrip and sent us to pick you up right away because—"

Matt shot his friend an angry look and Dylan stopped talking.

"Because what?" demanded Tess and Diane jointly.

"The search and rescue plane was about to land before we came to get you," explained Matt. "And we have also learned that another airplane has picked up your husbands and are now over the lake trying to land as well. . . . We think."

That disclosure raised the eyebrows of all three women.

Matt purposely left out any mention of an apparently crazy man on board with a gun. He wide-eyed Dylan to keep his mouth shut. "Dylan will escort you all to the van if that's all right. I need to quickly make a phone call before we leave." With that, Matt excused himself and turned tail for the nearest landline phone to call the Owensville Police Department.

Diane Jackson brushed past Dylan and knocked him slightly off-balance. "Let's go!" she commanded. "And I mean, now!"

* * *

Once the police heard the tale about the missing pilots being found and the gun-toting hijacker they were flying with, Matt fully expected cat-got-your-tongue silence, and he was right.

The duty sergeant on the other end of the phone grunted as Matt explained the offbeat series of events that were playing out at

Spruce Creek. After a few moments of dead air, the officer finally asked if Matt was telling the truth, intoxicated, or on drugs. He impatiently stated how the story seemed entirely fabricated and threatened to hang up.

But when Matt assured him the facts were the truth, the officer conceded and finally promised to channel the message to the inspector in charge of the diamond smuggling case. What really sold Matt's pitch was mentioning the type of aircraft, the gun and suspect on board. "Inspector Fenwick will blow a gasket," unintentionally stated the officer.

The call ended abruptly when Matt heard some sort of commotion through the earpiece. He stared at the handset curiously and hung up. When he turned around, Dylan and his entourage had all but vanished from the lobby. Matt pounced for the door like a sprinter exploding away from his starting blocks. Several people shouted for him to slow down, which he ignored. He hustled to the parking lot and found the group just climbing into the lodge van. "Hey, wait up!" he shouted, his chest heaving.

Dylan closed the side door and chuckled. "Relax. I wouldn't leave without you." Dylan lowered his voice. "This is one impatient group of women."

Matt aimed for the front passenger side door. "Can you blame them?"

"Nope. Not in the least."

In less than a minute, the van sped towards the airstrip with three anxious passengers squished shoulder to shoulder in the rear seat. Diane stared bleakly out the side window. Her logical side refused to believe the yarn coming from the mouths of men she just met. But if Jack Ward sent them, their facts must be legit despite such nonsensical claims.

To this point, Tess and Kim had not said a word; the blank stares on their faces said it all. The scenario seemed entirely cooked up. But in their defence, there really wasn't much to say. Somehow, a mystery airplane containing Paul and Dave were inbound to

Spruce Creek, and all that mattered was being there to offer whatever support they could.

For Diane, her emotions were already taxed to their limit. She struggled to not release another flood of pent-up tears, fearing that such a display would result in nothing but pity. That she did not need. It seemed mind-boggling how in one moment she wondered if her husband was alive, then to find out he's reportedly flying out of harm's way. And in a completely different plane no less?

As of late, it wasn't hard for Diane to notice that Paul's actions had changed. From her perspective, his business decisions seemed riskier than usual. She understood that income without risk was sometimes unavoidable, but Paul's eagerness for this trip felt more to her like a personal "I'm out to prove something" vendetta. At this moment, all she wanted was her husband back safe and sound. The frying pan across the back of his skull could happen later if that became necessary.

As the van rounded a snug tree-lined corner, the front wheels caught loose gravel and the van skidded sharply to the left. Dylan drove his foot into the brake pedal and whirled the steering wheel in the opposite direction to counter the sudden movement. The commotion resulted in a chorus of anxious gasps from the back seat.

"Slow down!" ordered Matt. "We'd all like to get there in one piece."

Dylan sloughed him off and apologized with only partial sincerity. "Sorry, ladies. I just want to get us there as quickly as possible. I'd hate for you"—*and me*—"to miss any of the—" he was about to say "action" but quickly decided that was an insensitive choice. Instead, he finished with "activity."

Matt jumped in to cover Dylan's foot-in-the-mouth awkwardness. "From what we heard on the search radio, your husbands are hot on the tail of the search plane, so that's why Dylan's a bit heavy on the gas."

"So, you spoke to them on the radio?" inquired Tess. "Do you have any idea how they ended up on this other plane? Or whose it is? You have to admit it all sounds pretty far-fetched."

"I'm sorry, but I don't have answers to those questions," added Matt. "And you're right. It's not a situation you encounter every day." Matt paused to change his thinking. "It was Rob Smith who connected with the search plane. The pilot was the one who passed along the information, but even he didn't have much to go on."

Diane looked at Tess, then to Kim. "I think I'm speechless. Thank God we at least know they're alive! That's such a relief and a huge weight lifted from my shoulders. From our shoulders."

"I told you they'd make it, Mom!" boasted Kim happily. "They always find a way to get out of trouble. They're like pilot MacGyvers! And besides, it's not like anybody has a gun to their heads."

Dylan's eyes widened. He glanced restlessly at Matt, the exchange not going unnoticed by Tess or Diane. Dylan swallowed hard and kept to the task of driving to avoid Kim's offhanded, bang-on remark.

Matt knew immediately the gig was up. He fended off the urge to smack Dylan for the giveaway, but the damage was already done.

Tess leaned forward; her stern voice capable of turning water to ice. "Why, gentlemen, do I suddenly get the feeling you aren't telling us the whole story here?"

Matt gave in and swatted Dylan on the arm anyway. "Good one, dude."

Dylan tried to change the subject. "We're almost there!" he reported cheerfully. "The airfield is just around these next few corners!"

Trying to stall, Matt gazed restlessly out his side window as tree branches brushed along the side mirror. He gulped a breath of air and slowly turned in his seat. "There is something else we chose to withhold for the time being," he awkwardly confessed. "Given the strain of what you're already going through, please understand we didn't want to upset you further."

"What?" boomed Diane angrily.

Dylan and Matt jumped in their seats from the sudden outburst. Even Tess and Kim flinched.

"I expect the truth," Diane demanded. "I've already been lied to by my husband, and I can't stomach more deceit from anyone else today. So, spill it!"

Matt knew the colour in his face resembled a red-ripe tomato. He side-glanced at Dylan who deliberately aimed his head forward in an obvious ploy to leave Matt hanging with the job of full disclosure. "Thanks for nothing," Matt whispered.

In Matt Hawley's budding career as a pro mountain biker and spokesperson, there were few instances where he found himself at a loss for words. Compared to this awkward moment, chatting to media or appearing on a TV talk show was a cakewalk. His throat constricted as if he'd just eaten a spoonful of dirt. "Well," he finally babbled. "As I'm sure you know, there is another person on board the airplane your husbands are in, and—"

"Well, duh!" chided Kim. "That's a given. The plane didn't just magically appear without a pilot."

"Well," Matt cringed. "Apparently, he's in possession of a . . . gun . . . and for reasons unknown, he's fired shots inside the cabin."

Diane felt the blood drain from her head. "Like, as in a hijacker?" she stammered in disbelief. "This better be a joke because that's the most insane thing I've ever heard! These are bush pilots for crying out loud! It's not like we're dealing with a Boeing 747 heading to Paris!" She gawked at Tess and Kim for support, both appearing too shell-shocked for words.

Wishing now that he had stayed with his fans signing autographs, Matt stared blankly out the window. He had no idea how to respond.

Dylan found his courage and stepped up to the plate. "No joke," he added quietly. "For once Matt's telling the truth."

* * *

Kevin did not have the usual luxury of floating 500 feet down a long-paved runway before dropping the wheels at his leisure on or after the touchdown markers. Here he needed the perfect culmination of airspeed, pitch and yaw, plus a boatload of good luck. During his training, he spent many hours practicing short field takeoffs and landings, but this demanding situation was unlike anything he expected so soon in his short career.

Though not overly bright, the two rows of lights mercifully outlined the north-south edges of the initial landing zone. Without them, finding the field would have been extremely hazardous. From Kevin's vantage point, the tiny bulbs angled slightly upwards, indicating to him an incline in the topography of no more than five degrees end-to-end. He checked his airspeed. Fifty knots and holding. With flaps set to full and the engine churning out sufficient power, he could get away with slower flight while maintaining a safe margin from a full-blown stall.

Kevin remembered his flight instructor telling him that a hard landing on a wet and muddy field could get an airplane good and stuck. The key he said was to keep the power on for a steady descent rate all the way to your aiming point. But to Kevin's way of thinking, this field looked too short and narrow to allow for any missteps. All he could do was land as close behind the approach end as possible, get the brakes on and pray he didn't flip.

Easing off the throttle, Kevin stole another glance at the airspeed indicator. "Forty-five knots. Close enough," he announced for his own benefit.

"What's close enough?" asked Susan, the alarm in her voice distinct.

"Brace yourself, Susan. I'll try to set us down like a feather but no guarantees."

"With you, there never are. But I'm bracing."

Kevin knew his approach was anything but textbook approved, but his priority was keeping himself and his spotter alive. And as much as he loved this airplane, he was no longer concerned if he dented a fender or two. He knew its quirks and felt confident he could get them both safely to the ground. Just then he thought of Carla, the paramedic who had treated his injuries at the airport. *Why now?* he wondered. Kevin genuinely hoped he'd get to see her again, but in order to focus on the task at hand, he willfully blotted out her pretty face from his mind.

As the Cub settled towards the shoreline, Kevin noticed a group of people standing near a huge pine tree. He'd find out soon enough who they were, but for now, his priority was balancing stick, rudder, airspeed and descent rate, the last factor a near-impossible feat given the unruly winds.

Trying to position the Cub's nose between the runway lights, Kevin noticed waves crashing into the shoreline. He weighed his landing options and knew that a controlled stall would allow the tail wheel to roll first with the mains succumbing to gravity immediately after. If he tried for a three-pointer, this meant a shorter stopping distance on the already compact field.

As the airplane dropped the last hundred feet, his headset unexpectedly came to life, the sudden intrusion unwelcome and distracting. "Looking good, Kevin," crackled Rob Smith's voice. "You got this."

Kevin ignored the encouragement as well-intentioned as Rob meant it to be.

When the Cub crossed the shoreline and the front wheels dropped closer to the visibly uneven ground, the airplane drifted sideways and over the long strip of white bulbs. Kevin immediately stomped on the right rudder and yanked the stick in the same direction. This caused the right-wing tip to drop sharply as trees at the end of the field rushed up to meet them.

As Kevin struggled to sideslip back to the runway, his peripheral vision caught sight of people running towards the airplane in reckless abandon. And it was in that dreamlike moment the freshman pilot wondered if they were the last semblance of humanity he would ever see.

* * *

Watching in alarm as the Piper Cub skewed away from the landing zone, Rob Smith froze mid-stride, the unforeseen stoppage causing Jack Ward to slam into him from behind. "Oh, dear Lord!" shouted Jack while regaining his foothold. "A bit of warning next time, please!"

Rob struggled a moment to regain his balance. He all but disregarded Jack's plight and turned his attention back to the plane. "C'mon, Kevin, bring it back!" he pleaded in desperation.

"Not good!" was all Laura Hastings could muster.

Tom stood shoulder-to-shoulder with Jack. He had never witnessed a plane crash and was morbidly certain he was about to do so now. "You okay, Jack?" he asked, not taking his eyes off the Cub.

"Never mind me! Worry about them!"

For a moment the Cub hung in the air as if suspended by invisible wires. Rob thought for sure the plane would plow wing first into the ground and that would be that—his pilot and spotter dead or seriously injured. As he swallowed down what little saliva he had in his mouth, the plane veered sharply off track and then to the right at what seemed a ridiculously impossible angle. To his utter surprise, the wing levelled out and the tale lurched back to its original heading, albeit noticeably lopsided.

Tom and Jack both gasped simultaneously. Laura was entirely speechless.

Rob never felt so powerless to help and yet at the same time, so mesmerized by the live-action spectacle before his very eyes. The people beside him bore the same wide-eyed expression he knew was on his own face, everyone frozen in place as if witnessing a spaceship trying to land.

Adding to the disarray of an already bleak situation, another freakish rush of wind blasted the field, its savage force knocking everyone off-balance as if decked by a huge invisible hand. As fallen wet leaves and small branches swirled into a huge column of air, everyone watching the Piper Cub momentarily turned their heads away to shield their eyes and faces. It was at that moment the Piper Cub nearly crashed.

* * *

It felt like a huge paddle had spanked the airplane. Kevin furiously jockeyed the rudder to correct the tail from its vicious left and right slide. As the wings lifted, a quick look at the airspeed indicator told him a stall was imminent. The Cub, now only a flagpole in height above ground, hung in the air long enough for Kevin to slam the throttle forward before succumbing to bone-crushing gravity. The surge in power was just enough to keep the plane aloft for the time needed to allow the nose to swing around before running out of grass and the trees swallowing them up.

"Hang on!" screamed Kevin, the panic in his voice surprising even himself.

"Yup!" yelled Susan.

With both feet jammed into the pedals, Kevin evened out the pressure and centred the rudder. He finagled the stick with rapid input corrections and yanked off the throttle to full open. On the cusp of a stall, the Cub shook as it plunged to the stubbly grass below. The left main wheel contacted the ground first, followed by the right and then the tail. All three tires lifted briefly and settled barely ten inches away from the edge of the runway lights.

In rapid succession, Kevin snapped the mixture to idle cutoff and applied pressure to the brakes as evenly as he could. For a moment the plane felt like it could nose over. He immediately eased off the brakes which helped glue the undercarriage to the grass just at the precise second the propeller stopped spinning. The Cub bounded hard another fifty feet before the wheels rolled to a jerky stop.

"We're down, Susan!" whooped Kevin excitedly.

Shaking from adrenaline, Kevin switched off the mags and master switch, then whipped open the door. The sudden inflow of rain and mountain air felt heavenly on his face. He breathed deeply and watched three men stride towards the plane, one being Rob Smith, the other two he hadn't the foggiest idea. A woman sauntered in behind the group, her face showing strain and relief all at the same time. *Laura!*

As Rob approached the plane, Kevin checked on Susan and noticed her eyes squeezed closed and her hands clenched to the sides of her seat. He was about to speak when she popped her eyes open, calmly removed her headset and seat belt, then leaned in and placed her palms on his shoulders. "Hey," she addressed him solemnly.

Kevin expected a tongue lashing for such a murderous landing, but instead, Susan broke into a genuine smile. "So, from where exactly do you want the gift card, I promised you? I think you just earned it."

Chapter 37

The Maule's wingtips rolled up and down through globs of murky grey clouds, their trailing edges leaving spirals of swirling condensation behind. Every couple of seconds the airplane jounced heavily from a pocket of turbulence, the sudden jolts adding to the challenge of rolling an airplane never meant for aerobatics.

After a third check of his seat belt, Paul Jackson motioned with his eyes for Dave to do the same. The last thing he needed was for them both to topple from their seats while inverted. Dave complied and discreetly yanked on his belt while an increasingly perturbed Gary Nordhavn spewed obscenities from the backseat. Too worked up to notice or perhaps even care, he remained unsecured from his seat. And for this plan to work, Paul needed him to stay that way.

The trick now was to convince Gary to set the gun aside, a task Paul wasn't optimistic about. If that occurred, Dave planned to roll the plane inverted for a few quick seconds, a ploy to hopefully catapult their troubled passenger onto the ceiling and the gun beyond his reach. With any measure of luck, Gary's shoulder would take the brunt of the upset and totally incapacitate the man.

But Gary was only half the problem.

The second complication lay in the Maule's carbureted engine. If upturned for too long, the apparatus would no longer be able to meter the gas passing through it. A rising float would effectively cut off the incoming fuel and the engine would quit. To make matters worse, if the airplane wasn't high enough to recover, then an engine restart and return to powered flight offered nil chances at best.

Admittedly risky, and by all rational accounts stupid, Paul knew the tactic could either save their lives by putting control back into their hands, or the airplane would enter an inverted spin, and they would all die regardless. *Either way,* Paul reasoned morbidly. *Crisis averted.*

Paul had never aspired to flip the wings of an airplane or be a passenger in one that did. He had long ago decided that such antics were best left to those with nothing to lose but their lives. He flew to sustain his business and support his family; end of story. But with the desperate situation he and Dave found themselves in, such a foolhardy act seemed worth the risk. And because Dave had experimented with aerobatics in the past, Paul felt bullish about their chance of success. With all his poor choices of late, Paul did toy with the idea of telling Dave to ditch the attempt, and they would take their chances.

Paul shook his head disgustedly. "Maybe I'm really not supposed to fly anymore," he grumbled aloud.

"Enough with the self-pity!" ordered Dave. "I'd rather not hear it anymore, Ace, especially now when we're about to hang ourselves."

"Sorry," Paul replied. "I was just—"

"I see a flat stretch of shore from here!" Gary hissed. "So quit stallin'. We can land right there or so help me I'll pull this here trigger again!" Trembling as though inside a deep freeze with no coat, Gary waved the pistol in Dave's direction and then over to Paul.

Dave nodded discretely at Paul to show he was ready.

Paul scribbled a note and showed it to Dave out of Gary's sight. WILL GET HIM TO SET THE GUN DOWN.

Dave rolled his eyes. "Good luck with that."

Paul turned his head towards Gary. "We aren't stalling, Gary. And you're right. I see that beach as well and agree it's a good spot to land."

Gary's loud huff and head nod indicated to Paul that perhaps through being validated, the man's eccentricity would soften. *But would that be enough*? Paul knew he'd have to play this hand carefully.

For Gary's benefit, Paul pointed aggressively out the window. "You see that spot along the northwest corner of the lake, Dave? That's our spot. That's where Gary wants us to land."

Dave faked a knowing glance without paying heed to the spot Paul pointed too. "Yeah," he remarked sourly. "Looks as good a place as any to dump this boat." *And its crazy owner.*

Paul shot Dave a nearly imperceptible wink. "Let's adhere to his wishes and this will soon be over for all of us."

Dave turned the airplane towards the clearing. "Amen to that," he agreed sourly.

Paul swung his head around and noticed Gary lean back in his seat, the gun clutched between his fingers. Paul watched him for a moment as Gary's face contorted in pain, his broken bone obviously causing him significant discomfort. Gary's eyes met Paul's for a moment, but then he looked away.

Finding it increasingly difficult to sort things out, Gary remained unwavering in his belief that he could fly the airplane by himself once these jokers got off. After that, he'd vanish from civilization and from those who inevitably would come for him. He knew they'd want their diamonds back, but the gems were gone and with them any chance of collecting the money needed to safeguard Cindy's well-being. But Gary figured she'd go too, that she'd never take him back after what he'd gotten himself involved in. He felt he had nothing left.

Gary scowled at the men up front but had trouble remembering how they got there in the first place. His turbid memory spit out only vague remnants of imagery from the past day's events, and he struggled to separate fact from fiction. He remembered fishing, taking off; the downed airplane he stumbled upon, and these men. Part of him wished he could simply push them from the plane to secure his own destiny.

Deep down, Gary sensed his irrational impulses weren't right, that his actions were deplorable. But despite a myriad of disjointed thoughts, growing contempt and distrust for these men, another part of his brain told him that his conduct was perfectly justifiable. He held the side of the gun up to his face, its barrel feeling cool against his skin. A delicious spike of adrenaline coursed through his body and Gary felt an overpowering sense of justification—that no matter their intent towards him, he would prevail.

The angle of bank on the wings rapidly increased as the plane turned towards the shoreline, the jarring movement interrupting Gary's delusional pondering. *That's good*, he decided. But there was no change in altitude and his fury spiked. He quickly and painfully wedged the muzzle of the gun into the base of Dave's neck. "What're ya doin'?" he demanded. "We should be goin' down!"

It took every ounce of resolve for Dave to restrain himself from reaching back with a balled-up fist and slamming it full force into Gary's head or shoulder. But recognizing a crackpot when he saw one, Dave knew that such a move could result in being shot a second time, and he worried the next bullet wouldn't be just a graze.

Hoping this plan wouldn't be his last in a cockpit, Dave held the turn for another few degrees on the compass, then levelled the wings. He knew altitude would be their friend if the engine quit while inverted, so he made no attempt to lower the Maule's nose despite Gary's insistence. Dave felt the cold end of the gun barrel pressing into his neck. He could not suppress a head to toe shiver.

"Down, I said!" shouted Gary.

Dave's silence and reddening face was Paul's cue to step in. He eased his feet from the rudder pedals and turned to Gary. The man's sweaty face had turned a shade of muddy purple. Paul wasn't sure how to defuse the situation, but he had to try one last time. "Please, Gary, lower the gun. You can't expect us to land safely with you waving that thing around. We're heading straight for the spot where you want us to land. Dave's keeping us up high until we get closer to the shoreline. Visibility is better up here."

Paul disturbingly found himself confronted with the gun's barrel. A massive palpitation ripped through his chest, and he flinched backwards to escape from the muzzle, but there was no place to go. Gary tried to strike Paul on the side of his head with the gun, but Paul managed to evade the blow which instead struck him full force on the top of his shoulder.

As Paul cried out, Dave's jaw clenched, and his hands strangled the yoke. With words unspoken, Paul clued into Dave's resolve. He set his feet into the rudder pedals and shored up his back into the rear part of the seat. As Gary shouted something unintelligible and continued to flail the weapon about, Paul and Dave ignored the tirade, glanced knowingly at one another and together sucked in two huge lungs full of air.

* * *

Dylan stopped the van a bit too aggressively, and everyone shot forward enough to warrant a collective rebuke. He spewed an apology, slapped the transmission into park and was out his door in a flash, not waiting for the others to follow. Matt watched his friend hightail it towards the airfield, got out of the vehicle himself and opened the side door for the women. "Sorry about that," he offered sincerely. "Dylan's a bit wound up, so I'll apologize for his manners."

"Well, that makes us all part of the same club, doesn't it?" stated Diane. "It's been a trying twenty-four hours for all of us."

Diane noticed the Piper Cub with its wings tipped at an unusual angle because of the uneven ground. Several people stood behind its fuselage and appeared to be hugging—but she couldn't be sure. She scanned the airspace above the lake but saw no sign of her husband's plane or whoever's plane it was.

As everyone exited the van, Matt spoke up. "Follow me, please. I'll lead you down to the airfield but watch your step. It's best to follow the path and stay out of the taller grass. You'll find Jack Ward in the red jacket by the Cub." Matt pointed. "That's Tom Sullivan from the TV station beside him." Matt watched as Dylan scooted in beside his dad.

Relieved to see the rescue plane had landed safely, Matt was equally disappointed that he missed the excitement of an obviously rough landing. Rain in the form of mist began to blanket the area, and as he started to walk from the van with his followers in tow, Matt stopped suddenly. "Sorry, ladies," he apologized. "But I remember seeing an umbrella in the van if any of you needs it." Matt scurried back, yanked open the rear door and produced a huge grey umbrella which he quickly opened. "This should help to keep the rain off if you all crowd underneath."

"I'm okay," reported Kim. "I actually like the rain." She pointed towards the small shed. "But I hate loud noises, so what's the racket coming from over there?"

Matt handed the umbrella to a grateful Diane Jackson before answering Kim's question. "There's a generator in the shed that supplies power to the runway lights and the beacon. Jack couldn't get the field lights to come on last night when your dad was trying to land." Matt smiled broadly. "But Dylan and I fixed them and—" Matt froze in place and squinted towards the lakeshore. "Did you see that?" he asked excitedly, his index finger aimed skyward.

Tess, Diane and Kim all turned their heads towards the lake as their eyes tried to hone in on the spot Matt was talking about.

"See what?" asked Kim. "All I see is a lake and clouds and rain."

Matt hustled closer towards the lakeshore, and then spun around. "I saw a white light high and way out to the left, just between those two big clouds. It was there for only a second, I swear." He spun back towards the water. "It must be the Maule! What else could it be?"

Kim squinted but saw nothing. "This is like trying to spot a fly in a hurricane."

Dylan hollered from his place near the Piper Cub. "Matt, did you see that?" he yelled excitedly while pointing towards the lake.

Fixated on the clouds, Matt waved back to acknowledge that he had. He no sooner dropped his arm when a high-pitched shriek erupted from behind him.

"There!" screamed Kim. "The light's right there! There's Dad!"

Tess and Diane were still unable to obtain a visual on the incoming airplane. Diane turned to face Tess. "Guess there's something to be said for youthful eyes," she quipped. "I see nothing but ugly grey clouds."

Kim pointed in exasperation, her index finger aiming towards a murky portion of the sky where a bright light shimmered on and off as it passed through chunks of clouds. "Right there, Mom! How can you not see that?"

"I'm looking," snapped Diane. "But I—" Then she saw it and her body began to shake with the sudden realization that her husband was on board that little speck of light and, in all likelihood, very much in danger. The joyful yet disturbing view rekindled the fear she had tried so hard to quell. As Diane looked away, Tess moved in and placed an arm around her friend's shoulder. "They'll be fine. They're almost here and this can end."

"But why are they up so high if they're planning to land?" asked Diane nervously. "For an approach, that looks totally wrong, Tess, and you know it. Maybe, they aren't landing at all. Something isn't right."

Just then the white light disappeared behind a ropy strand of dark nebulous clouds, the sight causing Diane to feel as though the gates to the underworld just swallowed her husband. "No!" she cried out. "Paul!"

"Don't worry," consoled Tess. "They'll pop back through the clouds in a second."

Kim tucked in on her mom's opposite side. "Yeah, Mom, don't worry. You can bet Dad's up that high for good reason."

"Why am I the only person here who's losing it right now?" asked Diane. "I'm feeling like a big baby, and you too aren't helping with your stoic 'we got this' posturing."

"We're just trying to be supportive," added Tess. "This whole ordeal is a lot to take in."

Diane tried to stave off her emotions and fix her eyes to the last spot she saw the plane. "But we have no idea what's going on up there," she added through gentle sobs. "Don't you guys get it? There's someone in that plane with a gun for heaven's sake! It's bad enough Paul's dealing with a medical condition, but now they've been high-jacked too, or maybe even shot!"

Feeling entirely awkward and unsure of what to do or say, Matt excused himself and walked towards the Piper Cub. Tess waited for him to pass beyond earshot, then sternly but lovingly spoke to Diane. "One thing at a time, Diane," she advised. "But either way, this is going to end here and now. I'm guessing the police will be here shortly to deal with this person, whoever it is. We'll get our men back, and we can all go home."

"Nice try, Tessa," countered Diane. "But you know as well as I do that it won't be that simple. The police will need statements and things will drag out forever, especially when they find out about Paul flying when he shouldn't be." Diane thought for a moment. "Although, I'd prefer that tidbit of information be withheld for the time being."

Just then another vehicle appeared through the tree line. From the large lettering and wavy stripes along its side panels, there was no mistaking it for CFCB television.

"Oh great!" snapped Tess. "Just what we need. Mr. Pretty-Boy reporter and his quivering cameraman."

"I thought they went back to Owensville," Kim remarked icily.

"Yeah, so did I," replied Tess, the exasperation in her voice open-and-shut. "But the flies are seldom far from the dung pile."

Diane couldn't suppress a smile. "The things you come up with, Tess."

Tess smiled and gave Diane another friendly squeeze of support. "I'll deal with the TV people. You keep an eye on the sky and pray our adventurous husbands make it down okay."

As Tess walked away, she failed to hear Diane muttering. "It's the how they make it down part that has me the most worried."

* * *

Jack Ward recognized Diane Jackson right away and his stomach twisted into a painful knot as he watched her approach. Even more agonizing was seeing Kim beside her, the mother-daughter combo almost too much to handle under these troubling circumstances.

Tom kept his eyes glued to the sky. "It's good they're here, Jack," he commented reassuringly. "No doubt they've already been through enough, and with that plane about to land, this whole ordeal can finally end for everybody involved."

But Jack wasn't so sure. He worried that if something bad happened to Diane's husband that he would need a lifetime of therapy to cope with his regrets. He nodded at Tom but said nothing. Jack commanded his legs to move and he began to walk forward, his limbs feeling as heavy as cement. He conquered only a few steps when Kim raced ahead of her mother to greet him, her arms open wide and a smile on her face. Jack's heart immediately softened.

"Uncle Jack!" Kim screeched. "It's so good to see you!"

Jack lifted his arms and met Kim's squeeze with equal force. "Good to see you too, kiddo." Jack's eyes drifted to Diane, hoping that her mood was equal to Kim's. But her face registered no emotion either way. Jack turned his attention back to Kim. "I'm so sorry for all this mess, Kim. If I'd done my job and fixed the lights when I should have, your dad would have been safely on the ground last night and none of this would have happened."

"It's okay," consoled Kim. "It's not your fault, Uncle Jack."

Diane closed down the umbrella and leaned in, her face inches from Jack's. "Still playing the blame game are we, Jack?"

Kim let go and indecisively stepped back. She held Jack's gaze as if to reassure him that things would be all right, that he didn't need to worry about her mom.

Jack's throat constricted, and he found himself unable to reply. Tears filled his eyes and he simply lowered his head. To his surprise, Diane grabbed him forcefully and hugged him like a mother would her own child. "Like I told you on the phone, Jack, I don't blame you for this. This situation isn't your fault and you know it. So, please quit beating yourself up. Paul brought this on himself, end of story."

Despite the rain on his face, Jack felt a tear roll down his cheek. He gratefully returned Diane's hug and found himself unable to avoid her piercing gaze. "Thank you, Diane, for understanding. It's been a rough weekend as I'm sure it's been for you and Kim. But all I care about now is for that plane up there to land safely."

"That seems the overriding sentiment here," agreed Diane.

Tom stepped into the fray, "I'm sorry to break up this reunion, but we should make sure we're all well back and out of the way."

* * *

"Hurry up!" barked reporter Dwaine Ennis as he jumped from the vehicle. "Clearly there's something important going on here because those are the wives of our missing pilots!" He noticed the Piper Cub being rolled off the runway. "And that's the rescue plane out of Owensville!"

"Yeah, yeah," the cameraman snapped back. "I gotta change the camera battery and format the P2 card. Plus, I'll throw on the camera's rain jacket. I'll need a few minutes. You go, and I'll catch up."

Dwaine's ears picked up the sound of a distant aircraft engine. "We don't have a few minutes!" he ranted. "This, whatever this is, is going down now! I need B-roll, and I need it yesterday!"

Dwaine popped open his umbrella, scanned the far shoreline and lifted his eyes towards the growing pool of cloud. For the time being, he decided he'd be fine without dawning the rain poncho stowed under his seat. Squinting, it was then his eyes spotted the prick of light. "There," he shouted! "I'd bet a week's pay that's why everyone's here!"

Not willing to admit it, Dwaine wasn't sure what was going on, and knowing that he'd never secure an interview, he despised basing his decisions on speculation. For all he knew the missing airplane and its two pilots were still lost in the bush. And yet he knew this gathering of people wasn't a co-incidence, which meant a story was in the making. Experience told him that whatever this was, it was about to happen fast as most extreme news events did.

Dwaine grabbed two wireless microphones and receivers from the audio bag, one a handheld, the other a small lavalier. He hot footed it to see Tom. "I want that camera rolling in thirty-seconds," he ordered over his shoulder. "Because this ballgame is all over in five minutes!"

As Dwaine sprinted towards the group of people at the far end of the landing area, he didn't notice the person closing in on his flank. It was then he nearly collided with a sudden blur of movement. He lost his balance and the handheld microphone slipped from his hands and fell into the grass.

"Going somewhere, Mr. Ennis?" asked Tess McMurray with arms outstretched to block his path.

"Oh, dear me!" huffed Dwaine while trying to regain his composure and retrieve his mic. "I'm so sorry; I didn't see you there."

Tess stood her ground and crossed her arms imposingly. "You should really watch where you're going next time," added Tess. "You could hurt someone."

"Yes, I suppose so," Dwaine distractedly agreed. "I was fixated on the sound of an approaching aircraft engine." Wasting no time, he pointed skyward. "Does that plane have anything to do with you all being here? And the rescue plane as well? This all seems like quite the coincidence."

Tess ignored the questions. "Why are you really here?" she asked curiously. "Other than lavishing kudos on yourself for self-professed exceptional journalism, I can't imagine your sudden arrival here will in any way benefit humanity. Would that be a correct assumption?"

Unaccustomed to being on the receiving end of a tongue lashing, Dwaine's throat promptly dried up. "Well," he finally admitted. "We drove back to Moger's Point after we filed a quick turnaround story. They told us you'd all gone to Spruce Creek, so we decided to drive up and see for ourselves."

Tess noticed the cameraman approaching at exactly the same instant he noticed her. The man froze in place and stared at Dwaine as if to say, "I'm not taking another step until she's gone."

Tess eyed him warily but said nothing. She looked Dwaine in the eyes. "We're not giving interviews, Mr. Ennis, so if you want to find out what's really going on here, I suggest you drop your pride and show some genuine compassion with your reporting of this, as you say, coincidence."

Dwaine cocked his head slightly and rubbed his chin. "So, you admit there is something of significance going on here?"

"I admit nothing," clarified Tess. "You're the reporter, so you figure it out. I don't want you pestering me or my friends on your quest for self-gratification."

"You drive a hard bargain," replied Dwaine. "But, please, let me assure you we're just here to report the news and present the facts. I want this to end well for your husbands. Nothing more, nothing less. I'm simply trying to do my job here." Dwaine motioned for his cameraman to shoulder his camera and begin shooting. "Now, if you don't mind, I'd like to get to work."

But the camera remained at arm's length, and the befuddled man carrying it dared not move despite angry verbal prompting from his now thoroughly agitated reporter.

Chapter 38

On the verge of rolling the airplane, Dave cussed when they suddenly entered into a thick blob of cloud. He checked his heading and vertical speed indicators, then tried blindly to steer the Maule in the general direction of Spruce Creek until VFR conditions returned. The rotating beacon, visible just a moment ago, was now hidden from view. And with rain pelting the fuselage and hindering visibility even more, situational awareness was nil at best. The compass showed a southwest heading, while the airspeed needle wobbled between eighty-five and ninety knots.

The airplane's tail yawed violently left and right, the unexpected movement sending a chill along Dave's already tense spine. *Now what?*

"Sorry," Paul confessed while exhaling loudly. "That was me. I needed to re-anchor my feet and check the rudder so—"

Gary bashed the front seat hard, the unexpected jolt causing Dave to bite his tongue. Almost of its own will, Dave's left hand balled into an angry fist. He looked at Gary with fiery contempt in his eyes, then somehow curtailed his anger before lashing out. "As soon as we exit this cloud, Ace," spewed Dave. "We go!"

In a last-ditch effort to override Gary's hostility, Paul swung his head around and again pleaded with him to calm down and lower the pistol. But the man was ostensibly no longer in charge of his faculties. Gary leaned forward slowly, but the fury in his voice

Deliveries

did not match his turtle-like movement. "I want my plane on the ground in the next five minutes or so help me I'll—"

"Okay, Okay!" shouted Paul. "We're about to do that Gary, so please, I beg you. Just take it easy! We flew into some cloud, that's all. As soon as we're clear, we'll descend and land."

But rather than defusing the situation, Paul's sudden outburst inflamed Gary's wrath. The man slid to one side of the airplane, glanced desperately out the window, and then shifted over to the opposite side. He pressed his nose to the glass like a child trying to see the world below. When all he saw was cloud, he slammed the butt-end of the gun against the window and howled in pain. A huge crack immediately appeared from one end of the window frame to the other, top to bottom. Gary slithered in his seat and began methodically swinging the gun about as if it was mounted to the end of a spring.

"Down!" screamed Gary, his face blotchy and red. All rational thought was gone. The only singular idea tumbling about in his mind was to land and be done with these men who played him for a half-wit. He suddenly remembered the defunct diamonds, that they were gone and with them any chance of fixing things right. Cindy would leave him too; of that he was certain. Stinging his eyes like whiskey on an open wound, Gary tried to blink away the sweat dribbling down from his forehead.

Paul watched Gary with a weird sense of compassion and disdain, both emotions rolled up into one caustic emotional ride. In all his life, never had he witnessed someone flip so quickly between moments of rational control to bouts of absolute hysteria and confusion.

Convulsing uncontrollably, Gary set the gun down beside his right knee. He brought both hands to rest on his collarbone and moaned quietly. It was then a sudden buffet of turbulence shot him out of his seat and pressed him back down. Gary screamed as the gun dropped to the floor. Panicked, he leaned forward as much as his body would allow, but his fingers could not find their mark. The gun was out of his reach.

It was then Dave uttered three simple words. "Hang on, Ace!"

* * *

Inspector Stan Fenwick never before had the displeasure of flying in the Owensville Police Department helicopter, that was until now. And given the choppy flying conditions to Spruce Creek, he wished that he'd driven his car instead. But in light of a recent call from the duty sergeant, and the relay of fresh information regarding the diamond case and the Maule aircraft involved, time was of the essence. Stan required rapid transit to where the action was and the chopper, unfortunately for him, was just the ticket, despite formidable opposition from a budget-conscious police chief.

With Stan sat two plainclothes constables he'd never officially met, one a burly man in his late twenties, the other an older fellow who looked as though he'd be more comfortable pushing a desk than in a field of operations. Both officers were "voluntold" to aid Stan with any arrests that may or may not be forthcoming. Admittedly, Stan hadn't the foggiest idea what to expect. All he had to go on was the missing pilots were now aboard the Maule aircraft, along with another person of interest who purportedly possessed a handgun and a very bad attitude. Stan also hoped for a convicting stash of real-live smuggled diamonds as evidence. "How much longer?" he asked impatiently over the voice-activated headsets.

The helicopter bounced sharply, followed by a bone-jarring slap to the left. It seemed to take a moment for the flight crew to regain what little control Stan felt they had. The machine settled into a calmer pocket of air before a reply came.

"You should be thankful Inspector that we were already sitting on the pad with the engines running when the call to arms came in," replied one of the pilots, a female who ignored Stan's ETA question. "You must have some clout with the boss for us to launch so quickly without a briefing. At any rate, we're hugging the river deck as it is, and visibility is marginal at best. And I can assure you we're at max throttle already. So, for your own safety, please ensure your seat belts are fastened and your tray tables are in the upright and locked position because our approach into Spruce Creek will be a guaranteed choppy ride."

And it isn't now? thought Stan moodily. "You didn't answer my ... oh, never mind. Whatever trouble is brewing at Spruce Creek could be over by the time we get there. Just hurry, please."

"Roger that," remarked the pilot sourly. "We wouldn't want you to miss the fun, so we are indeed hurrying for your sake."

Stan shook his head, made eye contact with both obviously miserable constables, and replied coldly, "No stewardess, we sure wouldn't."

* * *

Diane Jackson's legs shook beyond her control. She wanted to sit down, or at the very least crouch, but even if she wanted too, there wasn't as much as a stump to rest on. She forced herself to stay upright by leaning into Kim's left side for support. Tess moved in on her right for added stability. As soon as the plane set down, Diane intended to move in like a cat on the hunt. Foolish or not, she needed to get to her husband despite whatever dangers lurked in the shadows.

"Now we stress, watch and wait, eh girls?" announced Diane nervously.

"That's all we can do," agreed Tess. "But we're here and that's all that matters. I'd hate to be at Moger's Point knowing our guys are inbound here."

Diane thought it all surreal, like a dream—and by no means a good one. But this situation, in all its fervent reality, left her feeling like a chess pawn with no way to alter the outcome for her benefit or that of her husband. She closed her eyes and saw Paul's face, hoping that in the next few minutes she'd see him in the flesh, and not from her recent soiled memories.

Jack Ward stood well back of Diane and Kim Jackson, and despite assurances otherwise, he felt it best to keep his distance until the dust settled one way or another. Matt Hawley, along with Tom and Dylan Sullivan, positioned themselves to Jack's left, the four men seeking refuge from the rain under a pine-tree bough.

Search coordinator Rob Smith and his cohort Laura Hastings planted themselves under the left-wing of the Piper Cub, while pilot Kevin Davies and Susan McCutcheon hunkered down on the opposite side, both with arms pointing skyward over the lake. Rob tried to contact the Maule on his portable radio but received nothing but annoying squeals in reply. He threw his arms up in frustration and under-handed the unit to Laura. "Remind me to demand a new radio once when we get back to civilization," he grumbled. "This one I plan to throw into the lake."

"Mental note stored," replied Laura while inspecting the device. "But I'm not sure it's the radio. I doubt the pilots inside the Maule would be able to transmit a reply anyway, even if they wanted to. Assuming, as we've been led to believe, they're possibly being held at gunpoint."

"Yup, that's a valid point," agreed Rob. "I wish I knew for certain their intentions, so we could hatch a plan at our end. At this point, this is fast becoming a police issue and no longer a search and rescue. Wait until everyone back at Moger's Point hears about this."

Laura grunted and spoke quietly not to be overheard. "With no police here, I think we're acting law enforcement. Too bad we have no idea what's been going on inside that plane, but I imagine it's not been good."

Rob nodded in agreement. "I suspect our missing airmen wish they had just stayed home last evening. Lord knows that in hindsight, that would've been my personal preference too."

Deliveries

The umbrella felt heavy in Diane's hands, as though made from concrete and not fabric and aluminum. She tried to lift it higher for Tess's benefit, but in doing so, a strong wind gust sucked the handle from her hands and the wire frame smacked into the side of Tess's head.

"Here," urged Tess as she fumbled to grab the wayward umbrella. "Let me handle this for you. I'm taller anyway."

Diane tried to smile. "Thanks, Tess. I'm starting to feel like I've been hit by a freight train, as my dad used to say."

"All good," replied Tess. "The wind isn't helping matters, and yes, a train slam is a good analogy for our exhaustion levels. We've been through a lot, and the fun continues it would appear."

Confused, Diane looked at the sky. The plane was up high and aimed directly at Spruce Creek. "What's going on up there, Tess?" she asked. "I know I sound like a broken record, but I can't understand why they're up so high if they're trying to land."

Tess shook her head. "Wish I knew. You can bet the guys have a good reason if there's an unruly passenger on board who's calling the shots—quite literally. But then it's all speculation, so who knows for sure?"

Kim let go of her mom and stepped a few feet forward. "Do you hear that, Mom? I hear Dad's plane, but I think I also hear a helicopter. It's very quiet but it's definitely there."

At that moment Rob Smith jogged over, the excitement in his winded voice palpable. "Listen, folks, I just received a call on the Unicom channel that there's also a police helicopter inbound to the field. I have no idea how they got here so fast, but it sounds like they got word of your husbands and their troubled passenger."

"See, Mom. I knew I could hear a rotor system out there!"

Diane's eyebrows shot up in amusement. "Rotor system?" she asked smiling. "I think you've been hanging around your dad too much sweetie. But in any event, you were right. Seems as though things are really coming to a head now."

Matt smirked knowingly. "Sounds like the call I made to the police department got through to the proper channels—and fast. They must have taken off within minutes, and really booked it!"

"Would appear so," Rob agreed. "So, now we've got two aircraft inbound." Rob licked his index finger out of habit and held it aloft. "Given the wind direction from the west, the only place the chopper can land is right in front of us, so that puts us all too close to the action."

Laura Hastings picked up on the subtle head nod from Rob. She hurried in and promptly ushered everyone well back from either landing zone. Rob walked towards the lakeshore, all the while glancing up at the fast-approaching Maule. If, in fact, they were about to land, he too couldn't figure out why they were up so high. A chill ran along his spine, causing him to shiver.

"Are you actually landing?" Rob asked himself. *Or is this whole stinking ordeal going to drag on for lord knows how much longer?*

* * *

A glance at the altimeter showed the Maule at 600 feet, far too low for a harebrained manoeuvre never intended for the type of plane Paul Jackson sat in. He knew if the engine quit while inverted, they'd be in very serious trouble, as in very likely dead.

In back, Gary Nordhavn clutched his shoulder. His face exhibited both rage and physical pain, all rolled into one tortured expression. Paul watched the man a second longer when Gary suddenly locked eyes and began shouting demands oozing with condemnation. Paul knew that Gary could no longer be reasoned with, and for this situation to end with life and breath intact, he had to be repressed one way or another. Rolling the plane seemed their only viable option.

Paul thought of Diane and Kim, a blur of images cascading through his mind at breakneck speed. *You caused this mess, Paul, all of it.* Noticing Dave's hands and white knuckles clenched to

Deliveries

the yoke from squeezing so hard, it was then Paul's world slowed down; the only awareness of life and reality was his pounding heart. The drone of the engine eerily slipped away, replaced by a high-frequency ringing in his ears. Even Gary's thundering voice mercifully trailed off.

A breath away from Dave flipping them upside down, all Paul could do was brace his feet into the foot pedals and hold on for dear life. He felt like a player in a barbaric roleplayed video game, that a bevy of incorrect pathways led him to this moment, to the cusp of termination just before learning a personal life lesson. But if this real-world stunt failed, there would be no respawn for another go, and to Paul's dismay, a zippo percent chance to select the other fork in the road.

Paul gave his head a shake to displace the fog from his brain. He watched in fascination as Dave's hand slipped to the throttle and the plane's nose pitched up a few degrees. Paul locked himself in place for what he knew was coming.

Gary continued to flail about, yelling and demanding they land immediately. He booted the seat back with his feet, jarring Paul and Dave's upper bodies like someone kicking a theatre seat from the row behind. In all the raucous commotion, Gary somehow managed to retrieve the pistol from the floor. He scrambled furiously to spin it about in his hand, to use it once again as his personal bargaining chip. He found the trigger and popped off another shot through the left side door to emphasize his willful determination.

Dave and Paul shuddered at the firecracker sound and pungent aroma of gunpowder. The bullet casing spun towards the instrument panel, ricocheted off the upper dash and ended up on Paul's lap. He distressingly flicked it off and whipped his head around, where he found himself once again staring into a small black hole, the muzzle releasing a tiny wisp of smoke that dissipated before Paul found his next breath. His eyes wandered to Gary's lap. His seat belt remained unbuckled, and the crazed man was completely unaware of the pain and terror he was about to experience—just as Paul had hoped.

* * *

Those observing at ground level thought it peculiar when the approaching Maule appeared to climb and its engine revved up, especially since everyone assumed the plane was about to slow down, descend and land. The hairs bristled on Kevin Davies' neck. He suspected something unconventional was afoot and wondered if the Maule would skip out and leave the valley entirely or, God forbid, drop like a stone into the chilly waters of Bayshore Lake.

Beside Kevin, Susan McCutcheon's face revealed her concern. She leaned in so as not to be overheard by those standing nearby. "What's your pilot brain telling you, Kevin? To me, that airplane has no intention of landing here, unless they begin to spin wide circles and lose some altitude."

Kevin shook his head. "Wish I knew," he replied quietly. "Seems to me like they're about to hightail it away, which means we're all here for nothing and this mess drags out even longer."

"On the plus side though," added Susan. "Our job here would be done."

Kevin grunted. "Be careful what you wish for."

Chapter 39

Dave McMurray had not flown inverted for years, so he wasn't in any way surprised that his heart rolled cartwheels just milliseconds from performing a stunt that very well could end his life.

Shortly after acquiring his pilot's licence, Dave had become good friends with his flight instructor, an impeccably clean-cut man in his mid-sixties, named Benjamin Rudy, who was also a competitive weekend aerobatic pilot in his fire-engine red Pitts Special bi-plane.

Unconventional flight had always intrigued Dave, though it wasn't a pursuit he wanted to shell out extra money to embrace. But when the flying club took delivery of a new Cessna 152 Aerobat as part of its fleet, things changed. The Aerobat was a two-seat high wing airplane with tricycle landing gear and a frame certified for light aerobatics. This allowed an adventurous pilot the chance for more robust flying than with traditional aircraft.

One afternoon following a half-dozen circuits to bolster his logbook hours, Dave parked his Piper Cherokee and crossed paths with Ben on the apron who, with a clipboard and keys in hand, was on his way to flight test the new aerobatic Cessna. Shortly afterwards, Dave found himself anchored into the right seat with Ben at the controls, the two men smiling like school children as they gently rolled the airplane over the practice area ten kilometres west of the airport.

At Ben's prompting, it wasn't long before Dave tried the inversion himself. It wasn't pretty, but the sensation was exhilarating. He tried a few more times, and on his final attempt, he held the Cessna upside-down before rolling the wings to level flight. With an instructor beside him, his courage level far exceeded his ability. Dave wished Ben was in the plane with him now.

Horrified that Gary fired another shot, the blast served as a catalyst for Dave's nose to pick up on the acrid smell of fish. The scent had always been there, but the putrid aroma seemed especially rank all of a sudden when mixed with gunpowder. He tried to ignore the sensory overload by breathing through his mouth, and as he did so, Gary leaned forward. The gun's barrel passed briefly between Dave and Paul and then withdrew. Gary strung together a series of expletives, mixing them with words that made little sense to no one but himself.

Dave braced against his seat, planted his uninjured foot hard to the floor and tucked his pain riddled ankle in behind for stability. He noticed Paul's arms folded against his chest, his legs rigid and his feet cemented to the pedals. Paul turned his head to the left and nodded to get on with it, then faced forward and closed his eyes. For a fleeting moment, Dave thought it funny how a grown man facing certain peril would choose to shut his eyes to block out impending trauma. Admittedly, Dave wished he could do the same.

"Here goes nothing," Dave woefully exclaimed.

As he rotated the yoke through to vertical, and the wings rolled left beyond fifty degrees, a sudden slap of air pummelled the airplane hard. Anything inside the cabin that wasn't secured, lifted and fell, including a blindsided and still unrestrained Gary Nordhavn. A scream of pain erupted from the backseat as Gary pitched sideways into the door. Losing control of the plane, Dave quickly aborted the roll and brought the wings level. Their ploy was up.

Paul's eyes snapped open. He craned his neck around to see that Gary had somehow managed to retain the pistol despite his

Deliveries

contorted body position. Paul feared their upended passenger might accidentally or on purpose pull the trigger as he struggled to right himself. Instead, Gary looked down into his lap and his eyes widened as might a child discovering untied shoes for the first time. In a matter of seconds, his face converted from rage to genuine puzzlement when he discovered that his seatbelt wasn't fastened. The rapid physical transformation sent a hair-raising chill through Paul's entire body.

Gary set the gun down beside him and fumbled to grasp both ends of his belt. Despite bumpy air, he managed to grab hold of the receptacle, but the clip ended up wedged under his thigh. He reached for it with his free hand and tried to pull, but it wouldn't come free. His shoulder protested the harsh movements, but Gary ignored the searing pain. He leaned sideways to free the clasp, and as he did so, another sledgehammer of wind pitched the Maule sideways.

The gun slid to the floor as Gary thrashed behind Paul's seat. Yelping in pain, Gary abandoned the seatbelt and leaned forward in search of his coveted asset. His collarbone burned from scrunching over as his fingers grappled near his feet.

"Leave it, Gary," begged Paul. "This can end here and—"

Indignant, Gary frantically drew back his hand to discover the barbed end of a fishing lure soundly embedded into his skin. Blood trickled down his thumb, but he could not have cared less. Rather than remove the hook, Gary leaned over again, and this time his fingers discovered the weapon behind his right heel. He scooped it up and deftly aimed it at Dave McMurray's head. "Land now!" he snorted.

Helpless to do anything but stare, Paul watched in horror as the barrel came to rest at the base of his friend's neck. Dave froze where he sat, his eyes growing wide as his entire body began to shake.

Gary leaned forward even more. "Git this plane down now or you die!"

Paul Jackson wasn't typically an impulsive man, but the events of the last twenty-four hours systematically dispelled that shortcoming. In a blindingly fast upwards movement, he reached out with both hands and grabbed Gary's wrist, lifting the man's arm towards the roof and away from Dave's head. Gary squealed in agony and immediately countered the assault by pulling his arms back towards his chest with Paul's hands attached. In the scuffle for control, the gun discharged and sent another bullet into the roof, the lead passing dangerously close to Paul's left ear. The proximity blast was so loud, Paul thought his eardrums had burst.

Dave shuddered from the turmoil inside the plane, while also struggling to maintain flight control against increasingly unrelenting weather. With Paul's feet off the pedals, Dave felt the tail slide about on its vertical axis. "For God's sake," he pleaded. "Let him go, Ace!"

Fearing another shot, Paul's released his grip and backed down. He rubbed his ears while checking out Gary over his shoulder. Unnervingly calm, the man sat back in his seat and brought the gun to bear a second time, its muzzle aimed again at Dave's head, but this time from a safer distance. "You got five seconds ta cut the throttle and git the wheels aimed down, or—"

Dave suddenly felt the yoke move against his will. Stupefied, he tried to make sense of the unexpected deviation from his control. It wiggled a second in his hands before rotating fully left and forward. In a blur of motion, Dave felt his body weight slam against his seatbelt at the exact moment he noticed Paul's hands on the controls. The horizon spun on its axis and his world flipped upside down. Dave's voice gurgled out a faint protest as he instinctively wanted to counter the inversion to save his own life. Inwardly, he sensed the rogue move may have done just that, so he unshackled his hands from the controls and waited for the displaced earth and sky to right itself. But that never happened.

Everything not strapped in fell towards the ceiling, including the loose diamonds in Paul's shirt pocket. The small gems spilled out and scattered everywhere inside the cockpit. A frantic Gary Nordhavn screamed as his upper torso impacted the roof, followed by a sharp hit to his collarbone. Struggling to discern up from down, he flailed around about like a fish out of water, trying desperately to gain a foothold on anything solid.

For Dave, Paul's spontaneity was one thing, but he knew that keeping the wings inverted was a one-way ticket to the pearly gates. Waiting for the engine to sputter and quit, Dave held his breath. "Not good, Ace!" he groaned. "Get us . . . back around!"

The Maule's nose began to drop, and Paul added more forward pressure on the yoke to stay neutral. His eyes never left the overturned horizon. "Just a . . . second longer!" he grunted with his back screaming bloody murder. "Where's the gun?" he squawked at Dave.

As the blood rushed to Dave's head, he forcibly craned his neck around despite searing pain in his ankle. "How should I know!" he barked through gritted teeth. "Everything's messed up back there, and Gary's a pretzel! I don't think he's got it!"

It was then the engine sputtered, coughed and fell eerily silent.

* * *

Everyone on the ground released a collective gasp, followed by shrieks of horror from Diane Jackson as she watched her husband's plane unexpectedly flip upside down. "Oh, dear God," she cried. "What's happening?" The sudden deviation from normal flight was so unexpected that Diane caught herself blinking to be sure her eyes were seeing things correctly. They did.

As perplexing as it was to Tess, she grabbed hold of Diane's arm. "I'm sure it's for good reason," she tried to justify. "It's likely some crazy stunt to correct a bad situation. Dave and Paul have improvised before."

But this time Tess was anything but sure. She knew something was terribly wrong for such a drastic event to have so readily taken place, and what frightened her most was the underlying reason for such a stunt in the first place. The comforting thought, if one existed, was that instead of watching them plummet to the ground as one might expect, the plane hung there inverted, which meant that someone still held control.

"Why are they staying like that?" asked Kim. "Dad hates being upside down!"

Horrified, Diane replied nervously, "I wish to God I knew."

Standing nearby, Kevin Davies overheard the exchange between the women and decided to intervene. Rob Smith followed, his concern not only for the Maule and its occupants but that Kevin might spout off and further destroy the already toppled applecart. And to Rob's displeasure, that's exactly what he did.

"They better flip back over and quick," Kevin stated emphatically.

Diane looked at Kevin, her eyes wide with fear. "Meaning?" she asked nervously.

Kevin picked up on Rob's facial expression and thought it best to tread carefully with his explanation. "Older planes like that have a carburetor, and the engine can't handle inverted flight for long."

Rob glared at Kevin then back to the Maule. "What Kevin's trying to say, is that if they don't flip back around soon, the engine will—"

"It'll stop!" interjected Kim. "The engine will quit, Mom. That's what they're both getting at." Kim locked eyes with Rob. "Isn't it?"

"Yes," replied Rob. "That's it exactly. That could happen, but I'm sure it won't."

"And you would know that how?" asked Tess.

Rob swallowed hard. "Let's all trust it doesn't come to that, shall we?"

Kevin shared nervous eye contact with Tess, then timidly looked away.

Gawking in disbelief at the overturned airplane, Tom and Jack remained in place with their mouths agape. Jack wished he had not been privy to the bit about the plane's engine stalling out, but things being what they were, additional bad news seemed to fit in with the weekend's underlying theme of out-of-hand calamity.

Pointing to the sky as though witnessing a cataclysmic global event, Dylan Sullivan and Matt Hawley chatted away like two parakeets in a cage. Tom caught his son's eye and drew his pinched together thumb and index finger across his lips as a way of telling Dylan to zip it. The duo ceased their babble.

Distinct against the ambient sounds of wind, birds and rain, the Maule's engine could easily be heard by those watching from the ground. But another sound also reached their ears. The *thwop-thwop* of helicopter rotors grew steadily louder as the police chopper raced to the scene, low to the water and coming in unbelievably fast.

Rob lowered his gaze and quickly located the incoming helicopter. "Looks as though the cavalry has arrived," he said to Laura.

"Yup," she replied, glancing towards the machine. "They sure didn't waste any time getting here. They must have their jet packs lit. Whoever's in the Maule with our pilots must have really tripped their bad-guy radar."

Rob checked his portable radio and tuned it to the Unicom channel. He set the volume higher and jumped when a call blared through the speaker: "Spruce Creek traffic, OPD helicopter Air One, seven clicks east at 300 feet, inbound for landing south of the Spruce Creek airstrip."

* * *

As reporter Dwaine Ennis crassly barked commands, the cameraman tried feverishly to grab video of both incoming aircraft. At full telephoto, the inadequacy of the lens to get decent close-ups forced him to snap down the lever at the rear of the lens, which activated the two-times extender. This doubled the telephoto capabilities of the lens but also affected image clarity and the amount of light entering through the front element. The operator tried to adjust the iris, but it was already wide open.

From a video quality standpoint, the issues stacked against him made the task of collecting decent video nearly impossible. And now with blotchy patterns of rain collecting on the lens surface, seeing a clear image through the viewfinder sharp enough to focus on became another formidable challenge. The man grabbed a cloth from his coat pocket and tried to wipe the moisture off the glass surface as best he could. "I'm telling ya, Dwaine," he complained. "I can hardly see anything with this rain and the extender down. Plus, the video boost adds noise, so it really—"

"Do what you can," interrupted Dwaine. "And don't forget cutaways, especially shots of our hapless women. I need enough visuals to cover the entire story here!"

Under his breath, the cameraman mumbled. "I don't tell you how to report, so don't tell me how to shoot."

"What's that?" asked Dwaine distractedly, his attention forward.

"Nothing," replied the camera op sarcastically. "Nothing at all."

* * *

As Diane Jackson's eyes drifted between the two aircraft, her breath caught when she heard the sound of a sputtering engine. Dropping into the wet grass on her knees, Diane knew immediately the plane was in serious trouble.

"Mom!" shouted Kim as she bent down. "Are you okay?" But Kim knew exactly why her mother's legs gave out because she also heard the engine cough.

Jack scurried over to offer help. "Easy, Diane," he counselled. "Don't worry, they'll make it."

Diane looked up at Jack through growing tears. "I wish I could believe that, Jack," she sniffled. "Am I the only one who just heard their engine quit?"

"I heard it, Mom. But Uncle Jack's right. Dad will make it, engine or not."

Diane stood back up on wobbly legs, her arms supported with Kim on one side and Jack on the other. Tom Sullivan offered to help, but Jack shooed him away.

All eyes but Rob Smith's were on the Maule. His attention was on the police helicopter and its growing proximity to the plane. He adjusted the squelch on his radio and pushed the transmit button. "OPD Air One, Spruce Creek on Unicom. This is Rob Smith, Search Co-ordinator of Owensville S and R."

Rob glanced at the helicopter and then over to the Maule. He felt certain the helicopter crew was unaware of the inverted Maule or their proximity to it. "As you're aware, we have a situation here," he announced. "The aircraft you're looking for is slightly north of your position at, I'm guessing, a thousand feet." Laura Hastings moved in beside him. "And this is no joke, but they're currently inverted and apparently just lost power." Rob paused to let that sink in. "Recommend you stay clear of the Spruce Creek airfield for the time being and break off to the south, over."

* * *

"Did he just say inverted and without power?" asked Air One co-pilot Rhonda Wellington, with genuine surprise in her voice.

Pilot-in-Command Bob Walker shook his head. "I do believe that's what the man just said, though I can't imagine why or just what on earth is going on inside that plane."

Rhonda shrugged her shoulders. "Can't be anything good."

Both pilots glanced out the right-side front window of their Bell 430 turbine helicopter, but with low cloud scattered across Bayshore Lake, it was difficult to spot the plane against the ugly backdrop of white and grey.

Bob keyed his microphone button. "Air One, Spruce Creek. We're looking but don't have a visual on the Maule. We'll quickly set down in the open field south of the airstrip. And be advised we have an Inspector Stan Fenwick on board with two plainclothes officers, one of whom is experiencing a touch of air sickness. It's been a choppy ride out here, and I'm sure any further delay in landing won't sit well with him."

A jolt of rougher air butted the helicopter head-on, pushing the nose up and causing the tail to slide out to the left. Bob epoxied his hands to the controls and swiftly corrected the pitch while kicking in the perfect amount of tail-rotor to counter the onslaught. His gloved hand on the collective was especially stiff from already gripping so hard, but now was not the time to stretch his fingers. Having never before landed at Spruce Creek, he suspected the set down would be tricky given the snug confines, lofty pine trees surrounding the field, and typically unpredictable mountain winds.

Bob glanced at Rhonda and told her to buckle up. Then, he told his passengers to do the same before saying to nobody in particular. "This should be interesting."

* * *

Diane watched in stunned silence as the Maule flipped right side up, hung in the sky for what seemed an eternity, then side-slipped towards the lake directly into the path of the police helicopter. As she stood quietly, the faces of those around her displayed similar shock from being eyewitnesses to the oddball scene playing out before them.

The police chopper lurched once or twice from an obvious gust of wind, but stayed on course, its pilots oblivious to the airplane bearing down from above. Frozen in place, the only words spoken came from Diane's lips.

"Paul, I love you."

Chapter 40

Gary Nordhavn fell hard into his seat, his arms and legs floundering as he desperately tried to regain his stability. His head smashed into the side window, followed by yelps of pain mixed with raw fear. Lures, fishing poles, fish fillets and chocolate bars all succumbed to gravity, while empty water bottles ricocheted like tennis balls before settling to the floor. Gary's favourite tackle box caught him on the side of his left arm before crashing hard behind his seat. He howled in agony.

Dave thought it all sounded like cows trapped in a loading chute as they awaited slaughter, their hooves slamming into the steel gates of their enclosure trying desperately to escape. But there was no time to focus on their troubled passenger or even the gun's whereabouts.

With the propeller stopped and the engine starved of fuel, Paul levelled the wings and knew they had just moments to restart before stalling out. And without sufficient altitude to establish any sort of survivable glide angle to shore, their dire situation couldn't have been worse.

"Re-light the engine, Dave!" Paul shouted.

"Get the nose down!" countered Dave, his hands already on the yoke.

"I know that!" snapped Paul. "Let go, I got this! Crank the mags!"

Dave swore and pulled his hands away, but not before another wicked updraft hammered the plane, eroding what precious airspeed remained. Paul felt buffeting through the fuselage, followed by an illuminated red stall warning light on the instrument panel. "Not good!" he croaked, "that's not—"

The left-wing tip began to drop as disrupted airflow over the wing caused the aircraft to side-slip towards the lake less than a thousand feet below.

* * *

Bob Walker turned to his co-pilot. "We'll be on the ground in a moment, Rhonda, and then we can sit and wait for the Maule, wherever it is. I bet you're wishing you'd stayed a dispatcher than suffer through this ride."

Following an odd moment of silence from his co-pilot, Bob was about to repeat himself when his headset blasted to life.

"Oh, dear God!" shrieked Rhonda in horror. "Break left now!"

"What?" asked Bob. "What's the—"

Bob suddenly caught the flash of wings and the airplane slipping towards them. He roughly slammed the cyclic to the left and flipped the chopper on its side with no warning given to the three men in the back. Someone shouted a string of profanity over the intercom, but Bob was too busy to care. In his career, never had he come even close to a mid-air collision, and he wasn't at all willing to let that happen now and destroy an exemplary safety record.

"I take that back!" shouted Bob. "Screw dispatch!"

* * *

Without thrust, the Maule was now a glider, and a poor one at that. Paul eased the yoke slightly forward and applied right rudder to counter the dropping wing. He dared not remove his hands from the yoke. "Fuel pump, Dave!" he screamed. "Throttle, then crank it!"

It took Dave a moment to find the pump switch. He snapped it on, closed the throttle an inch and reached for the ignition. As he rotated to the start position, the propeller spun but never caught.

Paul's eyes grew wide as he strained to keep the plane under what little control he had. "Again!" he bellowed frantically.

"Ya think?" barked Dave. This time he rotated the ignition to off, then to the right through both mags, and finally to start.

Deliveries

"No, wait!" shouted Paul, his head aimed down. "Mixture!"

Dave shoved the lever to full rich and waited for a moment before re-engaging the starter. "C'mon you bloody thing," he pleaded furiously. "Fire up!"

The prop turned, sputtered once and remained still. Dave was about to try again, when something caught his peripheral vision out the left side window. It wasn't so much the helicopter's fuselage that caught his attention as it was its main rotor, the blades spinning circles of white from whatever paint scheme they came from the factory with.

Dave grabbed the yoke with his right hand and flipped it in the opposite direction. "Evasive!" was all he could manage to spew.

"What're ya doing?" screamed Paul as he fought back for control.

"Chopper!" countered Dave. "Right below us!"

Paul craned his neck to see for himself, but the helicopter wasn't in his line of sight. "A chopper?" he asked incredulously. "I never heard any calls on Unicom, so who's the bloody fool that—"

"Doesn't matter!" snapped Dave. "Give me the plane!"

Paul handed over control but kept his feet on the pedals.

As Dave rolled the wings through twenty degrees, he glanced out his window and saw the helicopter peeling away to the south. "They've seen us!" he called out. "They've turned away!" Dave brought the wings back to semi-level and cranked the starter a third time.

It was then Gary Nordhavn regained his balance and began frantically searching for his gun through a torrent of cussing. In doing so, he discovered several of his diamonds sprinkled about the cabin, including a full carat stone resting precariously on his lap. He knew immediately that he'd been lied too. Gary swore again and decided the deceptive men flying his plane would suffer, just as they made him suffer. But what he did not understand in his current frame of mind, was that in a matter of seconds, they'd all be dead anyway.

* * *

Flying, in general, was never one of Inspector Stan Fenwick's chosen things to do. In fact, he avoided air travel whenever possible, preferring ground, rail or water transportation over anything with wings or rotors. And with the sudden and violent departure from level flight, he despised flying machines even more—especially helicopters now.

Thrown sideways when the chopper tipped on its side, Stan's head bashed into something hard near the window, which resulted in an instant headache and a growing lump on his temple to prove it. He pressed his fingers against the impact point and was relieved to see no blood.

Even paler than before, the officer's pasty face lay covered in beads of sweat. Stan handed the man an airsick bag and was about to ask the flight crew what the devil was going on when the pilot's voice blasted through his headset. All three men flinched in their seats.

"Sorry about that back there," announced Bob Walker. "Evasive action and no time to give you fellows a courtesy heads-up."

"Evasive from what?" asked Stan cantankerously. "A flock of pelicans?"

"Not exactly, Inspector," replied the pilot. "But it was white. We just escaped from the clutches of a dive-bombing airplane, which I believe contains your diamond delivery man and your two missing but now found pilots."

Stan sat back in his seat completely dumbfounded. "I see," he replied. *Perhaps flying isn't so bad after all.*

* * *

Paul Jackson always wondered if he'd die in an airplane, and with a few hundred feet of airspace remaining between the Maule and the choppy water below, he was now more certain than ever that his time had come. With so much happening all at once, Paul's overclocked senses were on full alert. Chills coursed through his body—the pairing of adrenaline and fear producing the shakes and more nausea. He caught sight of the retreating helicopter to the south, while a delirious Gary Nordhavn held up one of the diamonds he found on his lap, examining it as though he had no idea what it was.

For whatever reason, Paul glanced out his side window. Bayshore Lake appeared cold and menacing, its waves a frothy mix of white caps sculpted into tumbling peaks and valleys from driving mountain winds. It was the last place he wanted to end up fighting for his life, assuming of course, he first survived the impact of smacking into its surface.

In a final effort to avert disaster, Dave frantically tried again to relight the engine. Paul rammed his feet hard into the pedals as if they were in some way linked to starting the engine. He frantically jockeyed them back and forth as winds buffeted the Maule from every direction.

"A little help here, Ace!" pleaded Dave, his hands split between the yoke and mag switch. "Take the yoke!"

As the waves rushed up to meet them, Paul grabbed the control with both hands. "Copy," he replied. "We're swimming regardless, so hold on!"

Gary kicked the seat back with both feet. "I don't wanna die," he screamed hysterically. "I don't wanna—" The toe of his left shoe brushed against a hard object. He froze, glanced down and saw the firearm. In one painful motion, Gary bent over and retrieved the weapon. His index finger curled around the trigger, and he cackled with delight. "Now I got ya my—"

"Shut up!" yelled Dave as he engaged the starter. "You're not helping you crazy—"

A savage updraft jetted the Maule higher, the gust throwing the left-wing down and launching the tail outwards. Like a rag doll, an unfettered Gary Nordhavn received the brunt of the impact, his upper torso in particular. He screamed, dropped the gun beside him and fell silent.

Without hesitation, Paul kicked in heavy right rudder and watched the propeller turn again—then stop dead. The airplane began to shudder, its wing entering a full stall.

"It's no use," bellowed Dave. "She won't start! Brace for impact!"

* * *

"You recording all this?" boomed reporter Dwaine Ennis.

Beside Dwaine stood his cameraman, the man squinting through the camera's viewfinder and his face scrunched in concentration. At full telephoto, the picture shook despite the camera being mounted on a heavy steel O'Conner tripod. "Yup," he replied. "But the wind isn't helping with image stability."

"It is what it is!" Dwaine remarked. "Just keep rolling and don't stop!"

Out of respect for the pilots' families and the visible trauma they were experiencing, Dwaine and his videographer chose to station themselves a respectful distance away from the group, but intentionally close enough to capture shots discreetly without being overly invasive.

Dwaine broke into a self-gratifying smile. He had always considered himself a persuasive reporter and wasn't above an occasional lighthearted bribe to secure what he needed. This time it was a bottle of red Moscato wine for his boss, Tom Sullivan.

At Dwaine's impromptu request, Tom begrudgingly agreed to wear a hidden wireless microphone to enable recording of conversations, even with the camera pointed away from the audio source. Dwaine fed on Tom's understanding of how important good quality sound bites were and how viewership ultimately drove news ratings—which translated to commercial revenue. So, with this being a lead story, Tom felt he needed to comply despite the backlash he knew would come from those around him when—not if—they found out.

The cameraman deftly panned the camera to grab a quick cutaway of those watching the drama, then aimed the lens back to the crippled airplane, now most assuredly committed to a watery demise. He noticed the police helicopter turning back towards Spruce Creek but staying clear of the struggling Maule.

It was then the camera emitted an audible warning beep through his headphones, followed by a flashing battery symbol in the viewfinder: the two signals an indicator that the battery was close to empty, despite a recent full charge. And to make matters worse, the spare cells were in the news truck. "Ah nuts," sighed the operator.

Dwaine leaned in. "Please tell me that beeping I hear isn't what I think it is?"

The cameraman kept his eye pressed to the viewfinder and reached into his coat pocket. He handed Dwaine the car keys. "Okay, I won't. But I suggest you hurry and fetch me another battery."

Livid, the big reporter snatched the keys and sprinted to the vehicle. On the way, he kept flipping his head around to catch the drama in the skies above and could not help but wonder if he had ever run so fast in his life.

* * *

"It's flooded," croaked Gary Nordhavn in a voice riddled with fear and pain. "You flooded it."

Paul swung his head around and zeroed in on the gun straightaway. This time Gary wasn't waving it around. Instead, the man pointed the barrel at his own temple, his eyes wide.

"Hey, man," spewed Paul. "Don't do anything stupid! It's not worth ending your life over." *Though we'll likely die anyway.*

"I already done somethin' stupid," Gary bellowed.

Dave wrestled with the airplane and tried desperately to keep from nosediving into the water. "No time for this, Ace," he gasped. "Let him shoot himself. He dies by gunshot or he drowns like us. His choice."

"Just fly, Dave!" ordered Paul.

"Fly what?" laughed Dave. "We're a rock with wings for crying out loud!"

Gary leaned forward, the sudden move causing Dave and Paul to lean in opposite directions. But the gun never came to bear. Instead, Gary's eyes swept over the instrument panel, his rapid personality shift leaving Paul more skittish than ever. Dave wanted more than anything to punch the man but kept both hands on the column.

"Flooded," quipped Gary a third time. "Too rich, the mixture—"

"Shut up!" Dave snarled. "I need to concentrate!"

Gary pointed at the engine mixture knob at the exact moment a violent pocket of air slugged the Maule sideways. He cried out in terror, fell back into his seat and began to whimper. "Flooded," he croaked indistinctly.

Dave countered with opposite pressure on the yoke, but with diminished airflow over the wings, the nose fell beyond his ability to control it. He extended his arm across his friend's chest like a parent protecting a child in a car accident. "Brace yourself, Ace!" he shouted.

As Paul leaned his back into the seat and thought of Diane and Kim, he unintentionally pieced together what Gary tried to say. With surprisingly rational behaviour from a man facing his own mortality, Gary knew why the engine would not start. "Kill the throttle!" Paul yelled. "Mixture's too rich!"

"What?" shrieked Dave. "What are you saying?"

In a flurry of motion, Paul yanked back the mixture and throttle. "Crank the mags again!" he bellowed.

Dave's hands were sealed to the yoke and Paul knew his friend wasn't catching on. With no time to explain, Paul reached down and deliberately turned the key to "OFF," then back through "BOTH" mags, and then to the "START" position.

Inside the engine block, the starter pulled electricity from the battery and began to spin, its gearing immediately catching the flywheel as the propeller rotated and the crankshaft drove the pistons up and down. Only this time with less fuel inside the engine's flooded cylinders, the magnetos fired the plugs and ignited a leaner mix of air and fuel. Paul held his breath but didn't have to for long.

The engine coughed as sooty black exhaust belched from the pipes. Then, blissfully, it fired up! With no time to gloat, Paul bumped the prop knob fully forward before going full rich on the mixture. He advanced the throttle to full power. The engine roared to life as the propeller bit into the air. Manifold pressure climbed and the RPMs rose swiftly into the green—the surge of thrust breathing new life into an airplane that just seconds ago, faced its demise. An ear-splitting "Whoop" escaped from Paul's lips as he waited for Dave to recover the plane. In back, Gary Nordhavn remained as quiet as a field mouse.

Paul's heart began rolling in his chest, the sudden hard palpitations stealing his breath away. Flooded with adrenaline and a body riddled with pain, he screamed at Dave through his panic. "Pull up!" But his friend seemed no more clued into the moment than a lobster being dropped into a pot of boiling water. Dave's hands clenched the yoke, but he wasn't responding.

"Dave!" shouted Paul a second time. "Engine's hot!" Paul forced his hands to the yoke in front of him and tried to correct their doomed flight attitude but could not find the strength against Dave's opposing force. "Pull us out of this!"

In apparent shock from the near certainty of his expiry, Dave remained stationary, his hands fiercely gripping the yoke, but unable to move. Horrified, Paul reached over and smacked the palm of his hand against his friend's cheek. That did the trick. The painful blow awoke Dave from his stupor, snapping his senses back to reality.

"Welcome back, amigo!" Paul yelled. "Now fly!"

Only seconds from slamming into the turbulent waters of Bayshore Lake, Dave noticed the Maule's nose-down pitch and severe bank angle on the wings. With lightning-fast reflexes, he rotated the yoke and strong-armed it back into his chest. The airplane seemed equally surprised at the sudden forces placed upon its control surfaces, its fuselage hesitating slightly before realizing it too had been given a second chance at life. Shored up by strong headwinds, the aircraft began a shallow climb to safety, then as lift took hold, the bird leapt into the sky like a jet.

"Ace!" Dave bellowed. "I'd kiss you if my lips could reach you!"

Chapter 41

From the wave riddled shoreline a hundred feet north of the Spruce Creek airstrip, it appeared to all watching that the small airplane would strike the water's surface at a significantly skewed angle. To its left, the police helicopter hovered a safe distance away from the stricken Maule, its crew no doubt watching the aerial drama with compelling interest.

Then, at the last possible moment, the plane's engine sputtered to life, growled to full power and climbed into a cloud-riddled sky as though lugged by an invisible tow-rope. The swift change in dynamics created such an unexpected turn of events, that everyone stood completely transfixed, if not paralyzed. The sobbing stopped, the gasps ceased, and the pointing fingers came to rest as might happen in a movie when a mammoth plot reversal catches everyone with their pants down.

Diane and Kim Jackson stared at each other in absolute disbelief, while a composed Tess McMurray shook her head and smiled as though she expected this outcome all along. To her left, an equally befuddled Tom Sullivan and Jack Ward watched in struck dumb silence as the Maule climbed to safety. As Dylan Sullivan and Matt Hawley squeezed in from behind, Tess thought the group of men resembled a recent photo she saw on Twitter: a shot of four large pelicans squished together on a tiny three-foot-square floating platform.

Everyone turned in unison when Search and Rescue Coordinator Rob Smith jogged over with Laura Hastings at his hip. "Okay folks," he loudly announced. "Crisis apparently averted. So, until we know what that airplane is up too, we need to vacate this area so the police helicopter can land." Rob spun to face towards the chopper, which coincidentally departed its hover and began to chase after the Maule. "Or not," he added cynically.

* * *

Completely winded and with camera battery in hand, reporter Dwaine Ennis dug his heels into the wet grass, stopping his forward momentum before bulldozing his annoyingly relaxed cameraman. "We still rolling?" asked Dwaine nervously. "Because that kind of action is never happening again!"

Without saying a word, the operator unlatched the depleted battery from his camera and handed it to Dwaine. "Nope," he replied coolly. "Camera died a minute after you left for the truck. Missed it all."

Dwaine had experienced his share of news stories when technical difficulties crept up. Such pitfalls were inevitable in his line of work. Sometimes, garbled audio was the culprit because of a flawed microphone, or a camera op who forgot to white balance, or completely disengage the macro lever on the lens, resulting in slightly soft footage. Such incidents were hazards of working with people of different experience levels. But a camera operator who failed to carry on his person a spare battery at all times? For Dwaine, such an omission was basic common-sense shooting, the offence deserving of a serious reprimand once they returned to the station.

Infuriated that footage critical to his story had not been recorded, Dwaine fought the urge to cuff his videographer across the back of his head with the microphone. Instead, he stepped back, sucked in a lung full of air to quell his anger, and then spoke in as even a tone as he could muster. "Get what you can. I'm sure they'll be landing in the next few minutes, and I'd rather not miss that too."

The cameraman nonchalantly powered up his camera and aimed it towards the Maule. He focused, set the lens aperture and hit the record button. Enjoying the moment, he felt certain that if his reporter possessed laser eyes, he'd have used them to melt his head into a pile of goo.

Attempting to conceal his growing smile, the operator happily left the big man to simmer in his own stew. It was a delicious moment to gloat over, and the perfect opportunity to exact revenge on a co-worker he never really cared for. *Ego comes before the fall*, he thought gleefully.

As Dwaine repositioned himself left of the tripod, he noticed a cheek-to-cheek smile on his cameraman's face. Instantly enraged, his face turned beet red. He leaned in towards the man and plucked the headphones from his head. "You find this amusing, do you?" he asked sarcastically.

Unflinching, the cameraman kept to task as he captured additional B-roll. "As a matter of fact, I do," he replied calmly. "Because watching you squirm just became one of my biggest and best career highlights!"

Dwaine's jaw dropped. "If I have anything to do with it, your career at CFCB is over. It's disgraceful for a camera jock to not have a spare battery with him and—"

"Chillax! Seems you're too self-absorbed to know when you're being duped," chuckled the cameraman. "So, now you can thank me."

"Thank you? What for exactly?"

"For expertly capturing every second of what happened over the lake just now."

Flustered, Dwayne stumbled back. "But . . . you said the camera died and that you missed it all."

The cameraman turned his head slightly and eyed Dwaine mischievously. "Yes, I did, didn't I? But I lied."

Deliveries

* * *

"It was Gary," stated Paul emphatically. "Technically, he saved our bacon, Dave. It wasn't you or me." Paul massaged his neck with both hands. "Sure, I clued into his rambling and got the airplane started. Then, I had to wake you from whatever terrified daze you were in. Sorry about the slap by the way."

Dave backed off on the manifold pressure and RPMs. "Apology not accepted," he chuckled. "Sorry I froze on you. Don't tell Tess or I'll never hear the end of it! I guess subconsciously I assumed my time had come, that all I could do was ride the ship down and meet my maker."

"I think it's safe to say we've been surrounded by guardian angels this whole time," stated Paul. "But the fact is, we both panicked and failed to use our brains. It was Gary who recognized a flooded engine when he saw it."

"Well, it's his plane, so that makes sense," added Dave. "I can't figure this guy out. One minute he's heck bent on trying to kill us, then the next he's saving our lives. He needs some serious help! But the fact remains he shot me, Ace, helping us just now or not."

Paul glanced over his shoulder to the backseat. Gary had curled himself into a ball with his knees drawn into his chest and his good arm wrapped tightly around. The gun was nowhere to be seen. He stared straight ahead with tears rolling down his cheeks. Paul thought he resembled a whipped pup who just received a chewing out for peeing on the carpet. He wanted to console the man but figured it wise to leave well enough alone. There was little to gain by poking a docile lion with a stick, even a well-intentioned one.

"When it comes to flying," acknowledged Dave, "sometimes the obvious is the easiest thing overlooked, especially when panic sets in and you think your life is about to end."

"Lesson learned for both of us. But we're still flying because of Gary, and that's a fact. When push came to shove, we pooled our meagre resources and are alive to tell the tale."

"Nobody will believe it when we tell them," replied Dave. "Especially the police when they look at the mess inside this plane."

Fishing lures and poles, fillets, chocolate bars, a torn open upended tackle box, and assuredly the screwiest of all, a diamond-littered interior would certainly raise eyebrows. Dave chuckled when he thought about the subsequent police investigation and how they'd be left scratching their heads over the mishmash inside. *No doubt one for the police history books,* he mused.

Dave levelled the plane at 500 feet and trimmed the nose as best he could. Given the rapid escalation of clouds amassing and drifting by on both sides, he still managed to find a narrow-uncluttered track of sky to fly through. The surprisingly unencumbered path reminded him of the bible story of Moses parting the Red Sea so the Israelites could escape Pharaoh's armies. A widening grin appeared on his face. *God really is the keeper of my soul.*

"What's so funny?" asked Paul.

"All I can say, Ace," Dave replied, "is that we should have bought the farm by now with all the trouble we've made for ourselves. But as you said, we had guardian angels in our pockets, not to mention a few stray diamonds!"

Paul glanced out his window. "Speaking of diamonds, the police chopper is in hot pursuit, coming up on my side."

Dave checked their airspeed. Ninety-five knots. Heavy grey clouds hung like appendages, reaching from above as though trying to grab the Maule's wing to exact revenge for eluding certain doom. Dave watched as the chopper pulled alongside a short distance away, its pilot visible and persistently tapping the side of his headset.

"He wants us on channel," observed Paul. "I'm not sure what frequency he's on." Paul fiddled with the Coms. "We never heard them before on Unicom."

"Doesn't matter anyway," noted Dave. "The radio took a bullet, and he's making it very clear that we need to land. I'm thinking he means this very minute."

Paul noticed the pilot's index finger, aggressively pointing down. "I couldn't agree more. The sooner I call my wife and daughter, the better." *If, they haven't left me for dead already.*

Dave offered a thumb's up to the chopper pilot, checked his compass heading and carefully brought the nose around, aiming it directly towards Spruce Creek. The helicopter stayed with them in perfect formation, its flight crew visible inside the cockpit with their glossy sky-blue helmets.

Setting the throttle to seventeen inches of manifold, Dave watched as the RPMs fell back. He grabbed for the checklist, but it wasn't in its usual place. "I don't know what happened to the checklist, so we'll have to wing it."

Paul looked briefly for it but gave up. "Pretty much like the 185," he guessed. "Besides, improvising procedures or forgetting them entirely is what we do best."

As the Maule's nose began to drop, Paul switched the fuel selector valve to feed off the right side, the fullest tank. The landing lights along both sides of the field at Spruce Creek provided a solid aiming point. Judging the glideslope would be the real challenge for Dave, as would the correct use of the rudder for Paul. The narrow field slopped upwards, and the wheels needed to hit the ground at precisely the right spot to avoid running out of turf. Regardless, Paul felt incredibly relieved that the lights were on, and he vowed to thank Jack once they landed.

"Airspeed falling through ninety," Paul announced casually.

"Let's go one click on the flaps," ordered Dave. "I want us low and slow before we cross the shoreline. Then, we'll need to drop in like a broken elevator."

"That's not an overly comforting thought," Paul remarked as he lowered the flaps fifteen degrees. "But I agree about low and slow."

As the Maule descended below 400 feet, the helicopter dropped in behind and out of sight. It was then Paul's side window flew open, the chilly blast of wind into the cockpit causing an unwanted distraction at the worst possible time. A blur of movement caught Paul's peripheral vision. He spun his head sideways in time to see a hand grasping a black object. *Oh, dear God,* Paul thought, *not the gun again.* But instead of the pistol coming to bear, Gary jettisoned the firearm out the window and it fell away.

The Colt struck the water's choppy surface within seconds, sinking like a stone to a depth of 210 feet, never to see the light of day again.

* * *

With the Maule on short final and the police helicopter on its tail, Diane Jackson broke away from the group. She walked to the beach area directly in front of the air strip's grassy thresh-hold.

Kim sprinted after her. "Mom!" she called out. "Wait for me!"

Seeing the immediate danger, Rob Smith started to pursue, but Tess grabbed his arm before he got too far along. "Let them go!" she insisted.

Rob tore his arm free from Tess's strong grip. "But it's not safe and—"

Tess glared disapprovingly, a strong signal to Rob that in no uncertain terms he was to back off. "After what those two women have gone through, and me for that matter, I think they're permitted to assume their own responsibility for being safe. And under the circumstances, I think they have every right to watch that airplane land and to do so from point-blank range if they so choose."

Rob eyed Tess angrily, but he conceded and backed off. "Fine, but the rest of us stay back until both those aircraft are safely on the ground."

"Sorry," argued Tess. "But, the rest of us does not include me."

With that said, Tess walked away to join her sisters in arms.

As her husband's plane grew in size, Diane Jackson wasn't sure what to think or feel. There were simply too many conflicting emotions coursing through her brain that she couldn't decide if she should laugh or cry. Reaching the spot along the shore where grass and weeds merged with loose rocks and lake water, Diane's feet began to sink into the moist sand as she approached the foamy surf. Waves splashed around her ankles, but she could not have cared less. Kim grabbed her mom's left arm and angled herself in for support and warmth. Both women stood their ground, unfazed at how close the plane would pass by as it set wheels down. At this conjuncture, all that mattered to Diane was an end to this entirely absurd charade.

Without saying a word, Tess crept up from behind and wrapped her long arms around both her friends. Together, the group of three focused on the stormy sky above, and the rapidly descending airplane smack dab in the middle.

* * *

"Close the window!" yelled Dave. "What are you doing, Ace?"

Paul grabbed the latch and re-secured it. "It wasn't me. Gary just tossed out the gun!"

"He what?" asked Dave—not believing his ears. "He threw the gun out? Oh, never mind! Just stay on the pedals because I guarantee this won't be one of my prettiest landings!"

Paul nodded. "Wouldn't be the first time today we—" A sharp stab of pain hit Paul in the chest. He fell forward, his hands clutched over his heart.

"Paul!" shouted Dave. "You, okay?"

Paul offered an unconvincing nod. "Yeah," he responded through obvious pain. "Just another physical reminder of my foolish ways."

"I'd really appreciate it if you'd quit doing the hands to your chest, lunge forward thing," implored Dave. "It scares the bejeebers out of me!"

Paul sat back up. "How do you think it makes me feel?" he sassed. "But for your sake, I'll see what I can do."

As the Maule slipped from the sky towards the shoreline, Dave lined up the nose with the converging rows of lights at the end of the airfield. From his vantage point, the landing area appeared unmercifully narrow and far too short for anything other than an ultralight. And with gusty winds slapping them around from all points on the compass, the usually simple task of maintaining a proper descent attitude was fast becoming a piloting nightmare.

Dave glanced at the airspeed indicator. *Seventy knots.* "We're too fast. One more notch of flaps, Ace!"

When Paul failed to comply, Dave tweaked the flap handle himself and waited a moment for the nose to lift and settle before adding trim. As he brought the RPMs back even further and watched the airspeed drop, the airplane skewed sharply to the left from a sudden crosswind. Instinctively, Dave brought his feet to the pedals when Paul made no attempt to correct the slide. Forgetting about his broken ankle, he howled as his foot contacted the hard surface. The Maule further drifted off target as Dave let up on the yoke. Feeling light-headed, he pulled his feet back and somehow corrected their track with ailerons only. "I know you're hurting, Ace," he grunted. "But believe me, so am I. You really need to put your feet on the pedals, and like right now!"

The tail slid recklessly left and right. "Copy . . . that," Paul moaned. "I . . . got it."

"How you feeling?" asked Dave distractedly. "Besides awful."

"I feel dizzy and light-headed," Paul replied. "I'll be fine. Just get us on the ground in one piece."

"That is my intent," assured Dave nervously.

For any pilot in command, flying stick and rudder went hand in hand. But with his ankle pooched, Dave needed Paul's full effort on the pedals. Like himself, Paul required medical attention, and Dave only hoped they would both survive long enough to receive it. "Just hang on," he pleaded. "We're almost done with this baloney." And truth be told, Dave couldn't have cared less if Gary buckled himself in or not for the approach and landing. In his opinion, the man deserved whatever additional wrath he had coming.

As the Maule trudged along at 300 feet above the lake, now less than one mile away, the beachhead raced towards them alarmingly fast. Paul's breathing increased to the point he felt he could hyperventilate if he didn't get things under control. He looked at Dave, and from the look on his face, knew he'd be unable to handle power settings. "I've got the checks," Paul offered decisively. "Airspeed holding at sixty."

"Copy," Dave replied as his eyes focused intently on the approach end of the runway. "Appreciate the help, Ace."

Paul slid the mixture knob to its full rich position and followed suit with the prop control. The propellers revved up towards full RPMs as the blades angled flat should they need to go-around, which considering the tall pine trees at the far end of the field, he decided would be a near-impossible feat. "Stupid place to build a runway," he protested.

Suddenly Gary Nordhavn leaned forward, his left index finger aimed towards the instrument panel. "Carb heat," he babbled. "Don't forget the—"

It was then the Maule's engine began to sputter for a second time.

Chapter 42

Mortified, Diane gasped and glanced at Tess, then quickly turned back to the stricken plane, its engine struggling to keep power. Despite the distinctly unique sound of the helicopter transiting across the lake, the sudden disconnect of sound from the other power plant seemed downright spine-chilling.

For Diane, the troubling sound triggered a flood of raw emotion and anger. With Paul so close, and the end of this fiasco at hand, another dastardly plot from the universe seemingly vaporized what little hope she retained. The very fact they managed to restart the engine following their bottom up antics was in Diane's opinion, nothing short of divine intervention. But she also understood that an engine out on final, and so low to the water, meant she may never see her husband alive again. There was usually no coming back from that, not twice, and the thought reduced her to tears.

With Kim's attention momentarily on the nearby television crew, she wasn't initially aware that her dad's airplane was again in trouble. She noticed the camera pointed towards the lake; no doubt focused on the aircraft as it descended towards the airfield. Beside the cameraman, the big reporter talked into a hand-held microphone while his hands flailed about with flagrant intent. Kim flinched when he slapped his cameraman on the shoulder and excitedly pointed in the Maule's direction. "You getting this?" he barked. "The engine's cutting out again!"

Kim whipped her head back around. The plane seemed to hang in the sky as though held up by a force field. It seemed close enough to reach out and touch, yet she knew enough about flying to realize they were out too far to make it. Feeling utterly helpless, Kim thought of her dad and what he must be going through. She wanted more than anything to let him know she was there, to show her support and remind him to push hard for her. *But how?* She knew if the engine quit and they fell into the lake, her dad would never see her or know of her desire to support him as he had done so many times with her.

Kim felt her mother's quivering arm slide around her waist. Without words, mother and daughter watched helplessly as the man they loved struggled for life before their eyes. Kim audaciously upraised her arms and waved them back and forth as she had done in a Taylor Swift concert. "For you, Daddy!" she shouted. "I'm here." Kim glanced fearfully at her mom and Tess, then to her dad. "We're all here!"

"We shouldn't be this close!" shouted Tess while stepping back.

"No Tess," stated Diane outright. "Kim's right. We hold our ground until this is over, one way or another. If Paul and Dave see us, then the risk is worth it. If they don't, then I can rest knowing I was here for my husband when he needed me the most."

"Alrighty then," conceded Tess, "so be it."

The Maule's nose dipped sharply towards the water. In those unendurable few seconds, Diane raised her arms like her daughter and began to wave. Tess immediately followed, and together they silently offered what they thought might be a final salute to the men they loved and the careers they adored.

At that moment of anguish, Diane Jackson uttered a simple, yet earnest prayer. "Please Jesus, save my husband."

* * *

"Seriously!" Paul calmly remarked as if engine trouble at low altitude happened all the time. Per Gary's advice, he snapped on the carb heat and immediately raised the flaps to reduce drag. "So close and yet so far!"

The Maule's engine coughed and misfired as though a tiny gremlin were under the cowling, mischievously and persistently crimping the fuel line to block the flow, then releasing the pressure as one might do with a garden hose.

Dave glanced at the airspeed. "We're barely holding sixty knots!" he rasped. "But if the engine quits for good, we drop into the lake with no paddle, Ace!"

"You're stating the obvious again, Dave," argued Paul. "We aren't done yet! We can make it. We're only thirty-seconds back, so keep flying!"

"Fifty-five!" yelled Dave. "And in the event you need clarification, we're falling more than we are flying! I feel like Buzz and Woody from the end scene of Toy Story, only they had a happy ending."

Gary Nordhavn wailed in fear, but Dave and Paul ignored him. Without the gun in his hands, the troubled man no longer posed a lethal threat, whereas the airplane itself, once a tool of liberation had now become their greatest adversary. Amid the chaos and the shoreline fast approaching, Paul noticed three figures clumped near the beach at the approach end of the runway.

Dave noticed them a half-second later. "Who's stupid enough to be out there when we're trying to crash land?" he asked callously. "And waving no less!"

"Doesn't matter now!" snapped Paul. "Ignore them! They'll move once they realize we'll slam into them if they don't; not that we'll even make it that far." Paul found the landing light switch and toggled it evenly to ward them off, but his effort proved futile. The onlookers were apparently oblivious to the danger they were in, or that the airplane in their path had engine trouble.

"Stupid until proven otherwise," grumbled Dave.

Another blast of wind batted the airplane sideways and dipped the left-wing. Dave rammed the yoke to the right, and Paul went as hard as he could on the opposite rudder. The Maule slipped roughly back to its original track, bucking like a car whose driver kept his foot on the brake and gunned the engine with on-again-off-again hits to the gas pedal. The engine seemed unsure of whether it should stay on or shut down. Either way, falling airspeed meant a nose-down pitch attitude and no more lift. Both men knew they weren't going to make it, but neither wanted to be the first to admit it or concede defeat to an airplane with an apparent death wish of its own.

Paul finally yielded. "Set us in the lake as best you can while we still have a bit of forward momentum and the props partly turning."

"There's no setting us in the lake!" grimaced Dave. "We fall as we stall!"

The airplane started to shake as the angle of attack on the wing exceeded the airspeed needed to generate lift and keep them aloft. Paul yelled at Gary without taking his eyes off runway lights directly in their path. "We're swimming in ten seconds, Gary. Brace!"

Other than a low moan, no response came from the back seat.

The engine belched for several seconds and briefly roared to life as though fighting to throw off the pangs of inevitable death. The Maule lifted marginally and the surge in power hurtled the plane forward like a burst of nitrous oxide into the cylinders. But it wasn't enough.

Now only a football field length away from the edge of Spruce Creek's airstrip, the propeller stopped its rotation and the engine fell hauntingly silent.

We almost made it, thought Paul. *To have come all this way, then to crash at the finish line.* As he braced himself, Paul decided to focus his eyes on the fools in his direct line of sight, the group carrying on as though at a rock concert cheering for their adored band. As the plane bore down from a steep angle, something about them seemed oddly familiar. It was then Paul fixated on one person's unique movement, and the two individuals huddled beside. "Oh, dear God!" he gasped in shock.

It was then Dave noticed Tess's stance and her blonde hair. Beside her stood Diane and Kim, the women in a self-explanatory show of support. Tears welled up in his eyes as the Maule slid towards the lake, the controls non responsive to the input he so desperately tried to add.

Gary Nordhavn heard the stall warning buzzer as the airspeed dropped below the minimum control speed. Knowing they wouldn't make it, he glanced out the side window at the choppy lake water rising to meet them. Coherent enough to know that his life might end, he somehow buckled himself in despite the pain in his body and an over-abundance of remorseful thoughts coursing through his mind. Gary closed his eyes and mouthed the words, "I'm sorry, Cindy."

Dave anchored himself as best he could, pressing into the seat back and tucking in his legs and feet. He bit his lip in pain as the sudden movement sent his ankle into the frame holding the seat in place. "Hang on, Ace!" he grimaced. "This is going to really hurt!"

"Yup!" grunted Paul with his own misty eyes focused on his wife and daughter.

Descending through forty feet and a breath away from smashing into the water, a fearsome upheaval of air all at once launched the powerless Maule and whisked it forwards. The aircraft shot upwards as if bounced off an invisible trampoline, followed by the rapid onset of positive G's pushing everything down inside the airplane. Dave's hands came off the yoke and fell heavily into his lap.

Dumbstruck, and bracing for a crash-landing he thought imminent, Paul yelped in fear from the unexpected jolt as white-hot pain tore through his body near his lower spine. He tried feverishly to stabilize the airplane's sliding tail, but any meaningful control was gone. It felt to Paul like riding in the backseat of a car at the onset of a brutal motor vehicle accident, where nothing could be done except holding on when outside forces conspire to destroy life and limb.

With no words spoken between them and both men trying in their own way to correct a hapless situation, Paul and Dave watched as the airplane strayed moderately left of the approaching runway lights, its fuselage caught in a battle between gravity and the forces allowing flight in the first place.

Dave watched in disbelief as the airspeed needle slipped below stall speed, while the vertical speed indicator registered a 200 foot per minute climb rate. In that bizarre moment where the pieces didn't add up, all he could think of was that no one would believe this was happening, that a sudden rouge gust of wind would be enough to keep the wings airborne just long enough to traverse the remaining distance to the shoreline. Dave noticed out of the corner of his eye the women scrambling for cover, obviously not expecting the sudden turn of events any more than he was.

Feeling like they were key players in a very lopsided ball game with diddly-squat chance of achieving victory, Dave fought to keep the wings level, while Paul quarterbacked the pedals left and right. But gallant effort on both accounts did little to alter the planes haphazard trajectory. Sliding forward and sharply down as though floundering on a steep water slide, the Maule lost its momentum and dropped from the sky, only this time the wheels were over solid ground, but outside the boundary of the lit airfield.

The left front tire found the grass first and thumped down hard to the left of the runway lights. The right side main and tail wheel plowed into the earth at the same time, resulting in a bone-rattling jolt to the airframe. Everything inside the cockpit violently slewed sideways. Gary Nordhavn shrieked as the landing gear buffeted across fallen branches, rocks, and brush.

The shift from an inevitable water crash to wheels on dry land happened so fast that Paul momentarily forgot he was responsible for brakes and steering, not that he felt either would do any good. The last thing he had focused on was Diane, Kim and Tess, all waving and then hastily ducking as the aircraft passed over their heads at thirty knots, crossed the beach and plunged from the air.

Dave's hands twisted the yoke around as if that would somehow cause the plane to go where he wanted. "Steering!" he screamed. His broken ankle received impacts from everywhere imaginable, but mercifully the pain was manageable from all the adrenaline coursing through his body.

"On it!" Paul shouted. "Hold on!"

Paul sunk his feet into the pedals just as the airplane started to careen sharply to the left. He pounded on the right pedal and applied brakes as much as he dared over the washboard, debris-laden terrain.

* * *

Jack Ward stood in fearful awe. It wasn't every day you witnessed a plane crashing into a lake, then just seconds before impact, it unimaginably launches skyward. As the machine reached its short crest and fell back to earth, he fully expected the craft to cartwheel as its wheels absorbed the impact of irregular turf. He fought the urge to sprint towards it, to offer whatever help he could. But until the plane came to a stop, however that came about, he realized such heroics were useless. Veering left, and then just as quickly drifting towards the edge of the runway lighting, hundreds of white lights snuffed out as the wheels tore through several strands of lights. "Ah nuts," quipped Jack as he impulsively jumped back.

"Back to the drawing board, eh Jack?" speculated Tom. "Though I'd say by the looks of it, our efforts with the lights paid off with two planes down."

Jack aggressively nodded his head. "Appears so. But that one hasn't stopped yet, and all that matters now is the safety of everyone inside."

The Maule bucked wildly along the ground before lurching forward. The tail wheel shot upwards as the main gear locked up, followed by the machine pivoting in a half-circle to the right as the gear snagged a twisted branch. The left-wingtip kissed the ground before settling back hard on its front wheels. Churned up from the tires, clots of mud, leaves and mangled branches all rose into the air and fell. Then, when everything settled, complete stillness. No doors opened or any hint of movement from the occupants inside.

"Everyone stays back!" ordered Rob Smith as he hoofed it forward. "We have no idea what we're dealing with here, especially if there's a gun on board!"

The police helicopter swung in low over the lake, kicking up huge amounts of spray, mixed with projectile-like vegetation. Everyone turned away to shield their faces as it quickly set down a short distance away. This close, the engine noise and the slap of the rotors were deafening. But seconds later, the engine spooled down, and except for light rain, wind in the trees, and bubbling surf slapping ashore, all fell quiet.

Unconcerned about their own personal safety, Tess, Diane and Kim sprinted towards the Maule from their place near the shoreline.

"Ladies, no!" shouted Rob. "It's not safe until the police say it is!"

But as the women dashed in, Rob figured it pointless to try to stop them. He watched a moment longer before deciding to move forward himself. As he did so, the side door to the police helicopter flew open and three men jumped out, two with handguns drawn, and the other an older gentleman with thinning grey hair at the sides.

The older man surveyed the scene for a moment then skittered forward with amazing dexterity. Rob froze and watched in fascination as the other two followed close on his heels, arms extended, and their guns pointed forward. One of them appeared wobbly on his feet.

Dylan Sullivan and Matt Hawley both uttered the word, "Cool!" at the same time.

Matt shifted around several pine trees to obtain a better view of the mesmerizing scene playing out in front of him. Dylan immediately followed.

"This beats mountain biking any day!" Dylan remarked distractedly. "But when this is over Matt, let's get back to the lodge and grab some food. I'm starving."

Matt rolled his eyes, "Dude, is that seriously all you ever think about?"

"Besides this, mountain biking and food," exclaimed Dylan. "What else is there?"

Matt boxed his friend on the shoulder, "I think you have a fair point."

Watching helplessly, search and rescue pilot Kevin Davies stood under the wing, his arm outstretched and finger-pointing, more for his own benefit than anyone else's. As the officers warily approached the Maule, Kevin heard the older man shouting. "You inside the plane! Exit slowly and place your hands on your heads! Do it now!"

Desperate to reach their loved ones, Tess, Kim and Diane all stopped in their tracks mid-stride, the moment surreal and completely beyond their control. Diane Jackson found it impossible to hold her emotions in check. She yelled as loudly as she could for her husband's benefit, inwardly praying that somehow her words would reach his ears. "I'm here, Paul! I love you!"

* * *

Inside the Maule, Paul's entire body shook uncontrollably. He ached from head to toe. Fumbling to unlatch his seat belt, the buzzing in his ears gave way to shouting from somewhere behind the plane, a pair of voices—both frantic in their own way. One male and one female, neither of whom he understood. Paul massaged his ears and tried to flip his head around to obtain a better view, but because of the plane's lopsided angle, he saw nothing but pine trees and vegetation.

Covered in sweat and in brain-numbing pain, Dave twisted his head to look at Paul. "Well," he scowled. "That was . . . fun. Let's do this again soon, shall we?"

Paul managed a weak smile at his friend. "You wanted adventure. I delivered."

"That you did, Ace, that you did."

Dave and Paul watched as three men stealthily approached from the rear of the plane. Two big guys slithered forward, one on either side and both with handguns aimed directly at them. One man's face was pasty white, the other bore an expression of "if you even blink the wrong way, I'll kill you." The third, an older chap who seemed less intense than the others but still clearly meaning business, scooted in closer as he barked instructions. "You, in the plane! I need you all to exit slowly and place your hands on your heads. Do it now!"

Dave reached for the door latch. "Gramps barking orders and the other dudes with guns are the only prompting I need, Ace. I've had enough expended bullets for one day; I'd rather not get shot again."

Paul nodded in agreement. "Let's do what the man says. We exit, but we exit slowly. No sudden moves."

"We can both hardly move anyway!" scoffed Dave. "Turtle speed it will be."

Opening his door in slow motion, Paul raised both arms to show he wasn't a threat. "We're unarmed," he shouted. "Even our"—he wanted to say hijacker but decided against it—"passenger. We all have injuries and need assistance exiting the plane, so please lower the—"

"Out now!" shouted the man again without listening. "For your own safety, climb out and place your hands on the back of your heads where I can see them. Exit slowly. No sudden moves!"

One of the two armed officers stationed himself left of the Maule's nose, the other on Paul's side of the plane twenty feet away, their guns trained on the cockpit. Paul thought the older man looked as though he'd be happier in a senior's home crafting puzzles, yet his hard-and-fast body position suggested he wasn't in the mood for being jerked around. Following a moment of painful struggle, Paul carefully side-saddled himself out the door and lumbered to plant his feet on the ground. Despite a pain-racked body, Mother Earth had never felt so glorious. He lifted his arms and placed his hands on the back of his head. "We're complying," was all Paul could spit out.

Livid at being treated like a criminal, Dave eased open his door. "We're the good guys here for crying out loud!" he angrily protested. "This cop has watched one too many crime shows," he whispered to Paul.

"Just get your hands on your head so you don't get us shot!" ordered Paul. Momentarily forgetting about their passenger, he glanced towards the rear. "You hearing this, Gary?" he asked. "We've been ordered to get out. All of us, as in right now!"

Slumped over in his seat, Gary Nordhavn was evidently incapable of hearing anything, let alone complying with police orders. Blood trickled down his face from a wicked gash on his forehead, and when Paul looked at the man's stomach for signs of breathing, he couldn't see any noticeable rise and fall.

"We might have lost Gary," noted Paul. "He's not breathing that I can see."

"I'm not trying to sound callous," replied Dave. "But karma sucks."

Dave turned in his seat, agonizingly guiding his legs to the side as carefully as he could to avoid smacking his ankle. "I'm coming out!" he announced. "We're unarmed and there's an unresponsive man in the back."

"That's our suspect?" asked the senior officer, his voice loud yet calmly authoritative.

"That's affirmative," Dave replied. "That's your skyjacker."

"And the gun?" asked the man in charge. "Where exactly is that?"

Deliveries

"Gone," Dave replied sharply. "Listen, officer, my ankle's messed up, so I could use a hand getting out." Dave softened his impatient tone. "Please."

Inspector Stan Fenwick walked slowly forward, his cohorts remaining where they stood. He cocked his head sideways and knew immediately these men were the missing airmen, and nothing more than participants slash victims in one of the most offbeat cases he had ever worked on. He couldn't help but wonder how these two pilots ended up inside the same airplane as a diamond smuggler, but he knew that in time, those answers would come.

Stan slowly but deliberately tread forward towards the passenger side of the airplane. "I'm inspector Stan Fenwick of the Owensville Police Department. You said you have an unconscious passenger, but no firearm on board? Did I hear that correctly?"

"Correct," grimaced Paul through clenched teeth. "The man responsible for all this and no doubt the one you're looking for is slumped over in the back with a nasty cut to his head. His name is Gary Nordhavn. He pitched the gun out the window before we landed. I'm not sure he's breathing."

Remaining sharp-eyed, Stan peered into the backseat and motioned for one of his officers to holster his weapon. He watched Gary a moment and turned back towards Paul. "His chest is moving, so he's definitely alive. Good to have you gentlemen back on terra firma," he offered sincerely. Stan noticed the carnage inside the airplane. "We'll help you away from the plane and arrange for the medical attention you need. Then, we'll deal with our innocent-until-proven-guilty diamond peddling friend."

Paul plodded away slowly by himself, and as he did so, Stan smelled gunpowder and noticed empty bullet casings and the holes in the roof, door, window and instrument panel. He scratched his head. "Are those impact points from what I think they're from?"

"Correct again," verified Dave. He pointed to his shoulder. "And this one too."

"He shot you?" asked Stan dumbfounded. "Are you okay?"

"Flesh wound," Dave replied. "And yes, he shot me."

Just then, a loud hacking cough erupted from the backseat, followed by shouting. Paul shuddered and a chill coursed through his body. As fast as he could, Dave limped painfully away with help from one of the officers. For him, separating himself from an unpredictable lunatic, gun or no gun, was worth the agony exploding from his ankle.

The other plainclothes officer immediately scampered in, re-aiming his firearm towards the back seat as Stan scrutinized his disgruntled culprit from a safe distance. Now very much alive, Gary Nordhavn wriggled about wildly. Stan tilted his head curiously and watched the man for a moment like a parent waiting for their child to settle during a temper tantrum.

Paul stopped and turned. "Hey inspector," he added. "In addition to the mess inside the plane, you'll find your diamonds scattered too, FYI."

Perplexed, Stan cocked his head sideways. "Pardon me?" he asked. "And why pray tell would the diamonds be scattered about inside the airplane?"

"I'll explain later," deflected Paul. "And a word of advice if I may?"

"Okay," agreed Stan curiously. "I'm listening."

"Tread carefully when you secure your prisoner," Paul suggested. "His collarbone is broken as you can see by what's left of his sling."

"I see," replied Stan as he noticed the tattered orange fabric. "Anything else?"

"And despite how emotionally messed up he appears to be," explained Paul. "He helped to save our necks up there. Otherwise, we'd likely be swimming, or maybe even dead. He's passive-aggressive or some such thing, but I don't think at heart that he's necessarily a bad guy. He confessed everything to us, and from what I gather, ended up bowing to pressure and the lure of easy money. Believe me, I can relate."

"I'll take that under advisement," acknowledged Stan before ducking into the Maule's cabin. "I suppose we all have skeletons in the closet."

Stan scrunched his nose from the putrid reek of fish, body odour and gun powder. Flung around the cabin from whatever maelstrom apparently transpired; lures, candy bars, water bottles, plus all sorts of unrecognizable debris were strewn about. Stan also noticed the spent bullet casings and decided the inside of the cockpit looked as though a bomb went off in very close quarters. The airplane had become a crime scene and would now be treated as such.

Crumpled in the rear seat, a noticeably tall dishevelled man with matted hair and glazed eyes stared back at Stan. He wasn't at all what Stan envisioned for a diamond smuggler and tough-guy hijacker. With glaring fear in his eyes and a creepy gash on his head, he appeared disorientated and unsure of his surroundings. He cowered back as Stan leaned in.

"Easy, pal," Stan ordered. "We'll help get you out of here. I just need you to settle yourself down first. Can you do that for me?"

Gary Nordhavn froze. He cocked his head sideways at what Stan thought an impossible angle. Watching the man's eyes darken, a sudden chill coursed along Stan's spine. It was then he realized this man did not want to exit his airplane.

* * *

Wanting to run to her husband, Diane's legs seemed unable to move as though restrained by an invisible band. She shifted her gaze to the police and the airplane Paul and Dave just emerged from. Both men had their backs turned away and seemed unaware of their loved ones' presence.

A scuffle ensued as the officers dragged a visibly distressed man out of the plane. Diane found herself stepping back several feet as the suspect went to the ground and was quickly handcuffed with his arms in front of him. The man let out a blood-curdling shriek, and it was then she understood what Dave and Paul had likely endured with their unruly passenger. Diane involuntarily shivered head to toe. More incredibly, the man she loved, and her best friend now stood before her. Pent up emotions bubbled up, and for the umpteenth time, everything slowed down, and Diane burst into tears.

"It's okay, Mom," blurted Kim. "Dad's back! He made it! No need to cry!"

Diane looked at her daughter and nodded. "Yes, he did make it back, sweetie, just like you said he would." Diane paused to process her feelings. "These are tears of joy, dear," she partially lied. "Just tears of joy."

* * *

Paul turned slowly away from the police and the now apprehended Gary Nordhavn. He genuinely felt sorry for the man, but at the same time he could not disagree with Dave—the guy had what was coming to him. And Paul knew that despite his attempted plea bargain with the Inspector, the charges against Gary would not be light.

Swallowing hard, Paul faced his wife and daughter square on, his thoughts towards his own impropriety chewing away any remaining confidence. *Does she know?* he wondered. Making brief eye contact with Diane, Paul found himself unable to hold her piercing gaze even from a distance. Instead, he looked down to his feet as he shuffled forward with awkward steps towards his wife.

* * *

Diane watched her husband tentatively approach, hobbling along with a prominent limp—his head blotted with dried blood. His apparent hesitation suggested he wasn't sure how he would be received under such dubious personal circumstances, and yet even with the distance between them, she recognized remorse when she saw it. Brushing aside her tears, Diane arched her shoulders and made a solid promise to set her grievances aside.

Kim let go of her mom and excitedly lunged forward. "Daddy!" she screamed. Something in Diane wanted to stop her daughter, to hold her back so Paul would understand the seriousness of his crimes. But she knew better than to try. In this window of time, Diane resolved that nothing else mattered; not Paul's medical restriction, nor his dishonesty. Instead, she reprimanded herself for not displaying the same kind of enthusiasm as her daughter.

Diane watched Kim wrap her arms around her dad's neck. The moment was bittersweet. As she soaked in the reunion, Diane noticed Dave's foot in a crude splint and his shirt covered in blood at the shoulder. With help from one of the officers, Dave trudged forward on one foot to where Paul and Kim stood embracing.

* * *

Not sure what else to do, Rob Smith and Laura Hastings both stepped forward to offer assistance when they noticed the group struggling to make headway through the thick grass. But when Rob stopped suddenly, he brought his arm up to halt Laura's progress. "Hold fast, Laura," he ordered. "I think we need to just let this play out without our involvement. Seems they have things under control."

Laura popped her chilled hands into the pockets of her vest. "Perhaps you're right," she agreed. "This certainly appears to be a family reunion moment, that's for sure. Nice to see things ending this way." Laura rubbed her neck. "Wow, I'm exhausted."

"Me too," agreed Rob. "But as soon as I get back to town, I'm heading straight for my garage. There's a certain blue ragtop convertible parked inside that needs a highway run in the worst way. I'll catnap later."

"You know," contemplated Laura, "not that you invited me or anything, but how about I spring for extra-large coffees, and you allow me to occupy the passenger seat. I could sure use the brain drain, and I've never been in a convertible."

Rob brought his hands to his face and massaged his cheeks. "That," he pondered thoughtfully, "might just be the best search and rescue strategy I've heard all day!"

"Excellent!" smiled Laura. "And I promise I won't say a word about your driving!"

* * *

With exhausted sandpapery eyes, Diane absorbed the entire scene all at once. Beside her, Tess made no immediate attempt to move forward. Instead, she stayed beside her "wingman," a mutual coping strategy between them that when life got tough, they stuck together. And this mess was by far one of the worst in their self-proclaimed, Pilots' Wives Club.

Two other people stood near the Search and Rescue aircraft—a man and a woman, their faces aimed towards the Maule, but neither stepping in to help. Their mellow, listless body language indicated to Diane that both were completely exhausted. Near the generator shed, Jack Ward and Tom Sullivan seemed unsure about what to do or how to involve themselves in the current situation. They simply watched as did Diane.

Diane thought Jack appeared completely worn, his physical stature hunched over and listless. But then she felt certain a mirror would reflect her own slouched shoulders, facial wrinkles and newly etched stress lines. She aptly decided it best to deal with her own insecurities before passing any further judgement on others, including her husband.

* * *

With Gary Nordhavn restrained on the grass, Stan Fenwick read him his rights before re-examining the Maule aircraft. Once inside, he noticed several diamonds scattered on both the front and rear seat, and also sprinkled about on the floor—their smooth facet's catching ribbons of sunlight streaming through clouds and into the cockpit. Stan picked up one of the gems and held it near his eyes for closer examination. "Well, I'll be a monkey's uncle," he declared. "This whole darn thing was true."

Gary tried to clutch his broken bone with both cuffed hands. He babbled disjointedly. Stan slid back out of the Maule and crouched down. "Easy there, partner," he stated. "We'll have you flying again in no time, only this time under police escort."

When Gary heard the word "flying," he became deathly still. He craned his neck sideways, and with piercing eyes and a lopsided expression, rasped a string of undecipherable words over and over.

With keen interest, Stan cocked his head at the sudden transformation in his prisoner's body language. He bent down closer to Gary's mouth to better hear what the man tried to say. Stan watched as Gary's pupils dilated and his face twisted into a mask of pained expression.

"What is it you're trying to say?" asked Stan. "Because all I hear coming from you is nonsense."

Gary shrunk back and his face eerily softened.

Despite the suspect being cuffed, the other two officers stood to the side with their hands ready to draw their weapons again if required. Both had faces reflecting a genuine look of concern mixed with weirded-out curiosity.

In a surprisingly articulate voice, Gary Nordhavn looked at Stan with pleading eyes, and repeated the word "delivery" over and over.

Stan Fenwick rose to his feet. He turned away from Gary, pulled his collar up and ordered his men to gently load their catch into the helicopter. "There won't be any deliveries today for you, partner," he articulated as he walked away. "Though I am insanely interested to hear all about it."

Chapter 43

Tess caught Dave's eye and waved. He smiled and waved back as if this sort of event happened every day between them and wasn't a big deal. Tess placed her hand on Diane's shoulder. "It's over," she calmly remarked. "At least this part is. I know stormy days may yet come for you and Paul, but for now, you don't look too happy about the way things ended."

Diane shrugged her shoulders. "I know my face doesn't show it, Tessa, but I'm elated our guys are safe despite their obvious injuries. I think I'm still trying to come to terms with all this. You have to admit the emotional roller coaster we've been on since last night is nothing short of unbelievable. I can't help imagining what they've been through, and that haunts me too." Diane leaned into her friend. "I'm just grateful we could be here when they landed, though neither of them seems too surprised to see us. Guess they may have actually seen us waving like absolute fools!"

"Well," laughed Tess. "It does seem that our prayers and show of support may have actually saved the day and earned our fearless Boy Scouts another adventure badge. What happened moments ago was pretty unbelievable."

"Certainly was," Diane agreed. "But I'm still angry at Paul, and from the look on his face I'd say he's fully aware I know what he did."

"Let that go for now," encouraged Tess. "Yes, it will need to be dealt with and there will be consequences but try to live in the moment. It's all we have, and things could have ended up far worse."

Diane smiled at her friend. "Right as always, Tess. I do have trouble focusing on the here and now, that's for sure. I wish I wouldn't get so worked up about things, though admittedly this ordeal was a biggie!"

"I think that's an ongoing issue we all need to work on," assured Tess.

"I suppose so. My father-in-law used to have a little wall plaque in his bedroom that read, 'Trust God and live one day at a time.' Though I realize that's easier said than done, I sure need to work on it."

"Indeed and Amen," nodded Tess. "So, are we just going to stand here and act like casual observers, or do we fangirl our husbands like Kim just did?"

Diane steered her feet forward. "For better or for worse, right Tessa?"

"Those I believe were the vows we both made when we hitched these guys," stated Tess. "So, let's try to focus on the better part."

* * *

Sheltered under the Piper Cub's starboard wing, Kevin Davies and Susan McCutcheon watched as the spectacle played out in front of them. Kevin glanced at the hole in the wing where the tape had let go. "Our wing held together!" he announced happily. "But I'll have to re-patch it before I fly back."

"Yes, looks like a reasonably happy ending for everybody this time around," acknowledged Susan. "And no offence to your flying, Kevin, but I'm hitching a ride back to Owensville by car. I've had enough airborne stress for one day. I need to go home and do something normal like make butter tarts for my little brother. He's always hinting."

Kevin laughed. "No offence taken to catching a lift back. I'm just glad everyone's safe and that the police showed up when they did. Things could have ended worse. And for what it's worth, I also happen to love butter tarts, so if you need the practice, I'm officially hinting."

Susan playfully fisted Kevin on the shoulder. "Good thing you have a praying spotter who's not above bribing her pilot to guarantee her safety. And I'll take your hint under advisement. My husband loves tarts of any kind, especially butter tarts. So, between him, my brother and you, you guys can fight over them."

"Speaking of your bribe," added Kevin. "I've decided I'd like my gift card to a restaurant, if your offer still stands."

"A restaurant? What about the aviator's watch?"

Kevin shrugged his shoulders. "Nah. I already have a watch. Besides, there's a certain paramedic I need to get hold of. I promised her a plane ride, and the way I figure it, she'll be more open to my advances if I can bribe her with dinner first."

Susan laughed. "I see you're a quick study."

"I learn from the best!" grinned Kevin broadly.

* * *

Ducking into the shed housing the generator, Jack Ward switched the machine off and went back outside. "Enough of that racket," he announced. "I think I've lost half my hearing. And half was all I had before."

"Agreed on both accounts," Tom jokingly replied. "With the runway lights ripped out, no need to generate power now, not even for the beacon."

"Nope," said Jack. "I've seen enough aircraft land here today to last me the rest of the year. I'm just glad this whole mess is over." Jack licked his lips. "I could sure use a scotch about now. And my bed and a sleep that never ends."

Deliveries

"If you drink enough, Jack, I guarantee you'll sleep well," acknowledged Tom. "But now that you mention it, I'd be happy to join you for a nip."

"I don't recall offering you an invitation," Jack remarked grumpily.

Tom smiled. "Always Mr. Generosity, eh Jack?"

Genuinely happy with the outcome, and that Kim and Diane Jackson had their loved one back safe and reasonably sound, Jack shuffled forward and looked back at Tom. "You know anybody wanting to buy this place?" he asked. "Because I'm thinking of selling. I'm too old for this kind of drama."

"Surely you don't mean that, Jack," challenged Tom. "Not after all the literal blood, sweat and tears you've invested here. What about your promise to Mildred?"

Jack turned towards the lake and watched Diane step cautiously towards her husband. "That's my point, Tom," he grumbled. "I have nothing left to give, and Mildred's not here, at least not physically." Jack thought a moment. "Whoever the buyer is can fix these bloody lights themselves and throw in a case or two of scotch as part of the deal. I'm exhausted and need to go play shuffleboard or something that doesn't boil my blood."

Tom shook his head. "You never change, Jack."

"You're finally figuring that out, eh Tom?" Jack retorted. "Certainly took you long enough, old friend. And don't worry, I'd share the scotch."

* * *

As Diane and Tess walked forward with arms linked, Diane fixed her eyes on her husband. Supported on both sides by Kim and Matt Hawley, his weathered face made him look years older than he was. To Paul's left, Dylan Sullivan assisted Dave as best he could. The sight reminded her of an epic seventh-century sword-wielding battle she watched on television a few weekends ago, where two best friends emerged from the trenches of battle, scarred and bloody, but alive and being held up by comrades in arms.

Like a nervous schoolgirl about to face a boy she adored, and yet one who caused her incredible heartache and suffering, Diane watched as Paul lifted his head and set his eyes on hers. Diane's heart fluttered like it did so often when he looked at her, that special feeling never going away in all their years of marriage. Smiling to herself and for Paul's benefit, Diane was about to leap forward to greet her husband when his legs suddenly faltered. He dropped to his knees as both hands wildly clutched at his chest. Seconds later his eyes fell away.

Diane gasped as she ran forward. *Oh, dear God, I'm too late.*

* * *

With only fifty feet separating himself from his wife, Paul could feel his heart beginning to flutter as several back-to-back palpitations impacted the muscle. As the blood drained from his head, the pressure on his chest cavity felt as though someone had clamped a vice and began squeezing tighter and tighter.

Raising his hands to his chest, another unseen force slammed his knees from behind, knocking his legs out from under him. Through fading vision, he saw Diane rushing towards him, calling out his name, frantic with worry.

The last thing Paul remembered before he passed out was his precious daughter leaning over him and his wife appearing alongside, both women uttering the same words at the same time. "We love you."

Epilogue

On the small bedside table beside her, Diane Jackson picked up one of the many get-well cards that lavished the drab pale-green room on the main floor of Owensville General Hospital. A large cluster of helium balloons floated nearby; the string attached to a bouquet of mixed flowers in a vase far too small. She read the sentiment inside the card, smiled, and then placed it back down with the others.

The setting sun cast the room in a warm glow as leftover sunbeams streamed in through the west-facing window. An IV-drip fed saline solution through a thin plastic tube and directly into the arm of her sleeping husband. A small clamp covered an incision point in Paul's wrist where a catheter was inserted into his artery and guided to his heart for the recently completed angiogram procedure. Respiration, heart rate and oxygen levels displayed on an LED monitor, the readings coming from a clip attached to Paul's right index finger.

Twitching, Paul's feet wiggled under the pre-warmed red plaid blanket, standard issue for patients in the cardiac wing of the ER unit, and for those in recovery. Kim stood near the door, her fingers busily tapping keys on her phone as she updated friends and family on her dad's condition. A few moments later, she walked to the foot of the bed and lightly massaged his feet through the fabric. "When's he going to wake up, Mom?" she asked. "It scares me that he's sleeping so much."

Diane looked at Tess McMurray and then at Dave. Both sat on folding chairs brought in by hospital staff because the compact room housed only one padded chair. Dave's arm and heavily bandaged shoulder hung in a blue cloth sling. Crutches leaned against the wall to his left and a smooth white cast graced his badly fractured ankle. There were already several signatures scribbled on the plaster with a black sharpie marker, one of the autographs belonging to Kim.

"Well," replied Diane. "They said he could be asleep for up to an hour, but after everything your dad has been through, I'll be surprised if he wakes up at all before morning. It's a long shot at best that he'll even remember the trip here to the hospital. The ambulance paramedics said he kept going in and out of consciousness and suffered from both dehydration and exhaustion."

"He's a tough old bird," assured Dave. "He'll get through this, Kim, don't you worry. In fact, your dad was the real hero up there. His rapid-fire instincts saved our bacon more than a few times."

"When he does wake up," stated Diane. "I'm supposed to call Inspector Fenwick. He needs to take more statements from Paul, though I wish he'd wait for another day or two. I don't expect Paul will be in the mood to answer questions."

Dave shook his head. "The Inspector tried to grill me after Paul regained consciousness. I told the guy in no uncertain terms that this wasn't the time or the place. He wasn't pleased, but he backed off. For an old guy, he sure has some gumption."

Tess spoke up. "And that reporter and his cameraman recorded everything. I tried to shoo them away but finally gave up once I had the upper hand and made sure they weren't leaving Spruce Creek any time soon."

Diane eyed Tess suspiciously. "And you would know this how, exactly?" she asked with one raised eyebrow.

Tess reached into her purse and brandished a set of keys that didn't belong to her. She held them up by the CFCB Television key chain. "Because," she proudly boasted. "I found their car keys in the grass and thought I'd be a good Samaritan and pick them up. I had planned on returning them right away." Tess exaggerated a wink. "But then I became distracted with the ambulance showing up and all the commotion with the police, and Paul being transported to the hospital. So, with any luck, they're still out there chasing down their keys and missed filing their precious story on the evening news."

Dave sat with his mouth open and his eyes wide in surprise. "You, my dear, never cease to amaze me! Wow, I'm lucky to have married such a bad girl!"

Tess smiled, "If someone does me or my loved ones *a bad*, I do them *a worse*! That's my golden rule!"

Diane couldn't suppress a chuckle. "Oh Tessa, whatever would I do without you? You will return the keys, won't you?"

Tess nodded. "Absolutely," she replied. "But not until tomorrow. I think our television crew deserves to sweat it out a bit longer, unless of course, someone from the station has already rescued them."

"No doubt they were in a tizzy," added Diane. She reached into her purse, grabbed her cell phone and began to dial.

"Who are you calling, Mom?" asked Kim.

"Bruce Macbeth. I want to give him an update on your dad. He was the air traffic controller who I visited at the airport, and the one who saw your dad and Dave fly off last evening."

Dave spoke up. "Bruce did try to talk us out of going, but stubborn, pig-headed Ace there knew best, or, so he thought. No offence, Diane. I even tried to talk him out of it, but he shot me down pretty quickly, no pun intended."

"None taken," insisted Diane as she waited for the call to connect through. "It's no surprise to me that my husband has a stubborn streak. And because he wasn't using his brain to the best of his ability over the past twenty-four hours, and because he's dealing with a possible heart condition to add to his broken airplane and broken pride …" Diane paused for air. "I'm definitely feeling overwhelmed and might just slap him first before kissing him."

"Dad's alive, Mom," reminded Kim, "and Dave. Isn't that all that matters? We just have to take things one step at a time. Dad getting better is priority number one, or are you forgetting that?"

Diane smiled at her daughter. "Oh Kimmy, right you are again. I'm sorry."

The call connected through and Diane heard Bruce pick up, but he didn't answer right away. She said hello a few times and could hear papers shuffling around and muffled voices. Then finally, "Hello, Bruce Macbeth speaking."

"Bruce, its Diane Jackson. Sounds like you're busy, so I won't take but a moment of your time." Diane repositioned her legs to get comfortable in her chair.

"Diane, so nice to hear from you! How are Paul and Dave? Quite the ordeal they've had from what I've been told."

"That's what I'm calling about. Paul's in the—"

"The hospital, yes I know. I just had a phone call from Inspector Fenwick. He had more questions for me and briefed me on the situation at Spruce Creek, as much as he was permitted to say. He's sure a feisty old guy."

"I see," Diane whispered. "Word does travel fast. Well, in answer to your question, Paul and Dave are both recovering. Dave's patched and bandaged, and Paul's sedated and sleeping from a heart test he just had. We haven't had any results yet, but the doctor will be in soon. We hope things work out on all accounts for him and that he gets to hold onto his flying status."

"That's good news," stated Bruce. "When he wakes up, give him my best. Also, be sure to tell him that the next time he heads out in bad weather against my recommendations, he'll owe my wife and me a belated anniversary dinner at the restaurant of our choosing."

Diane smiled. "I'll be sure to pass that along when he wakes up. Thanks for all your help, Bruce. Right now, he's out for the count and—"

"Pass what along?" Paul inquired in a surprisingly strong voice.

Startled, Kim jumped back. "Daddy!" she shrieked. "You're awake!"

Paul held up his free arm and grabbed Kim's hand when she stepped forward.

"Hey, princess," Paul grinned, "how's my girl?"

Diane jumped from her seat to join her daughter. "Paul, you're awake!" she gasped.

Paul chuckled. "That's what you both are telling me. And for the record, you might all want to curtail your scathing chatter unless you're sure the patient is out cold. I heard every hurtful word spoken, and here I thought we all were family!"

Diane leaned in and gently hugged her husband. "After what you put your family through, I think you should be thankful we don't find you a different family!" Diane suddenly remembered she was holding her cellphone and connected to Bruce. "Oh my, Bruce," she apologized. "I'm so sorry to leave you hanging like that. Paul just surprised us all and woke up from his slumber!"

"No worries," laughed Bruce. "I'll let you go. Again, please give him my regards for a speedy recovery. I better go and spend some time with Marilyn before I'm disowned! No doubt Paul and I are both in similar-sized doghouses and that begging for forgiveness might be the order of the day."

"You may just be right about that!" agreed Diane. "But thanks, Bruce, thanks for everything. And for what it's worth, Happy Anniversary!"

"Thanks," answered Bruce sincerely. "That remains to be seen," he joked. "But tell Paul that in the meantime I'll start on the suite and hot tub over my garage if you boot him out. I could use the rent money! Bye for now, Diane."

Diane ended the call and returned her attention to her husband.

Dave and Tess rose from their chairs to get in on the pleasantries. Dave leaned on Tess for support. "Welcome back, Ace," he grinned. "Now that you're awake, want me to bust you out of here? I'm sure the bucket of bolts that you call your airplane is being extracted as we speak and sold for scrap. But if it's still flyable after repairs, I'm sure we can be off again in no time on some other half-baked plan of yours."

Tess shot Dave a dirty look.

"What?" snickered Dave. "Getting into trouble is what we do best!"

Paul kissed his wife and smiled. He could tell from her facial expression that she remained angry, but he could also sense the compassion and forgiveness in her eyes.

Paul glanced at Dave. "What I really want delivered is a bowl of your wife's taco soup!"

"Taco soup?" repeated Tess.

"I'm not sure I understand," said Diane. "What's taco soup got to do with anything relevant here?"

Dave smiled. "It's a long story, but I assure you, it's a good story!"

"If it's as hot as Dave claims," recalled Paul, "then burning my face off is small penance for the sins I've committed, and for the one maybe yet to come."

Diane tilted her head sideways. "And what pray tell does that mean? You, my husband, are already in the doghouse, so there shall be no other sins committed until I say so."

"Well," answered Paul nervously. "Assuming I get patched up and cleared to fly, Inspector Fenwick kinda-sorta asked me if I'd consider piloting the Maule and the diamonds to their predetermined delivery point, in place of Gary. In a manner of speaking, I'd be the bait to flesh out the bad guys."

Four jaws dropped wide open.

"Good one, Ace," laughed Dave. "I see you haven't lost your sense of humour!" But when Dave saw the determined look on his friends' face, the blood rushed from his head, and he promptly sat back down. "You're serious, aren't you?"

Paul nodded at Dave, made eye contact with his wife and smiled sheepishly. "I resolve, from this day forth, to tell the truth, the whole truth and nothing but the truth, so help me God, and wife."

Diane scowled. "And when pray tell did the good Inspector have time to ask you such a knucklehead question?"

"Right before I went in for my angiogram," answered Paul timidly. "He was in the hospital when they admitted me and apparently sweet-talked one of the nurses to find me. It was simply good timing on his part."

Diane grimaced at her husband and stepped purposefully towards the door. "Oh, I bet it was all just a stunning coincidence that you two had time for a chat."

"Where are you going, Mom?" asked Kim.

"To find the doctor, or any doctor for that matter," Diane replied. "Or anyone else willing to accept a bribe to ground my husband for the rest of his God-given life."

Paul wanted to reply but thought better of it. Instead, he gazed at Tess. "Does this mean I don't get any taco soup?"

Manufactured by Amazon.ca
Bolton, ON